THE LEGEND OF

RANDIDLY GHOSTHOUND

BOOK ONE

aethonbooks.com

THE LEGEND OF RANDIDLY GHOSTHOUND
©2021 NORET FLOOD

ALSO IN SERIES

Want to discuss our books with other readers and even the authors like Shirtaloon, Zogarth, Cale Plamann, Noret Flood (Puddles4263) and so many more?

Join our Discord server today and be a part of the Aethon community.

CHAPTER ONE

*R*andidly Ghosthound took a deep breath to calm the buzzing in his chest and tasted the stale tang of disinfectant. The cold air in the underground dormitory tunnel stank of undergraduate excess and lazy cleanup. He paced along the corridor with decisive steps, quickly reaching the staircase at the end. Randidly raked his hand through his black hair, which was falling in a mess down to his eyebrows.

Rather than going up to his room, Randidly turned around and retraced his steps. His emerald eyes cut back and forth methodically, searching the emptiness for some method to move past this tension. When he reached the other end, he turned around and began again. He was going nowhere in this university, in his life, down this damn tunnel, and he knew it. Randidly mused over the physical act of going nowhere as he pivoted on his heel. Honestly, being physically stuck here wasn't so bad.

It was the suffocating, helpless sense of dissatisfaction driving him back and forth down the fifty-meter tunnel. His steps echoed in the enclosed space, sharp rebukes of the way he'd been living the first twenty years of his life.

I don't belong here. Randidly's eyes were red when he once again reached the grey cinder block wall and turned around.

That was when it happened.

System initializing...

"Huh...?" Randidly stopped midway through a step, pushing the horrible dissatisfaction in his chest to the side.

If he didn't know better, he would say a god-like entity had just spoken into his mind. Or he was suddenly in a videogame and received a system announcement.

Out-of-body situational awareness seemed to just appear in his mind. *System initializing.* "What was—"

The world warped. Randidly's body became sliced so thinly, his layers were insubstantial and infinite. Bewildered by the combination of unfamiliarity and awareness, he couldn't even scream. His already strained psyche was tortured by spatial forces beyond his understanding.

Without any of the delicacy of his disassembly, Randidly was slapped back together. He stumbled, hands trembling. The nervous energy transformed into a horrible certainty. His body felt strange and wrong, as though he lost something precious in that moment of separation. That something sinister slipped between the cracks as he had been reconstructed.

A Three-Horned Demon Ram spawned next to him, thrashing in pained annoyance where he had just been confused. The monster's movements launched Randidly face first into the stone wall. Luckily, the transfer of momentum was only glancing. The charging ram had spawned practically on top of him. But even the relatively light touch of the ram's powerful flank was enough to ensure the impact knocked him unconscious.

When Randidly awoke, it was to a headache and several blue floating screens.

Welcome to New Earth! Your world has been accepted into Nexus, and as such, is now running on a new System to give you the tools and Skills to survive and live a fulfilling life! Good luck. And know your efforts will always be fairly rewarded.

Basic Stats Set!
Randidly Ghosthound
Class: ---
Level: N/A
Health(/R per hour): 28 (16.5)
Mana(/R per hour): 17 (6.75)
Stam(/R per min): 16 (9)
Vitality: 4
Endurance: 2
Strength: 2
Agility: 3
Perception: 2
Reaction: 4

Resistance: 4
Willpower: 4
Intelligence: 3
Wisdom: 1
Control: 1
Focus: 2

**For more information, you can view your Stats anytime by thinking
"Menu" and then selecting "Status."**
Congratulations! The "Newbie Path" is open to you!

Congratulations! Due to you being the first player in your world to receive
damage, the **"P. Def Path"** is open to you!

Congratulations! Due to you being the first player in your world to observe
monsters, the **"M. Support Path"** is open to you!

Congratulations! For possessing only a single Health, the **"Risk Taker
Path"** is open to you!

**Warning! Your Health is extremely low. Due to your low Level, arrows
will guide you to the nearest Safe Zone in the Dungeon.**

The stream of flashing blue lights mixed with Randidly's concussion and
clouded his vision. Several seconds of staring at the sticky pool of drying
blood beneath him convinced him his headache wasn't one curable by
aspirin.

And these boxes...

The thought earned a frown from Randidly. *Are they really... notifications?*

A thick teardrop of blood oozed down his forehead and plopped onto a
partially dried patch of bloody grass. His vision slowly sharpened into focus.
For now, it seemed best to assume the notifications meant something. He
needed to head to a Safe Zone.

Having a single Health did not sound positive.

Trying his best not to panic or move too quickly, fearing vertiginous
repercussions, Randidly stood. Thick grass surrounded him. And only a few
meters away, tall ferns spread their leafy greenery. Beyond the ferns was
more grass, and beyond that—

Those trees look tropical. Randidly's mouth twitched. *Why the hell am I
in a jungle! What sort of engineering student belongs in a jungle?*

Randidly forced himself to turn away. Maybe he was hallucinating due to the concussion. He decided to take one step at a time, searching for the arrows referenced by the blue notification.

He saw grass and blood. Little else.

Randidly blinked several times, coming to a realization. The pool of blood was likely covering the arrow. He took several steps away from the site of his accident and a blinking red arrow on the ground revealed itself. It pointed backward, between his legs. Randidly turned around and looked up.

A faint glowing blue door in the stone wall of the underground tunnel stood directly above the pool of blood. Ironically, he cracked his head open on the door of the Safe Zone. Feeling slightly foolish, Randidly went into the room.

You have entered a Safe Zone! +200% to regeneration.

Randidly found himself in a rather large room with a pond and a small tree. Electric lights glared down from the ceiling. An uncomfortable sense of how strange this situation was struck him. Randidly had been walking home in the underground pathway on the Rawlands University campus. But this was definitely not anything close to that.

How could he possibly believe this was natural? Honestly, though, this room was about half the size of a football field and the area ended in stone walls. How did that tree get enough sunlight to grow?

Randidly was 90% certain this had been a maintenance room five minutes ago.

He rubbed his head and realized he didn't know how long he'd been sprawled unconscious in front of the Safe Room door. Sighing, Randidly sat down and brought up his Status Screen, waiting for his Health to regenerate.

In less than an hour, Randidly's Health rose from 5 to his max of 28. Inexplicably feeling quite a bit better with full Health, he decided to take a peek outside.

After carefully opening the door, Randidly scanned both directions. The wall looked relatively normal. Beyond that, some sort of underground jungle dominated what used to be a tunnel. Thick foliage from the ferns blocked most everything from his vision, except for a few tall trunks of tropical trees peeking through the gaps. The only clearing was the grassy area along the tunnel wall, which extended quite a long way on either side.

Randidly glanced back to the strange tree and pool of water. He decisively closed the door behind him. *I don't belong here either.*

There were no other discernible landmarks in the sea of shifting ferns and trees. Randidly kept to the wall, following the trail of grass along the fern buffer at the edge of the jungle, hoping to find the staircase up into his dorm at the other end. The fingers of his right hand trailed across the cement wall, taking comfort in the familiar texture of man-made, instant stone.

Twenty minutes later, Randidly sprinted back toward the Safe Room. His goal of escape had quickly given way to the simple desire to survive. His legs trembled as he forced himself to keep going. *It's funny how quickly you learn your place in the world when you have good teachers.*

His "teachers," two Level 24 Howler Monkeys, chased him with malicious intent. Bone-chilling howls, drooling mouths filled with sharp teeth, and bloodshot eyes left Randidly with little doubt how they intended to end their "lesson."

Randidly flung open the door and slammed it closed behind him, cutting off the nerve-racking noise of the monkeys' screeches. He bent over and vomited the contents of his stomach. Randidly blinked several times and tried to categorize the discoveries on his expedition.

One, this underground jungle area was incredibly large and not nearly as uninhabited as he thought.

Two, Randidly's Level of N/A was far from sufficient for fighting Level 24 enemies. Not that he tried. The way those bloodthirsty monkeys crossed the initial distance through the trees without him noticing spoke to their capability.

Luck had been with Randidly. Once the monkeys dropped from the tree, their speed plummeted to just slightly higher than his own, allowing him to escape by the skin of his teeth.

Third, the System also came with Skills. While fleeing certain death, Randidly learned the Running Skill and Leveled it to 3 during his mad dash to safety. With every increased Level, the System notifications informed him he'd earned a PP.

Randidly released a shaking breath and wiped the remnants of his vomit from his lips. Even with the Skill, his flight had been a close thing. By the time he made it back to the Safe Room, his Stamina depleted to 1. The thought of continuing to move for even a second longer made his vision go dark.

Randidly collapsed forward in the pond's direction, his low Stamina leaving him with no choice but to crawl the rest of the way. After slurping down water and catching his breath, Randidly opened his menu.

There were four options: Map, Status, Paths, and Friends List.

Both Maps and Friends List were greyed out. Randidly already knew what Status was, so he clicked on Paths.

A new menu displayed four Paths, each with numbers next to them, from which he could choose. Newbie Path was currently 0/7, while P. Def and M. Supp were 0/10. Risk Taker was 0/15. In the top right, there was PP: 2. *PP must stand for Path Points or something*, he thought.

After a slight hesitation, Randidly clicked on the Newbie Path, its numbers switching to 1/7.

Congratulations! For spending one PP on the **"Newbie Path,"** you have earned **1 Stat point(s)**.

Sure enough, when Randidly switched over to his Status, there was a plus sign next to all of his Stats. The interface seemed rather simple, if not for the sheer number of Stats from which to choose. Too many, in fact. Randidly looked at all twelve options in turn. They *could* be self-explanatory, but he could find no real information available regarding how they'd improve. He would have to learn through trial and error.

A frigid hand stretched its fingers around his heart.

If my Health wouldn't have stopped at just 1, would I have died, bleeding out in front of the Safe Room door?

Shaking his head, Randidly pushed that thought to the side. No use worrying over it now. Instead, he considered what to do with the Stat point. He was torn between something defensive like Vit or End, and something more active like Agi, which would let him run faster.

Struck by an idea, he went back to the Path screen and clicked on Newbie.

Congratulations! For spending one PP on the **"Newbie Path,"** you have earned **1 Stat point(s)**.

Now with 2, he put one of the Stat points into Vit and the other into Agi with a clear conscience. Randidly noticed his Health went up by 2 when he put the point into Vit, while his Health regen per hour went up by 3. Stamina regen increased by 1 per minute. Which, he supposed, was pretty small in the grand scheme of things.

His eyes went to the Safe Room door and he frowned. *I don't know how I ended up here, but I won't let this strange jungle be my grave.*

CHAPTER TWO

$\mathcal{S}$urvival became the central pillar of Randidly's behavior. He knew nothing about living in a jungle, but he understood video and tabletop games. Given the obvious method of growing more powerful through Skill Levels and PP, he laid out a bare bones schedule for himself.

Per that plan, Randidly began to jog, and was soon rewarded with a delightful notification.

Congratulations! You have learned the Skill **Physical Fitness Level 1**.

Will I just steadily accrue Skills by taking various actions? Randidly grinned. *That means the speed at which I'll gather PP will steadily increase.* He paused to scoop up a palmful of water to drink and returned to the grind.

Randidly quickly stumbled upon a problem. His schedule called for him to happily grind up his Skills while staying in the Safe Room for as long as possible, increasing his capability Stat by Stat. He started out quite well, jumping up to Level 4 in Running and Level 2 in Physical Fitness. He'd also gotten a more hands-on understanding of his Stamina, which had a powerful effect on his ability to move effectively.

But he was getting hungry. He stopped his exercise, a light sweat coating his body from the constant exertion.

Randidly sat down next to the pool and drank a few more palmfuls of water. He looked at his frowning reflection. The hunger had taken up residence in his stomach and was here to stay. It'd only been three hours since his first arrival in this Safe Zone, but already circumstance was prying him away from sanctuary.

Gritting his teeth, Randidly pressed his eyes shut and faced the truth. He knew where to find food. While he was lackadaisically walking through the jungle earlier, he'd spotted strange fruits and berries.

But going out there…

The twisted, drool-flinging faces of the Howler Monkeys flashed in Randidly's vision. Just as aggressively, his stomach rumbled. After much thought, Randidly put two more points for Levels into the Newbie Path, and added both of those free Stat points into Agi. His plan was to go in and get out as fast as possible.

Randidly experimentally hopped side to side while still inside the Safe Zone. He was pleased to find he felt a little quicker on his feet. With that extra bit of confidence, he approached the Safe Room door and opened it. The indoor rainforest swayed softly, almost invitingly, and Randidly shivered. He forced himself to creep out and tiptoe toward the tree line.

The forest rustled fitfully. As Randidly snuck through the open space toward the line of ferns, screeching calls wailed in the distance. Even more ominous, the immediate surroundings were completely silent and still. After staring at the ferns for some time, nothing changed. His stomach growled, prompting him to press on.

Several times, Randidly's instincts slowed his pace. Now sweating profusely, Randidly took several more steps and eased himself into the leafy greenery.

Once he was within the ferns, it was easier to see what they concealed. He took several careful steps around the feathery stalks to press up against the few trees at the edge of the rainforest.

Randidly hesitated, his hand against the rough-barked tree trunk. With his current position, the ferns still screened him from any watchers. His eyes rested for a few seconds on the open space beneath the trees, similar to the places where Randidly had seen berry bushes, further down the tree line. The problem was that this portion was empty.

Nothing moved. Yet further out among the trees, the rustling continued, like the constant noise of waves lapping against the shore. The longer he remained here, the more nervous he was becoming. He wiped the sweat from his brow.

When he closed his eyes, the snarling faces of those monkeys chasing him returned. He blinked those images away and refocused on his current situation.

Randidly could continue to move in the fern area, trying his best to remain quiet or step out into the small clearing, and dash in the direction he previously noticed fruits. When he found them, he would gather as many as he could carry and high-tail it back to the Safe Zone.

Because he couldn't quite remember how far away the berry bushes were, Randidly ultimately chose the conservative sneaking route. He slipped into a crouch and wove his way through the drooping ferns.

As he proceeded deeper amongst the shrubbery, Randidly learned Sneak Level 1. Although the first Level of a Skill didn't give a Path Point, it still boosted his confidence that he might be able to pull this off. Every careful movement would sharpen his capability, ensuring he'd be improving constantly.

The thought of continuing to grow made Randidly wonder what would happen when he finally *finished* the Newbie Path.

He wound his way forward, pressing aside the ferns and occasionally pausing to peek through the trees. He grew more certain with his foot placement the further he went. After moving for some time, Randidly glanced around a particularly thick trunk, scanning for any monkey threats. No animals, no movement. Randidly did spot a bush heavy with dark purple berries ten yards down near the edge of the tree line.

He crept in that direction, his breath extremely heavy in his ears. When he reached the berries, he wiped his sweaty hands on his pants. Should he eat a couple before trying to carry them away?

Randidly's stomach rumbled, settling the issue. The walk here made him hungrier. And that certainty from his stomach made the corner of Randidly's mouth quirk upward. *If these are poisonous, I'm so screwed.*

Well, first things first. Randidly eased himself out, glanced left and right, then scampered to the bush. He tentatively bit into a berry, which was a little bit larger than a grape. Sweetness filled his mouth, laced in a crisp taste that reminded him of strawberries. He spit out some seeds, pleased to find these were good for eating. Satisfied, he pulled up his shirt and filled it like a pouch.

When Randidly turned around, pouch full, he noticed he was being watched.

A lime green frog about as big as a small dog sat motionless on a low tree branch, gazing at him. Randidly might have already walked beneath it without noticing its presence. Above the frog hovered the label Level 27.

Randidly backed slowly away. Even if he had to take a different route back to the Safe Zone, he didn't want to chance being chased again. The frog watched him sidle sideways into the shrubbery layer, tilting its head. Receiving a notification that his Sneak Skill was now Level 2, Randidly turned and ran back through the ferns into the Safe Zone.

He sat on the ground and focused on his breathing, waiting for his pounding heart to slow. He ate about half of his gathered berries, spitting the seeds into the dirt by the small tree.

After eating, he collapsed onto his back and looked up at the stone ceiling. The fluorescent electric lights of this service-room must have been transformed when the rainforest took up residence. The light they produced felt a lot like warm sunlight on his skin.

Sitting up, Randidly went to his Path Screen and put the point he earned for Sneak Level 2 into the Newbie Path, getting a free Stat. He checked his Status screen immediately, and added the extra point to End, resulting in an additional 5 points of Health and 3 of Stamina, but only .25 Health regen and no Stamina regen. End was more base while Vit focused on regeneration?

If he had to choose between them, Randidly supposed he would probably prefer to buffer up his Endurance, for now. Increasing the maximum value of his Health and especially Stamina was more important than anything else.

But really, how useful is 5 Health going to be against a Level 27 Frog? Randidly reflected as he squeezed his eyes shut.

Lying back, Randidly did his best to fall asleep, half hoping this was all a dream, while the other half looked forward to tomorrow being filled with even more grinding. This was far from what he wanted when he said he didn't belong in his stressful engineering major at Rawlands University.

Even now, his own heartbeat felt strange in his chest. The Safe Zone helped, but his neck prickled with the sense of his own vulnerability. At the same time, there was something about this RPG setup he appreciated, even with the lurking presence of danger.

The simplicity, the systems, the Stats.

He hoped there would be a secret way of playing that allowed him to break this fucked-up game.

In life, there were no true short-cuts. Or at least no hidden methods that didn't leave you feeling slimy. The path to true self-improvement was murky and filled with dead ends. There was never any guarantee that effort would be rewarded.

But here, with the Skill Levels, although his heart was pounding…

Randidly felt anticipation.

CHAPTER THREE

*C*hen Randidly awoke from his fitful nap, unexpected blue notifications greeted him. He also didn't miss the way the lights above flickered on when he opened his eyes, as if they immediately shut off when he fell asleep. Shaking his head at the strange environment, he inspected the notifications.

His smile was one of pure elation.

Overnight, Randidly reached Level 3 in Farming. He was stunned to find several sprouts coming up out of the spot where he discarded the hard seeds from the berries. Excited, he got up and went over to inspect the growths. Although they didn't seem like much, if they started producing berries inside the Safe Zone…

Randidly shook his head. Though it might be safe, he didn't plan on remaining here forever. Not when he wanted to understand the limits of the System in which he found himself. In fact, the twenty-year-old Randidly knew that staying in the room and grinding would become a chore after a while. Still, Farming was a useful way to decrease the danger in the short term, allowing him to gather sufficient strength before venturing out.

"I wonder how Ace and Sydney are doing," Randidly muttered, his eyes going unfocused as he uneasily considered his two closest friends encountering the dangers with which he now wrestled.

He snapped back to the moment at hand, opening his Path screen and putting the final two points into the Newbie Path.

Congratulations! For spending one PP on the **"Newbie Path,"** you have earned **1 Stat point(s)**.

Congratulations! For spending one PP on the **"Newbie Path,"** you have earned **2 Stat point(s)**.

Congratulations! You have completed the **"Newbie Path"**! +1 to all Stats, **+1 Stat point per Level, +4 Health per Level, +2 Mana and +2 Stamina per Level.** You have learned the active Skills **Mana Bolt Level 1** and **Heavy Blow Level 1**!

Continue using Paths to explore this world! Remember, there will always be a path open to you. Rise and spread your Legend throughout the Nexus!

Randidly laughed. *It seems like completing a Path certainly earns a lot of rewards. The single Stats to get there were just breadcrumbs to lead me along.*

His eyes immediately went to the two new Skills. The +1 to all Stats was a holistic improvement, but the two Skills were the biggest gains. After all, how did he finish this Path? By accumulating PP by earning Skill Levels!

Randidly frowned when he read the middle of the notification. *The real problem is that a lot of these relate to Level-up gains, and my Level is still N/A.*

Did he miss something, or some option to earn a Class?

Randidly did a once-through on his menus, finding nothing that would allow him to select some milquetoast archetype like "Ranger" or "Priest." Considering how he was just rewarded with two Skills for completing a Path, such Classes would likely come along with relevant Skills of their own, making growth that much easier.

Grimacing, Randidly increased the volume of the small voice at the back of his head, born from his past experience playing games. If this strange new change that came to the world functioned like a typical game, there was likely a Newbie Area. Ignoring the jungle surroundings, the mid-20 Levels of the monsters Randidly encountered practically proved this was not a Newbie Area.

At this point, Randidly was primarily speculating. Perhaps this was a result of him being underground. He'd proceeded to the Dungeon Safe Zone, meaning he was in a Dungeon. He was just in the wrong place at the wrong time and missed the opportunity to earn a valuable Class.

Randidly focused on the spot where there was a series of lines instead of Class. He bit his lip. Typically, a Class was the most powerful weapon in a character's arsenal. Without that, his capability to grow and escape this Dungeon...

Compared to the +1 to all Stats he received for finishing the Path, how many Stats would he get from Leveling up a Class?

The contorted snarl of the monkeys flashed within his mind. Subconsciously, Randidly lowered his head and clenched his fist. The memories of waking up with only a single Health remaining were still strong. He admitted to himself his body had clearly informed him that losing that last Health would have been disastrous.

Randidly shook his head. He knew himself well enough to stop this downward spiral before it gathered too much momentum. *No need to worry about those things for now. I'm not improving as quickly as I can with a Class, but I'm improving, and that's enough. I have three more Stat points to put wherever I like and then two new Skills to learn how to use.*

Aside from the PP I'll earn, I suspect increasing the Skill Level boosts its effect somewhat. That's how Levels work. So if I get the Level of my Skills up to around Level 20 or 30, won't I be able to rival the monkeys?

Don't obsess over things you can't control. You've got this, Randidly Ghosthound.

Following his little pep talk, Randidly decided he was quite famished. After eating the other half of yesterday's harvest of berries, he closely examined his Status screen. He settled on putting 1 point into End, 1 point into Agi, and deciding to take a gamble, another point into Per.

Increased Perception would hopefully allow him to spot approaching enemies like the frog earlier. If it hadn't been willing to let him peacefully pass from its perch on that branch…

Randidly shivered.

After distributing his points, Randidly studied his Status.

Randidly Ghosthound
Class: ---
Level: N/A
Health(/R per hour): 47/47 (23.25)
Mana(/R per hour): 19/19 (8)
Stam(/R per min): 25/25 (11)
Vit: 6
End: 5
Str: 3
Agi: 8
Perception: 4
Reaction: 5
Resistance: 5
Willpower: 5
Intelligence: 4
Wisdom: 2
Control: 2
Focus: 3

Paths: *Newbie 7/7 | P. Def | M. Supp | Risk Taker*

Skills: *Running Lvl 4 | Physical Fitness Lvl 2 | Sneak Lvl 2 | Farming Lvl 3 | Mana Bolt Lvl 1 | Heavy Blow Lvl 1*

Putting several points into End improved both his Health and Stamina, which was important. Survivability was ultimately Randidly's main goal, but he was learning Stamina might actually be more important. If he collapsed from exhaustion while fleeing from a monster, Randidly doubted the amount of Health he possessed would be enough to survive.

Randidly squeezed his eyes shut and forcefully altered his thoughts to be more optimistic. He should not dwell on the image of a monkey ripping open his ribcage and rummaging through his organs. Doing so would only hinder him.

Randidly turned his attention to his two newly learned Skills. However, unlike the other Skills Randidly earned, these seemed like active Skills, only he had no idea how to activate them. Feeling slightly foolish, Randidly muttered, "Mana Bolt."

A screen popped up in front of him.

Mana Bolt: *Focusing your energy, you fire a bolt of pure Mana at your enemies.* **Costs 10 Mana. Damage based on Intelligence and Level of Skill. Damage, impact, range, projectile speed, and casting speed increase with Skill Level.**

Pleased at such an informative notification, he tried, "Heavy Blow."

Heavy Blow: *Concentrate your muscular force into one powerful attack. Will leave you slightly off balance.* **Costs 5 Stamina. Damage based on Str and Level of Skill. Damage, speed of attack, and accuracy increases with Skill Level. Recoil decreases with Skill Level.**

At least this is proof improving the Skill Level will directly benefit its power. Randidly forced himself to smile and rolled his shoulders. *Alright, let's get this show on the road.*

He spoke the rest of his Skills out loud, but nothing happened. Apparently, the helpful notification only popped up when he named an active Skill. Experimentally, Randidly raised his hand and pointed, focusing on his finger. He concentrated as hard as he could, scrunching up his forehead and squeezing his buttocks.

His hand began to tremble.

Nothing happened.

Feeling silly, Randidly concentrated again and tried adding a vocal component. "Mana Bolt."

Something *inside* of Randidly moved. A strange force he hadn't been aware of until this moment and one that he was *immediately* sure had not been inside of him before yesterday. This power boiled within his body, making his hair stand on end. Randidly couldn't help but look down below his stomach, where the feeling originated.

When the pressure built to a certain point, it exploded down his arm and blue energy condensed on his finger. It formed a gleaming sapphire marble and shot forward, or rather, downward, where his arm hung because of the distracting feeling of the Skill activating.

The ejected Mana Bolt struck him in the foot. And it fucking *hurt*.

Yelping and hopping, Randidly glared at the hole in his shoe, chiding himself for his idiocy. This was *exactly* why he needed to practice in a Safe Zone before letting his meager growth fill him with confidence. He checked his Status. His own Mana Bolt had done 5 damage to him.

At the base, the damage really is just Intelligence plus Skill Level, huh? At least that makes it easy to calculate. But how much Health does a Level 24 Howler Monkey possess?

Randidly wanted to try again. Due to his maximum Mana only being 19 and the Mana Bolt consumed 10 Mana, he would need to wait a bit. And with a Mana regeneration of 8, tripled to 24 inside the Safe Room, refilling his Mana would take a depressingly long time.

He made a mental note to figure out what the Wis and Int Stats did for his overall Stats. For now, Randidly turned his attention to his other new Skill, which utilized the much-quicker-to-return Stamina, Heavy Blow. Because the rate of Stamina regeneration was set to the unit of a minute rather than an hour, this seemed much easier to grind.

Feeling like he was in a martial arts movie, Randidly stood in front of the small tree in the room. He was increasingly aware at that moment of how he'd never done any sort of martial arts. But he bent his knees and lowered himself into a very uncomfortable half-squat. His legs trembled in preparation to strike.

His fist shot forward and impacted the bark. The tree shook slightly and Randidly winced.

Although not close to his full, desperate strength, Randidly punched like he meant it. His current situation ensured half-assing his preparations would result in feeding the constant low buzz of panic growing within him.

Randidly looked solemnly at his knuckles. Surprisingly, the uncomfortable throb in his hand wiped away the anxiety and completely cleared his mind. His worries and tensions were gone.

What remained was a dull ache, but even that began to fade. Randidly flexed his hand without any discomfort. Perhaps this was his Stats of Vit and End paying dividends.

When Randidly looked back at the tree, his expression changed. Doing something once made the second attempt that much easier. He once more settled into his best approximation of a martial arts stance and glared at his stationary opponent. He pictured the vicious face of the Howler Monkey.

His hand exploded forward and he half-shouted the Skill name. "Heavy Blow!"

Another new force moved within Randidly Ghosthound, this time originating from his heart. And where the other was cool, this was hot and demanding, filling his fist with heat that consumed everything but the pure mechanics of the motion. When this empowered punch reached the tree, the entire plant shuddered from the force.

There was a strained moment when Randidly felt oddly powerless, but the recoil was quick to pass. What remained were cleansing waves of pain radiating up from his knuckles, clearing his mind.

As he shook his head, Randidly's thoughts turned rather wry. *Why am I disappointed by this much? Even with the vulnerability afterward, the power is probably double what I managed before. And this is with a Skill Level of 1 and a Strength of 3. The more free Stats I get, the more Paths I complete, the more I'll improve. It's only a matter of time before I'm not just punching that monkey in my imagination.*

Randidly rid himself of the budding excitement. Positive spirals were better for his mental health, but they were just as ultimately fruitless. He forced his mind to turn toward setting a tentative schedule for himself.

He was in a venue where his death and his life were separated only by a single point of Health. He needed to stay focused. His stubborn streak emerged in the space cleaned by the pain from his knuckles, settling down in his chest and making itself comfortable. He refused to curl up and die. If he needed to push himself beyond his comfort zone to make that happen, so be it.

Hidden away in this corner of the Dungeon, Randidly Ghosthound would improve one Skill Level at a time until he could thrive in this new, gamified world.

CHAPTER FOUR

*T*he next few hours tested his commitment to his training regimen, but Randidly continued to push himself. He ran around next to the walls, keeping his pace above what was comfortable until his chest heaved unsteadily, forcing him to stop due to lack of Stamina. In between jogs, Randidly cast his mind back and did his best to remember a haphazard mixture of push-ups, squats, and pull-ups underneath the shady auspices of the Safe Zone's tree. Most were things he'd seen Ace do, which gave his heart another squeeze of anxiety.

How would his friends fare in the gamified world? The question floated back to the surface of his mind. Randidly gripped a branch and swung unsteadily back and forth, bringing his chin up to touch the bark. Ace was the type to roll with the punches and adapt quickly. Sydney on the other hand…

Finishing his tenth pull-up, Randidly let himself drop. *She might not know video games like I do, but she's strong. That's why I followed—*

Randidly grimaced. His history with Sydney was the least of his worries right now. She was dating Ace. The three of them were best friends. And that was that.

When his Mana unsteadily climbed back to 10, Randidly would walk around the pond and shoot a Mana Bolt toward the tree. Though the aiming was rather intuitive, Randidly kept missing the trunk by just a small amount. He mostly lay the blame for this at the feet of his Mana. If he could have a few shots in succession, he was sure he could home in on his target.

After carrying out his training schedule, Randidly gratefully collapsed. He'd improved his Physical Fitness to Level 3, his Running to 5, and both Mana Bolt and Heavy Blow to 2.

Surprisingly, though, Mana Bolt reached the next Level after only two uses. Heavy Blow took five. Perhaps the lower cost of Heavy Blow meant it took more to Level it. Unfortunately, Randidly's experience with Running and Physical Fitness meant the next few Levels would not be as easy as the first one was.

Reaching Level 20 in a Skill seemed very, very far away.

With a fist full of PP, Randidly opened his Path screen and considered his options. In the Path screen itself, the abbreviations were expanded for the Path names.

Physical Defense *0/??* | **Mental Support** *0/??* | **Risk Taker** *0/??*

Considering his stated goal of surviving, Randidly started down the P. Def Path. His *odd* points, the first and third, net him free P. Def Stats that could only be used on Vit and End. That suited Randidly just fine. Meanwhile, the *even* PP he added to the Path earned him regular free Stat points.

Randidly put one in each of Vit and End with the P. Def distributable points. With the totally free Stats, he put one in Int and one in Wis. Randidly scanned his Status screen, calculating the effects. Intelligence increased maximum Mana by 2 and Mana regen by .25. Wis increased maximum Mana by .5 and regen by 1.

Finally, 20 Mana. Randidly couldn't help but release a sigh of relief. Hopefully, the Mana Bolt target practice would go a bit smoother now.

However, his examination of his Status screen did stir other thoughts. Based on the abbreviations of Defense and Support Randidly had seen in his Paths, he suspected that a group of four of his twelves Stats would be considered "Offense."

Randidly wondered if part of the reason for his struggles to hit his target with Mana Bolts was due to a lack in the M. Supp category, specifically his Focus and Control.

However, he couldn't ponder forever. Randidly pushed himself up into a sitting position and focused on the base of the tree. The green sprouts were definitely growing, but they weren't growing quickly enough.

His stomach rumbled, reminding him he was out of berries.

After releasing a long breath and rubbing his knuckles against the tree bark for good luck, Randidly once more left the Safe Zone. He flickered across the bare grassy space. Once amongst the ferns, he calmed down, narrowing his emerald eyes. He ignored his rising pulse and crept forward through the shrubbery. Even if his heartbeat was erratic, his steps were firm and determined. He followed the edge of the tree line to where he previously located the berries. When he paused and peered around the tree trunk toward the berry bush he sought, Randidly was stunned to find it had been picked clean.

Nervous, Randidly's gaze slid upward to a familiar tree branch. Sure enough, the lime green frog was still there, looking quite a bit fatter than it had the day before. In addition, the frog had spun on its perch so it could watch Randidly's approach, rather than focus on the bush. Its unblinking eyes fixated on him.

For a second, Randidly froze, and he had to force his mind to whirr into motion. *Shit... well, I can circle around the frog and continue down the tree line. I definitely saw more than just a single bush—*

Burp.

The green creature shifted its slightly inflated body into a more comfortable position, its eyes grotesquely bulging. Despite his pounding heart, Randidly couldn't resist glaring in return. Forgetting about his plan of remaining relatively calm in the face of danger, he let the icy feeling of Mana flood through his veins. Raising his hand, he channeled Mana into his palm, preparing a Mana Bolt.

The cold energy gathered slowly. Randidly blinked in shock. He'd initiated the Skill non-verbally. The elation amplified when Randidly recognized the casting time had slightly decreased and would likely continue to shorten in the future due to increased Skill Level.

Given the current casting time, Randidly still had to wait for Mana to build in his palm, a long enough time for him to realize he was making a mistake. By initiating Mana Bolt, he'd antagonize this frog. Just as the realization seized him, the Mana Bolt shot forward.

Of course, this Mana Bolt spurred on by passion was the most accurate one Randidly unleashed to date. The projectile glided smoothly until it slammed into one of the frog's bulging sides. Almost immediately, the frog's eyes went wide, engaged in an internal struggle as it glared toward Randidly.

Randidly licked his lips, similarly torn between remaining still and bolting.

After a few seconds, the frog opened its mouth and vomited a cascade of half-digested berries and yellow goop that splashed on the tree next to Randidly. He jerked to the side, avoiding the secondary splash of bile.

A strategic retreat was in order. As Randidly turned to flee, the frog's eyes began to glow an ominous red.

Randidly took a step into the ferns and his hand spasmed. His gaze flicked downward to his palm. He hadn't escaped unscathed. Several small drops of the vomit were smeared on his hand. A loud sizzling caught his attention. His instincts betrayed him, making him glance behind to find the source of the noise. The unfortunate tree casualty was being eaten away before his very eyes, dissolved by the regurgitated yellow goo. The tree cracked, collapsing sideways while the remainder of the trunk steadily disintegrated.

Randidly's hand began to *burn*.

He put all of his vigor toward flight. His effort in sprinting back toward the Safe Room was so all-consuming that even the System recognized it. He earned himself another Level in Running. Ferns slapped his face and ripped at his shins. He barely even attempted to avoid the flora. Sweat ran down his face and forced him to blink several times to keep his vision clear.

The next notification he received during his flight made Randidly misstep and stumble.

Congratulations! You have learned the Skill **Acid Resistance Level 1.**

A splash only a short distance behind him, as if the frog spat again, urged Randidly to lower his head and push himself to go faster. That fiery energy originating in his heart spun out through his legs, making his muscles buzz with intensity.

Congratulations! You have learned the active Skill **Sprinting Level 1.**

Congratulations! Your Skill **Acid Resistance** has grown to **Level 2!**

Unlike the pain from punching the tree, the horrible burning on his hand struck a spark of agony as if to catch the flesh aflame. The sensation blazed up his arm and spread across his torso. Randidly's thoughts became desperate, barely able to register where he was. Abruptly, he realized he might have dashed too far.

He burst out of the ferns into the clear grassy area along the wall, wildly searching for safety. The pain drilled into his chest, making breathing difficult. He spotted the Safe Room door and dashed toward it.

Randidly didn't dare pause and examine the state of his Health.

Congratulations! Your Skill **Acid Resistance** has grown to **Level 3!**

Congratulations! Your Skill **Sprinting** has grown **to Level 2!**

Warning! Some of the acid has entered your bloodstream, causing you to be poisoned. Health will continue to decrease every five seconds.

Congratulations! You have learned the Skill **Poison Resistance Level 1.**

Randidly scrambled through the door, ignoring the continuing notifications. He was becoming distinctly dizzy. His torn shoes caught on the ground and he fell flat on his face. But his smarting nose was nothing compared to the pain of the flesh of his arm disintegrating. As he hauled himself back to his feet, his limbs trembled.

Congratulations! Your Skill **Acid Resistance** has grown to **Level 4!**

Congratulations! Your Skill **Poison Resistance** has grown to **Level 2!**

Warning! Your Health is extremely low. Due to being under Level 10, arrows will be on the ground guiding you to the nearest Safe Zone.

I'm already here, damnit! Randidly thought desperately.

Not breaking his twitching stride, Randidly transitioned from sprinting to blindly diving into the pool. Due to his worsening body control, he slapped against the water's surface before sinking into the cool liquid. On his way down, he began frantically wiping at his hand. That is, until his fingers caught in the quarter-sized hole on his melting palm between his thumb and pointer finger.

Randidly opened his mouth in pained shock, and water flooded his throat. Still, drowning was the least of his worries. His muscles and flesh were eroding. He opened his eyes to see if the wound looked as bad as it felt. The corrosion weakening the tendons of his hand was like taffy being pulled until, *snap!* The hole continued to deepen.

When his bone became visible, panic joined the water to strangle him. He was going to die today.

But just as his anxiety began to build up momentum, his stubbornness constricted his mind and squeezed out the distracting thoughts. Pain became the sharp prod to move himself forward. Randidly snapped back to focus. *I will survive. But I need to know how bad this is first.*

He first gulped down a mouthful of water and pressed his lips tightly shut. His brow furrowing underwater, Randidly checked his Status. His Health had sunk to 10, and then it ticked down to 9, and 8. Frantically, he opened his Path screen and dumped the 6 points he'd gotten on the trip into P. Def. Before he could switch back, he noticed another notification but ignored it.

He moved back to his Status screen, pouring all 6 points into End to buoy his Health upward.

His Health rose by 30—no, it was more.

Randidly blinked. *Wait, why was it not 30, but 44? Not that I'm complaining about the extra buffer...*

Still, the trial hadn't yet passed. Randidly returned to his intense monitoring of his Health, pushing his head past the surface of the water to gulp down several breaths. The boosted number continued to tick down, but it was slowing in its descent until it stabilized at 12 Health. Randidly dragged his waterlogged body out of the pool and pressed his face against the grass. He sucked in a delicious, still living breath.

Turns out the extra 14 Health I received mattered quite a lot. He dragged himself around and slumped onto his back. Now he considered the notifications he'd previously ignored.

He located the notification that likely saved his life. Turned out he'd thrown PP so frantically into the Path, he finished it.

Congratulations! You have completed the **"P. Def Path"**! **+2 to all P. Def Stats, +1 P. Def point per Level.**

Congratulations! You have learned the Skill **Iron Skin Level 1.**

Randidly couldn't muster a smile at earning another new active Skill. The determined part of himself took over, and he began plotting new ways to train these abilities. He idly scanned the rest of the skipped notifications.

Congratulations! Your Skill **Poison Resistance** has grown to **Level 3!**

Congratulations! Your Skill **Poison Resistance** has grown to **Level 4!**

Congratulations! Your Skill **Poison Resistance** has grown to **Level 5!**

Congratulations! Your Skill **Acid Resistance** has grown to **Level 5!**

The healing pool has cleansed your body. You are no longer poisoned. Health will no longer decrease.

Sighing, Randidly lifted his head, just to drop it back against the grass-covered floor. The ghost of the pain from the acid still hung over him. That had been too close. He wasn't yet ready to antagonize any lifeform in this place. The worst part was, he had only been splashed by a tiny drop. Even so little an amount ripped a hole in his hand, eating his flesh, and eventually poisoning him.

If it wasn't for this healing pool…

Shivering, Randidly once more recognized the unassuming specter of death waiting behind him for a fatal mistake.

Yet the stubbornness taking residence in his spine refused to take this lying down. Randidly leveraged himself onto his elbow, grinning. He survived. And as such, he benefited immensely. Not only had he finished the P. Def Path, but he now had 4 more PP to spend on the next Path.

That didn't even include the new Skill, Iron Skin, and all the PP he could earn from it to push himself along other Paths. Perhaps the Skill would even give him an edge against the frog's acid vomit.

However, no matter how useful Randidly's arrogant stubbornness was in the Safe Room, he'd learned his lesson about attacking monsters. Based on how quickly his Acid Resistance Skill Leveled compared to his hours of grinding Physical Fitness, Randidly doubted withstanding a direct blow from the acid would be possible, Skill or no.

Randidly put the 4 PP into the M. Supp Path. As expected, he received two freely distributable Stats and two M. Supp Stats.

Randidly see-sawed between his options, eventually adding both to Control, hoping it would increase the accuracy of his Mana Bolt. At the very least, with the boost of two, he'd gain a better idea of Control's effects, because it hadn't changed his Health, Stamina, Mana, or Regenerations.

For the two distributable Stats, Randidly was once again torn. He already experienced a huge boost in survivability with the End increase, but he was beginning to believe the Health he was accumulating was just a drop in the bucket. A direct attack would kill him several times over, even with 10 more End.

Decision made, one point went into Agi, and one into Per. Hopefully, he would have a little bit more of an edge avoiding the vomit next time. Sighing at his still growling stomach, Randidly reviewed his Stats.

Randidly Ghosthound
Class: ---
Level: N/A
Health(/R per hour): 12/98 (34.5)
Mana(/R per hour): 12/22 (9.25)
Stam(/R per min): 5/52 (14)
Vit: 9
End: 14
Str: 3
Agi: 9
Perception: 5
Reaction: 5
Resistance: 5
Willpower: 5
Intelligence: 5
Wisdom: 3
Control: 4
Focus: 3
Paths: *Newbie 7/7 | P. Def 10/10 | M. Supp 4/10 | Risk Taker*

Skills: *Running Lvl 6 | Physical Fitness Lvl 3 | Sneak Lvl 2 | Farming Lvl 3 | Mana Bolt Lvl 2 | Heavy Blow Lvl 2 | Acid Resistance Lvl 5 | Poison Resistance Lvl 5 | Sprinting Lvl 2 | Iron Skin Lvl 1*

"Too close…" he muttered, shifting himself into a sitting position. For now, he ignored his hunger. His life was much more important than going without a meal for a few hours. Logically, he understood the human body could survive a day or two without food, so long as he had plentiful water.

Plus, Randidly was tired. He needed to rest and steady his nerves before he returned to the outside world.

Randidly pressed his eyes shut and felt the strange automatic lights switch off as he did so. *One thing at a time. First, I need to recover. I can think about the rest later.*

CHAPTER FIVE

*R*andidly didn't truly sleep this time. His consciousness spiraled inside of himself, observing the pools of fiery Stamina and chilling Mana accumulate. Then he released a breath and opened his eyes. It took an hour and a half for all his Attributes to regenerate back to full, even with the bonuses of the room. It made Randidly more aware of the different uses of End and Vit. More Stamina regeneration would increase the efficiency of his training. He resolved to put a few more points into Vit when he had the chance.

Yet that thought made Randidly grimace.

He reached to touch his toes, stretching his stiff legs. Back at the pool, not a hint of his blood or the poison remained. He drank to quench his thirst, wondering if some kind of magic kept the Safe Room clean. He simply didn't have enough Stat points to assuage his worries. He needed to get his Agi and Per even higher.

And without more points in Int, he wouldn't have enough Mana to cast his Skills.

Five more Int would get him enough for another Mana Bolt, plus the increase in Intelligence would double the original value of its damage.

Which might not matter now, but these advantages accumulated.

Randidly slapped his stomach to quiet the needy organ and began to experiment with his newly acquired Skill.

Iron Skin: *Concentrate on your skin to temporarily increase your resistance to most forms of damage.* **Higher proficiency in utilization allows the user to more quickly activate the Skill and localize the application. Costs 10 Stamina per second. Defensive boost based on Level of the Skill.**

The cost meant it was more of a one-time use in battle, rather than a constant buff. Although, the quickness of his Stamina recovery meant Randidly could keep it on for six seconds, wait two minutes for his Stamina to recharge, and do it again.

Through the rough method of slamming his Iron Skin palms against the cinderblock walls of the Safe Zone, Randidly pushed Iron Skin to Level 3. This, in turn, gave him PP for his Paths, which earned him another point in Control and one in Perception. The cycle of rewards was honestly slightly addicting. There was no confusion or ambiguous responses from the System. You earned PP, completed Paths, then earned more Skills to grind.

Even working on an empty stomach, alone in the basement Dungeon, the prickle of satisfaction filled him.

Plus, this room was designed to be an area that allowed one to grind Stamina Skills efficiently. The regeneration tripling made Stamina fill up within minutes.

But Randidly's gaze turned heavy when he examined the sprouts from the berry seeds. The bushes were definitely growing much faster than was natural. Just not fast enough. By the time the berries would fatten on the branch, his days of fasting will have weakened him. He was honestly surprised he hadn't begun feeling twinges of weakness already, especially after the energy his body must have spent to recover from the acid.

Which brought him once again to the crossroad. He wasn't satisfied with his ability to survive, but he needed to risk it and leave the Safe Room anyway.

When his hand gripped the doorknob, it trembled, and Randidly closed his eyes. *I can do this. I've done it before. And even if things go badly... I've survived that too.*

With this small reinforcement, Randidly's eyes snapped open and he forced himself to smile. "I'm not just Randidly, I'm also the Ghosthound. And I will make these damn frogs pay."

Much, much later, obviously. From a distance, Randidly added inwardly. And with that, he pushed his way out into the underground Dungeon.

Every repetition of this dangerous emergence made him a step faster with a surer foot. He moved smoothly across the grassy space and slid amongst the ferns with only minimal sounds. With his guard raised by his previous expedition, Randidly eased himself up against the nearest tree trunk in the fern layer and scanned the surroundings.

Much to his surprise, he immediately saw frogs, although they didn't see him. Instinctively, Randidly stiffened. Not only was the source of his previous suffering present, there were at least a dozen more frogs releasing low croaks and hopping from branch to branch deeper amongst the trees.

Their eyes were damned near determined. It seemed as though... as though they were searching for something. Beads of sweat trickled down his back. A small breeze set the tree canopies to rustling, bringing with it another shudder-inducing gust of fear through Randidly. He quickly smothered it. He'd shot a Mana Bolt at one frog, but that attack hadn't even hurt it. At most, it had been annoyed. This frog army likely wasn't looking for him.

More persuasively, the frogs kept looking nervously toward the deeper parts of the forest. They weren't paying the shrubbery layer any mind.

Calming himself, Randidly crept away under the cover of the ferns until he could no longer see or hear their movements. His efforts even earned him another Level in Sneak, raising it to Level 3.

The ferns fluttered imperceptibly around Randidly as he moved. After creeping some distance, Randidly poked his head past a tree trunk and scanned back and forth. The berry bush that had been stripped of its precious fruit was in clear view.

If he continued to follow the peripheral layer, he would reach the dominion of the Howler Monkeys. Just like the frogs, those monsters were outside his ability to handle. When he craned his neck and scanned the area around the bare bush, Randidly was glad he invested a few of his spare points into Perception. Beyond the berry bush were a few trees with their branches heavy with small, dark spheres.

God, I hope those are fruit or nuts. Randidly's gaze sharpened. He carefully scanned the surrounding trees. The lower branches were blessedly free of frogs. Whatever the frogs were searching for pulled them away from this area. It was an opportunity.

I'm ready for this, Randidly told himself. *If they come back, I have the Sprint active. I can escape. And right now, I need food.*

He breathed in and out several times.

He silently stepped out of the ferns and took long strides toward a tall, slender tree about eight meters beyond the forlorn berry bush. Randidly's eyes brightened. The ground around that tree was littered with what appeared to be tan walnuts. He spared another glance through the shifting trees around him and picked up one of the nuts. His fingers squeezed the hard shell.

He pressed his lips together. If he failed to bring back food, he would be in an even worse position than he started. Randidly took the chance. He knocked his prize against the tree until it cracked and inspected the insides. Seemed like a nut.

He crouched beside the tree, listening for any signs that his noises were detected while he pried the rest of the nut apart and brought the core to his lips.

He nibbled it and was delighted to discover a savory, almost smoky flavor. He quickly cracked open several others, taking the edge off his hunger. Between each, he waited at least a minute, focused on the low hanging branches to spot any pudgy frogs. To his relief, no monster noticed the noise. Satisfied, Randidly prepared to gather more in his shirt to take back, when he caught a whiff of rotting flesh.

The smell was immediate and suffocating, filling both of his nostrils with the horrid scent of death. Instincts he didn't know he had drove him to press his body tight against the tree trunk and sniffed again, despite the newly arrived nuts in his stomach considering vacating their new home.

Moving carefully, he looked through the intersecting leafy branches in front of him. They revealed a small clearing he hadn't noticed earlier, about ten more meters into the jungle through the dense vegetation. Randidly's eyes locked on to a series of objects that appeared to be glowing red rubies hanging in the tree.

Randidly licked his lips and checked the surroundings for threats. He didn't find Howler Monkeys or frogs, or any other dangerous animal with a Level. He focused next on the ground. A long, scaly green body lay still in the clearing.

The source of the smell?

Following the firm impulse of his gut, Randidly pushed his way carefully through the complex maze of dense underbrush. Despite the threat of death, Randidly's intuition was sure this would be worth it to investigate. The trek to the clearing, at least, Leveled his Sneak to 4.

Still jumpy despite his heart's decision, he circled the area, moving on light feet. When Randidly finally turned inward to his destination, he understood why the surrounding trees were silent and still.

A strange humanoid creature with pointed ears was sticking out of the large snake's mouth. Its waist and legs weren't visible, seeming to have already been devoured. But even as the humanoid was being treated like a meal, it managed to drive a blade through the roof of the snake's mouth and into its skull. Based on the contorted and violent angles of both the half-swallowed humanoid and the snake's body, this blow proved deadly, either due to brain damage or blood loss. Both the corpses and surrounding grass were liberally caked in dried black blood.

Randidly couldn't take his eyes away from the dagger gleaming in the snake's mouth. The long and slender handle, wrapped in leather, was adorned with a simple amethyst set into the hilt.

Randidly shifted and suppressed the urge to scratch his neck. *I don't want to get that fucking close to these monsters… but a weapon would definitely make surviving down here easier.*

"Okay, let's just do it then." Deciding on the speedy route, Randidly sprinted from his hiding spot, reached into the massive skull, and pulled on the dagger while turning to flee back to the screening of the tree line.

Randidly lurched to a stop, the dagger stuck fast in the skull. Freezing, Randidly's eyes flicked back and forth, never once lessening his awareness of potential threats waiting to strike from the shadows. Seconds ticked past. To his distinct embarrassment, nothing happened.

The surroundings remained devoid of movement.

Slightly reassured, Randidly rocked the dagger back and forth, beginning the laborious process of removing the item from the snake's cranium. As he did so, his exertions shifted the motorcycle-sized head. Randidly was all too aware that one of this snake's fangs was about the size of his forearm. Being pressed up against the chilling scales did not help the fact that Randidly was forced to breathe shallowly so as not to gag on the thick perfume of rotten flesh.

The process took so long that, at one point, Randidly had to take several minute-long breaks to allow his Stamina to recover.

Eventually, Randidly was rewarded with a sickening pop—the dagger came free. Randidly admired the slightly curved blade with a wickedly sharp edge, despite the goopy chunk of red-black god-knows-what that remained affixed to the tip.

Randidly relished the feeling of tightening his grip on the leather handle. Weirdly, the weapon fit naturally in his hand.

Randidly allowed himself a soft smile, enjoying the tactile sensation of the weapon. Some of that faded when he turned to take a longer look at the face of the deceased humanoid in the giant snake's mouth. In death, the muscles of the humanoid's cheeks and jaws were tense and flexed. Randidly could practically see the effort of concentrated will it took to methodically strike up through the roof of the mouth, ensuring both would die.

Randidly bowed his head. *Thank you. I know you can't hear me, but—*

Movement brought Randidly's thoughts to a screeching halt. From the inside of the snake's mouth, a fist-sized black beetle scuttled out. Before Randidly recognized the Level 2 Corpse Beetle label hovering over the beetle's head, his body reacted.

"Heavy Blow!" Randidly gulped down air and his fist accelerated forward. With the fiery wave of Stamina fueling the movement, his fist smashed into the oversized beetle and squashed it against the snake's jaw. Even though his attack was slightly off target due to his hasty response, the beetle was quite weak.

It was merely a bigger than average beetle.

Congratulations! You have learned the active Skill **Spirit of Adversity Level 1.**

A strange sense of foreboding crept through Randidly when he saw the notification. The clearing around him remained still, despite his sudden offensive spasm. "Spirit of Adversity."

Spirit of Adversity: *Your thrilling battles against monsters of a higher Level have allowed you to develop a billowing spirit to challenge dangerous foes.*
When activated, gives you small Stats bonuses during fights against higher-Leveled foes. You will appear slightly more threatening to monsters of a higher Level. Effect and duration of the Skill increase with Skill Level.

Randidly's lips twitched when a few more Corpse Beetles crawled out of the dark throat of the giant snake, inspecting the squished body of their comrade. *Truly, my billowing spirit has given me enough confidence to face these Level 2 monsters. Such... thrilling battles.*

Randidly was about to distance himself before an entire army of the beetles marched out and posed an *actual* threat to him, when he spotted a satchel hanging over the partially swallowed humanoid's shoulder. It was pressed against the snake's rotting tongue, beneath his back. Randidly was torn. On the one hand, he didn't want to take more than what was necessary from this figure. On the other hand, the satchel could contain a clue that might give Randidly a method to pay the stranger back for this unexpected boon.

Ultimately, the decision came down to Randidly's pragmatism—there might be other tools to help him survive within the bag. He tried to carefully remove the leather parcel from its resting place. Because the flesh of the snake was starting to sag and rot, "delicate" wouldn't cut it.

Randidly did his best not to breathe too deeply and began wrestling with the dead body.

It only took a minute for Randidly's more irreverent approach to yield the satchel. He remained crouched next to the massive body of the snake for cover and opened his prize, revealing a swirling darkness. Frowning, he prodded it with the dagger, which instantly vanished into that strange space. Gasping, Randidly grabbed after it. He didn't consider the consequences at all, seized by such a horrible thought that his disrespect for the dead would mean nothing if he lost the dagger now.

As his fingers sank into that space, a strange knowledge entered his mind. He could see the one-cubic-meter space inside the bag perfectly. Randidly was also intimately aware of the objects floating in that zone. They danced across his mind as soon as his attention focused on them. Dried rations. A map. Some weird coins. A book in a language he couldn't understand. Fifteen empty vials. A bedroll of some kind. What could be campfire tools. And the dagger.

With but a thought, the dagger reappeared in his hand. Randidly gazed at the bag in wonder.

The stench of death was heavy, but Randidly's instincts also caught a whiff of an opportunity. The continued absence of any threat other than the Corpse Beetles gradually emboldened Randidly to seize this chance to gather resources.

Twenty minutes later, Randidly felt quite satisfied with himself. With his newfound dagger and bag, he gathered every useful article he could carry away with him. He took the glowing red crystals in the giant tree, as well as the blue ones that studded the roots. Plus, he harvested a sizable haul of the smoky nuts and several green banana-shaped fruits from nearby trees.

He used the dagger to carve out one of the snake's long fangs, which was as thick as Randidly's wrist at the base. The rotten flesh gave way easily beneath the sharp dagger. During the process, he squashed several more wandering Corpse Beetles, earning a second Level in Spirit of Adversity. He was about to start on the second, when a nearby bush rustled.

Having rehearsed this situation in his mind a dozen times, Randidly hopped over the snake's body, putting something between himself and the source of the noise. His legs pumped furiously beneath him, fleeing to the sanctuary of the ferns. His quick reflexes and exertion increased his Sprinting Level to 3.

Upon arriving back at the Safe Room, the first thing Randidly did was have a fine meal of nuts and off-brand bananas. For the first time in hours, his stomach no longer gnawed at the inside of his ribcage. Randidly lay back in the grass and smiled. Tension drained from his body and his eyelids fluttered steadily shut.

When he recovered, Randidly pulled most of the remainder of his haul out from the strange inventory-like satchel. He considered the nuts, bananas, and the blue and red crystals he'd taken from the tree. Randidly chewed his lip, eyeing the growing sprouts popping up from the discarded berry seeds.

Using the dagger, Randidly carved out nine holes, spaced several feet apart in a line. He buried three nuts, three chunks of the banana, one each of the red and blue crystals, and one with both crystals together. He was curious to see if he could grow a tree like the one outside.

Satisfied, Randidly lay down and stared up at the strange light sources in the ceiling. With food sources acquired, he could be a little bit more flexible with his planning. Plus, he could intensify his training regimen.

Humming to himself and feeling genuinely confident he would be able to survive this situation, Randidly gradually settled back toward sleep.

CHAPTER SIX

$\mathcal{R}$ andidly's eyelids fluttered. The sunstones embedded in the ceiling flickered to life, shining warm rays on Randidly's skin to lift him into wakefulness. What he found waiting for him were notifications.

Congratulations! Your Skill **Farming** has grown to **Level 4!**

Congratulations! Your Skill **Farming** has grown to **Level 5!**

Congratulations! Your Skill **Farming** has grown to **Level 6!**

Congratulations! Your Skill **Farming** has grown to **Level 7!**

Congratulations! You have learned the Skill **Plant Breeding Level 1.**

Congratulations! Your Skill **Plant Breeding** has grown to **Level 2!**

"Uh..." The bouquet of freshly picked PP left him speechless and rubbing his eyes. He rolled up into a sitting position and twisted around to look toward the row of buried seeds. "Plant Breeding?"

The area to the left of the tree was starting to look properly respectable as a garden. The current size of the berry bushes was only 90% of the height of the ones Randidly had seen in the jungle, but the leafy bushes filled him with optimism. His first harvest was quickly approaching.

It was at the purposeful plantings that Randidly now beamed. Thin sprouts from the first six of the holes rose up, the three nut and three banana trees. Perhaps it was because the final plant would be quite a bit taller than the berry bush, but the sprouts seemed quite a bit larger than the berry bushes had been after only a few hours.

I think they should still fit… Randidly thought, mentally judging the distance to the ceiling to be about three meters. *Maybe a bit cramped, but—wait, was the roof always this high?*

Randidly frowned up at the twinkling sources of sunlight inserted into the ceiling. The other tree had always been present next to the pond, but it possessed a rather squat and compact trunk. He eyed the distance between the roof and the treetop with uncertainty. He shook his head. His attention was drawn back to the final three places where he planted the blue and red crystals.

Disappointingly, nothing grew out of the crystals. Which honestly made Randidly feel quite a bit dumb. Compared to the seeds from bushes and trees, why the hell had he assumed something would grow from a glowing crystal.

Randidly rid himself of the negativity and focused on his precious pile of food. *There's still a lot to do. I was lucky the frogs were distracted last time. Before I go out again, I want to earn myself a few more assurances that I can survive…*

Randidly crouched next to his food, making some quick mental calculations. He had about a dozen of each color of the crystal, thirty nuts, twenty-five bananas, and some weird bread and dried meat from the humanoid who killed the snake. May he rest in peace. That was probably enough to keep him going for a few days, giving him the luxury of spending all his effort on grinding his Skills to increase his chances of survival.

Next, he went to his Path screen. This morning lifted his total to 9 PP, and Randidly used 4 of them to finish off the M. Supp Path. As expected, he received 2 M. Supp points and 2 free Stat points, which he put into Control and Vitality respectively.

With the Path finished, he examined the completion notification.

Congratulations! You have completed the **"M. Supp Path"! +2 to all M. Supp Stats, +1 M. Supp point per Level.**

Congratulations! You have learned the Skill **Meditation Level 1.**

Meditation: *Allows user to enter into focused state, increasing all Regenerations by 1% per Skill Level.* **May be knocked out of meditation by foreign forces and loud noises. As Skill Level increases, so too does resistance to having the user's meditation broken.**

Randidly tapped his cheek and opened his Status Screen. A 1% boost to his regeneration was currently less than 1. "The effect is small now, but hopefully, it will continue growing. And it's another active Skill I can do while resting. Huh, I wonder if it will stack with the bonus from the Safe Room?"

Randidly put the remaining 5 PP he possessed into the Risk Taker Path. Much to his disappointment, the first 4 PP did nothing. Contrast was the mother of stress. Aggravation filled him due to how easily he'd been earning Stat points. It was now clear to Randidly this wouldn't always be the case. Luckily, the fifth and final PP he placed into the Path earned him a notification and gave him hope.

Congratulations! You have earned **+1 all Stats.**

I guess it makes sense it will get harder to earn Stats as I continue to grow. Randidly grimaced when he noticed how many Stats were still only in single digits. *Hopefully, the bonuses every 5 PP, and for completing the Path, will keep giving generous rewards.*

Randidly kneeled down and pressed his knuckles against the sun-warmed grass. He breathed in and out. The fear Randidly felt from his close encounters with the Howler Monkeys and the frogs hadn't truly been vanquished; it'd just been tightly packed into the corner of his heart. His sudden realization that his growth wouldn't be as easy gave it license to spread its chilling feelers throughout Randidly's body.

I have active Skills. I can train and earn more PP. Randidly told himself forcefully. *This will work out. It has to.*

After a few seconds of strained kneeling, the tension in Randidly's heart began to ease. He took a couple of more breaths and turned his attention to other tasks.

Randidly spent some time familiarizing himself with his current state after the +1 to all Stats boost. He was glad he did. The exercise gave him some insight into what each Stat affected. Perception really did make his eyes and ears more sensitive, and the tiny boosts in Reaction he received enabled him to respond more immediately to threats.

Considering the landmine of a jungle outside the Safe Room, Randidly resolved to put a few more Stat points into Reaction.

After hopping around for a bit, Randidly tested his active Skills. The boost to Intelligence made his Mana Bolt slightly thicker, releasing a more intense light. It also traveled farther before dissipating. Randidly only stumbled upon this fact when he took a few extra steps back and completely missed his target of the tree.

Suddenly, another Stat occurred to him. Perhaps the increase in range was due to his Wisdom? He could only theorize for now, but it made sense to split up the attributes of magical attacks like that. Randidly settled into a sturdy stance and fired his second Mana Bolt.

This one *thunked* pleasantly into the bark of the squat tree.

The large boost to M. Supp he received let Randidly confirm that, while Control made his accuracy with spells better, Focus decreased the casting time. It now only took a few scant seconds to channel the energy for the spell. Though shorter, it was still too long in terms of what it would require to use mid-battle.

After his experiments, Randidly clapped his hands ritualistically to the audience of half-grown bushes and trees. "Alright, time to push my limits a bit."

Randidly didn't leave the Safe Zone for the next two days.

In pursuit of Skill Levels, Randidly Ghosthound became a training machine. In the mornings, he would jog, sprint, and do push-ups, interspersing that with Mana Bolts when he accumulated enough Mana. Then he would take a meal and start his afternoon by spending several hours grinding Heavy Blow. His new dagger soon created a dense network of scratches across the small tree. His continuous movements even earned him the Dagger Mastery Skill.

Randidly's frequent glances upward made him certain the roof was steadily rising to make room for the growing plants. This original tree seemed to be pulled upward by the retreating roof.

In the evening, Randidly shot Mana Bolts to burn his chilly Mana and used Iron Skin to deplete his fiery Stamina. After, he would sit and Meditate in order to regenerate it all back. Before starting back into his training routine, Randidly inspected his plants.

Small buds dotted the branches of the berry bush, hinting at the fruit to come. His trees were constantly shooting upward, quickly suppressing the bush in terms of height. Randidly filled vials with water and poured them across the base of the plants, oddly fulfilled in tracking their progress reaching upward.

Then he went back to work.

For two days, he threw himself into the exertion, suppressing the anxiety in his heart with food and hard work. Randidly ignored the notifications, continuing to grind. His knowledge and familiarity with his Stats-empowered body continued to improve. Every moment, Randidly felt himself becoming a more capable version of himself as he discovered new limits to his Stats-empowered self. It was intoxicating to say the least.

There was a cost to saving up PP. He wouldn't have access to a new Skill by completing a Path or using them in order to familiarize himself with newly acquired Stats. Regardless, Randidly allowed the PP to stockpile.

He wiped sweat from his forehead and continued to jog. Right now, Randidly found an almost perfect refuge from the emotions that plagued him since the System arrived.

He didn't want to let anything distract him from that sense of purpose and peace.

It was only at the end of the second day, while he used his teeth to gnaw at the last piece of jerky he obtained from the humanoid's satchel, that he allowed his elevated heart rate to slowly sink back toward normal speeds. It was time to tally his accumulations. Randidly looked at his Status screen and couldn't help but chuckle.

Farming Level 7 had increased to Level 11.

Running Level 6 had increased to Level 7.

Sprinting Level 3 had increased to Level 6.

Physical Fitness Level 3 had increased to Level 10.

Mana Bolt Level 2 had increased to Level 7.

Heavy Blow Level 2 had increased to Level 10.

Iron Skin Level 3 had increased to Level 7.

Dagger Mastery Level 1 had increased to Level 7.

Meditation Level 1 had increased to Level 5.

All in all, he earned 42 PP over the two all-consuming days. It was an amount superior to the total amount of PP he'd previously spent. When he first looked at his Status, he was intimidated by that number. He knew nothing about the mechanism one used to earn Paths.

Two things soothed his thoughts. First, when Physical Fitness reached Level 10, he unlocked the Basic Fitness Path, which would require 20 PP to finish. Second, Randidly remembered the few lines at the end Path completion notification for the Newbie Path.

Continue using Paths to explore this world! Remember, there will always be a path open to you. Rise and spread your Legend throughout the Nexus!

This System is almost too good to be true. Randidly gradually began to frown. *I can't really figure out a downside to this ability to grow, but maybe because of just how perfectly it works...*

For now, Randidly banished those thoughts. Higher order worries could wait until he escaped from this Dungeon. He finished off the Risk Taker Path, getting another +1 to all Stats at 10 and 15 respectively, and a Path completion notification appeared.

Congratulations! You have completed the **"Risk Taker Path"!** Not all risks are rewarded equally. Your willingness to expose yourself to danger and challenge your limits always increases the efficacy of your growth, but you have been rewarded with a **special bonus! +1% experience per each Level a defeated mob has over you.**

"Willingness to expose yourself to danger and challenge your limits, huh..." From the way it was phrased, this might be a larger truth about this new world. He certainly earned a lot of his Skills while in extreme danger.

Satisfied with the Risk Taker reward, Randidly poured 20 PP into finishing off Basic Physical Fitness. Like Risk Taker, only every fifth one granted him a reward. At 5, he received one point for P. Attack—which he put into Agi. At 10, a P. Def point—which he put into Vit. 15 points resulted in a P. Supp—which he put into Perception. 20 was a free Stat, which Randidly added to Wis to raise his Mana regeneration so his Mana Bolt wouldn't lag so far behind Heavy Blow.

Congratulations! You have completed the **"Basic Physical Fitness Path"!** Your efforts to improve your body will steadily firm up your foundation! Soon, even greater physical achievements will be available to you. **+10 Health, +5 Stamina, +1 Stamina per Level.**

Randidly couldn't argue that a Health boost was beneficial. Though considering how deadly Level 20 threats were, it was probably less useful than straight Stats. And he hadn't yet been able to benefit from the Level-up gains... Randidly stared at his reflection in the pool, contemplating all that potential that lay waiting for him in the domain of "Class." Increasing Level-up gains would be useful for him.

Hopefully.

Eventually.

Randidly went back to his Path screen. A sinking feeling wormed its way into his chest. It was empty. Despite the System's promise that a Path would always be available to him, no option was available.

A notification popped up.

You've taken your first steps into the Nexus! Continue using Paths to explore this world! Remember, there will always be a path open to you. Please select one of the Paths below for your continued journey!

And like magic, two options appeared in the previously empty space.

Trainee Path *0/15* | **????** *0/20*

That's one more worry I can consider addressed. Alright, now then... Randidly rubbed his chin while he examined his options. Although the second one would effectively be a random Path, considering its question marks, it seemed like a higher-level Path. The amount of PP it required was the same amount as Basic Physical Fitness. Still, Trainee Path felt like the natural continuation of the Newbie Path, which had granted him Skills.

And I can always use more Skills.

Deciding to play it safe, Randidly selected the Trainee Path, pouring his remaining 12 PP into it. To his surprise, he received a bonus reward for every PP he expended. Happiness washed over him. But that joy paled in comparison to the giddy response from the current "pessimistic" Randidly, used to earning nothing for his PP, when he received the reward for the fifth PP.

Congratulations! You have earned **+3 to Health.**

Congratulations! You have earned **+2 to Mana.**

Congratulations! You have earned **+1 to Stamina.**

Congratulations! You have earned **+1 Stat(s).**

Congratulations! You have encountered a branching Path. Choose either to immediately gain **+4 Stamina** and the Skill **Mighty Leap** or **+10 Mana** and the Skill **Entangling Roots**. *Warning! Your choice will affect rewards you will receive for Path completion.*

Branching Path... Randidly weighed his options. Essentially, he had to choose whether to proceed down a Mana or Stamina build. At least, his choice was between Skills and Attributes that leaned toward those options. Stamina was the obvious avenue for short-term survivability. Except Randidly couldn't deny his pull toward Mana.

A Stamina build would require up close and personal confrontations with monsters. That prospect *did not* fill Randidly with confidence. Especially when he considered those acid-spitting frogs. Relying on his physical body to close the distance seemed like a bad idea.

Overall, the associated Mana Skill appealed to Randidly's preferred operating procedures. Entangling Roots sounded like crowd control. Such a Skill could enable him to tie down the frogs or Howler Monkeys, enabling him to escape in a pinch. He could keep his distance and deal with his targets remotely.

Randidly's emerald eyes glittered, weighing the impacts between his two choices. *Plus, 10 Mana is one more Mana Bolt. And is there anything more satisfying than shooting blasts of energy out of your fingers?*

Randidly selected the Entangling Roots option.

Entangling Roots: *Summon roots from the ground to tie down opponents. Creates a dense concentration of roots in a small targeted area that will grab nearby threats.* **Costs 35 Mana. Duration of roots depends on Skill Level. Strength and size of roots depend on Skill Level and Intelligence. Accuracy of roots depends on Control. Mastery of the Skill will bring transformative benefits.**

"Well, shit…" Randidly muttered.

His heart ached as soon as his eyes landed on the cost. *35 Mana!* The greedy Entangling Roots would take almost all of his 42 total Mana in a single usage. Not only would he have less Mana to practice Mana Bolts, he'd need to spend more time meditating to recover.

Even relying on the tripled regeneration within the Safe Zone, Randidly's Mana regeneration was still short of 42. That meant it would take almost an hour and a half per use of the Entangling Roots to regain the expense. And he definitely needed to practice in order to have any confidence in using it in the underground jungle outside the Safe Room door.

Sighing, Randidly entered in the next 7 PP into the Path, emptying himself out. Luckily, the following notifications brought some measure of optimism back to his heart. The rewards were *extremely* timely.

Congratulations! You have earned **+2 to Mana.**

Congratulations! You have earned **+2 to Mana.**

Congratulations! You have earned **+1 to Mana Regeneration.**

Congratulations! You have earned **+1 Stat(s).**

Congratulations! You have learned the active Skill **Mana Shield Level 1.**

Congratulations! You have earned **+2 to Mana.**

Congratulations! You have earned **+2 to Mana.**

Mana Shield: *Conjure a thin shield of Mana a short distance from your skin.* **Effective against both magical and physical attacks. Will block 20**

damage, plus the Skill Level x 5. Costs 20 Mana to conjure. Size and control of the Mana Shield will increase with Skill Level.

After putting the two Stat points he earned from the Trainee Path into Wisdom, boosting his Mana regen a little bit further, Randidly felt slightly less cheated by his choice. His Mana pool was now at 51, and his regeneration climbed to 17 per hour. Inside the Safe Room, that 17 became 51 Mana per hour, just above the casting requirement of Entangling Roots. Training it by relying on one activation per hour, alternating hours dedicated to Mana Bolts, was barely enough for him to stomach.

Randidly closed his Menus, turning his attention to his depleted store of food. "And now… what's my next step?"

CHAPTER SEVEN

$\mathcal{R}$andidly eyed the leather satchel. He brushed his fingers across its smooth brown surface, allowing himself to briefly savor the tactile sensation.

Necessity dragged him out of the diversion.

He pulled the map from the satchel, his expression serious. After touching it, the map option in his menu screen became selectable. Randidly opened the map tab and scrutinized its contents. There was a general outline of the Dungeon, simply called "The Underground Jungle."

Randidly clicked his tongue. "What an unoriginal name…"

Randidly's heart sank the more he studied the visual in front of him. The Dungeon was enormous. Though he'd suspected this, having not seen any walls except the one he stayed near, it was particularly devastating to see the vastness laid out in front of him. He was situated in the Safe Room halfway across the southern wall, equidistant from the entrance to the Dungeon and the Boss area.

Randidly was about twenty kilometers from both destinations.

More disturbingly, while the boss's chambers were in the southeastern corner of the Dungeon, the entrance was in the northwestern corner, meaning Randidly had no other choice but to cross through at least some portion of the forest in order to reach the entrance. He wouldn't just be able to proceed along the wall.

Sighing, Randidly dismissed the Map menu. He had a long way to go before having any confidence in crossing the forest. Randidly put his chin on his hand and glumly viewed his Stats one more time before lying down for a nap.

Randidly Ghosthound
Class: ---
Level: N/A
Health(/R per hour): 138/138 (53.25)
Mana(/R per hour): 50/51 (17)
Stam(/R per min): 66/67 (20)
Vit: 15
End: 17
Str: 6
Agi: 13
Perception: 10
Reaction: 8
Resistance: 8
Willpower: 8
Intelligence: 8
Wisdom: 9
Control: 12
Focus: 8
Paths: *Newbie 7/7 | P. Def 10/10 | M. Supp 10/10 | Risk Taker 15/15 | Basic Physical Fitness 20/20 | Trainee 12/15*

Skills: *Running Lvl 7 | Physical Fitness Lvl 10 | Sneak Lvl 4 | Farming Lvl 11 | Mana Bolt Lvl 7 | Heavy Blow Lvl 10 | Acid Resistance Lvl 5 | Poison Resistance Lvl 5 | Sprinting Lvl 6 | Iron Skin Lvl 7 | Plant Breeding Lvl 2 | Meditation Lvl 5 | Spirit of Adversity Lvl 2 | Dagger Mastery Lvl 7 | Entangling Roots Lvl 1 | Mana Shield Lvl 1*

After careful consideration, Randidly convinced himself he was ready to truly "expose himself to danger and challenge his limits." If there was one activity he'd done more than anything else over the past two days, it was running. Randidly inwardly suspected his current sprinting speed was approaching the world record. He had no basis for this assumption, besides the liberating sense of speed he felt as the grass, trees, and his planted food sources stretched into blurs when he reached max speed.

Perhaps that sense of capability was why Randidly headed back to the Howler Monkey area. His Sneak Skill hadn't improved during training, but his Stats certainly had. He moved like a ghost amongst the ferns, periodically pausing to scan the surroundings. His progress was consistent and stable.

There were two reasons for this trip. One was to stop by the nut, banana, and weird crystal trees and stock up on more supplies. The other...

Am I really going to do this? the reasonable Randidly asked himself.

Confident Randidly's response was just as reasonable. *You managed to outrun them without any Skills. 5 Agility later and with additional Levels in both Physical Fitness and Sprinting, won't this be simple?*

Randidly intended to antagonize the close-range Howler Monkeys to check his progress.

He planned to lure one away and bind it with Entangling Roots, and then... something. A Mana Bolt smacking that vicious smirk off its face would do nicely. Then he would stage a strategic retreat.

He couldn't deny how much he had progressed, even if the prospect of this adventure left him slightly nauseous. The confidence he repeatedly instilled in himself demanded the opportunity to demonstrate its own truth. The training was fulfilling, but something new had steadily grown in Randidly's chest.

Randidly wanted to test himself.

Of course, this newfound desire to face his own fears was backed by hours of consideration. In retrospect, the most daunting aspect of the Howler Monkeys was their fluid and quick movements inside the tree line. Their long arms blurred, swinging from vine to branch, trunk to the ground, only a few meters away from Randidly. By the time he noticed their presence, they'd practically swam through the trees to arrive next to him.

Outside the trees, their stumpy legs could only carry them slightly faster than the Skill-less Randidly Ghosthound. He was certain his 13 Agility and Level 6 Sprinting would be enough to comfortably outrun them.

Randidly snuck to a position in the ferns corresponding with the location of the banana and nut trees, and the clearing beyond. The shadow of a tall and leafy fern concealed him while he honed in on the low branches of the nearby trees.

With his improved Perception, Randidly spotted two frogs slumped against the junction where branch met trunk. One was only a few meters to his right, partially hidden around the curve of the trunk. The other was eight meters down to his left, facing the deeper portions of the jungle.

If I would have rushed out there... Randidly gritted his teeth. He considered the distance between himself and the cluster of food-producing trees. With great effort, he forced down the memory of the acidic vomit eating away at his bone. *Okay, it's still doable, and the frogs weren't aggressive previously.*

One hiding spot at a time...

Randidly moved a little bit down to the left, away from his targets, distancing himself equally between the two frogs. Crouching, he stepped out of the tree line and scuttled forward until he could press his back against a massive, oak-ish looking tree.

Congratulations! Your Skill **Sneak** has grown to **Level 5!**

Buoyed by the improvement to his Skill, Randidly peered around the tree trunks and flitted from cover to cover.

Croak.

His heart pounded the moment he heard the distinctive sound. Randidly rolled forward behind a patch of nettles and settled up against the banana tree. He pressed the back of his head against the slender trunk and dared not move.

For almost a minute, he remained there, his blood pressure rising alongside the stretched moment of tension. Except, the splash and sizzle of acid that he feared never arrived. Randidly pressed his eyes shut. *Come on, Ghosthound. You can do this.*

He forced himself to twist and look toward the nearest frog. It was gone. He found it after a quick scan. It had hopped away from him to a new tree. Randidly huffed out a breath and gathered all the surrounding bananas into his satchel. He scampered forward to the nut tree and collected about two dozen little fallen seeds he'd missed on his previous swings through the area.

After a moment's hesitation, Randidly moved toward the clearing.

Congratulations! Your Skill **Sneak** has grown to **Level 6!**

This time, Randidly paused after the Skill Level-up notification. He settled on his haunches next to a gnarled and ugly tree that blocked the line of sight from both frogs. The jungle rustled and swayed around him, adding a constant thrum of tension to the brief break. Randidly tried to make himself as small as possible.

He opened his Path menu to spend his two new PP.

Congratulations! You have earned +1 to **Mana Regeneration.**

Congratulations! You have earned +1 **free Stat(s).**

The free Stat went directly into Agility.

Randidly circled around the clearing, making sure no frogs were in the area. He didn't see any frogs, but was rather surprised to see several larger-than-he-remembered beetles crawling out of the giant snake's mouth and around the grass of the clearing. The sunlight reflected off their glossy black shells.

"Those Corpse Beetles..." Randidly muttered to himself. "Are they getting bigger?"

One ambled across the humanoid's face. A strong impulse to go over there and squash the offending bug rushed through him. Pragmatic concerns stopped him. First, he had no idea how many Corpse Beetles were within the snake's body. And second, spending the time and effort to kill the beetles might attract attention to his position.

With a heavy hand of guilt squeezing his heart, Randidly ignored that portion of the clearing. He snuck toward the tree embedded with glowing crystals. Randidly pried loose the few that returned since his last visit. Although he didn't yet know the purpose of these crystals, how could a crystal growing in a tree not be valuable?

Randidly spared one last glance for the flagrant disrespect of the Corpse Beetles. Gritting his teeth, he pulled his gaze away and moved out of the clearing. He inverted his approach, taking the same movements in reverse. Only when he made it back into the ferns did he slightly relax.

Alright, first goal accomplished. And now...

Randidly Ghosthound moved toward the Howler Monkey's area.

As he made his approach, Randidly had the presence of mind to notice what he didn't even blink at previously—the type of trees changed in this area. Their crowns stretched higher and their trunks stood further apart. Most of the shrubbery had vanished, replaced with thick vines weaving erratically through the whole of the tree canopy.

There was only one problem. Randidly couldn't find any Howler Monkeys. He waited five minutes. Nothing appeared. Grimacing, Randidly firmly knocked his hand against a nearby tree trunk. The noise echoed outward through the still web of branches and vines. Still nothing appeared in the ten long minutes he stood frozen and vigilant.

Randidly activated Heavy Blow and slammed his fist against the tree trunk. The sound reverberated through the jungle. A few of the nearby vines swayed. Still no monsters revealed themselves. He'd been crouched there for almost a half hour and his palms were getting sweaty.

He felt slightly foolish for how much preparation had gone into this, only to be met with silence. Randidly came out of his crouching position in the ferns and walked boldly past the looming trees.

Nothing happened.

Randidly scratched his head. *Maybe they migrated? Dammit, I really don't want to test myself against frogs that can spit acid—*

Whoosh!

A blur at the edge of his vision was all the warning Randidly received. Had it been the him of a few days ago, this would have ended with him seriously wounded. Thanks to his constant state of tension and Stat increases, his senses were sharp. He summoned a Mana Shield in direct response to the noise.

The projectile smashed against Randidly's shield and the barrier broke open like an egg. Just as a sudden spike of pain ripped in front of Randidly's temple, a stone the size of an apple smacked into his shoulder. Even with the Mana Shield, the attack possessed enough force to stagger him.

Randidly recovered as best he could and whipped around to find the sniper. He quickly located two monkeys high in a nearby tree, chittering with laughter as one hefted another stone. The blood in Randidly's face drained into sour fear and embarrassment within his stomach.

It was such a stupid mistake. He'd been looking for the monkeys at the same height of the trees where he had seen the frogs.

Furious at the monkeys and himself, Randidly raised his hand and pointed. Mana gathered in his hand. The two monkeys chittered to each other, as if trying to decide which stone to throw at this pathetic human next.

Fwoosh!

With Randidly's improved control, his attack flew true and struck the Howler Monkey in the chest. With a squawk, it was dislodged from its position, descending until its back smacked against the ground. It hopped up almost in the same moment it crashed and rumbled toward him, fury written in capital letters across its contorted face.

That same sense of curdling fear Randidly felt during his first encounter with the Howler Monkey returned. He fled, activating Sprint to fly back into the ferns. Then he—

Tripped.

Ten meters away from the monkey, and Randidly tripped. So shocked by this development, he just went limp, tumbling forward with a blank expression. Until that blank face smacked into the ground. The realization of what happened tightened around his psyche like a deploying parachute. He had to move. He pushed himself to his feet, only to see—

Adult Corpse Beetle Level 6

The Corpse Beetles paused in their movements and regarded him curiously. Randidly twisted his head around. He'd tumbled right into the middle of a group of six Corpse Beetles. They had truly grown in size since he'd seen them last, from a fist to some being as large as soccer balls.

"If I would have just killed you earlier..." Randidly saw again the beetle crawling across the humanoid's face.

He scrambled forward on his hands and knees, and pushed himself into an erect position. He raised his fists and vented the fury pooling in his chest. "Heavy Blow! Heavy Blow! Heavy Blow! Heavy Blow! Heavy Blow!"

The first couple blows skidded off its exoskeleton. The third strike cracked the Corpse Beetle's defenses. The fourth and fifth punched a hole through the shell and pulped its innards.

Congratulations! Your Skill **Spirit of Adversity** has grown to **Level 3!**

Randidly might have continued to lose himself in the tactile sensation of grinding the Corpse Beetle's body to pus, if the ferns behind him hadn't rustled. The whole of his current predicament rushed back to him. With his hands caked in beetle guts, Randidly scrambled to his feet and prepared to activate Sprint to escape the Howler Monkey.

A familiar feeling of weakness greeted him. He was dangerously low on Stamina. He'd spent too much too quickly with his earlier Heavy Blows.

Randidly ran without activating his Skill, barely even cognizant of his surroundings. He exploded out of the ferns into the grassy area along the wall, his Stamina approaching zero. He was sweating bullets. In the last few steps before the Safe Room door, he ran out of Stamina. Randidly's feet got caught up on each other, and for the second time in under a minute, his face slapped the ground.

Wheezing, Randidly forced himself up and through the door.

He collapsed, chest heaving and his gore-covered hands shaking.

CHAPTER EIGHT

*E*ventually, Randidly rolled himself away from the door and unslung the satchel. *I should... get to work.*

He mechanically unpacked and sorted the gathered food. He munched on a few nuts until his mental state gradually recovered. Randidly took several deep breaths before looking through the notifications he earned in the blurry flight back to safety.

The first stone pierced his Mana Shield and inflicted a little over 30 damage. That meant the stone itself, thrown by the monkey, would have done about 55 if it hit him directly.

Obstructing the stone, even just for a fraction of a second, increased Mana Shield Skill immediately to Level 3, supporting the Path notification's claim— challenging his limits in dangerous situations would increase his Leveling speed. Even if the first couple Levels were the easiest, that was some quick growth.

Hitting the monkey in the chest with the Mana Bolt increased the Skill to Level 8. It was another shred of evidence demonstrating the downsides of simply holing up in a Safe Room and grinding his Skills.

But that's assuming I wouldn't immediately die in the outside world. With my current Classless state and the fact everything here is Level 20... The lines around Randidly's eyes tightened. *Each Skill Level is a step forward. I need to balance growth speed with my own safety.*

Each factoid burst within Randidly's brain. They became firecrackers brushing against each other, setting all his worries and trials within the Dungeon into a chaotic mess of flash and concussion. The arrival of the System and learning how to improve quicker by exposing himself to danger. His worries about Ace and Sydney. The fact that he was in a Dungeon and his lack of knowledge about the whole situation. Unimaginable pain when acid burned his flesh away and poisoned his blood...

Randidly heaved himself up and stumbled toward the pond in the middle of the Safe Room. He carefully lowered himself and splashed water on his face until the cool liquid smothered the roiling thoughts.

"Even if I can't handle everything right now, there are things I can handle. Just... focus on those."

Sighing, Randidly opened his Path menu and used a PP to finish off the Trainee Path.

Congratulations! You have earned **+2 to M. Stats.**

Congratulations! You have completed the **"Trainee Path (Mage Branch)"**! **+10 Mana, +1 Mana Regen, +1 Mana per Level.**

Randidly added the two stats he earned into Control and Intelligence. Although Randidly just talked himself out of thinking too broadly about the inexplicable changes in the world, he couldn't help but plan for the future. If Randidly wanted to leave this place, he needed to be able to utilize his Skills without the benefit of the Safe Room to boost his recovery. Bigger attribute pools and more power were a necessity. That way, he wouldn't need to use his Skill multiple times to defeat a foe.

Five Heavy Blows, with the bonus from Spirit of Adversity... Randidly thought with a frown. *And that Corpse Beetle was only Level 6.*

After finishing that Path, one choice remained for his PP—**????:** *0/20.* He clicked on it, and the name shifted to Wandering Survivor.

"Seems relevant." Randidly chuckled and put his remaining 3 PPs into it. To his surprise, he received something each time.

Congratulations! You have earned **+2 to Health.**

Congratulations! You have earned **+2 to Mana.**

Congratulations! You have earned **+2 to Stamina.**

Okay, my suspicions were completely misplaced. Randidly allowed himself a small smile. *This is exactly what I need right now.*

Finally feeling a bit more in control of his situation, Randidly inspected his growing plants. The buds on the berry bush were visibly larger. Fruit would come soon. The others were growing to a good size, except for one particular deviant.

Randidly frowned at the final banana tree. Its bulging trunk was absolutely hefty, swollen to double the girth of the others, and had reached twice the height of its brothers.

Randidly walked along the line of banana trees, poking and prodding them from different angles. He leaned back and tapped his jaw. *The change was sudden. Previously, the banana tree on the end was the same as the others. Considering the strangeness of this "System," I suppose it's possible for there to be a sudden mutation. After all, the Corpse Beetles seem bigger every time I see them.*

But that's such an unsatisfying answer. If only there was an environmental difference to explain—

A possibility occurred to Randidly. He got out his dagger and dug up the dirt in the three spots that yielded no sprouts. After five minutes, Randidly leaned back on his heels with a satisfied smile. As he suspected, the red crystal he'd buried nearest the banana pieces had vanished. Yet the lone blue crystal, and the combined red and blue were still there.

The red crystal had somehow been absorbed by the plant. That was likely the reason he'd earned the Plant Breeding Skill.

Randidly took a closer look at the ceiling and walls. This time, due to the explosion of growth from the red crystal-banana combo, it was easy to see the roof had been raised. Randidly swore the walls were further away as well. He hopped to his feet and jogged the distance. He'd practiced dashing around these specific distances so often, he confirmed the Safe Room was expanding.

Even if it isn't efficient, the System seems to be fine with me staying here to develop. Randidly rubbed his jaw. He went to the open side of the Safe Room and dug six holes, each at least three meters apart from one another. Three holes were filled with bananas, three with nuts. Randidly placed the same combinations of crystals for both tree varieties—one red, one blue, and one both—just to test the possible effects.

Satisfied, he laid out the bedroll from the satchel and prepared for a nap. The sunstones on the ceiling dimmed and quenched themselves.

Randidly awoke to a question his subconscious had been toying with for a while: how long did he sleep each time? He always woke up perfectly rested. As someone who had difficulties with insomnia, to suddenly have those problems alleviated was deeply suspicious.

He propped himself up on his elbow and looked around. Buds already sprouted from his six most recent plantings. The other food-producers also showed obvious signs of growth.

Perhaps the real reason Randidly wanted to know how long he slept was his worries about Ace and Sydney. Based on his sleeping, he'd been within the Dungeon for five days. If the rest of the world had also been overrun with monsters, five days was a long time. Randidly suspected the Newbie Zones outside the Dungeon would be more forgiving than this place, but he couldn't be certain if that were actually the case.

The not-knowing would consume his thoughts if he let it. The edges of those possibilities were so sharp, his mental fortitude would be bled dry by handling them.

Randidly shook himself and turned his attention to the notifications he earned while sleeping. Farming had risen to Level 13. Plant Breeding had increased to Level 5.

Expectantly, Randidly threw those points into the Wandering Survivor Path. *One Skill Level at a time...*

Congratulations! You have earned **+1 to free Stat(s).**

Congratulations! You have earned **+1 to Perception and Reaction.**

Congratulations! You have earned **+2 to Health.**

Congratulations! You have earned **+2 to Mana.**

Congratulations! You have earned **+2 to Stamina.**

Although not receiving a bonus Skill was somewhat of a letdown, Randidly wouldn't complain about more Stats and attributes. The extra Stat he put into Intelligence, committing entirely to his new raising Mana to grind spells plan.

Even if it wasn't the best choice, he made it, and it shaped his other preparations.

His morning routine remained unchanged. He dashed the creeping expansion of the Safe Room, taking pauses between heats to flare Iron Skin and expend his charges of Mana Bolt. Randidly was starting to get a better hang of the Skill's usage. Because the attack took a bit to charge, he started using his off hand to support the source of the Mana Bolt, and his accuracy steadily improved.

The feeling of progress rubbed salve across the bleeding sores of his anxiety.

Congratulations! Your Skill **Mana Bolt** has grown to **Level 9!**

Fwoosh!
Dunnnn!
A Mana Bolt zipped forward, impacting the original tree with enough

force its leaves rustled in protest. Randidly lowered his arm, frowning. Progress like this couldn't continue indefinitely. Even though he'd reached the point that Mana Bolt could be cast every fifteen minutes, Randidly could tell he was reaching the limit of "safe" grinding.

Mana Bolt earned 1 Level and Iron Skin had grown by 2. The amount he could perform each action basically doubled from prior training days. Even worse, Running and Physical Fitness didn't go up at all, even if Sprint managed to inch forward a single Level.

Randidly was somewhat distraught when Heavy Blow reached Level 10 and a Path didn't unlock for it. Randidly supposed it hadn't worked that way with Farming either. He could only shrug, caution himself not to get ahead of himself, and throw his 4 PP into the Wandering Survivor.

Congratulations! You have earned **+1 to free Stat(s).**

Congratulations! You have earned **+1 to Perception and Reaction.**

Congratulations! You have earned **+2 to Health.**

Congratulations! You have earned **+2 to Mana.**

Again, this free Stat was put into Intelligence to boost his Mana pool. Randidly sat down to Meditate, which thankfully earned him another Skill Level. This PP he tossed immediately into the Path.

Congratulations! You have earned **+2 Stamina.**

Randidly prepared for a new way to hone his Skills. He went to the water pool and splashed himself, washing away his worries. He carefully packed his satchel and Meditated until every Attribute was at their full values. He stood before the Safe Room door and slapped his face for good luck. *Every time you survive, you are a little bit more prepared. Just do it.*

His new afternoon grinding consisted of the fun activity of having rocks thrown at him by the Howler Monkeys.

Randidly carefully considered this, deciding it was a necessary risk. Although the rocks could do about 50-60 damage, Randidly believed, with the combination of an improved Mana Shield and Iron Skin, he could shrug off most of the damage. Now that he knew where to look in the tree canopy for the monkeys, the danger of being ambushed by several rocks at once could be lessened by preparation. The monkeys hadn't attacked him previously until he'd shown himself.

Despite being racked with worry, those emotions only consumed half of his heart. The remainder was a feral savagery he scarcely recognized. One that urged him to attract more danger and grow quicker. The raw pleasure at the growth provided by the System morphed into a masochistic desire to rush toward dangerous opportunities.

Randidly closed the door to the Safe Zone behind him with two feelings in his chest. The clammy memory of horror when he realized he'd burned his Stamina to crush a Corpse Beetle.

And a near salivating anticipation toward his own progress.

Although his goals were lofty and aggressive, he defaulted to his usual habits. He flitted quickly into the leafy layers of ferns at the edge of the jungle and examined the surroundings. Oddly, Randidly found no frogs in the nearby area. Even when he moved through the ferns and passed the original berry bush, there were no fat frogs standing watch.

Randidly continued further. The Corpse Beetles had improved again since he last saw them, reaching Level 8, even though they hadn't changed in size. They just wandered through the underbrush without trying to eat or attack anything. Randidly wondered if they were one of the base units in this jungle's food chain.

Finally, Randidly arrived at his destination. The trees in front of him were tall and strong, thickly layered with vines. He crouched and pressed his knuckles into the soft grass.

Three Howler Monkeys clustered together near the edge of the jungle. Now that he knew what to listen for, their low chittering communication stood apart from the rest of the ambient noise of rustling leaves. Randidly's emerald eyes were sharp as he scrutinized the three figures. With the distance between where they were standing and where he was, he could handle three.

Randidly pushed himself out of the ferns and stood in the open grassy area near the wall.

The Howler Monkeys spotted him immediately. They hooted to each other and bared their teeth in something akin to glee. One of the bigger monkeys shoved the smaller one, pointing and waving its arms. The smallest scurried its way to the ground, fetching as many rocks as it could carry. When the fetching monkey returned, the bigger two smacked it before taking the rocks. The two throwers chittered to each other and took aim.

They're fucking bullies, Randidly realized. The smallest Howler Monkey flinched and scrambled away from the throwers. The side of him that came here with anticipation shifted toward an emotion that was quite a bit heavier. Randidly's eyes narrowed.

The first stone was slightly off target, glancing off the shield without breaking it. The monkey's face twisted into a scowl. The other monkey took aim and its stone struck the shield squarely, sending long cracks through the Shield of Mana.

Randidly allowed himself a tight smile. His progress was real. His Skill Levels and growing Intelligence kept the shield from breaking.

The first monkey slapped its knee, hooting mockery at its fellow for failing to shatter the Mana Shield.

Chittering and gesticulating, the second monkey grabbed another stone and whipped it as hard as it could toward Randidly, which was a lot harder than he was ready for.

Crack!

He activated Iron Skin, but it didn't save him. Randidly's shield shattered and his chest ached from the impact. He was on the ground for almost a full second before he scrambled to his feet, anticipating additional projectiles. He glanced at his Status when he noticed the Howler Monkeys were taking their time picking their next stone.

In addition to his pounding heartbeat, Randidly earned himself rewards.

Congratulations! Your Skill **Mana Shield** has grown to **Level 4!**

Congratulations! Your Skill **Iron Skin** has grown to **Level 10!**

Randidly rubbed the aching spot right below his collarbone as he straightened. Receiving that attack once more restored the cautious part of Randidly to prominence. When the two monkeys both whipped their stones at high speeds toward him, he deployed a Mana Shield and threw himself to the side, landing and sending a jolt of pain through his chest.

Congratulations! You have learned the Skill **Dodge Level 1.**

The stones whizzed above him and clattered against the wall. The monkeys howled in annoyance that he dared dodge. One of the throwers turned and slapped their small companion to set it to fetching more stones. Randidly pushed himself to his feet, but more stones were already shooting toward him.

Hopping side to side to avoid another battering, Randidly felt rather glum. *Well, this at least counts as a Skill, and dodging should be useful against the frogs as well.*

When the Howler Monkeys ran out of missiles, and their tinier companion was forced to get more, Randidly took advantage of the opening. He sent a few whizzing Mana Bolts to knock them off balance. Randidly grew even more frustrated when his attacks failed to injure them. In turn, the creatures took their aggravation out on the tiniest, whimpering monkey.

The sight of it made Randidly's heart ache.

After ten suffocating minutes of this choreographed dance, one of the throwers could stand it no longer and dropped to the ground. It lumbered forward, with its furry features twisted. Randidly's fear had been tempered by exposure, keeping his breathing even. He checked his Mana pool and his expression soured. Only twenty-seven Mana currently remained, just short of an Entangling Roots activation. And that measly 8 Mana would take forever to regenerate outside of the Safe Zone.

Randidly carefully aimed and blasted the monkey twice in its ugly face before turning to run.

A stone struck Randidly's leg, sending him sprawling on the grass. He'd forgotten about the other large monkey still in the canopy. The monkey on the ground rubbed the spots struck with the Mana Bolts like they simply itched, and pounced forward.

Randidly's adrenaline spiked. His experience with the Corpse Beetles gave him the bit of experience he needed. He slapped the ground and dragged himself forward, just out of the way of the leaping Howler Monkey. While the monkey lashed out with its paws, Randidly rolled away, creating distance between them.

Because of his trembling hands, Randidly was slower getting back to his feet. Another stone struck his shoulder and he barely managed to stop himself from crumpling face first into the ground. That aggressive side of himself flooded his body with heat. Bent at the waist, he forcefully planted his foot and steadied himself.

Randidly could hear his own heavy breathing. He took another step forward and accelerated into a sprint.

The monkeys hooted and howled, but those sounds drifted away, replaced with a whooshing sense of freedom brought on by his improved Agility. His pounding heart settled back into a more sustainable rhythm.

At least until he saw the Corpse Beetles and dug his heels into the ground to slow himself down.

The Corpse Beetles clustered together around several small bodies. There were about a dozen within the grassy area, and from the way the ferns shifted nearby, there were hundreds more marching through the jungle. Their teeth clicked, merging with the wet squelching of flesh.

That was when Randidly noticed the frog bodies.

Some looked like they had been squeezed until their eyes literally popped out of their slimy bodies. Others were perfectly bisected, both horizontally and vertically. There were frogs whose legs were cut off alongside more who were smashed into oblivion.

At first, Randidly fought the horror swelling within him, assuming the Corpse Beetles had evolved and become a predator in the forest. Except, the Corpse Beetles in front of him were only Level 10. Not all of the beetles clustered around, trying to plant their eggs inside the corpses. Almost half of them were smoking and dying, eaten away by the acid present in the deceased frogs' bodies.

Randidly realized the bloated beasts were facing away from the jungle, as if they were fleeing from something. *No, the Corpse Beetles didn't do this. Perhaps... perhaps this is what distracted them recently. But what?*

Randidly drew lines with his eyes through the trail of frog bodies. His stomach bubbled. The path led directly to the Safe Room door. Their blood soaked so thoroughly into the grass along that stretch of ground, the small blades had been dyed maroon.

He licked his lips, considering not going back into the Safe Room and instead test himself in the wider Dungeon. Randidly immediately dismissed the idea. The only reason he could come out here and endure this confrontation with the monkeys and the beetles was he had a place to return to. A place where he could close his eyes and sleep without fear.

Yet now that a reaper seemed to have stalked through the jungle right up to the entrance of the Safe Room... A monster couldn't enter the Safe Room, right?

Strangely, it was the existence of Randidly's plants that urged him to take a step forward, smash a stray Corpse Beetle, and grip the doorknob.

As Randidly entered his previously sacred space, he froze. An extremely tall and broad-shouldered man was sitting in the middle of Randidly's pond, facing away from him. Drops of pond water beaded on his bare back. From the angle of his neck and head, it looked like he was studying Randidly's tiny stretch of garden. Based on the blood stains on the floor, the figure was heavily wounded and currently healing.

As quietly as he could, Randidly closed the door behind him.

Congratulations! Your Skill **Sneak** has grown to **Level 7!**

Despite Randidly's attempts to not draw attention to himself, the figure turned. He was bald and his skin had a strange bluish tint. Other than that, he was simply a stern-looking martial artist. Except for the closed third eye in the middle of his forehead.

The blue-skinned man said something in another language. A strange sensation crackled within Randidly's head. The sounds seemed to rip themselves apart and shift, suddenly snapping back together.

"—ah, you had not met travelers from other worlds before. There, now you can understand, yes? Hello, little friend. Are you the one who brought these things here?"

He pointed at the plants. Randidly barely managed a nod.

The man shook his head, laughing slightly. Randidly couldn't help but notice a bloodstain on his cheek. Probably frog blood. The horrifying trail of bodies outside of the Safe Room dominated Randidly's mind as the man spoke.

"Do not worry, friend, we are both travelers. And you are from one of the newly acquired worlds, yes? For you to proceed into a Level 35 Dungeon after such a short amount of time is truly a wonder."

Exhaustion overcame Randidly. He walked to the edge of the central pond and sat down, the stranger's words repeating in his mind. *Newly acquired worlds?*

This thing... is bigger than just Earth?

CHAPTER NINE

*O*nce Randidly started talking, he found it difficult to stop. As much as the heavy muscles of Shal's arms and the bloodstain down his cheek and jaw made Randidly nervous, he was also envious of this stranger. He could clearly move freely within the Dungeon. That sort of freedom was what Randidly sought.

He explained about the sudden notification, how many times he almost died, and how he established a base camp within the Safe Room. The whole time, Shal rubbed his chin and occasionally looked toward the growing plants.

When his admittedly brief story was finished, Randidly was met with silence. Shal's eyes were sharp, and Randidly couldn't help but wonder how easily this strange alien could kill him. But no matter what, it felt oddly freeing to share his experiences with someone else.

"Extraordinary…" Shal muttered, looking Randidly up and down. "You do not have a Class, then? Or a Level? Which makes your improvement… extremely troublesome. You cannot earn experience. Normally, I would not mind helping you secure some kills in the area, so you can find your feet, but…"

Randidly could practically see the wheels turning in the man's blue head.

"However, I could do you the favor of escorting you to the entrance if you would bring me food while I recover in this pool. It will take several days, and to rid myself of this curse, I cannot leave the pool."

"That would… be appreciated," Randidly said slowly. He felt a small flare of pride. No matter how easily this man had dealt with the frogs, he needed *him* now.

Satisfied with the exchange, Shal turned away, focusing on his recovery within the pool.

After meditating for about an hour, Randidly took stock of himself. During the last frantic few minutes by the monkeys, Dodge had grown to Level 3 and both Iron Skin and Mana Shield gained 1 Level. However, the biggest gain was Mana Bolt, which once more gained 2 Levels. Randidly hoped it was 1 Level for each impact against the bully monkey's face. With these 7 PPs, Randidly could finish off the Wandering Survivor Path. Randidly barely stifled a gasp as he read through the slew of notifications.

Congratulations! You have earned **+1 to free Stat(s).**

Congratulations! You have earned **+1 to Perception and Reaction.**

Congratulations! You have earned **+2 to Health.**

Congratulations! You have earned **+2 to Mana.**

Congratulations! You have earned **+2 to Stamina.**

Congratulations! You have earned **+2 to free Stat(s).**

Congratulations! You have earned **+1 to all Stats.**

Congratulations! You have completed the **"Wandering Survivor Path"!**
As you explore more places and Paths, your ability to survive increases. You are a resilient survivor. **+2 to all Regenerations.**

Well, thanks, random Path Completion Reward... While it wasn't a per Level-up gain, the increase in regeneration across the board was incredibly powerful, especially with strengthening his Iron Skin further. If his Stamina regeneration was high enough, he could maintain the Skill almost constantly.
Of course, that's only if I have the luxury of standing still...
Of the 3 free Stats points he got, Randidly bit his lip and put them all into Intelligence, boosting his Mana pool just a little bit more. He admired his new stats. Certainly, getting a +1 to all Stats was always a good feeling.

Randidly Ghosthound
Class: ---
Level: N/A

Health(/R per hour): 138/153 (58.5)
Mana(/R per hour): 50/84 (23.5)
Stam(/R per min): 66/78 (23)
Vit: 16
End: 18
Str: 7
Agi: 15
Perception: 14
Reaction: 12
Resistance: 9
Willpower: 9
Intelligence: 15
Wisdom: 10
Control: 14
Focus: 9
Paths: *Newbie 7/7 | P. Def 10/10 | M. Supp 10/10 | Risk Taker 15/15 | Basic Physical Fitness 20/20 | Trainee 15/15 | Wandering Survivor 20/20*

Skills: *Running Lvl 7 | Physical Fitness Lvl 10 | Sneak Lvl 7 | Farming Lvl 13 | Mana Bolt Lvl 11 | Heavy Blow Lvl 10 | Acid Resistance Lvl 5 | Poison Resistance Lvl 5 | Sprinting Lvl 7 | Iron Skin Lvl 10 | Spirit of Adversity Lvl 3 | Plant Breeding Lvl 5 | Meditation Lvl 6 | Dagger Mastery Lvl 7 | Entangling Roots Lvl 1 | Mana Shield Lvl 4 | Dodge Lvl 3*

Satisfied Randidly shifted back to the Path screen, where a new notification was waiting for him.

Continue using paths to explore this world! Remember, there will always be a path open to you. Please select one of the paths below for your continued journey!

??? 0/5 | ??? 0/5

Rolling his eyes, Randidly selected the second option.

You have selected the "Pathless I Path."

Well, at least it will be short. Randidly prepared to start his physical training. He glanced sideways toward the pool, hesitating.

Ultimately, Randidly felt quite uncomfortable with Shal's presence. He went around the original tree, which followed the red crystal-banana tree upward, blossoming into a medium-sized tree that could somewhat screen his activities. He practiced Heavy Blow, Dagger Mastery, and Entangling Roots. The more he practiced, the more comfortable the leather grip of the dagger felt in Randidly's hand. He laid into the tree trunk with enthusiasm, losing himself in the satisfying exertion.

He hadn't put any points directly into Str, but the +1 to all Stats from Path rewards were adding up. The blade sang as it cut through the air. Chunks of the tree were ripped out with each connecting blow. While he was catching his breath, Randidly turned toward the far wall of the Safe Zone and mobilized his Mana. After a few seconds of the chilling energy draining out of him, roots as thick as his wrist popped about a half meter out of the ground. They whipped around, seeking a target to entangle.

Congratulations! Your Skill **Entangling Roots** has grown to **Level 2!**

When he was out of Stamina and Mana, he recharged through Meditation. Randidly tried to ignore Shal's silent observation. With his Attributes full, he went to check on his plants. It was only when Randidly began to mentally note the minute and scientific differences between the breeds that he could truly forget his observer and immerse himself in the task.

Besides, today was a good day. The branches of the berry bush drooped underneath the weight of the first berry harvest.

Randidly ate several fat berries before taking others to plant by the far wall. He noted the taste was similar to what he remembered from before. The berries didn't appear to have changed. While he was planting the new berry section, Randidly squinted at the cinderblock wall. What sort of mechanism enabled this space to continue to expand? The walls remained inscrutable.

Randidly could only sigh and return to the tree trunk. He lost himself in the feeling of attacking the pacifist tree.

Congratulations! Your Skill **Dagger Mastery** has grown to **Level 8!**

Congratulations! Your Skill **Heavy Blow** has grown to **Level 11!**

Congratulations! Your Skill **Dagger Mastery** has grown to **Level 9!**

Congratulations! Your Skill **Farming** has grown to **Level 14!**

Upon seeing the notification for Farming, he ceased his training. Farming was his highest Level Skill at 14. The fact that it continued to improve was proof his ministrations were valuable. With a small smile, Randidly stored his dagger and brought out vials to water his plants. *Now I just need to figure out how this Plant Breeding works...*

Still, that was a problem for later. For now, he had enough PP to finish off the Pathless Path.

Strangely, he didn't receive anything for any of the points, even the fifth. Or perhaps, rather than strangely, Randidly admitted it was rather disappointing. He only received a benefit along with the completion notification.

Congratulations! You have completed the **"Pathless I Path"**! The world in front of you is wide and filled with wonders. But now you have discovered that even without a chosen Path, your efforts will carry you forward. **+1 Stat(s).**

Shal's voice cut through Randidly's considerations. "Food, please."

Randidly gathered an armful of berries and placed them on a wooden plate from the satchel. This had the benefit of floating, so Randidly set it on the surface of the pond and pushed it out across the water to him.

As the three-eyed man relaxed in the middle of the pond, ponderously popping berries into his mouth without opening his eyes, Randidly took the chance to examine him. His body didn't seem to be outwardly injured, but he hadn't forgotten Shal's brief mention of a "curse."

Randidly grimaced and turned away. *I mean, I can shoot bolts of blue power, so I suppose curses aren't too far-fetched. It just proves how many threats came to Earth along with this System. For all that it speaks of the rewards you can earn, how many will believe those words and die, blinded by their greed?*

Randidly's brow grew increasingly furrowed. *I'm lucky, for all that I'm not in the Newbie area. Monkeys and acid-spitting frogs... those are small potatoes compared to a demon. Or a fire-breathing dragon. Or a weird cult, or a thousand other fantasy threats that could be out there right now.*

Ace, Sydney... stay safe. I hope you're together. Protect each other, all right?

Randidly forced his thoughts to stop wandering. With two mouths to feed and only one berry bush producing food, he couldn't remain in here for very long. He would once more need to go out and gather supplies.

As soon as Randidly left the Safe Room, he knew something was wrong. His instincts forced him into a crouch, scanning the surroundings with wide eyes.

Everything was gone. The bisected bodies of the frogs being loaded with Corpse Beetle eggs. The decaying beetles that were partially eaten away by acid. Even the intestines and the thick path of blood soaking the grass.

Beyond that, there was the silence. Nothing in the jungle before him moved. The absence of the constant rustling did not feel natural.

His skin crawled. He tightened his hands into fists. *Something... something is definitely strange out here. But I need to do this. We have our roles. As long as I provide food, Shal will escort me out of this place. I might not have interacted much with him, but he seems like a man who would keep his word.*

So... I need to keep mine.

Randidly pressed his lips together and moved. He slipped amongst the ferns, traveling cautiously down the tree line. The jungle remained quiet around him.

He paused to examine the area around the first berry bush. No frogs were present. Everything was eerily pristine. Chewing on his lip, he slipped out of the ferns and took several steps toward the berry bush, which had newly grown fruit weighing down its branches.

Randidly harvested every berry he could.

Nothing happened when he reached the banana and nut trees either, and began harvesting. He almost wished a Corpse Beetle would wander into his line of sight, proving his previous encounters in this jungle hadn't just been a weird fever dream. Paradoxically, every moment without action left him even more anxious. He crept forward and peered into the clearing.

The long body of the snake was still there, its thick frame now beginning to sag. Likely, the Corpse Beetles had eaten their way out, consuming its muscles and organs in the process. Randidly's heart clenched to see the snake's mouth had collapsed across the humanoid, but at the same time, he was helpless to do anything.

He couldn't discount that what he witnessed was the Corpse Beetles evolving into some horrifying final form. Perhaps even now, a sinister monster lurked within that pile of snakeskin and rotting flesh, waiting for him to move too close...

Shivering, Randidly circled to the far side of the clearing away from the deflated snake on his approach to the crystal tree. The surrounding jungle remained motionless as he crouched beside the roots and prepared to use the dagger to pry out a blue crystal.

He received a notification.

Congratulations! Your Skill **Sneak** has grown to **Level 8!**

Huh, Randidly thought as he slipped the dagger between crystal and root. *That's a pretty random Skill Level in Sneak—*

Randidly froze. He raised his gaze, staring at the surrounding trees.

A black mass with eight legs perched on a web erected between two trees only ten meters away. The angle prevented Randidly from noticing it on his approach. Around that sea-turtle-sized body were several soccer-ball-like objects wrapped in spider silk.

The giant spider silently moved its legs, lowering its body from the web. Chilling Mana coursed through Randidly's body, fueling his Skill activation.

Just as the spider exploded into motion, roots ripped through the ground and seized upon its legs. Randidly was horrified when the spider only had to struggle for a brief second before the roots began to tear. He ignored the following notification, his attention caught on the hanging name above the spider's head.

Deadly Webspinner Level 30

Randidly's limbs finally caught up to his galloping heart. The Webspinner ripped itself free just as Randidly stored his dagger and transitioned between Running and Sprinting. The surroundings blurred in his acceleration toward the far side of the clearing, his path running parallel to the spider's web.

Randidly heard a wet hiss over the pounding of his heart. His instincts informed him a threat rushed toward his back. He forcefully broke off his Sprint, heaving himself to the side and rolling behind a tree. A large wad of what could only be spider silk exploded against the tree canopy above him. Lines bloomed outward like a chrysanthemum, its thick strands flinging outward and immediately adhering to anything they touched.

More than a direct threat like the frog's acid, this was a web bomb.

Randidly scrambled into the cover of ferns before the Webspinner could strike again and sprinted to the Safe Room door. He leaned his forehead against the heavy door. *This ecosystem is probably in constant rotation. A powerful monster moves into an area and scares away the small fries, but eventually, that monster dies and Corpse Beetles are born from its corpse.*

Then, while the smaller animals are spreading out and testing the limit, the Corpse Beetles lure over a more dangerous being that eats them... and perhaps that being lures something else, all the way up, until one of those giant snakes takes up residence.

Shivering again, Randidly pushed open the door and examined his notifications. In that final scrum, Entangling Roots, Sprinting, Running, and Dodging all Leveled up. Real experience really did do more than repetitive grinding. Still, confirming that wasn't as valuable as seeing his Sneak Level and realizing what it implied about his safety.

Within the pool, Shal seemed in deep contemplation. Randidly was happy to leave him be. Feeling slightly giddy, he sat down and Meditated. He quickly entered into an introspective state and stayed there until he regained all of his Mana. The cooling sensation of that energy helped him come to terms with the fact that every time he left the Safe Room, his life was in danger.

This is what the world has become, Randidly told himself. *You need to have the confidence to survive in a world like this. Each time you survive, you are a little bit more prepared and your Skills are that much higher.*

Worrying about the next unexpected threat is a waste of time. Instead, prepare. If you accumulate enough PP, you'll be able to handle anything.

Steadily, his persuasion worked and his heart ceased its trembling. When he sighed and opened his eyes, he noticed that Meditation had gained 2 Levels and reached Level 8. Randidly took the 7 PP this survival earned him and turned to his Path screen.

Once again, two question mark options were displayed, both costing only 5 PP. Feeling lucky, Randidly once more picked the second option.

You have selected the "Pathless II Path."

Are there really two possible choices or is this just subterfuge? Randidly speechlessly put 5 PP into his "randomly" acquired Path, gaining only the final completion notification.

Congratulations! You have completed the **"Pathless II Path"**! +2 free Stat(s). You have received 1 Random Chest.

Congratulations! You have received a **Tiny Chest (R).**

"Huh…?" Randidly rubbed his chin. "Something like chests exist too, huh? This really is like a video game."

In his palm, the sort of chest that could contain a necklace or a fancy watch appeared. Randidly ran his fingers across its ornate surface, wondering whether there was a connection between the size and the Rarity. Excitement bubbled in his chest and Randidly undid the latch, opening his Rare Chest.

Inside was a mortar and pestle. Both implements were solid white pewter. Blue lines were drawn on the mortar in a simple, looping pattern near the base. Randidly lifted the items out of the chest and the tiny box vanished, leaving Randidly rather confused, staring at his newly acquired item.

If I stay here farming long enough, I suppose I could grind up the crystals and experiment with different quantities… Randidly chewed his lip and considered the items. They definitely seemed to be high-quality, but he caught himself wishing he'd earned a Skill instead. Another avenue to gather PP would have been invaluable.

As it had this morning, Shal's voice brought him back to the present. "Come, bring me some of your food. Recovering has taken more strength than anticipated."

Feeling quite pleased he'd convinced himself on this foraging mission, Randidly arranged the bananas and nuts upon the wooden plate and floated it to Shal. Randidly didn't bother to keep much for himself. He might be forced to harvest with that Webspinner present, but he wanted Shal to recover as quickly as possible. Randidly was growing increasingly determined to leave this place and find Ace and Sydney.

His near-death experiences might have given him a bit of a boost. Perhaps he'd be able to protect them.

As for his family... Randidly shook his head, refusing to think much about them. All the family he needed he found at Rawlands University. Or rather, who he'd followed there.

Randidly distracted himself by sorting his haul from the day. He sighed when he realized he'd only managed to dislodge one blue crystal before he was forced to flee.

Then something occurred to him. Randidly turned to Shal. "Excuse me, do you know what this is?"

Randidly held up one of the red and blue glowing crystals.

In between the steady motion of Shal transporting food from plate to mouth, his eyes slid open, sparing the crystals a glance. "Yes, they are basic vigor crystals. They can be refined into Health and Mana potions. Although they were produced within an energy dense Level 35 Dungeon, the crystals are just the basic kind, put next to a Safe Room to help truly desperate individuals. I would say even a master Alchemist could only create potions that restore 100 Health or Mana from such things."

Randidly felt like an idiot. *Why the hell haven't I thought about that? If this is a game-style world now, then potions...!*

Randidly licked his lips. "H-how do you refine them?"

Shrugging, Shal gestured dismissively. "Such trifles are unrelated to my Class. I cannot learn this Skill. Now please, allow me to concentrate. I must heal."

Even in the face of Shal's dismissal, Randidly's eyes were bright when he focused on the crystals in his palm. If he had Mana and Health potions, despite them not being as efficient as Shal stated, the speed of his growth would skyrocket. Even if he only managed to make a potion that restored 20 Mana, that was two more Mana Bolts, ready any time he needed them.

Health potions would make it easier to survive something like the frogs' acid, Randidly belatedly reminded himself in the middle of his starry-eyed plans to reinvigorate his training regimen. *That's pretty useful too.*

CHAPTER TEN

*A*fter six hours, Randidly sat back and grinned at the vial in front of him with relish. The strange electric lights of the Safe Room caught the crimson liquid in the container and made it positively gleam. He'd experimented with the red crystals first, intending to make absolutely sure he didn't waste any of the materials for Mana potions.

The whole process was absurdly easy once he started playing with the crystals. The material was quite brittle. It took only a few knocks against the concrete walls to crack it.

His first experiment involved putting a pinch of the red crystal dust into his mouth. The particles dissolved, resulting in a flood of heat filling him. At first, he was quite pleased, until a notification popped up.

Congratulations! Your Skill **Poison Resistance** has grown to **Level 6!**

Randidly hastily coughed out a particularly large piece of crystal that hadn't yet dissolved. *Well, it's true that they say too much medicine is the same as a poison. I just need to perfect the dosage.*

Experiments two through seventeen involved consuming smaller and smaller pieces of crystal, which was surprisingly difficult without any sort of table or proper implements. When the seventeenth attempt earned him another point in Poison Resistance, Randidly admitted this method wasn't the correct one.

It was only after becoming dejected and rummaging through his satchel that he thought of a different way. He removed some of the vials he used to water the plants, his plan forming. Instead of letting the crystal dissolve in his mouth, what if he mixed it with water first?

Randidly filled the vial halfway with water from the pool and sprinkled a pinch of red crystal dust into the liquid. The water steadily darkened in color until it reached a crimson coloration. The real herald of victory was the resulting notification.

Congratulations! You have learned the Skill **Potion Making Level 1.**

The potion was warm in his hand. Randidly considered the process of testing its effectiveness with a sardonic smile. *Heh, does this mean I need to get beat up a bit, drink the potion, and compare how quickly my Health regenerates? Assuming it's a Health Potion...*

Randidly frowned at the potion in his hand, considering his options. Just as he was about to move, something about his gaze triggered a change in the vial. A small window appeared above it.

Amateur's Potion Level 1: Will restore **10 Health** over **5 seconds.**

Randidly hopped to his feet and laughed. He paused in his jubilation and looked toward Shal. The man was still recovering with his eyes closed. Randidly sat back down and rubbed his hands together. He wanted to make a few more practice potions, but the headache brewing between his eyes warned him he'd been pushing himself a little too hard.

He settled back against the grassy ground and closed his eyes. First, he needed to rest. Then he could continue to improve.

Randidly sat up and yawned, his arms stretching expansively. He hoisted himself off the ground and engaged in a few basic stretches. The funny thing was, he didn't feel cramped or uncomfortable in the slightest. There definitely must be some actual health benefits to earning Stats, because he was suddenly in great physical shape.

Shal's now familiar grunt pulled Randidly from his reverie and he split the remainder of their food. Most of it went to feeding Shal, though Randidly made sure he consumed enough berries, bananas, and nuts himself.

He moved to the first berry bush and plucked it clean. It wasn't enough for another meal, but it would certainly help stave off hunger for another few hours.

Randidly considered the rapidly ripening, growing line of trees. *Plus, I'm almost to the point of self-sufficiency.*

Only then did he turn to the task of Potion Making. His eyes glowed as he took stock of his materials. He'd only used a fraction of a single crystal to make his first Amateur Potion, and he had over fifty crystals of each color at his disposal.

There's just something about building and discovery. Randidly allowed himself a wide smile and got to work.

His initial goal was simple. What was the most powerful Health potion he could make? To that end, he arranged for five initial tests consisting of various amounts of water and red crystal to generate a result.

Thankfully, the process was simple. Randidly quickly identified the determinants of how successful the potion would be. Ratio of crystal to water and the uniformity of the crystal grain size.

Honestly, stumbling upon the second one was a fluke. Randidly grimaced as he sat back on his haunches and reflected. One potion had been much less successful than the others and he had no idea why. Luckily, he noticed a particularly large chunk amongst the powder he'd added to that vial, noting it due to its unusual size.

If I hadn't, I'd have likely wasted hours trying to figure out what went wrong... Randidly begrudgingly dumped out his results and began again. He put his Rare mortar and pestle to use, grinding the crystals down to a tiny, uniform size.

The ratio of water to material was also fairly simple. An almost full vial was ideal for a pinch of red crystal. The size was so perfect, Randidly couldn't help but wonder if these vials had been filled with potions in the past. He could picture that humanoid desperately slurping them down as the snake's fangs pumped poison through his veins...

Randidly shook himself away from those images and buried his uneasiness as best he could. *One foot in front of the other. Right now, I need to brew potions. Don't think beyond that.*

After two hours, Randidly reached the limits of what he could currently produce with his materials.

Congratulations! Your Skill **Potion Making** has grown to **Level 5!**
Apprentice's Potion Level 19: *A potion made by an inexperienced but serious apprentice.* Will restore **48 Health** over **3 seconds.**

Interesting that the Potion Level can be higher than the Skill Level. Randidly rubbed his chin. *Is it based off the amount of Health it heals?*

Although it was a far cry from 100, 48 Health was still quite a bit. Randidly was pleased with himself. He only used a dozen of the red crystals, resulting in a fair amount of potions that could restore 30-some Health in case of emergencies. The problem was he only had fifteen vials.

I want Mana for practice, but Health will keep me alive. Randidly turned the glimmering sapphire crystals over in his hand. He set them back down into the pile and sat on his haunches.

Ultimately, it was the shivering, fearful part of Randidly who decided the issue for him with a very morose thought. *If I'm hurt badly enough that I need more than two or three Health potions, won't it probably already be too late?*

Randidly tried not to think too closely about that. He continued to work on potions under the warm sunstones from the ceiling. Occasionally, he took breaks to harvest more berries and pour a few vials of water on his developing miniature orchard. By the end of three hours, he had four Health potions and eight Mana potions. Most restored about forty of each attribute. Randidly even somehow managed to make one that restored 61 Mana. He tucked that one away for emergency Entangling Roots situations.

One vial he kept for water. For the final two, Randidly experimented with different combinations of Health and Mana stones. This process was far more difficult. If the mixture wasn't *exactly* 50/50 or 75/25, the potion turned into a foaming grey mess Randidly hastily dumped out. The grass briefly turned brown in that region, forcing Randidly to move his practice a few meters to the side.

Congratulations! Your Skill **Potion Making** has grown to **Level 6!**

This is not really scientific at all... Randidly thought as he wiped sweat from his forehead between attempts. *Getting the ratios perfect with just my fingers is a matter of luck.*

Congratulations! Your Skill **Potion Making** has grown to **Level 7!**

Eventually, he did succeed. 75/25 with red in the majority was a Stamina potion, and it restored a staggering 80 Stamina. Randidly shook his head as he examined the meager result of his toil. After all, that amount would come back in four minutes anyway.

Another emergency potion, but one for basically just running away from slow threats. Randidly moved on to the other ratios, his hands beginning to ache from the repetitive motion of grinding the crystals.

Congratulations! Your Skill **Potion Making** has grown to **Level 8!**

Congratulations! Your Skill **Potion Making** has grown to **Level 9!**

50/50 created a liquid that could only be described as a concentration potion. After consuming it, even the tiniest detail seemed to stick out. While under its influence, Randidly's speed of Potion Making and accuracy of measurements skyrocketed. He remixed most of the potions, and soon each of his vials was filled with Health and Mana potions that restored between fifty and sixty of the attribute.

Congratulations! Your Skill **Potion Making** has grown to **Level 10!**

When the potion wore off, Randidly groaned from a sudden sense of dizziness. He rolled onto his back and covered his eyes. A pounding headache had taken residence between his eyes, inviting all its painful friends for a visit inside of Randidly's skull. It took almost an hour for the throbbing pressure to fade.

Never again, Randidly swore to himself. But when he tried to continue making potions, his hands were still shaking. Randidly huffed and used that time to practice jogging, sweating the remnants of the weird potion out of his body.

Despite the painful effect and his unwillingness to endure that horrible headache again, another part of Randidly saw several scenarios where such mental acuity would be useful. And as the effect lasted for almost an hour, he wouldn't have a harsh time limit to finish some necessary task. He filled one vial of that potion.

Congratulations! Your Skill **Potion Making** has grown to **Level 11!**

75/25 with blue in the majority took a bit longer. Perhaps because of some lingering mental exhaustion. Randidly kept working at it until he earned a notification and a cloudy-looking potion.

Congratulations! Your Skill **Potion Making** has grown to **Level 12!**

Lesser Restore Potion Level 27: *Weakens the effects of foreign influences on the body.* **Cures minor status ailments.**

That potion was not only the highest Level he'd made, but it also pushed his Potion Making to Level 12. Randidly stretched and rubbed his neck. From how sore his joints were, he must have been hunched over the mortar and pestle for several hours.

Randidly gradually frowned.

It's... strange that I'm not physically tired after today. Randidly chewed on his lip, staring at his hands. *I'm still mentally tired, but is it possible Vitality or Endurance affect exhaustion? Could it even possibly let me go for longer without sleep?*

Those thoughts would have to wait for another time. Randidly reeled back in his focus and considered the text of this new potion. He gripped the vial and its cloudy liquid, taking a few steps toward Shal.

"Uh, excuse me… Will something like this help you recover?" Randidly hated how weak he sounded, but he couldn't forget the trail of carnage leading into the Safe Zone. And this figure was the quickest method to escape this Dungeon.

Outside, Ace and Sydney had spent almost a week in whatever was occurring on Earth outside the Dungeon. Anxiety for his friends buzzed in Randidly's chest. The faster he escaped this place, the faster he could…

Thoughts for later, Randidly harshly chided himself. His hand on the vial tightened.

Shal spared him a glance, then beckoned him closer. Randidly applied a cork and tossed the potion, which Shal deftly caught. After a short inspection, Shal grunted and swallowed the contents, tossing the vial back to Randidly.

When Randidly caught the vial, all three of Shal's eyes were once again closed. Randidly scratched his cheek, wondering what this meant.

After a time, Shal opened his eyes, regarding Randidly, his head slightly tilted to the side. "In a small way, this does help, yes. If you had 1,000 of such potions, I would be cured almost immediately."

Shal didn't bother to wait to hear how many of those potions Randidly had. Randidly couldn't blame him.

Grimacing, Randidly walked back over to the intermittent patches of brown grass marking his Potion Making area. Accomplishment warred with disappointment within him. His potion had an effect, but it was miniscule. If he truly poured himself into the manufacture of potions, his Skill would improve and the total number he would need to make would be below a thousand. As for how much below…

Even though he'd expected a similar reaction, the sense of impotence was rapidly eating its way outward through his limbs. Randidly slapped his own cheeks to remain focused. *I'm improving. I'm taking steps forward. Trust the process. No great building was ever erected in a single day. You've got this.*

Shaking his head, Randidly refocused on the moment. Bringing up his Path screen, Randidly noticed he had two new options for the staggering 15 PP he gathered while making potions.

Seeing them elicited a sense of foreboding.

??? 0/10 | ??? 0/10

"Why did both change? Shouldn't I still have access to the old one? Unless they really were only one option…"

Resigning himself to his fate, Randidly randomly selected the second option.

You have selected the "Pathless III Path"!

Of course I have...

Randidly maxed out the path with his accumulated PP. He earned bonus Stats at 5 and 10 spent PP, in addition to his completion bonus.

Congratulations! You have completed the **"Pathless III Path"! +2 Stat(s).**
You have realized that while not all paths are the same, all paths will eventually lead you toward the same destination. Be careful as you wander farther afield. Danger lurks between your current position and the heights of power you seek.

Congratulations! You have learned the Skill **Pathfinding Level 1.**

Pathfinding Level 1: *It is very difficult for you to lose your sense of direction. Landmarks and interesting locations that you pass will be automatically added to any maps you possess.* **Your ability to remember your trail and make sense of new locations improves with Skill Level.**

Four Stats and a random Skill wasn't such a bad haul for this Pathless Path, all things considered. Without a second thought, Randidly dumped all the points into Intelligence. He needed his Mana higher so he could practice more with his various Mana Skills. Plus, the Stat points would boost his Skill damage too.

Randidly thought about the thick forearms of the Howler Monkeys as they whipped stones with enough force to break his Mana Shield. *I have some physical Stats, but let's be serious. I grew up in the modern era. I've never even been in a fist fight. Learning to fight up close and actually make use of this Dagger Mastery... that will take too long.*

He felt oddly sad at that thought. Like he was disappointing some sort of childhood dream of being a berserker, wielding a massive axe and continuing to fight despite increasingly grievous wounds. Randidly stifled that thought, returning to the Path Screen. Surprisingly, his new options weren't mirrors of each other.

$$??? \ 0/15 \ | \ ??? \ 0/10$$

Shrugging, Randidly selected the 15 options.

You have selected the "Pathfinder Path."

This Path comes from that Skill, huh... wonder what the reward will be.

With his few spare PP, Randidly started to work his way through this new Path based upon his Skill. The first 4 PP got Randidly nothing, but PP five got him +1 to P. Supp, which was acceptable. That point went into Reaction.

He Meditated for a while, going over his next move. They might have enough berries for another meal, but more food wouldn't hurt. With his new Skill and a few extra Stats, Randidly left the Safe Room, heading toward the monkey area with plans to stop by the banana trees.

Thankfully, the Deadly Webspinner stayed deeper in the jungle than Randidly needed to go. With the acid-spitting frogs still gone, he easily filled the satchel with food and proceeded to the Howler Monkey area. When he arrived, Randidly wasn't sure whether to be happy or sad when he spotted the same trio of monkeys lounging around.

One of the larger of the monkeys slapped the smallest to fetch rocks and the game was afoot.

By now, dodging was relatively simple. Instead, he kept still for a while, allowing the rocks to hit his shield, Leveling Mana Shield twice. The Skill almost had enough structural integrity to withstand a full power throw from the monkeys. His casual return fire earned Mana Bolt one Level. He didn't really wish to antagonize them too badly, but wanted to keep them honest.

It was when they finally dropped down that he tested the usefulness of the Mana potions. Randidly chugged several, casting Entangling Roots on an unfortunate Howler Monkey over and over again. The Skill was still barely enough to stop them for a split second, but it delayed them long enough to ensure he was never in any danger.

Besides, the exercise earned Randidly three enviable prizes.

Congratulations! Your Skill **Entangling Roots** has grown to **Level 4!**

Congratulations! Your Skill **Entangling Roots** has grown to **Level 5!**

Congratulations! Your Skill **Entangling Roots** has grown to **Level 6!**

The only disappointment was the Deadly Webspinner remained active around the crystal tree, covering the surrounding area with its thick web. He wandered somewhat close until the tingling hairs on his spine had him retreating back toward the edges of the jungle.

The only moment of horror came on the way back, as Randidly passed the area where he'd harvested bananas only an hour earlier. Thick ropes of web had sprung up around the banana tree, a veritable declaration of war from the spider who likely watched him move amongst the trees earlier.

Randidly repressed a shiver as he made his way back to the Safe Room. *Guess next time I'll need to go a little bit more out of my way to find food...*

CHAPTER ELEVEN

Congratulations! Your Skill **Farming** has grown to **Level 16!**

*B*ack at the base, Randidly catalogued the gathered food before inspecting his steadily expanding orchard. The first generation of trees was starting to produce food. Seemed his worries regarding the Deadly Webspinner were for naught.

Randidly pulled off a fresh banana from the Safe Zone tree and compared it to one he brought back. They were exactly the same. He rapped himself on the side of the head. *This is why you can't worry about things too far in the future. Worrying about hypotheticals that will never happen only wastes energy.*

The second generation of trees, in various stages of growth, had successfully mixed with the crystals. The trees with red crystals were larger and darker. The ones mixed with blue were slender and had pale bark. The seeds using both had grown vibrant and lush, with thick and heavy leaves. Perhaps in another day or two, the orchard would be fully functional.

With his 8 PP from the Howler Monkey expedition, Randidly continued the Pathfinder Path. At 10, he earned +1 all M. Supp, which was a nice benefit for his Mana Skills. After stretching a bit, Randidly served Shal another meal and lay down for a rest of his own. The combination of the Potion Making and the stressful journey to encounter the Howler Monkeys left him completely drained.

Yawning, Randidly's thoughts wandered. *I wish I had a clock…*

Congratulations! Your Skill **Plant Breeding** has grown to **Level 6!**

When he awoke, Randidly started with his typical jogging and dagger-work exercises. He went through another round of stretching, surprised to find how much more limber he'd become in the past few days.

How much the second portion of the orchard had changed took him by surprise. While he slept, small bulges rapidly grew out to become fruit. The trees had gained additional height, with the red crystal combinations dwarfing the others. They would be self-sufficient more quickly than he originally thought.

"Boy!" Shal called.

And that speed would be a good thing, considering how much of the food Shal consumed.

After feeding his ticket out of the Dungeon, Randidly returned to the fruit. He began with the bananas, knowing what to expect. He peeled one of the larger, freshly grown examples and took a bite. His eyes brightened. Not only were the red bananas bigger, they also had a strange savory spice that was a welcome variation from the regular sweetness.

The straight blue crystal bananas were tangy and strangely spongy, almost like a cake. They certainly seemed like they would keep longer without going bad. Randidly harvested those and created a new pile. The food depleted by Shal's meal was almost immediately restored.

Randidly paused with a frown. *Actually, do things simply not spoil in this room? Just... what exactly is going on in the world?*

Randidly ignored the notion and clapped his hands together, getting back to work.

The mixed crystal bananas were the true peculiarity. Each time he touched a banana hanging from the slender tree, they turned to ash. Except for one. That specimen seemed to pulse with light. As he studied it, Randidly realized juice was oozing out of the banana peel, leaving a trail of sticky, dripping residue on the trunk. Randidly eased the banana free and peeled it. The flesh was white like bleached teeth. Slightly nervous, Randidly took a small nibble of the fruit.

Warm waves of heat washed through his body. He smiled and flexed his hand, savoring the sensation. He felt... powerful. Acting purely on instinct, Randidly produced the knife and made it dance, slashing left and right.

Almost immediately, he gained a Level of Dagger Mastery, which made him smile wider. Soon he was leaping back and forth, cutting imaginary enemies to pieces with his precise attacks. Randidly was filled with a strange confidence that he was wrong about his disinclination toward hand-to-hand fighting. Although he wasn't experienced, that didn't necessarily mean he couldn't defeat a lousy Howler Monkey.

He was quick, strong, smart, and he could spot the monkey's weaknesses. With some proper image training, he could lay the groundwork for an easy victory. Randidly chuckled and his confidence began to swell, filling him with the certainty that the System gave him all the tools to grow strong, no matter what he chose to pursue. All he needed was time and attention, and he could solve any problem.

Even this Dungeon won't keep me trapped forever. Randidly's eyes flashed as he continued to hop back and forth, spinning the dagger and cutting the air. *And when I get out... heh.*

An increase in the Level of his Physical Fitness made his confidence swell even further. He definitely felt stronger and more resilient after biting into the banana. It wasn't just a change in Stats. It was the lifestyle, the diet. His body was changing, *he* was changing. The shaky confidence he had to slap into himself before leaving the Safe Room had finally, truly taken up residence in his chest.

Dagger Mastery gained another Level. He was so sure in that moment. He could walk out the Safe Room door, march to the Howler Monkeys, and cut them to pieces. Hell, on the way back, maybe he would stop by to check out the Deadly Webspinners. As long as he avoided their sticky webs, he could toy with them from afar.

Pah, I can't believe I've been wasting time feeding this man when all I needed to do was finally trust myself and—

All at once, the confidence vanished, leaving an empty coolness suffusing his body. Randidly shivered and dropped the dagger. *What... What was that?*

Trembling, he breathed in and out. The previous few minutes were a heady blur.

Perhaps the most disturbing thing about the whole situation was the infectious confidence that buoyed him after he took the small nibble. Randidly looked at the banana on the ground where he'd casually discarded it, with only a single bite taken. He would likely dispose of it altogether if not for the fact that he gained three Skill Levels in five minutes. Although it might have been a coincidence, it didn't feel like one.

At least this doesn't have the headache of the concentration potion. Randidly grimaced and rubbed the back of his neck. *But it's just as powerful. Is there some compound present that boosts Skill growth? Or was it because of how sure I was during my movements...?*

Being careful not to breathe any stray fumes from the banana, Randidly peered closely at the fallen fruit, trying to figure out why it had such a profound effect on him.

Congratulations! You have learned the active Skill **Analyze Level 1.**

Analyze: *Closely examine materials and rare items. Works primarily to determine the crafting potential of base materials. Can also give some* *insight into completed projects.* **Ability to discern materials and structure increases with Skill Level.**

Congratulations! Your Skill **Analyze** has grown to **Level 2!**

Lesser Origin Banana: *Made from a tree that grows rich in both yin and yang energies, only one Origin Banana blooms per tree.* **The concentrated energy within it has great potential to increase the efficacy of most effects.**

It could even increase the efficiency of training? But more than that, it doesn't explain that monstrous confidence that filled me.

Still, another Skill and the Skill Levels that came along with it were useful. Randidly tucked the banana into the deepest corner of the satchel for safekeeping. Meanwhile, he walked over to the middle of the nut trees, having high hopes for another origin food from the nut he planted with both red and blue crystals.

Unfortunately, his luck was not that good. When he pulled off a nut, an unpleasant scent wafted from it.

Warped Halnut: *Strange energies have warped this Halnut.* **Can be refined into a poison with unpredictable effects.**

Unpredictable wasn't exactly what Randidly was looking for. He turned to the blue Halnuts. Popping one off the tree, he cracked it open and gazed inside. Although the surface of the nut was oddly cool, it was otherwise quite normal. It did seem a bit oilier, with the flesh on the inside shifting when he pressed it. Randidly studied the nut until he Analyzed it, earning another Level for the new Skill.

Cool Halnut: *A variant of the Halnut with a unique taste.* **Its core is useful for crafting.**

Randidly nibbled the edge. To his surprise, it tasted oddly minty. He took a bigger bite, enjoying the strange, peanut-butter-like consistency combined with the minty flavor. He took another bite, his teeth smashing against what could only be the core.

A thread of cold energy spread within his mouth, numbing him. Randidly spat out the whole thing.

After the numb sensation went away, Randidly carefully cleared away the flesh, revealing a small blue bead.

Blue Energy Bead: *A refined version of a blue energy shard.* **Not edible. Useful for crafting.**

Ignoring the strange insult from the description, Randidly pulled out one of the glowing blue crystals he'd harvested from the tree. With the addition of the Analyze Skill, it was possible to...

Blue Energy Shard: *Basic, low-grade material. The energy will react unpredictably in various situations.* **Can be refined into various potions.**

With glittering eyes, Randidly turned to the red Halnut bush. *What a useful Skill. Let's see what else is going to enrich our diets here...*

For four hours, Randidly gathered information on the results from his plant breeding. He then went back through and examined all of his Potions with Analyze to see if he could see any changes. There were some small adjustments to the messages he received, but overall, everything was the same.

The process earned him another two Skill Levels in Analyze. What really excited him was a sudden thought when he examined the Origin Banana.

Immediately, Randidly threw himself back into the task of Potion Making. He concentrated as he carefully ground up the various crystals and mixed them together, seeking the perfect ratio. He failed over and over again, to the point Randidly bit the bullet and drank some of the remaining Concentration Potion.

For the result, I'll endure a little bit of a headache. Randidly gritted his teeth. *There's too much strangeness to this new world. The longer I stay here, the more things will develop in unpredictable directions. I need to escape the Dungeon as soon as possible...*

Congratulations! Your Skill **Potion Making** has grown to **Level 13!**

Congratulations! Your Skill **Potion Making** has grown to **Level 14!**

When he succeeded in his crazy idea, Randidly smiled with all the warmth of a Caribbean dawn. Thinking he would soon meet back up with his friends, some of the tension in his chest eased.

"Shal, I think this might be a bit more potent." Randidly's voice was controlled, because whatever it was that he'd created, it Leveled him twice in Potion Making in one go. And when he tried to Analyze it, he failed.

His Skill Level wasn't high enough.

Instead of regular red and blue energy shards, Randidly used the beads to form the base powder of the Lesser Restore Potion, and combined water with a few extra drops of the Origin Banana's juice. He failed three times, getting the ratios just slightly off even under the effects of the Concentration Potion. It seemed that as the Level of the potion increased, the requirements were even more exact. But on the fourth try...

Shal beckoned, and Randidly threw him the potion. This time, when Shal lifted the vial to his nose, he became serious, pausing to study the tiny potion. He took a heavy sniff.

"This... even I do not recognize it. But..." After a few moments of hesitation, Shal removed the cork, tipped his head, and threw back the unidentified concoction. Immediately, he huddled lower in the pond, completely submerged.

Shit. A dark thought occurred to Randidly. *Considering what happened to the Halnut tree... what if I made something poisonous? What if I killed him, and now his body is just floating in the pool?*

Or even worse... Randidly's expression twisted, picturing the bisected acid frogs leading to the Safe Room door. *What if the poison* doesn't *kill him and he's not pleased with me...*

For several seconds, nothing happened. Then the water began to bubble and boil around Shal. Randidly cautiously backed away, hoping this wasn't some sort of retribution for the vial he'd given Shal.

His retreat from the pool turned out to be a wise decision, but not for his paranoia-fueled fears. A giant black bat, made entirely of black mist, erupted upward from Shal's body. It screeched and its ethereal eyes found Randidly. With a roar, it spread its dark wings and charged.

Before it covered even a meter of the space between them, a spear shot out of the pool and skewered the specter's heart. Its spectral skin shredded and flaked outward as Shal's decisive blow impacted its capability to live, if not also its obvious animosity. With its body stretched beyond recognition, the hateful bat deflated and disappeared. All of its accumulated darkness vanished and the Safe Room returned to normal. With a huge grin, Shal leaped from the pool, laughing and shaking himself dry like a dog.

"Wonderful, wonderful! You have saved me many days in this boring room with that precious potion. I can repay you immediately. Are you ready to leave the Dungeon?"

Randidly licked his lips. "Yes. I'd like that very much."

The trip to the entrance was almost surreal. Randidly barely had time to harvest his plants before he was dragged out by his enthusiastic guardian. Shal explained, his voice booming, that you passively lose experience while in a Safe Room. Which was why no one in their right mind would stay there for even a second longer than they needed to recover.

Ah, experience... Randidly reflected, unable to yet worry about the volume of Shal's words. *Another aspect of this new System that matters not at all to me... At least not yet.*

For whatever reason, Randidly expected the journey to the front of the Dungeon to be stressful. He did his best to reassure himself repeatedly that he was ready for any potential ambush on the way. With his Skills and Shal's experience, they would take their time and get through the roadblocks.

But Shal moved too quickly for Randidly's worries to keep up.

Shal carried Randidly most of the way, leaping large distances through the forest without any incidents.

Shal explained the enemies around here were below 30, mostly meant to grind down weaklings' resources. It was only in the area right after Randidly's Safe Room, where the forest gave way to plains, that the Dungeon became truly difficult. It was there that Shal was cursed by an Orc Shaman Mini-Boss after sustaining serious injuries, leaving him in such a wounded state, he was forced to take shelter in the Safe Room.

At this point, Shal sighed. "However, it is hard to proceed. The mental attacks of the Shaman are too confounding. I might need to spend a few months Leveling to get my Willpower high enough to withstand his petty tricks."

After that ambiguous revelation, Shal was silent for the rest of the journey.

Covering that distance only took about five hours, with Randidly riding on Shal's back. To distract himself, Randidly Meditated, and even received a Skill Level. Either due to their speed or Shal's Level, they hadn't needed to stop and fight anything.

Hence, the strange sensation of disconnection from the world grew more all-consuming. After the week of struggling alone in the Safe Room. To Shal's arrival. The discovery of the potions...

Everything had happened so quickly. Too quickly. Randidly's emotions could have tied themselves into knots chasing after the parade of developments. But instead, they just left him exhausted.

Suddenly, they were standing before a set of huge iron doors. Randidly's heart pounded. He wanted so badly to leave the Dungeon and meet back up with his friends, but the nervous version of himself now balked at the very idea of leaving the Dungeon so quickly. Between the way his plants were growing, the experiment with potions, and training with the Howler Monkeys...

I have so much more growing to do.

"Here, friend, just press your hand against the doors and click *yes*." Shal smiled good-naturedly at Randidly.

Honestly, Shal's whole outlook changed since Randidly gave him that potion. Apparently, his recovery meant much more than any of the labor Randidly had put in fetching him food.

I should want to thank Shal. But suddenly... Randidly hesitated. His sudden desire to dig in his heels didn't make sense. Especially considering what would have likely happened if Shal hadn't arrived now that Deadly Webspinners had moved into the area. This action of bringing him to the entrance of the Dungeon likely saved his life. If he had been left to his own devices in here...

For all the liquid confidence he'd gotten from those potions, those agile Deadly Webspinners would have strung him up between the tree and sucked away his lifeblood until he was a husk.

Randidly urged his head to nod. He *should* want this. He *did* want this. The orderly and rewarding System wouldn't just disappear when he left the Dungeon. As for what he would find there... Ace and Sydney, together.

Numb, Randidly forced his body into motion. He pressed his hand against the door and a notification box flickered in front of him. There was a strange buzzing and Randidly could barely look at what was in front of him.

Randidly focused on the notification box. *Did the notification just... change?*

Strangely, Randidly heard a low female chortle. He must have imagined it, because when he looked around, Shal wasn't even paying attention to him. Scratching his head, Randidly turned to look at the notification. What he saw made the blood drain from his face.

You are unable to enter the Dungeon. Please choose a Class and reach Level 10 before proceeding. (*There is no further Level requirement, but please see Dungeon Level for a guideline of the necessary strength.*)

"But..." Randidly said aloud, as though the door to the Dungeon could hear him. "I'm just trying to leave."

Yet despite everything, he felt a small spark of relief.

CHAPTER TWELVE

"It seems," Shal said slowly, "this turn of events was never considered by the makers of this place. Hum… You must be Level 10 to use the door to a Dungeon. But while you are in here, you cannot gain a Class, and therefore cannot Level to the point that you can retreat through the entrance."

Randidly stared at the floor—he would be stuck here forever. His hesitation to leave and his desire to remain here with the plants and the Howler Monkeys doomed him.

The outside world weighed heavily on Randidly's mind. It'd been over a week since the change happened. He wasn't sure what was happening outside of the Dungeon, but it couldn't be good. Although the monsters out there, in a normal area, might be of lower Levels, they were still monsters. Monsters that tried to kill you.

Shal rubbed the back of his neck, regarding Randidly with heavy eyes. Randidly's heart felt heavy. He'd seen that expression enough on his father's face to know what was coming next. Shal owed Randidly for giving him that potion, but he didn't want to babysit him any longer. He had a life outside of Randidly. Randidly pressed his lips together and returned to boring a hole in the ground with his stare.

Shal released a gasp and Randidly looked up. The three-eyed man's gaze was blank.

"You have… no Class…?" Shal muttered, and his eyes sharpened. He barked out his next words. "Kid, what are your Skills?"

Randidly opened his mouth, then closed it. He knew he had no reason not to trust Shal, but revealing something like that so freely…

Shal was already waving his hand. "No, no, that's not it, you misunderstand. How many Skills do you have?"

After a quick count, Randidly answered, "Nineteen."

Shal burst out laughing, his face once more suffused with a grin. "Let me tell you a secret, kid. When you receive a Class, you're given a Skill cap. That becomes the maximum number of Skills you can learn. You can keep the Skills you have from before, but it ultimately limits what you can learn afterwards with the System. My cap is twelve, and my Class is rather rare. Yet you have nineteen Skills already..."

Shal paused to consider something, his expression soon brightening into a wide grin. "There is of course another way for you to escape this place, if you're interested in working with me."

Perking up, Randidly asked, "Is there another entrance? Won't I just have the same problem there too?"

"No, no, no," Shal said, waving his hand. "There are no more avenues of retreat. But you can always move forward. Such is the honorable way of the spear user." Shal extended his hand. "Help me defeat the Boss of this Dungeon, the Acid Salamander, and I will carry you out of this place."

"Defeat the Boss...?" Randidly looked at him in shock. Considering the monsters he routinely fled from thus far were just small fries, could he really stand against a Boss?

"Well, you personally won't be doing anything as grand as that. Before the Boss, there are those Orc Shamans that so grievously wounded me in the past. Your role will be to help me get past them. It shouldn't be that difficult. If we concentrate and get your Willpower up to 50, it will be a simple task to—Ah! I had forgotten! You can learn as many Skills as you need. A measly Willpower of 35 will be sufficient if you learn mental attack resistance and train it up some!"

"A Willpower of 35... How will we...?"

Shal patted Randidly's back, a strange twinkle in his eyes. "Now, now, don't worry about the details. But we must hurry. The sooner we begin, the sooner we get out, yes? And as you said before, you're desperate to return to your world, yes?"

Randidly forced himself to nod, despite the murky depths of his heart.

Within a single day, Randidly had been carried out to the entrance to the Dungeon and then back to the Safe Room. Shal still seemed to be in an immensely good mood. It made the storm clouds hanging over Randidly's head feel that much more isolating. His heart stubbornly refused to release any secrets regarding the sick feeling he felt when he tried to leave the Dungeon, followed by the sense of relief when he could not. The entire journey was Randidly chasing after the thoughts rattling around in his head, trying not to tremble.

After dropping him in front of the Safe Room, Shal put his hands on his hips and spoke, "How many more PP do you need to finish off your current Path?"

Randidly checked. "Two, and I have enough to do it now."

"Then finish it, but don't select another Path."

For the fourteenth PP he spent, Randidly received nothing, but the fifteenth gave him +2 Stat(s).

Congratulations! You have finished the **"Pathfinder Path"**! As you wander away from beaten trails, you discover the tools that enable you to thrive in these wild environments. **+2 Perception and Reaction.**
Congratulations! You have learned the Skill **Mapmaking Level 1.**

Mapmaking Level 1: *With the proper materials, it's possible for you to create maps of the areas you have traveled. As Skill Level improves, you will be able to notice and accurately catalogue smaller landmarks.* **It is possible to share your maps with others. Efficiency of mapmaking improves with Skill Level.**

When Randidly opened his Status screen, he hesitated, glancing sideways at Shal. *If I throw my lot in with him, I won't be able to put many more Stats into Intelligence, Perception, and Agility like I had been. Perhaps that's for the best. Shal has experience with the System. And considering his capability to move in the Dungeon...*

Randidly nodded, finally convincing himself. He put the two free Stats into Willpower. Then he shared his abilities with Shal.

Randidly Ghosthound
Class: ---
Level: N/A
Health(/R per hour): 157/153 [+4] (58.5 [+6])
Mana(/R per hour): 50/96 (25)
Stam(/R per min): 66/78 (23 [+2])
Vit: 16 [+2]
End: 18
Str: 7
Agi: 15
Perception: 17
Reaction: 15
Resistance: 9
Willpower: 11

Intelligence: 21
Wisdom: 10
Control: 15
Focus: 10

"Alright, now what?" Randidly asked.

Shal reached out and put his hand on Randidly's head. "Now we enter into a bargain. If I do this, you must promise to assist me in defeating the Shaman and all other troubles I encounter in the Dungeon. If we successfully escape, I shall consider your debt paid in full. It is not a casual thing, this bargain.

"But more important than even your agreement to help with the Shaman," Shal continued, "What I want now is to know that you possess the resolve to persevere through my training. It will not be easy. It will hurt, but you need pain to accumulate this strength. After the training, you will possess the strength to persist through the pain and to use the Skills I will give you. The act of defeating the Shaman isn't the only important thing. If I give you my Skills, you must use them with pride. You must honor the tradition of the spear. To this, do you agree?"

Randidly took in the whole of this strange alien man, his mind quiet and cool. And then one thought, unbidden, rose to the surface.

I want to be strong. I... I don't want to be scared anymore.

The other side of Randidly's heart shivered slightly. His aggressive side began to swell. *And if I can gather the strength to protect myself, to fight up close and not abandon those dreams I had as a child of being a hero...*

He didn't know what he would do when he exited the Dungeon, but some part of him was happy to have a current goal. He would train with Shal. The complex thoughts could wait until later. Randidly nodded his acquiescence to Shal's request.

But also... The tiny realist in the back of Randidly's head took the opportunity to speak up. *Are we really not going to question what he means by the training being painful?*

Shal's expression was serious. "Then go to your Path menu and select the option to be my disciple."

Opening the menu, Randidly did so, examining the newly-acquired option.

Disciple of Shal *0/X*

"It goes to X?" Randidly tilted his head to the side.

Shal nodded. "Yes, it will continue up to my Level. That is how the special Disciple Path of Tellus works. Currently, I am Level 36. When you catch up, you will receive a special Skill based on your effort and the Path will end. If your performance is sufficiently impressive, it might be a superior, evolved version of a Skill I have. You should have a few more PP, yes? You might as well put those in now. But do not finish the Path until I instruct you to do so. You must reach a certain standard first."

Randidly clicked the Path and dumped his points into it. What was shocking was that *each* PP spent earned him a distributable Stat point. At 5, he received a Stat point *and* 1 point in End and Agi. Immediately impressed, Randidly threw all the acquired gains into Willpower, pushing it up to 20.

If all I need to do is reach 35, this might not be so bad, Randidly reflected.

"Alright, now what?" Randidly looked to his teacher with expectation in his eyes.

Shal smiled. "First we rest. The work begins tomorrow."

Shal gave Randidly a spear, instructing him to familiarize himself with it while he made some preparations outside of the Safe Room. Randidly gripped the shaft, doing his best to imitate what he remembered from movies. He thrust the spear forward and swept it sideways. Occasionally, he slashed with it, tilting his body and awkwardly bringing the point of the weapon downward. He did enough correct movements to learn the Skill Spear Mastery Level 1.

As always, the presence of a Skill upped his enthusiasm. Randidly approached the movements more seriously, setting himself on the balls of his feet in order to put some power behind the attacks. While he waited, the Skill quickly grew to Level 3. At the same time, Randidly's plants earned him another Level in Farming.

The feeling of growth was intoxicating. But even more than the Skill Levels, the 3 PP he put into the Disciple Path rewarded him richly. Not only did he receive three more Stats to be put into Willpower, but at 10, he received +2 Agi, +1 Str, and +1 React, as well as the Skill Phantom Thrust.

Didn't Shal say I'd only get a Skill at the end? Or maybe I'd only get the chance for an evolved Skill at the end. But even for just the Skill alone, becoming his disciple was worth it. Randidly tried out the Skill, costing him 15 Stamina. Activating the Skill made the training spear Shal gave him move so fast, Randidly couldn't even control it. The stabs went wide of the pitted bark more often than not.

Randidly's lips curled upward, the sense of power as he activated the Skill warming his veins.

Around the time Randidly began to smile was when Shal returned and the training abruptly changed.

CHAPTER THIRTEEN

"*L*et us begin the training." There was something very different about
Shal's tone of voice now.

Randidly didn't pay it too much mind, too excited about his new
Skill. He was about to show Shal, but there was a coldness in the man's eyes
that stopped him.

"Put down the spear," Shal said coolly.

Randidly did so, but slowly, eyeing a box in Shal's arms he hadn't
noticed at first.

Shal beckoned him over toward the door to the Safe Room. "You must
do something for me. Come here and stay still."

There was iron in that voice, and the hairs on the back of Randidly's neck
sensed something was coming he wouldn't like. But he had chosen to follow
Shal, so he now literally followed him obediently out into the grassy space
right outside of the Safe Room. He hunched his shoulders, wondering why
Shal's expression was cast from steel. Randidly was still taken by surprise
when Shal dumped green goop on his leg, and his flesh began to flake and
sizzle.

Randidly screamed, all hopes to grow powerful and the pride from his
current growth wiped away by the bleach of agony. He crumpled to the
ground and clutched his leg. The pain became overwhelming, spreading to
his hands.

Shal nudged him in the side with his toe. "Stand. This is nothing. Did I
not warn you it would be painful?"

"Hah, hah." As the shock wore off, Randidly realized it wasn't as bad as
he initially assumed. Either due to his increased Stats or Skill Levels, his
flesh wasn't being burned away like it had the first time he encountered the

acid. A jarring burning sensation was all that remained at the edge of his consciousness. His leg shook and his hands were twitching.

Belatedly, he checked his Health. It was rapidly decreasing. With wide eyes, he looked at Shal. "My Health…"

"You have Health potions, do you not? And you have the materials and ability to make more. Stay here and survive."

Congratulations! Your Skill **Acid Resistance** has grown to **Level 6!**

Randidly licked his lips, steadily forcing himself to not think about the pain. He was acutely aware of the accord he'd made with Shal, recalling his desire to be strong. The fact that he hadn't questioned the offer was ridiculous. Of course growing more powerful was difficult.

If it wasn't, everyone would be powerful.

He needed to raise his Skill Levels, to train. Although it was slightly barbaric, Shal's method was undoubtedly effective. Randidly gritted his teeth and tried to focus on controlling his heavy breathing.

With forced calmness, Randidly hobbled over to a Health potion and drank it; relief a welcome pittance against the restored 37 Health. The shaking of his hands began to ease. The acid continued to rip away at his focus with renewed daggers of pain, but the rate at which his Health decreased slowed, giving him some hope. He still had 60-some Health. Just in case, he drank another Health potion to push himself back over 100.

Congratulations! Your Skill **Acid Resistance** has grown to **Level 7!**

Randidly cashed in both PPs, getting 2 more points of Willpower. Instantly, he felt slightly steadier, able to control his response to the pain. That earned a small smile from him. *Looks like there are benefits to all the Stats. Willpower seems pretty—*

Another splash of Acid from Shal hit Randidly, catching him in the chest and face, and some of it got into his mouth.

Trembling raced through his body, causing all his joints to creak and groan. His muscles began twisting him into knots. Randidly spat, attempting to get the poison out of his body. He was stunned to see blood stain the green grass. He wiped his mouth with the back of his hand, smearing it red.

Acid has reached your bloodstream! You have been poisoned.

Congratulations! Your Skill **Poison Resistance** has grown to **Level 8!**

"You better hurry."

It was slightly infuriating how calm Shal's voice was. At the very least, the anger gave Randidly something to focus on other than the pain.

"If you do not work quickly, acid and poison shall kill you before you can brew more potions. A true warrior must become numb to the specter of death hovering over his head."

Gagging on his own blood and bile, Randidly forced himself to drink two potions to restore his Health to safe levels. Even so, the acid and poison ate at him, pushing his Health back below 80.

Then 50.

Congratulations! Your Skill **Acid Resistance** has grown to **Level 8!**

At this point, not even a Skill Level was enough to cheer Randidly up.

With shaking hands, Randidly tried to mix another Health potion. The tremors in his body were horrible, but it just meant Randidly had to work for longer with the mortar and pestle to grind the crystals into a uniform thickness. The real difficulty was taking only a pinch of the crystal and adding the proper amount to a vial.

Ominously, Randidly stopped tasting blood. He could no longer taste anything at all.

Congratulations! Your Skill **Potion Making** has grown to **Level 15!**

Randidly examined the potion. It was only for 29 Health, barely above a failure. He drank it as quickly as possible and began work on the next one, his hands steadying through the repetition, the actions yet another distraction from the pain.

With a sigh, Shal grabbed Randidly and dragged him into the Safe Room. "Since it is your first day, and you are yet weak, I will be merciful. But you will regret forcing me to do this."

Even though the movement jarred Randidly's chemically burned skin, it was relieving to be back within the Safe Room where regeneration was increased. The poison barely took away any Health at all within the room, which was probably why Shal kept him outside for the training. Randidly brewed another potion, this time for 50, which he immediately drank.

Just as he began to work on the second one, an even thicker wave of acid splashed across his back. Randidly gritted his teeth and did his best to ignore it. Just when the pain subsided, and he began moving again, he was met with another wave of acid, basically covering every inch of him. The pain became an incessant buzz grinding away his focus. This didn't threaten to end his life with the Safe Room's regeneration boost, but it was another sort of mental torture. A thousand fire ants ripped his flesh from his body, one tiny shred at a time. His hands could barely move. He wanted to vomit.

Shivering, the best Randidly could do was simply continue to exist. Subconsciously, he leaned forward and hunched his shoulders.

"Three things affect how quickly you earn Skill Levels," Shal said, setting his box down and giving Randidly a long look. "First, repetition. More is better, that is simple. Second, the theoretical difficulty. The more difficult it should be to accomplish, the more of your effort goes toward raising the Skill Level.

"Finally," Shal punctuated this with another splash of acid across Randidly. "The actual difficulty. Extra training has meaning. Look, don't you feel yourself improving? Though in your case, it is the awkward crawl of a babe."

His chest heaving and eyes bloodshot, Randidly slowly began to move, carefully mixing the amounts of ground crystal. His fingers intermittently spasmed and twitched. Through every second of agony, he did his best to focus. He wanted to live. He needed to live. He needed strength to avoid fear and to protect the people he cared about.

Sydney...

Ace...

"There is some disagreement on *why* it is so. Some say the world knows your true plight, not just the theoretical one. Others say the more an individual wants it, *needs* it, the more the world responds. You warp the world with your wish. That image you have of the future... when you find it, hold on to it."

Randidly was practically deaf as he mixed. Any spare attention became consumed by the pain. A drop of goop slid down his face and dripped into his eye. It burned like a thin rod of iron had been shoved into the soft flesh of his tear ducts.

Even though it was twitching, Randidly kept the eye open. He gained the Skill Pain Resistance Level 1, but ignored the notification. It was just one more slap against his over-stimulated mind. His trembling hands were the center of his world. The cool feeling of the mortar, pestle, and glass vials were the only source of relief in his life.

"I believe that is what it is. The want. The need. Do you want it? What did you call yourself? Ghosthound? You, Ghosthound, do you really want to get out enough to push through this? Do you crave that strength?"

Randidly burned, inside and out. Deep down, a part of him grew to hate this entire situation. Why the fuck was he doing this? Why did he need to go through this? Every agonizing moment was longer than the previous one. What would be at the end of this road? Randidly questioned whether this would truly make him strong.

At the end of this, would he finally get a rest?

Congratulations! Your Skill **Potion Making** has grown to **Level 16!**

"No, it never ends." Shal answered as if he could read his thoughts. "If you start walking, you either continue to accelerate, or you die. You are consumed by those who are more willing to endure pain than you. They worked harder; that makes them superior. Let me ask you again, Ghosthound. Do you desire? Are you consumed by the wanting?"

I just want to fucking dunk you *a few times in a pool of acid!* Randidly finished the potion with gritted teeth. The result floated in front of him, taunting him with the result. His newest potion, one birthed by his sudden and all-consuming desire to harm Shal, would restore 71 Health points after drinking it.

Randidly downed it, stoically drowning his gasp when he was doused with more acid. This dose was seemingly more concentrated and vicious than the previous ones.

Congratulations! Your Skill **Pain Resistance** has grown to **Level 2!**

Randidly reached for a red crystal, but they were now out of reach. Ponderously, he raised his poison-dripping head. Everything ached. He forced himself to his feet and stumbled a few steps to the pile of red crystals. With trembling hands, he did his best not to spill acid on the crystals.

If I fucking survive this… Randidly swore quietly to himself. His thoughts stumbled and collapsed. Nothing was beyond this pain, beyond this moment. The aggressive Randidly boiled with indignation, lowering his head and concerning himself with the shaking grind of red crystals.

Randidly adjusted his thoughts with a scowl. *One step at a time.*

Randidly settled into a routine.

The morning became acid, agony, and potions right outside of the Safe Zone. He would make and make, attempting to keep up with the veritable vats of acid Shal hauled back, each a strange, painful variation on the common theme. Some days, he wouldn't be allowed to make potions, reduced to using simple Meditation, focusing on that hair-thin bonus of regenerations it granted him.

Several times, it was close to killing him. His Health slipped into the single digits on a number of occasions, then leveled off. Randidly would tremble, trying his best to ignore the tears in the corners of his eyes. Shal somehow knew the edges of his Willpower, his sanity and life, even as he pushed him.

Those moments were honestly the easiest.

The worst was when his Health plummeted below 20, crashing toward 0, and Randidly would finally manage to successfully finish a potion. He desperately gulped down the liquid, healing 40 Health and buying himself a brief respite. Shal would fetch more acid while Randidly sat there and breathed, savoring the sensation of being alive.

As days passed, more and more, Shal would interrupt those restive explorations of his mortality with another acid bath and Randidly would rush back to the task. Without potions, he would die.

And he wanted to live. No matter how painful it was, his desire to live remained pure and desperate. He clung to that resolve, even when strain weakened him past the limits of his mental clarity.

The afternoons were Randidly's favorite. It was Skill practice, with Shal as the target. A target who moved like a ghost, dodging Randidly's Entangling Roots and Mana Bolts effortlessly. He'd close the distance and brutally knock the wind out of Randidly, or forcefully pick him up and throw him into the forest. Randidly would be forced to jump up with a yelp, rushing back out, fearful of the silent hanging webs in the nearby trees.

This practice continued until Randidly ran out of Mana and Meditated back to full too many times for Shal's taste. Then came the third and final training period of the day.

The worst one. Spear training.

"The Spear," Shal explained, giving Randidly a simple, light weapon he'd been able to identify as being Level 10. "Is the greatest weapon. It is versatile. It can be quick and powerful. It can stab, it can sweep. But most of all, it is wielded by a Spearman, the most powerful warrior of all.

"You are weak. You have no hope of being a Spearman. Few can reach this level of perfection. But like my master still dutifully tried to drill the moves into my foolish body, I shall ravage you until it can perform the moves, even when you are no longer conscious. Even when pain is killing you."

Randidly fervently believed Shal wasn't being figurative when he demonstrated several movements and told Randidly how many times he expected each action to be performed.

"Is that how you become a Spearman?" Randidly asked uncertainly. A day's worth of being splashed with acid and knocked around had largely numbed his fear of pain. Still, the entrancing grace of Shal handling his spear gave him an instinctual pause.

Shal chuckled. "No. But it is a way that a non-spearman can slowly come to know the spear. Even I am not yet close to being a Spearman. I am merely a man with a spear. But to you…"

His spear blurred. Randidly felt his left arm, which was lightly holding on to his own spear, shatter from the impact of his shaft. "But to you, such concerns are too far in the future. For now, do your best to survive."

By retreating, throwing up Mana Shields and Iron Skin, Randidly truly did his best to survive the onslaught. Shal did not make it easy.

Yet some stubborn part of him, the part that desperately wanted to live, continued to entrench itself in Randidly's heart.

CHAPTER FOURTEEN

*T*ime lost meaning. Pain blurred the passage of singular moments, skewing one day to the next. There was only the opening of his eyes in the morning, the training, and closing his eyes at night.

And then there were the physical impacts through training with Shal that taught Randidly something unexpected. He could feel the way one muscle transitioned smoothly into the next. Being smacked in the forearm with a spear shaft echoed outward, stiffening his wrist and causing his elbow to ache.

Before the System arrived, he never really had the occasion to think about the way a body functioned. He'd always taken his own for granted. Shal pummeled that privilege into bruised understanding.

Randidly floated along, too exhausted to dwell very long in any one moment.

Randidly wondered whether his sense of the hours he spent awake was an accurate way to tell time. With one week of the hellish training turning to two, the time they spent training expanded without the usual hard limit of daylight. Randidly's body could simply endure additional abuse. Night never came before Randidly laid his head down on the ground.

There was a strange magic in the Safe Room. As if the day would continue for as long as necessary for it to be filled.

Which made him realize time meant increasingly little to him. When he eventually escaped, the initial stages of the monster invasion of Earth would be over. His friends wouldn't need his help as desperately as they would have previously.

Somehow, I doubt they've experienced something like this, Randidly thought numbly as he Meditated. *I should definitely have an advantage of Skills. Believe it, Shal says. Want it.*

I want to be powerful...

Even as his worries mounted, Randidly did not try and rush his training, nor did he ask Shal about upping the pace. The very thought of suggesting that made him shudder. It was all Randidly could do to survive the exponential increase in difficulty that was already occurring. And his Skills were growing at a prodigious rate under the strain. Each day, Shal found some new way to torture him and push his limits.

It was working.

Randidly swiftly gained the Skills Fighting Proficiency, First Aid, and Block from his struggles. Shal noticed these shifts, changing his strategies to isolate those new Skills, forcing each of them upwards in Level.

It only took a week and a half for Randidly to gather enough PP to finish off the Disciple of Shal Path. Shal told him to wait, recommending he refrain from putting the PP in until he said he was ready, so Randidly could experience how the Stat changes affected him all at once, rather than gradually.

They trained brutally for two weeks after that, concentrating more and more on spear movements. When he wasn't holding the spear, Randidly's hands ached. When he was holding the spear, his blisters popped and bled. Shal considered the pain proof that Randidly was properly putting effort into the growth.

That strange stubbornness that swelled in Randidly's chest, unlike the Stat increases for Willpower, was purely mental. Being exposed to intense amounts of pain and dangerous situations cooled his mind. His wits were sharpened and he no longer flinched when up against hard decisions. Several extreme weeks altered Randidly's behavior.

Shal begrudgingly put a stop to the intensive training. "Humph, well, you at least won't flee from battle now. Finish off the Disciple Path. Your foundation is barely enough to begin true combat with the spear, but we must know what Skills you have earned from me first."

Randidly obediently put the last 24 PP in all at once.

Starting with the 14 PP spent, Randidly earned:

Congratulations! You have earned **1 Stat point(s).**

Congratulations! +3 End, +2 Agi

Congratulations! You have earned 1 Stat **point(s).**

Congratulations! You have earned **1 Stat point(s).**

Congratulations! You have earned **1 Stat point(s).**

Congratulations! You have earned **1 Stat point(s).**

Congratulations! +1 Vit, +1 Agi, +1 Int, +2 Reaction.

Congratulations! You have learned the Skill **Spear Phantom's Footwork Level 1.**

Congratulations! You have earned **1 Stat point(s).**

Congratulations! You have earned **1 Stat point(s).**

Congratulations! You have earned **1 Stat point(s).**

Congratulations! You have earned **1 Stat point(s).**

Congratulations! +4 Agi, +1 Per

Congratulations! You have earned 1 Stat **point(s).**

Congratulations! You have earned **1 Stat point(s).**

Congratulations! You have earned **1 Stat point(s).**

Congratulations! You have earned **1 Stat point(s).**

Congratulations! +1 Agi

Congratulations! You have learned the Skill Eyes of the Spear Phantom Level 1.

Congratulations! You have earned **1 Stat point(s).**

Congratulations! You have earned **1 Stat point(s).**

Congratulations! You have earned **1 Stat point(s).**

Congratulations! You have earned **1 Stat point(s).**

Congratulations! You have earned **5 Stat point(s).**

Congratulations! You have earned **1 Stat point(s).**

Congratulations! You have earned **1 Stat point(s).**

Congratulations! You have completed the **"Disciple of Shal Path"!**

Congratulations! You have learned the Skill **Phantom Half-Step Level 1.**

He gained 24 distributable points in total. Upon Shal's urging, Randidly chose to put it all into Willpower. Shal had definitely been right about waiting to spend the points all at once. The sense of mental acuity he felt was stark. Suddenly, Randidly possessed a focus he hadn't been near achieving previously.

Randidly scratched his cheek, marveling over the acute sense of presence he felt while moving. *Focus is the wrong word. Even if just because of the Stat called Focus. This sensation... everything is so crisp. Clarity doesn't even begin to do it justice.*

With firm eyes, Randidly met Shal's gaze. He'd endured pain. Persisted through exhaustion. Earned over a score of Skill Levels and now had several new Skills to test out. He was firmly taking steps toward becoming strong.

A small portion of his stubborn refusal to give in was transmuted into a sliver of self-confidence.

Shal grinned like a wolf. "Good. Finally, some spunk out of you. What Skills did you learn?"

After Randidly listed them off, Shal grunted and rubbed his chin. "Your luck is pretty good. Those are all core passive Skills. Due to your lack of Class, your movement abilities will be useful. Now, show me this half-step. It appears to be an inferior version of the 'Step of the Spear Phantom' that I possess."

Randidly settled himself into the basic stance Shal taught him and demonstrated the Skill. It required a target, so Randidly targeted Shal. Randidly felt something strange within the hot Stamina settling around his heart. He could use Phantom Half-Step in two ways—away or toward. Deciding to do *toward*, Randidly stepped.

He immediately appeared halfway between his original position and Shal. He tried again, stepping backwards, only to stumble awkwardly. Unfortunately, the Skill took 80 Stamina and he barely had enough to use it once.

Shal grunted in a way that meant he was either pleased or annoyed. Grim-faced, he began the training once again.

Even if Shal displayed a noncommittal reaction to the Skill, Randidly could already see its benefits. He did his best to suppress a grin as Shal raised his spear and attacked. *Aside from the prohibitive Stamina cost, being able to control the distance between myself and a foe... heh. I'll prove it to you, Shal. You won't regret staying here to train me.*

Although Randidly's Willpower reached the Level Shal desired, the training continued, focusing on the spear and incorporating the new Skills he learned. Shal became the personification of the devil, pressing Randidly to squeeze every ounce of potential from his body.

It was brutal. Each day, the training ended not because of weariness, but because Randidly's injuries reached the point where he couldn't continue. The next morning, the bruises would have only just begun to fade when they started once more.

One small part of Randidly's heart was unsatisfied at the continued training now that he was improving. Shal seemed to sense this growing dissatisfaction one day and snorted in amusement. Instead of their usual spar, he took Randidly away from the Safe Room door to fight against a Howler Monkey.

The experience dispelled any lingering doubts Randidly held about whether the training was necessary. The thread of self-confidence was ruthlessly plucked out of him like weeds from a garden. He remained weak. Although he possessed Mana Skills to supplement his spear usage, the Howler Monkey's vastly superior Health forced health trades Randidly could not keep up with. Too soon, Randidly was out of Mana, reduced to Running and Sprint in order to escape.

Bloody and drained of Stamina, Randidly had to be carried back to the Safe Room to recover.

"Why did you lose?" Shal asked when he dumped Randidly unceremoniously in front of the Safe Room.

For several seconds, he could not answer around his panting. His body reverted to its typical behavior prior to the pain training—a constant state of trembling. Randidly gritted his teeth and forced out an answer. "The difference in Stats…"

Nodding slowly, Shal finally said, "It will continue as such until you leave this place and find a Village Spirit to give you a Class. Such is the way of the System. Those without a Class cannot hope to rival those with. So, what will you do in the meantime?"

Clenching his fist, Randidly said, "Raise my Skill Level to the point that Stats become meaningless."

Shall laughed. "It is a start. But Skill Levels are just the first step. Next is knowing how to *use* your precious Skills."

CHAPTER FIFTEEN

*W*ithout the Disciple Path, Randidly could freely peruse the mysterious options available to him and select one at random. His choices didn't seem to matter much. Each day, he gained enough Skill Levels that he routinely finished multiple Paths in a week. He began with Pathless IV, which gave him 1 free Stat point at 5 and 10 PP.

The Path Completion notification was more generous, but only barely.

Congratulations! You have completed the "Pathless IV Path"! +3 Stat(s). You have realized that all paths are the same, and all paths lead to the same place.

In a rare conversation between them during training, Randidly asked Shal whether he had any further recommendations about Stat distribution. Shal snorted and spun his spear, the spearhead ripping through the muscle of Randidly's shoulder. Barely able to utilize one of his arms, Randidly struggled to defend against Shal's quick stabs.

Such was the typical route conversations with Shal took. He was not a man who much valued conversation.

At the same time, Randidly appreciated the attitude. It allowed him to use his quiet moments of rest to think his way through the problems on his own. Shal was right: just as important as Skill Levels were Skill usage. The same rang true for Stats. He needed to adjust his Stat distribution to suit his role.

After careful consideration, Randidly decided to return to his initial plans of raising his Mana Skills. Of the three Stats, one went into Int, one into Control, and one into Focus.

And Pathless IV was just the beginning. The training continued to have truly unfathomable results on his Skill Levels. Randidly had more than enough PP to complete Pathless V, Pathless VI, and Pathless VII.

Altogether, those Paths and their completions blessed him with 30 free Stats that were entirely his to spend. 15 went into Int, and 5 to Control, Focus, and End respectively. Randidly chose Endurance due to his expanding Skills, and the increasing amount of Stamina he began to use in the course of fighting with a spear. The brief skirmish with the Howler Monkey had disturbed him.

That sense of helplessness when he ran out of Stamina and needed to be carried away was usually the last thought Randidly had before escaping into sleep every night.

Not that his dreams were any comfort. Sometimes Randidly saw Sydney and Ace, but most of the time, he was stuck in the same brutal schedule of training. He held a spear that came alive and swelled until it was a giant serpent that devoured him. He ran away from Howler Monkeys while dream Shal stood and watched with his arms crossed. Or he stood in a deep pit and a dozen faceless individuals dumped acid on top of him.

"I can—!" Randidly blearily gasped as he sat up from another nightmare.

For a few seconds, he looked around. Shal regarded him mildly over a banana before turning away to leave his student in peace. Randidly let out a shaky breath and rubbed his eyes. He pushed himself to his feet and started stretching.

He had no other choice. Training would start soon.

The day after he spent all those free Stats, Randidly unleashed his Mana Skills with wild abandon, throwing out Mana Bolts as fast as he could. Each one was either dodged or obliterated by a stroke of Shal's spear. Their strength definitely caught Shal's eye, and the boost in Randidly's aggressiveness gave Shal pause.

That day, Randidly's Mana-based training shifted. The Howler Monkeys became his new training partners. It was less of an exercise in him triumphing, and more about surviving the frantic encounters. Entangling Roots and Mana Shield underwent a baptism of constant use, their Skill Level rising quickly.

Which was important, especially for Entangling Roots. Only recently had the casting time been decreased enough for him to reliably catch a Howler Monkey.

Mana Bolt became Randidly's bread and butter in these desperate fights. His growth in Int was enough that a direct hit to the Howler Monkey's face would stun them, giving him time to scramble sideways and regain his footing. The monster's red eyes would bore into him, and the chase began anew.

Struggling in this new environment, Randidly completed Pathless VIII, which netted him 1 in Strength and Intelligence, 2 in Agility, and 6 in Willpower and Reaction. He would have preferred to put them into Control and ensure the heart-stopping mistake of missing a close-range Mana Bolt would become less common. Those were the moments where some part of Randidly genuinely thought he would die before Shal could intervene. He had to spend several trembling seconds afterward regaining his composure before he could fight another Howler Monkey.

In those moments, when Randidly's shoulders heaved, hand pressed to his chest to physically restrain his panic, he felt Shal's distinct brand of kindness. The three-eyed man was brutally demanding when it came to physical exhaustion. Though, when it was overwhelming emotion holding Randidly back, he seemed to look the other way.

I need to get up. One more training spar, then I'll take a break, Randidly thought almost a dozen times as he sat hunched over on his knees. If it wasn't a training spar, it would be one more progression through Shal's spear forms, or one more bout of acid exposure.

Randidly strangled any thoughts of the future and got to his feet.

When one Howler Monkey became manageable, Shal forced Randidly deeper and deeper into the monster's territory. Within those towering trees, out of the incongruous sight of the wall, it became a common occurrence for seven or eight monkeys to chase him down. Over and over again, he thanked his past self for the foresight to invest in Control.

Missing even a single Mana Bolt, with Howler Monkeys swarming through the trees behind him, swinging from vines and skittering over branches, meant being caught. And being caught would lead to only one thing as the monkeys scrambled on top of his body with bared teeth.

Death.

On one harrowing bout of training as Randidly fled, a combination of rock throws and an ambush by a monkey broke through Randidly's Mana Shield, bringing him to the ground. The Howler Monkeys wised up to his ways. During the chase, they must have sent one of their fellows ahead to ambush him.

He collided with the monster, their bodies tangling together and tumbling over roots. It came prepared with a rock and brought it smashing down on Randidly's head. Randidly reflexively activated Iron Skin, but he still felt something crack when the rock struck him.

Shit! Although Randidly was dizzy, he instinctively produced the dagger he found inside the snake. The monkey reacted just as quickly to his movement and its free arm caught Randidly's wrist in its powerful grip.

Randidly recognized the Howler Monkey in that moment. It wasn't just any monkey, but the scrawny one the original rock throwers beat and bullied into fetching stones. Randidly did nothing for several seconds. The recognition was so unexpected, he just lay there, gaping.

The Howler Monkey drooled, its eyes filled with hate and glee. No recognition of the empathy he'd shown by not shooting Mana Bolts at it during the earlier training existed within this monkey. It simply screeched and brought the stone cracking down once more on Randidly's skull.

Randidly activated Iron Skin, but the dizziness resonated from the impact point. The urge to throw up washed over him, and the vision in his left eye was fading to black.

For a split second, Randidly wondered whether this would be the point he died. Instinctively, he knew Shal would not save him.

Fuck. Fuck. Fuck!

Half-blind and scrambling, Randidly stuffed his left hand into the satchel and grasped around for anything to help. Tears streamed his face. This was it.

Randidly whipped out the first solid object he felt in a desperate swing. By some stroke of luck, the fang Randidly had cut out of the giant snake sunk into the soft flesh of the Howler Monkey's eye.

Congratulations! Your Skill **Spirit of Adversity** has grown to **Level 9!**

It screamed in agony. Randidly shoved the scrawny monkey off of him and scrambled to his feet. Gritting his teeth to resist the nausea, Randidly glanced at Shal, who watched him coolly in the distance. Randidly used the Phantom Half Step to cross half the distance between them. He turned to the right, using his good eye to land a couple of Entangling Roots on those monkeys close enough to be a threat.

He stumbled the rest of the way past Shal and back to the Safe Room, where he Meditated for several hours to recover.

When he opened his eyes, Shal was standing there.

"There was only one Howler Monkey. The rest were still far away," Randidly mumbled. His eyes fell to the ground.

Shal snorted. "Indeed. If you had died, it was only because you were too weak."

At around four weeks of training, a few days after the monkey incident, Randidly reached the point where he could Meditate while doing most actions. Using active Skills broke his concentration, but otherwise, he could maintain the passive bonus while sparring with Shal.

Sparring was a strong word for it, honestly. Mostly, it was Randidly blocking and dodging against a spear-wielding devil, although he could now survive a lot longer against the onslaught of Shal's attacks.

The next big change came when Randidly got his Mana Bolt Skill to Level 20, unlocking the Mana Bolt Path. Randidly continued down the Pathless Paths, feeling strangely connected to them, after grinding his way here for almost a month.

Pathless IX required 25 PP and earned Randidly 14 Stat points. After some thought, he threw all the points in Wisdom, providing a pretty significant boost to his Mana regeneration. Now that his Mana pool was higher and he could Meditate reliably, increasing the percentage boosted seemed like a good idea.

Pathless X jumped all the way up to an intimidating 50 PP to finish, and it filled Randidly with a thread of excitement. He threw himself into training. Randidly worked his way through the different spear moves, focusing on the Spear Phantom's Footwork and Phantom Thrust, and his confidence in the spear steadily accumulated. When he made mistakes, Shal thrashed him until he got back on track. Shal was never complimentary, but he no longer berated Randidly as much as he used to.

His rising abilities with the spear, combined with marginal improvements in the Level of Physical Fitness and Meditation, was enough to finish the Path.

Congratulations! You have completed the **"Pathless X Path"**!

Truly, you have found your way through the wilderness without difficulty. It is a rare achievement to reach this vista. Can you see it? In the distance? The Pinnacle of Strength that you are seeking? Good luck.

Congratulations! +2 Health/Mana/Stamina per Level!

Congratulations! +1 Stat per Level

You have realized that all paths are the same, and all paths lead to the same place. And that the path continues ever onward...

Randidly allowed himself a wry grin. *All per Level gains? Well, I suppose for someone with a Class, earning these extras would be valuable. And when I do eventually earn a Class... I'll be able to reap the true reward for all this work.*

Randidly wasn't very upset. The combination of Shal and the rewards from the System had toughened his outlook. For now, he needed to continue to train. Results would follow from his dedication to his own abilities.

Inside his Path screen, he now had access to the Path Pathless, without a roman numeral. His eyes bulged at the required 100 PP to finish. He glanced at his current extra PP—he had 4.

He laughed out loud. If he would get it, it would only be by going all the way, one step at a time. No reason to hold back now.

He put 4 PP into Pathless and followed Shal deeper into the forest to find more monkeys. Whenever Randidly improved, Shal always pushed him closer to the edge of death. It was somewhat horrifying.

But at the same time, Randidly accepted it. For good or for ill, his trembling episodes were becoming less and less common. Every emotion became tinder to toss into his mental furnace, driving him to push his limits.

CHAPTER SIXTEEN

*S*hal's spear slithered forward like a serpent. It smacked aside Randidly's spear and lunged toward the younger man's throat. Randidly scrambled backward, but his Stamina was exhausted. Mana Shield barely bought him half a second before Shal pierced his defense and ripped a gash in his shoulder. Blood erupted upward like the nozzle had been kicked off a water spigot.

The spray quickly ceased, but the wound still produced a steady pump of life-giving liquid. Randidly pressed his hand over the wound to staunch the blood flow.

Shal gave Randidly a long look and sighed. "I suppose it is time. You now have enough strength not to embarrass me. Let us leave this place. Or at least, you must now practice fighting against the genuine threats in this Dungeon."

Warm blood flowed between Randidly's fingers. He tightened his grip on the wound. Excitement, gratitude, and the familiar tingle of anxiety warred inside of him. He reached the point where he was about to fight against four Howler Monkeys and hold his own for several minutes. His current Mana Bolts sizzled their flesh and stunned them, while his Phantom Thrusts and Heavy Blows cut away enough of their Health that they no longer dared rush him.

In terms of defeating Howler Monkeys, Randidly had a certain amount of confidence in killing two.

Randidly glanced at his Status Screen. The past month with Shal's teachings had completely transformed him.

Randidly Ghosthound

Class: ---
Level: N/A
Health(/R per hour): 200/200 (63.75)
Mana(/R per hour): 139/139 (43.5)
Stam(/R per min): 105/105 (24)
Vit: 17
End: 27
Str: 8
Agi: 26
Perception: 18
Reaction: 23
Resistance: 9
Willpower: 50
Intelligence: 39
Wisdom: 26
Control: 21
Focus: 16
Skills: *Running Lvl 9 | Physical Fitness Lvl 17 | Sneak Lvl 8 |*
Farming Lvl 19 | Mana Bolt Lvl 20 | Heavy Blow Lvl 14 | Acid Resis-
tance Lvl 13 | Poison Resistance Lvl 9 | Sprinting Lvl 11 | Iron Skin
Lvl 19 | Spirit of Adversity Lvl 12 | Plant Breeding Lvl 9 | Meditation
Lvl 23 | Dagger Mastery Lvl 11 | Entangling Roots Lvl 21 | Mana
Shield Lvl 16 | Dodge Lvl 22 | Potion Making Lvl 18 | Mapmaking
Lvl 1 | Pathfinding Lvl 3 | Analyze Lvl 9 | Spear Mastery Lvl 33 |
Phantom Thrust Lvl 27 | Pain Resistance Lvl 9 | Fighting Proficiency
Lvl 19 | First Aid Lvl 13 | Block Lvl 23 | Spear Phantom's Footwork
Lvl 19 | Eyes of the Spear Phantom Lvl 9 | Phantom Half-Step Lvl 3

Randidly was close to finishing the Pathless Path, but the rate of Skill Level improvement was definitely slowing. Almost two months had passed since the training began. Whether it was physique, mindset, or work ethic, Randidly was incomparable to the way he was before.

I've improved. Randidly thought to himself. *Shal does not exaggerate. I will no longer embarrass him by fighting beside him.*

After storing as much food, potion crystals, and materials as he could carry within the satchel, Randidly followed Shal away from the Safe Room. To his surprise, they went toward the web-covered area, where the dangerous Deadly Webspinners had set up shop. As they passed through the groves of trees wrapped in webs, Randidly reflexively activated the Skill Eyes of the Spear Phantom. It constantly burned a small amount of Stamina, but sharpened his vision to a degree he would have believed impossible before the strange System descended over the world.

He could pick out every strand of spider silk draped over trees ten meters away. The Stamina was well spent, enhancing his already improved Perception so he could survive in such a dangerous world.

When the first Level 18 Webspinner Spiderling leapt from the brush, Randidly saw it coming a mile away. Just as Shal forced him to do thousands of times, he lowered his stance and used the training spear to pierce the monster cleanly through the chest. For several seconds, its many limbs flexed and flailed, until enough ichor drained out of the hole in its carapace, and it fell still.

Congratulations! Your Skill **Spirit of Adversity** has grown to **Level 13!**

Congratulations! Your Skill **Phantom Thrust** has grown to **Level 28!**

Shal paused in his advance as Randidly removed the corpse from his spear and carefully studied its body. The small things were relatively weak in terms of Health, but he made note of the sharp edges that ran along all eight of the spiderling's legs.

They proceeded deeper, and the Webspinner Spiderling's other advantage manifested itself—here were dozens of them. Shal didn't even bat an eye at their waves of attacks, calmly striding forward while the spiderlings leapt out in twos or threes. His spear flicked back and forth with a liveliness Randidly still struggled to capture with his own weapon. Shal felled them as quickly as the Webspinner Spiderlings made their presence known.

Such an easy journey did not last.

Shal glanced at Randidly, a familiar look appearing in his eyes. He stored his spear and folded his arms across his chest. "You may determine the speed of our advance. If even one so much as touches the hem of my cloak, perhaps we can revisit the sufficiency of your current pain tolerance training."

Had he been the same Randidly from two extremely long months ago, he might have paled before the challenge. If he'd been the Randidly a few weeks after that, when the training started, he might have gasped and gritted his teeth.

The current Randidly narrowed his eyes and got to work, his spear blurring to intercept all comers.

They stepped over dozens of spiderling corpses in their trek to reach the inner sanctum of the Deadly Webspinners. When they came upon that very same tree that grew the source of Randidly's potions, Shal gestured for Randidly to stop.

"You are running low on resources for your potions, yes? Fetch some. And bring me the head of the tree's guardian as proof of your growth."

Randidly cleaned the ichor of the spiderlings off of his spear while he tried to process Shal's words. His brain recognized the request, but all he could remember was the horrible quickness with which the Deadly Webspinner moved. Randidly imagined his leg being caught in the web explosion the monster spat out, struggling as Shal watched on and the Deadly Webspinner moved in for the kill.

Shal grimaced at his disciple and spat to the side. "Yes, the task became harder. What did you think would happen as you grow strong? That life abruptly becomes leisurely? Foolish. The stronger you become, the more you understand how weak you've always been. Yet you cannot stop struggling. Such a choice leads to death. He who stops improving dies. There are no exceptions. Have you resolved yourself to die, boy?"

I don't want to die, Randidly thought reflexively. And as he did, a switch was flipped. His face settled into a stern glower. He flexed his hands and tightened his grip on his spear.

He was the Ghosthound. And he would not flinch.

The wind swayed the draped spider silk and Randidly nodded in answer to Shal's challenge, slowly striding into the clearing. His sharpened eyes immediately picked out the camouflaged form of the giant spider, hiding within the canopy of the largest tree. The fearsome Level 30 hovered above its head alongside a strange purple coloring to its name.

The coloration made Randidly frown. *Is this a special enemy?*

As if sensing his thoughts, Shal spoke from the edge of the clearing. "The coloring is something you will come to know as you experience the System. White, Green, Blue, Purple, Red, Orange. Common, Uncommon, Rare, Ancient, Runic, Legendary. These are Rarities; they describe items as well as enemies. There is also Pink, which is Unique, reserved for extremely Rare spawns and the Dungeon Boss. The fact that an Ancient enemy is here, in a Level 35 Dungeon... Well, it must have wandered in from somewhere else. Just like you. It is clear to me that there exists some karma between the two of you. Good luck."

Without hesitation, Randidly stepped forward, raising his spear. After training with Shal's merciless attacks, he couldn't even help himself and moved aggressively. As he bridged the gap between them, Deadly Webspinner hissed, slowly climbing down, spiderlings skittering out of the surrounding trees to rush toward Randidly.

Did you think that relying on numbers would save you? Randidly's breathing became heavier. He trembled, but it was an entirely different emotion surging upward through him. Consuming him. His vision narrowed to just the foes in front of him, glaring at the spiderlings and their sharp forelegs. He warily regarded the sedate approach of the Deadly Webspinner positioning itself behind the minions.

I'm… excited, a part of Randidly realized as he spun his spear. *This is a chance. A chance to save my past self. To prove it was worth it. To prove taking one step at a time works. To prove I don't need to be afraid any longer. That no matter what happens, I have the capability to fight.*

Randidly huffed a breath and raised his right hand. With the increase in Skill Level, Randidly's mastery of Mana accelerated. Five Mana Bolts shot outward in quick succession, slamming into the giant spider. The Mana Bolts only left small dents in its armor. He would need to rely on his spear to finish it off.

Though its descent did slow; it clicked its two forelegs together in an animalistic wariness. Randidly stepped forward and thrust his spear through the first spiderling. He shifted his stance and stepped sideways, skewering another. His hand flashed upward, unleashing a Mana Bolt to knock a leaping spiderling backward out of the air.

Congratulations! Your Skill **Phantom Thrust** has grown to **Level 29!**

Congratulations! Your Skill **Mana Bolt** has grown to **Level 21!**

Every step pushed him forward. Rather than wait for the spiderlings to swarm him, Randidly cut a path to his target. He was vicious and brutal. He was sharp, doing his best to imitate his teacher. While he closed the distance to the waiting Deadly Webspinner, Shal's voice whispered in the back of his mind.

He who stops improving dies.

Randidly's skin tingled as he adjusted his grip on his spear. *And the Ghosthound isn't going to die here.*

Congratulations! Your Skill **Fighting Proficiency** has grown to **Level 20!**

When the road of corpses was paved, the Deadly Webspinner reared up and spat toward Randidly. For a split second, Randidly made to dodge, but his sharpened senses picked up a difference in the noise the spider produced. It was slightly different from when he first encountered its web grenade. Plus, the movement was quicker.

With narrowed eyes, Randidly employed the footwork taught to him by Shal, stepping to the side. The Deadly Webspinner thrust its body forward and released a basketball-sized glob of a familiar liquid: acid.

For a brief moment, Randidly lost the sharp edge to his movements. His body mechanically stepped forward and some acid splashed on him, gnawing at his flesh. The acid didn't impart much damage to him. It was this very same acid Shal routinely doused him in during the earliest bout of training.

I thought he found the frog population and harvested it from them. Randidly was trembling again, and not for excitement or fear. He felt oddly warm. *Shal took the acid from this Deadly Webspinner.*

Congratulations! Your Skill **Acid Resistance** has grown to **Level 14!**

Even from the beginning, he'd been preparing me for this fight. Randidly planted his foot into the grass and accelerated forward. His eyes hardened, all hesitations vanquished. The Deadly Webspinner screeched at his approach. It lashed out with one of its sharpened forelegs, scything diagonally through the air. Randidly stepped softly to the left underneath the blow and arrived next to the monster. He unleashed a Phantom Thrust and barely pierced the Deadly Webspinner's carapace.

The spider screeched, its eight legs blurred into whips aiming for Randidly's limbs. Randidly scrambled backward. One of the spider's legs cut the smallest divot from his side, prevented from doing a deadlier injury to Randidly's rib cage.

The Deadly Webspinner paid a price for that blow. Randidly unleashed another Mana Bolt that smashed accurately into one of the spots he'd hit earlier, cracking the carapace, if even just a small amount. Randidly grinned, adjusting his stance. *So you want to see who can bleed who dry first, huh?*

Try me.

Randidly removed a Health Potion and drank it. He activated Entangling Roots, using those few seconds of the Deadly Webspinner struggling against the restraints to close the distance and penetrate the monster's carapace once more.

Congratulations! Your Skill **Phantom Thrust** has grown to **Level 30!**

Congratulations! Your Skill **Spear Mastery** has grown to **Level 34!**

The Deadly Webspinner screeches grew louder, but Randidly knew the fight was just beginning. When it reared back, he recognized the movements of the silk grenade. Randidly shamelessly threw himself to the side and rolled to avoid the widespread explosion of sticky filaments erupting from the detonation point.

As he stood, he fired Mana Bolts with one hand while drinking a Mana Potion with the other. The Deadly Webspinner's body cracked in a few more places. The monster skittered forward.

Randidly's heart was pounding. He raised his spear. As his pulse rose in intensity, a strange new sensation seeped up out of the depths of Randidly's muscles. He ducked and advanced, thrust and retreated, dodged and attacked. This hidden emotion steadily grew until it consumed all of him.

He was fighting. He was struggling. He was growing.

Congratulations! Your Skill **Dodge** has grown to **Level 23!**

Congratulations! Your Skill **Spear Phantom's Footwork** has grown to \ **Level 20!**

Randidly Ghosthound was having fun.

The longer the battle stretched, the more Skill Levels he earned and the more a crazed smile stretched sideways across his face. Randidly couldn't help himself. The feeling was intoxicating.

An hour later, his satchel possessed less than half of his potions, and the Deadly Webspinner's body was covered in cracks and holes. Ichor constantly seeped to the ground, making his footing more precarious. Randidly was mentally drained, but the controlled movements taught to him by Shal kept his Stamina high enough for him to continuously perform.

Dodge, dodge, approach, thrust. Dodge, dodge, approach, thrust.

While each hit was negligible, the damage continued to accumulate. The spider's body was a coastal town ravaged by an earthquake. The plates shifted and buckled until the horrifying depths were revealed.

Congratulations! Your Skill **Phantom Thrust** has grown to **Level 31!**

His spear blurred forward. This time, when Randidly struck, he punctured deeply enough that a veritable geyser of ichor sprayed out. His hands and arms were drenched, tingling painfully. Apparently, even its bodily fluids were dangerous.

Randidly ignored the discomfort. He stepped backward, avoiding the Deadly Webspinner's counter-attack. He moved in closer.

Dodge, dodge, approach, thrust.

The writing had been on the wall when Randidly boldly thrust his spear into the Deadly Webspinner's mouth and punctured its acid sack. Its own powerful weapon ate through its body, opening a huge hole, which allowed Randidly to inflict more and more damage. The spider was forced to keep at least one of its forelegs over the wound in a desperate attempt to survive. Steadily, it began retreating, fear in each of its steps.

Randidly's joy had been eroded by exhaustion. But this was what Shal trained him for. No matter how tired he was, he never stopped moving forward, wielding his spear with deadly results. He'd been groomed for this enemy for months.

And Randidly refused to disappoint his master who had spent so much effort.

Two hours after the fight started, the spider began to tremble. A huge globe of spider silk formed in its mouth. As it was about to spit, something gave within its mandibles. The silk belched awkwardly. The Deadly Webspinner collapsed and the ground shook.

Congratulations! Your Skill **Spirit of Adversity** has grown to **Level 14!**

Congratulations! Your Skill **Spirit of Adversity** has grown to **Level 15!**

Congratulations! Your Skill **Spirit of Adversity** has grown to **Level 16!**

Congratulations! Your Skill **Spirit of Adversity** has grown to **Level 17!**

Randidly instinctively leaped backward, his mind dull, simply following the responses Shal drilled into him. When the spider didn't move, he blinked and straightened in confusion.

Shal rubbed the back of his neck. "Good. To have required over an hour against a foe you directly counter is embarrassing, but it is better to have a worthless pupil than a dead one. Rest for now; we will depart when you have recovered."

Boneless, Randidly fell to the ground. But in his mind, he felt a hint of glee.

I did well. And it is definitely possible, he thought to himself. *To make up the difference in power with just Skill... As long as I don't have a Class... with the variety of Skills I can accumulate...*

CHAPTER SEVENTEEN

When Shal kicked him awake, Randidly sheepishly smiled. He'd fallen asleep after Meditation, needing the mental break. He hadn't realized it during the fight, but he'd truly expended every ounce of focus he possessed. Shal snorted and gestured vaguely in a way that conveyed to Randidly he still had a few more minutes before they would depart. With that time, Randidly pulled out some of the spicy red bananas and ate while studying his Status screen.

Aside from the notifications Randidly noticed, he also earned some Skill Levels in Skills. Physical Fitness had risen 3 Levels to 20, Heavy Blow rose a single Level to 15, Dodge grew to Level 24, and Spear Phantom's Footwork grew to Level 22.

Throwing all these points into his Path earned him 2 Stat Points, which he put into Intelligence to increase his maximum Mana. Early on in the fight against the Deadly Webspinner, Randidly once more realized how important his Mana pool was against powerful foes. To take advantage of chances and inflict serious wounds, Randidly had been forced to use up his Mana Potions early. Otherwise, the fight would have taken even longer, relying solely on his precise and not very devastating spear attacks.

When he recovered, Randidly got to work looting. He used his dagger to saw off the least damaged of the Deadly Webspinner's forelegs and stored it in his satchel. He picked another twenty or so of both types of crystals from the Deadly Webspinner's base, and glanced at Shal.

Randidly cleared his throat and said, "Can I have some extra time to remake my potions?"

Shal looked at Randidly like he was a smelly homeless person who asked for his daughter's hand in marriage. Shal silently led Randidly to a nearby stream and kept watch while Randidly ground up crystals and mixed them with water.

Congratulations! Your Skill **Potion Making** has grown to **Level 19!**

Randidly followed Shal underneath hanging canopies of vines and through ominously silent clearings. For several hours, they were alternatively within areas of the jungle filled with raucous birdsong, monkey screeches, or silence. When weaker foes appeared, it was Randidly's role to keep them from approaching Shal. With the boost of confidence from fighting the Deadly Webspinner, Randidly accomplished this much easier.

I really can do this. Randidly clenched his fist as he stood over the body of a muscular Howler Monkey. *Even if I'm not strong, I'm changing. And that's a good thing.*

After a full day of travel, the trees started to thin. The constant ambushes from the Howler Monkey's ceased. Soon, they stepped out of the shadowy jungle and were beneath a wide blue sky. They'd arrived at the plains.

Are we really still within an underground tunnel between two dorms? Randidly sighed. *This System really takes the laws of physics quite casually...*

The plains were dominated by orcs. They wielded stone axes and rode a strange ram creature the size of a small car. Randidly abruptly realized those beasts must have been the Three-Horned Demon Ram that welcomed him to the System. Seeing the Uncommon Blue coloration of the Level 34 above even the mounts' heads, Randidly decided he would have to get one alone before he could have his revenge for that initial callous greeting.

Shal ripped through these enemies with ease, his body and spear flowing sinuously between attack and defense. Randidly had been impressed when Shal fought him, but now that he wasn't trying to teach, his movements were blindingly fast. The orcs fled in fear after a dozen of their fellows collapsed, their throats slit without ever seeing the attack coming.

Shal watched the orcs run away with a small frown. He gestured for Randidly to approach. "Unlike that spider, Resistance Skills cannot save you from these enemies. You may shoot your magic if you wish, but try not to catch their attention. I will not save you from your own foolishness."

"Only yours, right?" Randidly joked.

He wasn't surprised when Shal drove the butt of his spear into Randidly's diaphragm, knocking the wind out of him.

The duo steadily advanced across the plains. The benefit of the open sky and rolling hills was that you could see the enemies coming from a long way off. And come they did, in increasingly large numbers. Shal effortlessly cut down their smaller raiding parties. At first, Randidly dutifully stood around and did nothing. But a strange itch began to take hold of him. He wanted to fight.

He spotted an enemy staggering to his feet, heavily wounded by Shal's thrust. Randidly cast Entangling Roots, earning him a Level due to the Level of the target. With a combination of Mana Bolts, Heavy Blows, and Phantom Thrusts, Randidly killed the wounded orc, standing over it as the light in its eyes dimmed.

Congratulations! Your Skill **Spirit of Adversity** has grown to **Level 18!**

I won.

Inwardly, he felt nothing as he watched the fire of life flicker and die within the intelligent creature. That disturbed him somehow. Unlike the Howler Monkeys or the Deadly Webspinner, this creature contorted with fear as it died. Yet he simply watched. Randidly shook his head. These were just spawns inside of a Dungeon. He couldn't look any deeper than that. If he allowed emotions to cloud his decision-making, the orcs would not hesitate to slaughter him.

"Pupil, prepare. It is time to show your usefulness."

And just like that, an enemy with a blue-colored name of Orc Shaman was throwing a skull made of smoke at Shal. This skull was much larger than the one Shal expelled from his body with Randidly's homemade potion.

Feeling quite nervous, Randidly attempted to intercept the projectile with his spear. It passed right through and sank into the flesh of his torso. Randidly froze, strange thoughts flooding his brain.

Kill...

Kill now... Worthless.

Kill, self... Dead, worthless.

Kill now, blood... Cry, alone.

Die. Blood, kill self...

Randidly stared at the blade of his own spear, fascinated. His hands tightened against the shaft. His heartbeat pounded in his ears. Everything became hot and uncomfortable, as though his body were an itchy wool suit.

Congratulations! You have learned the Skill **Mental Strength Level 1.**

Congratulations! You have learned the Skill **Curse Resistance Level 1.**

Maybe... The blade of his spear grew to fill Randidly's entire vision.

Congratulations! Your Skill **Mental Strength** has grown to **Level 2!**

The familiar butt of a spear to his gut doubled Randidly over and woke him from his stupor.

"Good, you did not succumb. I was somewhat worried. You may have the same Willpower as me, yet you are so puny and weak. Who knew whether or not your will was as scrawny as your body? But your assistance allowed me to slay the foe. Let us continue."

Feeling more than a little disturbed, Randidly woodenly followed Shal. His mind was slightly fuzzy and his limbs were heavy. As he began to Meditate while walking, that feeling started to fade.

The PP he earned in these first initial clashes pushed him up to 90 in the Pathless Path, giving him two free Stat points. Randidly surreptitiously placed both into Willpower.

"Better safe than sorry," he muttered.

Randidly looked at the blade of his spear and shivered. For a few brief moments, nothing had been more beautiful than the razor-sharp edge of the weapon. He reminded himself that the scariest enemies were the ones that attacked in unpredictable ways.

Time passed strangely. The sunlight-until-you-drop climate threw off Randidly's understanding of how long they'd been fighting. It didn't help that Shal seemed to have limitless Stamina, thoroughly thrashing a group of orcs one second and marching determinedly forward to the next. Randidly supposed this brutal pace was part of the point, to keep pushing if you could go further. To extend your boundaries and make you forget your former limits.

Perhaps it was the accumulated fatigue, but there were times during his role as a Willpower shield that Randidly whipped around to stare behind him. He could have sworn some being leered at his back, smiling in satisfaction. He could only shake his head and do his best to dismiss those worries. It was probably just a remnant sensation of unease from being hit with the Orc Shaman's Curse. As a Rare enemy type, there were bound to be side-effects to taking multiple curses in a row without recovering to his peak state.

Randidly tried not to think too deeply about this and hurried after Shal.

They continued to plow through raiding parties of orcs at a rapid rate. Patterns began to emerge. None of the base wandering groups had Shamans, but after eliminating three groups, a group led by a Shaman would show up, and Randidly would offer his body to their strange curse.

Due to the exposure, Mental Strength grew to Level 7, while Curse Resistance rose to a meagre Level 3. For the life of him, Randidly couldn't figure out why the general Skill Mental Strength would grow faster than the specific resistance to curses. Running increased a Level as Randidly struggled to keep up with Shal's long strides, leaving him at 98 PP in Pathless.

Despite his jumpiness, nearing the end of the Path put Randidly into a pretty good mood. He didn't even really pay attention to the orcs Shal mowed down, instead doing some quick calculations in his head. Based on the map, if they continued to push through the orcs at this rate…

"Oy, worthless student."

Randidly looked up, finding Shal surrounded by three new arrivals, named Elite Orc Guards, their names green. Beyond them, two Orc Shamans chuckled, muttering to themselves and spreading a thick purple smoke on the ground around them.

Shal's expression was serious, gesturing sharply with his chin as his spear flicked out and knocked away one of the heavy axes of the Elite Orc Guards. "Get over here and distract them. I can overcome these three, but not if my legs melt off."

"Kekekeke…" one of the Elite Orc Guards sneered and stepped forward.

The monster yelped and jerked its head backward. Shal's quick attack left a trail of blood across one of its broad cheeks. Randidly's master jumped up onto a large stone, putting him out of reach of the strange smoke, and aimed a glare in Randidly's direction.

Randidly's palms were tingling as he nodded. *I'm ready for this.*

I have to be.

The three elite guards surged toward Shal with evil grins. Randidly cast Entangling Roots, taking them by surprise. One Elite Orc Guard's foot twisted in a root and fell on its face, alleviating some of the pressure Shal experienced. With that opening, Shal's spear carved its way into the unarmored portions of the guards' flesh.

Feeling a surge of pride, Randidly fired a few Mana Bolts at the Shamans, wanting to briefly distract them. He fired another at the back of an Elite Orc Guard's knee. It yelped from the unexpected concussive push and half fell forward. Shal's spear sliced downward and lopped off its arm. The tripped orc scrambled up and roared. Randidly rushed forward, activating Entangling Roots.

The purple mist reached the legs of the orc Randidly ensnared with his Skill. It tore at the conjured roots, unable to get free. The muscular orc was fast and strong, but did not work quickly enough to escape the creeping purple swirl. The mist curled around its legs, its flesh evaporating to reveal a yellowed bone. The bone cracked as the thickening mist obscured the rest of the details. With a scream, the orc fell face first into the knee-high mist, its cries abruptly silenced.

Sweat dripped down Randidly's back and he skidded to a stop in the face of the monster's sudden death.

"Bah, he has no Poison Resistance, worthless apprentice. You do. Go stop those two stick bags, and I will crush them all," Shal snarled as the two remaining Elite Orc Guards attempted to push him toward the creeping mist.

Randidly raised his hand and shot a Mana Bolt, narrowly missing the Shamans. They hissed at him. One lifted his staff and shot a grey skull at Randidly, which took him in the chest. For a second, Randidly was immobilized. He quickly banished the strange, violent voices, earning him another Level in Mental Strength.

Unfortunately, the purple mist had spread too far. He wasn't accurate enough at this range to simply snipe his opponents with Mana Bolts. With gritted teeth, Randidly stepped into the creeping purple mist. *I can do this. The pain I've endured… it has to have meant something!*

His leather pants disintegrated to nothing, and his shoes and socks were sucked away. Tingling came first, followed by a rapid increase in chemical temperature along his exposed skin. Randidly had to grind his teeth to withstand the pain.

Congratulations! Your Skill **Poison Resistance** has grown to **Level 10!**

Randidly moved forward on unsteady legs. Due to how quickly his Health was dropping, he whipped out and downed two potions. He raised his spear and tightened his grip on the wood.

Congratulations! Your Skill **Pain Resistance** has grown to **Level 10!**

Pain steadily narrowed his focus. As Randidly grew closer, the mist became thicker, taller, leading to increased pain and depletion of his Health. By the time it reached mid-thigh, Randidly stopped to down another Health Potion. His body was sweating every ounce of moisture it possessed in a desperate attempt to rid himself of the burning of his legs. There was still twenty meters to the Shamans, but if he went any deeper into the mist…

Congratulations! Your Skill **Poison Resistance** has grown to **Level 11!**

With a silent prayer, he raised his hand and shot off a Mana Bolt. It struck the Shaman in the chest, disrupting the spell and pushing the monster back. The purple mist began to thin and dissipate, and with it, the pain in his legs began to ease.

The other Shaman glared at Randidly. But as Randidly raised his hand for the second shot, the Shaman gestured sharply, speaking a strange incantation. The dissipating purple mist froze before rushing backward toward its hand. Above its palm, a huge purple skull the size of a fast-food restaurant swirled into existence. The giant skull's mouth opened soundlessly and the

Shaman pointed. The horrifying skull rushed forward, losing its shape, becoming a wide flood of purple energy as tall as a man.

Shal paled, swearing colorfully as he hamstrung another of the Elite Orc Guards.

The wave hit Randidly first, submerging him completely. The pain was horrendous, enough to make him sway, barely holding on to consciousness. His Resistances weren't enough. Randidly opened his eyes and immediately regretted it. The strange poison ate away at the sensitive membranes of his eyes, but he forced them to remain open. He used Phantom's Eyes to focus on Shal, waiting for… something.

Shal… Randidly's thoughts felt far apart. He knew his Health was rapidly dropping, but his body didn't have the energy to brandish one of the two remaining Health potions. *If it's you… you can definitely…*

With a frown, Shal ran toward the oncoming rush of purple smoke. At the last moment, he thrust his spear into the ground, vaulting up and over the devouring wave of purple mist.

The shape of the skull bulged outward, howling. All the while, the monstrous thing followed Shal's leap over its head with the empty hollows of its eyes. The shape dissipated, and the whole cloud rushed upward in pursuit of Randidly's master.

Randidly's bloodshot eyes widened. The skull reformed, growing from the middle of the purple smoke, rising up to devour Shal. Still far away, the Orc Shamans cackled, directing their cursed poison skull to reform at his landing spot.

With a worried expression, Shal considered his options as he arched through the air toward the steadily widening mouth of the skull.

The lines around his master's eyes tightened. Something bleak and vicious was forming there.

I need… to help… I can't just… be a burden again… His vision swam. Gritting his teeth, Randidly raised his hand and pointed, invoking Mana without relying on a Skill.

As Shal descended to the wide-open mouth of the poison mist, Randidly knew what he wanted. A weak and sickly series of vines existed beneath the purple skull from where he'd tripped the Elite Orc Guard earlier. Though they were rotting, Randidly mentally strained and gripped. The rotting vines wrapped upward, forming an ascending foothold. Shal landed on those roots and kicked off, leaping over the smoke before the vines collapsed under his weight.

It had been enough.

Shal spun through the air and flung his spear forward like an Olympic javelin thrower. The Shaman manipulating the skull was speared through the heart. Even through his disintegrating eyes, Randidly saw blood spurt from the Shaman's mouth, and it toppled over.

Shal hit the ground just as the purple poison dissipated. With a roar, he accelerated forward.

Randidly swayed and collapsed, unable to withstand the pain any longer.

CHAPTER EIGHTEEN

*R*andidly woke up with a start from another nightmare. He had been stuck inside a pit with acid showering over him. The waves were infused with grinning purple skulls that took huge bites out of his arms and thighs until he couldn't move. He simply collapsed into the mud and drowned beneath the flood of liquid.

His eyes were unseeing and painful. Randidly's chest heaved, struggling to control his trembling body. He only managed to calm himself when his vision cleared. Shal stood a little ways away, cooking stew. Seeing Shal's quirked eyebrow at his display, Randidly flushed and lowered his gaze. He controlled his breathing and began to Meditate.

Congratulations! Your Skill Meditation has grown to Level 24!

Randidly inspected his Status. Aside from his heart tightening when he saw how low his Health was, Randidly was pleased to see Entangling Roots gained a Level during those last desperate moments. And somehow he'd created a new Skill in the chaos, Root Manipulation.

Root Manipulation Level 1: *Control roots in the surrounding area by sensing them and infusing them with your Mana. Can cause them to deviate from their normal shape.* **Duration of control and distance from the user increases Mana expenditure. By using more Mana, you can increase the size and strength of the roots you control. Efficiency of Mana expenditure slightly increases with Skill Level.**

Before looking at his Path screen, Randidly took a few minutes to experiment with this new Skill, earning himself another Level in it. Although there was only grass in the immediate area on this strange plain, Randidly sensed several larger roots, deeper in the earth. Apparently, the Skill came with some ability to sense roots too. Moving them basically emptied his Mana pool.

I'll need to invest in Intelligence again... Randidly prayed that Attributes and free Stats would be easier to obtain once he received his Class.

Randidly pressed his eyes closed and Meditated for another half hour. Shal continued to stir the stew. Above, cottony clouds drifted across the sky. Shifting his attention to the smaller grass roots, Randidly marveled at his ability to control every single one. He urged them to reach up out of the ground and tightly grip the toes of his now bare feet and—

Randidly froze. A second later, he felt a bit better when he realized Shal had draped a blanket across him. The poison had eaten away his pants and most of his shirt. Beside Randidly was another pair of leather pants and an oversized shirt. There were no spare shoes, but Randidly didn't mind going barefoot.

Especially now. Pressing his feet against the ground let him constantly feel the presence of roots beneath him.

Ruefully, Randidly shook his head, moving past the sheer enjoyment of utilizing the Skill. Root Manipulation was basically useless at the moment. The Mana expenditure was much higher than Entangling Roots and it didn't yet have the power to stop even a freshly birthed Corpse Beetle. But at the same time...

Randidly inwardly shrugged. He kind of liked it that way. It was versatile and would only get stronger as he trained it.

It wasn't just a Skill within a video game system. It was magic.

With quite a lot of accumulated expectations, Randidly returned to the Path screen and placed the hundredth point into Pathless.

Congratulations! You have completed the **"Pathless Path"! You have realized that all paths are the same, and all paths lead to the same place.**

After that utterly worthless notification, another one appeared.

Although all paths will eventually lead to the same place, you have realized that different feet traverse those myriad Paths, and as different footsteps echo, the whole world shifts into a peculiar alignment.

Congratulations! You have unlocked the Soulskill **Green Spear Mastery Level 1.**

A Soulskill will gain a Skill Level anytime you consume a PP to move

forward on another path. PP cannot be used to directly advance a
Soulskill.
Remember that as the Path extends before you, ever onward, ever
changing, sometimes you will change too. Embrace your new strength
and you will thrive.

Rubbing his chin, Randidly brought up his Stat screen. Sure enough, he
had a new Skill, although it was displayed differently—it was underlined on
his Status screen. A helpful notification appeared as he stared at it.

Green Spear Mastery: *Utilize insights into the spear to understand the
earth, and insight into the natural world to advance with your spear.* **Success
at crafting with materials from the natural world increases with Skill
Level. High Skill Levels makes it marginally easier to learn spear,
crafting, earth, and life related Skills. As Skill Level increases, a minute
amount of natural energy will be added to your attacks.**

Just a passive buff? Although it would grow naturally, Randidly was
somewhat disappointed at the result. He thought it might be something
similar to a Class, but now it just seemed like an affinity Skill. Useful, but
nothing that he could make use of now to further assist Shal.

Still, like his new Root Manipulation, it would grow to be extremely
strong, Randidly hoped, after he'd completed other Paths. He forced himself
not to dwell on his disappointment, returning his attention to the rest of the
Path screen. He suddenly found himself spoiled with a plethora of different
options.

Physical Fitness Path *0/25* | **Mana Bolt Path** *0/25* | **Evasion Path** *0/35* |
Phantom Thrust Path *0/40* | **Spear Mastery I Path** *0/50* | ????? *0/??*

Six choices in total were arrayed before him. All of these Paths, except
the last one, must have been unlocked when he reached certain Levels in his
current Skills. The question was which one he wanted to complete first.

He immediately eliminated the mystery Path and Spear Mastery I. The
former because it was probably more Pathless stuff and Randidly wasn't
ashamed to say he was tired of that. The latter because it would cost 50 PP to
finish.

For the same reason, Randidly hesitantly set aside Evasion and Phantom
Thrust, even though those were the bread and butter of his short-range
fighting capabilities. The real reason Randidly leaned toward the smaller
Paths was the possibility they would reward him with a new Skill. Because
Mana Bolt seemed more likely to do so, and would probably give him Mana
as he spent PP, Randidly decided on that one.

But was it ever really in doubt? Randidly mocked himself. *I love Mana Skills.*

He put 5 PP into it, earning him 2 Mana on Levels 1-4, then 1 Mana and +1 of any M. Stat on 5. Randidly put that free Stat into Intelligence.

What was really surprising was the notification that followed.

Green Spear Mastery has reached Level 5! +5 Mana. Spear Affinity has slightly increased.

Randidly stared at the notification, barely even noticing the appetizing smell wafting from Shal's stew. *It really just… grows in line with PP spent? And you can get bonuses from it constantly? That can't be right. If I had Green Spear Mastery for the whole of the Pathless Path, wouldn't I have earned two hundred Mana? Heh, so this is another hidden benefit of having a bunch of Skills.*

Feeling oddly pleased with himself, Randidly looked at his Status screen.

Randidly Ghosthound
Class: ---
Level: N/A
Health(/R per hour): 94/200 (63.75)
Mana(/R per hour): 139/159 (44.25)
Stam(/R per min): 105/105 (24)
Vit: 17
End: 27
Str: 8
Agi: 26
Perception: 18
Reaction: 23
Resistance: 9
Willpower: 52
Intelligence: 42
Wisdom: 26
Control: 21
Focus: 16
Skills
Soulskill: *Green Spear Mastery Lvl 5*

Basic: *Running Lvl 10 | Physical Fitness Lvl 20 | Sneak Lvl 8 | Acid Resistance Lvl 14 | Poison Resistance Lvl 11 | Spirit of Adversity Lvl 18 | Dagger Mastery Lvl 11 | Dodge Lvl 24 | Spear Mastery Lvl 34 | Pain Resistance Lvl 10 | Fighting Proficiency Lvl 20 | First Aid Lvl*

13 | Block Lvl 23 | Mental Strength Lvl 8 | Curse Resistance Lvl 3 | Pathfinding Lvl 3 | Mapmaking Lvl 3

Stamina: *Heavy Blow Lvl 15 | Sprinting Lvl 11 | Iron Skin Lvl 19 | Phantom Thrust Lvl 31 | Spear Phantom's Footwork Lvl 22 | Eyes of the Spear Phantom Lvl 9 | Phantom Half-Step Lvl 3*

Mana: *Mana Bolt Lvl 21 | Meditation Lvl 24 | Entangling Roots Lvl 23 | Mana Shield Lvl 16 | Root Manipulation Lvl 2*

Crafting: *Farming Lvl 19 | Plant Breeding Lvl 9 | Potion Making Lvl 19 | Analyze Lvl 9*

His Intelligence and Willpower seemed pretty respectable, even if his physical Stats, especially Strength, had fallen to the wayside. What was really impressive was his long list of Skills and the prospect of how quickly his Green Spear Mastery could grow.

Randidly walked over to Shal. "Now what?"

Shal gave him a dismissive look. "Now, we talk. Take a seat. I think we should re-evaluate our working relationship."

Randidly's heart clenched and his skin prickled. He knew that strained expression. He'd seen it on several other faces in the past and knew the talk that it proceeded.

"What…?"

"You are too weak to be near the battle." Shal shrugged. "Even though I pulled both potions and poured them down your throat, there were moments I thought you would turn into a corpse. You have helped me through the hurdle that has long thwarted me; there is no need for you to fight with me any longer. After all, you have your own world to consider, yes?"

"But, I…" Randidly bit his tongue, hating how whiny his voice sounded. He let a few breaths pass before he tried again. "You… if it wasn't for that root foothold I made, wouldn't you be just as wounded as I am? Yes, maybe I'm not… not able to fight as easily as you, but your training paid off. I can do this. And you need my help."

Shal examined Randidly for a long time, from head to bare toes. He grinned wolfishly. "Heh. In this, you are correct. So now, we obviously continue until every enemy in front of us is dead. Together."

CHAPTER NINETEEN

*F*or the first few days, Randidly was deeply afraid Shal would change his mind and decide he was too much of a burden. He threw every ounce of himself into his daily training, pushing himself to the point of exhaustion. The fear of being abandoned unearthed new stores of energy. When they encountered orcs, Randidly became aggressive, often placing himself in close combat situations.

He'd come away from those fights with large gashes on his arms, shoulders, or thighs, surviving long enough for Shal to take care of most of the foes. With Shal providing a bit of interference, Randidly was even able to slay these Orc Warriors, gradually banishing the whispering fear of abandonment from his heart.

For now.

Shal was no fool to the increased desperation in his disciple, but didn't comment on it. He simply observed with cool eyes.

There were tangible benefits to this extreme method. With Randidly's accumulation of Skill Levels, he completed the Mana Bolt and Physical Fitness Paths, earning him the Skills Arcane Orb and Haste, respectively.

The Arcane Orb was a powerful attack spell, and Haste doubled normal Stamina consumption to slightly increase speed. Randidly was eager to test them both, raising them to Level 3. With those two Skills, Randidly could finally defeat an Orc Warrior without relying on Shal.

More delightful than Skills were the benefits of his Green Spear Mastery. Every 5 PP spent, he'd gain something on a 20 point rotation. First was 5 Mana, followed by a point in Vitality, then 5 Stamina, and finally, two freely distributable Stats.

As the duo progressed forward, the environment began to change. The long, rolling plains shifted, transforming into a murkier landscape. Small lands, ponds, and sluggish creeks crisscrossed their paths. The Orcs became less and less common, replaced by more poisonous creatures lurking underneath the murky wetland's water surfaces.

With his Poison, Acid, and Curse Resistance, Randidly became Shal's mineshaft canary, moving ahead to draw the ire of the monsters. Shal became uncharacteristically cautious, slowing their pace. When Randidly asked him about it, the blue-skinned man chuckled.

"To rush forward into the embrace of danger is certainly bold. But life is also precious."

Randidly tilted his head to the side. "I thought... it was important to push your limits?"

"Bah, fool boy." Shal shook his head. "A spear can only go forward, and thus a Spearman must hold tight to the shaft and support it, or he will lose it and become just a man. Shortly afterward, he will undoubtedly die.

"However, what we do now is exactly to avoid losing control of our spears." Shal's gaze was intense. "We must remain spear users, gradually building up speed through investigation and understanding. Disciple, never confuse moving slowly for remaining still. To do so would prove how numb and shallow an understanding you possess."

The distinction left Randidly confused, but he didn't press the issue, following his master deeper into the wetlands. Their slow, purposeful progress took them through swamps and across rivers, fighting serpents, poisonous toads, and aggressive alligators.

During that time, Randidly had plenty of chances to utilize his new Skills. Arcane Orb proved to be a Mana sink with actual destructive power. Meanwhile, Haste was the only way Randidly could escape the clutches of some of the more dangerous ambushes. He brushed up against the edge of death time and time again, barely surviving by sucking down Health potions.

Yet he did survive. And he steadily grew more competent.

Two months of toil later, they arrived at the Eastern edge of the Dungeon, dominated by a giant swamp. And there, sitting in the middle of the massive lily pads, holding court with its fellow aquatic creatures, was the being they had come to kill.

BLACK SWAMP SALAMANDER (BOSS) LEVEL 36

Shal and Randidly crouched at the edge of the swamp, peering through reeds. The loafing Boss was a salamander the size of a horse, lazily swimming between toads the size of boulders.

"I thought you said this was a Level 35 Dungeon?"

"And thus, the way out requires the power to kill a foe at Level 36. An extraordinary one at that," Shal grunted, scanning the surroundings. "Those lily pads seem large enough to bear weight, but those Guardian Toads around the Black Swamp Salamander… peh. Their poison clouds the black water of this swamp. Those are the true foes here. Come, we must prepare."

They moved some distance away from the swamp. Shal killed all the weaker monsters in the surrounding area before they set up camp. Then they slept.

That night, Randidly dreamt of a pair of eyes watching him. Every time he spun around, he found a blind toad behind him and the feeling reignited. A woman's faint chuckle echoed in his ears.

The next morning, they began luring away the massive Guardian Toads.

Attacking them directly infuriated the Black Swamp Salamander. It spewed a poisonous, sticky goop like a machine gun. At the will of the Boss, the Guardian Toads drifted through the swamp, releasing clouds of poison. Even Randidly's Poison Resistance couldn't withstand the stacking poisons, his Health far too quickly being dropped to dangerous lows.

Randidly and Shal were forced to retreat and wait for the monsters to calm down before trying again.

They realized the best way to grab one's attention without alerting the rest was for Randidly to fire a Mana Bolt. The resulting splash was small enough that most of the others overlooked it. If he hit near the Guardian Toad's skin, its curiosity drew it out to investigate without crying out in pain and alerting the rest.

The Guardian Toad drifted toward him, confusion in its massive eyes. Randidly wiped sweat from his brow, taking careful aim.

Congratulations! Your Skill **Mana Bolt** has grown to **Level 22!**

Randidly shot another Mana Bolt and lured it further and further into the shallows clogged with reeds. Finally, he drew it up onto solid ground, its massively fat body quaking in its attempts to figure out the source of the disturbance.

A grinning Shal waited beyond a copse of trees. Alone and taken by surprise, the Guardian Toad died before it could alert its fellows. A triumphant Randidly laughed and turned to lure another, but Shal stopped him.

His master pointed at the defeated toad. "If we lure them here again, the corpse will alert them to danger. We must move it first. I can cut it into smaller pieces, and with your Poison Resistance, you will carry them away."

Randidly's eyes twitched at the very idea. In the end, he couldn't deny he was the better choice. But carrying the stinking, painfully poisonous chunks of toad fat was *quite* unpleasant. *When I said I could be useful to you, this wasn't exactly what I had in mind...*

Congratulations! Your Skill **Poison Resistance** has grown to **Level 12!**

Randidly wrapped his arms around the massive frog leg. Even if the work was difficult, he understood its necessity and kept his mouth shut. Its poison decreased in effectiveness after its death, but the activity still left him slightly lightheaded. And the other notification he received aggravated him to no end.

Congratulations! Your Skill **Physical Fitness** has grown to **Level 21!**

This isn't weight training; this is just... Randidly looked at his ooze-covered and stinging hands sourly.

Still, the method was effective. Over the next several hours, they drew the remaining Guardian Toads away, slaughtered them, and disposed of their bodies. In the process, Randidly earned one more Skill Level in Mana Bolt and Poison Resistance.

They broke their fast at the edge of the swamp in silence. The remaining nuts and berries Randidly paused to cultivate at the edge of the plains gave them the energy they'd need to face the salamander.

Shal stood, dusting his legs. "Are you ready?"

"Yes," Randidly responded.

Shal gave him a long and contemplative look. "Do not die, boy."

The duo crept to the edge of the swamp, sizing up the Black Swamp Salamander across the murky water. Despite the disappearance of its eight Guardian Toads, the creature didn't seem too perturbed. It continued its lazily circles. It was the only creature who dared make ripples within its swamp.

"Distract it when you can," Shal said.

Without waiting for an answer, Shal took several steps forward and vaulted through the air to the first giant lily pad. He landed and immediately leapt to the next, causing a ripple to spread outward from the lily pad. The Black Swamp Salamander twisted its horse-sized body, its beady yellow eyes searching for the reason behind the disturbance.

Randidly released a hissing breath, raising his hand. *I may not need to be here, Shal, but since I am, I can give you the footholds you need. I can help.*

He unleashed a Mana Bolt while simultaneously activating Root Manipulation, shifting the plant matter within the depths of the swamp.

Congratulations! Your Skill **Mana Bolt** has grown to **Level 24!**

Just as the Black Swamp Salamander fixated on Shal, Randidly's Mana Bolt smacked the side of its head. Infuriated, it raised its head and roared for its Guardian Toads, except none remained to poison the area.

Shal took advantage of this chance, his body seeming to flicker and accelerate, covering three more massive lily pads. Something strange began to accumulate in the air around Shal. Randidly blinked several times and activated Eyes of the Spear Phantom to pierce the shadows around Shal.

Is that a phantom...? Randidly's jaw dropped. A spectral entity briefly flared behind his master as he raised his spear. As the Black Swamp Salamander lowered its head, Shal was there. The Phantom Thrust he used was completely different from Randidly's. The weapon was held at the ready and then simply vanished.

Blood spurted from the Boss's shredded left eye.

SCREEEEEEEECH!

The roar was a keening cry of pain. Shal spun, the shade behind him dissipating, and jumped off the body of the Boss. He was heading for an empty stretch of black water.

Randidly's heart leapt into his throat. Near where Shal headed, he poured as much Mana as he could into the few bits of plant matter he controlled beneath the water's surface.

Congratulations! Your Skill **Root Manipulation** has grown to **Level 6!**

Congratulations! Your Skill **Root Manipulation** has grown to **Level 7!**

Congratulations! Your Skill **Root Manipulation** has grown to **Level 8!**

A small sprout curled up out of the water just as Randidly's strained Mana pool emptied. Shal pressed his foot against the root and leapt back toward the thrashing Boss. His spear blurred. No strange phantasm hung behind him, but there was definitely something supernatural about his spear attacks. Whatever movements his master made were far beyond the limits of the Eyes of the Spear Phantom.

Randidly guzzled a Mana potion and urged himself not to get distracted.

Shal's strikes glanced off the Black Swamp Salamander's smooth skin. A second later, several deep gashes across its flank appeared before Shal kicked himself away.

In that moment, the Boss understood its help wasn't coming. It whipped around, sending a wave of dirty water splashing across Shal. Just as Shal landed on another lily pad, the Black Swamp Salamander opened its massive mouth and unleashed a spray of poisonous goop. Shal twisted and fled right, circling around toward its wounded eye.

SCREEEEEEEECH!

The Boss roared again, struggling to keep Shal within its impaired field of vision. Shal's complex Spear Phantom's Footwork left a trail of after images, further confusing the Boss. With his quick steps, Shal had enough time to circle most of the way around, attack the Boss's back, and flee, always remaining within its blind spots.

Even as Randidly prepared more footholds beneath the water, he marveled. *This... is this how powerful someone can become with the System? I knew I'd be beyond the limits of a human, considering my starting Stats were single digits, but this...*

Congratulations! Your Skill **Eyes of the Spear Phantom** has grown to
Level 10!

Randidly gained a Skill Level by merely trying to observe Shal's movements. His master was grace and violence personified—a being who could slay a Level 36 Unique Boss!

Randidly accepted his role as support, occasionally pushing out concussive Arcane Orbs to briefly distract the Black Swamp Salamander when Shal shifted his position. In addition to wounding the Boss, Shal was luring it more and more into the shallows. Furious, the Boss gladly followed. This made it easier for Randidly to intervene and cut down on its ability to eventually flee beneath the surface of the water.

Randidly steadily earned Skill Levels in Root Manipulation, Arcane Orb, and Eyes of the Spear Phantom. In addition, he made a mental note to emulate Shal's style. Although he was fully focused on the battle in front of him, he subtly adjusted the battlefield to his advantage.

That foresight and arrangement was even more useful than Stats.

Of course, a Level 36 Boss wouldn't fall easily. When the Black Swamp Salamander's eyes turned red, some part of Randidly knew immediately what was coming.

It was moving into its second phase.

Its entire body expanded slightly, sending a shuddering ripple through the swamp. The tail doubled in length, whipping back and forth and severely limiting the angles Shal could use to approach, despite the Boss being unable to find him. Even worse than the size increase was the arrival of reinforcements.

Randidly grimaced, spotting two bubbling trails of shadows cutting through the cloudy water toward the shallows. He prepared to unleash several Arcane Orbs to distract what must be Guardian Toads. But what surfaced were not Guardian Toads. Randidly's eyes widened at the notifications floating above the slithering arrivals.

Giant Serpent Level 32

These are... Randidly was stunned. That nameless humanoid corpse inside the mouth of the serpent came rushing back. He began to tremble, knowing that being had barely been able to inflict the killing blow before he succumbed to the poison. *These monsters...*

The Giant Serpents wasted no time asserting themselves in the fight. They slid into the shallows and reared out of the water, striking at Shal from behind. He spun away with his rapid movements, flitting across several root footholds to escape. The Black Swamp Salamander's tail tore through several of those root footholds, forcing him back. Both Giant Serpents aggressively charged forward.

Randidly licked his lips and downed another Mana potion. *One thing at a time. I need to help...*

Congratulations! Your Skill **Root Manipulation** has grown to **Level 10!**

Something vengeful rose in Randidly's chest. Shal might have been the one who taught Randidly to survive, building his foundation, but Randidly had an older debt to pay.

If not for finding that satchel and dagger...

Is that what had become of that nameless humanoid? He'd attempted to escape the Dungeon, reaching this phase of the Boss fight, only to be chased by the serpents all the way back to the area by the Safe Room?

He was certain his benefactor had once stood here, on the banks of this same swamp.

Randidly shouted, "Shal! They will chase you onto land."

Shal's face flickered. Randidly threw out several more Arcane Orbs to briefly distract the Giant Serpents. Shal landed on a lily, leaping back to shore in a silent show of trust in Randidly's words. As predicted, the furious Boss and Giant Serpents rushed after him.

Congratulations! Your Skill **Haste** has grown to **Level 5!**

Congratulations! Your Skill **Arcane Orb** has grown to **Level 8!**

Randidly used Haste to flee backward, firing Arcane Orbs over his shoulder. Shal landed on solid ground and spun his spear, deflecting a spray of poison from the Boss. The serpents arrived first, lashing out at him. Shal coolly ducked under their explosive bites and thrust his spear deeply into their tubular bodies.

Hissing in fury, the two snakes heaved their massive bodies, slithering forward. Shal's spear blurred from the strange phantasmal energy. The Black Swamp Salamander clambered out of the water, its limbs fat and heavy on land.

Randidly planted his foot and twisted around, blood roaring in his ears. Clear and focused certainty gripped Randidly. He knew exactly how he could help both his master and that unknown humanoid.

I might not know your name... Randidly's eyes flashed as he raised his spear. *But I sure as hell will make them remember what you've done for me!*

Randidly activated Phantom Half-Step, crossing the distance to the closest Giant Serpent. He hopped and dashed up its back with the aid of Spear Phantom's Footwork. Shal was below, using Sweep to open a deep gash in its body while Randidly crouched at the base of its skull, spear raised.

Haste. Phantom Thrust. Phantom Thrust!

Congratulations! Your Skill **Haste** has grown to **Level 6!**

All of the fury and raw aggression Randidly had been holding within him exploded outward through his spear. Again and again, he jabbed his weapon into the base of the Giant Serpent's skull. Randidly's feet smoked painfully from the poison in its skin. It didn't matter; the howl of his fury drowned out the pain. Shal noticed his actions and unleashed his own flurry of blows against it while dodging the Boss's spewed poison.

Randidly's eyes burned. He didn't know when, but he'd started crying. His shoulders heaved, his hands remaining firm on the spear. This was how he'd prove he was worth keeping around. He raised his weapon again. *Phantom Thrust. Phantom Thrust. Phantom Thrust.*

Congratulations! Due to your repeated actions, you have learned the Skill **Phantom Onslaught Level 1.**

Without missing a beat, Randidly unleashed his newfound Phantom Onslaught. Instead of a single thrust, Randidly unleashed six into the Giant Serpent beneath him. Flesh spattered and its bones broke. The slippery body beneath him shuddered. Randidly began to laugh then, activating Haste and using Phantom Onslaught as many times as his exhausted body would allow him.

Congratulations! Your Skill **Haste** has grown to **Level 7!**

Congratulations! Your Skill **Phantom Onslaught** has grown to **Level 2!**

Congratulations! Your Skill **Phantom Onslaught** has grown to **Level 3!**

Everything blurred. Randidly tried to activate Phantom Onslaught again, but his Stamina failed him. He swayed and was thrown off its back when the Giant Serpent collapsed.

Congratulations! Your Skill **Spirit of Adversity** has grown to **Level 19!**

Randidly blinked, examining the body of the Giant Serpent before him. Not only was the back of its skull cracked and ripped apart, but Shal had gutted it from the front. Randidly used his slowly recovering Stamina to smile. *Heh… Fuck you.*

In the next moment, Randidly stilled. The other Giant Serpent raised its body over the corpse of its brother. Its sharp eyes were fixed on *him*, who only had enough Stamina to sit and stare upward at the monster.

He'd exhausted his Stamina, forgetting about the consequences. Forgetting every lesson Shal drilled into him about fighting. The snake opened its mouth wide and launched itself down at him. Randidly knew he was going to die.

His face twisted into a snarl. *Fuck… you!*

Randidly was slammed to the side with enough force to briefly knock him unconscious. He woke with a start, bouncing and rolling across the ground. When he finally stopped, he pushed himself up.

Shal was there, a broken spear in hand and a baseball-sized wound through his bicep. The still living Giant Serpent flailed around in pain, the other half of Shal's spear driven through the side of its skull. Randidly noticed the flesh around Shal's wound from the serpent's fang was rapidly being eaten away.

"You…" Randidly began speaking, but flinched as the Black Swamp Salamander awkwardly clambered over the corpse of the first Giant Serpent.

Shal's face was impassive. "Boy. Your spear. Give it to me."

The instinct to follow Shal's directions made Randidly move. He scrambled back to where he dropped his spear and tossed it to Shal. His master caught the weapon and clicked his tongue.

"Hummm…" Shal flicked the weapon left and right, completely ignoring the screech of rage from the Boss as it surveyed its dead and dying subordinates. "I cannot utilize my own Style any longer with just a single arm. The Spear Phantom is too peculiar in its demands. But perhaps… yes, that old game."

Shal wiggled his arm and the spear came alive, slithering with the same sinuous grace the Giant Serpents demonstrated in the water.

The Black Swamp Salamander charged, raising its basketball-sized hands to smash Shal. Shal spun away, completely ignoring his wounded left arm. Somehow, even by only using his right arm, he flicked the spear and the weapon curved, ripping the Black Swamp Salamander's second eye to pieces.

SCREEEEEEEECH!

Now completely blind, its tail went wild, forcing Randidly to scramble away to avoid being crushed.

"And now," Shal grinned and flicked blood off of the tip of Randidly's spear, "you will die for me."

Randidly recovered from his stunned state when the bloody body finally collapsed. A weird, overwhelming sense of warmth suffused him. Wincing, he forced himself to stand and approach his master.

The Black Swamp Salamander Dungeon Boss lay dead behind them. A glowing yellow portal floated just beyond Shal, his eyes closed, focused on simply breathing.

Randidly pressed his lips together, looking from Shal to the yellow portal. Seven months had passed since Randidly started training under Shal. The ends of the plains had been a grind, pushing through increasing numbers of Elite Guards and Shamans. The Orc Chieftain left them stumped for a month before Shal gained 2 Levels. Plus, Randidly spent that time working on his Skills to finally allow him to take on several of the guards at once.

I was supposed to be helpful.

Even with all the improvements Randidly made in the fight against the Boss, he couldn't bring himself to view the notifications. His eyes kept going to Shal's left arm. The persistent internal acid kept his skin chemically burned and the muscles bared to the air. To save Randidly's life, Shal risked himself. If not for that strange, serpent-like flick of Shal's spear to blind the Black Swamp Salamander... would they have been able to survive?

Perhaps Shal was right when he wanted to talk after the first fight against the Orc Shamans. Randidly's hands tightened into fists, looking down at his own wounded body. The Poison Frogs were one thing, but he'd been rapidly overmatched by the Giant Serpents. His only use was as a distraction. *I became weight he needed to carry through the Dungeon...*

Randidly shook his head to disperse those thoughts. There was no point in thinking of that now. The past and the future were different from the present.

He faced Shal, feeling strangely reluctant. "Thank you, for everything. For teaching me how to protect myself. For pushing my limits. For helping me gather potion materials. For... fighting with me. If it wasn't for you, I—"

"It was nothing. It is every spear user's duty to tell the tale of the Spearman," Shal said simply. He raised his wounded left arm and moved the limb around, testing its limits. He cocked his head. "Why do you hesitate now? You have finally reached your goal. You can leave the Dungeon. Did you not worry for your friends?"

Randidly pictured Sydney and Ace. He smiled ruefully, shaking his head. "It's been more than seven months. If they still live, a few more minutes won't matter."

"Ah," Shal said, patting his gory shoulder, as he did when he noticed something. Then he winced as he aggravated his wounds. "Heh, you are confused, this makes sense. I was foolish and didn't connect the dots. Of course you would not know. Time in Dungeons flows differently. It is accelerated, so it's almost impossible for one to find an emptied Dungeon when entering it, and impossible to enter at the same time as someone else. I believe they are roughly one-thousand times faster than normal speed. The time that occurred outside is but a fraction of what you have experienced in here."

Randidly's jaw dropped. With his much higher Intelligence, he began doing some mental math, muttering to himself. "Some of the 'days' are long, but if the time I spent in here really is around seven months... Only about five hours have passed on Earth?"

For several seconds, Randidly stared at the ground. Five hours. Everything he'd accomplished compressed into five hours. It was just one more example of the System performing some impossible magic he didn't understand. Just one more example of how the world had changed.

He licked his lips. *If... if everyone else has only experienced the System for five hours, then the current me—all the hard work I've poured into training and preparing—will I be... strong?*

Randidly bowed once more to Shal. "I truly owe you."

He leapt through the portal without a backward glance.

Shal laughed at his disciple's impulsive actions. He tensed, looking at the portal with a guilty glance. He raised his good arm and rubbed the back of his head. "Ah, I should have told him about the System..."

"Well, it is no matter." Shal concluded, his eyes burning. "He has a spear. The problems he faces will sort themselves out."

With a slight feeling of nausea after passing through the portal, Randidly found himself standing on a road. A normal paved road. He fell to his knees and pressed his hand against the concrete. He flexed his toes and savored the familiar feeling. The sun was low on the horizon, bringing a slight chill to the air.

"Probably morning..." Randidly said. He rapped his knuckles against the road, unable to stop a grin from spreading across his face. "If what Shal said is true, then it's really been only a night since the System arrived!"

Randidly quickly came back to himself. The System meant danger. He examined the surroundings, picking out the sounds. Car alarms blared, and screams from several directions floated around him. A lower hum below that came the churning of mechanical engines and the roars of beasts.

Heat beyond the chill warmed his back. He turned to find the building behind him was consumed by flames. He stood at the edge of a small town dotted with houses, a general store, and a gas station within view. Chaos reigned within those streets.

The System's glorious arrival on Earth played out all around him.

Randidly's mouth formed a grim line. It seemed like the System hit hard outside of the Dungeons too.

A series of notifications popped up.

You are currently within an area of Newbie Zone inside of Earth's Zone 32! *Original geography within Zone 32 has been scrambled. Within the Newbie Zone, only monsters under Level 20 will appear.* **To survive, slay rare monsters to obtain Golden Coins, which can be used to found a "Newbie Village." At the "Newbie Village," you can obtain a Class, which will allow you to grow and obtain power! The Class is the first step to the Pinnacle!**

Warning! Founding a **"Newbie Village"** will automatically cause the **"Newbie Zone Level Restriction"** in the surrounding area to degrade within **7 days.** Grow strong quickly after founding a **"Newbie Village"** or you will die. **Monsters will invade "Newbie Villages" periodically, threatening its survival.**

Fallen **"Newbie Villages"** will become infested by monsters and turn into dangerous **Dungeons. Dungeons house great treasure, but also great peril, so enter at your own risk.** *If a village-formed Dungeon is not cleared within a month of its formation, a vast wave of monsters will spill out and attack nearby areas.* Such a wave of monsters will be beyond the ability of typical **"Newbie Villages"** to survive. **It is advised that you pacify Dungeons as quickly as possible.**

Randidly scanned the notifications. Then his eyes narrowed.

Congratulations! Your Skill **Eyes of the Spear Phantom** has grown to **Level 14!**

Randidly raised a Mana Shield, blocking a Fireball aimed at his chest. He almost felt like he was boasting by calling it a Fireball. The projectile was the size of a child's fist and fizzled harmlessly against the Mana Shield. Randidly located the monster, a small, imp-like thing with bulging purple eyes, and wearing a red robe, floated next to the burning building.

The notification above its head left Randidly a little underwhelmed.

Fire Imp Level 2

The imp revealed a wicked grin and began to chant. Randidly snorted. A sizzling Mana Bolt shot toward the creature. The projectile smashed into its chest. It crumpled and slammed backward into the building with enough force to punch its way through the burning wall. A gushing tongue of flame flailed out of the hole before everything settled.

Congratulations! Your Skill **Spirit of Adversity** has grown to **Level 22!**

Several seconds later, the monster didn't reappear. The house continued to crackle.

Randidly tentatively smiled. It was oddly satisfying facing enemies he was actually supposed to be facing. He didn't want to assume he was grossly overpowered right now. Especially if an enemy that could throw fire was supposed to be survivable with starting Stats.

Or is it purposely difficult to spur growth? Randidly wondered. *Like humans should need to hide for a while and make preparations before they try to kill monsters and found a Newbie Village. Which would explain why the Level protection falls off so quickly after the village is founded...*

Screech!

Randidly twisted around. Another Fire Imp rounded the corner of the burning building, spotting him. This time, he smashed it with a Mana Bolt before it even began creating its own meagre Fireball. The crumpled body of this monster skipped across the ground before coming to rest on the sidewalk.

On reflex, Randidly went over to the body and scoured the tiny pockets of its red robe. He was pleased to find several small red crystal shards. Honestly, the amount was somewhat shocking. But Randidly supposed most people wouldn't realize they were worth anything.

Not everyone would adapt as quickly to the System as he had, after all. Even in the proper area, greeted with the right sort of notifications.

Right now, Randidly had a few goals. The main one was to find Sydney and Ace. The second was to find his parents, depending on how large of an area this "Zone 32" covered. Finally, he wanted to kill one of the Rare monsters, suspecting it shouldn't be too hard. With that, he'd gain the key to obtain a Class.

Randidly planned on helping anyone he could. If he had strength enough to save someone, he wanted to do it. The System definitely offered benefits, but it was callous. He didn't intend to let anyone in front of him die unnecessarily.

He admitted he might not want to immediately create a Newbie Village. Randidly mused over the prospect of spending some time planting crops and building a base before he allowed higher Level monsters to spawn in the area. If masses of monsters mobbed him, Shal was no longer around to—

Shal! Randidly turned around, looking to the street, stunned by how quickly he'd abandoned his master to return to the world. Tentatively, he took several steps back onto the pavement. Gradually, Randidly frowned. *Shouldn't there be… some sort of obvious entrance to the Dungeon?*

Well, that can wait until later. The flaming house dragged Randidly's eyes upward. His mind whirred into planning mode. Of the tasks, finding his two best friends was the most important goal. With the Skill Levels he'd obtained in the Dungeon, Randidly was confident in dealing with the weaker monsters that appeared to be running wild in the area.

Unfortunately…

One phrase from the notification stuck out to him. *Original geography has been scrambled?*

For a moment, Randidly was stumped. Based on where he assumed the small town would be, the mountains should have loomed above them, not far to the east…

And he wasn't anywhere near the University like he should have been. He'd clearly been moved off-campus somehow. Perhaps it was a side effect of entering the Dungeon. Randidly walked around the block, covering a fair amount of ground.

The "block" itself was extremely strange. The area where Randidly had come out of the Dungeon was in the middle of the street. An apartment building was on one side and a flaming storefront on the other. Beyond the storefront was the gas station and the post office. Wherever the apartment building teleported from, nothing else had come. That whole side of the street was grass, aside from the one extremely tall apartment building. As though it had truly been randomly dropped here.

Randidly briefly tried to calculate the statistical likelihood of an apartment building being teleported next to a road, but knew it was a waste of time and stopped.

Meanwhile, the other side of the street appeared to have been taken from a small, sleepy town. He walked toward the end of the block where buildings were clustered more densely. On his way, he slaughtered three more Fire Imps, earning a Level in Mana Bolt. By this point, the screams in the distance had been cut off.

Around the corner, strangely named restaurants and antique shops stretched beyond the post office. Just as Randidly was wondering if he'd finally get the chance to use his Mapmaking Skill, the screams returned. Randidly activated Sprint and rushed toward the sound. When he saw the source, he skidded to a stop, ripping open his bare heels against the concrete.

Several wolverine-looking animals dragged a woman across the street. As she bled out, her midsection laid open by the monsters' fangs, she reached for a lone stroller.

Randidly activated Haste. With his accelerated movements, he practically teleported next to the Level 3 Wolverine Cubs. He lowered his spear and unleashed a Phantom Onslaught, tearing holes through their bodies. In a split second, all the Wolverine Cubs collapsed, their blood staining the concrete, mixing with the woman's.

Randidly was slightly disturbed by how warm their blood was as it seeped over his toes. More so that warm blood was warm blood. The two types were indistinguishable from each other.

"Ma'am," Randidly began awkwardly, but the woman didn't seem to notice him. As soon as the wolverines' claws released her, she dragged herself back toward the stroller, her tears drawing rivers across her blood splattered cheeks.

"My baby... My baby..." Her voice was raw and hoarse.

The earlier silence was probably her vocal cords giving out. Randidly knew he should do something, but he was frozen.

Before she could cross the three meters to the stroller, she collapsed. She coughed up blood, its pigment thick and dark, oozing as if by its own accord. With dull eyes, she rolled onto her back and died.

Solemn, Randidly finally found it within him to walk up to the stroller. What he saw made him grimace.

Inside was a silent, bloody mass of gore.

In this, I definitely have an absolute advantage in regard to the System. I've already realized the bloodthirsty sort of world this has become... I won't flinch from violence. Randidly's attention was grabbed by gunshots. They sounded reasonably near, just on the other side of the small town. When no screams followed, he wanted to test something before wandering near a panicked individual with a gun. Randidly moved to the end of the street and opened his Menu, selecting Maps.

As he'd hoped, his Mapmaker Skill was active. It'd already been pushing away the fog on the "map" of the area, marking things down and coincidentally labeling them exactly how he'd named them. He zoomed out and swore mightily.

The Newbie Area of Zone 32 was huge. Too huge. Based on what he could tell, it was at least a 200-kilometer by 200-kilometer area.

Perhaps if it'd been the Randidly fresh from the apocalypse, he would have hesitated, becoming lost for a while by the scope of the task he'd set for himself. But this Randidly had been tempered for seven months with death hanging over him. He'd been taught to recognize pain only as a sign of what he needed to accomplish. Trained in the ways of the spear by Shal, he'd stood against enemies far more powerful than simple distance.

"Guess we're just going to go out of order," he muttered to himself, hefting his spear and activating Eyes of the Spear Phantom. "Time to help some strangers."

Randidly walked confidently forward, spear raised and Mana swirling around in the palm of his left hand. It was not a good day to be a System monster in this area of the Newbie Zone.

CHAPTER TWENTY

*S*everal additional gunshots made Randidly pause, considering his approach. If these people had questions about his abilities, how should he answer? And should they join forces? If he could obtain some assistance, it would likely make searching the surrounding areas easier. At the same time...

Randidly wasn't sure what he should say to people to explain the System and what it meant for Earth. Especially when he didn't really know the endgame of all this. Should he encourage them to expose themselves to danger to grow more quickly in Skill Levels? The very real possibility that no one would even listen to him occurred to Randidly.

Suddenly feeling a bit leery of the gunshots, Randidly turned away, sparing the stroller a glance. The gore within that innocent basket reminded him this wasn't a nice world. Due to his lack of preparation in the Dungeon, he himself had faced death's doorstep more times than he could count.

With a hardened heart, he walked away from the town and headed into the wilderness.

Randidly settled down on his haunches, rubbing his chin while surveying the area. Having searched for a few hours and seeing no sign of the Rare Bosses, he decided to start a small base. He'd chosen this spot around two miles outside of town for several reasons.

The valley already contained a small cabin, which appeared to have been hastily abandoned when the strange wolverine creatures moved in. Randidly mopped up the wolverines with little effort, barely earning a Level in

Phantom Onslaught for his troubles. Most people seemed to have the crazy idea that fleeing to the city was the right answer, ensuring wild places like this were completely devoid of other souls.

His wider sweep of the surrounding hills brought him face to face with the horrors of the System. Whole families were cut down, left eviscerated in their cars. Homes were abandoned and burning. And even worse than the monster attacks was when Randidly found a few bodies clearly killed with bullets.

Suddenly, he was glad he hadn't followed the noises. Even with his increased Stats, Randidly didn't think he could survive a bullet to the temple.

The other benefit to settling here was the four different types of enemies that intersected in the area. The wolverines were the biggest presence, but Randidly killed dozens of them without finding any rare mobs. Also present were strange Komodo-dragon-sized lizards that belched thunder. Even those Fire Imps Randidly encountered when he arrived had taken residence. And while Randidly searched, he noticed small, sharp goblin eyes watching him from the brush at the other corner of the valley. All enemies were confounded by his Mana Shield and fled from his Mana Bolts.

The nearby exploration had gone smoothly, planting more seeds of confidence to germinate in his chest. Randidly still had vivid memories of his overconfidence endangering him. Thinking about how he'd stepped forward to face those Giant Serpents in the Dungeon...

Randidly shivered and refocused his thoughts.

The cabin and nearby farm attracted his eye. If he was going to spend some time here, he wanted to experiment with the System's properties. First to see if plants would grow as quickly as they did inside the Dungeon, but also to try experimenting with different combinations of crops for Farming. Randidly found some strange plants deeper in the Dungeon and was itching to see whether or not they could grow in this climate.

In the afternoon, Randidly began taking stock of the area, clearing out the wolverine bodies he'd taken down earlier. Randidly found a relatively clear tract of land and turned to the supplies he'd brought in his satchel. Some were poisonous, bits of things he wanted to experiment with in making potions. He focused on the food-stuffs.

The first two were the banana-style fruit and the Halnuts. As he was most familiar with their growth times, he planted them immediately. In addition, he had seeds for Stal Berry Bushes. Much more interesting was a plant he'd come across that grew almost like bamboo. Except the stalk could be eaten and tasted like radishes.

His ultimate find was tiny red potatoes. He spread them liberally in and outside the field. He definitely wanted to eat something other than fruits and nuts. Shal had taught him a lot about necessity while grinding nuts into a gruel that could be fried and kept for later, but Randidly sorely missed Earth food.

Randidly supposed he would need to learn how to clean and dress an animal for meat. Maybe even the wolverines, though they looked quite stringy. For now, he satisfied himself with his five crops in the areas around the wooden cabin. He sat and Meditated while practicing his ability to utilize Root Manipulation.

His progress from where he started was impressive, able to now transform tiny grass roots into knobby things the size of caterpillars by flooding them with his Mana. They extended upwards, waving softly at him. Randidly's mouth curved into a grin.

The sound of someone approaching made him look up. Slowly, Randidly stood, leaving his spear lying on the ground next to his satchel. If things went south, he planned to rely on his Mana Skills. He briefly considered hiding, but he was sitting in the middle of the field between his precious plants.

An extremely skinny looking teenager stumbled out of the woods, warily glancing around. He had small, beady eyes and thin brown hair. Randidly's eyes narrowed when he noticed the kid was using what looked like gloves with claws attached to the knuckles, which he'd seen drop from some of the wolverines he'd killed. When he picked it up, he was shocked to realize it was an equipment that granted +1 Strength. However, the claws kept getting caught on his spear and the bonus was minor enough that Randidly hadn't bothered to collect them.

He supposed that to a person who started with 2 or 3 Strength, +1 was quite a lot.

The kid gave him a surprisingly frank look, then narrowed his eyes. His voice was low and aggressive. "Oy, you think you can move in on my spot while I'm away?"

Randidly was honestly taken aback by the antagonism. Was this really the right time to quibble about a spot? Especially with the human race in jeopardy? All the advice Randidly had carefully considered and prepared to pass on to other people he encountered died on his lips.

Swaggering forward, the kid gave Randidly a dismissive look. "Weakling. If you must, you can hang around and do odd jobs for me, but get in my way, don't be surprised if I—well…"

The facade crumbled, unnerved by screeches coming from the nearby forest-covered hill. Stumbling forward, the kid ran to Randidly's side.

"Haha… as my f-first o-o-order, investigate that noise!"

Okay, back to my role as an experienced System-user… Randidly sighed, considering how to flush the monsters out of the tree line. A high-pitched, human yelp of pain staggered his thoughts. Picturing the eviscerated hunk of flesh in the stroller, Randidly trotted quickly forward, plucking his spear off the ground as he passed his satchel. Even if the earlier gunshots reminded

Randidly of the dark side of humanity, that didn't mean he was willing to let people suffer right in front of him.

Stamina exploded from his chest, activating his Haste Skill. In a mere second, he accelerated forward into the tree line, leaving the stunned kid staring blankly at his back.

Congratulations! Your Skill **Haste** has grown to **Level 11!**

I never really thought about this before, but it seems like this Skill looks quite cool. Randidly hesitated to push on. But at the moment, he couldn't afford to be distracted by this random teenager. He lowered his head and continued onward.

Just as Randidly passed between the trees, another thought struck him. He'd left his satchel lying on the ground back there. Randidly grimaced. He didn't turn around; the scream was more important. At the very least, hopefully the kid would keep wolverines from digging up the seeds he'd planted.

As he raced through the trees, sounds of combat grew louder. Deciding timing was more important than stealth, Randidly burst through a bush onto a muddy mountain track. A truck had been forced to swerve to avoid a falling tree and was now swarmed by goblins. Several hooded figures huddled in the bed of the truck were the source of the screams, batting the approaching goblins by desperately brandishing shovels. Meanwhile, a man near the front of the pickup truck swung a wood-cutting axe with more concrete effects. A shotgun and empty casings lay at his feet, as well as several moaning bodies of wounded goblins.

Still, the monsters didn't even notice their fallen fellows. Around four dozen goblins hopped and hooted around the sides of the truck, scrambling to climb on top of the vehicle. About six goblins twisted around and glared at Randidly the moment he arrived on the scene. They hissed, raising rusty-looking daggers.

Randidly's lip curled upward in derision.

He activated Phantom Onslaught and his spear blurred. Dozens of lightning-quick stabs ripped forward, goring the goblins that had the gall to glare at him. When those first several goblins collapsed, Randidly took advantage of the tail end of his Haste to plow through several others, taking them down before they realized the threat he represented.

Randidly was nowhere near Shal's effortless grace as he dispatched his foes, but his time in the Dungeon was not in vain. Just as quickly as he could attack, a goblin groaned and collapsed. Their tiny hands couldn't stem the flow of blood from their wounds.

Congratulations! Your Skill **Fighting Proficiency** has grown to **Level 28!**

As more and more of the goblins recognized the new threat and wheeled around to face him, Randidly poured mana into his palm, launching a large Arcane Orb into the densest cluster of bodies. The projectile slid forward, exploding with a wave of concussive force.

Those goblins nearest were torn to pieces, while the remainder were slapped with enough force that they collapsed, partially stunned.

Randidly, still wielding a spear like a God of Death reaping lives, stepped amongst the fallen bodies.

After he executed most of the indisposed bodies, Randidly noticed the axe-wielding man joined him in finishing off the weak goblins. The axe wielder had short grey hair, maybe about fifty years old. He had no problems using his axe to crush their smaller bodies, even without the Stats Randidly accumulated. The man was clearly used to working with his body. His movements naturally incorporated some of the tips Shal had imparted to conserve Stamina.

Unfortunately, the older man's experience didn't extend to battle. He didn't notice several goblins creeping up behind him, stone hammers in hand.

Randidly's emerald eyes glittered and he flicked his wrist. "Entangling Roots."

There was a small delay as his Mana mobilized itself, but soon, huge roots sprang from the ground. They slithered up the short legs of the goblins, gripping their necks. The roots squeezed with all the potency of Randidly's 42 Intelligence, shattering their spines.

Congratulations! Your Skill **Spirit of Adversity** has grown to **Level 23!**

Looking around at the mangled bodies and the few scared survivors, even Randidly was slightly surprised at his own strength. He trembled from the flood of adrenaline pumping through him, feeling slightly out of place by how quickly everything ended. He'd encountered several small groups of monsters when examining the area, but this was the first time Randidly challenged so many monsters at once and could completely overwhelm them.

I guess these monsters were designed just to be a threat to the average person, but still... Every glance identified one more corpse that bore the unmistakable wound inflicted by the spear Shal gave him. *I'm... strong. Heh. Finally. With this, as long as I find Ace and Sydney.*

The old man raised his axe and the few remaining goblins turned and fled. He set the head of the axe against the ground and met Randidly's eyes. Both were silent for several seconds.

The only sound was the pants of relief from the heavily garbed individuals in the bed of the truck.

Randidly's eyes flicked to the side. Those figures had pressed themselves down, out of sight. It was clear they didn't intend to reveal themselves. The older man was their representative. Randidly's eyes slid back to the grey-haired man, who noticed the shift in Randidly's attention, and had narrowed his own eyes.

As the older man opened his mouth to finally speak, Randidly threw something at him. He reflexively raised his hand to catch it. The old man was surprised to find a small bottle filled with red liquid.

"Health Potion." Randidly coughed awkwardly, realizing the older man might not understand the peace offering. After a second of thought, he added, "The world is like a game now. That will help you recover your Health more quickly."

"I'm uninjured," the man growled.

Randidly looked to the truck bed. He shrugged, feeling rather out of his depth. Honestly, the fight had been much simpler than this strained silence. Especially now that they were regarding him so suspiciously, even after he'd saved them.

His worries turned back to the teenager who remained near his satchel. "Then in case of future injuries. I'm leaving."

"Wait."

Randidly paused with his back to the old man, his senses sharpening. Randidly was far too aware of the shotgun shells scattered on the ground by the old man's feet.

The older man sighed and spoke in a very slow voice. "Where are you staying? The town… Is there anywhere safe from those monsters…?" Then the man's brows furrowed. "Did you get a Class at one of those… Newbie Towns? Is that why you're so strong and able to move so quickly?"

Randidly turned back around, his tongue feeling abruptly thick. *Is the reason that I have this power a Class? Honestly, I wish…* "I'm staying in a cabin in a nearby valley. After I heard gunshots earlier, I've been avoiding the town for now. But the truth is… I don't have a Class. I was just… lucky."

It made Randidly want to laugh as soon as he said it. There was a certain irony to calling Shal's forced acid baths and brutal sparring matches "luck." His bones had been broken and his skin left purple and bruised by such luck. Seven months of agony and strife were condensed into a single word. Randidly supposed avoiding the harsh truth of how to grow within the System was for the best right now.

Randidly saw himself in the tired set of the man's shoulders. His original fear and the version of himself that had awoken from nightmares. The one who sat trembling for several minutes. Being set before that familiar fear… Randidly had no idea how to help.

Randidly fled, returning to the cabin and his planted seeds.

CHAPTER TWENTY-ONE

o Randidly's dismay, the punk kid was not alone when he returned to the field. There seemed to be plenty of people in the area who heard the noises in the forest, even if they weren't brave enough to approach. Most importantly, his satchel still sat in the middle of the clearing, away from the confrontation.

The teenager was facing off against an Asian girl who looked to be around seventeen, with a chubby teen beside her. Those two new arrivals were both glowering at the punk.

"Back off, Tera," the punk spat.

Randidly made a mental note that these individuals knew each other. It was becoming more likely that Sydney and Ace would be within the area.

"This is me and my buddy's spot. We'll kick your ass if you hang around."

Randidly looked between the two individuals and the punk. *Wait, you and your... Am I...?*

Tera snorted and crossed her arms. "And what are you gunna do about it?"

The punk raised his hand in the clawed glove vaguely. "I—!"

Tera snorted. "Oh please. I saw you steal that claw off a dead wolverine. You probably haven't even figured out Skill Levels and Path Points yet, huh? You little pussy. That cabin is ours from now on."

"Fucking bitch!" the punk said, spitting at the ground, red faced. Both Tera and her companion's faces twisted into scowls at the insult.

At exactly that tense moment, the three teens noticed Randidly quietly sneaking forward, picking up his satchel. He felt a flash of embarrassment. He supposed, from the way their eyes widened, he struck quite a figure.

Barefoot, standing with a spear in his hand, and covered in a liberal application of goblin blood.

He pulled the leather strap of the satchel across his body. Even the punk, who claimed they were buddies now, looked at his blood-slicked form with obvious fear.

Suddenly, I'm the shotgun. Randidly's heart ached at their expressions. He regarded their wide eyes and felt extremely exhausted. None of the preparations within the Dungeon prepared him for the human element he'd encounter outside of the Dungeon. He had no Skill Levels for social interaction. He wasn't ready for this.

Randidly coughed and adjusted the strap of his satchel once more. When no obvious way to settle the standoff manifested itself for him, Randidly walked past the group. He busied himself with checking growth in his fields. Unfortunately, the trio didn't settle the problem amongst themselves.

The punk kid's face changed into a bright smile, hurrying after Randidly. Randidly couldn't help but be impressed by how quickly the fool managed to mask his fear to chase after benefits. *But then again, despite the gore I saw walking into the Safe Room when I met Shal... didn't I do the same thing? There is something just... compelling about strength that—*

The punk was about to gallop right over the spots where his seeds were planted.

"Wait!" Randidly abruptly said, jumping to draw several obvious lines in the ground with the butt of his spear.

The kid stumbled back out of the way, hands raised in surrender.

A twinge overtook Randidly's heart. He pointed to his field, speaking in a low voice. "Don't walk here. Plants."

He returned his spear to his bag and sat down. Only then did he notice the shocked looks they were giving him. *Ah, the satchel. They probably haven't encountered interspatial devices yet. In fact, if not for me finding that old corpse with the daggers and vials, I probably wouldn't have made it this far at all...*

The more I think about it, the more I feel like I owe a lot of people too much for surviving this long.

Randidly studiously closed his eyes, ignoring their curious looks. Tera and her follower were engaged in a heated, whispering discussion. The punk kid remained loitering around Randidly, looking unbelievably smug for someone who'd just gotten yelled at for walking.

Randidly slipped back into Meditation, practicing Root Manipulation. Simultaneously activating Iron Skin in preparation for potential threats that might be approaching helped calm him down. Raising Skill, he'd discovered, was about difficulty and the stress, but it was also about familiarity and practice. Even if the Skill Level didn't necessarily improve, just increasing the usage efficiency would benefit—

"Hey…"

The girl spoke, interrupting Randidly's train of thought. He glared at her, which caused her to stumble in her approach. Her mouth firmed into a line and she walked forward.

"Hey, you. You're strong. How'd you do it?"

Randidly inwardly sighed, though he felt somewhat relieved. It felt good that someone finally noticed he could help them. He opened his mouth to explain the lessons he'd paid for in the Dungeon with his sweat and blood, but he was beaten to the punch.

"Heh, you wanna talk to one of my minions? You need to go through me first. And make sure you don't walk on our spots." The punk kid puffed up, gesturing to the areas Randidly outlined on the ground.

Randidly was speechless. *Minion? Didn't you just flinch when I outlined "our spots"!*

Tera gave the punk a flat look, which probably meant she could read Randidly's disagreement on his face. "You must be joking. You're saying that *you* are in charge? You pissed your bed until you were twelve years—"

"I'm not… in charge," Randidly said slowly, inspiration awakening in him.

Randidly squirmed, recalling the strained silence between the older man and the individuals hiding in the bed of the truck, even after he intervened and saved them. He could readily admit all his preparations were unrelated to the challenge of involving himself with others. Continually interacting with people who came to him would also be quite distracting and ensure a drain on his training time.

Having this punk stay here and hold the base while Randidly searched for Rare mobs would kill two birds with one stone.

In the end, as long as I tell these few my tips, they can spread the word around, Randidly reasoned, his gaze shifting to the punk. *Even if his behavior is a bit extreme, he really was the first person I talked with… and he didn't steal my satchel, so…*

At Randidly's words, the punk kid chuckled coolly and raised his chin. "As I said, I, Dusk, am the boss around here."

Tera rolled her eyes. "What the fuck is that Dusk shit, Donny? Anyways, why's he so strong?"

Donny turned to Randidly, "You heard her; why you so strong?"

A vein in Randidly's temple began to throb. *I guess we need to set up some ground rules…*

After using an Arcane Orb to destroy a nearby tree and mildly remarking on the importance of respect, Randidly briefly explained Skill points, PP, and

Paths to them. In addition, he related his "theories" about how obtaining a Class from the Newbie Village would make them more powerful. He went on to his plan to set up a base here, making sure he had food and water covered, before founding a Newbie Village and obtaining a Class of his own.

In this regard, Randidly was finally rewarded with good news. The chubby teen, imaginatively dubbed Chubbs by the other two, said he'd seen a huge group of goblins further east, away from the city a little bit north from where they were now.

Donny's eyes were shining with excitement. He imperiously gestured and told Randidly to go get the item for the town so he could discover what extraordinary Class he was meant to have.

Randidly remained silent at the order, growing increasingly annoyed by this punk. He raised his hand, channeling Mana into his palm. A second later, a swirling Arcane Orb shot out and cracked the thick trunk of a tree at the edge of the valley. In stark contrast with the silence of the small group, the tree groaned and collapsed.

Congratulations! Your Skill **Arcane Orb** has grown to **Level 15!**

"You can chop firewood while I'm gone," Randidly said.

All three teens nodded emphatically. Tera and Chubbs brought out a backpack, producing a small tent and sleeping bags. Donny rubbed the back of his head and shyly asked Randidly if he could use the cabin.

The sun was yet to set, but they all seemed so dead tired, the time of day didn't matter.

The wide awake Randidly was confused by this until it occurred to him how the past several hours must have gone. The teenagers had probably awakened to the sound of flames and screams. They likely would have run from the monsters, desperately trying to survive and escape. The fact that they had enough foresight to grab a tent and sleeping bags was already impressive.

Randidly felt a smile tug at his lips, remembering his own desperate stumble to the Safe Room for the first time, unable to see the helpful arrow for all the blood he'd shed. *Besides, while they rest will be a good chance for me to lay the groundwork for this being the base camp. A good bit of training will work off some of the stress from today as well.*

I may be strong... but there are still things I cannot do. I need to remember that.

Before Tera lay down, she approached Randidly. "Should we... take turns keeping watch or something, like in the movies?"

Randidly considered it, then shook his head. "No, for tonight, I will be sufficient."

Giving him a weird look, Tera hesitated. She visibly decided not to say anything and walked back to her sleeping area.

Randidly honestly thought it would be fine. He'd more than likely be up all night training. He grossly underestimated the passage of time in the Dungeon. He came out several hours later than he initially calculated, and the only way to make up that time was to assume that days were longer than he believed. Almost double. Staying up a night or two would cause him no trouble.

Just as the sun was setting, a familiar pickup truck rumbled down the dirt track and pulled off the path, parking about thirty meters from the cabin. Chubbs, who had been kicked out of the tent by Tera, looked on curiously but didn't dare approach. After turning off the engine, the old man got out and ambled over to Randidly, who was fastidiously checking his plants.

After a glance and a nod, Randidly went back to work. Already, small sprouts were shooting up out of the ground, which was a relief. It seemed the System universally improved the speed at which plants grew. It wasn't just an effect for the Safe Room.

"Not many monsters to be seen on the way over," the man commented. "Those... goblins are staying away."

Randidly nodded, his mouth curling into a grin. "They may be monsters, but that doesn't mean they aren't smart. They possess pretty sharp instincts about these things. As long as I'm here..."

Seemingly satisfied, the man turned and headed back to his truck. "We're getting some shut eye, then. See ya in the mornin'."

CHAPTER TWENTY-TWO

Congratulations! Your Skill **Farming** has grown to **Level 20!**

A pparently, Randidly hadn't taught them as thorough a lesson as he thought. While he practiced his spear movements under the moonlight, they crept forward with the intention to attack the humans while they slept. However, it became clear what gave them such bold confidence. The approaching group was a column of goblins and wolverines, seemingly working together, led by a goblin with a green name.

Goblin Warband Leader Level 7

Uncommon, huh, he reflected. Randidly needed to kill a Rare monster to found the Newbie Village. At least this proved higher Level monsters among the goblins existed in the area. The Ghosthound grinned in the darkness. His challenges so far had been a little too simple for his liking.

Randidly admitted that Shal had given him the taste for battle. And he planned on sating himself on this night.

The murky shadows of the tree line at the edge of the valley were nothing for his Eyes of the Spear Phantom. He patiently waited as they crept closer. Wolverines on the edges, goblins and their stone weapons at the core. Randidly abruptly stood, shooting 20 Mana Bolts off in quick succession. In the cloudy darkness of the hours after midnight, the bolts burned like lightning. Those not struck and killed were blinded, screeching in confusion.

Randidly rapidly downed three Mana potions and strode forward. The goblins clustered tightly together.

With a grin, he shot an Arcane Orb, which exploded the group in a mass of pulped flesh and partially shattered limbs. The sounds of battle had finally awoken the people within Randidly's base. They emerged from their various shelters, confused and blinded by the dark.

The green-named goblin barked something in its language and most of the goblins turned and fled. Incensed by the smell of blood, the wolverines rushed forward, their eyes covered in a crimson haze. Randidly met them, calmly cutting the remaining monsters to pieces. With abundant Stamina, Haste gave him a small, decisive edge in any dangerous situation.

Not a single wolverine managed to lay a claw on him.

By the end of the night, Randidly was delighted to discover he'd gained points in Spear Mastery, Mana Bolt, and Haste. In addition to the other Skill Levels he'd gained today, he was able to spend 8 PP, raising the Level of Green Spear Mastery to 178, granting him another point in Vitality.

Randidly took a quick glance at his Status.

Randidly Ghosthound
Class: ---
Level: N/A
Health(/R per hour): 206/255 [+6] (102.75 [+9])
Mana(/R per hour): 139/228 (50.25)
Stam(/R per min): 105/186 (37 [+3])
Vit: 30 [+3]
End: 27
Str: 16
Agi: 40 [+3]
Perception: 22
Reaction: 24
Resistance: 9
Willpower: 52
Intelligence: 50
Wisdom: 30
Control: 21
Focus: 16
Skills
Soulskill: *Green Spear Mastery Lvl 178*

Basic: *Running Lvl 16 | Physical Fitness Lvl 23 | Sneak Lvl 29 | Acid Resistance Lvl 22 | Poison Resistance Lvl 14 | Spirit of Adversity Lvl 23 | Dagger Mastery Lvl 11 | Dodge Lvl 25 | Spear Mastery Lvl 39 | Pain Resistance Lvl 11 | Fighting Proficiency Lvl 28 | First Aid Lvl 13 | Block Lvl 24 | Mental Strength Lvl 8 | Curse Resistance Lvl 3 | Pathfinding Lvl 6 | Mapmaking Lvl 3*

Stamina: *Heavy Blow Lvl 19 | Sprinting Lvl 13 | Iron Skin Lvl 24 | Phantom Thrust Lvl 31 | Spear Phantom's Footwork Lvl 22 | Eyes of the Spear Phantom Lvl 14 | Phantom Half-Step Lvl 4 | Haste Lvl 12 | Phantom Onslaught Lvl 10*

Mana: *Mana Bolt Lvl 30 | Meditation Lvl 26 | Entangling Roots Lvl 26 | Mana Shield Lvl 21 | Root Manipulation Lvl 19 | Arcane Orb Lvl 15*

Crafting: *Farming Lvl 20 | Plant Breeding Lvl 9 | Potion Making Lvl 19 | Analyze Lvl 24*

Randidly barely worked up a sweat slaughtering the determined wolverines. Even without a Class, the addition of Green Spear Mastery giving him bonuses every 5 PP used was beginning to add up in terms of Stats. And with all his Skills adding passive bonuses to most of his actions...

The fire in his blood from battle still burned. Randidly settled back, slowly moving through the spear forms taught to him by Shal. The point he reached now was good for the current situation, but it wasn't enough. He needed strength. Strength to find Sydney and Ace in this huge area. Strength enough to support this growing sense of responsibility he felt toward the people who gathered around him.

And that would only accumulate through hard work and determination.

Roots wiggled underneath his feet, pleased to feel the flow of his Mana.

Randidly paused his training and looked around at his newfound community. It seemed that after investigating the commotion and seeing he had it handled, everyone had gone back to bed. He made a mental note to ask about glass containers for potions later and continued to calmly utilize his spear.

The greatest pleasure of the morning was when he got a notification that his Farming Skill increased to Level 21. Several sprouts had come up within his farming area.

Tera, Donny, and Chubbs looked with open mouths at the piles of bodies. The night masked the details of the skirmish. The old man folded his arms, his reaction even more inscrutable.

Randidly nodded in satisfaction. *The seeds are planted. Now I just need to wait for the crops to grow and gather resources. The biggest thing I need is the Golden Coin.*

Randidly announced to the group, "I'm going to go find the Goblin Boss."

"Uh, before you go," Donny said, his voice rather high-pitched. "Can you give us some pointers on Skill Levels? I know you said practice but… to get that strong…"

"Simply practice. Raise Skill Levels." Randidly scratched the side of his head. Other than the explanation he gave yesterday, he didn't have much hidden knowledge to give to them now.

Donny kept pushing. "Well, what sort of Skills are there?"

After a bit of hesitation, Randidly answered, "I believe Skills can be related to anything you experience. I have Skills for using the spear and for casting Mana Skills, but strange things too. Farming, Running, Physical Fitness, Potion Making."

"Woodcutting, Cooking, Cleaning, anything," the old man said noncommittally, spitting over to the side after he finished.

He nodded toward Randidly. "I'd like to speak with you when you return."

Randidly left the three teens with their thoughts. He hoped they would be able to find their own areas of expertise.

As he moved through the forest, Randidly considered offering them the vial of black acid he'd taken from the Black Swamp Salamander. Ultimately, he decided the teens probably weren't ready for such harsh training methods.

This is their first few days, Randidly reasoned. *At that time, I basically just farmed. I'll give them a week or so to get used to the violence before we press forward.*

Covered in gore, carrying a half-dozen new pieces of loot that weren't very useful to him, but overall very pleased about the whole trip, Randidly returned to the valley. Some very dramatic changes had occurred in the eight or so hours he had been gone.

Someone constructed a short wooden fence around most of the area Randidly planted his seeds in. They were already visibly sprouting, having grown a half meter. The fence even had small openings to enter the tiny field and the ground was beaten into a path between the various vegetables. A raised wooden platform had also been constructed in the center of the field area, providing a good view of the surroundings. Behind the cabin, Randidly saw what could only be the beginnings of a well. The surrounding area was strewn with large logs and piles of firewood. That made Randidly's mouth twitch. *Donny took me very seriously, I see.*

In addition, someone dug out a fire pit in front of the cabin and lined it with stones. A dressed and drained wolverine corpse was spitted over it, slowly rotating to roast. The smell was *quite* appetizing.

Most interesting was the bones of a second, smaller dwelling, had gone up next to the cabin. Tera, Chubbs, and Donny were furiously dragging smaller saplings to throw on a growing stack, which would likely be erected into walls.

Their constant bickering could be heard from far away, but Randidly ignored it, heading to the fire pit where the older man stood.

The older man grunted in acknowledgement as Randidly arrived. "Wood Cutting Level 4, Wood Working Level 5, Construction Level 3, Animal Skinning Level 4, Hunting Level 2, Axe Mastery Level 4. I currently have 16 PP, though I haven't spent any of them. Any recommendations?"

Randidly frowned, casting his memory back. "You have the Newbie Path available?"

The older man nodded. "As well as Woodsman and something with question marks."

Nodding, Randidly said, "Finish off the Newbie Path; it should only take 7 PP. Then you will get Mana Bolt and Heavy Blow, two active Skills that you can use while you raise your passive Skills. From there, you will just need to continue to practice."

"And for the Stats?" the old man asked.

Randidly briefly explained his understanding of what the Stats affected. "Is this what you wanted to talk about?"

"No, but..." The old man removed the skinned wolverine and checked it. "Perhaps it won't matter. Did you find whatever you were looking for?"

Randidly smiled and produced a glowing golden coin.

You have 1 Gold Nexus coin! Use? Y/N

Randidly intended to wait a while before setting up a base, but this man's capability changed that. He realized why a community was so valuable. They could assume certain roles and work together to achieve their goals. With the gold coin in his hand, and the changes happening in the area with only a few of them working...

Plus, monsters around Level 20 aren't hard for me now, but I'll have a Class. Randidly's fingers tightened on the golden coin. He could feel that part of him that got excited for the fights beginning to anticipate.

Without thinking about it too much, Randidly selected **Yes**.

CHAPTER TWENTY-THREE

A smartly dressed man appeared in front of him, smiling serenely at Randidly.

"Hello, I am your guide, Nul. Congratulations, you now have the qualifications to found a Newbie Village. To do so, you simply need to receive your Class. As the first person to receive a Class from me, you will receive the Village Chieftain Soulskill, which will help you survive in this world. Are you ready to proceed?"

Randidly's eyes were practically sparkling as he nodded. With a Class, he could finally Level. And then—

Another notification popped up.

You are about to be taken to the Class screen. Once you enter the Class screen, you cannot leave without picking a Class. You will have the option of choosing from three Classes. The first will be a General Class based on the System's initial impression of your Skills and personality when the System first initialized. The second will be a Random Class. The third will be a Class generated based on your current natural gifts and disposition. Do you wish to proceed? Y/N

Randidly frowned, turning to Nul. Some of Nul's words stuck in his head. He would receive the Village Chieftain Soulskill. Plus, the Class options.

"When it says current natural gifts, what does that mean?"

Nul gave him an innocent smile. "Different individuals are naturally blessed. At the time of the Class selection, the System will examine you and recommend a Class based on that."

"Do your natural blessings include Skill Levels? Current Stat Levels?"

Nul continued to smile, ignoring the question, which was the action of a man that didn't want to show his hand. Randidly was almost positive they did indeed improve the Class options he would have access to. Sighing, Randidly selected **No**. *The System is fair, but only to those who know its secrets. If you rush forward without preparation...*

If Randidly selected a Class now, it likely wouldn't be the first choice, because that Class would be based on the him from several months ago. Or at least that was how he read the vague textual description. Which meant he would receive a Class for a twenty-year-old who hadn't ever needed to really struggle in his life. Similarly, the second, random option seemed unreliable, and not a real choice at all.

The third option would be what he was betting on, a current scan of his "Natural Blessings." Anyone else fighting for their life wouldn't think anything of that phrasing, but Randidly noticed it immediately. If it scanned them now, perhaps scant days after the scan for the first choice, what was it scanning for?

If by Natural Blessings, they meant Stats and Skills bestowed by the System, it would likely take most people more time than Randidly to strengthen themselves and work up the nerve to found a Newbie Village. In this time, they would be relying solely on Paths to grow stronger.

Also hanging over Randidly's head was Shal's statement that you can only learn a set number of Skills once you have a Class. It occurred to him how limiting that experience would be.

Although likely less detailed, it seemed the old man's thoughts were on a similar track. "It's a game of chicken, huh. Are you gonna gamble on learning new Skills so you get a better Class option, or are you gonna take the immediate Class to try and grow strong?"

Nul turned from Randidly to the old man. "Since he has rejected this opportunity, I now offer it to you. Remember, gaining the first Class from me would mean that you also gain the Village Chieftain Soulskill—"

The old man snorted and spat. "Not interested. Let me reflect on my Natural Blessings a bit."

"Hey, who is that?" Chubbs asked, wandering over with a bickering Tera and Donny in tow.

Nul instantly beamed at the new arrivals. "Which of you would like to be Village Chiefta—"

"MEEEEEE!" Donny yelled, rushing forward to a bowing Nul.

"Do you choose to select a Class no—"

"I do!" Donny said, practically salivating.

Randidly and the old man exchanged glances. Ultimately, they shrugged and offered their condolences to the teenager who so willingly sacrificed himself for their benefit.

"Do you know anything about what a Class gets you?" the old man asked in a quiet voice.

Randidly shook his head. Since Randidly was already letting Donny be the one who dealt with people, he saw no reason to stop him from being the Village Chieftain. Although Nul was talking the position up, the slimy way they almost explicitly refused to indicate methods to get better Classes made Randidly rather skeptical. Plus, he already possessed a Soulskill. And his Green Spear Mastery had treated him pretty well so far.

If it did turn out to be a good thing, it's not like it would be that hard to kill another rare mob, once he found one.

Nul gestured, and a giant floating screen appeared in front of Donny, visible to everyone present. On it were three choices.

Lackey: Knight
Laborer

"The first choice is—" Nul began to explain, but Donny waved his hand, ignoring him.

"No need, I choose the second option. I am Dusk Knight! No, wait, Knight of the Dusk!"

Randidly had a hard time suppressing his smile based on the first and third options. He supposed it was a good thing the random Class ended up being so... official and gamey-sounding, like the rest of this world changed by the System. Hopefully, the Level-up gains would give them an idea of what a Class could provide in terms of power.

Motes of gold flew from Nul's hand to Donny and a short sword and shield appeared in Donny's hands. Grinning from ear to ear, Donny swung them around, promptly underestimating the weight, and fell on his face.

"What did the Class give you?" Tera asked, jealousy clear in her voice. She stared at Nul with obvious desire, but the pale fellow had fallen silent.

Even sitting on his butt, face covered in dirt, Donny glowed with glee. He waggled his fingers at Nul. "Show them the same notification you showed me, so they can stand and be awed in my brilliance."

Shrugging, Nul complied. Randidly looked closely at the notification that appeared.

Congratulations! You have received the Class of **Knight.**

Congratulations! You have learned the Skill **Ride Level 1.** You have learned the Skill **Honorable Charge Level 1.** You have learned the Skill **Stalwart Defense Level 1.** *You may learn 7 additional Skills to these and those you already possess. Skills may be forgotten to learn new Skills, paying 1 PP per Skill Level of the Skill you wish to forget.* **+12 Health per Level, +1**

Mana per Level, +7 Stamina per Level, +2 Vit, End, or Str per Level (these points may be distributed between 2), +1 Resist per Level.

The old man shook his head, looking to Randidly. "Those numbers just make my eyes water. How good is that? Seems like a hell of a lot to get per every Level."

Randidly nodded slowly. "That depends on how difficult it is to earn Levels, I guess. But once he completes the Newbie Path and gets that bonus, that's 16 Health, 3 Mana, and 9 Stamina, plus... 4 Stat points per Level? 2 among Vit, End, and Str, 1 to Resist, one freely distributed. Hard to gauge how much the Stats mean, but... all that extra Health and Stamina will add up quickly. It'll do a lot to keep him alive. After 15 Levels, he will have comparable Health and Stamina to me, and that's not even counting the bonuses he would get putting them into Vit and End."

Frowning, the old man nodded. "It really is hard to tell how useful it is. Well, I'll try the Skill Level route for a while and then revisit the issue."

"You must hurry," Nul said with a smile, returning his attention to Randidly and the old man. "Remember, the Newbie Zone protection will wear off on this area in seven days, and stronger monsters will come. You should select your Class immediately to make sure you don't regret your weakness later."

When he saw that neither of them cared, Nul turned back to Donny, smile attached. "So, where would you like your village to be?"

CHAPTER TWENTY-FOUR

*N*ul begrudgingly admitted the village would take up a fair amount of space when it was created. It would also have an indeterminate effect on the previous geography within its scope.

Buoyed by his excitement, Donny proudly marched half a mile up along the valley from their original spot with the cabin. As the new Village Chieftain, he eventually settled on an area on top of a low, forested hill, tucked between the higher mountains that hemmed in the valley.

Curious about the Newbie Village, Randidly and the old man followed. When Donny indicated the perfect spot, a blinding light robbed them of their vision. Acting on instinct built on months of struggle, Randidly dropped into a crouch and drew his spear, his senses sharpening. No attacks came. After several seconds, the light slowly faded, resolving itself into a clearing with several buildings. The trees that previously dotted the hilltop had been utterly banished.

Perhaps the strangest feature was the pillar of light rising from the center of the village. When Randidly saw the notification that appeared in front of him, and everyone else based on their expression, his visage darkened.

Congratulations! A **Newbie Village** has been founded near your location. *A pillar of light has been placed there and will remain there for 7 days, so it may be conveniently found.* Due to the founding of a **Newbie Village,** the starter protections in the surrounding area will disperse in exactly **7 days**. **At that time, monsters Level 20 and over will begin to appear. It is recommended that you proceed to the Newbie Village and acquire a Class as fast as possible to survive.**

The implications of this notification didn't seem to worry Donny, instead, he was laughing.

"Haha! This is so cool! Because I was the first one to found a Newbie Village, I get an extra 500 Soul Points toward upgrading it! I'm fucking first on the whole of Earth. This is so awesome!"

"Soul Points?" Tera asked.

Donny ignored her, continuing to giggle to himself. Instead, Nul stepped forward, his bland smile in place.

"Yes, Soul Points, which are used to strengthen and upgrade your Newbie Village. Besides turning in other golden coins for 500 Soul Points, you gain Soul Points for your village anytime you Level up. Eventually, the Newbie Village too can expand, giving greater benefits for the people who choose to have their Class based here."

"How much would it take to upgrade a Newbie Village into a…" Randidly hesitated, then went with his gut based on the Paths. "A Trainee Village."

"10,000 Soul Points." Nul gave Randidly a strange glance. There was something there, not fear but… almost annoyance. The bland smile returned, more blanketing and numbing than ever. "However, a Trainee Village possesses the possibility of allowing you to reclass, increasing your growth rates monstrously with the Stats and Skills you have gained by Leveling."

And instantly, he shifts what he is saying, trying to sway me to get a Class… This sort of character is very different than Shal, Randidly thought to himself, nodding calmly to Nul's enticement, and moved toward the tree line.

Casually, he looked over his shoulder and said to the surrounding people, "You all should rest now and prepare. I suspect we shall have a lot of company soon due to the pillar of light. Donny, you're going to need to decide about who you want to let into your Newbie Village."

Randidly walked away, wanting a bit of insurance for later.

Simultaneously, he was very, *very* glad he wouldn't be the one who had to deal with the rush of people who sought shelter after seeing the announcement of the Newbie Village.

Almost exactly three hours later, Randidly returned, having gathered his "insurance." The first items on that list were a Skill point in Running and a Skill point in Pathfinding. They were enough to finish his Spear Mastery Path, netting him two new Skills: Sweep and Spear Deflect. Sweep was a powerful area of effect attack, utilizing a wide swing of the spear. Spear Deflect was effectively spinning the spear in front of oneself, knocking away smaller projectiles, and reducing the strength of oncoming magical attacks.

Both Skills excited Randidly. First for their utility, but also for their ability to be Leveled. The higher a Skill got, the harder it would be to Level. That had become especially clear since he left the Dungeon. The monsters here were quite weak in comparison to himself. His Skill growth was rather stagnant.

Which is why limiting my number of Skills with a Class is something I should do purposefully, Randidly reflected.

Even just a few minutes ago, when he searched out the Mother Wolverine, which was Level 13. It was able to withstand several of Randidly's attacks, but was ultimately killed rather simply. He hadn't earned a single Skill Level relating to that fight.

As Randidly walked back to the cabin area, and the nearby obnoxious pillar of light, he considered his Path situation. He used all of the Paths he'd gotten by Leveling Skills and was now left with two similar options.

???? *0/???* | ?????

One included the zero, but they were essentially the same. Rather than overthink what was happening, Randidly chose the one with the 0 showing.

Monster Slayer I *0/1*

The one spare PP Randidly put into it was enough to instantly finish it off.

Congratulations! You have completed the "Monster Slayer I Path"! +1 free Stat(s).

Sometimes the path you walk is stained by the blood of those who would stand against you. But you must not falter, because to slow means to stop, and to stop means you die.

Randidly checked the path screen again, even though there was no more PP to spend at the moment. Sure enough, waiting for him...

Monster Slayer II *0/3* | Watcher: *0/??* | *?????*

Randidly tapped his cheek. *Another Path Series with Monster Slayer, eh? Cheap ones too. I didn't earn anything for spending the PP, but the Path Completion reward is tempting enough for the investment... Interesting that I suddenly unlocked this Watcher Path for finishing it... I wonder why. Tch, even Shal didn't have much insight into the mechanisms of the Path System.*

I'll just have to figure it out gradually. I just wish I didn't have this week time limit for the Level 20 limit hanging over me... Suddenly, Randidly's expression turned bitter. *I got so excited by the building of structures, but now that the Newbie Village is founded... I can't responsibly leave and search for Ace and Sydney. I'm the only reason these people had the ability to earn the Golden Coin in the first place.*

Hopefully, those two see the golden pillar and head over here on their own.

Shaking his head, Randidly walked out of the tree line toward the cabin.

The second group of things he brought back were various fruits and vegetables he'd found wild in the area. There wasn't anything exceedingly strange in the flora, but he came across a new variety of nut and a mushroom he was quite sure was poisonous. Still, growing it under the influence of the mana crystals would hopefully result in new species with interesting effects.

Randidly's biggest haul was a large quantity of red and blue energy shards he found in the local area, often guarded by more comically weak imps or wolverines. Even at the time, he grinned at the ease he could now harvest these crystals, when not guarded by Level 30 Deadly Webspinners.

He reached his hut and crouched next to it. He steadily knocked his knuckles against the dirt and abruptly stood. While considering his situation, he brought out a large stick he had found and began to crudely till the surrounding area by his first fields, which were beginning to grow upwards at a shocking pace. He wanted to get his new seeds down and growing as soon as possible.

An expansion of the farming area would be necessary.

Still, he didn't receive all good news from his wanderings today. Randidly was slightly disturbed to discover goblins had all but vanished from the surrounding area. Even the wolverines were currently on the decline. Apparently, defeating the Boss was a way to rip the varieties of monsters out of the area. Now the lizards and imps were growing stronger, both in numbers and in Levels, and were able to force Randidly to be wary of large groups.

Even if the individual projectiles were weak, withstanding a score of their scorching Fireballs at once would quickly deplete his Health.

He resolved to pay better attention to his surroundings, where his guard had begun to drop from his easy fights. After all, as far as he could tell, he was the strongest thing for quite a few miles. And honestly, Randidly liked the feeling.

At the same time, he never forgot the pain that birthed this capability. The edge of death he danced next to in the Dungeon was constantly there as a reminder of how quickly things could change. Nul's bland smile and subtle directions, woven together with the seven-day time limit, left him with a feeling of foreboding.

Randidly frowned at the pillar of light that rose from the hilltop. This

Newbie Town was not what he had hoped it would be. But perhaps it would be what humanity needed to get back on the right track.

CHAPTER TWENTY-FIVE

*R*aised voices distracted Randidly from his Farming. As he trudged up toward the Newbie Village, Randidly used the 2 PP he earned from Farming Levels, and the 1 Root Manipulation Skill Levels to open and instantly complete Monster Slayer II.

At the very least, Farming is still a reliable source of PP...

Congratulations! You have completed the "Monster Slayer II Path"! +2 Stat(s), +1 to Health, Mana, and Stamina.

Sometimes the path you walk is stained by the blood of those who would stand against you, but you cannot hesitate. But you must not falter, because to slow means to stop, and to stop means you die.

Snorting at the tiny gains, Randidly threw the Stat points into Agility and walked toward the source of the commotion. Several unfamiliar figures loitered around the now cleared hilltop. Inwardly, he said a quiet word of thanks to Donny, who chose to travel half a mile from Randidly's cabin before creating the Newbie Village.

He would have been quite uncomfortable to have so many strangers lurking around where he slept.

Even though he preferred smaller numbers, Randidly was confused that not many people turned up at the pillar of light seeking the ability to get a Class. There were only eight individuals at the moment clustered around the edges of the hill. Maybe he just underestimated and overestimated humanity simultaneously.

Underestimated by how much of a pack animal they really were. If there was a large group out there, it was sufficient to send a small group to investigate.

Overestimated, unfortunately, humanity's ability to cope with huge changes in their situation, and appreciate how necessary the thing called "Classes" would be. Or at least, their potential.

In addition to the skittish individuals who didn't even climb the hill, several bloody and gaunt-faced people remained along the tree lines at the edge of the valley, looking on warily. These were likely the lone wolves who killed the monsters before and came to seek more power. But they were not the source of the noise.

The Newbie Village couldn't really be called a village. It was simply a large building, seeming to be an inn, next to a statue. In a slightly disturbing twist, that statue was of the scrawny Donny, hefting his sword and shield, still looking quite a lot more mature and capable than he really was.

Donny stood before the statue, glaring at a tall, well-muscled, dark-skinned man.

That man also wore a police uniform and happened to have an assault rifle strapped to his back.

"I'm just saying, what do you expect," the man said with a shrug. "Sure, son, what you did was very admirable, and we are all very curious about what having a Class means for the world, but didn't you also recognize the danger? If in a week bigger and stronger monsters come, you—"

"Will kill them effortlessly! I'm going to Level up before then and handle it. And if you want to get a Class from my village, you need to agree that I am your boss beforehand. That's all I'm saying. We've got it handled, with or without you," Donny added pompously.

They're blaming him for the Level limit disappearing, huh... Randidly shook his head slightly. *Do they really think the System would just leave them be if they hunkered down and tried to ignore the changes?*

"Look, kid," the man said, losing his patience. "I've tried being nice. And I know a lot has happened in the past few days, so I'm willing to look the other way on some things. But don't be unreasonable. The Shellton Police Department has the situation controlled inside the town. Now we are looking into ways to protect the citizens. It seems like gaining a Class is an effective one. So I'll ask you again. Will you let me see this Class thing, without any of your stupid—"

Donny turned away. "Hmph, you'll be back."

Scowling, the well-muscled man walked away. Several of the more nervous-looking loners around the Newbie Village hurried over to him, their questions blurring together in their retreat. Compared to Donny, the man with the assault rifle definitely had a more reliable figure he could use to reassure these flighty individuals.

"He's right about one thing," the old man muttered, coming up to stand next to Randidly. "They certainly will be back. Especially as that seven-day window closes."

Randidly grunted, warily eyeing the rest of the loners. There was one in particular that caught his eye. As he examined him, the man moved toward Donny, a small smile on his face. Randidly could have mistaken him for a skeleton, he was so skinny. Greasy red hair adorned his head, and from his shirt, he worked in a fast-food chain before the System changed things.

The glassy look in the man's eyes put Randidly on guard.

"Excuse me, are you the guy who founded the first Newbie Village?" His voice came out high and nasally, but Donny visibly puffed up in front of his attention.

Donny grinned. "Hahaha, yes, I am. I'm actually looking for capable subordinates to handle some of the lesser matters, if you think you have what it takes."

The greasy man gave him a cheesy smile. "Oh, I'll do anything if it means working with you, boss."

Clapping him on the back with a happy laugh, Donny took the man to Nul near the central building. Several of the seedier-looking men standing around the outside of the clearing exchanged glances and trailed after Donny and the glassy-eyed redhead.

Randidly had a strange feeling about the group but set it aside for now. Donny was in charge of being the face of this Newbie Village and would need to learn to handle the dangers of that position. He turned to the old man, a question at the tip of his tongue. At the last second, he changed his mind, and asked a different one.

"What's your name?"

"Sam," the old man answered simply.

Randidly nodded. "I'm Randidly."

Randidly quite appreciated the fact that Sam's face never changed at all; he simply nodded in response.

"What do you plan on doing then, Sam? Choosing a Class or waiting? I cannot give any guidance on whether any advantages you can get by waiting will be worth it."

Sam grunted and then spat to the side. "At any rate, for now, I can afford to take my time. Raise some Skill Levels. Sound out the surrounding area and get in small fights with a few monsters. Those police types will be back, and honestly, we might need their muscle and central authority. A certain type of person thrives in this sort of environment. Letting those individuals run freely makes it more difficult for others. They build up momentum during wild times."

Randidly's gaze turned back to the central area, where Donny was introducing the seedy types to Classes. But at the same time, he couldn't help but remember the three hooded figures he'd seen in the back of Sam's truck.

"Are you just going to let them go like that?" Sam asked, tilting his head toward the gaggle of hungry and violent-looking men around Donny. They were rubbing their hands together and nudging each other with their elbows.

Randidly shrugged. "He deals with them so I don't have to. If he can't handle it, I'll find someone else."

Sam gave Randidly a long look. "Some would say that's a very cold view to take."

Again, Randidly shrugged. "Those people are welcome not to take it. But I think... if you don't take the cold, realistic view, the System will kill you far quicker than these suspicious thugs."

As night fell, Randidly began to move. Although he hadn't necessarily been slacking, being around normal people who bothered to sit and rest made Randidly stop training so frantically. That stopped tonight. He could imagine the expression Shal would be making at his laziness, the man's lips pressed so tightly together, they turned white.

He moved a bit away from where the others were gathered, ignoring the laughter of the group who gained Classes from Donny. He moved up the hill into the tree line, finding a deserted area where no one would bother him. Then he settled into the familiar stance Shal taught him, the basis for every move that followed.

He warmed his muscles and joints by moving through the spear forms. When he felt his heart begin to pump, he shifted to directly grinding his Skills.

Randidly spun his spear with Spear Deflect in one hand, while his other hand punched against a tree, utilizing Heavy Blow. He kept his eyes constantly sharpened with Eyes of the Spear Phantom. Due to his high Level of Meditation, he continued to boost his recuperative abilities with his Skill, increasing the rate of Stamina regeneration by 26%.

Congratulations! Your Skill **Meditation** has grown to **Level 27!**

One step at a time, Randidly thought with a smile. The warm energy around his breastbone and the cool energy in his abdomen flowed through his body, fueling these System-enhanced movements.

Meanwhile, Randidly alternated between Arcane Orbs and Mana Bolts, shooting his projectiles high into the sky in order to keep the noise to a minimum.

When his Mana or Stamina ran low, he once more worked his way through the spear forms, depicting the moves of a true Spearman. In a way, the slow, controlled movements became his baseline. Returning to those stances definitely grounded his mentality.

The exertion was hard, both mentally and physically. His breathing was heavy, and sweat dripped off his forehead onto the grassy ground. There were times that even Randidly's boosted Willpower wavered.

But he didn't stop or go easy on himself. The ghost of Shal seemed to hang over him, smirking and prodding him further, a contracted presence that gave Randidly a bit of a taste for masochism. His movements, as time passed, became wilder and more erratic.

While Randidly had been blessed with opportunities, he knew the reason he had his current power was because he seized the chance he was given. Randidly wiped the sweat from his brows and tightened his grip on his spear. *I have an advantage now, but how long will it last? Which is why I cannot stop preparing for the threats that I definitely know are coming.*

Who knows what the System will throw at us next...

Randidly pondered whether saving up and waiting for a Class really was worth it. Sure, best case scenario was he'd have the points from his large Skill list while reaching a high Level. It would give him a definite advantage when it came to fighting someone of a similar Level.

But what about the people who had been Leveling while he was training up his foundation?

It really depended on what kind of RPG game the System was based on, and how high the Level cap was. His experience with Shal raised more questions than it answered. Shal clearly had Stats much higher than Randidly's current physical Stats. Especially in Agility and Vitality. It was awe-inspiring how quickly that man could work his spear, and how he could recover from serious injuries faster than should be possible. Even if a foe managed to scratch Shal, Randidly's master always shrugged it off, counter-attacking, his body recovering to pristine form while his opponent bled out.

That capability also might have been exacerbated by the difference in Skill Levels. His current Spear Mastery Level 38 nowhere near demonstrated his finesse with the spear as Shal possessed.

That sort of familiarity and capability clearly wasn't something that could be made up with Class Levels.

Sighing, Randidly switched from Spear Deflect to practicing Sweep. It was comically easy for him to exert himself all night, carefully studying these different moves and improving them. It was becoming evident to Randidly that it wasn't just knowledge and capability that raised Skill Level, and Skill Level raising capability. It was a little of both. Training now, with some Skill in the spear, made these spear-based Skills increase by leaps and bounds.

An hour before dawn, Randidly's eyes snapped open. The training session had been quite fruitful.

He gained 1 Skill Level in Mana Shield, 2 in Arcane Orb, 1 in Root Manipulation, 2 in Eyes of the Spear Phantom, 3 in Heavy Blow, 1 in Physical Fitness, 4 in Spear Deflect, and 6 in Sweep.

Randidly put those PP on reserve for now, getting to his feet to glower at the darkness. The forest around him was still. Too still. Eyes of the Spear Phantom activated once more, piercing through the gloom.

Monsters were coming. And there were a lot of them.

Randidly Ghosthound's smile was wicked as he raised his spear. "Come, then."

CHAPTER TWENTY-SIX

*R*andidly removed some empty potion bottles and brewed three Mana potions while he Meditated after his earlier skirmish. An even larger grouping of monsters than he massacred in that clearing before dawn appeared to be massing on one of the ridges above them, some distance away. Inwardly, Randidly made another mental note to ask the others about glass containers.

After he finished, he padded quietly up toward Donny's Newbie Village. It seemed as if that was the monster's target. Randidly trusted Sam not to get himself ambushed more than he trusted Donny to make sure his unreliable "subordinates" would be ready for an attack.

Donny is in charge of the social aspect, but he's young, twenty-year-old Randidly justified. *Sometimes, he needs to be reminded of what needs to be done.*

Remnants of a fire had burnt low, and several men were sprawled around the light source, beer bottles rolling between them. The morning sun had done nothing to rouse them. Randidly stepped over them and headed to the main building. Neither Donny, Tera, Chubbs, nor the red-haired man were among the prone forms on the ground.

As he approached the main building, Randidly saw Chubbs sleeping with his back against the main door. Snorting at the quality of the "watch," Randidly hopped up to a nearby window and pushed it open, dropping to the floor in a dark room.

Two forms lay entwined in the darkness. Randidly felt a small pang of embarrassment for interrupting them. Despite the low lighting, he saw very clearly one pair of eyes flicker open.

Their gazes locked.

The figure stood, his emaciated limbs and red hair clear even in the darkness.

"I wanted to meet you. You have such a great smell about you. You were the one who hunted down and slaughtered the Boss to get the golden coin, weren't you? Are you strong? Donny is just there as a front, eh?"

Randidly ignored him, sparing a glance to the other person. Tera rolled sideways, yawning, and blinked upward in the darkness, frowning toward the man as she gathered the sheet to cover her body. "Decklan, wha—"

"What is your Class?" Randidly asked, looking back up toward the man. Although he gave him a distasteful feeling, his curiosity got the better of him.

His flash of yellowed teeth could have gleamed in the darkness. "See? This is why I liked you before I even knew you. You see and say the right things. What will you give me for that knowledge?"

After a thoughtful moment, Randidly removed the dagger he found stuffed into the head of the giant snake all those months ago. The dagger had served him well, keeping him alive in the early days. In addition, it had been the first note of "humanity" Randidly found. That mysterious corpse helped ground Randidly's shaky understanding of his Dungeon. If he hadn't found that corpse and its satchel…

Randidly admitted he wouldn't still be alive right now. Although this Decklan gave him a slightly feral feeling, he had been too shaped by Shal not to understand that this sort of ferocity was exactly what the Newbie Village needed to protect itself.

Besides, compared to the spear, my understanding of using this weapon is quite shallow. Randidly's eyes narrowed. *And should he turn this against me… I can see from their actions, they don't understand how much they waste their time with each other. Taking the dagger back won't be an issue.*

"Will this suffice?" Randidly flicked his fingers and the curved dagger sailed lazily away from him.

The man snatched it out of the air and ran the blade along his forearm, drawing a thin line of blood.

The man's body shuddered in the darkness. "Oh… Yes. This is perfect! Hahaha! My Class is Killer. Only a +3 to Stamina boost per Level, but… I steal the growth rates of the strongest thing I've killed since I last Leveled up, every time I Level. Hahaha, what a fun Class, right?"

Randidly nodded slowly. In a way, it made sense, and it was certainly versatile, especially if he could find powerful enemies, although Randidly wasn't disturbed by the Class as much as he thought he would be. Randidly's eyes sharpened, taking in every inch of this man. The feral sense he got from him grew stronger now that the air was tinged with the scent of blood.

Just the way he stared down monsters, Randidly met Decklan's eyes and spoke slowly. "Donny is… a buffer. I don't have time for most of these problems. I am the Ghosthound. And if you are excited about using it, you don't have long to wait. A wave of monsters is coming."

Decklan began to laugh and Randidly left, searching the rooms until he found Donny, shaking him awake.

"Up and at'em, Village Chieftain," Randidly said grimly. He slapped the teenager's shoulders several times. "We have company."

The rather drunk rabble that had taken an oath to call Donny "boss" were rousing themselves when Randidly left the inn. He slipped past the cabin into the small camp area Sam had set up by his truck. Randidly slowed as he approached, eyeing the wooden shelter Sam had made. He figured that whoever those figures were, they would be sleeping there.

The spot that would grant the watcher the most visibility was the bed of the truck, so Randidly headed there. The figure that sat up was small and covered in a camo raincoat.

For several seconds, the two regarded each other.

As Randidly opened his mouth to ask after Sam, the other figure spoke, the voice feminine and lyrical. "It looked like fireworks."

"Huh?"

"Fireworks. You were doing magic earlier, right? In the forest?" The girl's voice was a strange combination of eager and wistful. "Mine don't look like that at all."

As if it was the most natural thing in the world, she raised her hand. A thin bolt of energy shot forward from her palm and hit a tree with a dull thump, leaving a small scorch mark. Randidly tilted his head to the side.

Somewhat impressed that this young woman learned Mana Bolt so quickly, Randidly did his best to encourage her. "Your Skill Level is just low. As you raise it and your Intelligence, it will get stronger and brighter."

The hooded figure nodded as if he'd spoken profound wisdom. "I'm working on it. You want Mr. Hoss?"

Dubiously assuming Sam was Mr. Hoss, Randidly nodded. The figure hopped down off the truck and left Randidly to wonder about this masked girl. She was short, a full head shorter than he was. From her voice, she might only be fifteen years old. Randidly wondered why Sam kept her, and the two others, hidden with those baggy clothes.

Sam hurried out moments later, mouth open to say something, but Randidly shook his head. "Now's not the time. Something's coming. I don't think Nul has properly explained all the rules about Newbie Villages to us. In another hour, we're going to be attacked."

CHAPTER TWENTY-SEVEN

*S*everal hours passed since listening to the prophetic words of the man who called himself Ghosthound. With trembling hands, Decklan picked blood out from under his nails. He focused on his hands to keep his gaze off the bodies. The bodies of monsters stacked up in drifts. Not that long ago, the black-haired man had stood in that very location and fought against the waves of screaming enemies, his spear dancing.

Tera sat huddled up next to Decklan, dull-eyed and unfocused, her own blood-stained daggers lying beside her. To them, this had been a fight of survival. Wounds marked their arms and legs, each one a reminder of the close calls that could have spelled the end of them.

Decklan squeezed his eyes shut. To distract himself, he thought about Tera.

Although she was cute enough, Decklan was already tiring of her flimsy bravado and excitable personality. Still, if he were forced to wake up to a horde of monsters every morning, he definitely needed someone to help handle his nervous energy.

He licked his lips and forced himself to smile. *Yes. This is a good thing. I'll get used to this feeling. I am… a Killer…*

With those thoughts, he looked at his Status screen.

Decklan Hyde
Class: Killer
Level: 7
Health(/R per hour): 9/80 (44)
Mana(/R per hour): 22/33 (8.5)
Stam(/R per min): 14/50 (16)

Vit: 11
End: 4
Str: 9
Agi: 18
Perception: 7
Reaction: 9
Resistance: 5
Willpower: 2
Intelligence: 3
Wisdom: 6
Control: 7
Focus: 3
Skills: *Sneak Lvl 5 | Slash Lvl 7 | Dagger Mastery Lvl 5 | Backstab Lvl 12 | Feint Lvl 1 | Dual Wielding Mastery Lvl 4*

Most of his Stat points he put directly into Agility. This allowed him to barely lean beyond the claws of the three dozen or so wolverines that streamed out of the woods, coming for the Newbie Village. Eleven people had gotten Classes the previous day. Those eleven men had gained rather bland Classes like "Minuteman" or "Subordinate Thug." Still, they all gathered, nervous and excited at the prospect of strengthening themselves.

None of them had taken the Ghosthound's note of caution seriously.

Of those eleven, Decklan and Donny made it out all right. They stayed close to each other, relying on Tera to step up and push wolverines back when they were overwhelmed. As much as Decklan thought the little shit was annoying, Donny slowed several down with his shield work, handling the attacks of several at once.

A few of the other people who obtained Classes had broken and ran, quickly hamstrung and eviscerated by the wolverines. At the time, every bite into human flesh burrowed its way into his ears. Ferocious and unforgiving, the animals shredded the innards of those people, guzzling them down. At one point, Decklan considered fleeing himself.

That was when the Ghosthound finally rushed forward.

With a wave of his hand, blasts of energy accurately smashed several wolverines to the side. The guy moved like a ghost, his spear lashing outwards, leaving only dead bodies in its wake. He cleared out the bulk of their forces, leaving the exhausted survivors to thin out the stragglers.

By that time, only six of the eleven Classed individuals still breathed. Most of those who took formation on the left side were the ones who died, their vague blockade scattering when a few people caved and ran.

If he had been on the left side, Decklan wasn't sure he would have fared any better. Luck had saved him.

That was all.

After they killed the rest, Decklan followed where Ghosthound retreated to in the forest, curious where he'd come from and wanting to know why he waited to show himself. Although Decklan understood showing off and demonstrating how important Strength was, his shaky fear squirmed in his chest to think who would be left hanging next, to prove a point.

What he saw had even left the man with the Class Killer nauseous. Less than half of the wolverines had made it past the blockade set up by the Ghosthound to reach the rest of them. Their bodies caked the forest floor. Headless, blasted, burnt, impaled on thorns...

Some appeared to have been splashed with acid, leaving their bodies to melt away.

So now Decklan sat, not bothering to distinguish between the fear and excitement making his heart pound, barely keeping his hands from trembling. The Ghosthound was talking to the old man he was often with, whose axe was still wet with blood. They seemed to be discussing using the wolverine bodies for something.

The Ghosthound expertly slid his spear through the ribcage of one and held the corpse up for the old man's inspection.

"I've decided," Tera said next to him. "I'm going to get a Class from Donny and Nul. Even if I could get a better Class by getting stronger first... I need strength now."

Decklan nodded lightly, watching the Ghosthound. As the Ghosthound waved his hand, roots sprouted from the ground, slowly gathering the bodies of the wolverines into a pile. The old man indicated some messier corpses and those were then tossed into a different pile.

His face splitting into a wide grin, Decklan turned to Tera. "Good. Do it as quickly as possible and we'll go hunting immediately."

Her face brightened. "Really! Can Chubbs come?"

"Sure, sure, whatever," Decklan said, already turning back toward the Ghosthound, who seemed completely uninjured.

That Level of Strength. He would do anything to have it.

What was the Ghosthound's secret?

"You want to skin them?" Randidly asked hesitantly, studying the impressive pile of bodies. Even after the ruined ones were set aside. His eyes shifted to the spear holes ripping through most of their pelts, and he shifted uncomfortably.

And these are the good *ones...*

Sam put his hands on his hips and nodded. "Both for the skins and for the meat. I suspect we can get something akin to a Tannery Skill, which will be useful. Also, the rations we brought are starting to run low. Are your... plants safe to eat?"

"Yeah, the first batch will probably be done later today." The hairs on the back of Randidly's neck prickled upward as the instincts he honed in the Dungeon activated. Glancing over his shoulder, he caught Decklan staring at him again. Resolving to ignore it, Randidly turned back to Sam, who was making an uncomfortable expression.

"Hmmm... Then perhaps... you could come to my, uh, camp for dinner. We could have discussions." Sam finished speaking with atypical awkwardness, rubbing the back of his neck.

Shrugging in confirmation, Randidly switched the subject. "I did a rough count of the amount of wolverines that were here while I was fighting them. About eighty or ninety. How many did you get in your area?"

Sam grimaced. "Quite a few. Nowhere near what you had up here, just some stragglers. Maybe two dozen. Luckily you warned me in time. I was able to set up enough traps to stall them while I got to work with my axe."

Randidly said nothing about the numerous arrows he'd seen skewering the wolverines down by Sam's camp. "That puts it right at about a hundred. Just a theory, but I suspect there were a hundred and ten."

Sam's eyes sharpened as he made the connection. "Ten for each of the eleven people who obtained Classes?"

"I already asked Nul. He said we would be forced to discover the rules ourselves as we went along. But if this gets worse, or if more people come for Classes..."

"Or if you hadn't been here..." Sam muttered, his eyes glittering. "The village would probably have been wiped out before it even got off the ground."

"Well," Randidly said with a nasty glint in his eye. "Hopefully, most people wouldn't have gotten drunk immediately after obtaining a Class. If they Leveled a few times last night—"

"Enough to fight off ten wolverines each? All at once?"

Sam's statement hung in the air. They shared a long glance. Sam's eyes held more worry than Randidly's. He didn't have the Dungeon to teach him how callous the System treated human life.

"Then I guess it's back to work, so it doesn't happen to us next." Randidly said, raising his hand to block the rays of the rising sun coming up over the horizon.

CHAPTER TWENTY-EIGHT

*I*n addition to the 21 PP he gained from his training session in the clearing last night, Randidly also gained 2 more Levels in Sweep and 1 in Entangling Roots in the pre-dawn fight, putting him at 24 in total. Just looking at that number on his Path screen brought him satisfaction.

Monster Slayer III would take 6 PP. When he went to the Path screen, another option caught his eye. He unlocked the Heavy Blow Path 0/20 at Level 20 of the Skill. There was a high chance of him receiving another Skill if he completed it.

After a slight hesitation, he put 20 PP into it, finishing it instantly. He turned to the Monster Slayer III Path next, netting himself 2 Str and 10 Stamina for the PP he spent. Then he received his Path Completion notification.

Congratulations! You have completed the **"Heavy Blow Path"!** Your ability to carve a Path forward remains one of the most reliable methods to proceed. There are some impediments that will need to be dealt with using force, and for that you are prepared. **+1 free Stat(s) +20 Stamina.**

Congratulations! You have learned the Skill **Empower Level 1.**

Congratulations! You have learned the Skill **Calculated Blow Level 1.**

Empower Level 1: Cost 30 Stamina. *Infuse any physical movement with effort, very slightly increasing its speed and power.* **There will not be any adverse effects to the Skill activation. Effectiveness and potency of boost improves with Skill Level.**

Calculated Blow Level 1: *Passively begin to detect weaknesses of enemy creatures after fighting them for extended periods of time. Their weaknesses become visible to you. Hitting those weaknesses slightly increases the damage dealt.* **Effectiveness improves with Skill Level. Movement requirement to activate the bonus damage marginally decreases with Skill Level.**

Randidly was rather pleased with his decision to go for the Heavy Blow Path before continuing with Monster Hunter. Not only had it net him a fair bit of Strength and Stamina, it also gave him two Skills. The passive would slowly add up, especially now, while he was absolutely ripping through large groups of enemies. He would have plenty of exposure to fighting the different types. But Randidly was far more interested in the first Skill that would let him Empower any move.

It's a Heavy Blow without the drawback of being briefly vulnerable. Randidly rubbed his chin as he examined the Skill descriptions. *Based on the text, the bonus is much smaller, and 30 Stamina in the middle of a fight can add up quickly. But against a single powerful opponent...*

Randidly's mind briefly drifted back to his clash with the Giant Serpent. He pulled away from those images, forcing himself not to get distracted. He slapped his hands together to disperse the lingering sense of fear he still felt and got to work.

He experimented with Empower for a few minutes through strikes and leaps. Even with those few attempts, he pushed it up to Level 3. Although it was nowhere near enough to equal the extra strength added to an attack by Heavy Blow, it was just enough to give him an edge.

Randidly grinned, thinking of the possibilities when combined with Haste. He was willing to bet the sudden shift in speed might be enough to leave most enemies dazed. No longer would size and tough skin leave him completely helpless.

He was improving. He was moving forward.

Randidly used the remaining 6 PP he had to start and finish Monster Slayer III Path.

Congratulations! You have completed the "Monster Slayer III Path"! Do not hesitate as you continue forward, for a Path paved with blood still will lead you forward. +3 Stat(s), +3 to Health, Mana, and Stamina.

Sometimes the path you walk is stained by the blood of those who would stand against you, but you must continue.

Having a sudden thought, Randidly turned back and regarded the Newbie

Village. Decklan, Tera, and a few of the survivors had gone off together into the woods, yet Donny remained behind.

Donny had been rather unpredictable thus far. Randidly wanted the village to prosper, but more specifically, he wanted them to grow so he could learn more information about Classes and Villages for his own benefit. As it currently was, Donny didn't appear to appreciate the gift Randidly had given him, nor the dangers of the world, even now that he had a Class.

It's time to change it. Randidly's emerald eyes hardened. Behind him, the ghost of Shal's training methods flashed a knowing smile.

Although it would be a hassle, taking Donny monster hunting was the smart long-term play. The kid needed to survive. Honestly, with the gains he likely made last night and a few more Levels today, his increase in Health would be enough to sustain him.

As long as he didn't do anything stupid…

Sighing, Randidly walked over toward Donny, who was standing with Chubbs.

"Ahaha, well—" Donny was saying, his eyes brightening when Randidly approached. "Ah! Here, let Randidly handle this issue. I'm just off hunting—"

Randidly grabbed him by his dirty t-shirt before he could skulk away. "Perfect, I was just thinking the same thing. Let's hunt monsters for a few hours."

Donny nodded uncertainly. Randidly turned to Chubbs. While he was here, he might as well see if it was an issue he could help with. He owed them that much. "What is it?"

"Oh, I got a Class, and my first Class ended up being Quartermaster. The Stat gains are pretty small… but I got the Skill Insight. It lets me intuit things based on the amount of information I have about a subject. So I was wondering if Boss Donny had any ideas on what—"

"Track down everyone with a Class and interview them," Randidly interrupted him. It was easy to push Chubbs in the right direction. "Find out Classes and Stat gains. Also ask them about weird Skills they gained, and what Skills Level up the fastest. Then ask about Paths, and Skills gained from those. Then ask about any Class-specific Paths people have obtained. Then ask about the habits of enemies. Then local flora and fauna that have changed since the System appeared. Understood? Good, I will speak to you later."

Please work hard, my walking encyclopedia. Randidly pivoted on his heel and walked away, Donny trailing uncertainly along behind him.

Having Donny follow him was for the best. That way, he couldn't see the Shal-esque smile growing across his face.

Donny stabbed his sword into the neck of another lizard, its struggles completely helpless against the roots binding it.

A small ding notified him he Leveled up again and he brought up his status screen.

Donny Parke
Class: Knight
Level: 6
Health(/R per hour): 100/122 (22.25)
Mana(/R per hour): 25/25 (3)
Stam(/R per min): 11/70 (9)
Vit: 6
End: 5
Str: 15
Agi: 4
Perception: 5
Reaction: 4
Resistance: 11
Willpower: 3
Intelligence: 2
Wisdom: 2
Control: 2
Focus: 2
Skills: *Hiding Lvl 7 | Running Lvl 5 | Grappling Lvl 3 | Club Wielding Lvl 2 | Wood Working Lvl 2 | Construction Lvl 3 | Labor Lvl 5 | Heavy Blow Lvl 3 | Mana Bolt Lvl 1 | Ride Lvl 1 | Honorable Charge Lvl 2 | Stalwart Defense Lvl 5 | (1) Sword Master Lvl 3 | (2) Shield Mastery Lvl 6*

Even though Randidly told him to keep his Vit and End high for survivability, Donny decided what a true leader needed was not the ability to endure hardship, but the Strength to do something about problems. He would grapple with life and force it to the shape he wanted.

Especially with Randidly's support, Donny added hastily, sparing a glance for the meditating man.

Still, this sort of "hunting" was unsatisfying for Donny; he was bored. Seemed to be for Randidly too. No foes were worthy of his attention. Earlier, Randidly asked whether Donny wanted this to be hard or easy. Donny naturally chose easy and this was what followed for a boring forty-five minutes.

Looking at his double-digit Strength, Donny hefted his shield and bumped it lightly against a nearby tree, enjoying the way the trunk shook from his action. He turned to look at Randidly, who got up from his Meditation and moved into his constant state of motion.

Whether it was practicing with the spear, mixing weird chemicals, shooting off spells, or striking trees, he always maintained a fluid series of actions. No moment was wasted. Inwardly, Donny was slightly worried about Randidly's mental health at the constant exertion. Overall, he was pleased he had such a dedicated subordinate.

The Randidly of last night flashed before Donny's eyes. A man soaked in gore. Moving like the wind. He couldn't help but shiver.

Shaking his head, Donny said, "I, uh, changed my mind. This is too easy. Can we do this faster? The hard way maybe? Growing like this is pretty slow."

Randidly stopped and turned to Donny, his gaze placid, and his mouth seemed to twitch lightly. "Perhaps. But once you choose the hard way, you won't be able to stop it halfway. It might take a few hours, so you will be indisposed for that period."

"Ha, that's fine." Donny said, scratching the back of his head. "The longer I'm away from that creepy village guy, the better."

Randidly gave Donny a small smile. "Nul? I also find him rather... creepy. Follow me."

Randidly practically disappeared, even though he had been right in front of Donny not seconds ago. Somehow, the vanishing act was accomplished silently. Donny hurried through the brush, kicking it aside with a curse, trying to keep up. "Uh, Randidly... So, why are you helping us? You seem so strong already, and you don't want a Class. But you always patrol the surrounding areas—"

As if by magic, Randidly stepped out from behind a tree to Donny's left, causing him to jump. How had he...?

"I... am looking for my friends. But I don't know where to start. This 'Section,' as the announcement called it, it's too big. Trying to find two people..." Randidly shook his head. "For now, keeping the Newbie Village stable and growing seems like my best bet."

"So, you're giving up on them?" Donny asked, mouth gaping. Randidly gave him a sharp look.

"Of course not. But if I cannot find them alone, I have few options. One of them is to grow the village so much that it attracts them. Another is to recruit people to help me in my search." Randidly hesitated before adding, "Or I wait long enough that most of the population is concentrated, and then search those locations. After all, the Newbie Village mechanic will drive people to gather around an area they can receive Classes. Only, waiting that long worries me..."

Then Randidly grinned, turning to look deeper into the forest.

"Ah, here is the first batch. Let the hard way begin. Good luck, Donny."

CHAPTER TWENTY-NINE

*P*ain blurred Donny's senses. His lips were chapped and numb. The only times he bobbed up from his own situation was by hearing the words of the Ghosthound. Donny regretted ever suggesting the "hard" way. "Uh, my loyal minion, shouldn't we—"

"No, we continue."

"Ah, but my Health is low, and my regeneration—"

"I told you to invest in Vitality, did I not? When you Level next, do so. You need the regeneration. And it's going to get worse before it gets better."

Donny swayed, about to fall over. He sucked in a breath, doing his best to blink away his tears. He didn't like how whiny he sounded, but he had to reason with Randidly.

"Well, just for now—" The ground felt very solid beneath his face. "Gack! You *kicked* me!"

Donny considered lying there forever with the solidity of the ground seeping into him. Randidly reached down and yanked him to his feet.

There was no remorse in Randidly's eyes. "You would not advance. Raise your shield; the imps are coming."

Donny blearily twisted around. A dozen imps streamed out of the tree line toward their position. Donny forced his exhausted arm to raise his shield, desperately wishing for a break. Just as he opened his mouth to vocalize this desire, one of the imps threw a blazing spell.

After a few seconds, Donny's eyes went wide, his focus snapping to his burning leg while other Fireballs whizzed around him. "AHHHH! I'm on *fire!*"

Randidly snorted. "If nothing else, your Class gives you resistance, which should weaken the effect of magic—"

"AHHHH!" The pain was everywhere, rushing up his leg. Donny collapsed, slapping out the flames.

"—enough for you to survive this. Don't worry, ten more seconds and I will intervene."

"*What*! You're still just *standing there*?"

"How else would you learn how to defend yourself? Careful, they are circling around you."

More and more Fireballs impacted Donny's body. Everything blended together in agony. He groped the ground and locked on to his shield. He held the defensive equipment in front of him, feeling that it was simply too tiny. Through his tear-streaked vision, he barely managed to notice projectiles in time to crawl out of the way.

An eternity later, the Ghosthound was there next to him. Donny closed his eyes and something inside of him relaxed. He needed a break. Let Randidly—

"Guh!"

Donny rolled over a few times, sent sprawling out of his stupor by a kick.

The Ghosthound stood over him and shook his head. "Just barely passable. You survived for the ten seconds, but you passed out immediately afterwards. Drink this and then we continue."

"Nooooo-oooo… just let me die…" Donny flopped onto his stomach and curled into a ball.

"Did I hear you correctly? You wanted the difficulty raised and now you want to go again? Although your performance is shit, your attitude can be considered barely deserving of a compliment. Let us go, then." The Ghosthound casually pulled Donny up by his t-shirt.

"Put—Me—Down!"

The Ghosthound remained relentless, dragging Donny after him. "Ah, good, here is a large group. Careful of the lizard bites; their teeth are very sharp. Hum, perhaps we should gather some and take them back to Sam…"

"Do you really want to kill me!"

"Obviously not. But let me ask you a question." The Ghosthound patted Donny almost gently on the shoulder, only to shove the unsuspecting Donny forward.

The dog-sized lizards pounced on him.

Donny writhed back and forth, wildly waving his shield around to bat the monsters away. "SHIT! It's *biting meee!*"

"You want to be a Knight, yes? The Dusk Knight, I think you said? To have the strength to be the Village Chieftain and lead us?"

One of his wild strokes with the shield finally made the lizards scatter a bit, giving Donny some breathing room. Knowing they were circling around him, Donny rushed forward, smashing his shield again and again into one of the stunned lizards. "Ha-HAAA! *Die,* you fucking shit!"

Randidly continued to lecture. "With your Level of Strength, anything other than defense is inadvisable. You are like a turtle. Even now, you can only knock them backwards with your shield and wait for my help."

A lizard pounced on Donny from behind, biting into the flesh of his thigh. He wanted to tear his hair out, spinning around, trembling. "Because you bring twenty of them at *once*."

"Can you deny they are weak? They have no weapons, no Skills, they are common fodder. Yet you struggle. Is this what you want? To struggle against these forever?"

Donny avoided another pounce and pushed a third lizard away. It didn't matter how many times he swung; more and more swarmed him. His vision swam. Too much blood dripped out from the wound on his thigh. Donny was so exhausted. All he could manage in response was angry breathing.

"What I'm saying is this: we have a relationship. I have Strength, but no ability or willingness to deal with people. You have little Strength right now, but you can handle people. Well, handle might be a strong word, but—"

"Fuck…" Donny scrunched his eyes together. His arms ached. He couldn't keep this up much longer. "It hurts so bad…"

A lizard made the mistake of hopping toward the Ghosthound and was instantly skewered. The casual violence did not interrupt his lecture. "However, that was just in the old world. When that police officer came from town, he did not back down after you refused them. He postured with force. For sure, he will return, seeking what he wants. And what will you, as Village Chieftain, do?"

"Fuck…"

"What will you do?"

Donny's head was pounding.

"What will you do, Donny?"

There were too many lizards. Donny had bites on his shin and non-shield arm. It was too exhausting to react to these wounds. Everything was spinning. "Damnit…"

"What will you DO?"

"I'll fight if I have to! I'll stare down a gun! I'll throw him back until he agrees to call me boss!"

"Aside from the boss comment, good. But you remain too weak for me to believe you. I'll kill most, but these last five I shall leave for you. After you finish them, we immediately continue."

True to his word, the Ghosthound was there. His spear wove through their bodies, slitting throats and skewering their small bodies with every movement. When some turned to flee, the Ghosthound unleashed his powerful Arcane Orbs, blasting the cowardly monsters to bits.

Soon, there were only five left. Those lizards warily eyed the

Ghosthound, unsure of why his attacks stopped. Their nostrils began to flare, honing in on Donny's blood. They circled him.

Luckily, the Ghosthound's interference gave Donny a bit of time to catch his breath. "Is this... really necessary?"

The Ghosthound folded his arms. "Did you think it was easy? Finding strength, I mean. You must sweat for every ounce of it."

"Ugh..."

"Don't worry, that Decklan character seems promising. If you die, he will be the figurehead of my new Newbie Village."

"Ha! That prick...?" The lizards circled closer. Donny forced his eyes to focus on them.

"He seems charming enough. Did you know that Tera has taken to sleeping with him?"

"What! How did that—GAAAAAH!" One of the lizards darted forward, taking advantage of Donny's distraction, and bit into his shoe.

The Ghosthound chuckled. "That's what you get for letting your attention wander. Focus ahead; I've brought more monsters."

Although Donny was sure he was going to die at least a dozen times in the three hours of the "hard" way, he couldn't deny the training was effective. Still, he refused to ever, *ever* do such a thing again.

Donny Parke
Class: Knight
Level: 9
Health(/R per hour): 100/217 (52.25)
Mana(/R per hour): 25/45 (3)
Stam(/R per min): 11/120 (19)
Vit: 16
End: 5
Str: 18
Agi: 8
Perception: 6
Reaction: 5
Resistance: 16
Willpower: 3
Intelligence: 2
Wisdom: 2
Control: 2
Focus: 2
Skills: *Hiding Lvl 7 | Running Lvl 5 | Grappling Lvl 5 | Club*

Wielding Lvl 2 | WoodWorking Lvl 2 | Construction Lvl 3 | Labor Lvl 6 | Heavy Blow Lvl 5 | Mana Bolt Lvl 1 | Ride Lvl 1 | Honorable Charge Lvl 2 | Stalwart Defense Lvl 9 | (1) Sword Master Lvl 5 | (2) Shield Mastery Lvl 11 | (3) Shield Bash Lvl 3 | (4) Aegis Lvl 1

After looking at his Status Screen for a long minute, Donny turned to Randidly. "What Level are you?"

Randidly stopped moving through his spear forms and shrugged. "I do not have a Class, so I don't have a Level."

"Then…" Donny looked at him with wide eyes. "Your Strength?"

Randidly smiled and said, "Skill Levels. And practice fighting in desperate situations. Now let's head back. You need to rest before the people from town return. And tonight, well, you're going to demonstrate what hard work can accomplish."

CHAPTER THIRTY

*R*andidly didn't gain anything from those four hours, aside from the profound satisfaction of experiencing the perverse joy of forcing someone to go through the torment Shal subjected him to. It surprised him how quickly he embraced the role of stern taskmaster. There was definitely something cathartic about sharing that sort of experience. When he understood how not to let Donny sink into any real danger, he thought his screams were somewhat cute.

But then again, keeping myself on track is the most satisfying. Randidly slapped his cheeks to banish the strange thoughts.

It was reassuring that Donny wasn't just a sack of shit. Turned out, he possessed a backbone. Even if he wasn't an ideal choice, Randidly would ensure he rose to the role of Village Chieftain. Stepping into Shal's brutal shoes, bathing in the deep-seated joy, was just a side benefit at the end of the day.

Watching Donny struggle gave Randidly time to reflect on what areas he should focus on for Skill growth.

He decided to put more effort into increasing the utility of his Root Manipulation Skill, allocating Stat points into Control to increase the range of its applications. This earned him a small, positive effect on the Mana expenditure when using Entangling Roots. Once more, Randidly was left confused, unsure if Control made *him* more efficient with his efforts or if his higher Control made the Mana *use* more efficient.

Either way, decreasing his Mana costs was important. The rate he spent his Mana seemed to be increasing as he gained more Skills. After all, Randidly only had one mouth to drink Mana potions.

With concerted effort, Randidly earned himself two Skill Levels in Root Manipulation. He turned to Stamina Skills to give his meager Mana pool a break. Calculated Blow rose to Level 4, and Randidly was beginning to sense the weak points of the imps and lizards he fought south of the Newbie Village.

Randidly thrust his spear through a lizard and started to chuckle. *Although, to the current me, isn't the entirety of this lizard a weakness? Bah, well, when the Level restriction disappears, stronger foes should come. Six more nights...*

In addition, Empower grew to Level 6. From the experience, Randidly was swiftly learning that although the Stamina cost was pretty debilitative in an extended fight, it was oppressively powerful. He planned to practice using it while performing spear forms and spear footwork.

And if he could master it...

But Randidly knew the real way to grow was not training here. To that end, after dropping off a sobbing Donny onto Chubbs' lap, Randidly headed due east, toward what used to be a lake.

It had been transformed into sloping hills that gave way to a cracked plateau, noticeably devoid of people. Randidly suspected there must be an edge to the "Safe Zone." He didn't think the entire map was a Safe Zone, suspecting many such areas probably sprang up, giving people a chance at life.

But beyond that, in this wide area of the wilderness...

Randidly gained a point in Pathfinding and Mapmaking when he reached the edge of the safe area. Beyond that point, the map tinged red. The color reminded him of the pool of blood that covered the "proceed to the Safe Zone" arrow in the grass.

Grinning, Randidly stepped boldly over the line, falling back into habits he picked up in the Dungeon. Spear out, Eyes of the Spear Phantom constantly activated, he scanned the surrounding ground.

It was a good thing he was prepared. When the enemy came, it came for him rapidly.

A bolt of fur and snarls streaked out of Randidly's peripheral vision into his blind spot. He spun, Mana Shield activating instantly. The creature smashed through the shield with the force of its charge.

Randidly's eyes narrowed. A rushing crest of elation sang with the blood roaring in his ears. For the first time since leaving the Dungeon, he felt threatened.

His hands trembled, adjusting his grip on his spear. *Yes, it was always like this, wasn't it?*

His spear shot forward, utilizing Heavy Blow and Phantom Thrust. The attack was almost impossible to see with the naked eye. The black bolt of fur flowed around it, a flash of light on its claws the only signal that an attack was coming from a new angle.

Congratulations! Your Skill **Eyes of the Spear Phantom** has grown to **Level 17!**

Entangling Roots activated, bringing his weapon across his body defensively. Huge roots rushed upwards to grip the slippery thing. It hopped to the side, maintaining its momentum as it zigzagged through the roots.

This time, Randidly was ready for its speed.

As the creature made its leap to the side, Randidly attacked. Throwing everything he had at the monster. Phantom Onslaught, Haste, and Empower warped together into a storm of spear thrusts. A dozen stabs ripped toward the ever-so-slightly off-balance creature. Several long gashes struck true along the creature's body.

Congratulations! Your Skill **Empower** has grown to **Level 7!**

Blood spurted from the wounds on its side, forcing the monster to slow down and gather itself.

Entangling Roots began to stiffen, the mana supporting them now dispersed. As the wounded creature eyed him warily, Randidly activated Root Manipulation. The roots from the previous spell twisted around behind the creature, slamming down toward its fragile spine.

Randidly again underestimated its speed. It teleported forward, slashing at his throat before the roots could arrive. Now threatened, it aimed for the kill.

Randidly's adrenaline thundered through his veins. An Empowered Spear Phantom's Footwork enabled Randidly to dodge. Even then, a long gash was left in his shoulder, his Health dropping a good 30%.

Yeah. Just like this. Push me more! Randidly's eyes glittered as Mana surged in through his body.

The roots smashed against the creature. It swayed, concentrating on speed rather than strength. The black blur twisted, slashing at the attacking plants. The creature hissed in pain, its movements causing blood to pump from the long wounds Randidly left on its torso. That was all the chance Randidly needed.

With its focus to the roots, Randidly activated Phantom Half-Step. Suddenly, he was only half a meter from the speedy death machine. He raised his hand and activated Arcane Orb at close range.

Congratulations! Your Skill **Arcane Orb** has grown to **Level 18!**

Congratulations! Your Skill **Spirit of Adversity** has grown to **Level 24!**

Mana condensed and blasted outward, impacting the monster and the ground beneath it. Randidly's finger broke from the force of the explosion. When the smoke cleared, the residual damage proved to be worth it. The thing's spine shattered, finally killing it.

His shoulders heaved and he chuckled. Triumph rolled off of Randidly in waves.

He inspected himself, even while sparing the surroundings a quick scan. Around 60% of his Health remained, but his Mana and Stamina had dwindled to 20% and 5%. When those ran out, what Health he held on to would be swiftly devoured against another weird creature like this.

He swiftly picked up a small necklace it dropped, and slung the body over his shoulder. It only seemed to weigh around 80 lbs. Prizes in hand, Randidly returned to an area not marked red.

Licking his lips, Randidly couldn't suppress the strange emotions running through him. The thrill of a fight when his life was on the line. The fear of death. The responsibility he had toward the strange Newbie Town he created.

The need to find Ace and Sydney, and the slow-growing anxiety as no easy way to do so presented itself.

In the heat of battle, all these thoughts melted together into a palatable mixture he could sweat out, leaving himself clear-headed. All the complexities of dealing with people vanished, at least for the moment.

He sat down to Meditate, setting aside the body of the monster for now. Although the battle was short, it was incredibly fruitful. Not only did he sharpen the little bit of an edge he lost since coming here, he gained quite a few Skill Levels. In addition to the ones he noticed, he earned Level-ups in Physical Fitness, Iron Skin, Entangling Roots, Mana Shield, Dodge, Phantom Thrust, Spear Phantom's Footwork, and Root Manipulation.

All in all, that was 12 PP in twenty-three or so seconds. Randidly's lips split into a grin.

It was short-lived. A throb of pain spread upward from his shattered finger, twisting his grin into a grimace. He pulled out a Health potion and drank it to speed up his recovery. Although this was a good way for Randidly to improve himself, the problem was the risks associated with it. He wanted to continue to farm in this zone, but...

If he encountered two monsters such as this at the same time...

He remembered one of the last pieces of advice Shal gave him right before they made their final, successful attack on the Boss.

"A spear can only go forward, and thus a Spearman must hold tight to the shaft and support it, or he will lose it and become just a man. Shortly afterward, he will undoubtedly die."

Chuckling to himself, excitement coursing through him, Randidly looked out toward the cracked plateau with its strange cat creatures. His cautious side was steadily being overwhelmed by his primal desire for the simplicity of violence.

CHAPTER THIRTY-ONE

*D*uring the course of recovering from his wounds, Randidly gained another point in Meditation, which was always a pleasant surprise. Every point in that increased the effectiveness of his regeneration, especially while training, which would improve his other Skill Level growth.

As he prepared to head into the plateau again, his stomach rumbled. Annoyed, Randidly turned to the horizon. It was a few hours past noon, reminding him he hadn't bothered to take a break after training Donny, to eat. And he had not thought to bring food with him.

His stomach rumbled again.

Grumbling, Randidly turned away, making a promise to return tomorrow. However, his human needs were only one of several reasons he wanted to return early to the camp.

One was to witness Donny's resolve and the other was to hold up his end of the bargain in the fight against monsters. If it was a contest of strength, Randidly was not yet willing to let the Newbie Village be on the losing end of it. If it was to grow into a useful platform for him, it needed to survive these early encounters.

Randidly opened up his Path screen as he walked. He already put a few points into Monster Slayer IV, and the amount he currently had enabled him to finish it.

Congratulations! You have completed the **"Monster Slayer IV Path"!** +4 **free Stat(s), +.5 to Health Regen, Mana Regen, and Stamina Regen.**

Sometimes the path forward leads through blood and gore. Your progress displays your high adaptive abilities. Continue to improve,

sharpening your ferocity. Those who seek to survive in this place do well to embrace violence.

Randidly's eyes sharpened on the notification. *An increase in regeneration...?* The costs for the Monster Slayer Path were getting higher, but these increases... Even though the Stat was small, he'd never gotten regeneration before. It was an exciting development.

Interested, he poured the rest into Monster Slayer V, raising it to 7/25.

He took out the necklace the monster dropped. The cat-creature was a common Level 33 enemy, on par with what Randidly faced in the Dungeon. Its speed, though, was so overwhelming, it seemed more powerful than its Level revealed. That was compensated by having a relatively weak body. A single direct spell, applied to the back of the cat's fragile spine, was able to kill it.

Randidly's Intelligence had increased since the beginning of his journey, but it still wasn't oppressively high enough to one shot most monsters of that Level. Or any of them, to Randidly's knowledge. Considering this, Randidly examined the item.

As he stared, the explanatory notification appeared. Despite the fact that he usually didn't bother with System-dropped equipment, the natural unobtrusiveness of the necklace gave him pause.

That, and the bonus Stats.

Necklace of the Shadow Cat Level 20 (R): Vitality +1, Strength +2, Agility +7

Randidly immediately slipped on the necklace and enjoyed the feeling of capability that flowed through him.

But still, what I really want to know is how an item condenses from the corpse of a monster. Has the Earth really turned into a game world? Randidly wondered, not for the first time. He glided quickly forward, savoring the boost in Agility he received from equipping the Necklace.

Randidly arrived at the edge of the valley, the sun still high in the sky, before too many monsters accumulated. Randidly estimated it to be around 4 pm. For good measure, he slaughtered some wolverines he found clumped together before heading back to his cabin and his plants.

He harvested the ripe crops and replanted them, moving on to his second series of fields. Satisfied with his harvest, he started working the dirt for a third field, planting stranger combinations of plants next to each other. For this variety, he used some of his spare blue and red crystals. Although he didn't have much hope he would find more recipes for potions, it didn't hurt to experiment.

While munching on some Halnuts, Randidly considered his Stats.

Randidly Ghosthound
Class: ---
Level: N/A
Health(/R per hour): 206/262 [+1) (109.25 [+3])
Mana(/R per hour): 139/249 (51.75)
Stam(/R per min): 105/233 (39.5 [+2])
Vit: 32 [+1]
End: 27
Str: 18 [+2]
Agi: 42 [+7]
Perception: 22
Reaction: 24
Resistance: 9
Willpower: 52
Intelligence: 54
Wisdom: 30
Control: 31
Focus: 17
Equipment: Necklace of the Shadow Cat Lvl 20 (R): Vit +1, Str +2, Agi +7
Skills
Soulskill: *Green Spear Mastery Lvl 224*

Basic: *Running Lvl 17 | Physical Fitness Lvl 25 | Sneak Lvl 29 | Acid Resistance Lvl 22 | Poison Resistance Lvl 14 | Spirit of Adversity Lvl 24 | Dagger Mastery Lvl 11 | Dodge Lvl 26 | Spear Mastery Lvl 39 | Pain Resistance Lvl 11 | Fighting Proficiency Lvl 28 | First Aid Lvl 13 | Block Lvl 24 | Mental Strength Lvl 8 | Curse Resistance Lvl 3 | Pathfinding Lvl 8 | Mapmaking Lvl 4 | Calculated Blow Lvl 4*

Stamina: *Heavy Blow Lvl 22 | Sprinting Lvl 13 | Iron Skin Lvl 25 | Phantom Thrust Lvl 32 | Spear Phantom's Footwork Lvl 23 | Eyes of the Spear Phantom Lvl 17 | Phantom Half-Step Lvl 4 | Haste Lvl 12 | Phantom Onslaught Lvl 10 | Sweep Lvl 9 | Spear Deflect Lvl 5 | Empower Lvl 7*

Mana: *Mana Bolt Lvl 30 | Meditation Lvl 28 | Entangling Roots Lvl 28 | Mana Shield Lvl 23 | Root Manipulation Lvl 24 | Arcane Orb Lvl 18*

Crafting: *Farming Lvl 23 | Plant Breeding Lvl 9 | Potion Making Lvl 19 | Analyze Lvl 24*

Randidly knew, due to a variety of things, he'd grown much stronger than the average person. The sheer quantity of Skills he knew gave him a natural advantage over most others when it came to Paths. That was something he would never lose, even if his Skill number was later capped by a Class. He could always Level these Skills. Based on what he learned from Shal, he could forget them to learn others.

It made him wonder whether it would be worth it to take the time to learn a bunch of Skills and keep them at low Level until he had a Class. It probably wouldn't be hard to ask around. Having put Chubbs to work, he could more easily find useful Skills that wouldn't be too hard to earn. The question was simply whether it was worth the time spent to obtain ancillary Skills. Right now, he wasn't sure. It was only just now coming up on two days since he left the Dungeon.

In a way, Randidly was still playing catch up to the situation.

The list of things he had to do were piling up to the point he wanted to ignore them and throw himself into heart-racing fights. Which, Randidly admitted to himself, wasn't a very healthy response.

But it's the way I made it through the early days. Randidly rubbed the back of his head. *Training and focusing on the excitement... if I had stopped and thought deeper about what was happening...*

He shook his head. Even now, it wasn't a good idea to let his mind wander. He focused back on his own growth.

The other big help had been the addition of Green Spear Mastery and it Leveling when anything else Leveled. Every 5 Levels, he would get one of four rotating things—5 Mana, 1 Vitality, 5 Stamina, and 2 distributable Stat points.

And now that his Soulskill was past 200 hundred...

10 Vitality, 50 Mana, 50 Stamina, and 20 Stats he could add to anything had been given to him. He concentrated on Intelligence, Agility, and most recently, Control. Although it was slight, Randidly was really beginning to appreciate what Control could do for his Root Manipulation. Especially after that fight with the cat.

Speaking of the cat...

Randidly made a mental note to take the pelt to Sam later. That man was becoming increasingly interested in "high-quality" corpses.

His mind drifted back to his Status Screen. Although his current build made him strong now, he was slightly worried that if he attempted to keep this wide type of dabbling up, it would ultimately lead to weakness. He couldn't stay good at everything. Which brought him to the trouble of choosing what to specialize in.

Shaking his head, Randidly took a rare break, leaning back against the ground and enjoying the warmth of the sun and the calm movement of the trees. He stayed there, lying upon the ground, and simply breathed as afternoon turned to evening.

Men shouted good-naturedly around the Newbie Village. Randidly believed they were play fighting, trying to relieve stress and get a handle on the new determinative factor in their lives: Strength.

Randidly heard the steps before the body approached him, but Randidly didn't move. Chubbs sat beside him. It was easy to sense the apprehension the kid felt from the way he squirmed.

"Speak," Randidly said. Inwardly, he sighed. *Avoiding being disturbed like this is sorta why I let Donny found the Newbie Village in the first place... but I suppose I need to keep my cute little encyclopedia happy.*

"Um, I did as you requested, and asked around about—"

"Anything unexpected or interesting?" Randidly asked. "Any powerful-seeming Classes?"

Chubbs bit his lip. "Uh, well no. Donny's Class is the best, but I think Decklan's might even be better, if—"

"Anything else?" Randidly didn't really mean for his tone to come off as sharply as it did. He was coming down from the adrenaline high of the earlier fight and his finger still ached. His overworked mind needed a break, and hearing the mundane details wasn't something he wanted.

Chubbs finally said something that made Randidly willing to sit up and listen. "Actually, yes. I wanted to talk about the growth of the Newbie Village."

"Growth?" Randidly tilted his head to the side and turned toward him.

Chubbs nodded. "Yes. Nul, uh... doesn't like you. I think because you didn't get a Class from him, and I have some theories as to why that is. I also believe that 'cause of that, he has no need to be honest or forthright with you. But when I asked him things alone, he was more than happy to assist me.

"You see," Chubbs continued, "It's like a currency system. Donny, as the boss, gains points when people he gave Classes to Level up. When they kill monsters, those points can be spent on buying buildings for the Newbie Village or upgrading the village, which... I believe, is basically upgrading Nul. He's like the spirit of the village. Which is why he doesn't like you. Your strength does nothing to bring Soul Points to the village."

Randidly nodded slowly. "Buying buildings for the village?"

"Oh, yes. That's what I wanted to talk to you about. We have gathered around 500 Soul Points. That's enough to buy one of the basic shops. Weapons, Armor, Accessories, Potions, or the Marketplace. I wanted to know... well, Donny says he's going to save up for the upgrade, but I think it might be better—"

"What's your name?" Randidly asked, really taking in Chubbs for the first time. Although he was heavy for his age, he was still tall and appeared strong. His hair was light brown and his eyes were the same mild color.

He blinked at the question. "Ah... Daniel."

"Daniel, what currency would we spend at these shops?"

Daniel opened his mouth, then closed it. He got up and hurried up the hill.

Shaking his head, Randidly returned to expanding his fields and planting more food. He had a feeling that, soon, they would need it.

So many ways to improve, so many Paths forward... Randidly narrowed his eyes. *Just, which one is the right one?*

CHAPTER THIRTY-TWO

*A*s Randidly expected, the police officer returned as the sun neared the horizon. The eye-catching pillar of light remained a constant beacon, meaning it was impossible for the Newbie Village to hide. What he hadn't anticipated was the group of police officers driving over in a police van, spinning their tires and flinging pebbles as they bounced down the track to the base of the hill. They piled out of their vehicle in full SWAT gear. Randidly wondered how much protection the Kevlar gear would provide them in a System world, though it was a rather effective show of force. They strutted forward, heading once more to the main building where Donny stood, his arms crossed, looking petulant.

Randidly sat on the hill with his chin in his hand. He sighed, knowing he should be there for this, so he heaved himself off the ground and stifled his groan.

Shuffling closer, Randidly idly wondered how much Health a bullet would deplete. Probably not a large amount, especially if you had endurance to toughen up the flesh. A human started with something like 20 Health and was easily killed by bullets. It wasn't even the impact. It was the internal damage and the bleeding that usually killed someone.

That would be a debuff... So, maybe Vitality would be more useful for surviving a bullet?

Randidly checked his Health of 262 as he waited for the action to start in the area in front of the main building. *Does that mean I could have one of those action movie displays where I just soak up ten bullets before I deliver my dramatic monologue?*

Decklan lounged on one of the wooden chairs that Sam traded for a certain number of wolverine or lizard carcasses, considering the approaching police force. Based on their stature and stance, the first three or so were well trained. The rest...

Well, they were likely newly deputized. Their hands kept jumping to their guns, and their helmeted heads flicked back and forth, scanning the rather sizable crowd. He could see the tension in their bulging jaw muscles.

Decklan was extremely disappointed he missed the chance to be trained by Randidly like Donny had. He ended up distracting himself with other concerns as best as he could. He, Tera, and some of the other survivors from last night made rounds through the nearby valleys, looking for small hamlets that used to be there. Some homesteads were relatively intact, while others had been ransacked and stained with blood.

Even though he held the title of Killer, Decklan still averted his eyes from the corpses. He cursed himself for being a pansy, but his body wouldn't listen.

Sometimes they stumbled across lucky survivors, either regarding the pillar of light from the Newbie Village with suspicious eyes or cowering in their cellars. Either way, when Decklan arrived, he greeted them with a greasy smile and gave them something they hadn't had in a while—the chance for human interaction.

They managed to gather twenty-odd people during the day and about the same amount drifted in, seeking the light. At this point, pursued by monsters and harried by less scrupulous groups of survivors, even this hodge-podge gathering was the sweetest refuge most could wish for.

What was most pleasing, their group now numbered eight women, not including Tera. More disappointing was the fact that none were as young and fresh as Tera looked. Except for one who arrived firmly under the arm of a rather imposing and brutish individual who called himself Dozer.

Dozer was built like a linebacker and had a forehead that could crack granite. Decklan became even more annoyed when he obtained the Class "Brute." It apparently gave +2 Str per Level, +1 free Stats, and +4 Health/Mana/Stamina.

The flat Strength bonus was a lot less useful than Donny's split among three stats. Still, though Dozer might not grow to be able to endure very many attacks, he'd hit hard. And his quiet intensity had quickly found a place amongst the other fighters who chose to take a Class under Donny.

The police approached. Decklan, Dozer, and about a dozen others remained lazy in their seats on the logs and stumps they'd dragged on top of the hill. Fresh off their first few Levels of their new Classes, the group stunk of sweat and confidence, their feet up on a trunk obtained from one of the liberated houses in the surrounding valleys.

And there, at the center, with his palms across his belly, was Dozer.

Decklan and the other survivors hadn't joined in the sparring of the new arrivals, but Dozer had. Decklan had no doubt he put everything he could into Strength, what with the way he'd thrown another man like a rag doll, taking his cushioned armchair as "spoils." He joined Decklan's circle, his raven-haired female friend under his arm.

For now, Dozer didn't try to make a claim on Decklan's position of head honcho. If anything, that only made Decklan more wary. It showed his massive forehead wasn't just all muscle.

Despite the lurking threat of Dozer, Decklan was rather pleased by the other new arrivals. One of the newer individuals, a thin man with glasses, revealed himself to have the Class, Disciple. He possessed the Skill Healing Palm, which mended the wound and ensured a recovery that should take weeks would only take hours.

That man, Ptolemy, also sat in the circle of chairs, albeit nervously.

One of the newcomers shifted uneasily when the police stopped in front of Donny. He stood alone by the Village Chieftain's House.

"Think, uh… think we should… go help?" Ptolemy asked.

"They have guns. Just sit down; it'll sort itself out," another hissed.

Decklan chuckled and leaned back in his chair. "It's fine. Nothing will happen as long as the Ghosthound is watching."

The four individuals who had taken Classes to fight nodded fervently. They had firsthand experience in witnessing that man's strength. That kind of power had shaken them enough to forget about their fear toward monsters.

Dozer grunted and tilted his head.

"Who is the Ghosthound?" the girl under his arm asked, her voice slightly petulant, batting her lashes coyly at the surrounding men.

Closing his eyes, Decklan ignored the question. The talking ceased as the head police officer removed his helmet, revealing his dark skin and serious face. The men behind him stiffened, preparing to support their superior.

I almost hope this comes to blows. Decklan felt his lips twitch. *Ghosthound… would you kill another person, I wonder?*

Because if the Ghosthound could do it, so could Decklan.

The head police officer's voice was serious. "Kid, I'm only going to ask you once—"

"And I'm going to say this, *only once*," Donny interrupted, his nasally voice betraying his age. Yet the intensity in Donny's eyes was much more forceful than Decklan expected. "If you refuse to come under my flag, why should I help you? The more people who take Classes from here, the more monsters assault us every night. I can't just give them out freely."

The group around Decklan muttered, shocked by the news. Decklan noticed Dozer open his mouth in a tiny little toothy-smile. To Decklan's surprise, Donny continued to speak, wiping away any positive goodwill he'd built for his calm demeanor.

"We could barely make it through last night alive! It's too much of a risk to allow more people to get Classes."

"The answer is simple," the policeman responded. "Move into the city. We've set up a defensive perimeter. The monsters will be easily slaughtered with the weapons we have prepared."

Donny was already shaking his head. "The village itself needs to be defended. If the monsters make it to the center and destroy it, it becomes—"

The head police officer gestured impatiently. "Then we'll give you that protection. Police officers will be stationed out here. You may have Classes, but we have *guns*. Why are you being so stubborn? We are trying to help."

Donny stared him down. "You may have guns, but you are not strong. If you were, you would just kill a blue monster yourself and obtain a coin to found your own Newbie Village. Do you think you can hide and still benefit from those of us who risk our lives?"

"You fucking little—" The head policeman stepped forward, but his instincts stopped him dead.

"I think Donny's made his point clear. We aren't willing to take on the risks of being attacked by more monsters, just due to your assurances."

The voice was mild, but even Decklan felt his skin prickle when he looked at the Ghosthound, who suddenly appeared between Donny and the police officer. The Ghosthound casually leaned against his spear.

While the lead officer took a hasty step backward, his subordinates were whispering to each other. Decklan was able to make out one whisper in particular that made him smirk. "Is that the power of a Class?"

No, it isn't. Donny says the Ghosthound hasn't gotten a Class yet. Decklan licked his lips, rubbing the leather hilt of the weapon the Ghosthound gave him. *You've fought a few monsters, and you think you know what—*

The image of the Ghosthound releasing an Arcane Orb and blasting wolverines to pieces flashed in Decklan's mind. Pulped limbs had tumbled through the air, bouncing off the surrounding ground. Decklan pressed his lips together, suppressing an urge to be sick.

Even worse, Dozer noticed Decklan's strange reaction. He pinched himself to suppress his nausea and did his best to lazily wave his hand. "That... is the Ghosthound."

Dozer frowned and squinted at the figure. Decklan admitted he wasn't anything much. Tall, but not too tall. Athletic, but in a wiry way, with the long arms of a swimmer. Short, dark hair. Cold eyes the color of sunlight on grass; a vivid, warm green that strangely filled you with a deep fear.

His trademark spear was impeccably clean. Decklan's memories, however, were still fresh enough to cake the Ghosthound's entire person in blood and gore. He wore tan shorts and a brown shirt, with a satchel over his shoulder. His feet were bare and dirty, and it looked like he'd been bleeding, because his left shoulder was stained red.

"You..." The policeman hesitated over his words, eyeing the figure in front of him.

Decklan could practically feel the man's desire to force the point, struggling against his instinctual reaction to back down. The fact that he was trying so hard was honestly amusing.

"There is another option, of course," the Ghosthound said, flourishing his hand and producing a golden coin.

Most of the watcher's eyes went wide as saucers.

"I was worried you'd complain, so I brought insurance. There should be four blue bosses in the area that produce these. I've taken the goblin and the wolverines. The imps possess magic, and you are too fearful of the lizard's underground dens to challenge them, right? You were at a loss, so here, don't bother us again."

The police officer's face tightened. His reaction to the Ghosthound's dismissive words conflicted with his desire to obtain the coin. Randidly tilted his head to the side, looking at the police officers each in turn.

All looked away before he finally spoke. "You can have it. All I want in exchange is glassware."

"Glassware?" the head policeman repeated in a disbelieving tone. Randidly nodded.

"Beakers, vials, jars... That sort of thing. Anything glass and sealable. Plastic will not work. Deal?" The Ghosthound flicked the golden coin up in the air. There was still enough sun in the evening air to make it glitter before he snatched it.

The police officer stood still, towering a good five inches above Randidly. Decklan had watched people all his life. It was the officer who stank of fear. The Ghosthound waited, toying with the coin.

"What is your name?" the policeman finally asked.

"Ghosthound."

The word was soft, but Decklan felt himself and several others silently mimic the word, feeling it out with their mouth, echoing it so it hit the police officer again in a soundless wave.

Ghosthound. The hand Decklan had on his dagger tightened. He'd been referring to this man that way for a while. But this time, Decklan heard something new when the man himself said it. That name was an identity. Primal and ferocious.

The name was impossibly strange. Yet the cadence of Randidly Ghosthound's voice made the listeners shiver.

The head policeman sighed. "Fine, Ghosthound, you have a deal."

And with that, Randidly flipped the coin to the officer and walked away, heading toward Donny. After an unwilling few seconds, while the police officer struggled over the fact that he'd clearly been dismissed, he turned and walked away, the rest of his group following.

Decklan watched it all with sparkling eyes. Humans were complex and simple at the same time.

They had a thousand motivations. A thousand justifications. A thousand reasons. They either struggled and fought for all of them or none at all.

Sometimes, it only took one powerful ideal, one object, one symbol, for the complexity to fall into line. Everything else was swept away by the force of that one thing. It didn't seem likely anyone in the village would act out too much, especially with this powerful figure lurking in the shadows.

Decklan found his lips moving again, almost against his will.

Ghosthound.

CHAPTER THIRTY-THREE

*R*andidly approached Donny, annoyed he was forced to deal with the cop. Ultimately, he was glad the tension in the situation was solved by giving away the golden coin. He was slightly worried if the town would honor the deal and bring him glassware. If they dragged their feet, he could just start actively taking it and they wouldn't be able to say anything about it.

Mostly, Randidly wished the System included some Skills that helped with interpersonal Skills. At this point, it was halfway between something he didn't want to deal with and something he didn't know *how* to deal with. He'd been a quiet gamer before the System came. Struggling through his classes at Rawlands University with the realization that he wanted to break up with his girlfriend and run away hanging over him. He wanted to leave his life behind. In that tunnel, right before everything changed, he was certain he didn't belong there.

And now, thinking about that sense of addictive anticipation before toeing the line between life and death against a powerful foe... Randidly sighed and looked down at his hands. *Is this the sort of person I want to be?*

He quickly cut off that train of thought. Once he possessed all those containers, he could really up his potion production. Such a feat would benefit the whole village. If nothing else, Randidly was quite sure the soothing and pseudo-scientific arrangement and measurement of potions was an activity that brought him joy.

For now, Randidly went to speak with Donny. The Village Chieftain still glared after the police, mildly listening to Daniel rattle on. Awkwardly rubbing his neck, Randidly approached. After today, he was done interacting with people.

After a short discussion, Randidly believed he made himself clear.

The first building they would buy was the Recycler building. With it, they could purchase certain parts from the corpses of monsters in exchange for currency they could spend at other shops. It was the best starting point, because his walking, talking encyclopedia confirmed that Nul refused to explain where currency for the shops could be obtained.

Another trap. One that doesn't even teach a very valuable lesson, Randidly thought bitterly. *Unless the lesson is just how little the System cares about us.*

Plus, the Recycler would provide some sense of accomplishment while they accumulated more points for the Newbie Village. The building would create excitement for the eventual shops to come and give the people an immediate goal, keeping them satisfied.

These justifications were Daniel's, and Randidly agreed. In fact, he agreed so much, he directed Donny to concentrate solely on leadership, leaving Daniel to make the bland decisions about construction. Donny was only too happy to step aside, which filled Randidly with a desire to take him out for a "training session" again. In the end, Randidly supposed the fact that he hadn't folded before the police officer was a sufficient outcome, for the moment.

Besides, Donny seemed more concerned with recounting his heroic stand against the police.

The final order of business Daniel wished to discuss was food. Specifically, they had meat, but were any of Randidly's crops able to be eaten?

Annoyed, Randidly dumped most of his first haul from the farm land onto the ground, specifically, the non-Potion-Making items, and returned to his fields to recover. Somehow, handling the administrative and social tasks exhausted him more thoroughly than the ambush from the Shadow Cat.

Randidly gave himself ten minutes to simply exist. The cool dusk breezes and the smell of the dirt grounded him. Just as he calmed himself and settled into a spot next to his field to train, he noticed the corpse of the cat he killed in the cracked plateau lying against his cabin. He groaned, knowing there was one more discussion to be had before he could focus on training.

Maybe for someone else I would wait, but Sam… Sam at least is reasonable. Of all the people here, him I can trust.

Grumbling to himself anyway, he walked over toward Sam's campsite, the cat lying across his shoulders. He thought about the three crouching bodies as he neared, who he assumed were Sam's daughters. Unbidden, the words the teenager had spoken in regard to his Mana Skills rose to his mind.

It looked like fireworks.

Randidly studied his hands. He felt a strange sense of loss, thinking about those words. He never even stopped to consider the beauty of his magic while he had been in the Dungeon, just its utility. He came into this world with the System an inch away from death. It was hard to see these Skills as anything but tools of survival, and survival meant killing others for strength.

But they can be beautiful too... Randidly's expression was wistful, until a bit of Shal's sternness crept into his expression.

His strength remained insufficient to spend too much time daydreaming about how his Skills appeared. Outside of the Safe Zone, he had once more been only an inch from death. This small cat was enough to force him to go all out.

Sydney... Ace... I'm coming as fast as I can.

Randidly's hands tightened into fists. It was hard to realistically think he could find them before, knowing they were forced into situations where they could die. Adventuring to other low-Level areas would mean venturing through the den of those cats. And without Randidly here, this group probably wouldn't be able to defend the village for several days, even from other people, setting aside the waves of monsters.

In the end, Randidly being here warped the development of the area. That knowledge weighed heavily on his mind. Without him, the police would likely have made a concerted effort to hunt down the goblins at some point. It would have been a slow process while they acclimated to the System.

Thinking about what would have been made Randidly's heart tighten in what probably *was* concern to Sydney and Ace. If they were out there now, without Classes... There was no way to find them in the huge area of the map. In a way, that couldn't be solved by training or preparation. Randidly felt helpless.

It was better to operate on the assumption that they would survive. Both were strong. Far stronger than Randidly had been, prior to his experience in the Dungeon. They would live.

The logical conclusion was they would group up with people to survive. His best bet would be to find other Newbie Villages, looking for rumors of them.

Randidly stopped.

Honestly, he hadn't even thought to ask around here, or in the area the policeman controlled. They might even be there.

Feeling a small flame of hope for the first time in a while, Randidly crossed into the area of Sam's fire. As he did, a glowing blue butterfly floated up toward him.

Instinct took over and Randidly's spear appeared in his hand, a Phantom Thrust ripping through the unfamiliar thing. The butterfly dispersed into glimmering motes of light.

"Told you it was a bad idea." Sam stood over the fire, slowly rotating wolverine meat above the flames. Next to him stood two figures. To Randidly's surprise, neither were cloaked nor hooded. Instead, they wore strange dresses made from stitched together wolverine pelts.

"How was I supposed to know he'd freak out and attack it? What was up with that anyway?" The smaller figure spoke, tilting her head to the side, regarding Randidly with an intense stare.

She had medium-length blonde hair pulled into a ponytail. Her cheekbones were sharp and her lips were expressive. She was quite cute. To Randidly, it seemed like she was the same figure who spoke to him last night. And as Randidly suspected, she was young. Younger than he expected.

More intriguing than her prettiness was that it seemed like *she* created that strange butterfly. Randidly frowned. *Was it a construct of Mana? But why? Maybe some sort of scouting Skill...*

Randidly put his spear away, regarding the girl thoughtfully. She was starting to glare at him. Sam looked up from the meat, also regarding Randidly coolly.

Randidly opened his mouth to speak. "What sort of Skill was that?"

"Like what you see?" The second figure spoke tartly just as he finished, and then froze, hearing Randidly's words.

Randidly turned to regard the second woman, who stood six inches taller than the first, almost as tall as Randidly himself. Full-figured, with golden skin like honey, this woman was also inordinately beautiful. Her heart-shaped face was of the style that modern culture found most attractive, whereas the other girl's features were too sharp and impish. Even as she blushed after her words, she looked incredibly attractive.

An awkward silence stretched. The taller woman kept her gaze to the ground, clearly wanting to pretend she hadn't said anything. The younger girl snorted and rolled her eyes.

Turning to Sam, Randidly forced himself to speak. The best way he found to deal with beautiful women was to essentially pretend they weren't beautiful and weren't there. "I assume you made these clothes to ugly them up a bit? Really great effort. I can sorta see why you were... hesitant to let them just walk around."

Sam gave Randidly a wry smile. "That's my job. Even if... well. Even if things have changed."

Randidly turned back toward the younger girl. Compared to the heart-pounding woman next to her, she was much easier to deal with. "What was that Skill?"

"Oh, this?" she said shyly, raising her hand and producing a glowing orb. It instantly sputtered and disappeared, and she shook her head in annoyance. "Fuck-shit, out of Mana. It's called Mana Manipulation. I can basically do anything if I have enough Mana. Make any shape I want. Although only small stuff right now. Cool, right?"

Mana Manipulation? Is Mana something that is really that easy to manipulate? Randidly frowned. He basically just focused on the Skill and the Mana would follow his Willpower. His whole experience working with the cool energy was one of trial and error. He couldn't tell without looking at his Status where his Mana was at. There was no sensation of loss, just a weird sensation of inward movement. Even when his Mana pool was empty, he didn't really feel it, just noticed based on the ease of Skill use.

Setting that information aside for now, Randidly nodded and placed the cat at Sam's feet. He was weirdly aware of how awkward his body was. He couldn't remember the last time he took a bath. "You've been working on making clothes, right? Make me something with this. It should be a much higher quality than the wolverines. The fur is soft too."

Sam grunted. "Alright, I'll work on it tomorrow. For now, did you bring any food? You don't eat for free around here."

Helpless, Randidly promised he would bring a portion of his farmed fruits and nuts, making a mental note of establishing a fourth field. With how the population was growing, they would definitely need it.

Randidly allowed himself a single glance toward the tall and gorgeous woman before leaving. When he was out of sight of Sam's campfire, he picked up speed, rushing toward a nearby stream.

He was all too aware of how his clothes were covered in brown stains of various shades. Far too many days of mixed blood and sweat.

CHAPTER THIRTY-FOUR

$\mathcal{W}$hen Randidly returned, Sam asked if he would like to stay and eat with them. Considering the set of Sam's mouth, Randidly sensed this was a show of trust. And because he definitely felt Sam was one of the few people around the Newbie Village he could rely on, he accepted the invitation.

"This is Lyra," Sam said, gesturing to the blonde girl who was ripping chunks off her meat. She flicked her hand dismissively and continued to eat. Still, Randidly's Perception was high enough to catch that the girl peered intently at him while she thought he wasn't looking.

Sam pointed to the other woman, the luminous one who Randidly, in turn, was very careful not to stare at. "That's Ellaine. The other two... won't join us tonight. We were traveling together when the System came online. I hit a wolverine and got the Skill Driving Level 1. I knew something had changed and we... well... we were lucky to be away from the city."

Ellaine voraciously ripped through Randidly's fruits, glad to eat something aside from meat. Juice dripped over her lips, catching the firelight.

Besides that, the meal was relatively quiet, all three of them giving Randidly strange glances. He ignored it as best he could, preferring to wait for them to say what they were thinking. But considering their complexions, it didn't seem like they were Sam's daughters. Then who were they?

Randidly allowed himself another, singular glance. *Who is Ellaine to Sam?*

After the meal, Sam gestured him over to talk about equipment. They walked behind the truck to an area where several small wooden tables had been erected. It was almost a relief to be away from the women. Various garments made of wolverine pelts were strewn across the tables. Most of them appeared to be shoulder pads.

"It's surprisingly difficult to make armor from the body parts of these creatures. Part of it is the difficulty in manipulating the fur and scales, but the other part is my own body. I need points in Strength just to handle it. I've worked out a pretty good system for making them, and made a few discoveries…"

"Before that, try using this to cut the wolverine pelts." Randidly grabbed the paw of the cat he was carrying and held it up. He pulled, ripping out one of the claws. After brushing off the gore-covered tendon, he offered it to Sam.

Sam took it with a frown. He pressed the claw against one of the shoulder pads. It passed through it like it was nothing. He raised the claw up and squinted at it.

"Higher quality, eh," Sam grunted, shaking his head. "Higher Level, I suppose. Well, thank you. Anyway, I made some discoveries. Apparently, there's more value to making equipment than just having more padding. Take a look at this."

Randidly took the shoulder pad and examined it. His eyebrows rose.

Poorly Made Shoulder Pad Level 11: *An amateur's work.* **+2 Health.**

So, we can make equipment that can actually give Attributes, and possibly Stats, huh. But considering how high the Level is, +2 Health is pretty bad. Much worse than even a single Vitality.

"I did some experiments. The System definitely has some sort of criteria for grading the equipment. The relative damage to the materials determines the Level, even if my own workmanship is what affects the bonuses. I've made equipment for myself and the clothes for the girls. But of all of us, only I've received the Proper Utilization Skill. Despite the fact that we've basically worn the same stuff. Do you know what that means?"

For the first time ever, there was a hint of excitement in Sam's voice. "It means we influence what we can and can't learn! Simply by our beliefs and the way we think about the scope of our actions when we do something."

Randidly nodded slowly. That certainly made sense. "That Skill of Lyra's, Mana Manipulation, I've thought about it a bit, and I don't know if I could learn it. I've thought of this like a game, an RPG. You learn Skills and use Mana to cast them, that's it. I can't sense Mana like she appears able to. Just finding her own understanding made her discover her own Skill. Makes you wonder about the usefulness of trying to help others at all, when their perspective will open unique Skills."

"Exactly. Which is why I think we should keep the information we share with each other general, if we do it at all," Sam said. "I have an idea for what

I want to do. For how I want to grow before I accept a Class. And if it works out—"

A woman's hiss and hurried footsteps interrupted their discussion. All the excitement disappeared from Sam and he sprang into motion, rushing back toward the fire. Randidly followed closely, his eyes narrowing. They found a nervous-looking Daniel staring at the two women.

Luckily, it looked like they had gotten their hoods up in time, because Daniel turned back to Randidly rather quickly.

"Ghosthound! There's been... a-ahem. Sorry for disturbing everyone. We unlocked... Well, follow me, I'll show you."

The Killer, Decklan, stood smugly in the middle of a circle of people when Randidly approached. His eyes flitted across the surrounding men, almost fifty of them. More had shown up at the pillar of light after dark. Their group had really grown today. They all parted as he approached, finding Donny standing with Decklan and a mean, muscular man with dull, expressionless eyes.

"What's all this for?" Randidly asked. His skin prickled. If he had to fight them all, even he would have some difficulties. The limits of his Mana and Stamina would eventually drag him down.

Strangely, the thought excited him.

Nul stepped forward with a happy expression. "Finally, one of the villagers has reached Level 10. As such, I can now provide a new function for the Newbie Village and... other guests," he said with a distasteful look at Randidly.

At least he was willing to talk to Randidly. Having people here, getting Classes and Leveling, must put him in a good mood. Nul clearly valued the growth of the group too, even if he didn't care much if most people died or not.

"Players may use me to transport themselves into far off parts of the Nexus, competing in what are called Skill challenges. The Prizes are self-evident: Skills."

Randidly straightened, his eyes narrowing at Nul. After his conversation with Sam, there was something about this that made him wary. "We can learn Skills from you?"

Nul nodded with an enigmatic smile on his pale face. "But of course. However, my usefulness depends on how many Skill slots your Class provides. In that way, production-focused Classes have a definite edge. Often they have double-digit slots available. In addition, your options are limited by what Tier you are in."

"Tiers?" Daniel practically salivated at the thought.

"Yes," Nul continued. "No doubt you have noticed there are certain 'main' Paths that unlock naturally, based on total Stat value. For example, you start with Newbie Path and Trainee Path unlocks at 100. Apprentice is 400, Journeyman 750. Although the Skill challenges provide a wide breadth of Skills, they won't give anyone a Skill more powerful than your Tier suggests you are."

Nul made a strange gesture with his hand and a notification appeared before Randidly. From the way everyone was suddenly staring intensely at the air in front of them, it must be a mass notification. Randidly casually opened the Skill Challenge Menu.

Newbie: *Running 5 SP | Jumping 5 SP | Dodging 5 SP*
Trainee: *Slash 10 SP | Endure 10 SP | Roundhouse Kick 10 SP | Sneak 10 SP | Magic Missile 15 SP | Healing Palm 25 SP*
Apprentice (Locked): *????*

Quite interesting that the Skill here is Dodging when I have Dodge... Randidly tapped his chin. *Seeing these options will hem in people's ideas for what Skills can be, but also earning Skills can easily benefit us. The earlier we get the Skills, the quicker they can start growing.*

Randidly did some quick math. His current total Stats were 358, not including items, which Randidly suspected did not count toward the Tier. That meant he needed less than 50 to unlock the Apprentice Path.

Of the available Skills, some Randidly already had. Others, like Jumping, Slash, and Endure, seemed like they would be easy for some Levels, but he ultimately wouldn't use them. On the other hand, Roundhouse Kick, Magic Missile, and Healing Palm intrigued him. The first for some variance in his fighting style, the second for another Mana Skill to add to his repertoire, and the third for the utility it could bring. Should he ever be injured while exploring the area beyond the Level barrier, Healing Palm would certainly come in handy.

"How do you get SP?" Randidly asked, turning to Nul.

Nul's lips pursed in distaste. "Normally, you would earn it passively by gaining Levels and killing a certain number of enemies. You... well, you are a special case. You will need to trade in especially rare items in order to gather it."

"Will this suffice?" Randidly produced a third gold coin, taken by killing the Rare Boss of the lizards. Nul's eyes widened and he nodded, happily accepting it.

"Yes! This is good for 500 SP."

Randidly's eyes narrowed at the amount, but he didn't ask for the coin back. If Nul was so willing to part with SP, it was probably a treasure. For the Classless Randidly, these Skills were incredibly valuable.

Still, Randidly knew nothing about the System. It was hard to gauge the item's value. However, the smug grin on Nul's face did not sit well in Randidly's stomach. It basically gave him all the answers about the coin's value he needed.

"How does it work?" Daniel inquired.

Most of the other nearby people turned away, uninterested or currently unable to afford it. After all, although the Skills would give them variety, they would take up a valuable Skill spot. As their Class advanced, they would naturally unlock Paths relating to that Class, giving them Skills. As such, this was a cost they weren't willing to pay.

"Simple, just select the Skill and the trial begins. Time will flow differently there, so if you pass, others will think it took you but a moment. Of course, if you fail..." Nul snorted, giving Randidly a glance.

Randidly flashed him a grim smile and selected the Roundhouse Kick Skill.

CHAPTER THIRTY-FIVE

$\mathcal{T}$he world around Randidly warped as he found himself in an archaic stone room lit by torches. A notification hovered in front of him.

Defeat the Guardian and gain power! But be careful, it will not be easy to overcome this foe.

A figure in dark armor stood in front of Randidly, regarding him with indifference. His eyes glowed with a soft yellow light between the slit of his helmet. Randidly dismissed the notification and the figure exploded into motion, rushing toward him.

Or at least the figure "exploded" as much as he could with his obviously low Stats. Randidly stepped to the side, avoided the Roundhouse Kick the figure aimed at him, and lashed out, his hand slashing the opponent's throat.

When the blow landed, the dark figure shattered, turning into a black mist that flowed into Randidly's body.

Congratulations! You have learned the Skill **Roundhouse Kick Level 1.**

Congratulations! For being the first individual to unlock a Skill, you may attempt to unlock the **Special Tier Fireball Skill!**

And just like that, Randidly found himself back in the dark clearing, the group of people still dispersing. Daniel was giving him an uneasy look.

"Perhaps you should go first," he said, his brown eyes nervous. "If there is any danger... y-you're the one who can definitely survive."

Randidly snorted and resisted the urge to roll his eyes. "I've already returned from the Roundhouse Kick challenge. If you are prepared and have at least 10 in Strength and Agility, the Trainee challenges shouldn't pose a serious problem to anyone here."

To demonstrate, Randidly performed a slow and controlled Roundhouse Kick. He accelerated and released a few more, enjoying the explosive power flowing through his legs. He might need to increase his flexibility a bit to use this effectively, but otherwise, the Skill seemed incredibly useful.

Congratulations! Your Skill **Roundhouse Kick** has grown to **Level 2!**

Costs a decent amount of Stamina, though not so much I won't be able to release a few in quick succession without exhausting myself. Randidly thought in satisfaction. He looked around. Most of the group that had been leaving were now heading back. Apparently, the power he demonstrated tempted them.

Randidly sighed inwardly, not saying anything. Even if the Skill Level was low, his Agility of 49 was likely a higher Level than any present here were used to. They obviously hadn't seen Shal's casual grace, or the vicious speed of the orcs. Even the cat beyond the Safe Zone was an impossibly powerful existence for them.

Randidly wondered if it really was possible for Sydney and Ace to still be alive. Maybe, if they were at this Level of Strength... He quieted that thought and turned back to Nul.

After obtaining both the Magic Missile and Healing Palm Skills, earning the Fireball Skill from the unlocked Special Tier, and raising all three to Level 2, Randidly decided to take a quick nap before the monsters came.

The Fireball Skill produced a ball of flame that exploded on contact. Although the explosion was currently small, the heat was already impressive. Randidly was curious how much more powerful the explosion would get when the Skill Levels and Intelligence accumulated.

Magic Missile cost the same amount as Mana Bolt. It was slightly weaker, but the dart-like missiles could be controlled somewhat even after being fired, causing them to avoid shields, defenses, or terrain, and home in on the enemy.

Even though Randidly wanted to train these useful Skills, he firmly chose to nap. His time in the Dungeon taught him to make preparations as soon as possible, in case a Deadly Webspinner suddenly moved into the area. If the enemies would come at the same time as the previous day, they wouldn't come for six or so more hours anyway, which would give him time to rest.

Although it was clear Randidly didn't require nearly as much sleep as an average person, there was undoubtedly a limit to that. While he planned on once more going beyond the edge of the Safe Zone tomorrow, he didn't want to be forced to stay in his cabin during the daylight.

So he slept.

When he awoke, it was to a long, slow stretch and a familiar sensation of danger. Worried voices of the people of the Newbie Village reached him even from there. The monster horde was gathering in the hills above the valley. Randidly moved smoothly from his cabin, drawing his spear. Activating Eyes of the Spear Phantom, he scanned the edges of the tree line.

His frown deepened. Although he expected it, it was still somewhat intimidating to feel the movements of almost five hundred enemies beyond his vision. And the enemies were still gathering. Randidly spared a glance for the forces of the village.

Sam had been busy since the sun went down. It looked like he had help, because they managed to set up a fence around the entirety of the village, and had even dug a trench outside that. There was a wide gate area, but the rest would serve as a way to funnel the enemies into a single location, where they could be slaughtered.

Or at least that seemed to be the plan.

Turning away, Randidly sat and filled his empty potion vials, making as concentrated a Mana potion as he could. His greatest success was a potion that would restore 91 Mana, but he crafted several others with a restore of 80 at a time.

Congratulations! Your Skill **Potion Making** has grown to **Level 20!**

The movements of grinding the crystals and mixing it with water woke up his body, while the easy focus gradually warmed up his mind. By the time he finished, he felt refreshed and prepared for a fight.

Not today, because he wanted to go out beyond the boundary, but tomorrow. Randidly made a mental note to visit the village of the policeman and make sure he held up his end of the bargain, providing glassware to hold more potions. With those, Randidly could afford to be freer with his Mana Skills, making hordes of low-Leveled enemies like this a walking target.

Rising with glittering eyes, Randidly smiled toward the darkness.

Well, I should leave some alive anyway to fight me in close proximity. Otherwise, there isn't any tension to the experience, and without tension, it's hard to feel like I'm growing at all...

It's the after... Randidly went to rub his eyes but stopped himself at the sight of how caked with blood his knuckles were. He slowly lowered his arms and sighed. *Once the rush of accomplishment is gone, and the battle is over...*

What the hell am I doing here?

As the sun dawned, Randidly surveyed the battlefield with a bleak expression. The salvageable meat was being piled up by a few exhausted men while the rest were tossed onto a crackling bonfire. The air smelled of burnt hair and blood. They survived, which was a victory.

Except today didn't feel like a victory.

The fence bought the villagers time during the beginning of the fight, but the sheer number of monsters eventually pushed the fragile structure backward, reducing it to less than useless as it fell back on the villagers, hampering them. The desperate fighters of Donny's Newbie Village became swamped on all sides.

Surprisingly, they didn't break under all that pressure. Donny's Skills made him a great force for locking down large numbers, focusing their attention on his durable shield. Decklan came and went freely, wolverines, goblins, and lizards falling to the side, dead. Dozer wielded a huge club, smashing at least two or three enemies with every strike.

Randidly started the fight against the monsters by taking it to them, throwing Arcane Orbs and drinking Mana potions like they were water, rocking the seemingly endless enemy lines. Of the five hundred strong sea of snarling wolverines and hissing goblins, only two hundred made it past him to assault the village. That was still two hundred enemies rushing against fifty, with forty of those fifty freshly acquainted with their Class, and barely able to handle a single monster.

Casualties were initially prevented by Daniel bringing around Health potions Randidly provided and buoyed by a slight man named Ptolemy who gained the Healing Palm Skill naturally from his Class.

Randidly had paused his own slaughter when the wooden wall collapsed, initially planning on rushing back. When they initially held, he thought they would be fine and moved to clean up the remnants on his side of the battlefield.

But then something happened to the defenders, or at least most of them. They ran out of Stamina.

Most had followed in either Decklan's or Dozer's paths, focusing on Strength or Agility. Very few chose to invest a heavy amount of their points into Vitality or Endurance, resulting in a steep drop-off in their Skill usage after only a few minutes of hectic battle. Although they would only need about two minutes to fully recover their Stamina, there was no time for that with a wolverine slashing at your throat.

All in all, thirteen people died. The total number of individuals with

Classes now sat at forty-one. They recovered as many pieces of the corpses as they could to bury them, but the process wasn't pretty.

If I hadn't founded the Newbie Village so soon in my excitement to learn about Classes... if I had made sure they understood how horrifying the limitations of Stamina are... Randidly clenched his jaw so hard, his cheeks began to twitch. *These are lessons I learned with my body. This happened because I'm just...*

His heart fluttered, remembering Shal telling him it was best that he follow him no longer. He was a burden.

Randidly brought his spinning mind back under control and raised his head. With the sun at his back, Randidly forced himself to stand. He was stronger than any person here. He alone trained in the Dungeon with Shal. He used that strength to make something convenient for him, where he didn't need to be in charge. And his refusal to play a more active presence had directly allowed these deaths to happen.

I can be more than a burden.

With heavy footsteps, Randidly dragged himself down toward the Newbie Village. Most everyone was sitting, trying to steady their stomachs and ignore the smell of burning flesh.

The exhausted individuals soon noticed him standing before them, his own body covered in blood and grime. Randidly forced himself to keep his head held high.

"I'm sure you all noticed it," Randidly said, speaking softly. His heart was pounding, especially now that most of the people with Classes were looking up at him. "The limits of what you can do without a true tank. The limits of what you can do when you specialize without considering how everyone else is specializing. What you do is your business, but you need to be strong enough to defend the village. We need to work together."

Inwardly, something clicked, and the ghost of Shal inside of him smiled cruelly. Randidly forced himself to show that same smile he'd become so accustomed to witnessing. "I will not be present for tomorrow's horde. I hope you manage to survive in my absence."

Donny's face twisted in horror and several people gasped. Everywhere he looked, shock and worry consumed most faces. Randidly shrugged, turning away.

As he departed, he spoke once more over his shoulder. "Perhaps you should consider forming divisions, underneath Donny, Decklan, and Dozer. Specialize, but cover all your bases. And become familiar with fighting together. If you don't have sufficient individual strength, at least come up with a plan. Good luck."

Randidly knew this seemed like an impossible challenge to them, but a day's worth of Leveling, especially with some points going into Vitality or

Endurance, could do a lot. Without this prodding, they might grow too reliant on him, leaving them useless in the future.

And better than anyone else, he knew how much the desperate desire to survive would push them.

CHAPTER THIRTY-SIX

hat the hell am I doing?

Randidly sat by a creek, staring at his reflection. He could only shake his head at his previous behavior. One second he'd been racked with guilt for putting the people of this Newbie Village in this situation. From activating the Newbie Village too early before they had developed their base Skills and understandings of Paths, just to satisfy his own curiosity about Classes.

Then he panicked, attempting to solve the situation by telling them he was abandoning them?

If I really walk away, I'm not any better than my—Randidly pressed his eyes closed. He sucked in a breath and tried to change his train of thought. *If I don't follow through, they will be even more reliant on me. And if I don't follow through... Will they take me seriously in the future?*

Fuck. Fuck, fuck, fuck! Randidly stuck his face in the creek. The cool water did little to address the raging flames of embarrassment he felt. When it came to social interactions, pre- and post-System, Randidly Ghosthound was inept.

He threw the eventual decision of what to do about this thorny problem to a future version of himself. Instead, he inspected his Path screen. Randidly did his best to enjoy the sense of accomplishment for the night's haul, squashing the images of the human lives he paid to earn it.

Dodge, Fighting Proficiency, Spear Phantom's Footwork, and Haste all improved by 1 Level. In addition, Arcane Orb, Empower, and Sweep had grown by 2 Skill Levels. The biggest gains were in Roundhouse Kick, Healing Palm, and Calculated Blow, which improved by 4, 3, and a staggering 7 Levels, respectively.

Apparently, killing large amounts of low-Leveled opponents did a lot for Calculated Blow. As it was currently, it was almost effortless for Randidly to see through the weaknesses of the four different types of enemies that populated the area.

The Skill Level gains were enough for Randidly to finish off Monster Slayer V.

Congratulations! You have completed the **"Monster Slayer V Path"!** **+5 free Stat(s), +1 to Health Regen, Mana Regen, and Stamina Regen.**

Sometimes the path forward leads through blood and gore, and sometimes the path is long. But you cannot hesitate. Continue forward, carving your way through the flesh of your enemies.

Such a bloody image, but I suppose it's not wrong. Randidly shook his head, convincing himself it wasn't a shiver.

The completion of the Path left Randidly with several choices. He unlocked the Monster Slayer Path, which would take 100 PP, and he still had the Watcher Path. Even more interesting was the Potion Making I Path he earned after getting the Potion Making Skill to Level 20. It cost 25 PP. Though the low cost was tempting, it was the real possibility that a Skill related to Potion Making lying at the end of the Path that piqued Randidly's attention.

Farming is fulfilling, but too passive. At least when I measure and grind the different crystals, my mind feels clear.

Ultimately, the lure of that Skill was too great, and Randidly chose to pour his remaining 14 PP into Potion Making I. As he did, he was delighted to find that after putting 5 in, he got a point in Focus, and 10 gave him a Stat in Control. It was a pleasant surprise after the Monster Slayer Paths that only gave a completion bonus.

After Randidly put the 12 of his 14 PP into Potion Making I Path, something else happened that gave him pause.

Congratulations! Your Soul Path **Green Spear Mastery** has finally reached **Level 250.**

You have followed this Path for a long time, yet now it forks. On your left lies the Waning Rafflesia, and on your right lies the Blooming Hydrangea. You may only select a single option. The choice will affect the future development of your Soulskill. Please choose which side you wish to walk.

Randidly wasn't overly familiar with flowers, but he understood Waning and Blooming as adjectives. He briefly considered consulting Sam on what exactly the central flowers looked like, though he believed that didn't seem very important. Randidly also remembered the talk he had with Sam about the way ideas shaped the Skills they earned.

Randidly went with his gut.

His gut, and the scent of death he was having an increasingly difficult time enduring. It was not an easy and fun path he walked.

"Waning Rafflesia," Randidly said to the air.

The other Path seemed to encompass the softer sides of plants, focusing on aspects of growth and healing. Randidly knew that to possess the strength he desired to protect the village and find his friends, he needed the strength gained from rot and death.

Maybe the Monster Slayer V Path was right; Randidly Ghosthound would carve his way forward through the flesh of his enemies.

You have chosen the Path of the "Stinking Corpse Lily." Green Spear Mastery has become Spear of Rot Mastery. Skill Level has reset to 1. You retain all the benefits of Green Spear Mastery.

Congratulations! You have learned the Skill **Pollen of the Rafflesia (R) Level 1.**

Congratulations! You have learned the Skill **Edge of Decay (Un) Level 1.**

Congratulations! You have learned the Skill **Summon Pestilence Level 1.**

Pollen of the Rafflesia (R): *Release pollen from your spear, spreading the scent of spiciness and rot through the surrounding area.* **Area of effect grows with increased violence of spear movements. Enemies caught inhaling your pollen will experience drowsiness, nausea, and minor hallucinations. Costs 50 Mana. Effectiveness and severity of the poison grows with Intelligence and Skill Level.**

Edge of Decay (Un): Passive ability. *Wounds you inflict contain a hint of Rafflesia's Rot, often leading to increased infection and necrosis of the wounds.* **Accumulation of Edge of Decay on flesh in a short time period will increase its effects immensely. Frequency of rot and speed of rot depend on Skill Level.**

Summon Pestilence: *The Rafflesia has a strong relationship with hungry insects. Summon a group of those hungry insects to unleash upon your enemies.* **Number of insects depends on Intelligence and Skill Level.**

Concentration of Insects depends on Focus, Wisdom, and Skill Level.
Control over insects depends on Control and Skill Level.

My little encyclopedia was right when he speculated there were probably Rarities for Skills too. Randidly smiled reflexively upon seeing the powerful new abilities he gained. It didn't last long. He shook his head sorrowfully. There were just so many Skills he had to grind now. There simply wasn't enough time in the day for them.

At the moment, he would settle on any task as a distraction from his fretting heart.

Randidly adjusted his plans and looked south, toward the area the Fireball-casting imps came from. First, before he changed his training regimen, he planned on testing the limits of his new abilities.

Even through his sour mood, he was excited to test how his Rare and Uncommon Skills would change his fighting style.

Congratulations! Your Skill **Sneak** has grown to **Level 30!**

For the patron saint of rot and death, I certainly seem to creep around a lot. Randidly's mouth twitched and he settled next to a half-collapsed wall to examine the surrounding area.

After sneaking past their patrols, Randidly found himself within a ruined building that served as the Fire Imp's base. While getting in position, another pillar of light had risen up into the sky, and a notification about the policeman's Newbie Village appeared before Randidly. He dismissed it, focusing on the task at hand.

Hopefully, the town will be too busy guarding its own perimeter to bother us for a while.

He pressed himself against the wall. Hidden by the architecture, he activated Pollen of the Rafflesia. Randidly could sense, rather than see, a cloud of pollen spreading out around him. The faintest green tint swirled in the air. It began to drift into one of the main hallways within the charred building.

Randidly's eyes narrowed as two imps floated right into the pollen. At first, nothing happened, and Randidly was slightly disappointed. Then he noticed strange movements and activated Eyes of the Spear Phantom, and his vision instantly sharpened.

The left imp seemed fine, but the right imp was twitching and seemed to be talking to itself. As it moved deeper into the cloud of pollen, the twitching became progressively worse.

Two more imps, who had been out of Randidly's line of sight due to being around the corner, appeared, heading in the opposite direction of the first two. The twitching imps' response to their arrival made Randidly gasp.

The first raised its hand and blasted its compatriots in the face with a Fireball. The new arrivals fell back shrieking. The twitching imp giggled, unleashing another Fireball.

This is the power of a Rare Tier Skill... Randidly's skin tingled, stretched between morbid fascination at the display and excitement for how else the Skill could be used.

Congratulations! Your Skill **Pollen of the Rafflesia (R)** has grown to **Level 2!**

The right imp, finally responding to the horror of the imp-on-imp violence, grappled for the other imp's back. It missed in its haste and collapsed. When it began vomiting, it occurred to Randidly that it might not have been haste that made its grab so inaccurate. Meanwhile, the left imp continued to roast the other two imps. Randidly had seen enough. His Intelligence Stat probably made up for the lower Skill Level, but it was clear the Skill was pretty effective against the imps, especially when they didn't know what was happening.

Randidly flexed his hand and tried another of his new Skills. Mana condensed into his palm. A swarm of buzzing insects the size of his fist appeared above his hand. They instantly flew everywhere. Randidly pressed down with his will and they unwillingly gathered back up in a tight clump.

Congratulations! Your Skill **Summon Pestilence** has grown to **Level 2!**

Congratulations! Your Skill **Summon Pestilence** has grown to **Level 3!**

This Skill is much harder to control. Randidly grimaced when the insects began to wander outward again with even the slightest slackening of his focus. *Well, honestly, the pollen one I can't control at all, aside from letting it seep outward. The effects are powerful, but there are definite downsides to focusing on unruly organic weapons.*

Congratulations! Your Skill **Summon Pestilence** has grown to **Level 4!**

Noticing the quick growth, Randidly reasoned his relatively high Control was helping him gain Levels quicker. Randidly pointed and the Pestilence surged forward, albeit haphazardly, swarming the imp that was vomiting on the ground. The flies and wasps dug their greedy mouths into the imp's flesh. It screeched in pain, rolling around in a lame attempt to throw off the swarm.

The insects had no concept of a stomach at all. Randidly's eyes widened as the Pestilence ate and ate and ate, ripping away chunks of flesh and making them vanish. Within seconds, half the imp's head was missing.

The imp who was still flaming the other two turned, confused. Randidly reached out and *pressed*. The Pestilence rose off the first imp and attacked the second. At least most of the insects did. Some stayed, feverishly gnawing. Without glaring himself into a headache, Randidly didn't think he could dislodge them from their current meal.

Seventy-five percent of the insects were good enough. They obediently surged toward the unoccupied flesh of the imp.

Congratulations! Your Skill **Summon Pestilence** has grown to **Level 5!**

After studying them for several minutes, Randidly concluded it was a useful Skill, though currently not deadly. Although they could eat a lot of the imp's flesh, it was mostly superficial wounds, considering how quickly people healed with the System. He suspected the Skill would fare slightly better now that it was Level 5, but not enough to make a difference.

Plus, the foes I'm worried about won't be so easy to surprise and overwhelm.

Still, Randidly acknowledged the Skill could be excellent at distracting enemies and reaching hard-to-catch enemies, like the cat, when he spent enough Mana. With Magic Missile and Summon Pestilence, Randidly felt more confident about facing the enemies beyond the edge of the boundary.

He tried not to think of it as chasing after a distraction. He was merely heading out to train. Regardless of how he handled the coming night, he needed to be strong, first and foremost.

First things first, Randidly reassured himself by slapping his cheeks.

CHAPTER THIRTY-SEVEN

*S*weat dripped down Randidly's brow. He might have been slightly optimistic in his newfound ability to survive beyond the boundary. It was a forbidden zone for a reason.

If he encountered a singular cat, there was no doubt in Randidly's mind he would have been able to handle it easily. And there was only a single cat in front of him.

But, of course, there were also two lizardmen wielding scimitars, backing the cat up.

Randidly had stumbled across the lizardmen and decided to risk a fight. Coincidentally, Randidly and the cat appeared at almost the same moment, ambushing the lizardmen. Both froze. An uneasy and aggressive truce existed between the three parties as they eyed each other.

It seemed the lizardmen and the cat came to the same conclusion, turning their eyes toward Randidly. He was the weaker party. They advanced, rushing toward him, the cat transforming into a whirl of sharp claws and death.

After a half second of hesitation, Randidly gritted his teeth and removed something he hoped to never use again—the strange, invigorating juice of the origin banana. It would leave him extremely weak afterward, but...

He'd fought against the cat before and knew fleeing would be useless. Meanwhile, the armor and weapons of the lizardmen meant he couldn't simply offer up his body to inflict simultaneous wounds and use Health potions to grind it out. They looked uncomfortably sturdy.

"The only path for a spear is forward." In that tense moment, Shal's words echoed in Randidly's head. "A man holding on to a spear cannot hesitate. Or else he will die."

Randidly gulped the sweet-tasting potion down, and every muscle in his body relaxed. A smile spread across his face. Why had he even been worried?

The cat screeched closer, its claws ripping the air, followed by the grim-eyed lizardmen.

Spinning his spear, Randidly yawned. He considered several methods to overcome this trial. He stepped, activating the Phantom Half Step, closing half the distance to the furthest back lizardman, phasing entirely through the cat and appearing next to the closest lizardman.

Congratulations! Your Skill **Phantom-Half Step** has grown to **Level 5!**

Randidly made a pleased squeal. This Skill was very hard to raise. In his mind, drinking the potion had already paid for itself. It might have seriously depleted his Stamina, but he wasn't too worried about it.

The lizardman's eyes widened, then narrowed. Randidly delivered a kick to the side of its knee, sending it stumbling.

Randidly harrumphed, his spear stabbing forward, catching it in the shoulder. Although the lizardman was knocked backwards, there was only a small amount of blood that dripped from the wound. It seemed like the scales were tougher than Randidly anticipated.

Congratulations! Your Skill **Phantom Thrust** has grown to **Level 33!**

Just to be sure, Randidly unleashed another quick thrust on the same spot, further depleting his Stamina. He enlarged the wound, but not enough to make it a serious impediment. The lizardman scrambled backward. Randidly nodded to himself. *Yup, yup, what a pain. These are gonna be hard to kill.*

He glanced casually to the side, his left hand twisting and summoning Pestilence. The insects exploded toward the eyes of the second lizardman rushing to aid his fellow. He was caught full in the face, his scimitar raised. The insects sank into the soft flesh of its eyes and nose. It roared and the remainder of the insects ripped into the soft flesh of its mouth and throat.

Congratulations! Your Skill **Summon Pestilence** has grown to **Level 6**

It fell back, senseless and trying to scratch the hungry Pestilence from its sinuses.

Congratulations! Your Skill **Summon Pestilence** has grown to **Level 7**

...

Congratulations! Your Skill **Summon Pestilence** has grown to **Level 10!**

All in all, Randidly gained 5 Levels for Summon Pestilence in quick succession by controlling the insects so acutely in their feast. Raising a Mana potion to his lips, Randidly turned to regard the vicious black blur almost upon him. He couldn't help but sigh at having such a troublesome experience out in this dusty wasteland.

He activated Spear Phantom's Footwork and Haste, throwing himself to the side, almost amused by the cat whizzing past him. The Stamina he managed to recover was again expended, pushing him toward his limit. Disturbingly, the cat changed directions midair, rushing toward Randidly's face, its claws raised.

Randidly summoned Entangling Roots, filling the space between himself and the cat with thick plant matter. The cat slashed, cutting open a path through the roots.

Randidly anticipated this. An empowered Phantom Onslaught rumbled toward the newly made hole, the dozens of stabs ripping small gashes in the cat. Its preternatural grace overwhelmed the offensive. Though it sported several deep gashes, it managed to slip past and—

Congratulations! Your Skill **Magic Missile** has grown to **Level 3!**

—be smashed to the side by the Magic Missile Randidly summoned and left hidden behind the Entangling Roots. The cat hit the ground, off balance. Root Manipulation exploded upwards, grasping its thin limbs to pin it down.

For safety, Randidly hit the cat with two Arcane Orbs, emptying his Mana pool. At this point, both his two pools were almost completely depleted. One lizardman scrambled up, hurrying to his friends' side to figure out why it was screaming.

Randidly loomed over the cat and deftly cut off one of its claws, raising it to the sky, admiring his self-produced loot. The two lizardmen stared daggers at him. Either the shock of pain had passed or the lizardman's Vitality was more impressive than Randidly thought. His connection to the Pestilence had been cut. He considered summoning some more, then laughed.

Ah, looks like I'm out of Mana. Well, drinking another potion doesn't seem very fun. Let's see how confident these fools are in their scimitars.

Randidly spun his spear and smiled. His Stamina steadily accumulated in his chest, filling him with heat. The two foes spread out to surround him. Randidly rushed toward the left one, the one who he previously stabbed with his spear, lashing out with another Phantom Thrust.

The lizardman took it on the chest, pressing forward, swinging his huge scimitar. Randidly calmly deflected the attack with the shaft of his spear. In the next instant, he stepped to the side with Spear Phantom's Footwork, positioning himself to hinder the lizardman's ability to attack him. Randidly continued to attack, dodge, and block, weaving his way between the two opponents with Spear Phantom's Footwork.

Running low of Stamina, he spotted an opening and kicked a lizardman off balance, earning himself a few seconds to recover. When he was about to be pinned between them, he miraculously deflected a blow and forced them to block each other's attacks. The sense of capability he felt was incredibly delightful.

It was strange. This focus, this confidence. Everything was part of a grander system. Randidly felt like he unwittingly walked into a choreographed dance.

This was probably what Shal felt all the time, Randidly thought, his smile widening. *This is what I need, this strength. This is what it feels like to know you aren't useless.*

Randidly's smile never wavered, until one lizardman took a huge gulp of air and spat poison, splashing it all over Randidly's arm.

The lizardman's eyes curved upward in gleeful anticipation of victory. Randidly simply laughed, ignoring the poison and the lost Health. He had too much experience with that nuisance goop to have it distract him now. He stepped closer to the surprised lizard. Too close. So close that both the scimitar and the spear were useless.

The second lizardman circled around his fellow's back, trying to assist. The first didn't share its worries. It hissed in a gloating fashion, dropping its scimitar and reaching with its scaly hands, confident in its strength. It was right to be, Randidly reflected as he eyed those scaled hands. The strength of the lizardman was undoubtedly higher than his.

Randidly reached out with the claw of the cat and drew a smile across the lizardman's neck. The scales parted unwillingly but cleanly. Looking down at the blood spewing from its own neck, the lizardman stilled mid-grab, falling forward.

Randidly's close combat spared his Mana enough time to recover a small amount. He slipped out of the way of the body and cast Entangling Roots on the other lizardman.

It hissed, ripping the roots out of the ground with brute strength even as it surged forward. Randidly shook his head sorrowfully. There was no rest for the wicked, he supposed. Relying on the distracting explosion, Randidly used the rest of his Mana to hit the lizardman in the face with a Fireball. The act drained him down to exactly zero Mana. His abdomen clenched in an unpleasant twinge.

The flash of light, smoke, and heat caused it to stumble. Randidly rained empowered Phantom Thrusts upon it. The repeated strikes ripped hole after hole after hole through its thick skin.

After several desperate swipes, it gave up on Randidly as prey and fled, abandoning the body of its comrade. Randidly watched it go, admiring how much Health it must have for it to shrug off his attacks.

The timing was good too, because the last few Phantom Thrusts were just for show. Randidly's whole body trembled. He could hardly stand. His Stamina emptied just as the banana serum ran out. He managed to keep himself from swaying until the lizardman left his line of sight.

Randidly collapsed to his knees and retched.

He wiped spittle from his lips and tried to focus on not vomiting. Inwardly, he resolved to never use it again. It could become like a drug if he relied on it too heavily to get through difficult battles.

More than that, Randidly wanted that strength to be *his*. For the strength to succeed on his own, not by relying on a strange potion. This was the power of the origin banana.

Still, the results were pretty compelling. Randidly opened his Path screen to distract himself from his stomach.

Aside from the Skill Levels he noticed at the beginning of the fight, he also gained 1 Level of Haste, 3 of Spear Phantom's Footwork, 1 of Physical Fitness, 2 of Dagger Mastery, 1 of Phantom Thrust, 1 Arcane Orb, 1 Entangling Roots, 3 of Magic Missile, 1 Fireball, and 2 for Edge of Decay.

Randidly considered his status screen, feeling slightly disappointed the Edge of Decay wasn't as impressive a Skill at Uncommon, as Pollen of the Rafflesia was. Then again, he supposed the Level of his target might be part of the problem.

Randidly Ghosthound
Class: ---
Level: N/A
Health(/R per hour): 206/279 [+6] (114 [+9])
Mana(/R per hour): 1/273 (53.25)
Stam(/R per min): 48/247 (41.5 [+3])
Vit: 33 [+1]
End: 30
Str: 18 [+2]
Agi: 42 [+7]
Perception: 23
Reaction: 24
Resistance: 9
Willpower: 52
Intelligence: 56
Wisdom: 30
Control: 36
Focus: 19

Equipment: *Necklace of the Shadow Cat Lvl 20 (R): Vit +1, Str +2, Agi +7*
Skills
Soulskill: *Spear of Rot Mastery Lvl 11*

Basic: *Running Lvl 17 | Physical Fitness Lvl 26 | Sneak Lvl 30 | Acid Resistance Lvl 22 | Poison Resistance Lvl 14 | Spirit of Adversity Lvl 24 | Dagger Mastery Lvl 13 | Dodge Lvl 27 | Spear Mastery Lvl 39 | Pain Resistance Lvl 11 | Fighting Proficiency Lvl 29 | First Aid Lvl 13 | Block Lvl 24 | Mental Strength Lvl 8 | Curse Resistance Lvl 3 | Pathfinding Lvl 8 | Mapmaking Lvl 4 | Calculated Blow Lvl 11 | Edge of Decay (Un) Lvl 3*

Stamina: *Heavy Blow Lvl 22 | Sprinting Lvl 13 | Iron Skin Lvl 25 | Phantom Thrust Lvl 34 | Spear Phantom's Footwork Lvl 27 | Eyes of the Spear Phantom Lvl 17 | Phantom Half-Step Lvl 5 | Haste Lvl 14 | Phantom Onslaught Lvl 10 | Sweep Lvl 11 | Spear Deflect Lvl 5 | Empower Lvl 9 | Roundhouse Kick Lvl 6*

Mana: *Mana Bolt Lvl 30 | Meditation Lvl 28 | Entangling Roots Lvl 29 | Mana Shield Lvl 23 | Root Manipulation Lvl 24 | Arcane Orb Lvl 21 | Magic Missile Lvl 6 | Healing Palm Lvl 5 | Fireball Lvl 3 | Pollen of the Rafflesia (R) Lvl 2 | Summon Pestilence Lvl 10*

Crafting: *Farming Lvl 23 | Plant Breeding Lvl 9 | Potion Making Lvl 20 | Analyze Lvl 24*

Randidly certainly had a lot of Skills now, including some saved PP. He willingly embraced the next in today's series of tasks. He picked up the cat body and the lizardman, grunting at its surprising weight, and trudged back toward the boundary.

CHAPTER THIRTY-EIGHT

*A*fter meditating to full Health, Mana, and Stamina, Randidly distributed his PP, finishing the Potion Making I Path. As he suspected, he earned a Skill—Refine. This allowed him to use Mana to refine materials to more purified versions of themselves.

He sat next to his small hut, listening to the sounds of the Newbie Village making preparations for the night on the hill further down the valley. Several of the more proactive Classers sank axes into the scattered trees until they cracked and fell. Others had obtained nails from a group expedition to the north and hammered the logs into dwellings. Sometimes, Randidly noticed some of the "villagers" pause to look down at his hut. Each time, he lowered his head and very pointedly did not acknowledge them.

His palpitating heart couldn't handle it. He gathered the potion materials to bury it for another few hours.

Congratulations! Your Skill **Refine** has grown to **Level 2!**

Randidly explored his new Skill, making more concentrated versions of the potion ingredients. He produced a Mana Potion that would restore 130 Mana in a single drink. He swirled the mixture and grinned before making a few more.

He was really looking forward to obtaining more containers to hold potions.

Congratulations! Your Skill **Refine** has grown to **Level 3!**

Congratulations! Your Skill **Potion Making** has grown to **Level 21!**

Randidly started chipping away at the Monster Slayer Path, which would take 100 PP to finish. He was leery about committing to such a long Path, but the fact that the previous rewards were regeneration rates sorely tempted him. Fighting against multiple enemies beyond the Level suppression area required him to be at his peak over and over again. He needed to improve his potions and boost his regenerations to keep training there.

He put the rest of his PP into the Path and was pleasantly surprised to find he received 1 free Stat every 10 PP.

Even more surprising were the gains from Spear of Rot Mastery. Like Green Spear Mastery, it gave out benefits every 5 increases in the Skill Level. The rotation changed to 10 Mana, +1 Vitality *and* Control, +10 Stamina, and finally +2 free Stats. The only thing that hadn't changed was the 2 Stats. Everything else doubled in effectiveness. Randidly once more pulled up his Status Screen, and this time focused on the current situation of his Stats.

Randidly Ghosthound
Class: ---
Level: N/A
Health(/R per hour): 206/283 [+2] (120 [+3])
Mana(/R per hour): 139/291 (54.25)
Stam(/R per min): 105/267 (43.5 [+1])
Vit: 35 [+1]
End: 30
Str: 18 [+2]
Agi: 42 [+7]
Perception: 22
Reaction: 24
Resistance: 9
Willpower: 52
Intelligence: 60
Wisdom: 30
Control: 37
Focus: 19

His current Stat total was now at 378, putting him very close to gaining access to the Apprentice Path and the related Skills with Nul. What he needed to do now was focus. At the very least make a decision in regard to how he wanted to distribute his Stats from now on.

He had been putting points into Intelligence recently to keep the power of his spells high and raise his Mana pool. In addition, Spear of Rot Mastery would passively give him an acceptable amount of Vitality and Control as he spent PP. What was increasingly becoming clear was the benefits of not having a Class would become more and more evident as he gained more Skills, and accomplished more Paths in the same amount of time.

The Soulskill even guaranteed he was double-dipping with those Skill Levels.

Randidly became frustrated when he realized most of the higher-Level Paths gave out fewer rewards than the early ones everyone finished. In addition, unlike an individual with a few Skills they would polish repeatedly, Randidly spread his attention across a wide variety of activities with only minor overlap. For now, it was fine, though he was all too aware his advantage from the Dungeon would shrink as others trained for a similar amount of time. His Skills would ultimately be weaker, even if his bag of tricks was larger.

Sighing, Randidly settled back against a tree. That probably wouldn't be true until the next curveball he anticipated from the System, though it was good to be aware of the drawback now. He needed to choose his direction before he became used to juggling a bunch of things.

Randidly spent a few minutes examining his Skill categories.

Skills
Soulskill: *Spear of Rot Mastery Lvl 35*

Basic: *Running Lvl 17 | Physical Fitness Lvl 26 | Sneak Lvl 30 | Acid Resistance Lvl 22 | Poison Resistance Lvl 14 | Spirit of Adversity Lvl 24 | Dagger Mastery Lvl 13 | Dodge Lvl 27 | Spear Mastery Lvl 39 | Pain Resistance Lvl 11 | Fighting Proficiency Lvl 29 | First Aid Lvl 13 | Block Lvl 24 | Mental Strength Lvl 8 | Curse Resistance Lvl 3 | Pathfinding Lvl 8 | Mapmaking Lvl 4 | Calculated Blow Lvl 11 | Edge of Decay (Un) Lvl 3*

Stamina: *Heavy Blow Lvl 22 | Sprinting Lvl 13 | Iron Skin Lvl 25 | Phantom Thrust Lvl 34 | Spear Phantom's Footwork Lvl 27 | Eyes of the Spear Phantom Lvl 17 | Phantom Half-Step Lvl 5 | Haste Lvl 14 | Phantom Onslaught Lvl 10 | Sweep Lvl 11 | Spear Deflect Lvl 5 | Empower Lvl 9 | Roundhouse Kick Lvl 6*

Mana: *Mana Bolt Lvl 30 | Meditation Lvl 28 | Entangling Roots Lvl 29 | Mana Shield Lvl 23 | Root Manipulation Lvl 24 | Arcane Orb Lvl 21 | Magic Missile Lvl 6 | Healing Palm Lvl 5 | Fireball Lvl 3 | Pollen of the Rafflesia (R) Lvl 2 | Summon Pestilence Lvl 10*

Crafting: *Farming Lvl 23 | Plant Breeding Lvl 9 | Potion Making Lvl 21 | Analyze Lvl 24 | Refine Lvl 3*

All in all, he currently held a lot of combat Skills. That would be a good area to focus on. At the same time, he recognized the utility that being a Mage gave him, especially for now. No one else, aside from that young girl Lyra with Sam, could utilize Mana nearly as well as he could. It gave him a power no one else held.

It also wasn't difficult to practice Mana and Stamina things at the same time. The issue would be in learning to integrate them well.

From his Stamina-based Skills, he would continue to focus on the basic spear-work and the Spear Phantom Skills. In addition, working on Haste and Empower would yield benefits all around. The speed boost was better than Heavy Blow, especially when he didn't need to be briefly vulnerable afterward.

Crafting was a separate category. When he had spare time, he would work on Farming, Plant Breeding, and Potion Making to provide utility for the rest of his Skills. Those areas took him away from the surprisingly addictive dopamine cycle of fighting, almost dying, and growing in Skill Levels. Randidly was mentally tougher than he used to be, but sometimes he wondered whether he'd become numb.

His abrupt speech to the Newbie Town this morning practically proved that something a little erratic was happening within him.

The other decision lay within what he would focus on for Mana Skills. Randidly really enjoyed his new Skills from the change in his Soulskill and suspected they would Level up to become increasingly powerful. In addition, Entangling Roots and Root Manipulation were the things that led him down this path. He would continue to work on those.

What it really came down to was on which of the offensive spells would Randidly focus.

After quite a bit of thought, he chose Fireball, even though it didn't make sense. No, perhaps Randidly chose it *exactly* because it didn't make sense. A green Mage Spearman who also wielded fire? That was almost counterproductive.

Randidly smiled to himself. It seemed really cool. He supposed after all his hard work, he could choose to be willful at a time like this. He might have more Levels in Arcane Orb and Mana Bolt right now, but he needed to think long term. As soon as he gathered more Skill Levels in Fireball, he had no doubt he would earn a Path offering him other fire-based Skills to supplement his weaknesses.

With those Skills in mind, he would concentrate his Stats on Agility, Intelligence, and Control. He would harass and dominate with Skill Levels of spear Skills and follow it up with restrictive Mana Skills. Culminating it all, he would ensure he had high Intelligence to unleash powerful flame spells to crack open the enemies with tough defenses.

Randidly nodded to himself, satisfied. Looking to the clouds screening the sun in the sky, he assumed it was still before noon. He honestly couldn't believe so little time had passed from the speech he made.

Inwardly, he wavered. His eyes narrowed. The tremor in his chest was due to fear, but he focused outward without searching too deeply for the true cause. He could not run from danger. He would go back beyond the boundary and seek further challenges. That was the only way he could grow.

And growing was what was important now, no matter what he decided to do.

Randidly returned to the camp at around four p.m., hungry and exhausted.

Exhausted, partially because he dragged back two cat bodies, two lizard-men, and a strange scorpion the size of a large dog. Of them all, the scorpion proved the most dangerous. It stung Randidly before he even saw it, resulting in a creeping paralysis through his leg. His Poison Resistance had already been pushed upward, staving off the deadly reaction long enough for him to barely crack the scorpion's shell. Randidly didn't hesitate to burn its brain with a Fireball before his own body became rigid from the poison.

The paralysis lasted several minutes and put an end to the adventure beyond the boundary. He wiped sand off his knees and grimaced at the corpse. After the ambush, Randidly was ready for some rest.

This expedition earned him 2 Levels in Poison Resistance, 1 in Running, Entangling Roots, Summon Pestilence, and Meditation, and another 6 in Fireball. After all, he purposely focused on Fireball as he trekked forward, using it to secure kills and increase the Skill Level.

When Randidly returned to his cabin, he was surprised to find several men tending his fields. After watching them for several minutes, determining they weren't doing that badly of a job, Randidly retired to his cabin. He didn't think too deeply about why they would be trying to get in his good graces.

To his surprise, the cabin was already occupied.

Lyra sat on the pallet Randidly used as a bed in those rare moments he actually rested, multicolored balls of Mana moving in strange patterns before her. He coughed lightly to get her attention. She sat up, a worried look in her eyes.

"Did you get mugged on the way home?" She hopped off the bed and rushed to him, only to stop herself and sway at the last moment. Her brow furrowed, taking in his ripped pants and the swelling in his leg, around where he'd been stung by the scorpion. "You look like you spent a night wrestling your pants off."

Randidly ignored her, dumping his satchel in the corner. His clothes stank of blood and sweat, but with this girl here, it was a bit...

Actually, thinking about the blood on him made Randidly wonder if his Edge of Decay Skill would make the corpses rot faster. That was slightly worrisome, as he planned on handing them over to Sam to ensure he had plenty of good materials to experiment with in his craft. Sam mentioned something about a way to preserve the bodies, so hopefully...

Lyra gave the satchel a glance, taking several steps toward it, almost drawn to the otherwise unimpressive sack.

She instead circled around Randidly and headed to the door. "Sorry, by the way. For just l-letting myself in. Sam wants to talk to you. And Donny. And Daniel... Decklan has been making eyes at your cabin. You... are surprisingly popular?" And with that, she left.

Sighing, Randidly rubbed his head and grabbed a glass for water.

He noticed there were a lot more people hanging around the village today, almost a hundred at first glance. Which brought Randidly face to face with his own worries about how tonight would go. Not that all of them would receive a Class. And if just twenty did, they ensured two hundred more monsters for the group to handle without him.

Shaking his head, he picked the bodies back up and went toward Sam.

One thing at a time.

$\mathcal{R}$andidly was glad he went to Sam first. The crafter had good news. Sam successfully created boots from the cat fur and claws Randidly previously gave him, and they seemed to be of decent quality.

The horrible chilling guilt in Randidly's heart meant he swiftly turned down Sam's offer to take the equipment. He didn't even bother looking at them, refusing to allow himself to be excited over nothing. It was far better for someone else, someone who hadn't left the Newbie Village with a death sentence, to wear them.

He left Sam with the bodies, heading back toward the village. As he moved past his cabin, he once more gave the men tending his fields long looks. Ultimately, they seemed to mean well, having a basic grasp of harvesting the fruit without destroying the plants. They'd expanded the fenced-in area so all the fields were covered and all foreign weeds had been ruthlessly evicted. Randidly once more held his tongue.

Besides, Randidly thought with a mind fuzzy with emotional exhaustion. *The least I can do is make sure these Class-users won't need to fight hungry tonight.*

In the area between the cabin and the village, around a dozen lean-tos of a much lower quality than Sam's had sprung up. In addition, a more structurally sound wall was being erected around the village. One of the new arrivals must have some experience in the field of construction. The wall was made of stacked logs and mud, currently reaching chest height, with men and women hauling materials up the hill every minute. Even more impressive than the reinforced wall itself was the fact that the gate on this version appeared to be quite functional.

There were even a few people hanging around the gate, as if they were

age. Randidly felt
a more how quickly
wn guilt.

er him, hurried out of

ithin the wall. His initial
at a hundred. There were
sparring and brandishing
es, or talking freely to each

l silent.
of people, hurried over to him.
s. Apparently, the mayor over at
Class and is driving a bunch of
et a Class if they wish, but... it's
fine. I ac.. ght. Lots of people have experience
with Skill Levels..

He trailed off as thos. mism became too tiresome to carry
forward. Daniel focused on the gr. d when he finally said, "Are you really
not going to help at all tonight?"

For a moment, Randidly considered taking it all back. He wanted to
contradict his big, tough-love speech from this morning and agree to help.
Yet at the same time, Randidly was too aware of all the eyes on him.

More than three hundred eyes fixated upon his every move. Even if some
of these people didn't know who he was, they would soon understand what
he said and what he'd done. Their attention was overwhelming. The hairs on
the back of his neck prickled and his heart quickened, just like it had when
he was in danger.

"No, I'm not," Randidly huffed out, a flash of disgust raging through him
toward himself as he did so. He was turning his back on a problem he
created. He knew that.

He knew it, but he couldn't help turning away.

*Perhaps Shal had been right. Perhaps I'm still weak, despite my Skill
Levels...*

For all that admission of how weak he was, it should have thrown
Randidly back into the trembling nightmares of his early time in the System.
Instead, he found it oddly freeing. Once he acknowledged he wasn't strong
enough, physically and otherwise, to support a Newbie Village completely,
Randidly understood what he could do. The stark vision of the fighters
exhausting themselves and succumbing to the wolverines was extremely
sharp in his mind.

Even before he met Shal, Randidly survived in the Dungeon.

Randidly turned back to Daniel. "I didn't want to rush this, but talk to

Donny, get him to purchase the Miscellaneous Shop, and buy me as many vials for potions as you can afford. I won't participate in the fight, but that doesn't mean I won't help this village prepare."

Decklan narrowed his eyes, examining the tide of monsters rushing toward the village. The defenders were getting restless when the sheer numbers bore down on them. There were a lot of people—dead weight, in Decklan's opinion—who didn't choose to take a Class, attempting to grow stronger with just Skill Levels. These people were only here for a place to rest. The final count of individuals with Classes was seventy-seven. There were even several newcomers with rather interesting Classes.

Decklan didn't give them much attention. Not even the pretty girls who came over. After all, without the Ghosthound, this would be a long night. He couldn't afford to be distracted. It was hard to tell how many of the seventy-seven would remain alive come the morning. A monster wouldn't check how pretty you were before it ripped your face off and munched on your organs.

As instructed by the Ghosthound, they spent most of today sorting themselves into groups based on their builds. The results were skewed.

Thirty-four, most of which were people who survived the earlier days, were undergoing a Strength build. Those were under Dozer's lead. They were a rough-looking group. But honestly, everyone was after several days of killing monsters without showers. Those who stopped to grab their overnight bag when the System arrived didn't live very long.

And with all the work they did to reinforce the town today, there had been no spare time to go down to the river and rinse themselves off.

Decklan had twenty-seven men under him. They focused on Agility, scouting, hiding, and of course, assassinating. It wasn't true that Stats had to follow body type. It was slightly surprising how many huge men chose to build speed, their bodies stretching and limbering up with an unnatural grace.

Ten chose, or had been pressured into, the roles of damage soaks, most of their points going into Vitality and Endurance. They followed Donny and were standing behind the gate rather nervously with their newly created shields produced by Sam.

The remaining six were Mage types. Among them was an individual who gained a rare Weather Witch Class. She was a woman in her forties who had been a rather avid *Dungeons and Dragons* player at the local library before the System, and un-surprisingly embraced the new world quite quickly. She arrived this morning, chomping at the bit to get herself a Class. Two of the other Mages were Ptolemy and an individual who got the Class, Herbalist, which meant they would mostly focus on healing.

Ultimately, their long-range fire power amounted to three dunces throwing Mana Bolts and the Weather Witch tossing icicles. It was a far cry from the devastation the Ghosthound could cause with a single Arcane Orb.

That lack of firepower filled Decklan with anxiety. Hopefully, the walls would make the absence irrelevant.

The one bright spot was the Ghosthound provided quite a few potions. So many that Decklan seriously considered whether the machine was some sort of magical plant from the System. He'd done an impossible amount with only a few hours of preparation. Decklan felt the ten he'd slipped into his belt: 5 Stamina, 4 Health, 1 Mana.

Someone on the wall began beating a drum, signaling the monsters were coming.

"First group, to the front!" Donny shouted, leading a group of eight people, including Dozer. These were the veterans who could take the brunt of the damage from the first charge, while the twenty or so people behind them would rotate in to give the village's ringers a breather.

Behind them, the remaining Class individuals waited in reserve with Daniel, in case monsters scaled the walls. The NCCs, or non-Class characters, as most individuals had been jokingly referred to, huddled around the central building and the two strange shops Donny purchased thus far.

They held weapons, but from the way they cowered, it was obvious they wouldn't last long against an attack.

Decklan shook his head to rid himself of distractions, giving a hand signal to the twenty men with him. As a unit, they scaled the wall, which was rather easy from the inside. They crouched low once on the outside, waiting. Once the fighting started, Decklan's job was to sweep the stragglers who couldn't make it to the fighting at the gate, the ones who tried to surround the village.

Although the term used was stragglers, Decklan was under no impression his job would be easy. If anything, it would be the hardest. He just grinned. That was how Decklan wanted it.

He heard it the moment the fighting started. There was a slam. Defiant shouts from the defenders. Growls and hisses from the monsters.

A golden glow exploded from the gate. Donny used his Skill Aegis to boost the Health and Stamina of those around him. Decklan didn't like the punk, but had to admit his Class was incredibly useful. Especially in larger fights like this. Especially if they were supposed to survive this night without the Ghosthound.

After a few minutes, the sounds of approaching monsters pushing away from the direct battle at the gates neared his group. Smiling, he drew his daggers and gestured to his subordinates.

They had work to do.

Donny couldn't breathe. Hadn't been able to for a long time. He also didn't have time to check his Status. He kept his shield up with one arm, downing Mana and Stamina potions with the other, and activating Aegis over and again, ensuring the surrounding defenders benefited from a small amount of damage reduction and Stamina regeneration.

Congratulations! Your Skill **Aegis** has grown to **Level 14!**

Three wolverines and a lizard rushed into the man to Donny's left, sending him stumbling back.

I can't... Donny thought to himself, wanting to drop and let it all go. Instead, he found himself stepping forward. The step was unwilling and he could practically feel Randidly's foot smashing against his back, shoving him. The question that kept Donny up these past two days rang incessantly in the back of his mind.

'What will you do, Donny?'

His Shield Bash took the lizard in the side of the head, stunning it. His sword whipped out to stab its shoulder. Stab and retreat, sidestepping around the jaws of an aggressive lizard, and stabbing again. The man behind the guy who was knocked back had been blocked by the displaced person, but the individual behind Donny had not. They shifted into a new position.

Grecko, a grizzled man just south of forty, had been one of the first people to get a Class. When Donny shifted to the left, Grecko shifted up, his huge axe smashing down toward an unsuspecting wolverine that glared after Donny.

It was Daniel's idea, originally, to follow a front-line strategy similar to Roman legions. No one in the village was any sort of expert in history, but they muddled their way through to a working concept using the sweat-filled hours of the afternoon. It worked well enough for the first twenty minutes. But they were losing their edge as the battle dragged on longer than they anticipated.

Donny felt three taps on his back and gratefully stepped back. Two people moved forward to take his place. In his retreat, he activated Aegis one more time. After about ten feet, Donny felt confident enough to turn around, focusing on the resting warriors. Dozer was there, his chest heaving, throwing back two Stamina potions at once, his mouth stretched wide.

Seeing him do so, Donny considered his own status screen.

Donny Parke
Class: Knight
Level: 15
Health(/R per hour): 92/358 (63.25)
Mana(/R per hour): 8/75 (3)

Stam(/R per min): 11/211 (22)
Vit: 19
End: 13
Str: 20
Agi: 11
Perception: 9
Reaction: 11
Resistance: 22
Willpower: 9
Intelligence: 2
Wisdom: 2
Control: 2
Focus: 2
Skills
Soulskill: *Newbie Village Chieftain* Lvl 84

Basic: *Hiding Lvl 7 | Running Lvl 9 | Grappling Lvl 7 | Club Wielding Lvl 2 | WoodWorking Lvl 2 | Construction Lvl 3 | Labor Lvl 11 | Heavy Blow Lvl 15 | Mana Bolt Lvl 1 | Ride Lvl 1 | Honorable Charge Lvl 5 | Stalwart Defense Lvl 13 | (1) Sword Master Lvl 8 | (2) Shield Mastery Lvl 16 | (3) Shield Bash Lvl 9 | (4) Aegis Lvl 14 | (5) Legion Thrust Lvl 4 | (6) Sidestep Lvl 5*

No wonder he felt completely wiped; he almost used up all of his Stamina. He slowly removed his last three Stamina potions and drank them. Ptolemy trotted up to him and looked at him in askance, but Donny waved him away. One of the new recruits vomited off to the side.

Everyone's eyes were empty and spent, the way Donny felt inside.

'What will you do, Donny?' the Ghosthound whispered in his ear.

Despite almost dropping to single-digit Stamina, driven by the words of a man who earlier tortured him, Donny found his feet moving. His exhausted body neared Dozer. A notification popped up, but Donny largely ignored it, aside from an annoyed grunt that another of his Skill slots was taken.

Congratulations! You have learned the passive Skill **Leadership Level 1.**

"It's either this or death, and I refuse to die a virgin," Donny said awkwardly, patting Dozer on the back.

Dozer's body stilled. The other veterans, barely catching their breath without the aid of the Stamina potions, stilled and stared at the interaction.

They all began to laugh. Even if the sound was awkward, it lit the spark of something. A little of the numbness receded.

Congratulations! Your Skill **Leadership** has grown to **Level 2!**

"Don't worry; I'll have my girl personally suck your dick if we live through the night," Dozer said, slapping his knee and guffawing. The surrounding men chuckled. Even the few women seemed slightly amused.

"Uh…" Donny said, wondering if it really worked like that. Would a girl-friend suck the dick of other people if their boyfriend asked them to?

He shook his head and accepted a non-cracked shield from another NCC who hung around, as well as another Health and Stamina potion.

"This is the last of it," the NCC said, his expression nervous.

Donny smiled and turned to Dozer. "Ready to get back to work?"

Randidly returned to camp with a heavy heart, heedless of the wanton cele-bration around him. They won. He watched the entire night, his hands clenched into fists. With only marginal help from him, they survived.

He hadn't entirely kept his word. Though he wasn't there with his spear, Randidly used Entangling Roots and Root Manipulation to keep the monsters from spreading out too much in an attempt to scale the walls.

The tension he felt only began to dissipate when he heard from Donny that less than ten people died. For a System-enhanced world, that was worthy of celebration. People were already cutting down more trees and carrying bodies away, even though it was barely dawn.

Randidly ignored them. The exhaustion of the day finally caught up with him. He needed a break.

There was one last thing he needed to do before he allowed himself to rest.

As he moved through the dark forest, Randidly examined his Status Screen. He gained 2 Levels in Entangling Roots, 1 Level in Sneak and Eyes of the Spear Phantom, and finally 3 in Root Manipulation.

He moved west, cleaning up scraps from the monster horde that attacked the other town. However, Randidly soon tired and charged forward, leaving his Pollen of the Rafflesia hanging in the air behind him. Soon, he spotted the lights and approached the policeman's town.

Congratulations! Your Skill **Pollen of the Rafflesia (R)** has grown to
Level 3!

Glad to see they enjoy my dirt, Randidly thought. He kept accelerating, making a larger commotion to draw more monsters to feed him Skill Levels.

Congratulations! Your Skill **Pollen of the Rafflesia (R)** has grown to
Level 4!

Congratulations! Your Skill **Pollen of the Rafflesia (R)** has grown to
Level 5!

As soon as he arrived at the town, Randidly sucked in a breath. The roads leading into the town were caked in bodies. Based on the number of monsters bleeding out, the village must have let at least a hundred and eighty people get Classes. For that, Randidly felt some admiration for them.

It was obvious they hadn't used the individuals with Classes to defend against monsters. Randidly found the evidence smoking in chipped asphalt and embedded within tree trunks. They used guns.

Randidly spotted two heavy mounted machine guns sitting high on the buildings along the periphery of the town. Randidly rubbed his chin, unsure of how to react to the way they handled this. Although it seemed reasonable, based on Sam getting the Driving Skill, there were probably shooting Skills. Except guns required bullets. Unless something weird happened with the geography, there shouldn't be a facility to produce more bullets near here.

Randidly supposed this town being able to produce bullets was a possibility. They must have raided a military base near here or had a person who could mass produce bullets.

At the top of the town, there was likely a person who didn't care that they would soon run out.

Either way, it was a worrisome sign for the future development of this Newbie Village so close to his and Donny's. With a headache brewing, Randidly dragged himself back to his cabin.

A tall man stood in front of his cabin, leaning on the door. He wore one of Sam's sewed-together cloaks. Randidly recognized the cat fur he brought back had been used around the throat of the garment. This one was of much higher quality than most that had been passed out to the fighters.

Perhaps the most distinctive feature about the man was his face. He had deep, brooding eyes and a chiseled jawline. He also seemed oddly familiar, but Randidly set that aside.

"Yes?" Randidly asked. His muscles and mind groaned piteously to be forced to engage in conversation in this state.

The man chuckled; it was a warm and attractive sound. Inwardly, Randidly's dislike grew even through his exhaustion. "Maybe it's my vanity, but I'm surprised. Well, never mind. The world really has changed. I'm Kal Drake, and I was wondering if you could do me a favor."

A small lightbulb went on in Randidly's head at the name. He dimly remembered Kal Drake was a rather famous action star in…

For several seconds, Randidly's tired mind spun around in a circle. *There definitely was a movie, something about... weapons? Or was he the star of that racing movie?*

Seeing Randidly's confused expression, Kal smiled. "Seems that doesn't mean anything to you. Well, that's fine. It's simple. Sam seems to like staying with your group, but the rest of us aren't so comfortable here. I would like for you to take us to the other village in the morning."

After Kal left, Randidly Meditated to calm himself before sleeping, pondering Kal's request in the dark. This famous action star was one of the hooded figures Randidly had seen in the bed of the truck. It also explained why both Lyra and Ellaine were so attractive; they were probably all actors and actresses.

The fact that he came himself, without using Sam, probably meant this group wanted to leave without telling Sam.

Should Randidly let it happen like this?

Congratulations! Your Skill **Meditation** has grown to **Level 30!**

Randidly wondered if he would have an easier time thinking his way through this problem in the morning. The whole point of letting Donny be Village Chieftain was to avoid dumb problems like this. How did it end up happening anyway?

In a few hours, the fourth day of the Newbie Village would dawn. They were over halfway toward the end of the Level suppression protection. What lay beyond that day filled Randidly with fear.

But they are growing stronger. Just like I did. Randidly blew out a breath and proceeded inside the cabin to his palette. He made himself comfortable as best he could. *We just need enough time...*

CHAPTER FORTY

*D*ue to his high Vitality, Randidly woke a few hours later. The sun hadn't even dawned when he left his cabin and stretched. He loafed toward his farmland and found some well-shaped potatoes and citrus fruits to devour.

His mind began to buzz with thoughts. He considered the emotional aftermath of his guilt and the Newbie Village's success, the worrying trend of gun usage in the other Newbie Village, and finally the request from proba-bly-action-movie-star Kal Drake. He snuffed out all these distractions the old-fashioned way—sweating them out.

It was another day, which meant Randidly began it with training.

Spear first. Randidly moved himself through the almost relaxing move-ments Shal taught him. He slowed himself down, straining his muscles to control his body even when he wasn't utilizing momentum to throw himself forward. When he tired of that, he used Empower to add a little spice to the movements. His thrusts were quick and powerful, his sidesteps smooth and fluid.

Sometimes, for the briefest moments, he could see a bit of Shal in the way he performed a movement. That recognition filled him with warm satis-faction.

Congratulations! Your Skill **Empower** has grown to **Level 10!**

After he depleted Stamina in that manner, Randidly shifted to his Mana Skills. He fired each once, aiming for the trees along the edge of the valley. The process was noisy, but most of the people in the next-door Newbie Village were awake and training themselves. Mostly, he tested the accuracy and power, comparing Arcane Orb with the steadily rising Fireball. Satisfied with his magic-based growth, he conjured insects and tossed them at a tree. Compared to flesh, their gnawing progress was slow. Slow, but ravenous.

Congratulations! Your Skill **Summon Pestilence** has grown to **Level 12!**

After working up a nice sweat, Randidly headed to the river to rinse himself off. He soaked his sweat and blood-stained clothes while wading waist deep into the cool water. Randidly grinned down at his reflection. His hair was starting to grow wild, growing past his eyebrows.

Randidly dragged his hand back and forth through the water, the ripples shimmering in the pre-dawn light. His brow furrowed, considering Kal's request to defect to the other Newbie Village. It was not that he minded fulfilling it, but the real question weighed on him.

Randidly rolled his shoulders and stepped out of the water. One un-looked-for benefit of the System was temperature. With his Vitality, Randidly didn't feel very cold, even after soaking in the mountain run-off stream. He took his clothes from the small pool at the edge and wrung them dry. He put them on, confident the dampness would steadily evaporate throughout the day.

His eyes sharpened on his approach to his cabin. Randidly found Sam there, raising his hand to rap on the door.

Sam grunted and lowered his hand when he spotted Randidly. "Based on your face, Kal came and saw you, right? I bet you were wondering whether to tell me about his little ploy." He spat off to the side. "As if I give a shit about that prima donna. The real problem is he's insisting the rest of the girls go with him, so they don't get so 'separated from the real world that they start to think this is what life is like.' Kal thinks that while the monsters are a bother, I make it worse by insisting we camp."

Randidly chuckled. "What does he think is out there? A place where monsters don't exist? A place where the weak don't die? That... I don't know if Earth has places like that any longer."

Sam sighed. "Yeah... Honestly, he truly thinks things will change back to normal soon."

They stood in silence for several seconds. Randidly recalled the confi-dent expression on Kal's handsome face and abruptly felt a flash of irritation. He wanted to take Ellaine down his road of foolishness, huh? "I don't want to help him, but it's better I escort them, rather than wait until he's foolish enough to sneak off on his own. I'm going to the town to get those potion containers. The fifty we got for last night were helpful, but a surprising amount were dropped after use. If they want to come, I'll take them there. But... there is something strange about that town."

"You believe the rumors that the mayor's gone crazy?" Sam asked.

Randidly shrugged, remembering the caked bodies below the machine gun nests and the hundreds of bullets lodged into the surrounding tree trunks. "I guess I'll find out today. Let's be a good neighbor and bring a pie to welcome them."

Kal, Ellaine, and the fourth, still cloaked woman went with Randidly to the nearby town. Decklan caught them as they were leaving and invited himself along. It seemed to be a sore subject that Lyra wasn't coming, based on the grim line of Kal's mouth. Randidly made no effort to talk with the group anyway, and let it slide.

He was too busy not noticing the way Ellaine's curves were occasionally so undeniable in the way her robe flared outward around her hips.

Keeping himself in check was actually quite easy. Randidly was all too aware of Decklan, who closely followed him with his eyes the entire journey. It was honestly a relief when weak monsters tried to ambush the group. All he needed was a few Fireballs to roast the audacious lizards alive. Randidly didn't mind the admiring way Ellaine glanced at him when he easily handled the groups of a dozen or so monsters that leapt at them.

Congratulations! Your Skill **Fireball** has grown to **Level 10!**

Randidly flexed his hands, pleased with how well he could handle the attacks. Perhaps no one noticed but Decklan, but his Intelligence and ascending Skill Level were finally combining to reap a deadly efficient Fireball. One struck a lizard, smashing it into the tree. The tree cracked, setting everything on fire. The group watched the burning tree slowly topple.

They continued on in silence.

Randidly knew the town itself was back toward the location where he exited the Dungeon, and didn't have any better idea on how to approach to enter it. He led them toward the area with the machine gun nests. The rest followed like tourists, their heads whipping back and forth at the slightest sound.

Randidly clicked his tongue and chided himself. Honestly, it was something of an oversight they hadn't at least sent someone to scout the nearby Newbie Village. They needed more reliable information. Once the seven days passed, they would need to use the surrounding terrain to their advantage to survive.

As long as the other Newbie Village is willing and able to burn bullets, it shouldn't be hard for them to make it through the seven days as well... and suddenly, we have a political relationship on our hands. Randidly had a headache just thinking about it.

Nul's attitude toward the other village indicated there was some kind of competition between them. Randidly held no confidence reading the emotions of the Village Spirit. He still didn't act the same around Randidly as he did for the rest. Randidly mostly relied on secondhand accounts from Daniel to parse apart the traps laid by the System.

Nul was also completely tight-lipped about his own origins. Randidly didn't doubt his cute encyclopedia interrogated him on the subject at every chance he got. And if Daniel couldn't drag the answer out of him...

They crossed the final stretch of forest with only one small incident. A group of imps lurked below a hill, hidden from Randidly's sight. When they walked over the crest, the imps rushed outward with gleeful shrieks.

There were seven Fire Imps in the ambush. Two were close enough Randidly moved instantly to them, his spear flashing before they could raise their skinny fingers and conjure magic. Four more were instantly transfigured into miniature torches by his rapid Fireballs.

Only one had enough time to get off an attack in their doomed ambush. The blast of fire missed Randidly completely, rendering his peremptory Mana Shield useless. Instead, the fire rushed toward the still-cloaked figure. The lines around Randidly's eyes tightened.

At that moment, Decklan stepped forward and used his small buckler shield to take the brunt of the attack, flinching with a grunt from the heat, but surviving. Within a second, Randidly used Phantom Half Step and Phantom thrust, skewering the offending imp.

Congratulations! Your Skill **Phantom Half-Step** has grown to **Level 6!**

The issue arose when the surprise of having a ball of fire thrown in her direction caused the cloaked figure to shriek and fall backwards. Her cloak unraveled around her head, revealing long blonde hair and a striking, beautiful face.

Decklan turned with disdain toward the weakling he'd been forced to save, freezing when he saw her face. A very un-sinister flush came across his cheeks.

"You... aren't you Vivian Plath!"

Randidly scratched his head, unsure of what was happening. It seemed his suspicions were right. She was famous too, but he'd never been one to pay too close attention to actors. Besides, with the System taking over their lives, things like that seemed particularly unimportant.

Kal stepped forward. "Yes, but now's probably not the time for this. Let's continue to safety before talking further."

"Oh, yeah, I'm just such a huge fan of your... work," Decklan said lamely.

Vivian smiled politely in acknowledgement of his words, but kept her eyes on the ground as she stood. After she brushed herself off, she pulled her hood back over her face. Randidly couldn't help but notice Decklan's gaze followed her as they headed toward the outskirts of town.

Congratulations! Your Skill **Pathfinding** has grown to **Level 9!**

Randidly soon arrived in the area he'd first appeared, next to the building that had now entirely burned down. He was thankful someone else moved the woman and her stroller off the street. The group behind him wordlessly followed the weird half-street in the woods to a cross street, letting them head deeper into the town.

On the other hand, rotting bodies of monsters littered the streets, a testament to the town's victory last night over the monster horde. Odd silence hung over the group as they stepped over the rotting flesh. The smell quickly became overpowering as the day heated the dead flesh and concrete.

Pressing his lips together in a tight line, Randidly waved his hand, using Root Manipulation to lift bodies out of the center of the road, clearing a path. They walked for about three hundred meters before they came to a bus parked sideways between two buildings, effectively blocking the road. The area between the bus and the buildings was filled with boards, doubly and triply nailed to each other. It likely wouldn't withstand an actual assault by monsters, but it wouldn't need to. An intimidating mounted machine gun sat on top of the bus, a hefty warning to any who wanted to approach.

When they were about twenty meters away, the guard straightened, his eyes widening as the bodies in the road shifted, pressed to the side by Randidly's roots.

His voice was as shrill and sudden as a whistle. "Stop right there!"

Decklan was restless. The guard at the machine gun nest hailed them to stop, then sent for someone higher up on the food chain to deal with them. Even worse, the guard gripped the machine gun, staring them down with a horribly blank expression. The group who followed the Ghosthound were left standing in the street, slowly absorbing the stink of rot from the bodies around them.

That wasn't the only reason he was nervous.

Decklan glanced at Vivian again, his heart thundering in his ears. Never in his wildest dreams would he have imagined the weirdos that hung out with Sam were famous actresses and actors. And of all people, the sex-icon Vivian Plath...

Movement on top of the bus brought Decklan's attention back around.

The tall, black police officer that previously came demanding Classes looked over their group with an intense expression.

"You shouldn't have come," he said, a small hint of... something in his voice. It wasn't fear; it was more like dread. And a deep exhaustion.

It seemed the Ghosthound heard it too, because when he spoke, his voice was sharp. "Some of our camp preferred yours. And also, we had a deal regarding glass containers."

"That is true, but..." The police officer hesitated. He opened his mouth to speak, but another voice overrode him.

"Hahaha, we have guests? Well, well, well. How appropriate they would make a pilgrimage to the greatest kingdom in all the land."

An average-looking man stepped forward. His face was inoffensive but not very attractive. There were only two distinct features of his countenance.

The first was the sneer twisting his lips. The second was the huge, tacky crown he wore. It was gold but inelegantly made and imbalanced, as if the man robbed a jewelry store and melted all the necklaces and rings down to a lumpy crown approximation.

Almost unwilling, the police officer stepped to the side, and the crowned man took his spot at the edge of the bus. "Now, we get a lot of refugees coming to my town. What makes you worthy of being one of my adoring subjects? Why should I allow your entry?"

Decklan wrinkled his nose at the arrogance. It was obvious it didn't sit well with Kal either. The actresses exchanged annoyed looks. The Ghosthound seemed rather bored, his eyes scanning the nearby rooftops. He didn't intend to interfere on the issue of their relocation.

Vivian wasn't dissuaded by the crowned man's attitude, stepping forward and removing her hood.

"Please, there's no civilization out there. We just need a place to stay, that's all we ask." Vivian smiled.

Decklan didn't know how she did it in the post-makeup and hot showers world, but she looked so perfectly stunning, even surrounded by two stinking piles of bodies.

The crowned man was similarly taken with her. His eyes widened in a way that made something possessive growl in Decklan's chest.

"Oh, wow, you're beautiful. Hey, aren't you that actress?"

A satisfied smile spread across Vivian's face. "Those were different times. It's honestly embarrassing, I'm not sure what a woman like me can do when the world is like this..."

"Oh, no worries." The crowned man's smile was huge now. He gestured grandly. "You and your friends are more than welcome. Come in, all of you."

Eager, Kal and Ellaine walked forward, following Vivian. Decklan felt a strange regret followed by a weird compulsion to follow. He shook his head ruefully. Vivian really did a number on his head.

"Ellaine," the Ghosthound spoke shortly as the tall, honey-skinned woman passed him. She stopped, almost unwillingly, a hint of disgust turning the corners of her mouth down as her eyes scanned the Ghosthound's bloody figure.

"Yes?"

For the first time, Decklan saw the smallest hesitation in the Ghosthound.

The usually confident man licked his lips and spoke slowly. "I have two friends, Sydney Harp and Ace Ridge. While you're inside... ask around to see if anyone knows anything about them. Please."

Ellaine laughed, her eyes crinkling up at the corners. "You... honestly, every time I assume something about you, you end up proving me wrong. I feel like such an ass. From some of the looks you were giving me, I thought you had a crush on me. Ha! I'll look for your friends, but you protect Lyra, all right? I can't tell if she's spoiled or playing the fool, but she really has no self-preservation instincts with the world like this."

"I... ahem. I will."

The Ghosthound seemed like he was choking, but he eventually got the words out. Ellaine favored him with one last smile and turned to follow Kal and Vivian. The Ghosthound twisted and gestured to Decklan, who followed behind, beginning the long walk back through the rotting flesh-filled streets.

Decklan clicked his tongue. *What an oblivious bimbo. Someday soon, I bet you'll be begging to be the woman of the Ghosthound.*

Ehehehe... and as his right-hand man, it's only fair for me to take care of your friend Vivian.

"Oy, where are you two going?" The voice was cold enough to make the hairs on the back of Decklan's neck prickle. When Decklan glanced over his shoulder, the crowned man still leered at them. The Ghosthound didn't even bother to respond, continuing his trek.

"Hahaha! I give you a personal invitation and you blow me off? Interesting, interesting! How about you **Kneel** and beg for my clemency."

Decklan stopped abruptly and staggered for several seconds, as if his legs lost all their strength. He eventually fell, catching himself on his hands and knees.

Confused, he regarded his legs, which suddenly refused to move.

What, what's going on?

"Interesting," said the Ghosthound.

Decklan looked up.

The Ghosthound still stood, measuring the crowned man with his eyes. "I assume you would be the mayor? I've heard rumors about you. We should talk. Those rumors are not good ones. And I don't want to see more people needlessly lose their lives because of one man's foolishness."

The crowned man's face twisted in surprise. He adjusted his heavy and lopsided golden crown, glaring at the still standing Ghosthound. "Call me *King* Constance. I am your Liege. So, ***Kneel*** before royalty, peasant."

Congratulations! Your Skill **Mental Strength** has grown to **Level 9!**

*T*he notification took Randidly by surprise. A weird pressure wormed its way into his head. He hadn't imagined he'd encounter an enemy outside of the Dungeon that could use mental attacks. His heart sank. This "enemy" was the rumored tyrant that led the next-door Newbie Village.

He wanted to ignore the problem for now and gather more information. When he figured out what was going on, he could come back later to confront the authoritative police officer. The man was brusque. Though, through their brief dealings, Randidly had the strong impression he was honest and his heart was in the right place. Plus, Randidly was all too aware of the guard within the machine gun nest, observing every development.

From the way the policeman is standing, it seems like the rumors about him are true... Randidly's hands ached to be wrapped around the shaft of his spear. *If he is truly accustomed to using those mental Skills to target his fellow humans...*

Randidly recalled the hungry look this man gave Vivian Plath when she revealed her beautiful face.

"Interesting," Randidly said, meaning the exact opposite as the emotions in his chest spun together into a tight, dark ball. He studied the ridiculous man wearing the crown. A single look was enough to determine that he had, in fact, unleashed a Skill against Randidly. Just for walking away. This man was petty and Ellaine wanted to calmly walk into his kingdom?

If not for Decklan falling to his knees and the Skill Level increase, Randidly probably wouldn't have noticed it was a Skill. The combination of his high Willpower and the Mental Strength had been built up to handle Orc Shamans within the Dungeon. Even if this man had a Class related to these Skills, he hadn't had time to grow into a threat to Randidly.

But considering your behavior, you don't deserve time to grow into more of a threat. Randidly's emerald eyes hardened. *Yesterday, I failed in my responsibility to the villagers, because I was scared. Because I don't know how to handle these situations. But this time... considering the harm you could do with your capabilities...*

"I assume you would be the mayor? I've heard rumors about you. We should talk. Those rumors are not good ones. And I don't want to see more people needlessly lose their lives because of one man's foolishness." Randidly kept his tone light, even as the specter of Shal put his hands on his shoulders, urging him to eliminate the threat before him.

Even if Randidly remembered the sounds of humans shooting guns at other humans in the chaos of the initial arrival of the System, he didn't plan on making his decision immediately. Perhaps the activation was a subconscious thing.

Are you going to make me kill you? A tremor ran through his fingers.

Could he kill another person? Even if he knew doing so could save the lives of others? Of Kal, Vivian, and Ellaine... What sort of expressions would Sam and that girl Lyra make if they knew their companions were under the "protection" of an individual who could force them to kneel with a Skill?

An individual who wore a misshapen golden crown?

Randidly frowned and reined back his thoughts. For now, he should observe. He couldn't let himself jump to a conclusion based on a few seconds of interaction. No matter how deranged the man's eyes were.

The man bared his teeth, which did little to dismiss Randidly's growing sense of responsibility. "Call me *King* Constance. And I am your Liege. So, ***Kneel*** before royalty, peasant."

Congratulations! Your Skill **Mental Strength** has grown to **Level 10!**

A slight tremor went through Randidly's body. He laughed. The effect was mild at best. *Not a coincidence, then. A deliberate attack.* Randidly's mouth was dry.

So, this is a tyrant...

"Did you seriously call yourself king?" The tremor in his fingers spread to his heart, picturing blood spurting from this man's chest and down the shaft of his spear. His resolve didn't waver as much as he thought it would. He *could* kill another human, if he had to. "We now live in a fantasy world. But I don't think you're taking the right lessons from the shift."

A spear always advances. Shal's words echoed in Randidly's head.

Constance was shocked, seemingly lost at the sight of him not kneeling as he'd been ordered. Something in Randidly's mind abruptly came into focus looking at the thoughtless cruelty on Constance's face.

"Oh, your random Class from the Newbie Village literally ended up being King? That explains your strange Skills, but not your despicable behavior," Randidly remarked, shocking himself with how chatty he was today. His hand became heavy against his satchel, itching to remove the shortened training spear from the interior.

"A king has three burdens and three tools," Constance said slowly, his eyes malicious. "The first is the Will of the People. In my hand, I hold the Hammer of their demands! By their will, you will **Kneel**."

Randidly snorted, shrugging off the mental pressure almost as soon as it tried to worm its way through him. Those two Skill Levels pushed the mental assault from distracting to the territory of useless against him. "You can only throw as much of that Willpower as you can handle, and I guarantee you can handle less than I can. I was raised for this. I wonder… does that deplete your Mana or your Stamina? Based on how often you can use it… it's Stamina, right?"

This "king" paled, briefly lost by his failure and Randidly's comment about Stamina. Grinding his teeth, Constance stepped to the edge of the bus and pointed at him. "The King's second burden, the second tool, The Weight of their Country! On my shoulders, I bear its mantle. Every day, I wake up under this weight of responsibility. It will **Crush** you."

Randidly swayed, taken slightly aback by the immense physical pressure. Ultimately, it didn't seem as immense as it felt initially. The fact that it was able to catch him off balance was certainly impressive. Then again, this was a physical assault and Randidly's Strength was 20, dwarfed by his Willpower of 52.

The certainty in Randidly's eyes firmed with every order Constance barked. His expression warped into the twisting snarl of a hungry beast. *What do you know of responsibility? Because of you, this tyranny would not have happened if I hadn't casually given away that golden coin…*

Which means… my responsibility…

"Fine then!" Constance spat. "Just die already. Guards, **gun them down**."

The madness of Constance flung drops of spittle from his mouth as he shouted his command. Two guards stepped forward with submachine guns. The guard already fixed to the mounted gun pulled its barrel around, aiming toward Randidly and Decklan. The three actors heading into the embrace of Constance threw themselves into the piles of bodies lining the road, terrified by the scent of violence.

A familiar certainty overcame Randidly, one he'd only felt when the Giant Serpents ambushed Shal during the Black Swamp Salamander fight.

I will kill you. Randidly's eyes flashed. *And this time, I am definitely not biting off more than I can chew.*

Roots ripped through the bus and grabbed the ankles of the two submachine gunners, twisting and throwing them to the ground. Their poor response revealed how disappointingly low their Stats were. The roots continued to rise, gripping the mounted gun, and ripped the bullet belt, forcing the barrel to point toward the sky.

Congratulations! Your Skill **Root Manipulation** has grown to **Level 28!**

"You!" Constance's voice shook.

It was too late. Randidly's eyes were already cold and determined as he raised a Mana potion to his lips.

"No second chances," Randidly said quietly, his Mana pool rapidly rising to full. In his mind, he pictured the pained grimace on Shal's face as the Giant Serpent's fangs burned through his arm.

Following his instincts, Randidly produced an Arcane Orb in each hand and pressed them together. The combination sputtered and twisted violently. The Mana roiled and rebelled. Randidly didn't deny its nature, aiming it forward. The collision of energy exploded toward the bus. Randidly's Willpower wrapped around the attack, keeping it focused on his target until impact.

Congratulations! Your Skill **Arcane Orb** has grown to **Level 22!**

Congratulations! Your Skill **Arcane Orb** has grown to **Level 23!**

BOOOOOOOOM!

A wave of dust and bits of sizzling metal ripped outward. The explosion rocked the road, turning most nearby corpses to mush. The bus was thrown backward, ripping the hastily made boarded walls from the buildings. The bus crashed about five meters away, a huge hole burned through the middle of it.

With a grinding noise, the bus rocked on its heavy axles and stilled.

Through it, Randidly spotted the crumpled form of Constance, thrown off the bus and onto the ground. Without the weight of this tyrant's Skill on his shoulders, Randidly wasted no time rushing forward. He whipped his shorter training spear from his satchel.

The King would die this day.

He burst through the hole in the bus and was met with a hail of gunfire. The nearby guards had enough presence of mind to pull out their small caliber weapons. Randidly's Mana Shield took most of the bullets, breaking after ten or twelve impacts. By then, he was already through the choke point and rushing toward Constance.

The head police officer was off to the side, scrambling to his feet, but he wouldn't make it in time.

In a move that required more dexterity and bravery than Randidly would have ascribed to him, Constance sprang to his feet, whirled around, and grabbed Randidly's hand.

"The Final Burden! The Final Tool! The Mandate of God, Geas. On my head, I wear their crown. **You belong to ME.**"

Congratulations! Your Skill **Mental Strength** has grown to **Level 11!**

Randidly went rigid as a huge mental attack slammed against him. Grunting, Randidly tried to withdraw his hand, but the flesh of his and Constance's seemed to have been bonded.

For several seconds, he struggled to create distance. Whatever it was, this Skill somehow prevented it. The mental attacks were growing stronger at a steady beat, originating from that hand contact.

Congratulations! Your Skill **Mental Strength** has grown to **Level 12!**

Ceaselessly, the attacks came, narrowing the distance between Constance and Randidly's Willpower. Narrowing his eyes, Randidly focused and poured all his Mana, funneling it into Summon Pestilence. He created a huge, humming cloud of flesh hungry insects around his entire arm.

Congratulations! Your Skill **Summon Pestilence** has grown to **Level 13!**

Randidly shuddered against the sense of weakness originating from his empty Mana pool when he directed the insects at their magically cemented hands and ordered them to devour.

The bugs attacked the flesh of both their bodies. Constance screamed. The mental attacks faltered. The bugs were deaf to his cries as Randidly's powerful Willpower pressed them onwards. Even as he maintained his will, Randidly swayed unsteadily at the combination of pain and dizziness. He gritted his teeth and marshalled himself, enduring the next wave of mental attacks.

The insects ripped and tore, digging their pincers into the flesh to rip it away. Bit by bit, bite by bite, they feasted.

Their hands finally parted. Constance's hand had been reduced to mere bone. The insects hadn't left Randidly alone either, but his superior Vitality and Endurance ensured he was only gashed and bleeding in comparison.

Randidly directed the insects to continue attacking Constance. He focused on his hand, steadying himself. The sense of dizziness gradually faded.

In comparison to Randidly, it was obvious the insects preferred the soft flesh of Constance's body.

"Wait! You must stop!" the policeman shouted, running forward.

Randidly regarded him coolly, his head still pounding from whatever Skill Constance tried to use on him. Constance clawed at his mouth and nose, the bugs burrowing their way into them, directed by Randidly's vengeful Willpower. The beast inside of Randidly's heart growled at the retribution. He pressed them onward, aiming to devour the so-called King's tongue completely.

Congratulations! Your Skill **Summon Pestilence** has grown to **Level 14!**

"Please! You must let him live. He is the only thing holding this town together. If it falls... Do you really want the burden of all these refugees on your shoulders?"

The bugs continued to buzz, ripping small pieces of Constance's flesh away. The beast was in its throes of passion. But the other side of Randidly's heart began to assert itself. His sense of responsibility hesitated.

"You want the glassware, right? That is only possible with him. If he dies, the community will be too fractured for you to get your glassware."

Randidly thought about it but did not call off the insects. He'd already resolved himself to take the items he needed anyway. The screams from within the buzzing cloud grew louder and louder.

The police officer stared on helplessly.

A new voice cut across the chaos. "Let the man live and I will give you this."

A strange man with skeletally thin limbs appeared with a serious expression on his face, offering Randidly a large black coin. There was something familiar...

Randidly stilled. This was the same emblem on the golden coins used to found Newbie Villages. Except the design on this coin was larger and more complex. The man spun the coin in his hands, catching the light.

A black Nexus coin?

Randidly studied the figure, realizing why he looked familiar. Even though this figure had different mild features, the same vacuous smile played on his face with the same empty eyes. This was the Village Spirit.

"How will that help me?"

The screams grew hoarse, the volume dropping precipitously to rasping moans. Steadily, the wrath of buzzing and the clicking of insects strangled out all other sounds.

The Village Spirit paled, shaking his head. "I-I cannot... Please. You must understand, we can only walk on the Paths in front of us. To tell you is not my Path. I am but one half of a whole. But if this man dies…"

Something cracked on the Spirit's face. His whole form shimmered, then refocused. "Please."

The only noise Randidly could hear was the buzzing of insects. Like cicadas in summer, the sound was somewhat hypnotizing.

Constance is likely the Village Chieftain. Randidly realized. *Losing that, the Village Spirit seems afraid of something.*

The damage this man could do would easily spread from his own village to theirs, if he was allowed to grow and get more Skill Levels. To his own surprise, Randidly sighed and snapped his fingers. He didn't know why, really. One part was the lack of threat he sensed from the silhouette within the insect cloud. Another was the glassware. And some lingering portion was the sliver of him that hesitated in taking another's life.

The biggest piece was this Spirit being gripped by sadness over its own fate. Though he might regret this action, he relented, for now.

Plus, the greatest danger of this confrontation was the strangeness of the Skills that Constance the King could unleash. Now that those were no longer surprises, Randidly was confident it wouldn't take nearly as much effort to kill the man in the future.

"Even still," Randidly rumbled, taking the coin. "You owe me."

"This!" Nul's eyes widened at the sight of the black coin.

Randidly felt somewhat relieved to see the stoic Nul react so violently to the coin. He'd spent most of the walk back to the village worrying about Constance and his growth. Steaming from battle and violence, he was assured a follow-up was easy. Though the more Randidly thought about it… If his Skill was already at a point that it could threaten him…

"I hope it's worth the trouble that asshole is going to be," Decklan mumbled, his arms folded across his chest.

"Of course it is!" Nul insisted, his eyes glittering. "This will let us found the Town's Dungeon an entire Tier early. With this, our future is assured! You must give it to me!"

CHAPTER FORTY-TWO

"*A*nswers first," Randidly said firmly, tightening his grip on the coin.

It was around 10 a.m. by the time they made it back to their village after his light assault of their next-door neighbors. Hopefully, that demonstration was enough to cow Constance. Randidly wouldn't bet on it lasting for too long, although, in the short term, his revenge was not likely to be forthcoming. An arrogant man like him would want to grow stronger before he dared reveal himself in front of Randidly again.

Do you think you can match me for speed of growth, Constance? Randidly flexed his hands. Plus, his eviscerated tongue and vocal cords would give him pause.

Nul nodded rapidly. "Yes, yes! Each village may form its own 'kept' Dungeon, typically in the Trainee Tier—"

"No." Randidly slowly shook his head, his gaze never leaving Nul's eyes. "Bigger answers. How could their guide have this coin?"

Nul stilled, his expression becoming bland and noncommittal. "I don't know what you mean."

"I think you do." Randidly saw Daniel gasp, making the same realization he did. He held up the coin. "I haven't seen one of these. And not to be arrogant, but if I haven't been able to find whatever is making these and kill it, I doubt anyone over there has either. If it didn't come from any of the people here…"

Nul looked troubled. "This… is not something I can speak of, I promise you. I am bound. But suffice to say, your suspicions are not unfounded. All guides are not created equal. Which brings me to the perfect opportunity to bring you the good news! I, too, have a gift, and it has just been unlocked as your Village Chieftain got his Soulskill up to Level 100."

Nul's smile did nothing to dispel Randidly's suspicions. If the item didn't come from the people of the other Newbie Village, it came from their guide.

Nul's *answers* were remarkably poor at handling the questions that quickly bubbled up in Randidly's mind.

Randidly supposed it would end up being worth it, if the Dungeon they obtained warped time like the Dungeon he'd been stuck in. He waved the coin. "What is your gift? Is it as valuable as this?"

"Perhaps you should be the judge of that; you seem rather intelligent," Nul said smartly with a smirk. "It is something called Class Inheritance. Very simply, due to my influence, there is an item you can purchase from the Accessory Shop called a Mentor Stone. Using that will force a connection, giving an individual a Path Disciple of the Individual who used the stone. When that Path is complete, if you bring them to me and the mentor is from my village, I can make sure they can obtain a similar Class."

Randidly stilled. This was obviously a similar method to what Shal used with him. If it were true, they could reproduce Classes with more powerful growth rates. With the information Daniel had been gathering…

The fact that Shal could activate the process without the Mentor Stone made Randidly's eyes narrow with suspicion. Was it really something due to Nul, or was it something every village unlocked at a certain Level?

"What do you mean by similar?" Daniel asked.

While Randidly's encyclopedia caught on to the positive implications of this process, it would seem he didn't have as much innate suspicion toward the Village Spirit.

The Village Spirit that would have let us gorge ourselves on obtaining Classes, only to be overwhelmed by the monster tide he didn't mention the first night, Randidly reminded himself.

Nul shrugged mysteriously. "It is hard to say. There is some potential for change. The higher ranked the Class, the higher the possibility the Class might degrade into a less powerful subset. But conversely, the lower-tiered Classes might evolve into something wondrous."

Nul turned to Randidly. "Will this gift of mine be useful?"

"Do you have nothing else?" Randidly asked, his voice light. He suppressed the urge to pat down the Village Spirit and look for other contraband.

Nul's face soured. For a long time, he said nothing. And then he finally said, "There is a Path you may take, where balance is ended, and one half may feed off the other to grow stronger. If you do so, and afterwards I am still alive, I will be able to answer your questions."

At the end of this small speech, Nul's face was red, and his whole body trembled. Randidly suspected it was a ruse. In a way, there were similarities to what the other spirit said about being one half of a whole. Thoughtfully, Randidly handed over the large black coin.

"The easiest way is to give the different ranks tiers of equipment, but I simply don't have enough high-quality materials," Sam said unhappily.

Randidly rubbed his chin. Though he planned on training for longer beyond the boundary today, it was clear he needed to go on a more harvest-focused mission. Sam required supplies to test his new theories about preserving bodies. Brooding, he turned, only to find Decklan still followed him.

Randidly's eyes brightened at the sight of the perfect pack mule. The best part was, the pack mule was glad to agree to Randidly's proposal.

After assuring Sam he would handle it and requesting Decklan's aid, Randidly left the village, glad to be away. Their village now swelled to around six hundred people. Based on the talk, more would be coming. The most recently arrived said they were in a moderately-sized city to the south when the System appeared, and had largely hid within their homes during the initial few days. When the first pillar of light appeared with the notification, they were the brave souls who ventured forth, seeking the method to survive.

They believed more would follow. When the second pillar rose, the monsters only grew more powerful.

That meant there were more varieties of monsters and golden coins just four days' travel south. Randidly grinned. Four days for an average person. He hadn't been doing it much, but his Physical Fitness and Running, combined with his current Agility, meant he could make the journey in a much shorter amount of time.

Randidly pressed his lips together. *And another city means another group of people who might have seen Ace and Sydney... But the problems with these two Villages are too pressing for now.*

The other strange part about the influx of people was the entire valley around his house was slowly being cleared. Alongside that, a Non-Class Character village had sprung up near his cabin. They relied on the Skill system for strength, and were ultimately scared away from getting a Class based on the responsibility to fight for the town that was involved.

Most people didn't have the guts to fend off a horde of monsters at two a.m. every night. That might change as Daniel figured out the logistics of the Class Inheritance method Nul talked about. And that would take time.

In addition, there were about a dozen full-time farmers who completely took over the care of nurturing and harvesting Randidly's plants. A pang tore at his heart from the missed opportunities for Skill Levels. When he really thought about it, other Skills he possessed were more necessary to push upward. Survival came first. For all that Farming was oddly soothing, it wouldn't keep him alive.

The farmers were doing a good job too. The fields spread to five times the size of Randidly's original four fields, creating a huge sea of rapidly rising food.

As they left the village, an annoyed voice stopped the duo. "Someone else beat me to offering my services, huh? Well, whatever. Wherever we're going, I'd like to go along with you. I'm ready, I think."

Lyra stepped out from behind a tree, her gleaming hair pulled up into a practical ponytail.

Decklan gaped at her. "Lyra Silver!"

Randidly's lips twitched. *Surprisingly, Decklan is quite the movie buff, huh?*

The young girl gave Decklan a dismissive look and held up a hand to Randidly, silencing him even before he spoke. "I know what you're thinking. I probably can't pull my weight in a fight. But look."

Just like that, Lyra teleported five meters to the right, her body instantaneously switching positions. Some of the shock value was lost when she swayed, falling to her knees. After an embarrassed glance around, she got back to her feet.

"My Mana pool is big enough to do it twice, as long as I'm casting nothing else. I can control the direction and distance, although this is about my limit. Should be enough to stall long enough for you to protect me, right? So lead on, leader," Lyra said with a shy smile at Randidly, her cheeks still somewhat flushed from the embarrassment of falling.

Randidly studied the teenage girl. Her smile was sharp, sweet, and sour, like drops of sweetness glistening on a silver blade used to cut the flesh of a mango.

Randidly opened his mouth to say something, but something in Lyra's eyes gave him pause. A fear of rejection. Suddenly, he was standing in his own memories in front of Shal, although the roles were reversed. His heart tightened with something akin to anxiety. Almost helpless, Randidly turned away and began walking. He decided to give the girl a chance.

She laughed quietly and followed. A few seconds later, Decklan saw through the stars circling in front of his eyes and hurried after the other two.

'*Watch out for her*,' Ellaine had said to Randidly. And because he asked her to look for Ace and Sydney, he wanted to fulfill that request.

Of course, the first thing Randidly was doing was taking her to the most dangerous place he currently knew of. He scratched the back of his neck, feeling slightly guilty.

CHAPTER FORTY-THREE

*U*ltimately, Randidly decided to skirt the edges of the boundary. He headed toward the area he knew to be controlled by the lizardmen before venturing any deeper. Although they were strong and resilient, the lizardmen didn't possess the oppressive speed of the cats. They would be the easiest opponents if Randidly meant to insulate Lyra and Decklan from danger.

Despite being confident about their chances, Randidly spared his followers a worried glance. He'd given them both a max strength Antidote purchased from the Newbie Village Miscellaneous Store, in case they encountered one of the scorpions. Randidly wondered if either would even have time to drink it, considering it was a strong enough poison to paralyze him for several minutes.

Some of Shal's callous acceptance settled over him, and he stopped fussing. They would either grow stronger or die. He was here to push them toward the path of living. He couldn't guarantee anything. That final bit of distance between life and death needed to be crossed by each person individually.

Surviving underneath the oppression of the System took resolve.

"We're out here looking for lizardmen. The couple I encountered used scimitars, which we should gather and carry back. Mostly, we want their scales. Incredibly hard to penetrate, great for cushioning blows too. Other than that, we might see scorpions, which you should avoid at all costs. Their poison is extremely insidious. I was stung once and it soon rendered me immobile. Then there's the hyper-quick cats. They're probably way too fast for your eyes to follow. Honestly…"

Randidly hesitated, then said, "If we encounter them, just turn and flee. You being here will only make things more difficult for me."

He narrowed his eyes, activating Eyes of the Spear Phantom and began to search for an appropriate group of foes.

They found a pair of lizardmen rather quickly. Randidly rushed forward and distracted them while Decklan danced around and slashed with two small knives made from the claws of cats Randidly killed. Even with Decklan's low Strength, they were enough to leave shallow cuts in the lizardmen's scales, which was a testament to the sharpness of the claws.

With some of his spare moments, Randidly took in Decklan gracefully utilizing the claws. *Perhaps after we've gathered enough bodily materials for Sam, I should harvest a few more of the cats.*

Lyra surprised him with her usefulness. She created a realistic bird of Mana that flitted around the heads of the lizardmen, distracting them.

Randidly kept them mostly at bay with spear movements. When they lapsed their guard, he blasted them in the face with a Fireball, leaving them snarling and singed.

After five minutes of tussling, they managed to kill both lizardmen. Randidly even let Decklan finish one off, which let him gain Stats from killing the stronger enemy. The growth rates weren't much higher than the lower-Leveled enemies, but every step forward mattered.

"Now what? Head back with the bodies?" Decklan asked, panting.

Randidly snorted and gathered the bodies into his satchel. He'd cleared out the interspatial space this morning so they wouldn't be slowed by the first couple of corpses they gathered.

"Mana potion," Lyra said, holding out her hand.

Randidly gave her a slightly surprised look at her boldness, in the end handing several over. Keeping her with a full Mana pool meant keeping the teleportation option ready, which ensured her survival.

And a living Lyra was another thing Randidly could talk to the lovely Ellaine about.

"I'm always surprised how great the Mana potions taste. You... are quite good at making them," Lyra said, wiping her mouth and returning the empty vial with a smile.

Randidly nodded absently, squinting at the sun. The temperature was quickly rising. He could already tell it was going to be a long day.

Daniel considered his options. Donny spent most of his time training with the recruits, leaving all the decisions up to him. Nul sensed this, allowing Daniel access to all the Village Chieftain functions without having to receive constant permission.

They were currently at a staggering 2400 Soul Points. The points accumulated whenever a person who received a Class Leveled, whenever they killed a monster, or when they brought back certain items to trade.

It didn't seem like possible items to trade were dropping, but Nul assured Daniel such treasures existed. He also informed him stronger enemies gave more Spirit Points, but your average enemy at this Level was only 1.

The problem was how to spend the Soul Points. 10,000 would upgrade them to a Trainee Village. Daniel dismissed unleashing such an upgrade too soon. He was the type to build a solid foundation, rather than rush toward the next goal.

The most attractive choice lay in the Mentor Stones. They cost 100 SP a pop, but they would allow more people to inherit Donny's Class of Knight. There were other valuable Class options, like Ptolemy's Disciple or Clarissa's Weather Witch. Daniel was all too aware, though, that the men clamoring for Classes wanted to take a more physical role. Plus, more Knights would make surviving the nightly monster hordes that much easier.

Nodding to himself, he moved to the Shop and purchased four before he could second guess himself. They needed the bulk at the front lines. He already talked to Donny about it, identifying likely candidates, three men and one woman. Tall and grim, steadfast in the face of danger, even before they'd gotten a Class. They were some of the first to move their families up from Franksburg, the city to the south.

Based on their firm expressions, it was clear crossing such a distance in the System world wasn't a peaceful process.

Which left 2,000 Soul Points in their coffers. Sam recommended earlier to Daniel they purchase the Weapon Shop. Although he was getting pretty confident shaping armor, making weapons required a forge, which they weren't currently equipped for. The Basic Weapon Shop would cost 500 SP.

Sighing, Daniel wandered around, studying their bustling village. The outer wall had been raised to two meters, giving additional protection to those within the village. They even had mini ramparts in several places that defenders could stand on to attack invaders. From there, the few individuals with functioning guns or bows and arrows could provide ranged support.

An archery range had been set up in the far side at the urging of Sam. Those who willingly wanted to wait a bit and Level Skills before getting a Class attempted to gain archery Skills. Even if they didn't end up having a Class related to archery, having the Skill meant they would keep that and could continue to grow it.

Based on his talks with Randidly about the power of Paths, Daniel really wanted someone to unlock and finish the Archery I Path. Even though it was a little much to ask for quick results from absolute beginners, it would be easier if someone with experience arrived and could impart critical pointers.

Most of the NCCs moved down to the farming area, lower in the valley.

Groups of them walked around with the newly minted role "One Shoulder Pad Warriors" as work groups. It was how the NCCs could earn themselves food while staying here.

Daniel made a mental note to talk with the man they put in charge of farming, to see first-hand the daily yields from the various fields. Sure, the crops grew fast, but Daniel wanted to save up food for when the Newbie Zone dropped in case monsters didn't stop in just attacking the village, aiming their ferocity to cut off their food supply. He already consulted a few people about where to set up a defensible perimeter around the NCC area.

Daniel sighed and rubbed his cheeks. It seemed like all he did these days was plan for future troubles.

A group of Two Shoulder Pad warriors walked past, heaving huge logs like it was nothing, laughing all the while. The current Class system in the village was simple, though he did speak with Dozer and Donny about raising the criteria, especially now that there were so many people showing up. There was effectively a two-day waiting period, provided you were seen participating in the nightly defense.

If you lived through your first night, you got the first shoulder pad. You lived through the second, and either Dozer, Decklan, Donny, or Daniel himself noticed you, you received a second shoulder pad. Above that opened the tooth necklace Level group, which currently only included Decklan, Donny, Dozer, and Sam. Those with tooth necklaces were an integral part of the Newbie Village, ensuring everyone else knew they needed to listen to their orders. They also had plans in the works to make that the Level of the squad leaders.

One Shoulder Pad could be trusted, Two Shoulder Pad are as close as we have to veterans, necklace wearers have some authority, and then there's... Daniel sighed.

Randidly didn't really fit into any of the typical classification systems. He really didn't have to. Anyone who saw him fight knew why he didn't need to be classified like the rest.

It was a rather loose hierarchy, but it worked for now. Daniel couldn't help but wonder how long that would last. Such was his penchant for worries manifesting itself. He'd voiced worries to Sam that someone could steal the items to signify higher status, but Sam just snorted.

"Maybe that would have worked a week ago, but now, without the strength to back it up, they would get seen through instantly. It's a mark of pride earning it. Don't treat it like an ordinary item."

That brought Daniel to the other issue. A growing number of thefts had been rising in the village. The community's reaction, as far as Daniel could discover *any*, was strange. Rather than getting angry, they shrugged and stole whatever else they found unattended. It was an open secret that basically everyone would take something of yours if you left it alone. It worked currently because no one really had anything worth getting upset over. Left-over food, building materials, and bits of monster corpses could be easily replaced.

Plus, there were the rather encouraging signs of growth the System gave individuals when they Leveled up. Those small victories were enough to keep everyone from dwelling too much on the disappearances of their trinkets.

Daniel rubbed his eyes. They only just started exchanging things by bartering, which encouraged another vote for securing the Basic Weapon Shop. Most people traded excess monster bodies into the Accessory shop, earning small amounts of bronze and silver coins they were currently casual about. All that would change once they could be used to purchase weapons.

The economy would come alive, which would unfortunately drive up crime, bringing Daniel back to the need to create a firmer hierarchy.

Looking up at the glowing pillar of light broadcasting their position to the world, Daniel sighed again. *Bahhh... If I don't start brainstorming tonight, with all the things I need to do tomorrow...*

Ugh... how are we going to get anything done?

Daniel went to Nul and bought the Basic Weapon Shop. He wandered past the group training area to a jutting pillar of stone that sprung up next to the statue of Donny after Nul activated the black coin. In it was a large wooden door covered in runes.

Their "kept" Dungeon.

Ten people could go in at a time, and time was so accelerated within that it basically didn't pass. However, if they didn't complete the Dungeon within twenty-four hours, they would get kicked out. Completing the Dungeon earned a number of points equal to the Level of the Dungeon for the town. It was currently at Level 1. Randidly recommended raising it to 12 before he'd left for his own daily training regimen.

Daniel grimaced. Raising it to Level 2 cost 200 SP. Level 3 would be 300 SP...

Daniel supposed he wasn't doing anything else with the SP. He raised the Dungeon Level to 5, spending 1400 SP. Daniel went over to Dozer, who was throwing large boulders gathered by his crew, to raise the Skill, Herculean Strength.

"The Dungeon is up to Level 5. Don't take anyone near that Level in with you, all right? Test things out and make sure there are no casualties. If there's danger, just wait out the twenty-four hours."

Dozer snorted and gestured. Eight of his subordinates swaggered forward, heading toward the Dungeon. Surprisingly, the tenth was Clarissa, the Weather Witch. Daniel supposed Dozer wasn't as dumb as he looked.

The whole party disappeared through the door into a glowing portal of light.

As soon as the door closed, it opened back up, the group trotting smartly out. They were all there. The only difference Daniel could see was Dozer now held a large wooden club, caressing it even.

"Loot?" Daniel asked excitedly, and Dozer nodded.

"Pah," Clarissa spat. "God, it smelled horrible in there. Got some silver coins too. No wands, though. Or staves. Or crystal balls or magical talking pets…"

"I've got a pair of meaty balls right here, if you need them," a man muttered and the rest guffawed.

Clarissa pointed at the speaker's feet, freezing them to the ground, moving coolly away with a snort. The men around the guy laughed even louder as he flushed, struggling to break the ice.

"We have the Weapon Shop now, so the money has its uses. Although the cheapest weapons looked to be 30 silver," Daniel said.

Dozer grunted and went back to the Dungeon pillar, touching the door.

"Bah, twenty-four-hour cooldown. Alright, rest up, you lot. Next big thing is the horde," Dozer said, wandering away.

His men dispersed and a few wandered toward the Weapon Shop. Most headed out to gather wood and build themselves some sort of house. Sam had a few assistants with architecture and construction background, and they were becoming efficient at throwing shacks up to put a roof over your head.

But it would cost you something. Whether it was labor, money, or monsters.

Daniel looked down at the NCC village made up of mostly tents, as if it would blow over any moment. He wondered whether in a month if there would be something like an aristocracy here. Technically based on merit, Daniel supposed, but still. The world was evolving.

That didn't mean there wasn't plenty of work to do. Donny informed him earlier they had two interesting Classes come up, Brawler and Ranger. Daniel wanted to ask them about their Stat gains and Skills.

CHAPTER FORTY-FOUR

*A*fter killing their ninth lizardman for the day, Randidly settled into the routine of their battles. They'd been lucky enough to have only encountered lizardmen, and almost farmed enough corpses to return to camp. Even more promising, most of the bodies were intact, although there had been a couple times they had to flee.

All in all, it had been fruitful for Randidly. The day saw him grow 2 Levels in Spear Mastery, 1 in Phantom Thrust, 1 in Spear Phantom's Footwork, 2 in Eyes of the Spear Phantom, 1 in Fighting Proficiency, 3 in Block, 1 in Haste, 1 in Sweep, 3 in Roundhouse Kick, 2 in Edge of Decay, and 4 in Empower.

Entangling Roots, Root Manipulation, and Mana Shield rose 1 Level, while Fireball rose a staggering 5 Levels. Using it as the finishing blow on lizardmen certainly boosted its growth speed.

Meditation, Spirit of Adversity, and First Aid each increased a Level. The biggest increase for the day was Pathfinding, which rose 7 Levels.

Randidly supposed they covered a lot of ground in seeking isolated groups between the lizardman patrol, but the enormous rise in Pathfinding was a bit ridiculous. He had to assume the difficulty of the enemies in the area had something to do with it.

And likely because the average Level is so much higher than my Levelless self. Randidly's lips twitched as he looked at his Status screen.

"Ghosthound, how high is your Agility?" Decklan asked timidly.

Randidly saw Lyra roll her eyes. Randidly felt slightly awkward that the man called him by his last name. He scratched his cheek, musing over how it wasn't his fault he inherited a weird last name from his father's family.

Randidly considered lying, but decided it wasn't worth it. "46, plus a few bonuses. Why?"

Decklan shook his head wonderingly. "My Agility reached 39 with that last Level. But it's basically my only Stat that far above 20. Still, you seem… quick. Impossibly quick. Those few points sure mean a lot."

"No, I suspect it's not the reason the difference feels so large," Randidly said simply.

Decklan frowned. "Then what is—"

"Ugh, it's the Skills, obviously," Lyra interjected. "Ghostdoggy, you have a Skill to speed up your movements, right?"

A vein in Randidly's forehead twitched. He slowly rounded to stare at the golden-haired Lyra. "Are you talking to me?"

The younger woman flinched and blushed furiously. "Ah… I s-s-suppose I am! But… I'm right, aren't I?"

Slightly confused by her sudden bashfulness, Randidly nodded. "Yes, actually. I have two passive Skills boosting my speed in fights."

"Uh huh, and you have other active physical Skills, right? I've been watching you closely," Lyra announced. "There are times when you're just… extra quick in setting your feet. Other times, your attacks suddenly accelerate. It's… well, it looks kinda cool, you know?"

Randidly decided to ignore the final part of Lyra's little outburst. Honestly, he was rather impressed she managed to see through his Skills so quickly. "Yeah, I also have two active Skills I can use to give myself an edge in fights."

Lyra beamed in pleasure when he told her she was right. "And what Level are those?"

Randidly paused, considering. "Around 30."

Lyra nodded sagely, pointing at Decklan. "No one else is as advanced as him in Skill Levels, not even Sam, so it's hard to tell. But past 20 seems to be where Skill Levels really start to shine. Taking a Class gives you fast growth, but Ghostdoggy here has top end utility. Your Stats might be similar, but he will have four Skills enhancing his movements at all times. It's hard to tell what the conversion is between these, but those small advantages in Skill Levels add up."

Decklan nodded, thoughtful, as though he just experienced a great epiphany after a lecture from a learned professor, which swelled Lyra with pleasure. Sighing, Randidly used the break to take the last of the materials out of his satchel and craft more potions to enable them to gather a few more bodies.

Congratulations! Your Skill **Refine** has grown to **Level 4!**

Congratulations! Your Skill **Potion Making** has grown to **Level 22!**

A tingling sense of peace flowed through Randidly when he finished the grinding and mixing. He smiled, even as the other two's conversation slowly filtered him back to the present. *Truly, there is just something cleansing about the intensity of focus required to make potions. Especially because... violence, or excitement, or fear aren't relevant. All that matters is preparation and precision.*

"You... aren't wrong." Decklan's voice drifted over Randidly and attracted his attention. The two were still discussing Lyra's earlier words. "But we also receive Class-related Skills every 10 Levels. We've tried a couple times already and it doesn't look like these are Skills you can learn through practice. You can get variants, sure—"

"Okay, well, I didn't say there weren't benefits to Classes," Lyra responded testily and crossed her arms. "What I was just pointing out is that he—"

Randidly refocused on his potions, tuning the two of them out. Academically, he was interested in Classes, but for now, he wanted to find out how long he could survive without one. The accumulation of Skills and Skill Levels was truly addicting. He wanted to savor that feeling before adding Class Levels into the mix.

Halfway through the seventh Mana potion, he froze. It'd been a good thing he sat on the ground for his work. Otherwise, his bare feet and calves wouldn't have transferred the subtle vibrations up to his body and tipped him off.

Randidly activated Haste and Empower, pushing Decklan to the side and wrapping his arm around Lyra's waist, leaping across the dune to avoid the incoming attack.

The sand underneath where Randidly had been sitting exploded, revealing a huge, flailing centipede. Its legs made a vicious grinding noise that set Randidly's teeth on edge. It screeched in its failure to successfully rip into vulnerable flesh and shot toward Decklan.

"Excuse me, but the first dance is mine," Randidly said.

Roots burst from the ground, wrapping around the centipede's trunk. After a slight struggle, it managed to tear through them. That moment of immobility was enough for Randidly to drop Lyra and cover the distance back to the centipede. He unleashed an Empowered Phantom Onslaught directly onto its head.

Randidly's brow furrowed when most of his blows skittered off its chitinous shell. Even the direct attacks barely cracked the monster's defenses. He needed a few direct hits to get through. The centipede spun, its body smashing outwards. Randidly easily dodged it, landing on its back. Its head twisted and smashed toward him, and was met by a Fireball in the face.

Only then did Randidly get the chance to examine it closer and see the green, and therefore Uncommon, label above its head.

STONEJAW CENTIPEDE LEVEL 31

While the centipede hissed in pain, Randidly shouted to Decklan, "Keep your focus on its legs. When it's looking at me, get close and try to cut them off. Watch out for when its body spins."

"It's legs?" Decklan said, confused. "But there's so many. Cutting off a few—"

"I'm not talking about a few!" Randidly dodged out of the way of another diving bite.

Somehow, he sensed this fight would not be a quick one. The head twisted and spat acid. He spun his spear in a Spear Deflect, knocking away most of it, but some still landed on him. Randidly grimaced as a very familiar pain flared along his left hip.

Why can they always spit acid? I guess I should be thankful; variety might be deadly.

Congratulations! Your Skill **Acid Resistance** has grown to **Level 23!**

"I'm talking about them all," Randidly finished. "It's gonna take a while to wear down its Health, even if I go all out. If we can manage to bring it back, I feel like this will finally shut Sam up about his needing new materials. And you..."

He spared Lyra a glance. She flushed and waved her hands, as though to say she understood a close-range fight would be deadly. Somehow, Randidly didn't believe that was the case, but he didn't have time to be distracted. "Well, don't do anything stupid."

The centipede screeched and attacked again. Randidly spread his hands wide, urging his roots to seal its movements. A fire in his hands caused it pain. A small smile played across his lips.

His heartbeat quickened with the familiar dance of violence. It invigorated him. This was what he lived for now, this thrill.

Carefully keeping an eye on his Stamina and Mana Levels, Randidly loped forward, dodging its flailing legs and acid loogies, to get closer. The centipede was certainly powerful and resilient, but it was clear its move-set was repetitive.

Decklan stayed to the side, rushing in to sever one or two legs with his cat-claw blades, then hurrying away. If the centipede noticed, Randidly hit it in the mouth with a Fireball, earning its ire.

The battle dragged on, minutes crawling past. Frantic collisions and hasty dodges clumped together to illustrate the movement of time, until the total duration of their fight neared a half hour. The only reason Randidly continued to be in a reasonable condition was due to the Mana potions he made and the emergency ones he kept within his satchel. That, combined with his Regenerations, was just enough to steadily break down this Uncommon foe.

Every few minutes Decklan stopped to take a break, his chest heaving. Randidly didn't fault him for it. In fact, he was pleased Decklan didn't try to push himself. Only after the man's Stamina recovered did he rejoin the battle.

There were several large holes on the Centipede's torso now, ichor oozing from its broken armor. The wild hisses became more and more wrathful, and that fury toward its attackers overwhelmed any self-preservation instincts.

Randidly was reaching the end of his potion-fueled Stamina when the creature swayed and fell, one of Lyra's birds perched on its head.

Randidly collapsed in relief. He pushed his Stamina pool to a ridiculous degree and it earned him 2 Levels of Physical Fitness. In addition, he gained 1 of Spear Deflect, another 2 in Fireball, 2 in Haste and Empower, and 1 in Running.

Which left him with just enough PP to finish off The Monster Slayer Path.

Congratulations! You have completed the **"The Monster Slayer Path"!**
+10 free Stat(s), +5 to Health Regen, Mana Regen, and Stamina Regen.
+.5 Health, Mana, and Stamina Regen per Level.

Although the path before you is long, you cannot stop. You can only drink the blood and bathe in the gore. You may emerge from these crimson pools changed, but at least you will be alive.

Here, to live and continue down your Path is the ultimate victory.

A growth rate that includes regen Stats? Randidly clicked his tongue. Although this wouldn't help him currently, the other bonuses were enough of a boost to his current abilities that he didn't mind. 10 Stats would have been plenty, but +5 to all regenerations was quite useful. It was a good haul.

After expelling several large gutfuls of air, Randidly got to his feet. He grimaced when he took in the sheer size of the monster corpse in front of him.

Honestly... Randidly forced his body forward and crouched next to the corpse of the Stonejaw Centipede. He poked the dead monster with his hand. Its marred carapace was weirdly warm. *I might need to spend those free Stats on Strength just so I can bring it back to the village.*

It started as a low background noise of rough grunting and dragging. Easily enough to overlook, as it was pretty similar to the usual bustle of activity at the Newbie Village, which people began calling Donnyton. Except it spread. As if everything in and around the source was being pressed into silence.

The grinding steadily approached, pushing all surrounding sound of everyday life out of the way.

Daniel reeled in irritation, doing his best to ignore it and focus on the schedules for the Dungeon. They split their now almost 200 strong Classers into 20-person groups. The grouping ensured veterans were paired with fresh blood. Together they entered the Dungeon for tempering, as most of the nearby monsters had been pushed back by their expansion.

There had been a few casualties, which filled Daniel with regret. He reminded himself not to take it to heart. So many people died since the System came to this world, and more would die tomorrow. That was just the way the world worked. Repetition pushed their recognition of death toward nothing but a numb acknowledgement.

The sudden absences reminded everyone why exposing themselves to risk was necessary. They needed to gain strength to survive.

Now, though, Daniel was stuck with the annoying task of scheduling those rotations for the Dungeon. Theoretically, they could almost have it in use constantly, except for the twenty-four-hour cooldown. They would also need more people to fill the few gaps.

Daniel looked up when the strange dragging reached the front of the village, unable to push the distraction away any longer. Everything around him had fallen completely silent, save for that incessant noise. Guards and NCC laborers paused in their work and peered over. Annoyed, Daniel went to see what all the lack of fuss was about.

The sight made Daniel just as speechless as the rest of them.

Randidly walked forward, like a veritable Atlas, carrying a huge centipede body across his shoulders. He'd even looped it several times around himself in order to carry a larger portion. The whole of the body was thicker than most men's torsos, and stretched for thirty meters. The tail end dragged along the ground behind Randidly for about twenty of those, and an exhausted Decklan pushed from the back.

A lovely girl with blonde hair napped on the middle section of the thing's back.

Randidly looked casually around and grunted. "Dozer, give me a hand. Decklan isn't pulling his weight."

The joke earned a few nervous chuckles from the crowd. Dozer walked forward, gesturing for several people to follow. Dozer went to the middle of the body and lifted like he'd been doing all day long with logs and various other materials. The weight was enormous, made more so by the sheer size, changing his confident expression to a grimace. He shifted his stance and picked it up again, taking the weight onto his shoulders. Two of Dozer's men nervously approached the lovely girl, unsure of whether to help or leave her alone. Her eyes snapped open and she flinched, surprised to find the surroundings had changed.

Hopping off the centipede, she looked over at Randidly. "It's been fun. You... you take me to the most interesting places. So... feel free to come ask me out again." She flushed and hurried away.

Decklan collapsed the moment he noticed Dozer's men, grateful to have someone else take over his portion of the exertion.

Randidly grunted again and started forward. "Taking this to Sam's. Let's see him complain about materials after I drop this on his fucking doorstep."

Almost all of Dozer's men who grappled a portion of the centipede gulped, already sweating under the exertion.

It wasn't a far walk, but...

How the hell far did Ghosthound bring this thing, all by himself?

Daniel heard it too. The whispers.

Ghosthound... Ghosthound...

That's the Ghosthound.

Those individuals who were new to the town looked on with bright, awestruck eyes. They finally realized the pillar propping everything up.

Gritting his teeth, Daniel turned around and headed to his desk. He couldn't observe the contribution Randidly Ghosthound was making to the Newbie Village, even if he didn't fight at night, without being driven to throw himself back into his work.

CHAPTER FORTY-FIVE

S am didn't bat an eye at the size of the corpse; he just scratched his ear noncommittally.

"You're gonna have to take it around back. Can't work on it out here," Sam commented. "Dozer, stay for a bit too; gonna need you to smash the joints so we can work on it one segment at time."

Scowling, and more drained than he'd felt in quite a long time, Randidly left them to their work. Sam could have at least been a *little* surprised. At the same time, Randidly had gotten his own reward on the way back, so he wasn't too peeved about the noncommittal reaction.

Congratulations! You have learned the Skill **Mana Strengthening Level 1. Mana Strengthening:** *Channel Mana through your body to slightly increase physical attributes.* **You may experience a slight decrease in flexibility due to the energy being channeled through your body. Boost of physical attributes increases with Skill Level and Intelligence. Mana cost decreases with Skill Level.**

Just on the walk home, chugging Mana potions, he boosted the Skill to Level 7. It was the only way he managed to drag that huge body to the Newbie Village.

It also made Randidly excited for the future. When he had Haste, Empower, and Mana Strengthening going, his consumption of Mana and Stamina would be prodigious, but his abilities also became impressive. The stiffness from Mana Strengthening was noticeable, but he was confident his other Skills could make up for it.

After returning to his cabin, extremely conscious of the wondering and slightly fearful gazes of the population of the Newbie Village, he collapsed. Once alone, something tight and determined unraveled in his chest. It was surprisingly stressful to be responsible for the lives of two others. He recalled the horrible flash of fear when he felt the centipede's approach. If he hadn't moved in time...

Randidly's expression was bitter. *What sort of expression would Ellaine have made if I had to tell her I let Lyra die?*

Yet the experience wasn't all bad. Slowly but surely, he was finding strength. Still lying on the ground, he reached for the ceiling.

Step by step, things were progressing, both for him and the Newbie Village he supported. More people poured in every day. Each person was a chance to hear information about Ace and Sydney.

Most likely I'll hear bad news, or nothing at all... I still need to keep looking.

And beyond that? Once I find them, what will I do? What am I looking for?

The answer rose unbidden.

Strength. Only with power would he have the freedom to escape his fears and anxieties.

The answer was simple, learned from seven long months of struggle in the Dungeon with Shal. It was the answer that had been laid starkly bare before him when his own weakness forced Shal into dire straits. Randidly shook his head, a rueful smile forming. He opened his Path screen and was quite pleased by the available options.

Watcher *0/??* | *?????* | **Entangling Roots** *0/40* | **Meditation** *0/35* | **Heretic I** *0/???* | **Oathbreaker** *0/25* | **Apprentice Path** *0/50*

The Watcher and ????? Paths were there before. All the others were new arrivals since starting the 100 PP Monster Slayer Path. Entangling Roots and Meditation came from Skill Level, Randidly guessed. Apprentice unlocked when his Stat total reached 400. But Heretic and Oathbreaker...

Randidly grimaced. Once more, he would wait before completing the first two Paths. While he had so many options, the ones with an unknown source probably weren't worth the PP investment at this point. That narrowed his choices to Entangling Roots, Meditation, and Apprentice.

All three had their strong points. Apprentice would likely give Skills, but was the most expensive. Meditation would likely further improve his regeneration abilities, which he needed. Though it likely wouldn't result in a Skill, nor give many bonuses until the completion. Thirty-five PP would be quite a few Skill Levels to wait for any bonuses.

Meanwhile, Entangling Roots was Randidly's go-to Skill when encountering a new opponent, slowing and tying down the enemy while he repositioned and adjusted. Any improvement in that Skill, or availability of a similar, more powerful Skill, would be worth it.

He could only pick one and each held a significant investment. The lowest being Meditation at 35 PP.

Randidly rubbed his temples. *Let's look ahead a bit. What will I be doing tomorrow?*

Now that the Newbie Village had been broken of its initial reliance on him, forming its own formidable squads, Randidly planned on actively helping more with the monster horde. After that, should he return to the other Newbie Village for the glassware? Perhaps not so soon. Give them time to gather and forget he attacked their boss.

Instead, returning to the boundary seemed to hold more immediate benefits. He could explore in a different direction than their patrol through the domain of the lizardmen. Take a more tank-based group with him and fight cats.

No, that might be getting ahead of himself. The cats would probably kill most people instantly, aside from Donny. Even Randidly felt chills as those claws ripped toward him. Back to the lizardmen then... Which was fine. He'd gained a lot of Skill Levels fighting against them. Perhaps he could rely more on his Mana Skills and let some people practice taking the precise and targeted blows of the anthropomorphic lizards.

And if he wanted to focus on his Mana Skills...

Randidly set the Apprentice Path aside. Better to focus on improving his current Skills, either by Meditation or Entangling Roots, over learning new Skills. Right now, he needed to see immediate improvements in his strength if he wanted to survive for longer beyond the boundary.

For several long seconds, Randidly teetered between the two options. He settled on the Entangling Roots Path. His immediate concerns were increasing his combat ability and harvesting more materials to keep the rest of the people in "Donnyton" alive. Randidly put his 6 leftover PP into the Entangling Roots Path.

At 5, he earned himself 1 in Control and Focus. At least the Path was going to be a rewarding one. Randidly grinned in pleasure before checking his full Status Screen.

Randidly Ghosthound
Class: ---
Level: N/A
Health(/R per hour): 206/291 [+2] (137 [+3])
Mana(/R per hour): 139/347 (60.75)
Stam(/R per min): 105/307 (53 [+1])
Vit: 39 [+1]
End: 30

Str: 27 [+2]
Agi: 47 [+7]
Perception: 23
Reaction: 26
Resistance: 9
Willpower: 55
Intelligence: 68
Wisdom: 30
Control: 43
Focus: 20
Equipment: *Necklace of the Shadow Cat Lvl 20 (R): (Vitality +1, Strength +2, Agility +7)*
Skills
Soul Skill: *Spear of Rot Mastery Lvl 120*

Basic: *Running Lvl 19 | Physical Fitness Lvl 28 | Sneak Lvl 31 | Acid Resistance Lvl 23 | Poison Resistance Lvl 16 | Spirit of Adversity Lvl 25 | Dagger Mastery Lvl 13 | Dodge Lvl 27 | Spear Mastery Lvl 41 | Pain Resistance Lvl 11 | Fighting Proficiency Lvl 30 | First Aid Lvl 14 | Block Lvl 27 | Mental Strength Lvl 12 | Curse Resistance Lvl 3 | Pathfinding Lvl 16 | Mapmaking Lvl 4 | Calculated Blow Lvl 11 | Edge of Decay (Un) Lvl 5*

Stamina: *Heavy Blow Lvl 22 | Sprinting Lvl 13 | Iron Skin Lvl 25 | Phantom Thrust Lvl 35 | Spear Phantom's Footwork Lvl 28 | Eyes of the Spear Phantom Lvl 20 | Phantom Half-Step Lvl 6 | Haste Lvl 18 | Phantom Onslaught Lvl 10 | Sweep Lvl 12 | Spear Deflect Lvl 6 | Empower Lvl 16 | Roundhouse Kick Lvl 9*

Mana: *Mana Bolt Lvl 30 | Meditation Lvl 31 | Entangling Roots Lvl 33 | Mana Shield Lvl 24 | Root Manipulation Lvl 29 | Arcane Orb Lvl 23 | Magic Missile Lvl 6 | Healing Palm Lvl 5 | Fireball Lvl 16 | Pollen of the Rafflesia (R) Lvl 5 | Summon Pestilence Lvl 14 | Mana Strengthening Lvl 7*

Crafting: *Farming Lvl 23 | Plant Breeding Lvl 9 | Potion Making Lvl 22 | Analyze Lvl 24 | Refine Lvl 4*

His Intelligence was already impressive at 68, making his Mana Skills pack quite the punch. Perhaps it was time to funnel some points into his other Stats to keep his physical capabilities high. In the fight with the centipede, if he hadn't been as fast as he had, the overwhelming power of that large body would have definitely killed him.

And since he wanted to gather more materials from the Shadow Cats...

Randidly walked outside, grounded with a sense of direction. The rare sort of peace he usually only felt while making potions filled him. For now, time to train. To his annoyance, people scurried around like diligent worker ants near his cabin, making preparations for the night. Even the farmers continued their grim-eyed vigil in nurturing the plants. The presence of others reminded him of his social anxiety, and his peace steadily dissipated.

Everyone gave Randidly a wide berth.

Sighing, Randidly slipped away through the trees into the darkness, following a path up the nearby mountain. When he found a relatively clear area, he began a new type of training. It made him nervous.

He blasted himself in the chest with a Fireball.

The first explosion sent him stumbling. A large chunk of his Health dropped, leaving in its stead an inflicted burn status. Touching the wound, Randidly used Healing Palm twice, restoring the Health and removing the burn status. The skin still stung.

He repeated his self-inflicted blow. Somehow, he had the vague sensation Shal would be so proud in witnessing this training method that he would wipe a tear from his eye.

After ten repetitions, Randidly was forced to take a break to hit up all the places where blue energy shards grew within the strange, System-planted trees. He previously marked them on his map for ease of gathering. After mopping up the monsters that inevitably cropped up around them, he returned to the clearing.

He took a short break to brew another few batches of Mana Potions and continued.

Fireball.

Congratulations! Your Skill **Fireball** has grown to **Level 17!**

Healing Palm. Healing Palm.

Congratulations! Your Skill **Healing Palm** has grown to **Level 6!**

Fireball.
Healing Palm.

Congratulations! Your Skill **Healing Palm** has grown to **Level 7!**

Fireball.
Healing Palm. Healing Palm

Fireball.
Healing Palm.

Congratulations! Your Skill **Healing Palm** has grown to **Level 8!**

Fireball.

Congratulations! Your Skill **Fireball** has grown to **Level 18!**

Congratulations! Your Skill **Pain Resistance** has grown to **Level 12!**

Healing Palm.
Potion Making.
With the skin of his torso stinging, Randidly practiced Empowered Spear Phantom's Footwork to break up the monotony and burn through his Stamina. When he exhausted himself, he forced his attention back to the training.
Fireball.
Although Randidly already earned several Levels in Fireball and Healing Palm, now was when he got the notification that made him smile the widest.

Congratulations! You have learned the Skill **Fire Resistance Level 1**.

Chuckling, Randidly continued the rotation, firm of mind with the knowledge that his method of moving forward was the correct one. The pain was difficult, but compared to his goal, it was a small thing.
Strength. For everything, he needed strength. He could not slack off now.

CHAPTER FORTY-SIX

*A*nnie batted her eyes, pretending to just wake up. She felt no qualms against putting on an act of adorable sleepiness for Dozer when he pressed himself up, holding his forehead. Although Dozer fell asleep earlier the previous night, mostly due to her intimate ministrations, it was obvious he still found getting up in the middle of the night for the beast horde to be difficult.

Annie squirmed. She rubbed her body against him without being too honest about the fact she was doing it purposely. But still he stood, strapping on his leather and furs, lowering his necklace of teeth over his head. His jaw was strong and stark in the shadowy lodging. This was how Annie liked her men. Big, brooding, and direct. She admitted to herself this made them quite a bit easier to control, though that wasn't *the reason* she liked men with those certain traits.

Although it was a nice side effect.

Yawning for effect, she allowed part of the blanket to slide off, her left nipple poking out from behind the blanket. She liked the way his eyes followed it for several seconds, before grunting and turning away, scratching his groin.

Not that she would have let him take her right before he needed to fight against the horde. She liked to make him want it. Give him a reward so he would work hard.

Dozer reached for the huge club he found within the Dungeon. "Stay here," he intoned seriously, giving her a look over his shoulder as he left. "Wait for me."

Annie was the picture of solemn obedience, nodding, her eyes bright.

As soon as he left, she snorted, kicking off the blankets. She found some of the spandex she had scrounged up since the System came. Not that furs weren't great for the whole tribal vibe, but she felt next to naked without her leggings.

Tying her hair up in a practical ponytail, Annie left the hut and went around to the small space in the walls where she stored her bow. She didn't like to brag, but she was probably—no, obviously—the best archer in the village. Sometimes other people got lucky and hit the target, but she could loose an arrow and hit a target at—

She scratched her head, then shrugged. Basically, further than anyone else. In her mind, her judge of distance was great, mostly because she felt that *everything* she could see was within her distance.

She even started gaining Skills for it. Archery Mastery, Hawkeye, Snipe, Power Shot.

She hurried toward the wall, as if she would stay in and let her Dozer handle the problem himself.

She was a woman, not a pretty doll.

After several awkward bouts of flirting with Daniel, he finally succumbed and allowed her to be up on the new ramparts. She *was* the best archer, after all. They both mutually agreed not to tell Dozer. The big, blunt, strong man was surprisingly sensitive about certain things.

Annie arrived near the gate, where groups of Classers stood, faces grim. For some, it was the first time standing on the front lines. Annie had half a mind to seek out Decklan and inquire where the underground betting pool had placed the over/under for deaths tonight. She decided it wasn't worth the trouble.

Sam shouted for Classers to gather, passing out new shields he managed to make from the giant bug the Ghosthound brought back. It was honestly kind of cute the way so many crowded and jostled to get a piece of dead bug skin.

Largely ignored in the milling crowd of warriors, Annie gathered arrows from Sam's people and climbed the side of the ramparts by the gate, lifting herself onto the vantage point. To her surprise, there was already someone there.

It was the older magician lady who had gone into the Dungeon with Dozer and his men. Annie smiled sweetly at her but said nothing. Clarissa nodded before turning her attention back to the valley. In the NCC village below, one by one, the fires and lights were being snuffed out, so as not to attract the monster's attention.

"Alright! First Squad to the front. Second Squad ready to switch," Donny shouted, sporting a shiny black bug shield and a mean-looking iron sword he probably got from the new Weapon Shop. He turned to the milling group behind those first ten squads. "The rest of you, listen to Daniel. He'll set you up in groups. We'll do one full rotation with the regulars, then work in the fresh meat from every other squad, all right?"

Daniel acknowledged the order and Donny turned back to the front squads, grinning from ear to ear. Most people had to stand on tiptoes, straining to see his gangly teenage form. He lifted the huge shield, almost three-fourths the size of a door, like it was nothing, revealing his power. Even if his body didn't show it, his Stats were real.

"So, now," he drawled slowly, moving to the front. "You regulars. The final count is two hundred and sixty Classers here. Honestly, we might have bad news for the fresh blood. Who knows if there is even going to be any monsters left by the time we get through a full rotation, right, boys?"

They howled and hooted, men and women, young and old, pounding their chests. In that moment, donning their makeshift weapons and armor, the tribal vibe was quite strong. Even Dozer joined, his adorable smile stretched wide as he pounded the ground with his club.

Annie shook her head. If he gathered enough ambition, Dozer could be double the leader the little dweeb Donny was. But honestly, he was happy now, so it was fine. And if they ever wanted to take out Donny—

A figure strolled up from the NCC village. She narrowed her eyes, just making out the shape after she caught movement in the corner of her eyes. To her surprise, he kept to the shadows, spear spinning, as relaxed and casual as can be. The Ghosthound. If someone didn't have a vision Skill like Annie, they likely wouldn't even be able to see his approach.

Not only did this strange founder of Donnyton have a Stealth Skill, his Stats and body control were impressively refined.

She pushed back a wave of shock. There was another person suddenly with him. A lithe girl, her blonde hair pulled into a bun. The Ghosthound gave the girl a somewhat helpless look.

The two were quick. Within ten seconds, they crossed the distance from the village to the wall, silently scaled it, and dropped onto the ramparts further down from where Annie and Clarissa stood. Calmly, the Ghosthound walked over, his eyes flicking past Annie and Clarissa, scanning the waiting Classers.

The noise attracted Clarissa's attention. When she turned, she hopped slightly, shocked by their sudden appearance.

"Ah-oh, it's you. You... You're the Ghosthound, right?" Clarissa said nervously, fear, wonder, and excitement warring across her face. "I'm uh, Clarissa. The Weather Witch."

She extended her hand. The Ghosthound glanced to the hand and nodded slowly. After a few seconds, the blonde girl stepped up, taking Clarissa's hand.

"Ah... I'm Lyra. I can see you have very dense Mana around your body, so if you have any tips you could share with me…" the girl said brightly, flashing a cheeky smile.

This was the first time Annie had seen the Ghosthound up close. He was tall, but not too much so. Obviously athletic, but not overly muscular. There was something else. She could feel it. Maybe it was the way his eyes swept over her, registering and dismissing her instantly. Maybe it was the unnatural stillness about him, like he was asleep or dead even while standing. At least until he moved with an unnatural speed. Maybe it was the piercing green of his eyes. They could almost rip through your soul and rifle through your thoughts at will.

When the Ghosthound turned away from her, Annie released a breath she hadn't realized she'd been holding. The blonde girl gave her a knowing smile, tinged with the slightest bit of powerless jealousy.

Interesting. Annie narrowed her eyes a bit and regarded the Ghosthound again.

"I've distributed some to Daniel already, but…" The Ghosthound nodded toward Clarissa and Lyra. "It looks like the two of you are the most capable with Mana amongst the Classers. Do you have enough Mana potions?"

Clarissa thanked the Ghosthound, taking a few from him.

Lyra shook her head. "I, uh, I think it would be better for me to get more Mana potions from you as I need them…"

"You won't be able to keep up with me," the Ghosthound said bluntly. "And I don't want to stop mid-fight to babysit you."

"You won't have to—" Lyra flushed.

Annie noted how the younger girl forced down her irritation. It was clear she wasn't used to needing to do so much work to earn attention from a boy.

Lyra frowned for several seconds and tried again. "How will I grow if I don't push myself just a little beyond my comfort zone? And imagine how epic a moment it would be, for you to pass me the Mana potion right when I need it, and then I cast the best spell ever and wound a monster that's about to attack you! You'd be so thankful that you'd have to—Ah, well… B-b-besides," the blonde girl blushed, "I bet it's lonely, right? Always fighting alone in the middle of the monsters. So…"

For a second, their eyes met, and this time, Annie was the one to flash the blonde girl a knowing smile.

Ah, to be young, Annie thought rather smugly. She heard the girl was actually a pretty well-known actor, but this wasn't a sterile set environment. This was real life. It was all too clear the girl was nursing a crush.

Scratching his head, the Ghosthound nodded to Lyra, acknowledging he heard her.

He stepped to the edge of the ramparts. "Donny, Daniel, Dozer."

It was in his voice too, a low, resonating baritone. The crowd fell silent, staring at the figure who appeared above them, holding a plain-looking spear, with serious eyes.

The three men walked forward.

"Randidly," Daniel said. "Are you fighting?"

"Just as artillery," the Ghosthound replied with a smirk.

This was the first time Annie heard his real name. She should have known Ghosthound was fake.

Though it fit him. The strangeness of the System somehow made it reasonable that someone with a name like that would become influential.

"There's something else. The enemy is bringing air support. I suspect we won't be able to keep them outside the wall as much as we have previously. I'll thin the numbers, but you'll need to handle the extra pressure."

Daniel's eyes went wide, his panic clear. The Ghosthound had already turned away. Donny and Dozer were both nodding, eyes firm.

What Annie didn't expect was that Randidly would turn and look her straight in the eyes. "You're an archer?"

To her surprise, his firm and demanding tone set her heart beating quicker. Annie tried to sound cool and tough as she nodded and spoke. "I... don't have a Class, but..."

He shrugged, his emerald gaze returning to the darkness. "That's fine. But when I point it out, I'd like you to make the shots. Prepare your bow."

He glanced at her and added, as though her dazed expression and still hands annoyed him. He had a *very* good disapproving scowl. "They're coming."

Sure enough, when Annie looked out, a veritable sea of monsters rushed forward. Above them, smaller, swooping forms could be seen amongst larger, colossal shadows that glided down from the mountains.

"Those..." Annie muttered.

All of the strange excitement she felt from the Ghosthound's intensity fell away. How the hell was she supposed to affect those things with a bow?

"Looks like giant condors, right? They're pretty tough too. Randidly's Fireballs don't take them down in one shot, and those things have some *juice*," the blonde girl said with a shake of her head.

The Ghosthound was already looking at Clarissa. "Use your Mana sparingly on the ground; the warriors below can handle it. Take out the air support. If you need more Mana potions, just say the word. We're gonna be the wave break to keep them from being overwhelmed."

The Ghosthound pointed. A bright flash of fire shot from his hand at the approaching mob. When it hit the monster's line, it exploded outward in a blast of flame, knocking away everything within a three-meter area. Smoke and debris blasted outward and the monsters in the epicenter of the blast were burnt to a crisp.

Annie was amazed. *It really looks like artillery struck...*

The Ghosthound pointed again, and again, and again. The front-line charging toward them was ragged and scattered.

Donny sighed theatrically below. "Welp, let's pack up, boys; looks like this is going to be an easy one."

There were a few chuckles, and the tension was largely out of the first few squads, but they weren't relaxed. They stretched muscles and tightened shield straps, squeezing the shafts of their axes and adjusting their fur and snakeskin armor to better cover their joints. They knew their business. These were the warriors that survived at least two nights.

Although they hadn't been at this for long, they knew this initial display was only the beginning. They needed to keep their guard up. If they didn't, they would have been dead already.

The front runners of the monsters slowed, scared.

The second wave surged forward, running past, screaming their fury. Again, and again the Ghosthound pointed, his finger the sizzling harbinger of death. Annie shivered as she watched him continually drink Mana potions to fuel his slaughter.

For the third wave of monsters, the fourth, and the fifth, the Ghosthound possessed a Mana potion and broke them all.

Due to their high numbers of Classers, the waves of monsters were endless. The shadows grew larger the closer they came. Grim-eyed, Randidly reached up and cracked his neck. He raised another potion to his lips and guzzled it all down. Above, a bird screeched, and a strange winged creature with a woman's head and torso dove toward them, talons flashing.

"Clarissa—"

"Ah!" The blonde girl twisted awkwardly, forcing herself forward. "How about you let me go first?"

A strange, glowing hawk condensed on the girl's outstretched arm and threw itself up with a few beats of its powerful and luminous wings. It streaked upwards, meeting the harpy creature midair. The screeching was abruptly cut off. The harpy fell in two bleeding pieces. The hawk swooped around, ripping through more of the approaching harpies, but there were dozens.

The Ghosthound rolled his eyes, looking surprisingly human when he grinned at the blonde girl. "Very impressive. You're definitely a glass cannon. If that's all, Clarissa—"

"Would it be that uncomfortable to give a compliment every once in a while? The stoic type is cool and attractive, but a lot of people are drawn to the gap too," the blonde girl muttered.

Annie's lips twitched. The girl's awkwardness was starting to be rubbed away by the lack of response from the Ghosthound.

Lyra stamped her foot and waved her arms. A crow, hummingbird, goldfinch, and an eagle sprang into existence above her head. All the conjurations were made of that strange glowing energy. They flew up, joining the hawk in sweeping attacks against the monsters.

Each of them was more weapon than natural creature, ripping holes through the harpies just by flying into them. Harpy bodies fell like rain across the stretch of ground between the forest and the Newbie Village. The girl's glowing bird bodies sizzled and flickered, silently screaming their fury in their slaughter.

But as soon as they appeared, they faded, the blonde girl collapsing in a sweating heap. "Ugh... I... those potions... please..."

"I suppose that's my cue." Clarissa stepped forward and summoned icicles, expertly spearing a flying harpy before it could approach.

"You too," the Ghosthound rumbled.

Annie started. She was genuinely shocked by his faith. *Me? You want me to shoot wildly flying birds?*

At night...? While they swoop down and try to kill me!

Admittedly, the Ghosthound took care of any monster that came too near, all the while throwing Fireballs at the ground army, leaving wide gaps in the flood of monsters. It wasn't like she was in any danger.

Gritting her teeth, Annie nocked an arrow and raised her bow, taking aim. When she tried to track the harpies, her vision blurred, their movements too confusing.

She closed her eyes and loosed, hoping for the best.

She was rewarded with a screech. Annie was shocked to find her arrow through the eye of a harpy, the body crumpling and falling to the ground. She'd hit and slain a harpy.

Congratulations! Your Skill **Archery Mastery** has grown to **Level 12!**

All through dumb luck.

Feeling giddy, she nocked another arrow, taking the time to aim and trust her instincts. That one ripped the throat out of one harpy and ricocheted away, taking another in the chest.

Congratulations! Your Skill **Archery Mastery** has grown to **Level 13!**

Congratulations! You have learned the Skill **Ricochet (R) Level 1.**

That first portion had been properly aimed, and the fact that it Ricocheted...

The Ghosthound gave her a long look, as though he hadn't missed that she closed her eyes to start. "Nice shots."

Then he glared at the sky and the bigger shadows closing in. "Still too far away..."

"Aegis!" The call came, a golden light suffusing the first squad as they ripped through the first wave of enemies and the beleaguered second.

As more came, they came in thicker groupings. Wolverines, lizards, and imps all running together like one mass. Due to the flying groups, the Ghosthound couldn't deplete them as easily. The Classers below were left to take the brunt of the strain.

At this point, the people in the first squad were all above Level 10 and able to take on several of each enemy at once. But if there were a hundred enemies pressing in around them?

They responded to numbers with discipline. The weapons of the Classers slashed in short, brutal strikes. Admittedly, they were still pretty clumsy, but they were getting the hang of Roman-legion-style fighting.

Annie took out another harpy and shook her head sadly. That was another reason why her Dozer wasn't in charge. His fighting style didn't match the strategy. He couldn't charge outward and smash the enemies to bits. Her man struggled just as much to *not* harm the humans next to him as he fought against monsters.

"Finally," the Ghosthound said, fixated on the sky. "Here they come."

CHAPTER FORTY-SEVEN

*R*andidly gathered fire in his palms and released it up into the thick mass of flyers. When he missed, he threw more Fireballs into the sky. He didn't bother with calculating wind or speed. He simply adjusted the flight path with his extremely high Control Stat, backed by his Willpower.

His latest Fireball struck the wing of the first huge condor. The bird screamed, falling sideways, unable to glide with a huge chunk of its feathers burned away. Dozens more cruised lower, aiming for the base with their fork-like talons.

"First Squad, switch!" Donny called, his squad sliding back one individual at a time, replaced by a member of the second squad. It was a smart ploy. Having the first squad at the back to deal with airborne threats was a good way to balance their rest with the most pressing threat.

Randidly threw several more Fireballs upwards. The first condor crashed, its thirty-meter wingspan smashing dozens of monsters it carried into the dirt. It didn't appear to have a high Level, or any offensive weapons, but it was able to support the weight of many monsters on its back while gliding. Randidly had seen them hopping off the mountain, looming above Donnyton to get up to speed before slowly making their way down here.

Transport jets... Randidly grimaced.

It was annoying, but the condors themselves weren't too big of a problem. It was what they represented that was scary. Randidly activated his Eyes of the Spear Phantom and scanned the back of the horde. Low-Leveled monsters rushed out unendingly. Fighting against foes numbering in the thousands was exhausting.

No end in sight yet, huh?

Randidly drank a Mana potion and tossed a dozen more Fireballs up into the air, ripping holes in wings and blowing heads entirely off bodies. Most crashed into the rumbling monster charge, sowing chaos.

There were far too many of the condors.

Several times, a condor crashed on their side of the wall, delivering around two dozen groggy monsters. They staggered off the condor and were met by the newer squads backed by the first squad.

The only problem occurred when a condor slammed into the wall, splintering the thick logs and giving the monsters handholds to scale. Despite their low intelligence, these creatures noticed the opportunity and swarmed like maggots on rotting meat.

Decklan's group appeared like ghosts, ripping through the distracted monsters. Sam gleefully had his men drag the condor over the wall, screeching about not damaging its feathers. Sam cut a small gash on his hand and rubbed the blood on the bird's body, looking at it with greedy eyes.

Randidly admitted to himself that Sam's pursuits were getting decidedly strange. The way he looked at a fresh monster body he'd never seen before... it wasn't moral.

Randidly continued to rain fire down, his Skill Level increasing, the explosion getting marginally larger, inch by inch. Each Skill Level was a slight increase. With the monsters so densely packed, such an increase was extremely important, earning him more valuable Skill experience. The sensation of growth was intoxicating, despite the danger.

Congratulations! Your Skill **Fireball** has grown to **Level 20!**

Congratulations! Your Skill **Fireball** has grown to **Level 21!**

The squads rotated, the fresh recruits stumbling during their first brush with danger, but surviving. Ptolemy was there, healing scratches, bandaging wounds, replacing any wooden shields that broke. Randidly's potions were distributed freely, bolstering their Attribute Pools during the most frantic clashes.

Randidly spared a glance for the Weather Witch and the Archer. Both possessed a surprising amount of mettle, standing tall while harpies attacked. Not that he would let any get close enough to matter, but still. Both were accurate. Both were practical. Both were blessedly silent.

"Mana potion!" Lyra chirped from Randidly's side, holding out her hand like a proud dog waiting for a treat after performing a trick.

He tossed her a Mana potion. A long, slow smile formed on his face. *She might be a little oblivious to threats on her life, but she's pretty adorable when being obedient. I can see why Ellaine was so worried about her.*

Still, Randidly kept his attention fixed at the oncoming horde. Looming at the back, crouched down but abundantly clear given its size, was a large wolverine. Even from this distance, it was too large to be normal. Randidly could clearly see its glowing blue name and Level.

Godmother Wolverine Level 21

Not a Stonejaw Centipede, but still a troublesome foe for the Newbie Village. Randidly prepared to go meet it, then thought better of it. Instead, he turned toward the forces below. Even if he was to take the lion's share, keeping them involved was important to prevent any more reliance. Half of the Classers were fighting, the others were bent over panting.

"Dozer, time to live up to your namesake. Clear a path directly forward, into the enemy. Donny, get your most durable people and follow him. Looks like we have our first Boss," Randidly announced.

A ripple ran through the fighters below.

Dozer's squad wearily got to their feet, hefting their shields and drawing their short swords. Randidly chuckled then shook his head. "No, no, leave those twigs here. I said clear a *path*, not thread a needle. Give Donny a hole large enough to stumble through. I might need to use him as a distraction."

The whole group stilled. Dozer shifted, looking up at Randidly. Then his ugly, flat face split into a huge grin. He dropped his short sword and shield and drew the huge club from where it sat at the back of the group. All around him, men shed armor and small arms, drawing axes, clubs, halberds, and spears. Huge, weighty weapons that were meant more to bash and slaughter.

Although the legion-style tactics were effectively keeping them alive, they lacked a certain flair.

Dozer strode forward with his weapon across his shoulder, his ten-man squad following him. The fourth squad currently held the front, holding back the monster horde.

"SQUADS six through ten," Dozer bellowed. "PART."

Confused, they shuffled to the side, revealing squad five, who nervously glanced backwards, while the fourth squad struggled with grim expressions. Donny formed up a group of twenty-five or so people, hurrying after Dozer.

Dozer and his group bounded forward, gripping their heavy weapons with both hands to keep from injuring themselves.

Randidly threw down handfuls of fire, not at the area near the gate, but in a line directly forward, thinning enemies in the way. The monsters screamed and collapsed, easing the burden on the charging group of Classers.

His huge thighs bulging, Dozer crouched behind the fifth squad and leapt, his huge, two-meter club held high overhead. His squad loyally followed, roaring. Their huge, muscled forms reached the apex of their leap, then they were falling, weapons swinging in dangerous and glittering arcs.

Most nearby wolverines and lizards were meat paste before they under-stood what was happening. Dozer rumbled forward, his huge club swinging back and forth, four or five monsters crushed or smashed backwards with every blow. His men charged after him, swinging like mad themselves, and the monster horde was quickly bulldozed before them.

Donny followed, the golden glow of Aegis suffusing his group as they moved, mopping up the mess left by Dozer. Feeling the time was right, Randidly bombarded the area around the Godmother Wolverine with flames, killing the weaker monsters and antagonizing the Boss.

The thing was the size of a bus. It roared and stood on its hind legs, shouting its challenge toward the sky as it waved its clawed paws. It charged forward, heedless of the minions it crushed. With both rushing toward each other, Dozer soon caught sight of the charging wolverine and laughed wildly, raising his club.

The two forces met with a boom. Dozer staggered back several steps. The Godmother Wolverine stopped dead. Its face was confused, then furious. It reared up again. But Donny was there, shield blazing with golden light, and Shield Bashed it directly in the chest. His practiced Skills combined with the Boss's previous confusion was enough to get an edge. Stunned, the thing stumbled. Decklan swept in, his knives leaving long scratches on its flank.

Their squads spread out around them, knocking the other monsters back and forming a loose defensive circle, letting the powerhouses meet.

Randidly was slightly disappointed he *actually* didn't need to be part of the struggle. Until he sensed this enemy was not one that would get his blood flowing. Although it was as high a Level as the things beyond the boundary, most of that appeared to give it a prodigious amount of Health. It was enough for the three of Donnyton's finest and their squads to defeat it. Also, they would be further reassured of their ability to survive without him. That was very important for the future.

It turned out to be an appropriate Boss for the Newbie Village. The System hadn't attempted to blindside them this time.

Because he wouldn't fight the Boss, Randidly drew his spear and hopped off the wall. He glided forward into the snarling mass of common enemies that filled the space in front of Donnyton.

Now was the time for him to play.

Randidly held a satisfied expression when the sun rose. For one, there were only three deaths this morning, and one of them was an NCC who got too curious, wandering too close to the horde. Only two people who had *expected* to face danger were overwhelmed by it and fell.

In addition, Randidly experienced a satisfying amount of Skill Level gains. Spear Mastery increased by 2, Phantom Thrust by 1, Spear Phantom's Footwork by 3, Heavy Blow and Fighting Proficiency by 1, Haste by 2,

Sweep by 4, Empower by 3, Calculated Blow by 8, Roundhouse Kick and Edge of Decay by 4.

Fireball also increased by 3 more Levels during the mop-up portion of the fight, with Root Manipulation going up by 1, Pollen of the Rafflesia and Summon Pestilence both by 2, and Mana Strengthening by 3.

Randidly adjusted his Shadow Cat necklace, which was sticky with dried blood. As he did so, something occurred to him. *Was the reason they started using necklaces to denote authority, because I've been wearing this?*

There's no way that's the case... Right?

CHAPTER FORTY-EIGHT

*R*andidly earned quite a lot of PP in the battle. He supposed that was understandable. Part of it was the huge library of Skills he currently possessed. Odds were one or two would Level up constantly, especially when he slaughtered his way through big groups of wolverines or lizards.

Additionally, no matter how strong you were, being surrounded by enemies added a lot of mental pressure, raising the stakes. A small mistake or shift in stance could be deadly. In addition, his higher regeneration rates, combined with his constant potions, meant he could continue far longer than others, out-grinding Skills Levels with the sheer amount of time spent fighting.

At this point, Randidly had become a Skill Level factory.

Still, the rewards this time were large. He began spending PP freely. The completion notification for the Entangling Roots Path was a welcome sight, followed by a flood of additional notifications.

Congratulations! You have completed the **"The Entangling Roots Path"!**
+3 Int, Wis, Control, and Focus; +25 Mana.

Where you walk, the earth comes alive, heeding your beck and call.
With your bare feet, you steadily come to understand the Soul of the
World.

Congratulations! You have learned the Skill **Wall of Thorns Level 1!**

Congratulations! You have learned the Skill **Soul Seed (U)!**

Wall of Thorns: *Produces a bristling wall of thorns.* **Size and sharpness of thorns based on Intelligence and Skill Level. Shape of the wall and distance away based on Wisdom and Skill Level.**

Soul Seed (U): A rare skill that will not Level. *Nurture the seed with the essence of your other Skills and different plants will grow.* **Effects of the plants will be determined by the Level of Skills used to nurture them. Plants grown from Soul Seeds will have intelligence and Level, and will be capable of growth once they sprout. Amount of Soul Seeds you are able to support depends on certain intangible factors. Current limit of Soul Seeds:** *0/2.*

Congratulations! As the first member of your race to unlock a **Unique Skill,** you have received the reward Path **"Frontrunner** *0/100.***" Use this Path to lead your race to salvation. The Path to the Pinnacle is long, but you have already taken the first few steps forward!**

For finishing the Entangling Roots Path, your Skill has evolved! Synchronicity with Soulskill "Spear of Rot Mastery" detected.

**Calculating mutations
mutations found.**

Forking Path! Choose which Skill **Entangling Roots** shall take on characteristics of: **Pollen of the Rafflesia, Edge of Decay,** or **Spear Mastery.**

Warning! Change will be permanent and affect the usage of the Skill.

The new Skills intrigued Randidly, especially the label of Unique, for Soul Seed. By what Randidly heard from Shal, Unique was a designation usually only applied to Dungeon Bosses. Looking at Wall of Thorns, he was excited to go cat hunting today. Depending on the size of the walls he could make, he would be able to hem the Shadow Cats into a smaller area where their high Agility would be less overwhelming.

Randidly's confidence was boosted by the "reward" Path he received. Although he was a little leery about another 100 PP Path right now. The memory of the long slog to finish his first 100 PP Path made him sigh.

For the moment, his attention was on the ways Entangling Roots could evolve. He hesitated for a few seconds, even though he knew exactly what he would choose.

Grow slowly, but always advance... Randidly pressed his lips together and made his selection. He truly had been taught well by Shal.

Congratulations! You have chosen **Spear Mastery.** Your Skill has evolved into **Spearing Roots. Level has been reset, but benefits from the original Skill's Skill Level have been retained.**

Congratulations! You have learned the Skill **Spearing Roots Level 1.**

Randidly moved into the forest and tried his new toy. The sight of a dozen sharpened roots shooting upward, boring holes in the wood of an unlucky tree set him laughing. Although he would need to rely on Root Manipulation for his Control of the Skill, the increased strength and power of the stabbing roots were more than enough to make up for it.

Besides, he'd been using Root Manipulation to touch up on the accuracy of Entangling Roots anyway. And now, for the big control, he gained Wall of Thorns. Slowly, his fighting style was coming into proper form.

Curious, Randidly next tried to use Wall of Thorns. A short, waist-high hedge of sharpened thorns sprang up. Randidly pressed his finger against one and pulled back, impressed. If it was sharp enough to get through his Endurance, most low-Leveled monsters would tear themselves to pieces on it. The Mana cost was less than Spearing Roots for this small amount, but could scale up if he wanted to increase it in size. He would need to Level it a bit before it was truly useful against the Shadow Cats.

Randidly looked at his hand, concentrated, and summoned a Soul Seed. A small, weirdly maroonish-colored, wizened-looking nut appeared. A small bar hovered over the seed.

Soul Seed: 0% Nurtured

Randidly scratched his chin. *Nurtured, is it? The notification said I nurture it with Skills, so do I just...*

As he focused on the nut, he felt a strange connection forming. Instinctively, he knew that while he kept the seed on his person, it would grow based on any Skill he activated, even passive ones. He put the seed away and turned back to his spare PP. He poured it into the Meditation Path and was rewarded at 5 spent PP with 15 Mana, and at 10 PP with +2 Wisdom.

Yawning, Randidly rubbed his stomach. Today was a good day. And every good day deserved a good meal followed by a short nap to reinvigorate him.

An hour after he closed his eyes, Randidly bolted upright. Sweat coated every inch of him, his heart racing. The tight fear of helplessness consumed him, the same sweeping hold he felt when facing the Giant Serpent and Shal saved him.

Gradually, he calmed down.

It'd been the sort of nightmare he hadn't had since he left the Dungeon.

He'd fought against a bunch of Constances while the weirdest feeling of something sinister watched his every move. Whenever he noticed those eyes on his back, he'd spin around. Each time, there was nothing out of the ordinary. Just more scowling Constances.

Right before he woke up, something oddly familiar hummed beneath the throng of battle—the low chuckle of an older woman.

Why is a woman laughing at me? Am I really that stressed... Randidly shook his head and went to the barrel of water in the corner of his cabin. After splashing his face, he felt better. The cloud of paranoia hanging around him after the nightmare parted.

Randidly couldn't bother with being distracted.

It was time to train.

Leaving by a side path, Randidly escaped from Donnyton without facing more questions from Daniel about Skills or intercepting strange followers clinging on to him for the journey.

Decklan was quick and determined. It wasn't like the man was that much of a burden. Even Lyra was useful with her Mana Skills. Lyra was an NCC like he was, which meant she could learn as many Skills as she pleased. For that reason, Randidly vaguely felt he should pour some effort into her growth.

Considering his earlier stress from the nightmare, Randidly let himself off the hook as he loped along the game trail through the forest. *I wouldn't mind taking her along, but maybe protecting her for Ellaine was why my dream this morning was so weird, so for now—*

Randidly froze when he topped the hill. He'd caught something out of the corner of his eye. A shadowy figure with a sharp smile on her face, sitting on a stump, watching him intently.

He spun around, expecting to see Lyra with her Mana birds fluttering around her. There was nothing. The path was deserted and the stump was just a stump. Randidly chuckled nervously.

Okay, I'm definitely stressed. Randidly kneeled to Meditate for a bit and balance his mental state. Even if he had grown definitively stronger, he wasn't so strong that he could allow his mind to roam the clouds while searching for these cats.

Today marked the fifth day of the week of monster hordes. There would likely be additional Boss monsters tonight he would need to be prepared for.

Looking at the sun filtering through the leaves, Randidly wondered what waited for the Newbie Zone once the walls fell, and the monsters from beyond the boundary roved toward the village.

His eyes snapped open. Clenching his fist, he turned and began to walk. He would meet whatever came with strength.

And he would work on sharpening that strength.

Daniel glanced up at the nervous man, annoyed. Considering how much work he had to do before the next monster horde…

"What is it?" he snapped when the man simply rubbed his hands together.

"Uh, S-Sam wants to speak with you, sir," the man stuttered and hurried away.

Sighing, Daniel wiggled his fingers at his assistants, who tiredly took the paperwork from him. Despite what the rest of the people here seemed to think, a society required bureaucracy to function. You couldn't steal whatever you needed from wherever you wanted. That wasn't a sustainable economy.

However…

On his walk to Sam's settlement down by the farming area, Daniel rubbed his temples. It was becoming increasingly difficult to find a way to *actually* base their economy on something. Some people pointed out that maybe that wasn't such a bad thing. Donnyton had no real production besides food and animal pelts, and the slightly more sophisticated armors Sam produced. Otherwise, all they had were Classers.

Gold was becoming increasingly popular as a currency, yet paradoxically, none of the Classers took it seriously. They gambled it away on dumb, ridiculous bets like arm wrestling contests or who could cut down more trees with a single swing. They behaved like children, and their increased physical prowess was their shiny new toy.

"Sir Daniel," a woman said, hurrying next to him, struggling to keep pace with his long strides.

Although Daniel hadn't gained very many Levels, he gained quite a few Skills during his various duties. As such, he'd seen it prudent to put some into physical Stats. The woman, one of the designated NCC representatives, thus struggled to keep up.

He had to admit, being called Sir Daniel certainly was better than "Chubbs." In a way, all the long hours he put into keeping Donnyton on track were worth it.

"What is it?" Daniel said, lengthening his stride.

"We would like permission to extend the current farming plot. Probably by doubling the current size and moving further south down the valley. A recent arrival brought coffee seeds, and—"

"Fine, fine," Daniel said, waving his hands. "Draw up a new map and send it over for approval."

"Yes, sir," the woman said, peeling away gratefully. She shouted to the nearby Classers, offering food bribes for labor. A lot of One Shoulder Pad Classers, having nothing better to do, agreed and followed her.

That certainly *was* an advantage of the current Donnyton. The simplicity and efficiency of accomplishing a task through labor was refreshing.

Daniel arrived at Sam's area, shocked by the changes that occurred. The ground had been flattened. Around a dozen wooden tables were covered with monster parts. Some tables were laden with monsters being skinned, others with drying skins, more with stacks of sorted bones, and some even had men stitching away on top of them, creating armor and clothing from the furs of monsters.

A lot of people had taken to wearing the equipment, especially the Classers. Daniel still preferred the feel of processed cotton. At this point, the Stat benefits from their wares were marginal at best.

Sam and Dozer stood to the side, surrounded by several of Dozer's brutish henchmen. Dozer hefted what looked like the giant skull of the wolverine he killed last night. Dozer lifted the object onto his head. He rapped his knuckles against the side to prove its defensive capabilities.

Narrowing his eyes, Daniel walked closer. Although it was definitely a wolverine skull, there was no way it should fit his head so regularly, with the eye holes conveniently wide and spaced perfectly to see out from within.

"Heh, as expected, you can see the problem immediately," Sam said, positively glowing as he regarded it. He jerked a thumb at the skull-covered Dozer. "That's the work of my new Skill, Bone Shaping. Can't do much of anything impressive with it yet, but if I keep working at it, we'll have whole suits of armor soon. Imagine, heh-heh. But I need a few more skeletons to test the limits."

Dozer grunted happily, clearly excited.

Daniel rolled his eyes. "How quickly can things like that be made?"

"Well, like I said, I'll need a few more bodies to figure out the concrete details," Sam said. "It's not like it takes too long, but it's not short either. It needs to be personalized by me."

Shaking his head, Daniel reached into his spatial backpack, which he purchased with 50 SP, and removed a pile of folders. "I look forward to seeing your bone armor in widespread use. In the meantime, I took the liberty of drawing up some evaluation forms for you two and Decklan, to handle."

"Evaluation?" Dozer muttered, staring uncomprehendingly at the tiny words covering the pages handed to him.

"Yes, evaluation. I know you're tired of me harping on the ranking stratification, and I am too. I made a rubric for you to grade each Classer by.

Strength, Utility, Teamwork, Leadership, etc. Just fill all the columns in, and add them up. You'll have a number between 1 and 100. Obviously we will just be going by the 10s digit for the specific rank, but specificity is always preferable," Daniel explained with a smile.

He turned and walked away, leaving the piles of paper with the two men.

Daniel called over his shoulder, "Oh, and I expect it done by the end of today. Until it gets done, I'll probably be too busy to work out the schedule for the Dungeon."

The cat sidestepped, avoiding the Wall of Thorns. Spearing Roots ripped upward and left several scrapes across its body. Its blood dripped from the gashes, staining the sand.

In that moment of pained distraction, it stumbled.

A Phantom Thrust ripped into its neck and sprayed more of its blood across the ground. After a few wobbly steps, it collapsed, spent.

Pleased, Randidly kneeled down and allowed himself to rest. After scanning the surroundings, he pulled out Blue Energy stones and began refining them to make higher tiered Mana potions. He'd been tracking cats for around two hours and hunted six with pelts in various stages of being intact. The Wall of Thorns really helped, but even more important were the points he started putting into Strength. Whereas before, he could only leave small scratches, now his blows sent the cats stumbling from the force. His spear-work was becoming an increasingly deadly force.

Honestly, it was mostly perception and reaction holding him back. He was slowly beginning to realize his body was faster than he could properly control. Ruefully, Randidly put that on the list of things that needed to be worked on as he progressed.

That was an easy fix. He just needed to dedicate some time to training. But at the moment, there were far too many demands on his time.

So far today, he gained 3 Levels in Wall of Thorns, but only 2 in Spearing Roots, even though he used it more frequently. In addition to the Skill Level bonuses carrying over, the difficulty in Leveling also increased. Haste went up by 1 Level and Refine by 2.

Randidly noticed that although evolving the Skill increased the Mana cost to 45, with his Mana pool of 450, it still meant he could cast it ten times before needing to take a break for Mana potions. The rate at which he could improve spells was improved enormously by the larger Mana pool.

As he moved forward through the strange wasteland, he wondered if he'd reached a Level of Strength that would earn him an impressive Class. Randidly couldn't help but smile at the prospect. So far, the System clearly demonstrated it closely observed and rewarded good behavior. Considering how much time he poured into training, Randidly trusted he accumulated a few accomplishments. The Class would probably be something related to his Spear of Rot Mastery.

He still wanted to push his fire magic Skills to a higher Level before trying it. The combination would be deadly if condensed together in a Class. Normally, he would be utilizing Fireball as much as possible to earn Skill Levels, but today was a bit special. He had other concerns in mind.

Randidly removed the Soul Seed from his pocket and inspected it.

Soul Seed 22% Nurtured. *Strongest Influences*: 1. Spearing Roots | 2. Wall of Thorns | 3. Haste | 4. Refine

Randidly wasn't sure what to make of the Strongest Influences information. He supposed it was still interesting. More interesting was that it had gotten to 22% in two hours. Roughly eight more hours to be nurtured.

And after that...

Randidly scratched his cheek. *I guess I have to plant it?*

CHAPTER FORTY-NINE

A quick movement caught Randidly's eye. For the first time, two cats streaked across the wasteland together. He supposed they had to breed somehow, so it shouldn't be strange to see them socializing. He hunkered down behind a stone. When he thought about it, it was honestly more surprising he hadn't seen it before.

Monsters *did* breed. Some of the Classers had captured wolverines and lizards and were starting a ranch for meat along the west side of Donnyton's valley, as the trees in that area were cleared for their lumber. The captured monsters seemed to be accepting domestication well enough. As long as someone with a Level over 10 was present, or equivalent strength, to suppress them. The monsters showed some instinctive intuition regarding who could kill them.

Randidly chewed his lip. He wanted more pelts and claws from the Shadow Cats. Two together made his hunting more dangerous, but also doubly as efficient.

They hadn't appeared to notice him.

Randidly crept forward, moving around the rock and keeping to the shady side of a large crack in the earth. As he settled into a position for ambush, he released a silent breath. His body stilled, allowing himself to completely sink into his environment.

Congratulations! Your Skill **Sneak** has grown to **Level 32!**

I can sneak without moving? Randidly's lips twitched, mobilizing the Mana in his body. As the two Shadow Cats came hurtling past, a Wall of Thorns sprang up in their path. The first one plowed into the thorny impediment, releasing a series of long yowls in its struggle to disentangle from the thorns. Spearing Roots rushed up, permanently silencing it.

Congratulations! Your Skill **Spearing Roots** has grown to **Level 4!**

The other dodged, narrowly avoiding the trap. Spearing Roots tore through its back leg when Randidly changed targets. The next Spearing Roots sought its hobbled form, but this cat did something Randidly had never seen before.

It swayed its upper body, receiving some scratches, but largely dodging the attack. Then, contrary to form, it leapt away, streaking back from whence it came, leaving a trail of blood.

That gave him pause. He tilted his head and watched the blur flee across the wasteland. *Strange; usually, they would attack me, regardless of their injuries…*

Is it like the domesticated animals? Is my aura growing too dangerous?

Randidly clicked his tongue and collected the body of the first cat, storing it away. He squinted at the bloodstains left by the fleeing one. Shrugging, he decided to follow. Although it would be increasingly dangerous if it returned to a den or warren of the things, it could speed up his hunting.

A smile tugged at the corners of his mouth. He admitted he was slightly hoping there was some danger waiting at the end of this rainbow.

Dozer, Donny, and Decklan glanced fearfully at each other and down at the stack of papers in front of them. The immaculately designed forms were soggy and wet from coffee.

When the man who wanted to grow coffee arrived, he sweetened the deal by offering some of his already roasted beans. Naturally, those bribes slowly percolated up the chain of command until they arrived at Donny.

Only sixteen years of age and not such a coffee drinker, he turned to Decklan and Dozer for their expertise on the subject. These mid-twenties men had engaged in frantic coffee drinking more frequently than him and were happy to help. After several piping hot cups, the two assured Donny it was an excellent strain.

Unfortunately, they knocked over the pot, spilling the remaining coffee across the table.

The sheets they were supposed to rank all the Classers with were ruined.

"I mean… What can he really do? I'm the Village Chieftain," Donny said with uncertainty.

"Good, you take the blame," Decklan said, crossing his arms. "Well, since we're done here—"

"He distributes the food…" Dozer mumbled. "He controls who gets weapons from the shop with SP, rather than having to save up gold themselves. Wood that comes up from the NCCs? He controls that. You wanted to start to build a house, didn't you, Donny?"

Everyone grimaced, returning their stares to the coffee dripping off the edges of the table. The three considered the issue solemnly, picturing Daniel's pudgy face contorted in fury. It was honestly difficult to imagine. It really couldn't be that bad, right?

"Well…" Dozer said, unsure. "He did mention all he really needed was a 1-10 ranking. We could just…"

"Rank everyone? Today?" Decklan snapped.

Donny laughed. "Yes! That's exactly what we do. With the most efficient method for determining strength!" His smile widened and he spread his hands. "With a tournament! Let's just all fight each other!"

No longer slumped over in shame, their worried looks turned into flinty, evaluative ones.

"A tournament…" Decklan said calmly, his blade flashing hypnotically while he made it dance across his hands.

"A tournament," Dozer agreed, his chest heaving and eyes bright. From his flexing fingers, he clearly wanted to heft his massive club.

"I'll go tell the squads and grab Sam. I'm sure we can assemble a stadium or something by the time we get to the top sixteen. People who lose in the preliminaries need to build," Donny said, picturing himself being crowned champion.

"Ah… Will the, uh… Ghosthound be participating?" Dozer asked.

They mulled this question over for several seconds.

"Let's not bother him with this," Donny said. "After all, it's purely administrative work being done to rank the Classers, nothing more."

"Nothing more," the other two echoed, eyeing each other.

Randidly followed a trail of blood, scratches, and disturbed sand to the edge of a small path, leading downwards into a ravine. He crouched and pressed his fingers against the blood, feeling its heat. Randidly hesitated. The hair on the back of his neck tingled. There was something… strange here. Something was wrong.

That unerring sense of self-preservation Shal had beaten into him was wildly against him proceeding forward.

Randidly pressed his lips together, weighing his options. The steep sides of the ravine as the trail wound its way downward through the rocks didn't reveal any lurking traps, even when he activated Eyes of the Spear Phantom. A familiar thrill grew in his gut as his instincts warred each other. Against his better judgment, he padded softly down, around twisting turns, through meandering paths, until finally, deep within the gorge, Randidly arrived at the entrance to a large cave.

Is this really the breeding ground for those Shadow Cats?

The trail of blood had long since disappeared. Randidly anticipated an ambush. He activated Eyes of the Spear Phantom and scanned around. The darkness of the cave's mouth slowly parted before his scrutiny. Yet even Randidly wasn't prepared for the enemy within.

It lounged just out of reach of the sunlight, as large as a mini-van. It possessed the body of a lion, head of a woman, and wings of an eagle. Its eyes opened, the amber irises drifting toward him.

The floating text above its head dominated Randidly's focus, freezing him solid. In a bright yellow color Randidly didn't recognize from any of the Rarities, he immediately understood he might be facing a being that was far more deadly than its Level implied.

The Hungry Tribulation, Ep-Tal Level 30

"My, my, my," the creature murmured, getting to its feet. Randidly didn't miss the long claws that briefly unsheathed when it pressed its paws into the ground. The thing lifted its head and sunlight glittered off its mane. "It seems the sheep have wandered quite far from the shepherd. And what *soft* wool you have, little man. Haven't even received a Class yet. Well, well, well…"

Its slow and considered movements did little to assuage Randidly's fears. If anything, its display of intelligence made him absolutely certain he stumbled across something he should not have. At least not yet. Perhaps this was the System's inevitable curveball.

"What… are you? Your name is yellow—"

"Ah, ah, ah," the creature said, seeming pleased. It sat on its haunches, regarding him with a glimmer of interest as it shook its gorgeous mane. "The fat sheep does know some truths of this world. Yes, I do not fit into the normal hierarchy of enemies you would face. I am… special. I am the Tribulation that waits outside the edge of the Newbie Zone for freshly formed villages. A desolation, but perhaps also a blessing, should you survive our inevitable tryst. The Hungry, Hungry, Hungry Tribulation."

The sphinx flashed its yellow teeth. Due to its oversized human head, the sharpness of its maw was especially horrifying.

I… don't belong here… Randidly Ghosthound shivered, taking in the stains of blood, gore, and ichor that marred the thing's enamel.

Randidly remembered now. The fear he first learned in the Dungeon, surrounded by enemies more powerful than himself. That aggressive, dopamine-fueled part of himself that chased after Skill Levels receded.

Although this enemy wasn't as high as the Level of the Boss of the Dungeon, the suffocating aura was ten times as great.

There was no Shal here to take the brunt of the damage. No Shal to use his arm to buy Randidly's life.

What remained was the original feeling. That vague sense of mistake somewhere along the line that led him here. Was it his refusal to help Donnyton pass its own monster horde two nights ago? Was it when he didn't think deeply about that strange woman's laughter earlier in the forest?

Or perhaps, was it all the way back in the Dungeon, when he didn't believe Shal that he would be a burden?

If I die here, what will happen to Donnyton? Randidly's skin tingled. The feeling came, wet and raw and fresh. The old dread of a predator, looming above him. The Deadly Webspinner, the Howler Monkeys, even the acid-spitting toads. Though his hands shook, his smile grew wider, his eyes bright.

After withdrawing for a bit, the half of Randidly that went a little mad underneath the influence of the System returned with a horribly vicious thought.

I might die today... but I'll definitely feel alive for a while, too.

In a smooth motion, Randidly drew his spear and leveled it toward the sphinx with the harsh yellow name. He tried to keep his voice light. "Aren't you supposed to tell me a riddle or something?"

Its smile widened and it lowered its stance into a crouch. "No, no, no... But we shall enjoy our time cavorting together. To a wandering, lost sheep, there are quite a few lessons I am willing to teach, teach, teach."

The final repetition of the word was a signal. Ep-Tal leapt forward and Randidly dodged, activating Haste, Empower, Footwork of the Spear Phantom, and Mana Strengthening all at once. In terms of physical ability, this was his peak.

His eyes narrowed, sensing rather than seeing he wouldn't make it in time. The sphinx Ep-Tal adjusted mid-motion, its paw sweeping outward to squash all his hopes of escaping.

He instantly used Phantom Half-Step, creating plenty of distance between them. Randidly's bare feet skidded across the dusty stone ground. He weighed his options in that brief moment.

Whereas the cats had only been annoyingly fast, this creature was mind-bogglingly fast. Already it crossed the distance to him, a huge paw swiping sideways. His blood froze to ice even as he belatedly reactivated his Skills.

Congratulations! Your Skill **Haste** has grown to **Level 22!**

Congratulations! Your Skill **Mana Strengthening** has grown to **Level 11!**

Randidly got his spear up in time to somewhat deflect the blow, but Ep-Tal's Strength was overwhelming. He was forced to grit his teeth and activate Mana Shield and Iron Skin to withstand the strike. At the same time, he used Spearing Roots, aiming for its underside while it was distracted attacking him.

The beast laughed and sidestepped so fast, it seemed to vanish before Randidly's eyes, avoiding the roots in the process. Its mouth gaped open and belched fire.

Sweat coated his brow. He raised his hand and simultaneously channeled Root Manipulation, unleashing a Fireball to intercept the larger fire cannon spat by the sphinx. Randidly didn't doubt he wouldn't be able to take many of those Fireballs due to his low Fire Resistance.

For now, he needed to buy time to escape.

At the same time, he was grinning. The thrill of the fight and the flood of adrenaline through his body was not something he could easily deny.

The Fireballs met in a huge explosion of roaring flame and Randidly confirmed his was slightly weaker. He leapt to the side under the cover of the smoke, taking the chance to pull out and down a Stamina and Mana potion. He scanned for the sphinx.

Right before it struck, he knew where it would be.

"Here, here, here..." It cooed from behind, its paw smashing into Randidly's back. He instinctively activated Mana Shield and Iron Skin, even while knowing it wouldn't be enough.

Congratulations! Your Skill **Mana Shield** has grown to **Level 25!**

The impact was brutal. Even with Iron Skin, several of his bones snapped. Some other internal agony informed him his organs hadn't escaped the impact unscathed. For the moment, he simply pressed his hands to his chest and activated Healing Palm through his forced tumble. He hit the ground and barely managed to keep his Health afloat. Staggering to his feet, he drank two Health potions in quick succession and his body snapped back into place. Quite painfully, but otherwise without any repercussions.

A realization came to Randidly. It wasn't that this sphinx Ep-Tal was fast; it simply used the same Skill Lyra did. That was why his Eyes of the Spear Phantom were rendered completely useless.

It could literally teleport anywhere around him. He felt it move right when he heard its low chortle.

Rather than trying to track it with his eyes, Randidly raised his spear and prepared to receive its attacks. If Lyra had taught him anything in the past few days, it was that the things she did came at great cost. It was not a move that could be used indefinitely.

And when it ran out of Mana, that was his chance to strike or flee. He simply had to survive.

Perhaps originally this sense of powerlessness would have broken his spirit. Not for the current Randidly Ghosthound. He raised his guard and gritted his teeth, his emerald eyes bright. No matter what it took... he refused to stop struggling.

Even here, with this Tribulation who possessed a yellow name, he would survive.

CHAPTER FIFTY

For several long seconds, Glendel remained frozen in the brush. His heart pounded, imagining every horrifying monster that might be pushing its way through the nearby underbrush. An eyebrow itched, but the slender 28-year-old remained completely still. Thankfully, the rustling moved away from him. When the sound vanished completely, Glendel fell on his hands and knees and spat out a fat wad of phlegm.

After wiping his mouth, he stood unsteadily and continued deeper into the valley.

On behalf of Glendel's group leader, he'd been sent to investigate two Newbie Villages that sprang up close together. Glendel watched the barricaded city, annoyed. This couldn't be a coincidence.

In the winding, fifty-mile trek up the mountainous region, their group hadn't crossed a single pillar of light. Imagine their surprise when they arrived and found two.

Perhaps these players knew some secret of growing with the System.

Their leader was cautiously pessimistic. Something was certainly different here. And thus, Glendel planned on making contact with both Villages.

He approached the more civilized in appearance village first. From shouting distance, he was told to turn around and leave or they would shoot. Upon trying to explain himself, the men sitting in the machine gun nests fired off warning shots, sending him scampering back.

Although he put points into End and Vit from finishing Paths, he didn't think he could do something as ridiculous as survive bullets.

Disgusted, Glendel was about to give up. At least until the bus acting as a gate pulled to the side and a truck drove out, carefully driving through the small, thin path free of monster bodies. Maybe they sent someone out to talk with him.

When it pulled off the road and onto another path, Glendel walked out cautiously, waving his arms.

The truck was ready to pull right past him and only stopped when Glendel shouted, "Hey!"

Glendel moved to the driver's side and peered in. A tall, athletic black man dressed in a police uniform met his eye. Next to him was a beautiful woman with honey-colored skin. A woman who looked oddly familiar.

Glendel offered a nervous smile. "Hey, uh, again. I was just wondering… how do you get into the city?"

The two exchanged a heavy glance. The woman's frown crumpled further and the officer gave her a sympathetic nod.

Their private communications lasted several seconds before the officer turned back to Glendel. "Unfortunately, we aren't accepting any more refugees at this time. If you want shelter, we recommend you head to Donnyton to meet up with other… survivors. Actually, we're heading there now, if you need a ride."

Glendel nodded and got into the back of the cab. The truck pulled away, driving around the hill in a long loop. The man and woman up front talked in tones too low for Glendel to hear. Instead, he turned and took in their cargo.

Glendel frowned. *They're transporting glass jars…?*

Randidly's left arm hung useless at his side. Four large furrows in his flesh kept him from being able to move it. No doubt the muscles were completely severed. And without a long stretch of time to recover…

The slashes from the sphinx came faster and faster, ensuring his other limbs would end up the same. With only one arm, he blocked as well as he could, dispersing the force.

When Randidly began to find his rhythm, the sphinx would teleport, attacking from an unexpected angle. His only warning was a mere glint of the beast's golden fur.

Randidly gritted his teeth, urging Spearing Roots to activate behind him and rush toward his back. He held his ground, masking the move from the sphinx's vision with his body. As the huge paw descended toward him, Randidly raised his spear with his good arm. Simultaneously, he guided the roots around him, hugging them against his form as closely as he could before guiding the sharpened stakes of plant matter at his foe.

In his chest and abdomen, both his fiery Stamina and cool Mana were running low.

Because of his desperate subterfuge, Ep-Tal's attack hit him almost square on. The training spear, given to him by Shal, bent dangerously beneath the force of his swipe.

At the same time, several of the Spearing Roots dug into the soft flesh of that deadly paw, finally marring the sphinx. The Hungry Tribulation tsk'd in annoyance, shaking free the roots. Randidly used that opportunity to withdraw several potions, downing them all.

With his Health surging upward and his arm healed, Randidly leapt forward. His body hummed with the furious heat of Stamina, unleashing an Empowered Phantom Onslaught.

The moment it was free of the roots, it teleported away again, his attack hitting nothing but air. Panting, Randidly adjusted his stance and waited for the foe to reveal itself. When it did appear, it was back in the shadows of the cave. It licked its paw, giving Randidly a disappointed glance.

"Heh, heh, heh, you are likely waiting for me to use up my Mana, correct? But it is in vain. Before the Newbie Barrier drops, I have unlimited Mana to ensure I never accidentally succumb to any of the other monsters out here. I may not have any regeneration, but my well of Mana and Stamina will never run dry. And for the plotting, struggling you, that is bad, bad, bad…"

Randidly lowered his spear, far too many questions swirling in his mind. "And what about your Health?"

The sphinx threw its head backwards, laughing. "Hahaha! From your face, you are wondering if it is a trap, yes? That I claim to have no regeneration and fail to mention infinite Health, just infinite Stamina and Mana. It is no trap. Although I am bound, I am still a sphinx. I have my pride. No challenger will be clueless around me. Although that is a term broad enough to get lost in, isn't it, little sheep? Clueless, clueless, clueless…

"But that is not to say I cannot heal myself," it continued. "Yet, until the barrier drops, I am stuck out here. I might as well play with you for a while. It gets so dull out here beyond the wanderings of the adorable sheep of the System. And the only way to amuse myself… is to eat, eat, eat."

The Hungry Tribulation stretched in a very catlike manner and walked toward him, its eyes gleeful.

A tireless foe with infinite Mana and Stamina… Randidly didn't have time to recognize how tired he was or check his Status Screen. Such a task would take too much time and inevitably inform him he should have collapsed by now. Only the echo of Shal's dismissive snort kept him standing, even as his trembling hands gripped his spear. *A tireless foe… keeping me alive out of boredom.*

Randidly looked down the length of his weapon, studying the lazy smile of his opponent. The Hungry Tribulation, Ep-Tal, blinked out of existence. Randidly forced himself to relax, waiting for the sign. Tensing, as Shal told him so many times, was an unnecessary waste of Stamina.

Its presence returned. He whipped his gaze upward.

Several Fireballs shot down toward him. Randidly went numb, taking in the light and heat of the flames. *I really wish I had a few more days' worth of training up my Fire Resistance. Next time... if there is a next time.*

He raised his gifted weapon and shifted his stance, spinning the spear in a Spear Deflect. The Fireballs crashed against his defense, almost causing it to falter. The skin of Randidly's arm burned until it warped and bubbled. The pain was nothing compared to his concern about how much Health that cost him.

Congratulations! Your Skill **Spear Deflect** has grown to **Level 11!**

With no more luxury to think, Randidly willed his Mana into motion. Spearing Roots shot upward in the area obscured by the flames. The area that whispered to him by the instincts Shal instilled in him.

"Gah!" the sphinx spat.

Randidly grinned. *Didn't feel like repeating that, huh? About fucking time you took me seriously.*

Shal's hand was now on his shoulder. *A spear can only go forward, and thus a spearman must hold tight to the shaft and support it, or he will lose it and become just a man. Shortly afterward, he will undoubtedly die.*

It was time to attack. His singed fingers did their best to tighten on his weapon.

Randidly rushed through the smoke. The sphinx hopped backward away from the roots, revealing several long scratches ripped into its side. Randidly planted his foot and forced his exhausted body to pursue, raising the spear.

The sphinx teleported a dozen meters away. Randidly activated Phantom Half Step, covering most of that distance. His spear lashed out. He ignored the cool hole in his chest left by his nearly depleted Stamina.

Congratulations! Your Skill **Phantom Half-Step** has grown to **Level 9!**

Roaring its fury, Ep-Tal spat several more Fireballs and reared up onto its hind legs, ready to meet him.

Randidly took the opportunity to hop behind a nearby rock to drink several potions thanks to the sphinx screening its vision of him with its own attack. Only when the flames impacted the ground and flared outward did it realize his feint.

"You, you, you..." the sphinx said, amused.

Ignoring it, Randidly opened his menu. He'd seen some of the Skill Levels he earned, but he hadn't anticipated the sea of PP waiting for his acknowledgement.

Spear Mastery had gone up by 1, Eyes of the Spear Phantom up 1, Spear

Phantom's Footwork up 2, Phantom Half Step up an additional 2 from earlier, Dodge and Block both up 2, Haste up 1, Spear Deflect up 3, Empower up 2, Spearing Roots up 1, Root Manipulation up 1, Mana Strengthening up 3, Physical Fitness and Running up 1, Sprinting up 2, and Fire Resistance raised a meager 1, considering how badly he'd been burned.

31 PP in all, combined with his earlier Skill Levels. He dumped enough of that into the Meditation Path to finish it off. *Not exactly an active Path, but whatever I can get right now...*

Congratulations! You have completed the "The Meditation Path"! +5 to Perception and Reaction. Your mind is clear and your eyes are focused as you continue forward.

The Path that lies ahead may be fraught with difficulties, but you will meet it directly. The inner peace you find will continue to guide and heal you.

Effectiveness of Meditation has slightly improved. Regeneration of Skill has increased to +1.5% per Skill Level.

Randidly hesitated, trying to consider what to put his PP into next.

That horrible voice spoke again. "My, my, my... What is taking so long? Don't you want to play, play, play?"

He didn't have much time to consider his options. Grim-eyed, Randidly scanned his available Paths and locked on to the Frontrunner Path. *This is a Reward Path, right? Time to show me, System, how well you truly mean to reward those desperate fools that manage to impress you.*

He had 17 PP leftover from the Meditation Path and threw everything into this lifeline.

To his delight, he received 8 distributable free Stat points, one for every two PP. If this continued, this Path would be worth 50 Stat points, without including the completion bonus. He beat down that long-term optimism, tempering it against his current situation.

Movement urged him back to the present. Randidly dumped all his free Stats into Agility. He needed the edge in speed or he wouldn't be able to handle the constant teleportation. Improving by 8 Agility might not be much, but it was a step ahead of those brutalizing lion claws.

To further confuse the beast, Randidly lowered his head and charged to meet the sphinx. His Health, Mana, and Stamina rapidly filled as those potions finished their precious work.

His heart pounded wildly, dancing between adrenaline and oblivion as he raised his spear. He missed this. Hanging on by a thread, fighting for his life.

In moments like this, he could forget how much life was lost due to the System and enjoy the primal simplicity of it. Failure resulted in death. Achievements earned rewards. Moving forward was the only choice.

He held on to his spear and advanced, so he would not die.

CHAPTER FIFTY-ONE

*R*ubbing sweat from his brow, Glendel finished helping the beautiful woman, Ellaine, and the police officer, Kraig, unload the cases of beakers, test tubes, and seemingly hundreds of other glass articles. With the final package the duo brought along delivered, Glendel took the chance to take in Donnyton.

The initial signs were encouraging. Honestly, while the other city had the advantage of being based in modern buildings, Glendel noted barely any movement from within the well-defended walls. The heavy machine gun nests left a slightly bitter impression, where here, people swarmed around with the very noticeable intent to make the space livable. Some carried building materials while others shouted for assistance. Groups gathered to head into the Dungeon while others crowded around a fire roasting meat.

Glendel stood in an area that was beginning to form into a small town square. Several work teams in sweat-stained shirts dug out the foundation of buildings along the outskirts of the area. They weren't beside the pillar of light, but at the base of the hill, along a dirt path, that to Glendel was the main flow of traffic.

A group of three women rolled huge tree trunks to a large pile next to one of the foundations before chatting and wandering away. Glendel's eyelids twitched when another group started wrestling, dropping their tools and slamming their bodies against one another with a low grunt.

Kraig tapped Glendel's shoulder, dragging his attention back. The policeman jerked his chin toward a tall longhouse, the only completed building in the developing town square. "Work's not done yet, unfortunately. We need to talk to Donnyton's Supply Manager."

"This place…" Ellaine mumbled, joining the two men and soaking in the same sights that held Glendel's attention. "It's a lot bigger than the last time we were here."

"Good. It's for the best if humanity has several housing options," Kraig said, moving toward the longhouse with the other two trailing after him.

Their glassware was accepted by a stern woman with a clipboard, who took everything in with a glance before turning around and whistling. A dozen dust-covered youths stampeded out of the depths of the warehouse. They danced slightly, clearly nervous. She frowned at them all.

The woman shook her head and sighed. "Fine, fine, finish taking these back to the vats in the back and *then* you're all free to go watch the spectacle up there."

Whooping, the youths swarmed around Glendel. The crates were moved in short order, and Kraig and Ellaine got back in the truck, the latter gazing wistfully across the grounds, locked on another large building farther down the valley. She shook her head and settled into her seat.

Before they left, Kraig leaned out the window and gave the woman a serious look. "Make sure the Ghosthound knows we aren't going to seek any sort of retribution for what happened. Let's take a non-interference policy from now on, all right? We each... we each have our own troubles and our own way of adjusting. So... Good luck."

And with that, the duo drove off. Glendel made a mental note about the term "Ghosthound," as if it was a proper noun. Just like the machine gun nest, that name... The impression it gave him was strangely heavy. Was it a monster of some sort?

Had this village tamed a monster? Is that why they formed so quickly? Glendel speculated.

Not that it would likely be difficult to fight down one of the blue monsters in their area now that they had banded together with a leader and a common goal, except his own group hadn't accomplished such feats. There was always another emergency, another problem that seemed more important.

Yet these people had the spare attention to kill the monster and take the first steps toward civilization at a speed visible to the naked eye.

The woman snorted, which made Glendel realize he was just standing there daydreaming. She crossed her arms and examined him. "What, are you defecting? Well, I'm just a bit busy, so—"

"Oh no." Glendel shook his head. "I'm, uh, from a group traveling up from Franksburg. About sixty of us. Those two from the nearby village simply gave me a ride. My group wanted to establish relations for... trade."

"Trade?" Strangely, the woman's eyes began to sparkle. "What are you looking for?"

"Food, but also partly a place to stay. Or some protection so we can set up our own community," Glendel admitted. "And also access to... whatever it is you do to get a Class. Information too, if that's possible. We're willing to give supplies we've gathered in exchange. Clothing. Tents. Tools.

"And," Glendel added, saving the best for last. He'd considered withholding this information for now, but if this woman was in control of this bustling new town's supplies, having her on his side would be a good thing. Glendel licked his lips, letting the tension build. "...Medical supplies."

"Hmm... I'd be willing to talk about the clothing and tools. We're probably past the tent stage. As for medical supplies..." The woman shrugged and flapped her fingers dismissively. "I don't think anyone's gotten a cold since they've gotten Stats. They just raise their Vitality and Endurance. But definitely more modern-made clothes would be a relief."

Glendel blinked, slightly surprised. "I mean... even without infections, keeping Health high should be something you'd be interested in, right? Certain medicines have relevant benefits to Health."

Perhaps we miscalculated, Glendel thought when the woman remained unswayed by his words. *Perhaps... perhaps obtaining a Class comes with more benefits than we thought. If they really have moved beyond needing medicine...*

Before the woman could answer, a snort of laughter picked up from behind him. He turned to find a lovely girl with sharp features and blonde hair to her shoulders. She covered her mouth.

"Ah, I shouldn't laugh. I'm just here to pick up some extra Mana potions. Ahem. You... you haven't done much experimenting with the System, have you?"

Embarrassment rushed through Glendel in having to acknowledge she was right. His group took the stance that gathering information was more important than immediate experiments.

Meanwhile, the stern woman offered a playful curtsy to the girl. "Miss Lyra, is there any reason why you should be given special treatment in regard to Mana potions?"

Lyra scrunched her face up and huffed, folding her arms.

The woman straightened and smiled, returning her attention to Glendel. "If you have any examples of clothing, I'd love to see them. Numbers, sizes, etc. I'm willing to buy in bulk, if food and information is what you want. As for getting a Class, there are some restrictions related to that. You'll have to go check up at the Classer portion of Donnyton."

"Classer...?" Glendel shook his head, refocusing. Feeling slightly nervous, he couldn't help but ask, "First, I guess I just don't understand why medical supplies aren't more attractive. You probably didn't know this, but certain plants can be mixed to create potions—"

Lyra burst out laughing again, slapping her knee. Considering they had been talking about "Mana potions," Glendel's stomach flipped unpleasantly. Were their potions not restricted to Mana?

The woman gave Glendel a kind smile. "Mister…?"

"Glendel," he said, straightening and folding his hands behind his back.

"Mr. Glendel, why don't you follow me. It would be easier than explaining."

Glendel followed the woman into the longhouse. The interior was filled with an eclectic mix of metal and freshly hewn wooden shelving, filled with various supplies. They passed dried meat, dried fruit, nuts, furs. Glendel's eyebrows rose. Perhaps the woman was right about not caring about food. He'd only seen a few dozen people working around the square, though, so it was strange they had so much.

They passed through to the back where the space opened up. Around twenty people stood by large vats, filling the glass containers. Some were filled with red liquid, others with blue, and the rest with yellow. Glendel gasped.

To the left of the vats were several long tables. The workers moved rapidly about their business, grinding, measuring, pouring water samples. All of them mixed endlessly.

Flashes of joy swept over some faces, while disappointment colored others. Several carefully filled buckets with powder from the ground-up energy crystals, struggling to maintain the equality in quantity while upping the scale.

No wonder they weren't interested in medical supplies. Based on the Attributes Glendel studied on his Status Screen, one restored Health, one Mana, and finally, Stamina. With huge vats of each, they had enough potions to solve any problem that might come their way.

Glendel bit the inside of his lip. The medical supplies his group wasted days gathering and transporting were almost useless.

It suddenly made sense why they were more interested in the tools portion of the offer. Most of the measuring equipment at their disposal were rather archaic analog scales. They had to balance the two amounts of powder on the trays until they reached an equilibrium. Only then would they mix. No electronic scales seemed to be present in the room.

Plus, they were gathering more glass containers. Perhaps… perhaps if they returned to the hospital.

But that seemed like a bad idea. At least until they learned more about the System. For now, they would trade clothes for information. Plus, as an extra sweetener… Glendel mentally thanked Alana for insisting Regina bring a few generators. Really, the only thing this place seemed to lack was electricity. Hopefully, that would be enough to trade for access to Classes.

Feeling curious, Glendel wandered closer to the mixing tables. Seeing that the stern woman didn't stop him, he examined what exactly they were doing. His mouth fell to the floor. *The speed their hands are moving… They probably all have double-digit Agility!*

Lyra chuckled and the woman looked on with a tight-lipped smile. Glendel picked up a vial of the finished potion, examining it. After gripping it for a bit, he was surprised when a small explanation appeared in his vision.

"68 Health...?" he muttered, shocked. The highest they'd been able to achieve with herbs was just over 50. And that was only when Regina—

The woman coughed into her hand, embarrassed by Glendel's reaction. "Yes. Unfortunately, mass-producing the potions hasn't been as effective as we wished. Hmmm... but since we'll soon be business partners, I cannot let you leave empty handed."

She moved to a smaller space to the side, where a cooler sat on the table. She filled a vial with liquid from the cooler, the drops glimmering azure even in the dim light of the longhouse.

"Here, consider it a gesture of goodwill. This was personally mixed by the Ghosthound. Maybe this will help you understand why we don't need medical supplies."

Ghosthound... that name again. Glendel narrowed his eyes. At least until he saw the explanation for the potion he now held and could no longer stay calm.

"This restores—" Glendel gasped. "199 Mana! That much Mana... from just this small amount of liquid? Can you even have that much Mana? This isn't... this can't—"

Glendel stuttered to a stop, wanting to deny it, but unable to refute the notification floating in front of him.

Lyra wiped the tears from her eyes. "Yeah. The Ghosthound... he's special."

CHAPTER FIFTY-TWO

*S*till slightly shellshocked, Glendel followed Lyra, who promised to take him to someone who could talk to him about getting a Class. Through her rambling filling up the silence, Glendel figured out NCC was what they called those without a Class, while Classers obviously had one. He wondered if there was any tension between the two groups.

"This is the NCC village," Lyra explained, a strange bitterness to her lyrical voice as she gestured around the blooming town square. "All the buff and glorious Classers live up there above us, on high in Valhalla."

"What, uh... What's it like, having a Class?" Glendel stammered. The past half hour had gone not at all like he'd expected.

"Oh, I don't have a Class. I just rely on my charm to get around." She winked playfully and continued forward.

She doesn't have a Class? But... she needs Mana potions that restore so much Mana?

At a loss, Glendel followed her up the hill toward the fort, whose walls kept growing in their approach. It was a lot bigger than he realized. Lyra continued past the gate and Glendel paused to glance curiously in. It was almost completely deserted. A small group of people chatted at tables, but other than that, the interior of the walls were completely empty.

Do they really have all that food in the longhouse just for so few people...? Glendel hurried onward after the girl.

They proceeded out the backside of the walls, through a smaller gate. The sounds of shouting grew louder the further down the hill and around the bend in the valley they went. They rounded a corner, revealing a sea of people.

Probably just short of eight hundred people stood, watched, or worked.

Directly in front of them was a downward slope until it leveled off. Glendel surmised the area must have previously been a quarry. People lined up around the outside, cheering at those fighting below in the center. Around fifty people were off to Glendel's right. Some of them were bandaged, focused purely on recovering. Others ran around, dragging felled trees and stacking them, constructing what appeared to be a rough-looking stage surrounded by bleachers.

An old man raised an axe. With a single swing, he cut a ten-meter-tall tree in half right down the middle. Several men took the two halves and began assembling the seats, while several others set up another section of tree for him to cut.

"What... What is going on?" Glendel gasped.

Lyra shrugged. "A tournament, obviously. Want to compete?" She studied him for a second and shook her head. "Well, you don't seem like you've taken many Paths. Maybe it's best to watch until Donny is finished here."

It's coming. I need... to MOVE.

Gritting his teeth in the face of his own exhaustion, Randidly stepped backwards. The sphinx's claws raked through his previous position, gleaming with enough sharpness to rip through Randidly's Iron Skin.

Congratulations! Your Skill **Dodge** has grown to **Level 32!**

With a grin, the monster teleported forward mid-slash, putting Randidly back in the path of the attack.

Randidly had been fighting this beast for almost an hour now with no injuries to it, but that didn't mean he wasn't making progress. The sphinx's patterns were becoming familiar; he'd predicted this very attack. Once that malice in its expression hardened, he knew Ep-Tal would strike. Ignoring his aching limbs, Randidly stepped forward under the slash and unleashed a Phantom Thrust to meet its torso.

The movements were so perfect, that no sooner had the sphinx activated its blink Skill then Randidly accelerated forward. The attack drew a long but shallow scratch across its chest.

Just as quickly as he was in, Randidly planted a foot and hopped backward. The power in the sphinx's limbs would snap him like a twig if he let it. The Hungry Tribulation hissed its fury and spun around, lashing out with its hind legs. Raising his spear, Randidly dodged the left foot and deflected the right, but was still sent tumbling by the impact.

His training spear groaned in protest. The weapon likely couldn't endure many more blows like that.

Randidly created a wall of thorns between them. Green branches bristled upward. Mana was harder to recover, but he had no choice. Time seemed to slow within those precious seconds as he considered his options.

Health was still fine, though at the rate he needed to periodically burn Mana to buy himself a moment like this, his regeneration wouldn't be able to keep up. And already he needed to ration the few Mana Skills left in his tank for the foreseeable future.

Stamina, on the other hand, regenerated at about 1 per second. Only, he was constantly depleting it as he attacked, dodged, and blocked the fearsome attacks of the Hungry Tribulation, Ep-Tal. Randidly dearly wished he had a Class. He could gain a few Levels and push his regenerations up even higher. He resolved himself to take any Paths, whenever he could, that would benefit regenerations in the future.

Perhaps the real danger was mental. Randidly's body felt like soaked wool left out in a rainstorm. He fought against a sense of inevitability from the sphinx's attacks, just as much as he fought against the monster. Even if the thing didn't really have infinite Health, it was becoming obvious Randidly needed more than a few more Agility to match up against it.

He was helpless to wound it.

Stewing in fear, Randidly's mind briefly turned to the addictive potion of the origin banana.

Randidly's jaw flexed so aggressively, one of his teeth chipped. *Stamina it is. I don't need... I cannot rely on foreign influences. I... if I'm not enough...*

I'll just die. I can only blame myself.

As quick as possible, Randidly withdrew a Stamina potion and drank it. He leaped away from the Wall of Thorns just as it went up in flames with a roar of heat. The necessity of the potion blasted through Randidly's system like a numbing agent, washing away all his guilt, worry, and fear. All that remained was a high-strung humming as his muscles coiled into readiness.

He knew a single mistake would cost him his life. A single misstep and he would be dead.

He retreated further, using the cover of flames to run a small distance up the path, away from the sphinx's cave. Fleeing usually caused the creature to teleport behind him, but he took the chance to push their fight here, where there was more space for him to maneuver.

When the Wall of Thorns collapsed in a poof of char and soot, the sphinx returned to the front of the cavern, sitting calmly. It winked at Randidly before padding back into the dark depths. Several seconds later, it returned, a half-eaten cat in its mouth. It made a show of gobbling the thing down, presenting itself as its wounds healed.

Ep-Tal yawned and grinned. "See, See, See? Plus, you are not one of mine, so there are certain... consequences associated with killing you. Feel free to run away, away, away..."

Randidly was torn. He furiously examined the sentence for any sort of trap. Ultimately, he lowered his head and slowly backed away. The Hungry Tribulation's eyes followed him the entire time, delighting in the obvious tension throughout Randidly's body.

This was really just a game to you... Randidly thought bitterly, steadily retreating out of the ravine. No matter the why, Randidly took this opportunity.

Because now that he'd fought against the sphinx once...

Only when he was out of sight did he allow himself to turn. He Sprinted for ten minutes across the wasteland, returning to just inside the edge of the Newbie boundary. The entire way, his Stamina scraped near single digits. He didn't dare stop. Randidly held no trust in the creature, not for a minute. He did, however, believe the notifications that appeared told the truth. He would be safe within the Safe Zone from monsters of that Level.

Up until that last second before he left the wasteland, he half-expected the creature to suddenly appear in front of him and smash him with its over-sized paws. He downed his last Mana and Health potions in preparation of that very development.

Nothing happened. He slowed to a walk, moving into the relatively safe cover of trees.

Did it really just let me go? Randidly furrowed his brow. *Does it really not care? Does it not think I can improve enough to threaten it?*

That earned a low chuckle out of him.

Randidly sat and Meditated to recover quicker and began making plans. He thought of several adjustments he could make to his training schedule. Randidly wondered what might have happened if he hadn't followed the cat to find the sphinx today. In two days, that horrible creature would have simply shown up at Donnyton.

Even if its Mana and Stamina were no longer infinite, it would have ripped through them, especially the NCC village below. Considering it seemed to recover Health by eating, all the people that had come to Donnyton to seek shelter were practically walking Health potions.

With just its body, it'd carve a path of blood through the remnants of humanity, laughing and crooning the entire time. The more Randidly thought about that, the more furious he became.

He didn't examine too closely why he would rather be mad right now. Instead, he tried to estimate what their response could have been.

Ultimately, Randidly felt he and some of the other elites might escape. Perhaps they'd be able to hold it at bay when it no longer had access to the infinite Mana and Stamina. Either way, most of the village would be ripped to pieces. Their farms would burn. Their potion-brewing enterprise would be derailed and the workers transformed into corpses. The wolverine butcheries would just be a source of flesh to the Hungry Tribulation.

All the NCCs who worked for Sam, raising Skill Levels before trying to get a Class, now dead to the monstrously fast Ep-Tal. Hundreds of people wiped out without truly understanding how horrifying the System was.

They would likely survive, but the village would be reduced to a few dozen individuals at best. The peace they currently built by holding on to the past would be shattered. Surviving such a slaughter would no doubt change them too.

Why gather other survivors if they would ultimately be slaughtered by the next raid the System sent?

Narrowing his eyes, Randidly bared his teeth with malice. *But that didn't happen. I was forewarned. And now that I know of the threat... I will prepare. Even with two days, I will teach you regret, Ep-Tal.*

The phantom of Shal behind him nodded in approval. Randidly Ghosthound would murder this threat to Donnyton. He'd rip the creature to pieces before the Newbie Barrier dropped. He had no other choice.

It was necessary to save lives. He was the strongest person in Donnyton, by far. This was his responsibility.

Randidly removed the materials from his satchel, beginning to refine and brew more potions. He was running low on almost everything. Gathering supplies was his first step before remaining in the forest to engage in preparations to take down the sphinx. It would be slightly slower than just returning to the village and obtaining supplies there, but Randidly feared if he returned, someone would want to follow him to train.

He'd been able to scrape by and survive with Decklan and Lyra, but that was against the lizardmen. Their weaker Physical Stats and limited Mana pool meant they would be crippled instantly.

Besides... Donnyton has already proven it doesn't need me. And right now, to be the shield the village needs, I have to focus.

Congratulations! Your Skill **Potion Making** has improved to **Level 24!**

A throbbing pain right behind his eyes refused to give him even a second of peace, probably due to the extended bout he just endured against the sphinx. Even if his Mana and Stamina were filled, he was missing something. A mental spark that slowly dimmed the more he had to draw from his exhausted body. A light that waned in his use of Willpower to keep himself from revealing a weakness.

There was a lot of time in the middle of that hour that was blurry in his memory. Randidly set down his potions and shook his head, taking several breaths. Above, the sun began to sink toward the horizon.

The headache remained.

Randidly opened his Path menu. *I need to rest... but first, let's see what else I can earn from this.*

Randidly gained 1 Level in Spear Mastery, 2 in Phantom Thrust, 1 in Phantom Half-Step, 2 in Iron Skin and Dodge, 3 in Block, 1 in Spear Deflect, 1 in Empower, 2 in Edge of Decay and Spearing Roots, 1 in Healing Palm, and 3 in Fire Resistance.

While examining his gains, another notification popped up.

Congratulations! Your Skill **Meditation** has grown to **Level 32!**

Randidly dumped those PP into the Frontrunner Path and earned a free Stat every 2 PP spent. With those Stats, he raised his Reaction by 11. As the fight dragged on and he'd gotten used to his increased speed, he realized he wasted quite a lot of time calculating his response. His body was fast enough to barely keep up with the sphinx, but the monster's preternatural reactions continually caught him by surprise. That ability to teleport with infinite Mana was unfair. But with an increased Reaction, hopefully the gap between them would narrow.

Randidly considered his Status Screen.

Randidly Ghosthound
Class: ---
Level: N/A
Health(/R per hour): 311/303 [+2] (155 [+3])
Mana(/R per hour): 501/512 (71.5)
Stam(/R per min): 357/357 (59 [+1])
Vit: 45 [+1]
End: 30
Str: 28 [+2]
Agi: 57 [+7]
Perception: 24
Reaction: 41
Resistance: 9
Willpower: 55
Intelligence: 73
Wisdom: 39
Control: 55
Focus: 26
Equipment: *Necklace of the Shadow Cat Lvl 20 (R): (Vitality +1, Strength +2, Agility +7)*
Skills
Soulskill: *Spear of Rot Mastery Lvl 228*

Basic: *Running Lvl 20 | Physical Fitness Lvl 29 | Sneak Lvl 32 | Acid Resistance Lvl 23 | Poison Resistance Lvl 16 | Spirit of Adversity Lvl 25 | Dagger Mastery Lvl 13 | Dodge Lvl 32 | Spear Mastery Lvl 45 | Pain Resistance Lvl 12 | Fighting Proficiency Lvl 31 | First Aid Lvl 14 | Block Lvl 29 | Mental Strength Lvl 12 | Curse Resistance Lvl 3 | Pathfinding Lvl 16 | Mapmaking Lvl 4 | Calculated Blow Lvl 19 | Edge of Decay (Un) Lvl 11 | Fire Resistance Lvl 8*

Stamina: *Heavy Blow Lvl 26 | Sprinting Lvl 15 | Iron Skin Lvl 27 | Phantom Thrust Lvl 38 | Spear Phantom's Footwork Lvl 31 | Eyes of the Spear Phantom Lvl 21 | Phantom Half-Step Lvl 10 | Haste Lvl 23 | Phantom Onslaught Lvl 10 | Sweep Lvl 16 | Spear Deflect Lvl 12 | Empower Lvl 22 | Roundhouse Kick Lvl 13*

Mana: *Mana Bolt Lvl 30 | Meditation Lvl 32 | Spearing Roots Lvl 7 | Mana Shield Lvl 25 | Root Manipulation Lvl 31 | Arcane Orb Lvl 23 | Magic Missile Lvl 6 | Healing Palm Lvl 8 | Fireball Lvl 24 | Pollen of the Rafflesia (R) Lvl 7 | Summon Pestilence Lvl 16 | Mana Strengthening Lvl 14 | Wall of Thorns Lvl 4*

Crafting: *Farming Lvl 23 | Plant Breeding Lvl 9 | Potion Making Lvl 24 | Analyze Lvl 24 | Refine Lvl 6*

Spear of Rot mastery was getting close to 250 again, which was where it evolved last time. Randidly suspected it would wait longer the second time around. Perhaps he might even need to get it to 500 before it would shift and bless him with additional Skills.

Now that his Reaction was 41, Randidly had more confidence in his ability to keep up with his own Agility of 57 without making any mistakes.

He shook his head ruefully. Contrary to his plans, he was still simply raising every Stat, staying good at everything. Except in this case, he had no choice. His most powerful weapon, his Mana Skills, just weren't able to cope with an enemy that could freely teleport. A single moment was enough for the sphinx to Dodge. He needed to lock it down before he could smash it with the heavy hitters.

And that required him to use his body.

Randidly would need to rely on closing the distance and attack first in order to seize the momentum. To do that successfully, he needed Physical Stats. Or at least a way to increase his Stamina regeneration to use Haste and Empower regularly.

Struck by a sudden thought, Randidly checked his pockets and found the Soul Seed, inspecting it again.

Soul Seed 91% Nurtured. *Strongest Influences*: **1. Spear Mastery | 2. Spearing Roots | 3. Empower | 4. Fire Resistance | 5. Refine**

It appeared that while he fought the sphinx, the seed neared completion. Although he had no idea what sort of result would occur because of it, Spear Mastery and Fire Resistance becoming stronger influences, due to the nature of the fight, were not lost on him.

So many different things I need to do and preparations to make... Randidly pressed his eyes shut. He leaned back and allowed the last rays of the day to caress his skin.

Not knowing exactly when the Level Barrier would fall also bothered him. When the last monster of the horde was killed? Was there a Boss death to trigger it? Or even worse, would it begin to fall right when the final horde came for Donnyton?

There were two more hordes left. Without a firm answer, Randidly would rather react proactively, even if it meant he had less time.

It would be a long night.

Because by tomorrow morning, he would go sphinx hunting.

CHAPTER FIFTY-THREE

*D*ozer put his hands on his hips and laughed enthusiastically. He raised his arms and flexed before the Classers crowded around the quarry. "Kukuku, what other outcome but this was possible? Bask in my radiance! I am the strongest!"

Donny and Decklan gazed hatefully at him, but kept their mouths shut. Both Decklan's speed and Donny's Endurance, alongside his ability to interrupt tempo and survive damage, were intimidating. During the monster hordes, their individual contributions were greater than Dozer's.

However, this was not a battlefield. There was nowhere to hide. There was no press of bodies ensuring Donny's devastating Shield Bashes could be brought to bear. This was a duel.

In an open space, Dozer's larger weapon held the advantage. After a long struggle, he prevailed. A tired crowd of Classers lay around, nursing their wounds, knocked out of the competition by Dozer's enormous swings. By the end of it, they cheered for Dozer, savoring the moments when other Classers were beaten by him and forced to join their cause. In their eyes, the only way to accept their defeat was to have all others be similarly defeated.

"The strongest? I would probably rate you as fifth most impactful in a battle, overall. But your raw power has no rival. I suspect even the Ghosthound would struggle to clash directly with you."

Dozer frowned, his moment passed, and turned to face the speaker. Sam walked forward, examining the surroundings. Both because of his role as the head blacksmith for Donnyton and the fact that he hadn't bothered to participate in the tournament, Dozer didn't attempt to contradict him. Behind Sam, the young teenager, Lyra, looked around with obvious interest. Small animals that were composed of Mana flittered and capered across her fingers.

Gasps sporadically escaped from the surrounding Classers upon seeing the girl for the first time. Just as quickly, more experienced Classers with two shoulder pads whispered caution to those men. The girl was beautiful, but there were two problems. First, she was young. She might look mature, but she was likely only sixteen. Second, her relationship with both Sam the armorer and the Ghosthound meant that anyone who wanted to pursue her needed to step very, very carefully.

Honestly, Dozer knew of no one aside from Decklan who possessed the nerve to talk to her. And the conversations between Lyra and Decklan were mostly about training methods. They'd gone together with the Ghosthound one day and that experience formed the basis of their relationship. And also…

When Decklan returned, he shared with Dozer how the girl shredded powerful lizardmen with her Mana animals. From the pale set of Decklan's face as he explained, she was perhaps just as much a monster as the Ghosthound.

The men whispered uneasily about the last monster horde. When the blood of harpies rained from the skies, there was only one culprit—Lyra.

The Ghosthound could reduce a horde to nothing with a blast of fire, and Clarissa was extremely accurate with her icicles. Those still didn't hold the same visceral intimidation as having blood rain upon you while fighting. The looks pointed to Lyra changed when people realized that ominous red rain was the signature of her cruelly silent birds.

"Who's above me?" Dozer grumbled, looking away to show he wouldn't fight over this.

Sam grunted and halted his approach. It was almost worse that he considered the question so seriously. "Me, Clarissa, Annie, and Donny." He glanced at Lyra. "Can you think of anyone else?"

Lyra shrugged and smiled. The Ghosthound hung between them, a name Dozer would easily admit was more powerful than he. But at the moment, subjected to her small smirk, a hot spark of dissatisfaction slammed within Dozer.

Something else occurred to him and he frowned. "Annie? What are you talking about? She doesn't even have—"

Sam held up a hand. "You should speak to Annie about it directly. I'm sure she'll answer your questions. Anyway, Donny, I'm here for you. There's a guest."

Lyra stepped to the side and gestured theatrically to a thin man with long black hair tied up in a bun. The man looked around nervously, stepping forward without hesitation when he was indicated. The Classers regarded him curiously, their instincts likely giving them the same message as Dozer's. This man was not a threat.

He waved vaguely. "Hello, I'm Glendel. It's nice to meet you."

The discussions hadn't gone as well as he would have wanted. But they were able to quickly come to an agreement.

Glendel returned to the basecamp of his group, hurrying forward through the lengthening shadows. It had been ten days since the world changed. Now it seemed like these changes were merely the prelude. Even more sweeping forces were coming.

How strange that between leaving and returning to the group, so many of the impressions I had shifted... Glendel thought that as a general rule, his group was probably more adaptable than most and had done well for themselves. Yet the sight of Dozer wrapping his arms around a thick tree trunk and simply ripping it out of the ground still made him shiver.

The power of Classers was overwhelming.

Even still, across all the amazing feats Glendel had seen, the shadow of a single word lay: Ghosthound.

This is only just the beginning. Glendel's nerves had him chewing the inside of his cheek. He was very glad he'd set out when he had.

While others wanted to sit inside and wait out whatever happened in the world, Regina had taken a more sustainability focused outlook on the whole situation. She pushed for gathering individuals into a cohesive group, accumulating medicine and food, defending themselves actively, and methodically clearing out monsters in the hospital where they used to work.

She led them in this frantic first week, inspiring them to greatness, discovering Potion Making and the magic of Skills with the System. It was because of her they knew everything they did about this world.

The casual way the people of Donnyton talked about these things shattered Glendel's worldview. They were strong. Far, far stronger than Glendel believed possible. Partially, it was Classes, but it was also clear Donnyton experimented even more aggressively than Regina encouraged. During the tournament, Glendel watched as many fights as he could. The casual strength even the one-shoulder-pad Classer could display was breathtaking. The variety of Skills and fighting styles was humbling.

Approaching the camp, Glendel stopped between a tree hewn by a lightning bolt and whistled, as agreed. The trees around him were silent for several seconds and he feared the worst.

The counter whistle came at last and he hurried forward, happy to be back. He had so much to share.

The group set up shop at a gas station, their convoy of tractor trailers and ambulances pulling over, surprised at how few monsters they encountered in the area. In retrospect, the reason was obvious. The Newbie Village of Donnyton was already dominating the nearby landscape. When even the

NCCs had enough strength to handle themselves around a monster, the wandering creatures would thin out rather quickly.

Remembering the pens where there were some enterprising individuals trying to breed monsters for meat, Glendel shivered. *One step ahead of us, in so many ways…*

He nodded to those he passed by and received weary nods in return, their eyes hollow, following his bulging backpack with small frowns. Unfortunately, in this group of sixty, the food he'd been given from Donnyton wouldn't do much to satiate their hunger. Though it would bring hope.

Alana, the tall woman who handled most of the dirty work of monster fighting for the convoy, looked up as Glendel hurried toward Regina's RV. After a second of terse silence, scrutinizing his current condition, she waved him into the interior.

Slightly breathless, Glendel stepped forward. He couldn't tell if he was nervous or excited.

Regina Northwind, former surgeon and current iron-handed leader of their expedition, frowned at a ledger in front of her. She didn't immediately notice his presence, and Glendel hesitated, unsure of whether to disturb her. She coughed lightly into her hand and said "Report" without looking up.

Glendel sucked in a breath to steady himself and considered where to begin. He did his best to recount his experiences of the past several hours.

Most of the other refugees apparently flowed into a village called Donnyton, whose occupants easily numbered at least a thousand. The other town, currently closed to new residents, refused him entry. Although Donnyton's people were more tribal, they appeared more active.

He brought out the powerful Mana potion, and detailed examples of the different crops the administrator woman was willing to trade for tools and clothes. He then explained their other food harvesting preparations.

At this, Regina sighed. "Not interested in the medicine at all, huh? I suppose it makes sense. How much of this did you say they had?" Her finger tapped against the powerful sapphire Mana potion.

"Around a cooler full. From the way they talked about it, it wasn't too difficult to create. They're even harvesting the energy crystal trees and growing a grove near the edges of their fields."

Regina's eyes narrowed. "And they have Classes, yes? What do Classes do? How strong were the people that obtained one?"

"They didn't all have Classes," Glendel explained. "From what I could gather, Classes give you something like a special Path that also provides Skills. In addition, you get extra Stats per Level, so it doesn't make them immediately stronger. As for how strong they were once they gained a few Levels…"

Glendel hesitated. After a long pause, he shook his head. "I don't know how to explain. Strong. So strong I can't comprehend their strength. More monstrous than monsters."

Regina was silent for a long moment. "Compared to Alana, how strong are they?"

Glendel reflexively looked back toward the door where Alana sat, methodically sharpening metal bars into knives. He released a long sigh. "As far as I can tell, there are three ranks of people, with special individuals above that. Alana is likely comparable to the first rank. Maybe a little stronger, more skillful with her spear. But the people at the second level… they surpass the human limits. They could crumple her weapons with their bare hands."

The air was very still. It didn't even seem like Regina breathed. She leaned back in her chair, biting her lip. Glendel was all too aware of the web of wrinkles across her face.

Regina broke the silence. "How are women treated there?"

"It seemed normal. There were female warriors. The head of the NCCs, what they call non-Class characters, was also a woman. I met a very strange young woman named Lyra. She seemed to have a fair amount of influence. There were definitely more men than women. I think they outnumber them about two to one."

Regina rubbed her forehead. "If that's the case, we cannot afford to be left behind in this new world. There's no reason not to trade with them. Let's gather everyone up and head closer tomorrow."

"Ah, there's one more thing, but I don't know what it means," Glendel added.

Regina arched an eyebrow, and he continued. "They kept referencing something called a 'Ghosthound.' At first, I thought it was a monster or something, but the more they mentioned it, the more I think they were talking about a person. Not to judge their appearance, considering the certain state of the world… but a lot of the men there seemed like brutes or thugs. A lot of tattoos and primitive tooth adornments. But as soon as the Ghosthound was mentioned, they became quiet and as well-behaved as Christian school children."

"You think this Ghosthound is the reason these villages formed so quickly?" Regina asked, rubbing her chin.

"Maybe. That's the only thing I can guess."

"Thank you for your time, and for agreeing to scout ahead for us. It is appreciated. Try and get some rest. We won't move for a few hours."

Glendel backed out of the room, a lump in his throat. She made it sound pretty now, but Glendel would rather have not been the scout, even though he knew Regina had a very compelling reason as to why it had to be him.

He was the only remaining male in their group.

Immediately after the System arrived, most of the male doctors stormed out of the hospital, demanding answers with half-assed plans of action, only to be mauled by the waiting monsters. Regina gathered up most of the nurses and organized them, working through their new series of problems. Just by statistical anomaly, most of the remaining men either died or ran off, unsatisfied with taking orders from Regina.

CHAPTER FIFTY-FOUR

*D*awn spread its arms wide and welcomed the new day. The coming night would be the final monster horde to ravage Donnyton before the Level barrier dropped, and an even more dangerous foe was allowed to roam free.

During that time, Randidly would rip out the threat at the roots or die trying.

I am not afraid. Randidly told himself. And in those moments, it was true. His words stilled his heart. He'd spent the past twelve hours frantically preparing, honing the particular Skills he needed. More than the preparation, it was the looming necessity that urged him forward.

He did not wish to let Ep-Tal, the Hungry Tribulation, loose upon Donnyton. Everything he managed to help build was threatened by the presence of this monster. Randidly clenched his hands around his training spear, stalking through the dusty badlands toward the ominous ravine. *A spear can only advance. If I let go, I will die. I have no choice.*

When Randidly proceeded down the long path to the base of the canyon, the sphinx raised its head from the depths of the cave.

The inhuman woman showed its teeth in the approximation of a smile. "Oh, oh, oh, you came back so soon. Did you miss me, me, me?"

Snorting, Randidly drew his spear. He stared at the first rays of the day reflecting off the blade. He was not afraid. Because right now, he needed to be the one who wielded fear.

Only if he could force Ep-Tal to unthinkingly take a particular action could he inflict the sort of blow that would threaten its life.

For now, Randidly didn't advance or use any Skills. He adjusted his stance and calmed his heartbeat. He allowed the pounding excitement at gambling with his life to rise and drown out all other emotions.

The trick to this fight would be seeing how far Randidly could push the sphinx with small and painful wounds before it would inevitably take him seriously. To slowly whittle away at its Health and all at once drop the hammer in the very moment it realized he represented a legitimate threat.

To wield fear like a blade, but only at the right time.

Randidly didn't deny the hidden dangers in escalating the conflict. He sincerely doubted the Fireball was the most powerful spell in the sphinx's arsenal. If Randidly had a weakness, it was to magical attacks. Especially unexpected ones.

I doubt I'll be lucky enough that it's a poison-based attack. Randidly thought grimly.

He leveled his spear and the sphinx regarded him with a lazy expression and languid posture. Currently, he wasn't a threat. He was the same toy the Hungry Tribulation batted around last evening. He could only advance, pressing himself beyond this "safe" designation, and into a capable threat.

A transition with enough momentum to crush the sphinx's resistance and finish it off.

Or die in the process.

His grip would loosen from the spear, his debt to Shal forever unrepaid. His friends, Sydney and Ace, forever alone out there in this System-dominated world. Donnyton, left without any knowledge of the threat that would soon approach on silent wings.

I am not afraid, Randidly told himself again. Even as he thought it, a small twinge of regret surfaced. He should have left word with Donnyton about his plans. He'd been so caught up in his training, it completely slipped his mind.

The sun dawned completely, shedding flowing waves of light that dripped down the canyon walls and gradually illuminated the battleground. The eyes of both combatants abruptly narrowed.

With a smile, the sphinx teleported closer and pawed casually at Randidly. This time, his boosted Reaction meant his Agility also gained an extra boost. Randidly easily sidestepped the blow, his sharp movement creating a sizable distance between his body and the razor sharp claws. Heat rose through his limbs. Rather than the wild roller coaster ride his body had been previously, he finally felt under control.

Time to begin.

To start out on the right foot, he spent extra Stamina to activate Haste. Randidly stepped forward into the wide space his sidestep created, meeting the sphinx with a Phantom Thrust to its side, drawing a long scratch.

Congratulations! Your Skill Phantom Thrust has grown to Level 39!

The sphinx hissed in annoyance and glared at Randidly. In his heart, Randidly no longer had to tell himself he was not afraid. The truth spoke for itself. Previously, he'd taken an hour of bitter struggle to get such a blow.

Ep-Tal's grin widened and it teleported. His increased resistance excited it. Suddenly, the games it could play with Randidly were more thrilling.

Do you feel it too? Randidly wondered around the sound of his pounding heart. *This addicting heat?*

He couldn't remain distracted for long. The sphinx reappeared directly behind him. With tingling hands, he spun around. The sphinx teleported a second time, now in the sky above him. It belched a Fireball.

Reaction jolted him into motion a few fractions of time more rapidly. Rolling to the side, Randidly managed to avoid the Fireball, only to be met by another paw strike when he hopped back to his feet.

Too close to Dodge... unless I want to use both Haste and Empower.

Randidly gritted his teeth and met the casual attack with a Sweep, strengthened with Empower and Heavy Blow. The sphinx chuckled and teleported backward. All that Stamina Randidly used simply swung his body into a pirouette. Meanwhile, the sphinx lowered its jaw for a Fireball.

This time, Randidly was ready. He knew the creature would try and make him feel helpless after he made it bleed. He was not afraid of this petty sort of foe who behaved so predictably.

Congratulations! Your Skill **Empower** has grown to **Level 24!**

Randidly spun the spear back into a ready position with the aid of another Empower. He activated Phantom Half-Step and crossed most of the distance separating them. The fire still formed in its mouth. Randidly took another step forward and pierced the air with a Phantom Thrust, right into its open jaw. The half-formed fireball sparked fitfully and collapsed the moment the spear pressed through it. The blade of his spear sank into the soft flesh of the roof of Ep-Tal's mouth.

Congratulations! Your Skill **Spirit of Adversity** has grown to **Level 26!**

Congratulations! Your Skill **Edge of Decay (Un)** has grown to **Level 12!**

There was a moment where Randidly had a second of clarity. The Fireball spell backlash was disintegrating and his spear cut deeper. The sphinx's eyes widened.

All that image training I did was more effective than I thought. Randidly was almost aghast at how well he anticipated and practiced this exact series of moves. *It's really because this bastard doesn't take me seriously. Its responses have been so lazy. Even against a powerful foe, a well laid plan will prove effective.*

Just like Shal guided the Black Swamp Salamander into the shallows, as long as I can keep guiding the sphinx...!

But there was a problem. For all that the extra Skill Levels were useful in narrowing the gap between man and monster, he was progressing too quickly to stick to the original plan. The advantage of that was his Mana was still completely full, which Randidly hadn't expected.

Then, in the sphinx's widening eyes, he recognized its genuine pain. If he didn't up the intensity right now, Randidly would lose his tenuous grip on the weapon of *fear*.

The Fireball completely sputtered out. Randidly twisted his spear to rend more flesh and promptly yanked the weapon free. The sphinx's expression twisted, catalyzed by an overwhelming ancient anger and a willingness to slaughter, all its killing intent concentrated on the black-haired Randidly Ghosthound.

In the face of that incensed Tribulation, Randidly grinned.

Tsk, at the very least, I was hoping to get more cuts active for Edge of Decay... Even to his own mind, Randidly's thought felt reckless. His heart alternated between pounding and fluttering. His own pulse beat within his tight grip on the wooden shaft of his spear. He didn't shy away from that strange relish.

Randidly had felt before how influential confidence could be. To the System, belief mattered. And he was now armed with the purest belief that his plan would work.

First things first... Before the rage in the sphinx's eyes could turn to action, Randidly tightened his grip on his weapon and cast four Mana Skills at once. The cool Mana in his navel swirled wildly as so much drained at once, causing his stomach to do flip-flops.

He summoned Spearing Roots, ripping them up from the ground into Ep-Tal's stomach. Better to sharpen its sense of pain as much as possible right now. Then he activated Root Manipulation to create another Spearing Roots. Only this time, he pushed them up to the sphinx's head height and wrapped the roots around its mouth, surrounding the hinge of its jaw.

Congratulations! Your Skill **Root Manipulation** has grown to **Level 34!**

His Mana drained rapidly, pushing the movements of the roots to its limits. This was another portion he practiced quite extensively over the past several hours.

Randidly's high Willpower and Control were brought to bear as he *pressed* with everything he had, rapidly effectuating his will and speeding the roots' movements until they blurred.

With an audible click, the sphinx's jaw snapped shut. Its eyes bulged. Randidly wasn't sure if its mouth was always the source of its offensive spells, but better safe than sorry. He knew it could break out rather simply, but all he wanted now was to buy time.

A slight headache began to develop along the bridge of his nose. He pushed its existence to the side, not daring to slow the frantic pace of Skills.

Summon Pestilence came next like a wave, most of which Randidly used to attack the still shocked eyes of the beast. It took everything he had to direct a small number of insects to an unobtrusive mission elsewhere. The headache rapidly grew more demanding. Randidly gritted his teeth.

Congratulations! Your Skill **Summon Pestilence** has grown to **Level 17!**

Mana Strengthening rounded out his four Mana Skill attack. Randidly unleashed a physical assault on the sphinx's bound head and neck, his spear flashing in the spreading light of the dawn. Blood spurted across the ground.

Congratulations! Your Skill **Edge of Decay (Un)** has grown to **Level 13!**

Unfortunately, the pain and shock could only keep the monster still for so long. The sphinx reared back on its hind legs, seeking escape from the roots spearing into its stomach and wrapping around its mouth. Randidly pressed his lips into a thin line and rushed forward, quick as a ghost. Every step bloomed hot with Empower and Haste, invigorating all across his body. He raised his spear and launched a full power Phantom Onslaught on its chest. *I just need a few more attacks!*

Shal once told Randidly that his spear was dull. At the time, he hadn't understood it. He did now. His emerald eyes burned, vengefully plunging the head of his spear into the golden fur of the sphinx's lion body. Desperation and joy fueled his limbs. If Randidly failed to inflict enough damage, he would die.

His spear was now sharp. It cut because he needed it to. His spear bit like a rabid dog. And the Hungry Tribulation, Ep-Tal, bled.

Congratulations! Your Skill **Fighting Proficiency** has grown to **Level 32!**

Before, Randidly's attacks would leave long, shallow scratches that only annoyed the sphinx. At the time, Randidly had been struggling to survive and conserved his Stamina. He fought to flee. Now he fought to maim, spending Stamina freely. Empowering each ability to maul.

Furious, the sphinx tried to roar and ripped through a portion of the roots binding its mouth. Randidly's Intelligence was high enough now that the roots were incredibly resilient. The strained roots barely managed to endure. He still had a few more seconds.

Even better, the sphinx seemed stunned that its attempted roar failed. This created the perfect opportunity for an Empowered Sweep to rip a large gash in the sphinx's exposed throat.

Congratulations! Your Skill **Sweep** has grown to **Level 17!**

So worried with establishing superiority, a sadistic part of Randidly observed. *If you had just charged forward and relied on your body to knock me over, would you be this miserable? Fuck you for underestimating me!*

The sphinx bucked wildly, ripping the roots out of its stomach. It desperately slashed at the binds around its jaw, shredding them. To avoid the sphinx twisting and smashing him to the side, Randidly retreated a few steps. With a small break, Randidly brought a Mana potion to his mouth and drank it. By the time he downed it, Ep-Tal had freed itself.

Just as it turned its bloodshot eyes on Randidly, irritated and inflamed from the bites of the Pestilence, another wave of Spearing Roots slammed into its left thigh. Randidly surged closer, even as the monster's unbound mouth allowed it to roar in fury.

Even if you're a special Tribulation with bonus Mana and Stamina, you're still only Level 30. Randidly's gaze fixed on the blood pumping from the sphinx's wounds. *Is it fun playing around with me now?*

The sphinx only slightly recovered from its shock this time and twisted out of the way when Randidly thrust his spear. Even though its body was huge, it managed to Dodge and deflect most of the roots. Despite some missing, Randidly activated Root Manipulation and brought them around to wrap around the sphinx's body. Unfortunately, it kicked backward and destroyed the roots scratching its flank.

Randidly kept his crazed grin plastered on his face and summoned another wave of Spearing Roots. When the creature was distracted, he peppered its massive body with Phantom Thrusts.

Congratulations! Your Skill **Spearing Roots** has grown to **Level 9!**

Randidly never allowed himself a break. Stamina drained rapidly out of his body. This was a chance he needed to seize. Every spurt of the sphinx's blood was another step—

Just as Randidly pulled his spear free from the sphinx and prepared another thrust, the monster threw itself backwards, forcefully ripping all the roots to bits. Its eyes practically spit sparks as it briefly inspected its own gashes.

It bore a hateful glare at Randidly. "You, you, you… A toy like you needs to be—"

Ep-Tal's body stiffened. When nothing happened in response to calling on its most agile Skill, its eyes widened.

Congratulations! Your Skill **Summon Pestilence** has grown to **Level 18!**

Randidly activated the Pestilence he'd hidden on the sphinx's body, sending it viciously biting into the open wounds of the creature. Now that it was discovered, it wouldn't be long before the monster dealt with it. Randidly's original intention had been successfully accomplished.

He confirmed his theory that no foreign materials could be touching the sphinx's body for it to Blink. That final tension in the frantic battleground eased his pounding heart. He hadn't been certain the conjured bugs from a Skill would count.

The sphinx might be frozen, but Randidly was not. The split second bought by the shock of the teleportation failure allowed Randidly to down a Stamina potion and take a quick step forward. The additional Skills of Haste and Empower transformed Footwork of the Spear Phantom into an impossibly fast and smooth movement technique. His spear blurred into deadly motion.

Congratulations! Your Skill **Empower** has grown to **Level 25!**

Randidly didn't dare commit too fully, but he wanted to keep the pressure rising. He flicked his spear out in whip-like blows, slicing at the sphinx's gaping wounds across its shoulders.

Thankfully, its predictability continued. Hot on its own fury, the sphinx opened its mouth and shot a Fireball. The combination of anticipation and his higher Reaction meant Randidly could simply sidestep. He kept attacking, spending his Mana just as quickly as he recovered it.

It followed up with a swipe of its paw, but the wounds to its muscles were beginning to dull the edge of those weapons. Randidly danced sideways, his spear flicking back and forth. The monster raised its head and roared, giving Randidly the opportunity to square his shoulders and thrust his spear deeply into the flesh of its left forearm.

Congratulations! Your Skill **Spear Phantom's Footwork** has grown to **Level 32!**

The sphinx was simply too big. The weight of its flesh and the Health it contained made this process mostly a way to cause pain. There was no way for Randidly to inflict a deadly amount of damage in a short amount of time. But in terms of shaking the Hungry Tribulation…

Even through his own adrenaline-fueled spree, Randidly noticed the wildness taking root within the sphinx's eyes. Randidly's Cheshire smile stretched even wider. *You don't remember what it's like, do you? To fight or die?*

The sphinx finally spread its wide eagle wings, releasing a blast of air that stumbled Randidly. It shuffled forward on bleeding legs, its eyes red and its wings beating frantically downward, forcing gusts of wind to pummel him.

Although Randidly was initially shocked, it quickly became clear the sphinx possessed no special Skills to utilize through its wings. The air was annoying but posed no real threat. They were massive and beautiful, and ultimately irrelevant.

On the next beat of the sphinx's wings, Randidly stepped sideways, avoiding the blast of wind, and cut into the gleaming white feathers with the blade of his spear. From the resulting screech, these wings were quite sensitive.

The sphinx belched out two Fireballs and spat them not directly at Randidly, but around him. Randidly pressed his lips together and lowered his head. Rather than Dodge, he accelerated forward and did his best to ignore the flash of pain along his arms from the Skills' detonation.

Congratulations! Your Skill **Fire Resistance** has grown to **Level 9!**

Having earned himself another stunned look from the sphinx, Randidly's confidence received another boost. While the heat dissipated, Randidly conjured more Pestilence and smashed a locust-covered fist into the beast's nose.

As the monster reeled backward, Randidly saw his chance. The monster swiped halfheartedly at him and beat its massive wings, spraying blood with the motion. With the sphinx briefly blinded by the insects eating its eyes, Randidly jumped forward and thrust with the spear.

Every Skill he could think of was contained in that basic thrust.

He activated Haste, Empower, Mana Strengthening, Heavy Blow, and Phantom Thrust. In addition, his body had been honed to a reliable machine by Shal's intense demands of repetition of the basic thrust. Randidly's eyes gleamed. *This is the proof! Proof that I'm growing stronger! That with preparation—*

Randidly's strike smashed into the sphinx's forehead, eliciting a roar that sent him stumbling backward. All his fury, fear, and his deep sense of guilt toward Shal drained through his spear and into the wound. Randidly retreated, feeling strangely exhausted.

Inwardly, Randidly grimaced at the result. He'd drawn a deep gash, right above the left eye. He had been trying to blind it, but it'd jerked to the side at the last second in its panic. He began to tremble. He still had plenty of Mana, but the confidence he gained in leading the sphinx by the nose was thoroughly shaken that such an attack only ripped through its eyebrow and scratched its skull.

Blood rapidly bubbled up from the head wound and dripped down across Ep-Tal's face. Randidly couldn't decide how to proceed. All that momentum, all that planning to get the sphinx afraid. Should he press again and—

The blood flowed quicker, coloring the sphinx's left eye. Its breath quickened.

From stillness, the sphinx exploded into motion. It did not like its blood staining its eye. It spun around and leapt toward the cave. It didn't even bother to release a Fireball to keep him at bay. At the moment, it was completely consumed to return to where bodies were waiting for it to recover.

Randidly's grin crept higher. Even if his confidence didn't return after failing to inflict a significant wound, his plan finally worked.

Gotcha. Who's the toy now?

Randidly stalked after it, removing a Mana potion from his bag and drinking it. The tingling coolness of the liquid was more refreshing than Randidly remembered it being in a long time. Then, as his Mana pool began to fill, he mobilized his energy in preparation for what was to come.

Just as the creature reached the mouth of the cave, Randidly spent all five hundred or so of his Mana on Spearing Roots. When one Skill activation was done being fueled, he created another one, pouring himself totally into this one massive blow.

Despite the stone and dirt of the cave's mouth trembling, the sphinx stepped across the threshold.

Though Spearing Roots was normally an incredibly powerful, penetrative attack, it had a significant drawback. Spearing Roots could only originate from the ground. Except against the flying monsters, most of the foes Randidly encountered remained on or near the ground. Even if the angle of attack from the Skill wasn't normally an issue, this unforeseen flaw limited the avenues of attack Randidly possessed. And on a monster with a huge body like the sphinx, also limited the areas he could damage easily.

Which was why its stomach and back legs were currently the most gored.

The sphinx took another step forward, its head, front arms, and the tips of its white feathered wings moving past the threshold.

Randidly's Mana pool was quickly emptying out. His smile sharpened as the first tremors shook the cave's mouth. Where normally he could only produce the roots from the ground, a cave meant the ground was all around you. And all according to plan, the sphinx ran right into the large mouth of its cave, with only a meter or so of space between its head, sides, and the earth.

Congratulations! Your Skill **Spearing Roots** has grown to **Level 10!**

An onlooker could perhaps believe the cave had been a mouth this whole time, with viciously sharp roots for teeth. Just as Ep-Tal surged forward, the cave bit down upon its soft, vulnerable wings and stomach.

Congratulations! Your Skill **Spearing Roots** has grown to **Level 11!**

Thorned roots burrowed into flesh wherever they could find it. The mass Randidly created were so densely packed, the initial crash against the monster's torso knocked the wind out of it. The aftermath was strangely silent.

My Strength is only about 30, but my Intelligence is 73. Randidly swayed slightly, hit by a wave of lightheadedness. He used his spear as a cane to hold himself upright and drank another Mana potion.

Finally, the sphinx caught its breath.

SCREEEEEEEEECH!

The roots thoroughly tunneled into its upper torso. Only its head likely made it safely through to the cave proper. Once it was immobilized, the second wave of Randidly's Skills arrived and ripped the wounds even deeper. Attacks came from the sides and below, burrowing long holes through its flesh. No spot on its body was safe from the invasion of the roots.

Blood at an entirely different magnitude of volume gushed through the small spaces in the roots. The sphinx twisted and bucked, instinctively digging its feet into the ground and forcing itself backward. The more pained it became, the more frantic its movements, until its limbs twitched around its desperate yowls.

That said, Randidly held no hopes this would kill the monster. Especially considering the way it could devour flesh to heal. He utilized Root Manipulation to twist the roots toward the front, digging those thorns as a warning of what Randidly could produce with a second wave if the sphinx tried to force itself forward.

Guzzling another Mana potion, Randidly targeted the pristine portion of the sphinx's wings. Any place not stained by blood was ruthlessly punctured and shredded. Still half-mad with pain, the beast dug its feet into the ground and ripped off huge slabs of gore to extricate itself. Randidly released a sigh of relief. He brought the roots down fully, effectively blocking the cave.

Congratulations! Your Skill **Root Manipulation** has grown to **Level 35!**

If the sphinx was determined, it wouldn't be stopped very long, but it was more than enough to slow it down while Randidly ripped into its back.

Mewing in agony, the thing staggered to its feet. Its wings hung limp over its sides, blood flowing down each and every feather, pooling where the tips trailed over the ground. As the sphinx straightened, its eyes acknowledged the gauntlet Randidly had thrown down. Randidly couldn't help but recognize that while the attack was effective, so much of its body still functioned.

Its back legs were scratched, but comparatively unharmed. Stretches of rippling muscle across its legs and torso weren't yet wounded enough to affect its movements. Only its wings were truly broken.

And as the Level Barrier hadn't yet lowered, its Mana and Stamina regeneration were still incredibly boosted.

A storm brewed on the sphinx's silent features. Although the head of the monster was human, all humanity drained out of its feral expression. Yet Randidly couldn't waste this opportunity. The more he allowed pain to sharpen the sphinx's mind toward the threat he represented, the more he needed to apply pressure.

I can do this. Randidly told himself. He tightened his grip on the spear. Before Randidly attacked, a notification popped up.

Congratulations! Your **Soul Seed** has been completely nurtured. **Upon being inserted into fertile soil, the seed shall grow.**

Randidly snorted and pushed the Soul Seed to the side. Honestly, he'd forgotten about it during the extended training session of the past twelve hours. He could experiment with it when he wasn't fighting for his life.

"You will die, die, die," the sphinx said, lowering the lids of its eyes until only half were showing.

"Sure, sure, sure." Randidly injected as much confidence as he could as he moved closer.

The creature opened its mouth and Mana flowed rapidly to fill it. Instead of a Fireball, a milky wave of gas spread and covered a five-meter area around the sphinx, submerging Randidly within its depths.

The Skill had come so quickly that even Randidly's Reaction didn't catch up. Or perhaps in this case, Randidly's expectations meant the variation in the Skill Ep-Tal used caught him completely by surprise.

If you accelerate too much and lose grip on your spear, the specter of Shal whispered in his ear, *you will die.*

Within a second, the milky air began to vibrate. In addition to whatever nefarious effect was coming, it completely destroyed Randidly's visibility. He flared his Eyes of the Spear Phantom, but the surroundings remained just as murky and obtuse.

Randidly began to backpedal and a ripple ran through the milky substance. It began to twist and rip. A horrible shriek blasted outward, somehow magnified to an overwhelming degree. Jarring, jagged vibrations hit Randidly's ears. Strange movements in the air made it unbearable to be within. Randidly stumbled to a stop before he'd taken a single step, struggling to collect himself.

Randidly was numb. He fell to his knees. His eyes were blank as he looked at his hands.

Shal's phantom grunted, *Get up.*

The horrible screeching continued. Randidly's arms began to shake in his attempt to push himself up. He pressed his hands into the dirt and stared at the grains between his fingers. The noise robbed Randidly of something vital. And that valuable essence was being sucked out of him.

Get up. This time, it was Randidly, urging himself.

Still, he could not move.

Although he'd been through a lot, this was the most painful experience Randidly ever encountered. Numbness and agony twined through his entire being. It made his bones ache and his marrow roil, while simultaneously making Randidly feel like he was staring over his own shoulder.

Congratulations! Your Skill **Pain Resistance** has grown to **Level 13!**

After what felt like an eternity, it stopped, and Randidly collapsed, coughing up blood. It hadn't done much actual damage, but the pain, combined with the strangeness... Even now, his ears rang and his vision swam.

The shaken Randidly looked up just in time to see the sphinx leaping at him, mouth wide and teeth bared.

CHAPTER FIFTY-FIVE

*P*ain made him groggy.

Survival ensured a proficient means to spark movement.

Rolling to the side, Randidly managed to get out of the way. He Empowered his hands and pushed off the ground, throwing himself up to his feet. He swayed and staggered, all too conscious of a dull ring coming from his ears.

The sphinx's paw smashed the ground, leaving a huge crack in the earth. A wave of concussive force blasted outward. Randidly was still too dizzy to react in time to the fallout. The shockwave sent him staggering. Blood dripped from his left ear, where the painful ringing became sharper.

His ass hit the dirt and he knew he could not stay there long. Gritting his teeth, Randidly forced his trembling hands to still just as another paw swipe ripped past his nose. He jerked back in time to avoid having his head torn off. The huge claws instead ripped through his shirt. Tattered cloth and flesh fluttered as he reeled and attempted to stabilize himself.

Congratulations! Your Skill **Dodge** has grown to **Level 33!**

I need... I just need a moment... Randidly's hand wandered into his satchel for a Health potion.

Blood oozed in a small waterfall from the wound on his chest and he took several steps backward. A notification came up that his Health had dipped below 20%. Randidly couldn't focus on it, his eyes narrowing to view his current enemy. Although the sphinx had seized the initiative, now that he really looked at it, Randidly could tell it was also slightly off after using that strange spell.

The monster shifted its weight as it swayed, its movements nowhere near as sharp as they were previously. In addition, Randidly noticed blackening around the edges of the sphinx's wounds. Both panted, staring each other down in a moment of stretched time.

Congratulations! Your Skill **Edge of Decay (Un)** has grown to **Level 14!**

The moment passed.

The sphinx hissed at his close viewing, following up with a Fireball directly aimed at his face. Randidly rolled to the side once more. Partially through the motion, his adrenaline-crazed senses noticed a small black object that slipped out of his pocket in the roll. Reflexively, he scooped it up.

The Fireball burned into the ground and sprayed Randidly with shards of partially molten rock. The sphinx hustled forward, swinging its paw. Again it staggered, allowing Randidly to completely avoid the blow. While one hand went up to pointlessly press on his chest wound, the other wrapped around the small, completely nurtured Soul Seed.

Randidly's expression was bitter, wishing by some miracle it was a Health Potion he picked up. In the future, he sincerely planned to practice pulling potions out of his satchel while performing all sorts of different maneuvers.

Randidly glanced down at the seed. *A throwback to Farming, the lifeline that supported me until Shal showed up and told me how to truly thrive in the System. Unfortunately for Farming, you need to plant a seed before it can be useful. In this case... this seed needs to go in "fertile soil." Whatever that means...*

Another Fireball belched by the sphinx forced Randidly back even further. He was stunned to discover that the spear he dropped earlier was by his feet. The sphinx noticed it too.

With a surprisingly adroit motion, considering his current dizziness, Randidly snuck his bare toe underneath the shaft and kicked it up into the air. His hand closed around it. In one hand he held a weapon, in the other he held a seed.

The sphinx rumbled forward and Randidly was struck with a crazy idea. As the sphinx opened its mouth to unleash another Fireball, Randidly followed the impulse without thinking about it too deeply. He whipped the small Soul Seed into its mouth with a sidearm throw. Luckily, the passage of even the seed was enough to throw off the flow of Mana for the spell. Once more, the fire energy dispersed before it could be released at point blank range.

Randidly didn't have enough time to pull out a potion with the sphinx charging toward him. He put a foot back and slightly bent his knees, settling into one of Shal's basic stances. His Health was ticking downward, but retreating further would only make it worse.

A spear must advance. Randidly sternly told himself.

Randidly met the sphinx's charge with a Hasted and Empowered Phantom Thrust. Such was the speed of their collision, that after the tiny Soul Seed dispersed the Fireball and bounced off the roof of the sphinx's mouth, his spear tip caught up to the tiny projectile. With so much dexterity that even Randidly was surprised by his own movement, Randidly hit the Soul Seed directly and pressed it forward, driving it up and into the soft flesh of the sphinx's mouth.

There. Randidly grinned with the heady rush of triumph. *Planted.*

The sphinx's woman-head slammed into Randidly's chest. Blood burst from his wound and Randidly wheezed in pain and stumbled backward, his spear still stuck in its mouth. Ep-Tal was just as thrown by the impact. Its face was spattered with blood and its neck awkwardly tilted backward from the wedged spear.

Ignoring the pain in his body, Randidly stepped back up to the stalled sphinx and drove his weapon deeper, ripping upward through the top of the jaw, hoping he'd hit something vital.

The sphinx began to tremble, mewing through its propped-open mouth. Randidly took that time to plant his feet and shove the spear even deeper, cracking against something hard with a wet thump.

Just when he thought the creature might collapse and die, its mouth slammed shut, snapping the shaft of the spear into pieces. Randidly was sent stumbling backwards. It raised its head and howled, and Randidly spotted the other half of his spear was still sunk into the roof of its mouth.

With the brief distraction, Randidly dropped the remnants of the spear and withdrew several potions. He gulped down two Health potions and one Stamina, hurriedly raising himself back up to something nearer to his full strength. This was definitely the decisive blow he needed, but in terms of inflicting more damage...

Randidly's fingers flexed, considering his half-full Mana pool. *I definitely regret turning down Daniel's offer of a spear from the weapon shop. Having a spare is a good idea for situations like this.*

Realizing it couldn't do anything about the pain, the sphinx turned its red-rimmed eyes on Randidly, all pretense of playing gone. An extremely large, angry monster that would kill the source of its misery before anything else charged.

It was met by a buzzing, swarming cloud of Pestilence to the face. The locusts were only too happy to take advantage of its wounds to inflict even more damage, but the Skill barely slowed it down. Its long claws shredded the air where Randidly had been standing. He'd already rolled to the side and popped back to his feet.

While hungry insect mandibles ripped out chucks of the sphinx's cornea, Randidly cast Spearing Roots to rip into it at a sideways angle. This time, his target was the tendons of its back legs. As long as he could further lower its mobility, Randidly wouldn't need to worry about it running away by foot to hunt down monsters to eat.

It whipped around, likely following its sense of hearing to locate him. Randidly anticipated that. Root Manipulation made minute final adjustments and the Spearing Roots punctured the thighs of its back legs.

Congratulations! Your Skill **Root Manipulation** has grown to **Level 36!**

The sphinx kicked backward and freed itself almost immediately, but Randidly's smile curled wide again to see one of the legs twitch an extra time, as though the core muscle screamed from the movement. Leaping to the side and gathering more Pestilence, Randidly felt a hint of confidence that he might be able to pull this off.

Of course, that moment was exactly when the sphinx twisted midair and leaped after the shocked Randidly with an extra bit of malicious sharpness. Its eyes glowed golden and that light burned through the vicious insects of his Summon Pestilence. Randidly could do little more than scramble backward. The huge body smashed into him and knocked the wind out of his lungs. The two of them crashed into the ground, with the sphinx partially on top of him. Randidly's ribs screamed in protest.

Although wounded and dripping blood from the holes the bugs dug in its face, Ep-Tal leered down at Randidly. Its breath was hot and hungry against his cheeks.

"Now, now, now, wha—"

Using a chunk of his Mana to fuel Root Manipulation, Randidly urged several to wind around the sphinx's feet and drag it off of his body. As soon as he could, Randidly gasped and wheezed, trying to get his breath back. The sphinx turned to face the roots, kicking and ripping itself free. It didn't take long. Randidly didn't go for a potion this time. When it turned back to him, he crunched its nose with a Roundhouse Kick.

The pain strengthened the growing fear in Randidly's chest. The best way he knew to push that down was to struggle.

Congratulations! Your Skill **Roundhouse Kick** has grown to **Level 14!**

Congratulations! Your Skill **Roundhouse Kick** has grown to **Level 15!**

Breaking its nose wouldn't inflict significant damage, but still it fell back, slightly stunned by the impact. Plus, the strike clearly jostled the spear in its mouth. It reverted to the strange mewing noise.

At that moment, Randidly poured all his remaining Mana into Spearing Roots. Exhausted and with its legs wounded, the Hungry Tribulation crouched back on its heels. Its stomach was not prepared for the several sharp spears ripping upward from the ground, this time gleefully digging into the torso of the monster. Through the slight sensation of Root Manipulation, Randidly felt how they ripped through the stomach, puncturing holes in the sphinx's damnable lungs.

Congratulations! Your Skill **Spearing Roots** has grown to **Level 12!**

The sphinx opened its mouth to scream but only expelled blood around the shaft of the broken spear.

That horrible milky, pearlescent air spread from its mouth and covered Randidly. He made to dash away, but his body was too exhausted. He Empowered his first step and felt his Stamina nearing dangerous levels. Before he could recover, the air once more began to hum, then distort. The shrieking noise returned, just as the ringing had finally left his sensitive ears.

As the first blast of noise hit him, Randidly gritted his teeth to stay standing. A notification popped up that made his current dilemma so much worse.

WARNING! YOUR HEALTH HAS FALLEN BELOW 10%!

Randidly glanced down at the deeply gouged flesh of his chest. *Damnit... how long have I been bleeding now?*

The noise intensified, causing the back of his head to throb. The pain was definitely worse. Randidly hoped his Health wasn't decreasing at a commensurate amount. Randidly only realized he was crumpling when his knees hit the ground. His hands felt numb and distant. Blackness ate at the corner of his vision. He groped the ground for something, anything.

A stone, a weapon, something to strike this beast. The monster was right there, only an arm's length away. But a dark fear gnawed at the bottom of Randidly's heart. It'd been lurking recently, waiting for the right moment. And now it chose to spread its clammy fingers.

You're going to die because you're weak, the voice whispered. *Because you're a burden. And because you failed, all of Donnyton will follow. Devoured by this Hungry Tribulation. Because do you think, after killing you, it's fury will be sated?*

Perhaps it will torture the entire town to vent its wrath...

Randidly's vision swam. His palms touched the ground and he flexed his fingers ineffectually. He remembered the gaping mouth of the Giant Serpent, its fangs dripping venom. His mind scrambled, thinking of his different Skills. This time, there would be no Shal to save him. He desperately wanted to not need saving.

I just... Randidly's green eyes watered. The sensation of dirt between his fingers grew distant. Only the vibration remained, coiling through his entire being from that horrible noise. Some part of him wanted to give up, to just collapse.

But as Randidly's head fell forward, he caught himself. Shal's phantasm was there, glowering at him, demanding he perform one more set.

This...! Randidly flexed his hands. Both his Stamina pool in his chest and his Mana pool in his navel held the barest hint of energy. Randidly flared Iron Skin for a few seconds, hoping to protect himself from the noise. *Not like this!*

It worked, just barely. And soon, his Stamina once more had been completely depleted. He collapsed, his forehead pressing against the ground. The pounding in his head intensified. *After all this time, all this struggle... am I going to let it end like this?*

Sydney... I just wanted... to be strong for you...

Somehow that thought gave him the energy to push up onto his hands and knees. He twisted, bringing his head around to look behind him. The ghost of Shal crossed his arms in the way he did when he was pleased, but he didn't want to show it. Something vicious rose in Randidly's chest, the horrible vindictiveness of the Ghosthound.

Biting his lip to keep himself conscious, Randidly cracked his knuckles against the stone ground and swayed slowly closer to the sphinx. Even if he had to rip out its spine by hand, he—

At that moment, the spell broke. The sphinx collapsed, rolling onto its back and scratching at its own face.

Randidly blinked several times, even now only a thread away from losing consciousness. His strained senses had no way to process what he was seeing. A long, thorny bramble erupted from the sphinx's eyeball, spurting blood and matter everywhere. As soon as he saw it, Randidly felt a strange connection to this plant. This vine had hatched from his Soul Seed.

Fertile soil indeed. Heh, am I going to be saved once more by Farming?

While Ep-Tal was distracted, Randidly forced his numb and tingling fingers to grope at his satchel until he blindly pulled out a potion and downed it. It was a Mana potion, which helped with the headache but did nothing to rid him of the very real concern that he was about to die.

Still, the vindictiveness of the Ghosthound was currently in the driver's seat. Randidly narrowed his eyes as it panicked, trying to reach into its mouth and pull out the thorny root creature growing in its skull.

Randidly had enough Mana to utilize Spearing Roots, ripping them into its broad back. Rather than aiming to inflict serious damage, Randidly guided the first three Skills to force the roots up and then wrap as best as they could around its spine, forcing it to remain on its back. The final

Spearing Roots ripped into its side, aiming to penetrate as many organs as possible.

Congratulations! Your Skill **Spearing Roots** has grown to **Level 13!**

Congratulations! Your Skill **Spearing Roots** has grown to **Level 14!**

Seeing that the bleeding from his chest had mostly scabbed over, he had the gall to purposefully pull out another Mana potion. A second barrage of roots pierced into the sphinx's side, amplifying its agony.

Only then did the woozy Randidly bare his teeth at the massive thing writhing on its back and drink a Health potion.

After being the recipient of several targeted Mana Skills, which left the dusted stone ground covered in thick, brown-maroon gore, the sphinx twisted and fixed its eyes on Randidly. The thing looked quite ridiculous, its mouth propped open by the spear, its left eye being drawn back within its body by a thorn creature. It was more zombie than sphinx at this point. Its bared stomach was as filled with holes as a honeycomb.

"I'll... k-k-kill you..." Ep-Tal whispered. It spat something at Randidly, infinitely faster than a Fireball. Its punctured stomach heaved and out of its mouth fountained a gallon of blood, splattering over its upside-down head. Then it collapsed. Notifications sprang into existence around Randidly, but at the moment—

His Stamina was still empty. Even with improved Reaction and Agility, his movements were sluggish.

He had barely enough time to twitch before the impact slammed against him, spinning him around. He looked uncomprehendingly down. A long, thin, pink thing, like a giant leech, stuck out of his left shoulder. The weirdest part was the strange markings covering its form.

It was the sphinx's tongue.

The thing quivered once and started to wiggle. It narrowed from the bloated size of the sphinx's head to something closer to a cigar. The movement allowed the tongue to work itself deeper into his flesh with a malicious intensity. Swearing, Randidly tried to get a grip on the thing with his other hand, but that had been the arm struck by the sphinx's claws. The arm at first spasmed, refusing to listen. Only after he narrowed his eyes and slowly worked his will against the failing flesh did he get the hand to move where he wanted it to.

The pain was excruciating. Something, or more likely several some-things, was definitely torn in his shoulder, even beyond the lacerations.

His fingers were wet with blood, and by the time he grabbed at the vibrating tongue, his fingers slipped off and the wiggling pink thing vanished into his shoulder. Almost non-comprehending, Randidly looked down at the gaping hole it left by its passage.

He was all too aware of its alien presence in his body, and a horrible sense of wrongness spread out. It began to move, working its way through his muscles toward his chest cavity.

Randidly began to sweat. *Removing it right now… by myself…*

As he considered the problem, a small vine-like bramble crawled out of the sphinx's body and hurried toward Randidly. The connection was immediately there, marking it as his Soul Seed. Randidly was shocked to find he could feel it, even what it was thinking. Just barely, but that came with the knowledge that this plant had thoughts.

At the moment, worry radiated out from the rolling, thorny tumbleweed. It seemed to understand something was wrong with him.

Looking down at the small vine, an acorn-sized chunk of grey, green, and red flesh with several thorn-covered tentacles stretching out a half meter in several directions, Randidly felt oddly touched by its concern. The pink tongue moved deeper into his chest, and he grimaced in pain. Without many other options, Randidly once more trusted his instincts.

"Crawl in. Find it. Stop it. Go on," Randidly encouraged, offering the open wound the tongue used to climb into his body, pulling the gory hole open with his free hand. The thing rolled around on the ground, confusion radiating off of it.

Grimacing, Randidly vaguely reached out and grasped at the connection between them like he did to utilize Root Manipulation. The Soul Seed creature stilled. With all the force he could muster, he pictured what he wanted and projected that thought toward it. Instantly, it understood and climbed into the open wound, wriggling after the first interloper.

This… Randidly looked down at his shoulder, feeling too exhausted to acknowledge how many strange occurrences the System brought into his life. The sensation of thorns tearing through his flesh brought back the horrible realities of the present.

Honestly, the vine creature was even more painful than the tongue, leaving huge gouges in his flesh as it moved in pursuit. With his good arm, Randidly lifted his last Health potion to his lips. His Health stabilized, but he still felt a deep sense of dread toward how close to death he'd come. Even now, he avoided looking at the sphinx, lest it hop to its feet and cackle at Randidly for being fooled by its ruse.

Luckily, the pursuer could take advantage of the hole already dug in his flesh to catch up. Randidly knew the moment the vine reached the tongue. Just as the pink creature was about to move out of his upper torso, the vine wrapped around it, its thorns digging into the struggling tongue.

He sensed from the vine's projected impressions it was having difficulties subduing the intruder. Randidly could only smile grimly. At least he bought himself some time.

He looked to the sky. The sun had steadily risen, filling the ravine with light. Hopefully, the village had fared well in his absence last night during the monster horde. There were probably more Boss-type monsters, but Randidly assumed they would be fine. The enemies they faced might be numerous, but they were low-Leveled. With this fight, he realized just how wide a gap in Stats was created by a huge Level difference.

If he had a Class himself, plus his many Skill Levels... this foe would have been so much easier. A wave of weak monsters was a course designed to fatten people so that this Tribulation could come and reap them.

Need to watch out for high-Level solo monsters... Randidly thought groggily, trying his best to ignore the sensation of the small thorny bramble fighting against a pink cigar in his shoulder.

Congratulations! Your Skill **Pain Resistance** has grown to **Level 14!**

He heaved himself to his feet, trying not to jostle the tiny battleground. Randidly spared Ep-Tal a glance, then sat down and painstakingly began to brew Health potions with a single arm. With the constant thrum of pain, the process was especially aggravating. After observing his Status, it was clear the conflict would sap away his Health before he could return to Donnyton and get help.

As a brief and frantic surge from the tongue intensified the pain and forced him to stop grinding red crystals, Randidly found his face twisting with a smile. *Heh. Shal did it because he wanted to prove how much of a hard-ass he was... but shit, knowing I can do that, it's not the only reason I haven't given up right now...*

The pain eventually passed and Randidly returned to work. Even now, the calm and exact process soothed him, giving him a mental escape, even if not a slight physical one.

Congratulations! Your Skill **Potion Making** has grown to **Level 25!**

When he finished three mediocre Health potions, he moved over to the sphinx and placed it into a larger spatial storage ring he had Daniel buy exactly for these hunts. For a long time, he stared at the enormous bloodstain on the ground. His eyes narrowed, surveying the entire battlefield. Stones were shattered and scorched by Fireballs. Others were covered in blood. Places were marred by thorny roots poking out of the ground, scraggly and tufted like unkempt hair.

Perhaps the most horrifying portion was the cave mouth, still thick with roots. Drops of blood oozed and dripped from their tips.

Randidly looked back at the place where the corpse collapsed. He licked his lips. "I may still be weak, but I'm not a burden. I can protect Donnyton."

He turned and began to trudge home, not daring to move too fast, lest the tongue slip free and rip through his heart and lungs. Although his Stats had improved, Randidly was under no impression he could survive that strange thing reaching his heart and running amok.

CHAPTER FIFTY-SIX

*R*egina Northwind looked around the battlefield in the wake of the monster horde. Her eyes did not miss the professional way people moved among the bodies, selecting the ones with salvageable pelts and dragging the rest to large piles. Apparently, those would be sold to a magical store that made them disappear.

"Remarkable," Regina said calmly, her hands folded behind her back.

Glendel looked around nervously beside her. Of all her people, only she, Alana, and Glendel chose not to gather with the NCCs below.

Regina was glad she'd come. In the case of benefits provided by Classes, seeing was believing. Glendel hadn't been exaggerating their exploits at all. If anything, the man underestimated what these people were capable of.

Of course, there is a third option. Regina shook her head slightly. *Perhaps with a Class, with Skill Levels, this group of people is just growing faster than we can follow. They only had the capability that Glendel described yesterday, but only a day later... It was definitely worth it to rush here as quickly as possible.*

Glendel made a small noise to grab Regina's attention. Two leaders from Donnyton were walking over, the sixteen-year-old Village Chieftain and a huge brute with a steel club the size of a support beam for a house. Both took root in the thickest of the fighting, settling Regina's internal question about why they had chosen someone so young to lead them.

Alana hurried over to stand behind Regina, bearing brand new animal hide armor and a sharp spear. The people of Donnyton gladly accepted her assistance in the fight, even if she, as an NCC, would only fight to spell the front lines and plug gaps in the defenses. From the drying blood of her foes on her armor, it was obvious Alana had given herself several small promotions during the course of the fighting.

And from the way both the teenager and the brute nodded to her, she'd done enough to become memorable in their eyes.

But that's the problem, isn't it? Regina kept her face even. *They possess power. And to a strong individual, they greet her with justice and comradery. But how much of that masks a darker agenda? With the Stats of some of these Classers... if someone had malicious intentions toward one of my nurses...*

Bitterness bubbled up through Regina. She tried to focus that energy into studying the two men in front of her. Their rough tribal armor and dented weapons didn't make Regina feel any better. The people here seemed perfectly content to abandon their previous life and pick up this new one, filled with violence and struggle. This group certainly benefited. They were leagues ahead of any of the other small survivor groups they'd encountered.

After all, they were the first ones to establish a Newbie Village.

Perhaps in a stroke of luck for Regina's paranoia, the NCC woman Glendel talked to strode over to join them. She was talking with a pudgy man with an irritated expression. Both groups from Donnyton arrived at once, the two duos nodding to each other. Then they all turned to the hospital group.

Points for that, Regina observed. *They trust each other. But when you fight for your lives every night... Heh.*

"My name's Donny, nice to meet you. You're the group that's looking to trade clothes?" the skinny kid said with a surprising amount of confidence and maturity. He offered Regina his hand and she shook it. His fingers were calloused and warm.

The big one grunted and gestured to himself. He didn't bother to offer Regina his hand. "Dozer. Strongest Warrior."

Alana relaxed in a dangerous fashion next to Regina and began studiously inspecting the sharp head of her spear. On the other side, Glendel shivered.

"I'm Daniel, and this is Mrs. Hamilton. Do you really have clothes? God, I want to be in something other than furs so badly," the chubby one said with a shiver. He offered Regina his hand, but his handshake was quick and awkward. Of them all, he was the easiest to read.

"Yes, we do," Regina said with a slight smile. "And you have two things we need very badly—food and access to a Class."

Donny's mouth twisted slightly. "It always comes down to that, huh? But the food..." Donny and Mrs. Hamilton exchanged a long glance. "That portion is relatively simple. Mrs. Hamilton has authority to trade as much as she deems fit. We'll take as many articles of clothing as you can spare. We haven't yet found anything like cotton in the area or a monster to farm for wool, so we basically can only make rough clothing from fur. It's been—"

"Itchy," Daniel interjected with a small titter.

"As for Classes…" Donny continued. "There are a few more… strings attached to that. For every Class given out, the village will be attacked by more monsters at night. For now, we can manage, but we don't wish to take on undue risk."

Regina's smile didn't change. "In terms of clothes, most of what we have are scrubs used in the hospital, but we also have the hospital's stock for special guests. We managed to hit up a department store on our trek up here. You say strings, though. Such as?"

Donny opened his mouth to answer. A shout came out from the group of gatherers, over by the monster bodies, and the group turned to look.

From years working in the ER, Regina had a good ear. That was not a shout of surprise, horror, or pain. Instead, the yeller sounded excited, even though she was quickly shushed by the tribally garbed Classers around her. Regina's features worked into a frown, looking for the source of the trouble. The Classers were now looking away, down past the edge of the hill on which the Village of Donnyton sat. They had an angle to see something Regina and Donnyton's leaders couldn't quite make out.

"What was…" the nervous Daniel demanded, but the others gave him the sort of look that said 'what do you expect it is?' Daniel closed his mouth.

Even more strange were the expressions on their faces. They were… expectant?

The Classers at the edge of the hill shuffled out of the way, as docile as lambs. Finally, the object of their attention was visible to Regina.

Walking slowly across the battlefield was a tall, athletic man. He was young too, probably only in his early or mid-twenties. The combination of the firm line of his mouth and his piercing green eyes made him stand out.

Regina noted the exchange of an excited glance between Dozer and Donny, and narrowed her eyes to examine the newcomer further. *This man is also part of the leadership of Donnyton?*

However, Regina's attention was immediately grabbed by the long, jagged wounds on his right shoulder and across most of his chest. It was the sort of wound that, if left untreated like it clearly had been, he would have bled out and died prior to the System's arrival. His entire torso was revealed, his clothing in tatters. His pants were covered with dried blood and his hair was matted and sweaty. Even his feet were bare.

The man's green eyes swept to the side and he beckoned two lounging individuals, each who wore two shoulder pads. The group this man gestured toward was the wounded area. Most of the individuals there had been recuperating from the injuries they received during last night's battle.

They leapt to their feet like the ground beneath them became lava and hurried to his side. The young man said something to them. They saluted and dashed off.

Regina began to hear it then, the whispers. A crowd was steadily forming across the edge of the hill and next to the walls.

The Ghosthound.
That's the Ghosthound...!
He's wounded?
What sort of monsters...
Did he attack the other town again!
But since he made it back... then they...
The Ghosthound...

So this was the Ghosthound. Regina heard from the stammering Glendel about the way the village treated this man. She wasn't sure what she'd been expecting. Although the bloody man before them certainly seemed like an intense person, he didn't appear worthy of the near worship she noticed in the gazes of nearby people.

The Ghosthound was heading directly for their group, his gait still slow and even. Strangely, the hand of his wounded right arm was up, gripping his uninjured left shoulder. By the time he arrived before Regina and the leadership of Donnyton, the two men he'd sent off returned with a large table made of thick wood, carried between them like it was cardboard. It looked like a worktable used to hammer and shape metal.

The young man spared a curious glance for Regina, but that was it. Apparently, she wasn't the reason he'd come here. As she watched, the Ghosthound climbed onto it, his breath hissing through his teeth in the process.

"Dozer, you have an axe?" He leaned back on the table, staring up at the mid-morning sky. The entire time, he continued to apply pressure to his left shoulder. That was when Regina noticed the strange circular wound he was covering.

The muscular man stiffened and blinked several times, clearly giving a lot of thought to the question that was answered by the weapon strapped to his waist, beneath the massive club. "Uh, yes—"

"Good. Split open my chest. Right about here. You're going to have to pull back the bone, but try and snap the ribcage cleanly, I don't want any more internal damage. Oh, Miranda, good. Heh, you should see the shit I've had to make do with, brewing potions with just one arm. Send someone to bring me several jars of the high-quality Health potion, just in case."

His emerald gaze slashed left and right across them all, seeming to weigh the watchers. "Those of you who are squeamish... probably shouldn't watch. It won't be pretty."

As Regina listened to his words, the strangeness about the young man finally settled into place. *This boy... is in shock. He's running on mostly instinct right now. Just what sort of ordeal has he gone through, to hobble back here and casually order these people around?*

And just... Suddenly, Regina shivered. *This System. How much will it change us all, by the end of it?*

While the rest of the people looked stunned, Mrs. Hamilton bowed and made several quick hand gestures at those standing behind her. Instantly, several people dashed down toward the NCC village. Of them all, Miranda Hamilton was clearly the most decisive. Regina hadn't missed the way the woman's face blanched when he said her first name. She might not even have thought the boy knew it.

Behind her, Glendel became even more nervous. And his nerves in turn made Regina abruptly conscious of the fact that everyone in the area was slowly drifting closer, looking intently at the Ghosthound. Apparently, not a single person present thought they were squeamish enough that they should turn away. Even the NCCs stared at the young man with rapt attention.

The glassy-eyed Ghosthound turned to stare at Dozer. "Well?"

The large man was shedding his massive club, which dented the ground when it fell, and pulled out his axe. "Uh, okay, I just—"

"You shouldn't do that. If the strike doesn't kill you, the blood loss will," Regina finally spoke up, drawing the Ghosthound's attention.

They made eye contact and held it for several long seconds. The situation was strange and they hadn't quite joined Donnyton yet, but this young man held influence. In addition, Regina had simply seen too many young men foolishly believe in the reliability of their own bodies over the years to remain silent when the patient was clearly in shock.

This examination from the Ghosthound was much more intense. He might be in shock, but there was still something ticking behind his eyes, weighing her.

"If you want," Regina offered into the abrupt silence around her, "I could handle it. I was a surgeon, before the world changed. I still am."

The Ghosthound hesitated and shook his head. Regina was honestly surprised he heard and understood her words so quickly. "It would be impossible. Time is of the essence. Dozer, cut me open. Right here."

The Ghosthound jabbed at his chest with his thumb, right above his heart. Dozer obediently raised his axe, but Regina stepped forward with a frown on her face. Alana stepped with her, lending her support with her presence.

Regina cleared her throat. "You've lost a lot of blood and are behaving foolishly. If you insist on this, you will die, and will have no one but yourself to blame."

The air around them stilled. Regina didn't balk—this was her job. She was used to the looks from disgruntled friends and family.

To her surprise, the Ghosthound chuckled. For someone in shock, he was certainly very aware. "You won't understand easily, will you? Fine, stranger. Cut me open. Right here, I need something removed. You have my permission."

The Ghosthound pointed to that same spot midway through his right pectoral muscle. Regina nodded and removed several instruments from her bag. A needle, scalpels, rubbing alcohol. Even though they hadn't brought the medicine to this meeting, Regina brought her travel bag, just in case.

Just like with Classes, seeing was believing for how valuable a surgeon could be, especially now.

The Ghosthound leaned back as Regina approached and once more looked up at the cloudless sky. "Don't worry about the delicate instruments. Just cut. This thing has been in me for too long already."

Regina bit her lip, torn between stubbornness and acknowledgment that the System made many of the traditional elements of her craft obsolete. She set the alcohol and needle aside. Instead, she held firm her scalpel and stood over the patient's body, her emotions falling away, taking on a practiced stance and pressing down with her scalpel. Her movements were skilled, even if the venue was unusual.

Her scalpel slid over the young man's skin. Regina clicked her tongue inwardly. He must have put some Stats into Physical Defense. She used her shoulder to cut again. The blade pressed against his skin.

And pressed.

And pressed.

The pressure she exerted neared the physical limits of her body and her eyes bulged.

The Ghosthound chuckled, not even looking at her struggles. "Now do you understand? Yes, you would be more exact. But you have no Strength to wound me, even when I'm lying still like this. Even with the sharpest knife, you cannot penetrate my skin. Now, Dozer… *Cut me.* Then open me up."

Regina stepped back, her face stiff. Dozer took her spot and raised his axe. He brought it down in a smooth arc, the blade sinking about an inch into the Ghosthound's stomach. Everyone in the surrounding area heard the weapon chip off the bone of his ribcage.

Hissing, the Ghosthound narrowed his eyes at Dozer. The glassy-eyed shock parted for a moment before that pain. "That was close. You took it too easy. Hopefully, you can fit your hand in that small cut to break my ribs, yeah? Reach in and pull them, snapping them open. Shouldn't be too hard. They're already partially fractured."

Dozer's hands trembled, reaching in to grip the inside of Randidly's ribs, sending the man on the table into a tense groan. Dozer tested his strength, but to his obvious surprise, found the ribs resisted him. He pulled harder and then harder. He shifted his hand, tearing open the wound on the Ghosthound's stomach further. Blood spurted over his fingers, but he ignored it and focused on his work.

This is madness… Regina couldn't help but think.

Dozer readjusted his hands and yanked with all his might. He was finally rewarded with a loud snap, the Ghosthound's ribs cracked at the side and opened up, bulging against his skin. Now perfectly content to ignore the blood, Dozer continued to extend the gash up across his chest, so he truly could pull the shattered ribs aside and reveal most of Randidly Ghosthound's chest cavity.

The man on the table beckoned and a jar of Health potion was brought to him, which he guzzled down. About halfway through the jar, he paused his consumption and said to Dozer, "You should see a pink tongue wrapped up by a thorny vine in there. Pull them both out and throw it on the ground. Stay away from it afterwards, and don't touch it for very long."

Regina wasn't sure what surprised her more, the strange things the patient was saying, or that Dozer really did reach into the man's chest and pulled out those very objects, both of them wiggling wildly. Dozer hastily threw them to the side. The nearby people scrambled backward, opening up a large space so those things could roll and roam.

Dozer scratched his cheek, spreading blood across his jaw. "Do ya want...?"

The Ghosthound nodded, eyes still fixed upward. How he ignored the pain, Regina had no idea. After a nod of his own, Dozer pushed the cracked ribs down, back into a semblance of place, and removed his axe.

The Ghosthound drank the rest of the potion and the wound slowly healed. He must not just have Endurance, then, but also plenty of Vitality to make his wound heal so quickly. Only when the wound mostly knitted together did some of the tension in the Ghosthound's body ease, his breathing becoming more rapid and shallow.

"R-Randidly... how much of that is your blood?" Unbeknownst to everyone, a young blonde girl had snuck through the crowd and was staring down at the injured Ghosthound. From Glendel's report, Regina recognized her as Lyra. Her face was creased in tight but controlled worry, even as her clasped hands trembled behind her back.

The edges of the Ghosthound's mouth quirked up in a grin. "Less than half, only the fresh drops."

With what seemed like a great effort, he heaved himself to his feet. Regina suppressed the desire to step forward and tell him to rest, as the young man began to do some torso rotations to test his range of motion. At the very least, he was taking his time and moving slowly. Contrary to every instinct Regina had honed over her long career, the wound didn't burst open.

Due to the System... will this boy even bear a scar? Regina wondered.

"And where is the thing that did this to you?" Lyra's voice lowered to a dangerous note, her eyes beginning to glow a clear blue as she fixated on the inflamed flesh on the boy's chest.

Strangely, Regina felt the strangest urge to take a step backward away from the girl. She easily quashed the abrupt instinct to flee. Meanwhile, the

Ghosthound paused in his tentative inspection of his body and waved his hand.

There was a flash, and suddenly, Regina's nose was filled with the scent of blood. The space directly behind the table, which had been left mostly empty as a courtesy to the Ghosthound, was now filled with a strange creature of mangled flesh, the size of a small van. It resembled the top half of a lion, with the bottom half of a jellyfish.

Regina sucked in a breath. That wasn't a jellyfish. Most of the bottom half of the body had just been reduced to hanging, torn strips of pink flesh, its luxurious coat of fur rendered to vicious mutilation. Atop the lion's body sat a swollen woman's head, battered, with one of her eyes popped.

Lyra stilled, then shook her head slowly, the tension sliding out of her. "You save all the fun things for yourself."

The Ghosthound snorted, walking gingerly toward the two strange entities that had been removed from his body. The tongue's struggles seemed feeble now, and as the Ghosthound approached, the thorny thing slid off of it and rolled over toward him, climbing up to curl around his shoulders.

A strange, unassuming man with dull red hair appeared above the tongue. His eyes sparkled as he stared down at the wriggling thing. Slowly, he reached to his waist and pulled out a dagger. There was a strange hunger in his gaze.

The Ghosthound snorted and flicked his fingers, an explosion of heat and flames spread out in a wave. Beneath that onslaught, the tongue wizened and shriveled, disappearing to nothing,

"My kill," the Ghosthound grunted before returning to the table and lying back with a sigh. "Man... I have such an annoying headache..."

CHAPTER FIFTY-SEVEN

*G*lendel sat very still inside of Regina's RV. Regina's brooding form and Alana's pacing made him extremely nervous.

The negotiations for food had gone relatively smooth, but the Classes didn't come cheap. Everyone with a Class was required to assist with the monster hordes for now. Once the Safe Zone for Newbies dropped in the area, they would likely have similar duties. From the casual words of the Ghosthound, it might even be worse for the Newbie Village once the Level Barrier dropped. The young man, likely with complete honesty, waved everyone away without giving more details. He'd been exhausted from his ordeal and needed to rest.

Still, even the vague suggestion from the Ghosthound held a profound effect on the leadership of Donnyton. The lack of information made Donny unwilling to commit to anything specific in regard to options other than Regina's group officially joining with Donnyton. At least for now.

Glendel rubbed his hands together underneath the small table. Taking a Class was a path to power, one that progressed more rapidly than the actual Paths, though doing so meant tying themselves to this place. In a way, agreeing to join Donnyton meant Regina would likely be subordinate to someone else, thus Alana's insistent prowling back and forth through the cramped interior.

"We should try the other village again, before we commit," Alana said decisively, finally stopping from the endless loops.

To Glendel's surprise, Regina shook her head.

"No, this is honestly better than I had hoped for. I plan on accepting their offer for now. Settling down will be good, especially because they at least take the task of protecting their members from external threats seriously. The problem is the social structure…"

Rubbing her head, Regina gestured at the notes she had Glendel make regarding his observations. "As far as we can tell, they don't appear to really have any strict hierarchy. Warriors are rated on a 1 to 10 scale. Miranda Hamilton is in charge of the NCCs. Daniel is in charge of information gathering and the village growth. They have their three leaders for the warriors: Donny, Dozer, and Decklan—"

"And why do they all have D names?" Alana muttered with the smallest bit of venom.

Regina ignored her and continued. "They have some Mages, Healers, Archers… but right now, it's all working. And the only reason is because of that man. The Ghosthound. He's the glue that holds everything together. He's the reason they obtained a village so early, and now they are bounding away and gaining more and more advantages. The problem isn't him, but… it also *is*."

Glendel spoke up for the first time. His mind drifted to the bloody and miserable figure, carved open on a worktable with an axe. "Do you think… he will abuse his power?"

Regina hesitated. "I don't think so. Honestly, from the way most people reacted to him today, he isn't usually like that. His forthrightness was likely a result of being in shock. But like I said, it's him, but it's also not. The village is growing strong because he's the pillar that keeps them going. But that is also their weakness. If he weren't there, it would all come tumbling down. Some of the others would want to step into the space he left, but none could fill it. There would be infighting."

Leaning back in her chair, Regina sighed. "In addition to that… the way they treat him, well, I suppose there was no other avenue. He's their savior. They revere him. Although he remains fine for now, attention like that can change a person."

"You aren't making me very excited to stay here," Glendel said. Alana slowly returned to her pacing.

"It's best to face the ugliest truths first," Regina said grimly, her eyes narrowed. "That way, you aren't surprised by what you wake up to find one otherwise uneventful morning. You become ready for it when it happens."

After an extremely long day, Randidly finally had a moment alone to turn to his notifications. He eased himself down on his palette in the small cabin. Someone, probably Mrs. Hamilton, thought to place a few pillows in it for him. The whole setup was more luxurious than the base palette he was used to.

Still, Randidly remained afflicted by a sense of weakness. His Attributes were all full, but he couldn't shake a strange chill through his body. It was like some core part of himself refused to warm up, no matter what he tried.

Randidly looked down at the healing skin of his chest. *Probably I just need sleep. The System can replicate a lot of healing, but I'm still a human. After running so high on adrenaline, it would be shocking if there wasn't some sort of hangover...*

Still much better than using the Origin Banana potion.

He ignored the Skill Level notifications and focused on the unfamiliar ones.

Congratulations! Your **Soul Seed** has sprouted into a **Soul Plant Level 1!**

The Soul Plant has begun its own journey through the Nexus! Due to the circumstances, the Soul Plant grows by feasting on: Blood. The Soul Plant option has been added to your Menu. The Soul Plant can only Level when you direct it to Level, after it has accumulated enough food. Based on the "blood" absorbed, the Soul Plant will have different options for growth.

Congratulations! Your **Soul Plant Level 1** has absorbed enough blood to **Level!**

Congratulations! Your **Soul Plant Level 1** has absorbed enough blood to **Level!**

You have slain **The Hungry Tribulation, Ep-Tal!** Due to you not belonging to the **Newbie Village** that corresponds to the **Tribulation**, bonuses for slaying the **Tribulation** have been halved. **All parties involved receive +5 to all Stats!**

Congratulations! You have learned the Skill **Agony (Un) Level 1.**

Agony (Un): *A double-edged sword used to hurt your opponents.* **Spend Health to inflict Mental and Physical damage on all beings in a small area around you. The ratio of Health lost to damage dealt improves as Skill Level increases. *Warning: you will experience the pain as well. Warning: it is possible to completely spend your Health and die from the activation of this Skill.***

Randidly smiled bitterly. So that was the Skill the sphinx started using at the end, or at least a version of it. He was lucky Ep-Tal hadn't used it the entire time. The sphinx undoubtedly had more Health than him. The Hungry Tribulation could have simply ground him down to nothing.

Of course, Randidly knew why it hadn't. If it was experiencing the same pain Randidly endured, it likely only considered the Skill as a last resort. Taking into account how it toyed with him, it likely hadn't occurred to the sphinx to use it until it was too late.

Randidly set that train of thought to the side and considered one specific line amongst that notification. *Pah, so I would have gotten additional Stats if I had taken a Class and belonged to the village? That stings a bit... An additional five to all Stats...*

Shaking himself, Randidly turned to the other notifications.

Due to its Tribulation being defeated, all individuals within the Newbie Village receive +2 Levels. It's pillar of light will now pulse blue, to warn of the impending collapse of the Newbie Barrier, which will fall in exactly 24 hours, regardless of how much time remains on the seven-day grace period.

Warning! A Newbie Barrier near you will fall within 24 hours.
This means several things. First, monsters over **Level 20** may periodically spawn in your area. Specifically, **Tier I Raid Bosses** will now periodically appear within your surroundings. These **Raid Bosses** are extremely powerful, and if not eliminated quickly, will form a settlement and spawn additional high-Level monsters. The longer they are allowed to develop, the stronger the **Raid Bosses** will grow and the more powerful subordinates they will spawn.

However, Raid Bosses have a higher-than-normal probability of dropping either unusual materials or equipment.
In addition, a **Wild Dungeon** will form near the **Newbie Village** that has survived past the fall of the **Newbie Barrier**. *The Dungeon Level will grow depending on time and the Level density of monsters and individuals with Classes in the nearby area.*

Upon clearing a **Wild Dungeon**, a "time" will be recorded. *The quickest time to clear the Dungeon will receive SP for their village once a day, depending on the Dungeon Level.*

Wild Dungeons that have not been cleared in a week will periodically spawn monster hordes. As the time the Dungeon hasn't been cleared grows, so will the frequency of monster hordes.

Please note, a monster horde from an un-cleared Dungeon is much more destructive than the monster hordes during the seven-day protection window.

In addition, new options for spending SP have appeared in the **Newbie Village** that has survived its **Tribulation!**

Congratulations! You are the first person to slay a **Tribulation** on your world. **You have taken the first steps to joining the Nexus. More rewards to follow in 24 hours, when the Newbie Barrier falls.**

Randidly frowned and his headache returned to go along with his strange weakness. It wasn't that the new changes were especially dangerous, especially if they kept up good scouting in the surrounding area. What bothered him wasn't that the rules were weirdly formulaic and game-like.

Daniel would be excited about the new source of SP by clearing the Dungeons with the best "time." The danger of monster hordes could also be controlled somewhat, due to frequent Dungeon clears, and that would allow the village to relax. Of course, the non-specificity of the time limit for clearing the Dungeon was a bit of a typical move for the System, but…

Although the lion's share of the danger would depend on what exactly a Raid Boss entailed, Randidly felt this change would shift the village in a positive way. Mostly, he predicted the non-combat Classes, and the non-Class Characters, without the worry of a daily horde, would explode in number.

The Classers would grow quicker. If the current batch could handle the Dungeons, the rest wouldn't be pressured into getting a Class themselves. And enough individuals accumulating Skill Levels could match that growth rate. Most of the expansion of the Newbie Village would be in non-combat areas.

They still received a daily trickle of refugees from nearby areas. Those people would have the choice to either take a Class or take their time. It would be good for the town.

The more Randidly thought about the coming changes, the more he was bothered that none of the people of Donnyton seemed to be aware of these notifications. Randidly's expression turned strange. *Shouldn't they have all gotten the notifications? At the very least, they would have noticed if all of the Classers Levels jumped up by two…*

Brooding, Randidly sighed and pushed himself up from his cushy perch on his palette. He hobbled to the door and opened it to look toward the pillar of light rising majestically out of Donnyton proper.

For a few moments, Randidly legitimately couldn't make sense of what he saw. The color of the pillar hadn't changed. A raw possibility occurred to him and the blood drained from his face.

Perhaps the villagers of Donnyton hadn't gotten the notifications, because they weren't within the area where the Newbie Barrier would be falling ahead of schedule. It was now the sixth day, and a golden pillar of light still stood tall and luminous over the village, even during the day.

Slowly turning, Randidly gazed at the pillar over the neighboring village, where the "king" was likely sitting on his throne. The pillar pulsed blue.

After all that effort... Randidly's exhaustion made his vision swim. *And I ended up protecting... the other village?*

Just as quickly as he allowed those bleak thoughts to dominate his mind, Randidly shook himself. He refused to give up because of a small setback. If he did it once, he could do it again. And this time, with more opportunity to prepare.

Still exhausted, Randidly narrowed his eyes at the pulsing blue pillar and began to consider. *With this, the Level 20 restriction will drop around the same time for both Newbie Villages. The problem is whether our lovely neighbors will come out of their kingdom long enough to fight against the Dungeons and Raid Bosses.*

The king hadn't made a move since Randidly went to his village, broken the gates, and urged Pestilence to eat through his tongue and vocal cords. Non-interference policy, the policeman had said when he dropped off the glassware. Randidly sighed. It didn't seem likely that all of their Classers getting a 2 Level boost would do much to change that.

Hopefully, the new buildings wouldn't give them any ill-advised ideas.

Although, having more help for the hordes and Raid Bosses would be helpful. Especially since two Dungeons would likely spawn, one for each village, as the Level restrictions fell.

He shrugged. *We can only fight one foe at a time. Focus on the one in front of us. And in the end, so what if they stay turtled up? That just means more experience for Donnyton's Classers.*

CHAPTER FIFTY-EIGHT

*T*he longer he pondered, the worse his headache became. Randidly put it off for a little bit longer, looking instead at his Skill Level notifications. The fight against the sphinx had certainly been quite generous in that regard.

Even setting aside the Skill Levels he noticed during the fight, he received 2 Levels in Spear Mastery and Phantom Thrust, 1 in Spear Phantom's Footwork, 2 in Phantom Half Step, 3 in Fighting Proficiency, 1 in Haste, Sweep, and Phantom Onslaught, 2 in Empower, an impressive additional 2 in the already quickly growing Spearing Roots, 1 in Fireball and Physical Fitness, and 2 in Mental Strength.

He continued down the Frontrunner Path, which generously gave free Stat points as rewards. These Stats he poured into Intelligence, Strength, and Control, raising his ability to do damage, which had been slightly underwhelming during the fight against the sphinx. If not for the cave, and then for the final appearance of his Soul Plant, Randidly likely would have failed to kill the Tribulation.

Now that he knew he might have to fight another, he planned on relying less on the environment and more on his own power. The Frontrunner Path settled at 70/100, meaning he still had 15 more Stats to get from it. And his Status Screen was already becoming monstrous.

Randidly Ghosthound
Class: ---
Level: N/A
Health(/R per hour): 311/340 [+2] (175 [+3])
Mana(/R per hour): 501/534 (77.75)

Stam(/R per min): 357/392 (65 [+1])
Vit: 51 [+1]
End: 35
Str: 38 [+2]
Agi: 62 [+7]
Perception: 29
Reaction: 46
Resistance: 14
Willpower: 64
Intelligence: 86
Wisdom: 44
Control: 64
Focus: 31
Equipment: *Necklace of the Shadow Cat Lvl 20 (R): (Vitality +1,*
Strength +2, Agility +7)
Skills:
Soulskill: *Spear of Rot Mastery Lvl 259*

Basic: *Running Lvl 20 | Physical Fitness Lvl 30 | Sneak Lvl 32 | Acid*
Resistance Lvl 23 | Poison Resistance Lvl 16 | Spirit of Adversity Lvl
26 | Dagger Mastery Lvl 13 | Dodge Lvl 33 | Spear Mastery Lvl 47 |
Pain Resistance Lvl 14 | Fighting Proficiency Lvl 35 | First Aid Lvl
14 | Block Lvl 29 | Mental Strength Lvl 14 | Curse Resistance Lvl 3 |
Pathfinding Lvl 16 | Mapmaking Lvl 4 | Calculated Blow Lvl 19 |
Edge of Decay (Un) Lvl 14 | Fire Resistance Lvl 9

Stamina: *Heavy Blow Lvl 26 | Sprinting Lvl 15 | Iron Skin Lvl 27 |*
Phantom Thrust Lvl 41 | Spear Phantom's Footwork Lvl 33 | Eyes of
the Spear Phantom Lvl 21 | Phantom Half-Step Lvl 12 | Haste Lvl 24
| Phantom Onslaught Lvl 11 | Sweep Lvl 18 | Spear Deflect Lvl 12 |
Empower Lvl 27 | Roundhouse Kick Lvl 15

Mana: *Mana Bolt Lvl 30 | Meditation Lvl 32 | Spearing Roots Lvl 16*
| Mana Shield Lvl 25 | Root Manipulation Lvl 36 | Arcane Orb Lvl 23
| Magic Missile Lvl 6 | Healing Palm Lvl 8 | Fireball Lvl 25 | Pollen
of the Rafflesia (R) Lvl 7 | Summon Pestilence Lvl 18 | Mana
Strengthening Lvl 14 | Wall of Thorns Lvl 4 | Agony (Un) Lvl 1

Crafting: *Farming Lvl 23 | Plant Breeding Lvl 9 | Potion Making Lvl*
25 | Analyze Lvl 24 | Refine Lvl 6

Randidly's Intelligence, Agility, and Control were well over 50, which
was probably a line none of the other members of Donnyton had passed,

even if they focused completely on one Stat. Combined with a total Vitality of 52, Randidly continued to excel in any task required of him. Even tanking damage. He likely did them all much better than most of Donnyton's Classers could manage.

But mostly, that was a result of how broadly he developed his Skills.

It was still something of a disappointment for Randidly that his Resistance was still so abysmally low. 14 looked very sad surrounded by 46 and 64. Though his speed was currently so high, and he possessed enough defense Skills to survive most attacks, that he didn't want to invest the points into it currently.

Randidly walked back into his hut, satisfied despite himself. There were so many things to do. Despite that, he needed to listen to what his body was telling him. He was neither in fighting nor training condition right now. He made himself comfortable and closed his eyes.

As soon as he was asleep, Randidly dreamed. He was lying on that worktable, surrounded by the people of Donnyton. Only this time, it was a cloudy night with no stars. The face of every watcher was blank and empty, as though they'd become mannequins rather than people of flesh and blood.

The only individual who seemed to move was the surgeon, Regina. Except her eyes were too bright, too hungry, too sinister. She leaned over Randidly, spinning her scalpel across her fingers as she examined his chest.

Randidly groaned softly and tried to roll or sit up, but he couldn't; he was too exhausted.

In the depths of his chest, the smallest thread of warmth began to flow out from the wound inflicted by Ep-Tal's tongue. First one and then a dozen. Those threads of warmth flowed through his body, alleviating the horrifying chill Randidly had felt since the fight against that monster.

"Well, well," the dream Regina whispered, leaning closer. Her eyes twisted into that of a predator. "What have we here?"

In his cabin, Randidly's eyes snapped open. He sat sharply up, partially to prove he could and partially to shake himself out of the cold grip of fear. Randidly gritted his teeth as he rubbed the healing flesh of his chest. *I'm not weak. I won. It wasn't for Donnyton... but I am* not *a burden.*

No answer came to Randidly's thoughts. Even his heart, usually so torn between fear and wild aggression, remained silent. The strange emptiness of the moment allowed Randidly to notice his fingers could barely find the remnants of his wound. Maybe in another day, all traces of his fight against the sphinx would disappear.

Which left him outwardly unmarred, waiting for his next challenge from the System.

Shaking his head to dispel his thoughts, Randidly left his cabin. The sun was high overhead, signaling he'd probably slept only three to four hours. Still, he felt refreshed and recovered, his feet carrying him behind his cabin where he left the thorny vine to play. Now, as he intended to Level his Soul Plant, he wanted to be able to see it.

When he came to the glass container, one he politely asked it to remain in, he found the strange being had left it and was instead clambering around. It froze the second it felt his approach, aware of its disobedience. Randidly was more surprised to find Lyra crouched nearby, examining the container.

"You have weird taste in pets," she informed him, wonderment in her eyes as she gazed down at the wiggling creature.

For the first portion of their interactions, she didn't seem awkward or shy, just present. The girl didn't even seem to mind the long scratches the thorny vines left on her hand as it tentatively climbed off her arm and back into the glass container.

Randidly smiled slightly, mildly embarrassed, and elected not to respond. Instead, he sent a mental impression to the Soul Plant that it could wander freely while he was in the area. Randidly felt somewhat awkward to do his experiments with the girl here, but her genuine interest in the plant was enough that he didn't want to engage in the awkward conversation to ask her to leave.

Instead, he opened his menu. Sure enough, there was a Soul Plant option. He clicked it and a small Status Screen appeared.

Soul Plant (Blood) (Click to Rename)
Level 1 (Click to Level Up)
Survivability: *6*
Physicality: *4*
Magical Aptitude: *1*
Brain Function: *3*
Particularity: *2*
Battle Ability: *4*
Special Skills: *Flexibility*

Randidly scanned through the explanations for the Stats. They were all pretty self-explanatory. Survivability was defense, Physicality was physical Strength, and Magical Aptitude meant magical strength. Brain Function was how intelligent it actually was, like what sort of complex concepts and orders it could wrap its mind around. Particularity, on the other hand, counted any characteristics that made it unique and gave it a capability not really covered by the others. Battle Ability was a combination of all the above scores, which would equate it to what Level monster it could hold its own against.

Starting out able to fight Level 4 didn't seem very impressive, but Randidly supposed it was currently only Level 1. It had time to grow. Although, it was pretty impressive this small, weird plant with foot long tentacles could manage to surround and strangle one of the Level 4 wolverines that were as numerous as fleas in the valley.

After a slight hesitation, Randidly renamed the plant to Thorn, due to its prickly appearance. Then he clicked Level-up.

Congratulations! Your **Thorn Level 1** is ready to **Level up! Due to its nature, your first choice to guide its growth is set: Make Thorn either** *Hungry* **or** *Thirsty*.

No explanations provided, huh... Randidly sighed. *Not just the dangers, but also the benefits are hidden behind ambiguity. But I suppose that's just what it means to follow your own Path.*

The Level-ups for the Soul Plant were even more opaque than the split Path options Randidly had encountered thus far. On a whim, he clicked Hungry.

Thorn is now **Level 2. Survivability has increased by 2. Physicality has increased by 1.** Thorn has learned the Skill **Strangle.**

Congratulations! Your **Thorn Level 2** is ready to **Level up! Due to absorbing the blood of The Smiling Tribulation, Ep-Tal, please choose whether Thorn shall absorb its** *Body* **or its** *Mind*.

After a second of hesitation, Randidly decisively selected Body. After all, he didn't really need a strange Mage plant. Although having it be a little bit more intelligent would undoubtedly be useful, it was its limbs and dangerous thorns that allowed it to rip apart the Tribulation from the inside.

Thorn is now **Level 3. Physicality has increased by 2. Due to increased size, Particularity has increased by 2.**

A gasp took his attention away from the notifications. Thorn had swollen into a fat bush about three feet in diameter, bristling with thorny tentacle vines. Lyra stumbled backward, dropping the Soul Plant directly on top of the glass container. Underneath the weight of its new body, the glass container cracked and shattered. Simultaneously, Randidly felt Thorn's pleasure as it stretched its new body and flexed its powerful muscles.

"That..." A shocked Lyra looked at a long gash on her arm, to Thorn, and to Randidly, before looking back to Thorn. Her eyes narrowed. "Did you do that on purpose? Shit..."

Lyra hopped to her feet and glared at Randidly for several seconds. He scratched his head, feeling vaguely responsible for the injury, but he'd honestly forgotten she was holding Thorn. Before Randidly could decide what to say, she spun on her heel and harrumphed to the tree line.

It was only at the edge of the clearing that she paused and glanced over her shoulder, her blonde hair swishing across her shoulders. "I'm glad you made it back."

Then she was gone.

While Thorn wandered off a bit to experiment with its new body, Randidly grimaced and looked down at his hands. *Yeah... this is exactly why I left the running of the village to Donny. Sometimes, I just don't understand what exactly people want from me.*

However, Randidly's self-pitying musings were soon broken by a sound of scuffling nearby. Randidly looked up sharply but was greeted by a notification.

Congratulations! Your **Soul Plant Level 3** has absorbed enough blood to **Level!**

Bemused, Randidly moved out of the clearing and deeper into the trees until he stumbled upon the source of the commotion. He saw his plant some distance away. It was next to a worn stump, ripping through two or three imps with its long and thorny limbs.

Congratulations! Your **Thorn Level 3** is ready to **Level up! Due to exposure to the forbidden tongue of Ep-Tal, he has gained profound insights into the world. Shall he have mastery of the *Land* or *Sky*?**

Thorn did enough with the tongue to get an extra bonus, huh? Randidly shook his head again at the extremely vague options presented to him, though he saw no reason to hesitate. As for the choice... Although Thorn flying would be amusing, wasn't this also a pretty straightforward selection? Randidly chose Land.

Thorn is now Level 4. Magical Aptitude has increased by 1. Brain Function has increased by 1. Particularity has increased by 3. Thorn has learned the Skill **Dig.**

So now it can dig? Shrugging, Randidly looked once more at its Status Screen and opened up the Soul Plant Menu.

Thorn (Blood)
Level 4
Survivability: *8*
Physicality: *7*

Magical Aptitude: *2*
Brain Function: *4*
Particularity: *7*
Battle Ability: *11*
Special Skills: *Flexibility | Strangle | Dig*

It had certainly been effective at Level 1, when it grew within the skull of the sphinx. Randidly hoped for more impressive feats from his new companion in the future. What was pretty interesting was that its Battle Ability now put it on the same Level as something Level 11, even though it was only Level 4, by its own standards. That was reassuring, although it was hard to tell how accurate a measure that was.

And can it train and hone its abilities? Or does it do everything by instinct... Randidly rubbed his chin and examined the most recent change, which had lengthened its thorny appendages and left the size of its main body the same. Obviously, Randidly had no Level and could handle a hundred Level 11s. It was a question of quality of the fighter, rather than Level against weak monsters. It did serve as a decent way to understand Strength.

After playing with Thorn a bit, and impressing on it the importance of not eating humans, Randidly left, heading to talk with Daniel and Donny about what was to come. He needed to warn them about Donnyton's Tribulation and what he learned fighting the sphinx. *Better invite Sam too, and Decklan and Dozer. They would be the ones on the front lines...*

Randidly grimaced. *Why does it feel like the stronger I get, the more people I have to talk to? At this rate, Donny just needs to sit back while I take care of most of the big picture arrangements.*

The group of six stayed after the Ghosthound left. Daniel, Donny, Sam, Dozer, Decklan, and Mrs. Hamilton. They were silent for several seconds, listening to the young man's departing footsteps.

The first to speak was Donny, who turned to Sam. "Have you had a chance to look at the body he brought back?"

Sam grunted. "Yeah, and what I've seen... Let's just say that unless you have the Strength of Dozer, it's a real chore to cut the thing up, even the hide. And that was mostly turned to Swiss cheese, almost useless now besides making bandages. The bones and claws are a different story, and I have a few ideas about how I can use them..."

Daniel coughed. "He means... if what Randidly says is true, and there is another one of these out there, waiting... can we handle it? Would we be able to endure without him single-handedly pinning it down?"

After a few seconds of thoughtful silence, Sam said, "If we're there to meet it, in formation, probably. But out of all of us… Only Dozer, Clarissa, and Lyra can damage it. If we can keep it locked down for long enough, sure. If Randidly is there to take the brunt of it, definitely. With a limited Mana pool, a Level 30 monster will be mortal."

The room fell silent at the unspoken truth of that statement. If it came upon them in the night, while they weren't ready…

Decklan smiled crookedly. "We still have a day. Let's up the training. Daniel, how much can we improve the Dungeon?"

Daniel checked his notes. "We are currently just short of 9000 SP. In another hour, we'll get there. If you prefer we focus on the Dungeon, instead of upgrading the village itself… we can push it up to Level 14. That's almost a three times increase in difficulty. Is that what you all want?"

Donny, Dozer, and Decklan made eye contact and nodded. Mrs. Hamilton closed her eyes and shook her head.

"This might not be quick enough to help prepare for a threat tomorrow," she said when she opened her eyes. "But if Ms. Northwind's group joins us, perhaps some of them can supplement the squads. A lot of them used to be nurses. They could be taught Healing Palm and become a healing corps. Having a designated Healer with each squad would increase the success rate."

"That's a good idea," Daniel said slowly, rubbing his chin. "In addition, I think we should initially raise the Level to 10, to let most people go through the experience of being isolated in a different dimension. But we need to acknowledge… if we make it any more difficult, I expect some casualties. You can't account for everything. For the more elite troops, they can wait and head into the Level 14 Dungeon."

Donny laughed awkwardly, shaking his head. The rest of the group looked at him, confused.

"It's not the Dungeon plan. Well, not the method. It's just…" Donny, looking suddenly like the teenager he really was, scratched his ear awkwardly. "Can you believe we're talking about this? Risking our lives? If this had been two weeks ago, I would just be…"

Everyone remained silent while Donny grasped for his thoughts.

"And yet… I can't stand still and avoid these hard decisions. Because I know if I wait or hide, something big and mean is eventually going to show up, and I won't be ready for it. So, I train and take risks, just to prepare. It's like the Ghosthound says, 'The only thing a spear can do is move forward, thrusting into the future.' It's just strange how much we've changed in such a short amount of time."

After that, the group dispersed, drifting apart. Each turned away, alone with their thoughts, considering how the world changed.

And changed them in the process.

CHAPTER FIFTY-NINE

*I*t was around two o'clock in the afternoon when Glendel's group drove their convoy down the road to officially settle in Donnyton. While the lower portion of the valley and the road through it had been cleared by some enterprising individuals in preparation for Donnyton's expansion, it hadn't been very professionally done. The vehicles thumped over the road's bumps. Glendel gripped his seat to keep from being thrown off.

They ignored the observation from Donnyton's patrols, determined to make it without incident. Alana recognized someone from last night's monster horde and walked up to explain the situation. Regina, Alana, Glendel, and the rest of their group of sixty-some women unpacked the remnants of their lives and made the space a bit more livable.

Later, they sent a group into town to officially trade their clothing. To their surprise, the attitude at Donnyton was grim. Almost the entirety of the village, some twelve hundred people, gathered around a tall pole that was erected on the slope between the NCC village and the Classer Compound.

Through the crowd, Regina saw Mrs. Hamilton and moved to speak with the quartermaster of Donnyton. "Miranda, what's going on?"

Miranda Hamilton turned to the group of new arrivals and smiled. "I apologize, this has just been a very intense morning. The kept Dungeon was improved to Level 10. Only, when it reached that Level, there were some changes. Increased difficulty, but also increased time compression. So now you need to spend more time in there. Apparently up to a week. The first group to go in, when they realized they weren't going to be kicked out after twenty-four hours, started rushing for the Boss, to escape before they ran out of food.

"Ultimately, they were able to make it, but…" Mrs. Hamilton's eyes were slightly wet as she looked to the monument, where three names were being carved into it by a serious-faced Sam.

Glendel spotted a few others rubbing away tears. Every face he looked at was bleak.

"Their squad leader died defeating the Boss. He was… He was one of the original twelve that received a Class from Donny on the first day. It's just… a sobering experience."

Regina nodded slowly, a sympathetic expression on her face. "Death is always difficult—"

"Especially when it comes so cheaply. The System changed the entire economy of life," Mrs. Hamilton said bitterly and wiped her tears. "But I won't trouble you with the details. Come, I'll take you to speak with Donny and Nul. Let's get you Classes."

Regina saw Alana stir next to her. Although Alana usually kept herself unexpressive and at arm's length, she'd always been universally praised as the most comforting nurse on staff by patients. She glanced at Regina and Regina gave her a tight nod. In the face of this tragedy, Alana reached out to a few of her acquaintances from the fight last night, murmuring quietly.

Regina's group followed after Mrs. Hamilton up onto the hill.

When they got to Donny, Daniel was also there. Daniel took the time to explain the information they gathered in regard to Classes, what little they knew about the three options and where those options originated. He also went over the mentor system, which gave a bit more consistency to Classes. Then he proceeded on to why some individuals were currently raising their Skill Level, in the hopes of getting a better third option from Nul.

"Actually, Ma'am," a voice interrupted, "if you would like to wait a few minutes and let us ahead of you in line, we can finally test one of our theories about the third option for Classes."

An older man with short grey hair and two axes strapped to his back walked up with a portly bearded man at his side. They nodded to Daniel, but the man with the axes kept giving Regina sidelong glances.

"What do you mean, Sam?" Daniel asked.

Sam didn't respond, his focus entirely on Regina. He smiled slightly, and she even smiled back, her mouth creeping ever wider. In general terms, the smile was small. But compared to the expressions Glendel usually saw from her… Alana hadn't missed the exchange either, looking at Regina with obvious shock.

"As long as it's no trouble," Sam said slowly. "I don't want to insert myself in a situation needlessly."

Regina controlled her face, her smile fading to twitching lips. She gestured theatrically and gave the man a half bow. "No, be my guest."

Is Regina really… flirting with a stranger? Glendel pinched himself.

"Ah…" Sam said, turning to Daniel. "Well, Jerry just insists he has to know whether this means anything, raising Skill Levels without getting a Class. I'm telling him to exercise patience, it's only been a week, but—"

"Someone has to be the first." Jerry stepped forward toward a blandly smiling Nul. "I'm willing to do that. And a week was a short time with how things used to be, but now… with how easily we can die… I don't want to waste any more time."

Nul stepped forward. "You have made an excellent decision."

Glendel didn't like the look of Donnyton's Village Spirit. Although the man looked human, there was something impossibly thin and delicate about his frame, as though he were a doll made to look like a person. Still, it was a small issue compared to being murdered by monsters. Everyone was quiet for several seconds as Jerry examined the notifications in front of him. Then the man swore quietly.

"Well shit. Now I feel like an idiot. The current third option for me is Leatherworker. This shit fucking works. Fucking hell, man, why didn't you stop me?"

Jerry wore a wide grin when he turned and faced Sam, who slapped him on the back. "Ya think I didn't try? Alright, I'll leave the skinning to you in the future."

"Bah, I'm gonna stink like a tannery," Jerry grumbled. Daniel offered his congratulations and the man grinned again.

As the two left, Sam repeatedly glanced over his shoulder toward Regina. Regina's group took this opportunity to discuss their options for obtaining a Class. To know they could direct at least one option with their Skill Levels was extremely valuable. By the end, everyone decided to wait, working their Skill Level up by helping out around the village.

Everyone except one. Glendel flushed to feel the stares of so many of his former coworkers and superiors.

"Are you sure?" Regina asked with curious eyes.

Glendel nodded. "Yes. If we're going to be here, I want to get strong as quickly as possible. I know I might be able to find something more suited to me if I work at it for a while, but… I'm just going to go for it."

Alana seemed dissatisfied, probably because she also wanted to try and accumulate power as quickly as possible. Nervous, but feeling hot with emotions, Glendel went up to Nul and asked for a Class.

Again, there was a long silence. Finally, Regina asked, "Well?"

Glendel shook his head slowly. "My first option is Lackey, my third is Assistant. But my second, random option…"

Feeling almost embarrassed to say it, Glendel finally stammered out, "I'm, uh, p-probably taking the second option. And it's… it's called… S-s-sovereign of G-Ghosts. That seems strong, r-right?"

Randidly looked up, surprised that someone knocked on his door. He set aside his ingredients, giving up on figuring out how to craft the next tier of potions for now. He supposed just under 200 was still a lot of Health or Mana, even though his Mana pool was over double that.

If it's a matter of concentration... I'll need to raise the Skill Level of Refine... Randidly mused on his approach.

When he opened the door, he found all of the important figures of the village: Sam, Donny, Daniel, Decklan, Dozer, Mrs. Hamilton, and Annie. Even Lyra, who was poking an unnerved Thorn. To his surprise, Regina, the surgeon who recently had her group join Donnyton, was there, alongside that tall, pale man Glendel, who always seemed to be lurking around.

Dozer hefted a large package across his shoulders, but it was Sam who Randidly turned his attention to. After thinking how aggressively he talked when he walked up to Donnyton earlier, desperate and delirious from pain, his stomach twisted itself as though it was trying to wring out water.

Randidly tried not to blush, faced with all these people. "Yes?"

"You've done a lot for us, kid, no two ways about it," Sam said gruffly. "We thought we'd give you something in return, to show our appreciation. You said your spear had been broken by that monster, right?"

Randidly nodded slowly. Dozer lowered the large package and unwrapped it, revealing a towering, eight-foot-tall spear, made entirely of bone. Randidly's eyes widened. He stepped forward and took the monstrosity from Dozer, feeling its significant weight. Without a Strength of at least 30, utilizing this weapon would be impossible. Randidly made a mental note to invest a few more points in Strength, so he could control it better.

The shaft appeared to be made entirely of linked vertebrae, grafted and shaped so each piece flowed smoothly together. A sharpened spike of bone ran sideways across the right side, leading his sight up to the head of the spear. On its own, it was a beautifully fanning bone, sharpened to a razor edge.

Randidly stepped past them into an open space and performed several simple spear moves, marveling in the power he felt behind every movement. He checked its Stats. Despite his nerves about the watchers, his lips curved into a smile.

The Spine-Spear of Ep-Tal Level 30: Agility +2, Strength +10. *If you crave something, take it.*

Randidly looked for a long time at the sentence that followed the Stats. Right now, this was exactly what he needed. He already invested so many

Stats into offensive ability, but this spear would raise that even further. A boost of 10 Strength from an equipment was monstrous.

"You made it from that monster's spine?" Randidly asked as he turned to look at Sam.

Sam nodded, seemingly pleased with himself, and put his hands on his hips. "Heh, don't think you're the only miracle worker, kid."

"Thanks. Thank you all," Randidly said, truly meaning it.

It was a beautiful weapon, one that would help him make up for his previous lack of power. The next Tribulation would be that much easier. Even if he didn't have a potion to completely fill his Mana pool, he wouldn't need to rely so heavily on his Mana Skills.

He could merely shove this giant spear down the throat of the next sphinx trying to shoot Fireballs at him.

Everyone drifted away after the gift had been given, chatting with each other as they went. Randidly followed the larger groups with his eyes. He stored the giant spear in his Interspatial Ring, noting how they clustered. Some must have rather pressing matters to attend to. Donnyton continued to swell like crazy as more and more people were attracted to the pillars of light.

Truly, thank god I didn't try and become the Village Chieftain. Randidly shook his head. He was surprised to see Sam giving several long glances toward the surgeon woman. *Plus, who knows if I could have kept my current Soulskill while taking that one...*

At first, Randidly intended to go back to work after getting the spear. If not on the potions issue, then he wanted to begin a new training regimen. Seeing the surgeon reminded Randidly of how wildly he behaved while half-dead after the fight with the sphinx. He clenched his fists and walked up to Regina and Glendel.

"I apologize if I was short with you. Having that inside my chest... wasn't enjoyable," Randidly said, bowing his head, nerves buzzing in his chest.

Regina nodded calmly. Her even expression did a lot to ease Randidly's anxiety. "I apologize as well. Perhaps I am just too used to dealing with hot-headed young men, I didn't even consider that you might know more about what you were talking about than I did. It was a humbling welcome to Donnyton, that's for sure. Although most of whom we dealt with were people from the hospital, right after the System arrived, we did see a lot of injured people from Rawlands University. Heh. Some of the things they claimed when they demanded treatment—"

"Rawlands... University?" Randidly spoke slowly. His heart began to pound in his chest.

"Oh, yes, portions of Rawlands' campus were teleported down there, mixed within the limits of Franksburg. Do you know it?"

Randidly's gaze sharpened as he turned away from Regina and looked to the south. Suddenly, he didn't want to spend time training at all. A bigger mission called to him.

"Yes," he said, his gaze unwavering. "I used to go there."

And so did Ace and Sydney.

CHAPTER SIXTY

$\mathcal{R}$andidly paced back and forth through the interior of his cabin. He tried making attempts with his new spear, tried distracting himself with Root Manipulation and playing with Thorn. He had even attempted to lose himself in Potion Making. Nothing could pull him away from the sudden urge to abandon everything here and head south to Franksburg. Just in case Ace and Sydney needed him.

Even now, he did his best not to think about the phrase that popped up in his mind during the worst of the sphinx fight, right as he was collapsing.

Sydney... I just wanted... to be strong for you...

Not even the occasional fantasies Randidly indulged about Ellaine did anything to distract him from rushing to investigate this first lead regarding their whereabouts.

And Randidly probably would have left immediately, if not for three things.

First, he could easily imagine how disappointed Shal would be if he let his emotions get away from him. Especially with it only being a possibility about Ace and Sydney. Shal would insist he take this seriously, and be firm on the point that if they survived this long, they would continue surviving.

The second was about Donnyton and its Tribulation. He made this town, long before they accumulated enough Skill Levels to be ready without them. With some intervention and luck, the Newbie Village was thriving. But Randidly's presence would drastically reduce the amount of damage a Tribulation could inflict.

That spine-spear shaped by Sam became an anchor. It was the proof of his bond to the town. Randidly could not leave before he helped them truly establish themselves.

And finally…

The expression on Sydney's face when she found out he was also going to Rawlands University. She had given him a long look, as though checking if her childhood friend was lying to her.

Then she shook her head slightly. "You know… their engineering program isn't very good, right? Are you just doing it to follow me?"

Randidly hadn't answered. He hadn't needed to.

Sydney sighed. "Your life shouldn't be that weightless, Randidly."

Now, pacing around the interior of his cabin, Randidly huffed. He didn't bother to wait for which of those thoughts was the most persuasive. "I just… I need to stay until we deal with Donnyton's Tribulation. And since tonight is the last monster horde, it will probably be in the next few days. But also… my fight against the sphinx proved how important preparation is. Then it's settled. I'll train. I'll make sure that when I find my friends—" Randidly's hands tightened into fists "—I *can* protect them."

The final night came.

Donnyton triumphed over the ten Boss-type monsters that were thrown at it. Time passed. The town prospered, spreading its reach into the surrounding area. Sam straightened and wiped the sweat off his forehead.

He grimaced at the numerous shacks erected around his workshop. *Of course, "prosperity" just means there are larger and larger piles of tasks for us each day…*

Twelve days passed since the Newbie Barrier had fallen around Donnyton. It had been an extremely busy time for Sam. Much to his disgust, Daniel was strongly pushing for an increase in the differentiation between ranks. Thus, Sam received the task of creating a new ranking system for the village.

Outwardly, he was grumbling, but inwardly, he was rather smug; he had another chance to put off all the other busywork Daniel demanded. He could just experiment with Bone Shaping while he assented to the newest request. He pulled out some of the finer bones brought in by the Ghosthound and began his work.

This push for a more complicated ranking system stemmed directly from some of the other more pressing activities in the recent weeks, such as the consolidation of the squad system and the constant vigilance for the incoming Tribulation.

The former was going quite smoothly. By and large, all Classers were separated into groups of ten, comprised of nine squad members and a leader. There were a few exceptions to the numbers, based on need and special interest, but all squads were of this same composition.

With the constant influx of refugees to the area, combined with the fact that the other Newbie Village was extremely selective in who was allowed to enter, Donnyton continued to grow. Thus far, there were twenty-two solidified squads. There was also a pool of regular members and "officer track" Classers who were randomly grouped together and made to play war games under the watchful eye of Dozer, Decklan, and Donny.

If a squad seemed to gel, they would become an official unit and receive their call sign and current number. The call sign would never change, but their number could. It was based on the ranking of their perceived strength. Which meant it could go up or down depending on the situation.

Regina commented that while currently effective, the squad system was only a short-term solution. As the number of people in the village increased, they would likely need groups to have experience fighting as a larger unit. Better to start looking for another tier, a company of men, and train someone to manage the larger lot. She also pointed out the great flaw of the current system is that oftentimes, the strongest or second strongest person is the squad leader. Those individuals constantly put themselves at the front lines of fighting, resulting in very little tactical deviation once the fighting starts. There is just no way for a person fighting to have the vision to spot the enemies weaknesses and exploit them.

She even pushed for another specialty role, a tactician, to be included with most squads. That had been shelved for the time being.

Sam thought she had a point, but Dozer and Donny were nonplussed by her words. Sam almost laughed aloud at their expressions. Sure, they were strong, but they still seemed so young at times. They had no sense of the long-term consequences of the choices they made now.

They just hadn't had the experience of time to understand the specific ways life usually worked.

Not that he could blame them for their confusion. If things stayed as they had been, they wouldn't need a company. The fall of the Newbie Barrier meant more and stronger monsters spawned in the area, occasionally double as strong as the wolverines. After a few close scrapes, they hammered out a rough patrol schedule and dealt with most of the incursions.

Other than that, very little changed in the last twelve days. Raid Bosses were a concern, but Glendel's new abilities had proven invaluable at finding and identifying them, rendering them pretty harmless. His ghosts served as excellent scouts, able to phase through solid objects and turn near-invisible.

Other than the occasional mobilizations against Raid Bosses, there just wasn't a unifying foe anymore, like the monster horde had been, to keep them on their toes, making them work hard to survive.

There was of course the looming Tribulation. Up until now, no one had seen it. No matter how frantically the Ghosthound combed the surroundings, not even he could find any trace of it.

And his tension, with no monster in sight, Sam reflected, *is starting to have a strange psychological effect on Donnyton.*

They were constantly training and grinding themselves to a point, ready for the oncoming vicious sphinx. Vigilant patrols scoured the area. Any non-domesticated monsters were killed seconds after they spawned. All in all, Donnyton had become a safe and orderly place.

Still, everyone was waiting for the hammer to fall. And through that orderly town, the Ghosthound never faltered in prowling or training. Sometimes it seemed the young man did both at once. He was a constant presence.

Sam pushed all that aside, focusing on his current task. In order to provide at least a little differentiation in the upgraded ranking system, he was making several types of pendants through his Bone Shaping. For the general groups not yet part of a squad, they were given a bone pendant in the symbol of their use.

A flame-shaped bone for the Mages. A cross for the Healers. An axe for Dozer's squad, a shield for Donny's, and a curved dagger for Decklan's. This group of pendants were annoying to make, due to their group size. Just to continue on with the project, Sam was forced to spend most of his Mana pool and replenish it with Mana potions.

Bone Shaping by itself was simple. Sam used his hands, infused with Mana, to rub the bones. It was a gradual process. Some of the Mana would sink into the surface of the bone, and Sam would still maintain a certain measure of control over it.

After a sufficient amount of Mana was rubbed into the bone, he *pressed*, driving the Mana up and forward into the shape he wanted. The bone slowly twisted and stretched to fill that shape.

Not enough Mana and the Skill failed, leaving him with a strangely twisted bone. Too much Mana and the bone exploded. Press too hard and the bone exploded. Press too soft and for several seconds nothing would happen, until the bone ultimately dissolved into powder as the Mana diffused.

Sam practiced obsessively these past few weeks, reducing the percentage of bones he wasted through his Skill.

Although it wasn't outwardly obvious, Sam was a prideful man. Early on, when the village had been established, his Skill with an axe and construction gave him what he thought was a pretty significant head start in terms of Paths, which translated into higher Stats.

It was nice, in a way, protecting the girls and even that asshat Kal, by wielding his axes with wild abandon, running solely on the thrill of adrenaline while monsters rushed him.

But as the Classers Leveled, that Stat advantage he accumulated disappeared. Then Vivian, Ellaine, and Kal left, wanting to flee to "civilization." All he had left was Lyra. Of course, by that point, she no longer needed his protection. Sam couldn't fathom the extent and methods of her Skills, but he couldn't deny the results she achieved.

In fact, she'd been visiting the Ghosthound these past weeks, giving him lessons in the control of Mana. Out of everyone in Donnyton, Lyra was the only one who wasn't driven away by that crazy obsession he had with finding Donnyton's Tribulation.

She was also the only one willing to "play" with the Ghosthound's strange, thorny pet.

Sam chuckled despite himself, his smile grim. Was even *he* beginning to call Randidly the Ghosthound? It was a sobering thought. Although Randidly was clearly the most powerful and versatile person in the village.

That kid is bearing so much weight on his shoulders. Sam could only shake his head and get back to work. Donnyton being strong was the best way to help Randidly with his stress over the Tribulation.

Sighing, Sam turned back to his final project for the new stratification system. For the squads, he made the numbers fifty through eleven. Simple, plain numbers on bone worn by the squad leader. For the final ten, the highest ranked of all the squads, he used larger pieces of bone, to be worn on those squad leaders' back. These took a few tries, but make them he did. Resplendent as graceful bones, displayed in roman numerals.

X, IX, VIII, VII, VI, V, IV, III, II, and finally I.

These will be the pride of Donnyton, Sam hoped as he looked at his curved and primal creations. *The honor that all the Classers strive for. Something to give structure to this strange, System-governed world.*

Also achievable by the non-Classers, Sam supposed. There were several competing for spots in squads, although there was sometimes some grumbling when they were included on *your* team. The battles against Classers did raise their Skills more quickly, which was helpful. It also was becoming increasingly obvious that having an NCC gave squads certain advantages.

Often, they knew most basic combat Skills of all varieties and could fill multiple roles in combat. Healer, Mage, Tank. This capability was part of the reason Regina used to argue for a tactician position in every squad.

Unfortunately, this versatility came at the cost of low Health, Mana, and Stamina pools. They usually had to rely on potions to stay relevant in fights. Aside from Randidly, all of the NCCers were rather easily winded.

After shaping the others, Sam drank another Mana potion to begin the final piece at his best.

For the I, the top-ranked squad, Sam reverently used a bone from the Tribulation Randidly killed. They were darker than normal bones, a grey-blue, almost resembling metal. This, after all, was the pinnacle. It should be worth striving for.

Sam examined the piece of equipment he made, then chuckled.

Livery of the First Squad Level 29: *A sigil made for the best of Donnyton.*
Within it is a small echo of the Pinnacle. Wearer receives +50 Health,
Mana, and Stamina. Those under the command of the Wearer receive
+10 Health, Mana, and Stamina.

Sam nodded, pleased with himself. The others granted small amounts of Health or Stamina, but this was a much more significant amount. There were perks to being on top. And the fact that he pushed a piece of equipment to Level 29 was a good sign.

They already arranged a system of challenges, so the lower squads could fight to gain rank, but it hadn't been used overmuch thus far. Now the pendant wearers would try to obtain a top ten ranking to achieve those extra bonuses the larger pieces granted. And those in the top ten...

Would aim for the top.

Wistfully, Sam wondered how he would fare, should he join the pool to be placed into a squad. Although he felt he was slightly inadequate in comparison to the top tier, he thought he matched up pretty well in comparison to most people's physical specs. He was nearing 20 in almost every physical Stat, which he'd done while putting a significant amount of Stats into Wisdom and Focus. Perhaps the total was not super impressive compared to what someone could accomplish with a Class, but still...

A cleared throat caught Sam's attention and he twisted around. Daniel stood behind him, fidgeting with a dagger tied to his waist.

Sam chuckled as he saw the bored expression on the kid's face. "How long were you waiting?"

"Almost five minutes," Daniel replied, probably only half joking. Although with Daniel's patience, it would no doubt get spent after even that short amount of time. Judging by the way he was bouncing from foot to foot...

"Well?" Sam asked, folding his arms.

"The first stage of the Class Trials happened today," Daniel gushed, his eyes bright. "I have the results."

The Class Trials, as Daniel called them, were his brainchild. He would take volunteers and oversee their training, promising them support in exchange for all the information concerning their Paths and Stats choices, and having control over when they chose a Class. Daniel had taken in twenty individuals, seventeen men and three women, and had been working them to the bone since the Newbie Barrier had fallen.

Based on the original plan, one half was long term, while the other was short term. And since he was here now, he likely made the short-term group take a Class recently. With the relative peace of Donnyton, it made sense.

Before Sam could say anything else, Daniel handed him a clipboard. Upon closer examination, it was covered in Stats, lists of Skills, physical descriptions and measurements, Paths, and general psychological assessments. Sam felt a begrudging respect for how neat and tidy the handwriting was. Unfortunately, most was marred with underlines, circles, and random lines drawn around between strange bits of information.

Sam gave Daniel a level look.

Shaking his head, Daniel said with an annoyed expression, "Okay, okay, the short version, right? The total Stats, rather than the distribution, made a difference in quality of the Classes received. Due to variables I haven't been able to identify, some individuals Level Skills faster generally, while others displayed particular affinity toward a certain Skill and Leveled only that rapidly. It was only two weeks, but I was surprised that the difference between the lowest individual and the highest was approaching 20 Stat points—"

"Focus," Sam growled, rapping his knuckles against the wood of the worktable. Daniel's propensity to get lost in thought and ramble was now famous in Donnyton.

Daniel opened his mouth, then closed it with a scowl. With an exaggerated sigh, he said, "Alright, fine. As I stated, total Stat amounts made a difference in terms of quality, but Stat distribution doesn't seem to affect Class type. A person with high Intelligence could still become a Berserker. Class type stems from the Skills you've Leveled. Heavy Blow leads to Warrior, Herculean Strength to Defender, Mana Bolt to Mage, Healing Palm to Acolyte.

"Perhaps unfortunately," Daniel continued, "the one individual who was best at Leveling probably got the worst Class out of everyone, Jack of All Trades. The Stat gains are fine, but the Skills he's gotten have been lackluster so far. Just general proficiencies. Since he was good at everything, I had him Level *everything* he could. Spells, fighting Skills, Cleaning and Cooking, Construction, Potion Making, and so on. But because he had everything, he had no dominant Skills that led to his Class. As such, I've agreed to take him on as an assistant. It seems that in terms of Classes, what really matters is the flavor of the Skills."

"An assistant will be useful for you," Sam said half-heartedly, mulling over the results of the initial group.

The Stat total increasing the quality was good, but the general Skills making Classes more difficult was not great news to hear. After all, all of his production Skills were spread out quite a lot. In addition, he had a fair amount of combat-related moves. If he took a Class now, what would he get?

"Not really," Daniel said with a smug grin on his face. "Ever since my Class granted me the Memorize Skill—Wait, you were being sarcastic, weren't you? Well, I'll be leaving, then. No need to stay around and be mocked."

Daniel's affronted expression as he turned and stalked away was so comical, Sam had to laugh. They were embracing this world quickly, Sam thought. Perhaps too quickly. Becoming too used to their positions of power. Hopefully, this strange pseudo peace didn't last too long.

Besides, Randidly really needs to work off some of that tension… Otherwise, he might buzz himself to pieces.

"Oh, one more thing," Daniel said, still hurrying away. "I'll leave the pleasure of speaking with the Ghosthound about this piece of news to you. Good luck."

Now it was Sam's turn to scowl. As much as he wished for the kid's mood to ease, interacting directly with him wasn't pleasant. His dedication to catching the Tribulation was anxiety-inducing at a distance, and downright infectious during a conversation. Sam knew he wanted to go out and hunt it down, but didn't know where to start, leaving Randidly forced to wait. All the while, his gaze turned toward the south.

In one of their evening strolls through the area, Regina confided in Sam that the strange, wistful gaze had started when she mentioned Rawlands University. Perhaps there was a connection or relationship hidden there, the past of the man who would become the Ghosthound. One that even now could draw him.

What exacerbated that wistful mood was apparently the Mana lessons with Lyra weren't going well.

It wasn't like he could ignore this task. For all that his energy was a pain, the Ghosthound remained extremely knowledgeable about the System. More so than even Daniel. Perhaps he could look at the data provided by the experiment and have some other insights. Sam left the bone articles to cool and headed down the valley past Randidly's cabin.

This time of day, he would not be sitting patiently within, unfortunately. He was either brewing potions or training in some of the eastern woods. Sam's journey took him past several farmers who were tending their fields. Sam noticed the tension in their posture and sighed, continuing forward. It didn't take long before raised voices picked up on the breeze.

"What do you mean you just do it?" Randidly growled.

"I just do it, so why can't you? What do you want me to say!" Lyra answered with a rare hiss of irritation.

Sam could picture her furious face and mouth pressed into a thin line. Sam hurried closer before the conflict could escalate.

"Some *instruction* would be a welcome change of pace," Randidly said with just as much heat. "But I guess what else could I expect from a child—"

"*What* am I supposed to *teach* you! I have a Skill that lets me see Mana. You don't. After I earned the Skill, I just reached out and played with Mana, shaping it into whatever I wanted. I figured you could skip the seeing step and just control it, but I didn't realize you had a giant turd for a brain."

Randidly snorted. "I can feel the Mana is there, sure. But I haven't been able to touch it! Can you just... explain what it's like to touch it?"

"If you can feel it, aren't you touching it already? Just do it, want it, feel it!"

The farmers were beginning to flush. Sam arrived at the small gated area Randidly built to grant himself some privacy during his training session. Sam let himself in, making as much noise as possible. He was met with two hostile glares and a rather destroyed stretch of ground.

Even if they hadn't been progressing well through the specific lessons, it was clear the duo's Skills were extremely effective.

Their glares switched back from Sam and settled on each other. Sam felt helpless watching these two oblivious youngsters interacting with each other. The Mana training was obviously a front. The Ghosthound wanted a distraction, one that would make him feel like he was accomplishing something, while his gears spun from being unable to find the Tribulation and his heart ached from not being able to follow his desire to head south.

And Lyra...

Lyra thumped her foot against the ground. She wasn't getting what she wanted from the arrangement either. "How can you call me a child when I'm doing something you can't manage to do? This isn't my fault! You're just so stubborn—"

"My fault? Do you think I'm not putting enough effort into this?" Randidly's voice dropped dangerously.

Sam realized his earlier thoughts about being impressive for an NCCer were rather foolish. If it came to blows between Randidly and Lyra...

"Can you just listen to what I'm saying and stop getting so angry? I'm doing my best." Lyra's lips trembled, knowing the reason he was so angry had nothing to do with her at all, not really. "I'm trying..."

"You know what's annoying? Your attitude. *How* do I just 'do it'? If you behaved like a reasonable person, just once—" Randidly spun around and walked across the smoldering training field, heading for a barrel of water.

Lyra stamped her foot and followed after him. Their earlier Skill confrontation left her leather and fur armor singed. "Would you even listen? Aren't you too busy treating me like a little girl to take me seriously? Oh, there's Lyra again, just joking around, she's so snarky and unapproachable, I'd rather pat her on the head and leave her alone so she just—"

Randidly ducked his head in the water, blocking out her voice. For a few seconds, Lyra stared at his back. She spun on her heel and walked toward one of the walls. With a wave of her hand, she conjured a bear made of Mana that smashed its paws against the wall, ripping a hole through it like it was made of gauze. Lyra calmly stepped over the broken section without altering her gait and proceeded away, passing the area now completely vacated of farmers.

Sam sighed. He hadn't known Lyra well before the System arrived, but he'd spent a good amount of time with her since then, and Randidly too.

Lyra was always raised to be an actress, and the best actress. She grew up under constant pressure and observation. She felt *seen* and judged constantly. Only a stubborn disposition and her natural talent and intellect helped her through it.

Now, facing Randidly, a person who she was obviously attracted to, she was infuriated he wasn't behaving how she expected. She simply wanted to be viewed as a woman and a peer. To him, she was a teenager. Seventeen might be a respectable age for some people, but to an admittedly distracted and stubborn twenty-year-old Randidly, she was a kid getting mad at him for reasons not on his radar.

Honestly, Sam respected how much Randidly Ghosthound gave himself to the task at hand. But the problem in this case was the lack of development around the Tribulation. Sam sensed things would get worse before they got better.

Randidly finally pulled his head out of the barrel, flinging water in all directions. He glanced around and stiffened when he didn't find Lyra and only the hole she'd made in the wall.

Randidly glanced to Sam. "So, what did you come here for?"

CHAPTER SIXTY-ONE

*R*andidly Meditated in his cabin. Slowly, his eyes opened. He twisted, his piercing green eyes, burning a hole through the wall as he found himself drawn toward the south, where his friends might be waiting.

It had been three weeks since the Safe Zones around theirs and the neighboring village expired. During that time, scouts combed the surrounding area. They found the two Dungeon locations, the one near them being Level 20. The one west, past the other town, was only Level 14.

They also encountered a few Tier I Raid Bosses, the most troublesome of which ended up being a Level 25 Rhinoceros Pack Leader, surrounded by a few dozen of its Rhinoceros children. Unfortunately, Glendel's ghost scouts missed the early signs of this foe because they ranged quickly across the badlands, gathering strength before thundering back to attack the Villages.

Almost the entirety of their force had mobilized. The second unit of tanks and both Decklan's and Dozer's personal units moved to kill it, with support from Clarissa. Ultimately, it was overkill, but Dozer did earn a belt that gave him a huge boost in Health Regen. They also brought several powerful Rhinoceros bodies back with them. Sam was delighted to have new quality materials to use in his armors.

The leadership of Donnyton called a meeting, which Randidly attended mostly as a way to distract himself from the frustrating lack of a Tribulation. Everyone agreed the next time they found a Raid Boss, as long as it hadn't established itself, they could probably handle it with one elite unit and Mage support.

Randidly remained silent in the second part of the meeting, where Donny awkwardly brought up the fact that perhaps they should change the methods they were using to search for the Tribulation. Daniel kept giving him nervous looks, irritating Randidly further.

Most people weren't briefed on the details of the Tribulation, just informed about the new dangers that could appear at any time. The greatest change in the past week was the completion of housing for almost everyone involved.

Sam's builders were starting to click into an efficient groove, able to throw up enough rooms to house an extended family in an hour. Some of the more enterprising, and fed up, individuals amongst Donnyton's residents worked out a pretty sophisticated plumbing system, which finally eliminated the need for latrines. Mrs. Hamilton visibly beamed at the shift.

In between briefings and meetings, Randidly rushed through the surrounding hills, killing any monster he found. Sometimes he would wound the monsters he encountered, hoping they'd flee and lead him directly to the next Tribulation. Like how it'd happened with the sphinx.

They never did. Randidly grew irritated with trailing them and would finish the miserable monster off. Staring at the corpse, the fearful part of Randidly asked why he allowed it to endure such pain.

Once he returned to Donnyton, he received more briefings on the progress of the Newbie Village. They even figured out how to get a pretty sustainable and working power plant out of mages, but they didn't really have the infrastructure here to make use of it. Nothing required power.

The one change Randidly did appreciate was that budding mages were forced to repeatedly heat water with Fireballs, resulting in a functioning bathhouse. It made a world of difference to wash with hot water. Those moments were some of the few that allowed him to relax.

Due to rising demand, an NCC woman gathered herbs, planted a garden, and began selling soap. For the first time in a long time, the people of Donnyton were clean.

One night after scrubbing and scalding himself, Randidly climbed the height of the rolling hills around Donnyton and looked up at the gleaming stars. *I... I know I shouldn't be this tense. It's definitely slowing down my training. I know that whether Ace and Sydney are still alive, hurrying and worrying does nothing. But... what does my resolve mean if I can't prove myself? I just feel... Why am I working myself so hard like this?*

The addictive cycle of improvement of Skill Levels and danger slowly receded. None of the foes Randidly met posed a threat. And without the constant dangers, Randidly felt lost.

He took any method to distract himself from his aching heart and growing sense of unease.

Donnyton had grown to house almost three thousand people, with around eight hundred of them taking Classes. Most of the Classers were men, although an increasing number of women who had been training up Skills were getting interesting Classes. Many of Regina's group received healing-style Classes and were now fully integrated into the regular squads. There was even one woman who received the Class Green Mage, and had shyly come asking him for advice.

He stoically told her "Practice" and returned to his own training. Even if his distracted heart meant his Skill Level accumulation had slowed to a crawl, he didn't dare take a break. If he did, his nerves would be even worse.

This is preparation, Randidly told himself. *And without preparation, the next threat will be even worse. Because it's definitely coming... that's the sort of place the System is.*

Except everything moved so quickly since the change; since Randidly woke up in the Dungeon. Somehow, this extended period of calm dominated his awareness. Even the painful fight against the sphinx seemed like a dream.

In the meantime, Donnyton continued to prosper. Those of Regina's group who hadn't chosen Healer usually went a Mage route, bolstering their previously pathetic Mage corps. Just recently, after obtaining a specific Skill they wanted to base their Class on, and Leveling it a decent amount, people were taking Classes and receiving even more specialized Skills. Many were preparing to be an active participant in the village's defense.

Over the past three weeks, Randidly took Thorn hunting several times. The little bugger was vicious, moving invisibly underground and springing upward, sinking its many thorny vines into the victim's body. It'd wrap the unfortunate monster in a death grip on its throat before it even knew what hit it. Unfortunately, it seemed like it had become picky about blood after eating the sphinx, and hadn't Leveled since then.

Driven by his restless spirit, Randidly had taken to ranging further and further through the wilderness with Thorn at his side. Randidly practically buzzed with the tension running through his body. The sounds at night echoed across the whole valley. He felt like he could hear every Classer laughing uproariously and every monster raising its head and howling at the moon. Those constant noises of life within the valley only made it worse.

So he fled, taking Thorn to hunt. He prowled through the tree lines and chased down any monster he encountered. Thorn acted like a bloodhound, catching the scent of clashes between monsters and guiding Randidly unerringly to the site of the action.

On that night, twenty-two days after his fight against the sphinx, Randidly stalked between the long shadows of the trees after a shrunken version of an ostrich. The Level 19 Feathered Runner had been wounded in a clash against a Raid Boss. Randidly was hoping it would lead him to the breeding ground of its kind.

Or to a Tribulation. But it seems like I won't get that lucky twice in a life-time, Randidly thought with a bitter expression. A flash of anger swept through him and he couldn't resist raising his hand and pointing imperiously at the Feathered Runner. "Fireball."

Sparks flew from the tip of his finger and a soccer ball of flame shot down the slope at the fleeing monster. To Randidly's surprise, the tiny ostrich abruptly changed direction. Although the projectile was fast, its movement was agile enough the Fireball missed completely.

BOOOOOM!

A belch of flame licked up from the impact point and singed the branches of the lower canopy. A hole was now punched through the trunk, and although the tree didn't catch fire, there was a crunching groan as it collapsed sideways.

Randidly narrowed his eyes and activated Phantom Half-Step twice in quick succession. He wove through the last few intervening trees and raised his hand again. The Feathered Runner reached the base of the slope and found a game trail. It lengthened its stride to speed away, but it was too late.

"Fireball."

The Feather Runner jerked again with its Level 19 Stats, but this time, Randidly was too close. The Skill hit its compact body and its feathers lit up like a torch. After several unsteady steps, it collapsed and skidded across the forest floor. The flames steadily dimmed, but not before illuminating the uncaring bark of the surrounding trees.

By the time the light had gone out, Randidly realized he was breathing heavily. He flexed his hands and walked forward, inspecting the beak and claws. *Probably not even worth bringing them back to Sam. The materials... fuck. What a waste of time.*

Just as he turned away, Randidly heard something that made him stiffen. Someone was singing in the surroundings. The slow, sad song had Randidly pivoting and turning to look deeper along the tree line. Some of the tension in his chest eased at the beautiful soprano. Randidly's feet carried him closer. At the base of the slope there was a small creek bed, and when he followed that to the northwest—

Randidly stepped out into the clearing. Ellaine spun with her hands raised toward the sky. She wore a white dress, and suddenly, the lonely moon was warm and loving. Its light hit the soft fabric of her garment and made her luminous. Even more unusual were the strange yellow butterflies that fluttered around her as she sang. They seemed to be proof, proof that this woman was beyond the limits of this world.

Randidly couldn't breathe.

As she continued to croon out the words to a song he didn't recognize, he felt increasingly awkward standing several steps out into the clearing. If she turned and saw him...

Abruptly, the singing stopped. Her gaze was locked on to him. Her eyes tightened in fear. The glowing butterflies fluttered in the air for a bit, then began to wander away.

Seeing the fear in her expression, Randidly's heart twisted. "I just heard singing—"

"Oh, thank god!" Ellaine laughed, bringing a hand to her chest. She collapsed forward, putting her hands against her knees. "I thought... I definitely thought you were something that was going to eat me! Or you were his—"

Ellaine shook her head and straightened. She moved across the clearing, and to Randidly's almost horrified surprise, wrapped her arms around him in a hug. She smelled like wildflowers and grass. He stood very still before awkwardly patting her on the back.

Randidly licked his lips. *Were we... really this close?*

She took a step back and beamed at him. "Anyway, it's so great to see you, Randidly. I feel like all I've heard about Donnyton has been so impressive lately! How have you been?"

"I've..." Randidly tried to think of how to answer that question, looking back over the past few weeks. Perhaps because of the innocuous way Ellaine said the question, he really examined his recent behavior. The more he thought about how tense and irritable he'd been, Randidly slumped, though he still tried to keep his expression even. "I've... I've been okay."

Ellaine's arm curved in a perfect arc and she lightly punched his shoulder. More than any force, the strange suddenness of their physical intimacy made Randidly sway. "Ha! Don't you dare bullshit me. I've seen that look in your eye. You're burning out."

"I..." Randidly scratched his cheek. Even now, the back of his throat tasted like bitter acid. He wanted to deny Ellaine out of hand, but the combination of his desire to look for Ace and Sydney, the threat of the Tribulation, and his sense of responsibility toward Donnyton had begun to strangle him.

Ultimately, Randidly couldn't finish his sentence.

Ellaine laughed again, the corners of her eyes crinkling in the moonlight. "See? I told you. That's why I... why I come out here sometimes. When the System arrived, I almost immediately got burnt out. Life changed too drastically, but now—you saw them, right? Here, I'll bring them again."

Ellaine took a few steps away and began to sing. Randidly allowed himself to relax, slightly. Her voice rose through the night, stilling even the breeze. As she sang, those luminous butterflies returned, fluttering down and settling on her arms and shoulders.

After the slow and sweet final notes, the butterflies awoke and departed again. Ellaine winked at Randidly. "Do you see them? Those definitely weren't native to Earth before the System arrived. Even though so many things have changed in horrible ways, there are beautiful things that are different too. There is... a beauty in the new perspectives."

Randidly allowed himself a long look at Ellaine's side profile. "You have a beautiful voice. I'm envious. I'm... pretty tone deaf."

"Well, thank you." Ellaine's smile faded a fraction before she theatrically pointed at him. "But you! Don't *you* dare talk about envy. Aren't you basically the strongest guy right now? Which is why you can just wander around on a dark night and I'm constantly flinching at shadows. I... really wish I had your strength."

Randidly's heart twisted again. Thinking about the constant state of vigilance Donnyton had been forced into, Randidly could only shake his head at Ellaine's words. "I... I'm not all that strong. There are... a lot of things I can't do."

"Of course. I said you're strong, not God." When his expression remained stiff, she stepped forward and punched his shoulder. "Yeah, you're definitely crispy from taking things too seriously. Sure there's things you can't do; that will always be true. But don't let all the things you can't do bother you. There are too many to count. Instead... be empowered by the things you can do."

Randidly didn't bother to stop himself from staring at Ellaine this time. He practically drank her in. Her eyes in the pale light of the moon were glittering and amber. She was... one of the most beautiful women he'd ever met.

"Thank—" Randidly began, taking the initiative to take a step toward her, but his head whipped around.

"What is it?" Ellaine whispered.

Randidly tilted his head to the side, relaxing when he identified the source. "Humans. Walking through the forest in a line. Probably searching for something."

"Ah. That's probably for me..." Ellaine spared a glance at Randidly. Without giving him time for his heart to react to each individual step, Ellaine pressed herself up on her tiptoes, brushed her lips against his cheek, and took a step away.

She waved with a half-smile. "That's a tiny thank you for getting us safely to Turtletown. What a funny name, right? But the King loves it. We... we were pretty rude about leaving Donnyton. But you put up with it and protected us. We were burnt then, like I was saying. But we really appreciated what you did for us. We—well, I, didn't forget it."

Ellaine turned away, pausing before she got much further and glanced over her shoulder, her white dress still nearly blinding in the moonlight. "If I had the chance to choose again whether to leave..."

She snapped her mouth shut, offering Randidly an awkward smile. "Well, anyway, take care of Lyra, will you? She's always had such a big crush on you."

Then Ellaine was gone, walking confidently toward the line of police officers creeping through the woods.

Randidly pressed his fingers against his cheek. His thoughts whirled around in his head and heart, but it wasn't a chaotic, bouncing-off-the-walls sort of feeling. No, this was a bathtub when the stopper was pulled out. Everything swirled and all the chaotic emotions tormenting him for the last three weeks were finally draining out of him.

Be empowered... by the things that you can *do, huh...* The moonlight felt cool on Randidly's skin. He closed his eyes and savored the peace of this moment. If he concentrated just right, he could still hear the sound of Ellaine's singing. *A spear must always advance... yes, that's right. I shouldn't dwell, I shouldn't falter. I should just... focus on what I can do.*

Some part of Randidly felt several of Ellaine's silences in their strange conversation were a little awkward. She was clearly hiding something about her experience in this Turtletown. Randidly let that drain away too.

He should set aside worrying about things he couldn't do. Plus, he didn't want to create trouble just on a hunch. For now, he would leave the issue of Turtletown alone. Instead, he wanted to think about what he could do to prepare.

As he sorted through his thoughts, Randidly called out to Thorn and headed back toward Donnyton.

Perhaps the only area where Randidly currently felt content in his own training was with his new spear. The exertion required to master the strangely rigid and heavy weapon would allow him to bury his anxiety in sweat.

It wasn't a change reflected so much in Skill Level, but comfort in battle. More than anything, Randidly focused on solidifying the foundations of his spear techniques, practicing the strange forms and exercises Shal taught him. In repetition, he found a brief respite from the sense of failure that plagued him with Donnyton's Tribulation remaining a no-show.

If the skulking Tribulation had the nerve to finally reveal itself, Randidly had no doubts in his mind his powerful spear blows would rip wide holes in its body, even without relying on his impressively powerful magic.

I'm stronger. Randidly told himself with each repetition of the basic thrust with the heavy spine-spear. He twisted his body and twirled the massive weapon over his head. *I'm taking steps forward.*

Hearing those affirmations helped ease Randidly's anxious heart.

In terms of productivity of Mana Skills, these weeks were spent mostly focusing on Fireball, trying to raise it to the point that it was comparable to Spearing Roots. However, it seemed like that wouldn't be the case for a long time. Although Fireball had a Level comparable to Spearing Roots, the plant-based Skill had its Level reset when it changed, retaining the benefits of its previous gains. In terms of power, Fireball still lagged behind.

Instead of fixating on Skill Level, Randidly hoped to get a Fireball Path and obtain a more powerful fire-based Skill. Whether it was an evolution of the Fireball Skill or a new one altogether, the Skill Paths hadn't let Randidly down thus far.

He did have the option of going and checking if there were any Skills he could learn from the Skill Challenges, but until he went through the Apprentice Path himself, he was leery about spending SP to learn something he might be able to get on his own.

Randidly sighed and lowered his spear. What was significantly slowing his progress was... everything else. Randidly knew logically his attitude was getting worse and worse. He continuously failed to refine energy shards to a stronger version of themselves, the very thing he needed to discover the next tier up in potions, which was one more source of doubt in him, making him wonder if he was really improving at all.

Since their fight a week ago, Randidly no longer bothered with lessons with Lyra in regard to Mana control, and she hadn't bothered to come and ask about it. Both appeared to be in agreement, at least on this subject. For some reason, it annoyed Randidly even more than the fight had.

He could sense the cool Mana and warm Stamina flowing through his body, strengthening him, being used for his different Skills. He just couldn't affect it at will, and Randidly didn't know why. To him, it felt akin to trying to affect the flow of his blood. Yes, he could feel his heart pound and the blood flowing through him. That didn't mean he had a method of interacting with the blood and controlling it.

These frustrations, and the lack of the Tribulation, sapped away the effectiveness of his Skill training. It just hadn't been increasing like it used to. Something needed to change. He needed to move in a new direction.

Sighing, Randidly returned to the present. He'd waited long enough. He was now quite sure of his theory. It was time to talk to the Donnyton Council.

Although Donny was the nominal Chieftain, Donnyton was essentially run by three people: Daniel, Regina Northwind, and Mrs. Hamilton.

Although on paper she was in charge of supplies and the NCCs, Mrs. Hamilton had the most influence overall. Mostly by dint of the rapidly inflating population of people who chose to not yet take a Class, or ever. She controlled access to coffee, the baths, soap, mass-produced potions, and the food.

Needless to say, she usually held the deciding vote on the issues of Donnyton.

Plus, no one fought her for this responsibility. Even more convincing was how everything in Donnyton was coming together, despite how many complex systems were at play between the Classers, supplies, NCCs, the issues of security, experimentation with Skills, and the new arrivals. Someone needed to keep everything on schedule, and Mrs. Hamilton never gave anyone a reason to doubt she was that person.

Daniel was the expert on Paths, Skills, and Classes. He also did most of the work regarding the Newbie Village. By contrast, it was harder to define why Regina was part of the group. However, she had good instincts for people and assessed tough choices well. Her insight proved extremely valuable.

Every night, the three of them met to discuss the direction the town was headed, what resources they needed, and what the big project for the following day would be. There was a standing invite to Donny and Sam, and though they showed up occasionally, they remained largely absent. Dozer and Decklan held zero interest, preferring to spend their nights training.

They also never invited Randidly. He assumed this was because he made his unwillingness to be involved in the small details quite clear. Even he admitted some of his moods at the meetings in the past three weeks had been somewhat disruptive.

Which was why, when Randidly showed up dragging a confused Donny, the three blinked in surprise. The normally cool Mrs. Hamilton did a double take and rubbed her eyes.

Regina, Daniel, and Miranda glanced nervously between each other over their mugs filled with the new trendy strain of coffee, and plates laden with a luxurious meal of baby wolverine, garnished with freshly harvested saffron.

Of them all, Regina recovered herself the quickest. "Ah, Ghosthound. Lovely for you to join us. Would you like some—"

"No, and I'll make this short." Randidly's face was grim. "I've put it off for some time, but I think something needs to be done. I will lead a caravan south, to gather additional refugees in Franksburg. The Tribulation... I suspect will not be attacking anytime soon."

"You—without you here... if the Tribulation does show up..." Daniel blubbered.

Randidly grimaced. His mind went back to the way the shadow cat suddenly turned and ran away from him after being injured. At the time, he hadn't thought about it much. But with three weeks to reflect...

"That's the whole point. I... suspect this Tribulation won't come as long as I am here. In fact, I suspect it was the reason I discovered the other Tribulation in the first place."

Perhaps what I really overlooked was the naming. Ep-Tal was the Hungry Tribulation. It was a monstrous sphinx, and I just assumed all Tribulations would be like that. But if it's not... When Randidly arrived before Ep-Tal's cave, he hadn't seen the wounded shadow cat. The blood-stained trail had vanished at the top of the canyon. He'd merely followed his prickling instincts when he found Ep-Tal.

He assumed it had just been eaten. But what if it hadn't?

What if the "shadow cat" had only been there to lead him to a foe? And when it had, it vanished.

"At any rate, we can't keep up this constant state of readiness forever. I'm... well. I suspect it's a different variety of Tribulation than the other village experienced, but no less dangerous. Just less confrontational than the sphinx. For the trip south, I think Alana, Clarissa, and Devan will suffice."

The three main members of the council remained silent. Not because the choices were bad, but because the choices were some of the hand-picked few they were already considering sending south. Had he been monitoring their communications? Not that there was anything to hide from him, but...

Meanwhile, Randidly simply chose those three because it made sense.

Devan was the first person to successfully complete the mentor system with Donny, and achieved the highest Level of Knight, other than Donny. His squad, which would accompany him on the journey, was currently ranked 16th. Alana obviously knew the path, and would be a good guide of the area. Randidly was impressed by her ability to pull her weight in a fight, even though she hadn't yet received a Class. And Clarissa's magic would be useful, as well as giving her a taste of danger. From what Randidly observed, though she was a bit reckless in battle, she'd remained largely shielded from the consequences due to the squad around her.

Since Randidly couldn't protect Donnyton in a traditional manner, he wanted to improve it more obliquely.

They could take one of the junior squads for manpower, enabling them to handle basically every foe Randidly had seen thus far.

Besides, they were traveling back into a zone covered by the Newbie Level Zone. Any more would be overkill.

"I'm glad to see you agree," Randidly grunted, and left them.

Donny, feeling awkward at being thrust into the situation, sat down and began to eat.

"So," he asked mid-chew, "what were you guys talking about? Wow, this is good!"

CHAPTER SIXTY-TWO

*I*n the predawn light on the morning before the caravan was to depart for the south, Randidly's lips cracked into a smile. He'd just gained a Level in Meditation, and with it, he finally gained enough Skill Levels to finish off the Frontrunner Path. After applying the final PP, he received a notification.

Congratulations! You have completed the "The Frontrunner Path"!

The odds were stacked against your race with the arrival of the System, but you rose above the trials and tribulations to give your people a safe place to stay. Being the first in any accomplishment brings great power, but also places a great weight upon your shoulders. Others are raised, but only because you drag them upwards with your existence as proof of what may be possible. Let this Path give you the tools to share some of this weight. Because beyond this Path, there always awaits another.

You have become Unique in many ways. But that does not shorten your journey.

You have learned the Skill **Blessing of the North (U).**

You have learned the Skill **Blessing of the East (U).**

You have learned the **Skill Blessing of the South (U).**

You have learned the Skill **Blessing of the West (U).**

You have learned the Skill **Inspiration (U).**

The explanations for the first four Skills were useless. Just text about blessing a worthy subordinate and granting them power relating to himself. Randidly read the description of Inspiration with a bit more interest.

Inspiration (U): *The next spell you cast will be Inspired. You will be able to accomplish feats far beyond the limits of your normal Mana pool.* **All Mana will be consumed when you cast an Inspired Skill. You will not regenerate Mana, for any reason, for twenty-four hours after completion of the Inspired Skill. That Skill cannot be used in conjunction with Inspiration for 30 days.**

Randidly rubbed his chin in contemplation. *One big Skill... Hard to say how big. Only, I'll lose access to Mana for a full day? And then I won't be able to Inspire that same Skill for a month...*

Heh. Having this as an ace against any high-Level foes...

Randidly supposed how excited he should be depended on the effectiveness of the Inspiration. Making a mental checklist of the two things he still had to do before the caravan headed south in an hour, he walked outside of his cabin and winced.

Make that three things. He made the promise again to Ellaine under the moonlight to look after Lyra, but Randidly still didn't know how to respond to the suggestion that all of Lyra's behavior... was because she had a crush on him.

"Hey..." Lyra stopped petting a luxuriously stretching Thorn and straightened. She waved and hurried over, too quickly lowering her hand and wrapping it up behind her back with the other one. With the seed of that knowledge planted within him, he could see it. He was no longer quite so oblivious to her obvious nerves, or the way she searched his face for any response as she fidgeted.

Randidly felt frozen. He had no idea how to handle this affection. This girl was only seventeen years old, no matter how mature she looked.

On the other hand, Randidly was twenty. Or he was, if the time in the Dungeon didn't count toward his age. Based on the calendar, it was still two more months until his birthday. Randidly wasn't sure exactly how much time had passed, but he suspected it was enough to make him officially twenty-one. Which didn't make him feel any better about this strange situation.

With Randidly stuck in his own thoughts by the sudden appearance of Lyra, she was the one who broke the silence. "I... just wanted to apologize. For our fight about the Mana thing. I can be... pretty harsh. I don't mean to be. I was just... this was the way I was raised, you know? You either improved or you lost everything. And—"

"No, no, I'm sorry," Randidly interrupted. "I've... I've been way too... something about the Tribulation. About heading south. My friends might be there. I probably... took that out on you."

"Apology accepted?" Lyra smiled.

For a brief second, he understood why Daniel always loved to wax poetic about Lyra's roles as an actress in cult classic sci-fi films. She really did have an unearthly wattage to her smile.

She coughed lightly. "So...?"

"So, what?" a bewildered Randidly asked.

Lyra gave him a pleading glance. "Do you... forgive me?"

"Oh. Yeah." Randidly rubbed the back of his head, feeling even more strange about the situation when her expression brightened. Then he blurted something out without thinking. "Would you like to come south with the caravan? To look for other refugees? Maybe we could... try the Mana lessons again."

Lyra grinned and made a dramatic flourish in pulling a modern plastic exoskeleton rolling suitcase out of her Interspatial Ring. When Randidly blinked in confusion, Lyra blushed a bit. "Ah... actually, I was sorta hoping you would ask me exactly that, so... yeah, I'd love to come with you."

Randidly rubbed his jaw. "Well yeah, it's not a big deal. You're definitely the best in Donnyton at using Mana... and anyways, I was talking with Ellaine the other night and I promised to look after you—"

"Wait." Lyra's beaming smile slowly faded. "You talked with Ellaine? When was that? You went to the other town?"

"No, no. We just... happened to run into each other in the wilderness. It was over by the other village... when I was combing the area for the Tribulation." As Lyra's frown deepened, Randidly became more and more confused. "It was good, though. We had... a really good talk. And she just said I should—"

"Take care of me, I got it," Lyra said coolly. "Like you would a child."

"You are a little—" Randidly paused when Lyra looked at him with burning eyes and licked his lips. "We... with monsters. We have to look after each other, right? So—"

"You know what? I'm not feeling well." Lyra spun around on her heel and her suitcase vanished. "Go on without me. I don't need a babysitter."

Randidly scratched his head when she stalked away from him. *Was she... upset that I'm trying to keep her safe?*

But there were more important things to focus on than Lyra's feelings. In an attempt to distract himself from the confusion of that interaction, Randidly brought up his Path menu. Now that he'd gotten through the Frontrunner, he could choose a new Path.

Watcher *0/??* | *?????* | **Heretic III** *0/???* | **Oathbreaker** *0/25* | **Apprentice Path** *0/50*

His options decreased, but he'd already made a decision. It was time to head down the Apprentice Path. So far, Paths like this had been very generous with their Skill rewards. And more Skills meant faster gathering of PP, which was Randidly's current way of gaining strength.

I'll get a Class someday, but for now, I'll continue to sharpen my Skills. Randidly clenched his fists. *From the Encyclopedia's research, I need to push the Skills I want to determine my Class to the highest Level. I'm doing pretty well with spear Skills and Spearing Roots... now I just need to find my flame based offensive Skill.*

Randidly turned to the final item on his agenda and removed a small seed from his pocket. When he'd come back from his talk with Ellaine, he realized the Skill changed to allow for a second use.

He'd spent the last several days nurturing the thing.

Soul Seed 100% Nurtured. *Strongest Influences*: 1. Fireball | 2. Meditation | 3. Potion Making | 4. Refine | 5. Calculated Blow | 6. Root Manipulation

The influences were a bit... strange. Especially for what was clearly going to become a plant. Let alone Fireball, how could a plant use Meditation, Potion Making, Refine, and Calculated Blow? He simply let the plant observe his training, and so much of his current effort was on discovering potion recipes. Otherwise, after he stopped forcing himself to seek out the Tribulation, he spent most of his time mopping up random creeps in the area with Thorn.

You know what I'm missing for this strange plant? Lyra's Mana Manipulation, Randidly mused. He was still somewhat irritated he hadn't managed to generate the Skill, no matter how often he focused his Willpower on his Mana pool.

Randidly admitted to himself that any further attempts without a Skill to observe Mana were useless. Lyra seemed to think observation was a pointless step. Maybe it was, for her—the strange combination of frustration and inexplicable talent that she was. Randidly figured he needed to see it to get a handle on using it.

Feeling it wasn't enough.

Thinking about Lyra's departure made Randidly oddly morose. He turned and gazed at the bear-sized hole in the fence around his training area. A ghost of a smile flitted across his face. It was *very* impressive she managed that with only Mana. And during the short time he had submerged his head in water, no less. No wonder she'd been insulted when he said he wanted to protect her.

She didn't need his help. At least not against monsters short of a Tribulation.

Randidly heaved out a sigh and turned to the south. His training sessions were over. He'd chosen his new Path and begrudgingly acknowledged his own improvement. He was ready to move on from these strained few weeks and head toward an actual goal he cared about.

Finding Ace and Sydney.

Randidly smiled as he pictured the two of them as he best remembered them, walking ahead of him and arguing with each other. Those were precious memories of his time at Rawlands University. Maybe Sydney was right. Randidly made his decisions whimsically, following the currents of his emotions. But there were also times like that where he made a choice and been both surprised and delighted by what he discovered by following his impulse.

Be safe, guys. Randidly clenched his fists and looked in surprise at his left hand. What he found there made him chuckle. He had completely forgotten he still held the small, strangely nurtured seed. Since it was finished being nurtured, he intended to plant it, but some part of him hesitated. He was about to head south, after all. And Randidly wasn't sure when he would return.

He studied the tiny seed in his hand. It would work out somehow, even if he wasn't around to see it.

As Randidly walked out to the slope between the NCC village and the Classer compound up on the hill, he was surprised to find two small children crawling through the fields, picking weeds. He recognized them too, Nathan and Kiersty. They were twins and the youngest members of Donnyton at eight.

Even seeing them made Randidly's expression somewhat heavy. The System hadn't been kind to children. Although from what Regina said, it was less that they were killed, and more that the parents of these surviving children weren't willing to travel with them, and bunkered up in their homes.

Ultimately foolish. Randidly supposed he could understand the sentiment of wanting to protect those precious to them.

Struck by a sudden notion, Randidly walked over to the children. When they saw him approach, the two dropped several woven grass dolls, as though embarrassed to be caught with them. The girl wiped her nose on her sleeve. Randidly crouched before them.

"I need a favor."

CHAPTER SIXTY-THREE

*T*he group made good time heading south, mostly because everyone other than Randidly sat in the tractor trailer and drove down the deserted road. He roamed through the forest, slaughtering any monsters he came across. The foes he encountered through the area where the Newbie Zone had fallen were relatively strong for a while, possessing Levels in the teens. During that time, Randidly mostly worked on his Fireball and Summon Pestilence, gaining 1 Level in the former and 2 in the latter.

When night fell, the group camped out under the stars. Randidly's newfound peace allowed him to calmly sit with the others, listening to Devan and his squad joke around. In his heart, he was excited to finally be taking a concrete step toward locating Ace and Sydney. It filled him with happiness.

After the third day of travel, they entered the Franksburg Newbie Zone and the common Level of enemies halved. The most intimidating foe Randidly encountered was Level 8. Against these weaker foes, Randidly trained Agony.

It was a vicious, brutal Skill, driving him insane with each and every use. By the same token, he wouldn't have continued to hone the painful Skill if he'd also bore witness to it ripping apart the will of his enemies. He also didn't have that big of a Health pool to draw from. At least against these low-Level enemies, especially in groups, it was more than enough to decimate them.

By the end of three days, they reached the spot on the highway where they would need to turn east to Franksburg. They camped below the curving on-ramp of the branching highway, taking in the crumpled and abandoned cars along the edge of the road.

Randidly gained 1 Level in Roundhouse Kick, 2 in Pollen of the Rafflesia, 1 in Wall of Thorns, 3 in Mapmaker, 1 in Physical Fitness, 3 in Running, 4 in Sprinting, 2 in Pain Resistance, 1 in Spirit of Adversity, 2 in Pathfinding, and an impressive 8 in Agony.

Randidly had a hunch that the pain he went through in using the Skill increased the effectiveness of the Leveling simply by stressing the body. Either way, his growth was an impressive feat.

Randidly poured his PP into the Apprentice Path. At 10 and 20, he received 2 distributable Stat points each, along with a familiar and exciting notification at 25.

Congratulations, you have encountered a "Branching Path"! Choose a Patron from the following list, and complete your apprenticeship.

Randidly scrolled through the list and his eyes widened at the options. There were a lot of unexpected terms on the list.

Patron of Silence. Patron of Frostbite. Patron of Nightmares. Patron of Crystal. Patron of Zephyr.

Honestly, this seemed like another instance where the System gave him no guidance. Being the first one to reach this point came back to bite him. Sighing, Randidly went with his gut. He chose the Patron of Ash. If he really was going to commit to fire as his damage-dealing spells...

The Path you walk has become littered with ash. The sky darkens. The fire stands before you, and you do not blink as you walk toward it. Ash fills your lungs with every breath, but you dare not falter.

Other than the cryptic notification, nothing changed with his body. Randidly shrugged, setting it to the side. He returned to the group, who were gathered around the back of the truck, all thirteen "ambassadors" from Donnyton. They stood when he approached, the squad saluting him, Clarissa, Alana, and Devan simply nodding.

"You should figure out what your plan is when you enter the area, and who your leader is. I will not accompany you to speak with the representatives of Franksburg. I have... other business," Randidly announced.

Although Alana seemed slightly unsettled, she said nothing. The rest nodded calmly, as if this was expected.

"Anything else?" Randidly asked, feeling quite strange. Although he supposed everyone at Donnyton always listened to him, to have them be so deferential to him now was a bit... complicated.

It made him think about how his departure of Donnyton probably gave the other Tribulation license to strike.

"Ah, actually..." Devan spoke up, adjusting his pendant numbering 16, his eyes bright and nervous. "We were wondering… if perhaps you could give us some pointers. On fighting."

Compared to discussing things, the black-haired young man was eagerly willing to engage in a spar with the group. Alana was against joining the rest in coming at Randidly Ghosthound all at once, but at Clarissa's insistence, she relented.

"You'll understand after it starts," Clarissa assured her.

Alana pressed her lips into a thin line. Even though she understood he was more powerful than anyone else in the Newbie Village, how much could they learn just by overwhelming him with numbers?

Still, Alana didn't vocalize her concerns. After watching Randidly get his ribcage ripped open, she'd been curious about him. No matter that the circumstances weren't ideal, she wasn't willing to miss the opportunity to fight him.

In the meantime, Randidly cut down a sapling, whittling it into a good approximation of a spear. He spun the weapon, flicking it back and forth as though he'd borne the weapon his entire life. Compared to his huge spine-spear that Sam made for him, it was a weapon much more appropriate to use in a training spar.

Randidly used Root Manipulation to clear cars out of a twenty-meter circle and stood at the far side, calmly drinking a Mana potion. After restoring himself to prime condition, he added, "I won't use active Skills to start. If you touch me, that will change. Deal?"

Alana's eyes were burning, but Devan nodded seriously. Randidly was slightly worried it would take a while for them to start, but Clarissa was not a shy woman. After her shout, an icicle zipped toward his head.

Grinning, he spun his sapling spear and knocked the projectile harmlessly away, eyeing the rest. They surged forward in neat lines, the front with shields raised, moving to encircle him. As they neared, he stepped forward and delivered a non-Roundhouse-Kick to the one on the far right, throwing him back several meters.

Those with Classes might catch up to him eventually. Right now, Randidly still held a dominant amount of Strength, combined with his plentiful experience fighting over the past several months…

In those opening clashes, Randidly strolled through their midst, lashing out with his sapling. He adjusted his positioning when it was necessary to keep the rest at bay. Another icicle rushed for his head, which he again knocked away. His spear crashed against weapons and shields, keeping the struggling group just off balance enough for him to slip through the cracks.

He lowered himself and rushed forward, putting his significant Agility to use. Clarissa would make this fight annoying if they ever locked him down enough to use her powerful spells.

"Gotcha!" Alana growled, lunging forward, stabbing toward his side with her spear.

Randidly chuckled and spun the sapling to his left hand. He used the butt of the weapon to jab backward, expertly knocking the spearhead harmlessly to the side. He spun his weapon in the same fluid motion and smashed Alana in the shoulder.

As Randidly turned to face forward, he found a Shield Bash rushing toward his head. He swayed his torso, straightening and spinning, avoiding it completely. He twisted around Devan to have a straight shot to Clarissa, who stood with her hands raised above her head, a ball of glowing blue energy held at the ready.

"Frost No—"

Clarissa stuttered to a stop. Upon seeing her, Randidly knew what spell she was casting, and leapt back toward the ten-man squad who were hurrying behind him out of formation, desperate to assist.

Randidly clicked his tongue. *Your stance is always your first priority. If you are going to hold yourself open like this...!*

Randidly had been probing and playful before, but now his sapling spear became the medium of a lesson on preparation. The blows he unleashed were fast and brutal. Three strikes knocked three men to the ground, with a fourth and fifth soon following. At that point, Alana barreled toward him swinging her spear in a powerful sweep.

You came prepared. Good form. Randidly admired Alana's careful footing. His eyes narrowed imperceptibly. Since he had a foe worth facing, it was time to get more serious.

Randidly calmly blocked the sweep. She tried to kick him in the chest. Randidly sidestepped and cut sideways with his spear. Alana scrambled backward, but it was too late. He knocked her legs out from under her and she collapsed in a heap. Before he could deliver a blow, knocking her out, a shout dragged his attention back to Devan.

Grimacing, Randidly rushed forward. Challenging Shout was a bitch of a move. He felt as if he could overpower the compulsion to attack the user with his high Willpower, but there was no harm in going along with it to demonstrate the difference in strength between them.

Randidly thrust, his sapling sliding cleanly through the air toward Devan's shield, having no other choice but to attack directly. The wooden imitation spear and the reinforced iron shield collided with a dull boom, the force large enough to throw out a shock wave. Eyes wide, Devan stumbled backwards, his stance completely overpowered by Randidly's strike.

Randidly's thoughts were dismissive. *You get surprised too easily.*

"Lightning Bolt!" The spell shot out, catching Randidly in the chest.

Karma cackled at his behavior. He gritted his teeth slightly to withstand the weird tremors, and rushed toward Clarissa.

She, at least, approached the problem of restraining him with workman-like efficiency. Ice once more gathered into her raised hands. "Frost Nova!"

Randidly hopped off the ground, using the moment of his earlier dash to carry him the rest of the distance toward her. A wave of cold hit him, creating a layer of frost over his skin, but his strength was more than enough to overpower it.

He landed and casually punched her shoulder. She squawked and fell backward.

He looked around, nodding.

"That should be about it then, right?"

Alana's gaze was clouded and focused on their small campfire.

Devan sat down next to her, offering her a mug of coffee, which she took. The heat started to ease the ache in her fingers that lingered from the earlier fight.

"You've never seen him fight before?"

Alana shook her head slowly. "No. I've seen the monster he killed and brought back, but... I didn't know..."

"Ah, that's right. You were out on patrol the day he fought against the Kill squad," Devan said.

The Kill squad was the nickname for Dozer's personal squad. It could also include Donny, Ptolemy the Healer, and Paolo the Brawler, depending on what they needed. It wasn't ranked, both because it included people from multiple squads, and because Dozer and Donny didn't join the squad competition. Its strength, however, couldn't be denied.

"Who was there?" Alana asked.

"Everyone from the Kill squad participated." Devan's eyes reflected the flickering light of the campfire, his tone bitter.

Alana licked her lips and asked her question, even though Devan's blank expression hinted at the answer. "How... how did they do?"

"Better than us. They started out being brutalized, but Donny was guarding Ptolemy full time. They managed to slowly box the Ghosthound in while getting healed, and the Brawler was able to touch him. After that... he used one of his basic Skills. Phantom Thrust. It was... *impossible* to see. He'd raise his arm and then you'd wake up hours later with a headache. The attack is fast and versatile. Same thing happened to everyone."

They sat in silence for several minutes, Clarissa drifting over and settling down beside them. She leaned forward conspiratorially. "He hasn't told anyone, but Daniel says that based on his talks with Nul, the Ghosthound's Spear Skills should be around 30. Maybe even higher than that."

"Is he..." Alana digested the information for several seconds. Considering the way Skill growth was fickle but definitely slowed as it rose, being Level 30 already was very impressive. Alana hesitated, then said, "Is he ever gonna take a Class? If his Skills are already at Level 30..."

Devan shrugged noncommittally. "Does he need to?"

CHAPTER SIXTY-FOUR

$\mathcal{R}$andidly watched with amusement as the group moved toward Franksburg. He detected the enemy scouts around them and faded away, avoiding their notice. His party would be ambushed, but he wasn't worried.

Alana was a capable leader, and Devan's eyes missed nothing when it came to approaching threats. They would find their way out of it.

Besides, despite Daniel's groanings, they were all provided with Spatial Rings to store their supplies. They would probably be searched, though Randidly didn't think the world had degraded to the point that people would steal dingy rings off of captives. All their hidden supplies would be safe.

For himself, Randidly circled around to the far side of Franksburg, his heart beating wildly when he saw more and more Rawlands University buildings. Some of them were strangely split in half with only part of them remaining, the rooms exposed. It was like a giant sliced them and moved the pieces. One thing was certain, some of those from Rawlands definitely made it here.

Cautiously, he revealed himself and began walking toward the interior of the city, trying to appear lost. There were no people openly in the out portion of the city, but Randidly occasionally picked up movement in the windows of the surrounding buildings. Monsters had been cleared out in this area, although they were thick outside of the city limits. There was nothing that would force him to reveal his true strength. Eventually, a group of people in police motorcycle helmets and full body camo trotted around the corner.

A patrol. Perfect. Randidly thought as he tried to seem hungry and lost.

When they saw him, they froze. The people in the back ran into those in the front. Randidly raised his hands, doing his best to look unthreatening. He supposed he should have changed out of his shirt and pants made of wolverine fur. At least he stored his spine-spear.

Before anything else happened, one of the figures in the group took a step forward and spoke. "Is that... Randidly...? I can't believe you're alive!"

The girl removed her helmet and rushed him, wrapping him in a hug.

Randidly coughed awkwardly. Suddenly, he was teleported back to the certainty he felt in that underground tunnel, the night this all started. He reached up and patted her back. "Uh, yeah, I made it. It's good to see you too, Tessa."

Tessa was Randidly's ex-girlfriend, although it was hard for him to think about her as that presently, primarily due to the time-warping effects of the Dungeon. After all, Randidly had been walking back from breaking up with her the moment the System initialized. To her, it had only been about a month.

A crazy month, but the memory was probably fresh in her mind.

Tessa wasn't a woman who addressed things like that directly. She gladly partook in the excitement of the reunion without acknowledging Randidly's awkward expression. She chatted the entire way back, hanging right next to him. Randidly was curious that none of the other members of the group seemed to care about his presence. In fact, they didn't really seem to care about patrolling at all. There was no real formation, just them wandering around in a large square.

Although it was... slightly strange, Randidly was reassured by her presence. She was an influence from before the System came. She also was proof that Rawlands University had been here, which gave him hope for Sydney and Ace. Plus, she knew them. Likely, she would be a good source of information.

A few times, Randidly opened his mouth to ask about his two friends that he chased to come down here. Only, he couldn't bring himself to say the words.

Tessa had never been comfortable with Randidly's relationship with them. Especially Sydney. He was finding it difficult to bring up the subject. Even though he'd broken up with her and didn't have any lingering feelings, he felt himself falling back into her tempo of conversation.

Tessa noticed his frown and gestured awkwardly at the group. "Oh, this sort of job is just a commission thing. When they have need, the government offers food and people do tasks. It's actually my first time patrolling like this, haha. I don't know if I could actually kill anything, even if a monster attacked me... oh! But don't worry, I'm still pretty strong! I have a Skill

Level of 84, so I'm pretty tough. Most of those are just normal stuff, but all together—"

"Skill Level?" Randidly's focus sharpened. All of his pride at his own accomplishments vanished. *You have a Skill at Level 84!*

"Yeah, like, the total Level of all of your Skills Leveled up, added together. Because that's how many points you have to put into Paths. For people who are lucky enough to get Soulskill, that means quite a lot! So, what's yours, Randidly? Since you've survived in the wild for so long, you must be pretty tough, huh?" Tessa reached over and rubbed his arm affectionately.

Randidly nodded slowly. Oddly, her touch made him want to recoil, but he felt bad about that sudden, harsh rejection. He forced himself to keep still and instead considered her question. It made sense they needed a way to gauge strength without Levels here, because they didn't have access to a Class. He decided a lie would be easiest. He wasn't here to attract attention. The looks he got from the people of Donnyton were bad enough. "I'm a little over 70."

With just two of my Skills, Randidly thought to himself, but let the number sit out there. Not everyone had as many Skills as him, so it wasn't fair to count everything.

"Oh wow! That's pretty high, actually. I guess you'd need to get Skills, to survive. It's been weeks! What have you been eating? And what are you wearing anyway?"

As she spoke, she reached over and began to play with his fur armor. Randidly suppressed the impulse to pull away and tried his best to give reasonable responses. He'd grown crops or found berries. He had also killed some wolverines for meat and roasted them over a fire.

The conversation was starting to wear on Randidly, and apparently, the leader of the patrol too.

He turned around, took off his helmet, and sneered at Randidly. "Don't let her sweet talk you. Skill Level 70 is nothing here. I'm 91, and I'm still stuck patrolling around. Some people are born lucky, and others aren't. Levels don't mean anything in front of fate. If you don't get a rare Skill or a Soulskill—"

"Oh, fuck you, Alex," Tessa said, partially glaring at him, partially glancing nervously at Randidly. "He was alone. It makes sense if he hasn't had an easy time."

Randidly shrugged. It would take a lot more than this to offend him, especially knowing his Intelligence Stat was only 1 lower than the total number of Skill Levels this guy gained. Still, he had to admit that compared to the awe-struck way Donnyton's people looked at him, this was equally as uncomfortable.

In an entirely different way.

The group lapsed into silence. Soon they arrived at a gated area, which Randidly recognized as part of the Rawlands campus. A bored-looking man let them through and handed out small bags to each in turn.

When her turn came to receive a bag, Tessa stepped forward, pulling Randidly. "We, uh, found someone. An outsider."

The man's eyes widened, and he moved over to a little kiosk. "Been awhile since we've seen one of those, figured most everyone outside was dead or holed up somewhere… Here, take this."

The man handed him a bundle of stapled papers. Randidly flicked through it. It contained general information about Skill Levels, monsters in the area, how to find work and food in the city, and more.

Apparently, they'd gotten so many refugees, this had been necessary at one point. Randidly had to admit that Franksburg was a pretty big city, at least for the post-System world. People probably flooded here, rushing to escape the monsters running rampant in the wild. If nothing else, there was safety in numbers.

The man wished him luck and Randidly drifted after Tessa.

He spared her a glance. She had shoulder-length brown hair and glasses, and a face with high cheekbones. What originally attracted Randidly to her was the small frown she perpetually wore. As if every moment was a struggle against the injustice of the world, constantly battling with the same unhappiness Randidly underwent for the longest time. That he didn't belong here.

That frown disappeared when she talked. To him, it was as though she were scared to show that part of herself to anyone else. As the months of their dating passed, and Randidly's awkward attempts at opening up hadn't resulted in her doing the same, his attraction steadily evaporated.

The first impression Randidly had of Franksburg was the people. Whereas Donnyton had become cozily crowded, tucked into a valley, here, there were people everywhere. Filling the streets, hanging out windows, calling and cooking, selling food for tokens that Tessa explained were from the government.

Eventually, after squeezing through the hot crowds in the streets, Tessa stopped in front of a building, her mouth twisting. "This, uh, is where I live. I have a bunch of roommates, but since you probably need a place to stay, you could—"

"Thank you very much," Randidly interrupted, and Tessa's smile widened. And so incredibly fake, to his eyes. Compared to Ellaine, this woman…

The words to ask about Ace and Sydney came to Randidly's lips once more. As previously, they sank back down into him. This time, it was for an entirely different reason. What if he asked and heard the worst?

You're being foolish. Randidly helplessly chided himself.

"But for right now," he continued, looking around, "I haven't seen this many people in... what feels like forever. I kinda just want to explore the city. If it's not too much trouble, how about we meet back here tomorrow morning, and you can show me what living here is like?"

Tessa's face fell slightly, but she maintained her smile. "Yeah, sure. You should be safe inside the city. But my apartment is #576, if you get cold and, uh... need a bed."

After she left with several glances over her shoulder at him, Randidly wandered through the streets. He sought the path of least resistance and moved into areas that were definitely seedier. Several men in trench coats talked quietly on the corners. The rare pedestrians lowered their heads and strode quickly to their destinations. These people didn't even glance at Randidly, which was a relief. He found himself a bench and read through the packet. After reading the entire thing, he rubbed his neck and looked around.

Honestly, it was similar to the way Donnyton operated, just on a much larger scale. There were a lot of large, short-term projects, and every day new jobs would be announced for different times. People would go and work, and receive food or tokens for their efforts.

Randidly was curious about whether the "government" was making any moves to find a gold coin and found a Newbie Village. He assumed they had to be. They should have enough strength to do so after five weeks. It was only a matter of time before this place became a village too. With the booming population, it would gather SP extremely fast. The pamphlet said the population was around fifteen thousand. Randidly had no doubt it'd grown precipitously since the pamphlet was made. He wouldn't be shocked if it was more like fifty thousand.

For now, Randidly wanted to do several things. Meet more people and gather information on Franksburg. And the easiest way to do that... was to blend in and listen.

Or at least, the easiest way for me to do that... Randidly felt somewhat helpless at his own social anxiety.

Randidly stood and walked around, heading for a Job Cryer to find a job for the night.

Karen frowned at her two children, Nathan and Kiersty. They stood guiltily in front of her, their faces smudged with soot.

"Where have you two been? And how did you get so dirty? Did you wander over by the forge again?"

Both children shook their heads, kicking the ground. Karen upped the voltage on her glare.

Kiersty mumbled unintelligibly.

"What was that?" Karen said.

"We were taking care of a special tree for the Ghosthound."

"You were... what?" Karen asked skeptically and snorted. "A special tree, huh? Where is it? Let's see how special it really is."

Karen had been expecting her overly curious twins to take her to an old log half buried in the ashes of a long dead fire. To her surprise, they led her behind the farms, past the area where the domesticated wolverines were raised, and into a small clearing hidden by a low hill that should really just be called a mound.

There, standing in the middle of the clearing, was a tree. Its bark was black and appeared to be covered in soot. It bore no leaves, despite having a trunk and branches, just like a normal tree.

The thing was only about as tall as her chest. It swayed lightly in the breeze. Karen reached out and touched the bark. Her fingers came away covered in soot. The tree began to sway more rapidly, buffeted by the wind.

Karen let out a relieved smile. At least it was just a tree, even if it was a scrawny, weird one.

Karen froze.

There was no wind. There had been no wind this entire time. Karen stumbled backward, afraid this strange tree was some sort of horrible new monster. She almost tripped over her children standing behind her, arms raised, swaying side to side in a strange mimicry of the tree.

"You—" Karen paused and looked from the children to the tree. The children moved left and the tree mirrored them. They moved right and it followed. The kids weren't mirroring the tree. The tree was mirroring *them.*

"What... what are you doing, honey?" Karen gasped.

Nathan turned and said matter-of-factly, "Dancing. The tree likes it when you dance with it."

Karen made a choking sound, unable to decide how to respond.

An hour later, after taking Nathan and Kiersty home, Karen returned to the clearing with Mrs. Hamilton in tow. To Karen's surprise, Mrs. Hamilton insisted they wait a bit before confronting it. The portly boy who ran the Classer compound came down to meet them.

The three of them proceeded to the clearing and stared at the tree for a while.

"So..." Daniel coughed impatiently. "What is this about? I received some new data earlier today that is *quite* fascinating."

"Apparently, the Ghosthound gave two children a seed, and it grew into a dancing tree," Mrs. Hamilton remarked with a bemused expression. "Do you know how to make it...?"

Karen shrugged helplessly. "You just... dance, I guess?"

Daniel snorted and stepped forward. He began to perform the robot.

Mrs. Hamilton chuckled. "You are surprisingly talented, Daniel."

"Oh, shut up, I just—"

They both stopped, shocked. The tree, jerky and slow at first, but then with increasing proficiency, imitated him, replicating the robot. Flakes of soot fell off as its branches twisted and bent with increasing confidence.

"Well, fuck," Mrs. Hamilton said, her eyes wide.

CHAPTER SIXTY-FIVE

*A*lana glared up at the man in front of her, her hands handcuffed behind her back. Although she wasn't quite sure whether she could break out on her own, she was positive Devan and the rest of the squad could. Their Stats were high enough to completely rip through the restraints of the old world.

But they all remained silent, looking to her. Sighing inwardly, she kept a stern face to hide her indecision.

"Let me ask again," the heavy-set blond man asked. He wore a police uniform and regarded them all with suspicion. After being tossed into the cell, he was the only individual who attempted to speak with them. Not that he listened to what they were saying. "Where did you come from? How did you survive out there with the monsters?"

Alana did her best to remain calm. "Like I said, we came from a town to the north. We've already established a Newbie Village, and so we have Classes—"

The man made a disgusted face. "Bah. Don't play dumb with me. You sound like the Freedom Fighters. Guns, where are your guns! The only way to beat back these monsters is with bullets. If you survived, it was due to guns. Did you hide them before you came close, looking to fool me? As if! I'm no fool."

Alana rolled her eyes, and the man leapt forward and slapped her.

It felt like a child's slap to her enhanced body. Still, her eyes narrowed. The flesh of her cheek tingled, and a horrible, vindictive anger rose in her heart.

The man stood, straightening his jacket, and said, "Fine, keep lying. We'll let you starve a bit in your cells, see if you change your tune. If by the end of the week, you still refuse…" The man's smile turned sinister. "Well then, don't blame me for being impolite."

Randidly, to his own amusement, was Sewing. The opportunity was especially ironic, considering everything he'd learned about fashion came from Tessa. There was a big event tomorrow night and they needed quite a few costumes. More costumes than made sense to him. Sam recommended that Randidly learn more basic Skills recently, for PP, but Randidly had been so frustrated these past few weeks with the Tribulation, compacted by the frustrating lessons with Lyra, he hadn't been able to calm himself down enough to try something new.

Strangely, after traveling around and seeing so many people, running into Tessa, feeling close to finding clues about Sydney and Ace… the half-relaxed Randidly finally released his remaining bit of tension. He was moving. He was improving. He didn't need to be so hard on himself. Ellaine had been right.

Randidly sat hunched over in a dimly lit warehouse, stitching clothing together. Occasionally, he glanced around at the vast piles of material, thinking how ecstatic Mrs. Hamilton would be to obtain even a fraction of these. He supposed the pre-System resources available in cities were incomparable to the empty countryside.

Congratulations! Your Skill **Sewing** has grown to **Level 3!**

The act of Sewing was quite soothing. He also activated Root Manipulation, making the small plants in the area dance as a way to spend his Mana while his hands were occupied. It wasn't quite as efficient as he normally would want to be, but Randidly supposed this was something of a break anyway.

He initially asked those he encountered if they knew someone named Sydney or Ace from Rawlands University. Blank stares from his fellow workers were all he received. Shrugging, he focused on the cloth and tried to remember Tessa's long-winded rants on hemming. He also kept his outlook positive. Randidly supposed it wasn't surprising they didn't know anything. There were a lot of people in the city, and only a few dozen people here Sewing. This would take time.

Randidly's eyes narrowed. *And the other reason for my departure… I need to cool my heels and see if this fucking Tribulation finally shows itself. And for that, I need to give it time to act.*

Mostly, he listened to the people around him talking when they would walk around and stretch their sore hands before sitting back down to continue their work.

Congratulations! Your Skill **Sewing** has grown to **Level 4!**

Randidly's movements were becoming more natural, his loops tighter. Compared to Shal's draconian expectations, the managers of this job were kindly grandmothers that worried more about his health than how much work was being done.

"I heard they are leaving tomorrow morning," one woman said. Another sighed in response and shook her head emphatically.

"They *always* say that. The mayor can't work up enough balls to actually do it, and the fire department isn't going to volunteer to do it on their own. That's just the way the world works. Until their money is threatened, they won't move."

Another woman chimed in, "The Freedom Fighters would do it, if they got enough volunteers."

The second woman fixed the first with a long stare. "And do you know what volunteering means? Being a meat shield for the gunners. The mortality rate for which is very, very high. No amount of food is going to make people leap to their deaths. Not when easy work like this is available. Better just let the monsters have the wilderness, that's what I say. Especially when we get to keep a portion of what we make."

The second woman gestured to the piles of finished clothes beside them. Her own pile was rather large. Every other nearby person had about 70% of hers. Except for one.

Randidly's was about double the size.

They glanced at him but ultimately ignored him. The women didn't seem to take his presence seriously. To them, he was just one of those weird shut-in types who would come out at night to work, and return to their room to eat.

Randidly equally ignored their stares, waiting for the talk to continue, intent on his stitching. A notification popped up, and he smiled.

Congratulations! Your Skill **Sewing** has grown to **Level 5!**

Seems like with my higher Agility and Control, I do have some sort of natural advantage when it comes to the movements of Sewing. That thought gave Randidly pause. *Hum. A portion of Leveling comes from doing the action well... so does that mean those with higher Stats have a slight edge on accumulating Skill Levels?*

Time passed, and Randidly's stack of clothes continued to grow. After a while, a portly man and a taller woman walked around, picking people for a special job. About one out of every dozen were chosen. The second woman, and, to Randidly's own surprise, himself, were chosen for the opportunity.

"Those that were picked," the man announced, "follow this woman. The rest of you, come collect your pay."

The woman manager introduced herself as Cassie. She took them back into another portion of the warehouse, where the bolts of fabric appeared flashier and more valuable. She pointed to a few other people already present, who were doing embroidery. "This needlework requires a bit more finesse, but the pay is better. If you're interested, I want you to try learning this stitching method."

Randidly mastered it the quickest, within about fifteen minutes. After an hour of impeccable work using that method, Cassie hovered over his shoulder with a stunned expression. "I... cannot believe you started out as an amateur with this. If I didn't watch you learn, I would think you've been doing this for years."

Congratulations! Your Skill **Sewing** has grown to **Level 7!**

"Thank you," Randidly said. Though he was really thanking her for giving him a more difficult task, which helped boost the speed at which he gained Skill Levels. Each PP mattered.

Randidly noticed the gossiping woman from earlier glance his way with a sneer. With her competitive spirit rising, she began working her needle furiously, attempting to keep up with Randidly's precise movements.

After another hour, they asked if anyone needed a break. A few of the workers gratefully set down their work and stretched their arms. Randidly continued to stitch, heedless, working on an elaborate hoop skirt. The gossipy woman, her eyes bloodshot, looked on helplessly. She bit her tongue and shook her head, returning to the Sewing. She had too much pride to stop.

Congratulations! Your Skill **Sewing** has grown to **Level 8!**

Another hour passed with Randidly humming softly to himself. His hands burned with the activation of new, minute muscles, but he liked the feeling. *Aaah, this is actually quite refreshing. After worrying about Ace, Sydney, and the Tribulation for so many weeks, it's nice to give my mind a break and just work my body.*

Nearby, the competitive woman's chest heaved, her eyes bulging. He wondered if he should offer to take a break, to ease her mind. Before Randidly could do anything, the woman hunched over her own station, never wavering with her needlework.

By this time, Cassie returned and asked them both if they would like to stay on for another four hours, doing a different type of embroidery. She cautioned them that if they started, they would need to finish or they wouldn't get paid. It was a rush job that had to be done immediately.

Congratulations! Your Skill **Sewing** has grown to **Level 9!**

Randidly simply nodded and followed after her. He could already feel he was approaching the limit of his growth in this manner of needlework. Behind him, the gossiping woman collapsed into a coughing fit.

Alana looked curiously at the bound Devan. "You don't want to escape?"

He shrugged. The rest of them seemed similarly relaxed. Even Clarissa had frozen and shattered her handcuffs after the guards locked them in the room, pulling a pallet out of her Spatial Ring to take a nap. Whenever someone was hungry, they removed food from their Interspatial Ring.

"It's not that I don't want to escape. I want to efficiently accomplish our objective. Their leader is paranoid and stressed beyond what he can handle. He's worried about everyone taking his power and thinks guns are his only salvation. I have no doubt that such a desperate, worried man will want a display of power. So, we wait, and try to recruit there," Devan said.

Alana asked in a confused tone, "What do you mean, display of power?"

"He means," one of the squad members interjected, "that the idiot might publicly torture us or some shit, maybe try to execute us. He'll bring a big crowd together to do it. Better to let them do the gathering and cash in on it. We're only here to advertise for Donnyton, yeah? And these fools aren't scary at all compared to a Raid Boss."

Alana blinked at how calmly they were handling the situation. Clarissa rolled over on her pallet, snoring loudly.

"Thank you so much for the work," Cassie said, handing Randidly several food tokens.

He looked at them rather nonplussed. He supposed they were for meals, but it wasn't like he needed it, what with his satchel space full of consumables.

"Uh, thank you, it was… enlightening," Randidly said, meaning it. His Sewing reached 11 by the end of the night due to the various different projects. Cassie was more than willing to teach such a studious pupil more and more complicated needlework, which hastened the rise of his Skill Level.

"No, thank *you*. If you hadn't shown up, I would have probably needed to work alone by myself for the rest of the day to catch up," she said, beaming. Then she had a sudden thought. "Oh, actually, take these too."

She offered two slips of paper. Randidly took them, unsure of what he was holding. "Uh..."

"Don't look so confused," Cassie said with a laugh. "You must have noticed the costumes were for—oh god, you really didn't, haha. It's for the concert tonight! Those are backstage passes. Feel free to come and visit. It's supposed to be a good show."

Cassie waved as he left, and Randidly wandered away, bemused. *A concert, huh... This city really wants to basically ignore the arrival of the System.*

He supposed live music was a fine way to relax. For now, he walked briskly back to a Job Cryer, looking for something to do until the time he had to meet Tessa.

Hopefully, there would be more knowledgeable people at this new job. And additional PP to earn.

CHAPTER SIXTY-SIX

*D*aniel looked over the report, slightly disappointed in his most recent project. It couldn't be considered a total failure, though the result left him as deflated as an old and dirty pool floatie. In the wake of Glendel acquiring such a powerful-sounding Class, he dedicated a lot of resources to Leveling him up and finding a suitable protege to use a mentor stone and gain the same Class.

They'd done it, but the difference in Classes was staggering. The notifications sat before him, frustrating him endlessly.

Congratulations! You have received the Class of **Sovereign of Ghosts!**

You have gained the Skill **Spiritual Communication Level 1.** You have received the Skill **Spiritual Merger Level 1.** You have received the Skill **Spiritual Summoning Level 1.** You have received the Skill **Spiritual Bestowal Level 1.** You have received the Skill **Aura of the Spirit Sovereign Level 1.** You have received the Skill **Soulbind Monster (U).**

You may learn **12 additional Skills to these and those you already possess. Skills may be forgotten to learn new Skills. +6 Health per Level, +20 Mana Per Level, +4 Stamina per Level, +4 Per WP, Wisdom, or Focus per Level (*these points may be distributed between 4*).**

Glendel's Class was truly impressive. He received six Skills, one of them being what the Ghosthound called a unique Skill, along with a 20-point boost to Mana per Level in addition to 4 Stats per Level, although they were distributed to some weird areas.

Meanwhile…

Congratulations! You have received the Class of **Spirit Caller!**

You have gained the Skill **Spiritual Communication Level 1.** You have received the Skill **Spiritual Summoning Level 1.** You have received the Skill **Ghost Claw Level 1.**

You may learn **6 additional Skills to these and those you already possess. Skills may be forgotten to learn new Skills. +8 Health per Level, +10 Mana Per Level, +7 Stamina per Level, +2 Per, Wisdom, or Focus per Level** (*these points may be distributed between 4*).

Nul said they could obtain greater or lesser versions of Classes through the mentor system, but this result was depressingly lesser. To be fair, Glendel's Spirit Sovereign was the highest tier of the Classes they had. Spirit Caller seemed to be an acceptable option. It allowed them to summon and bind lesser ghosts, which were excellent scouts. In addition, it also came with Ghost Claw, an offensive move that summoned an ectoplasmic ghost hand to attack with. It was scary-looking. Even at Level 1, it appeared powerful.

But it was clear that while Glendel obtained something overwhelming, the Spirit Caller was a high-ranking foot soldier at best.

Looks like we won't be able to mass-produce these sorts of Classes then… Daniel rubbed his eyes. Although increasing his Stats meant he could stay awake for longer, that didn't mean he should skip resting too often. The reason he was up now was because the hordes used to come around now, and he was just used to it.

Inwardly, Daniel should be pleased at their progress in Donnyton. If anything, he felt listless. They survived, but more problems kept cropping up. The Tribulation hung over their heads with no change. The village was growing and prospering. Businesses were forming. There were weird dancing trees popping up. It just felt—

Daniel turned to Nul. "What should we be working toward right now?"

Nul remained silent and utterly unmoving without the slightest twitch.

"Will we eventually have more direction?"

This time, Nul acknowledged him. "It is hard to say, but… perhaps."

"When will that happen?"

Again, silence. Daniel studied Nul's reactions for a long time. He only chose not to speak when there was a direct answer he was somehow kept from saying. If the answer was vague, he felt no compunction from droning on and on about a subject. When the answer was too simple…

A lightbulb went on in Daniel's head. He planned on purchasing a second kept Dungeon with the 12k SP they had, but…

"Nul, let's upgrade to a Trainee Village."

Nul's smile stretched wide, his white teeth glittering in the candlelight. "What a wonderful idea."

"Dammit!" the man swore, his chest heaving, dropping his knife and resting his forehead against the cool counter.

Randidly ignored the melodrama and continued to consistently slice carrots and move them into the bin. He gained the weirdly specific Cutting Vegetables Skill, but it was currently only at Level 2. Apparently, cutting carrots was nowhere near as good an experience as Sewing. The other problem with the job was that everyone remained tightlipped in the cramped kitchen, merely furiously chopping carrots.

The sound of which was almost soothing. After briefly inquiring to his nearby cutting mates about Sydney, Ace, and other portions of Rawlands University and receiving no relevant information, Randidly settled into the monotony of the task without much complaint.

Which made him face a rather unfortunate truth. *I'm… flinching away from actually finding them. Now that I'm here and might run into them.*

Tessa reminded him of things he would rather have forgotten. The long talk with Sydney, before Randidly broke up with Tessa. The moments waiting in front of Tessa's door, when he wondered the entire time what sort of face he should make when he eventually had to face Ace, his best friend.

They were the two people he was closest to in the world. But relationships weren't simple things. Randidly preferred as little public interaction as possible, even at the best of times. Randidly pressed his eyes closed. *If I show up, will Sydney just say I chased after her again? Will Ace… understand why I had to say those things to Sydney that night?*

Randidly looked up, glad to be dragged out of his own head by a strange pounding noise. The man next to Randidly growled in agitation and looked up when he noticed Randidly's attention.

He gestured to the carrots in front of him. "I've been putting most of my points into Agility, yanno? But… It's like I hit a wall. Even though my Stat is still going up, I can't get any faster. Just a little more and I bet they would move me up to kitchen duty…"

Randidly stayed silent for a long moment. The rest of the workers in the kitchen kept their eyes on their own table, continuing to cut. Feeling bored, Randidly began to randomize his cut locations, starting in the middle, then hopping to one side, then back, then between them, while simultaneously keeping all of his carrots an even size.

It was disappointingly easy. Randidly showed his teeth at the vegetable. *Stats really start to mean a lot, huh? Compared to the average person, I've already moved closer to being a superhero.*

Knocking another two cut carrots into a bin, he gave the muttering man another glance, realizing he hadn't continued to work.

"What's your Reaction Stat?" Randidly asked, trying to sound casual.

The man didn't move, still mumbling to himself. Around them, the soothing sound of knives hitting cutting boards buried most other ambient noise.

Randidly flicked a carrot at him and it ricocheted off the man's head. He straightened, shocked.

Randidly asked again, "What is your Reaction Stat?"

The man shrugged. "What does it matter? I'm just trying to move quicker."

Randidly sighed. "Reaction improves your nerve endings and increases your sensitivity to tactile feedback. You feel better. More than that, you might not be able to control your speed without Reaction. No matter how good the acceleration is, a car that can't turn in time won't win many races."

The man gaped. Randidly resisted the urge to scratch his cheek.

A small Asian woman to Randidly's left regarded him. Compared to the man, her hands were defter in their movements. "Did you hear that at one of the university lectures?"

Randidly shook his head. "No, just from my own observations."

The woman muttered something and looked away, ignoring Randidly again. Randidly made a mental note to ask Tessa about these lectures and to attend one. Why hadn't the woman mentioned it when he asked earlier? Was the university in question not Rawlands? There might be more people he knew there, if it was actually sponsored by Rawlands. Maybe people who knew Ace and Sydney.

Randidly pictured Ace's face and shivered. The two of them hadn't had a chance to speak. Only hours after Randidly confronted Sydney, the world was irrevocably warped. He reached into his bin and found nothing. "Where do I get more carrots to cut?"

Everyone perked up in shock. The supervisor saw the situation and came over, scratching his head. "I... I guess you can go? If you're finished with your work."

Nodding, Randidly walked out, relieved.

"Wait, you forgot your tokens—" But Randidly was already gone. Shrugging unhappily, the supervisor returned to his spot, wishing he'd thought to ask the guy to come back again tomorrow.

The man who put all of his points into Agility looked at Randidly's neatly cut carrots, his eyes bright. "Reaction, huh..."

A notification popped up in front of Randidly.

Congratulations! Your **Arbor Level 1** is ready to Level up. **Due to its nature, your first choice is set: Give Arbor either *Vanity* or *Sloth*.**

A vein in Randidly's temple throbbed considering the two choices. It was bad enough when he checked the seed he left behind, which he named Arbor, and saw what it grew off of. Suddenly, he felt rather foolish for trusting the raising of the plant to children. Randidly brought up its status screen again.

Arbor (Attention)
Level 1
Survivability: *2*
Physicality: *1*
Magical Aptitude: *3*
Brain Function: *7*
Particularity: *6*
Battle Ability: *1*

The fact that it was based on Attention was a hard thing to stomach. Randidly wasn't sure where he went wrong with this Soul Seed. Perhaps it was the weird Skills that nurtured it, or the abandoning it and leaving it with those kids. This one had an extremely low battle ability.

Randidly swore to himself to not make another Soul Seed, even if he developed more uses of the Skill, until he had time to purposefully, and personally, nurture it.

Randidly raked his fingers through his hair. *And now I have to choose between Vanity and Sloth... What a day.*

With a sigh, Randidly selected Vanity. It was better it liked looking at itself in the mirror than it being unwilling to work in the future. He supposed Vanity wasn't that bad of a flaw, for a plant creature.

Arbor is now **Level 2. Particularity has increased by 2.** Arbor has learned the Skill **Elaborate Dance.**

Randidly closed the notification and the Soul Seed menu before he did something stupid in response to the "Skill" his Soul Seed learned. With a brittle, twitching smile, he arrived outside Tessa's apartment, settling down to wait. He hoped no one gave Arbor any sort of weird attention that would warp its growth.

Looking around at the passing people, he considered asking about Sydney and Ace. It was a different time of day from when he'd arrived previously and the bustle was mellow. The owners of the different stalls didn't quite seem as desperate as they had before. Randidly squeezed his eyes tightly closed.

I'm just throwing myself into dumb tasks to avoid the hard decisions about Ace and Sydney. I need to consider this more directly. But this place... Randidly studied his surroundings. Ten-story buildings rose above him, stretching higher as one headed toward the city center.

In a way, maybe he was lucky he had been teleported directly into the Dungeon that day. That way, he wasn't given the option to try to cling to the pre-System world. There simply weren't any remnants of it in the Dungeon.

Randidly supposed as a practical matter, he could ask one of these people if there was a missing persons board or something. In the end, he decided it was fine to wait for Tessa and ask her. His time alone was nice, being alone and just one of the crowd, without people freezing up in some strange mixture of awe and fear when he passed.

He was anonymous here. No one here looked at him with eyes filled with expectation. All of his capability meant nothing in the city.

The bubble of voices up and down the street was peaceful. For a while, Randidly enjoyed the simple feeling of being treated like a normal guy in a normal town.

CHAPTER SIXTY-SEVEN

essa pulled her ponytail over her shoulder nervously, spinning in front of the mirror. The sleek, matte-black material of her dress swished around her. After biting her lip, she reached behind her back to unzip the dress and toss it like a dozen discarded others beside her bed.

The walls of her room were covered with various cut-outs from magazines and scraps of fabric. Everything seemed textured.

Her room appeared cluttered at the best of times, but now it slid toward the garbage can at a craft store. To the left of her mirror, the black and orange prototype uniform for Missy's, the bar where she worked, hung half finished. A thick black ruff ran from the left shoulder to the right hip, but it still didn't feel quite right to her. She knew in its current state, Missy would eat her suggestion alive and not bother to spit it out. Tessa had only one shot to—

That can wait. Right now, I just need a dress. Tessa decided on a white dress with blooming sunflowers along the top half and regarded her reflection with a frown. She felt... strange. Except the world *was* a strange place now, wasn't it? She didn't follow that thought any deeper. Despite the strangeness, she had nice clothes and the weather was agreeable.

That was enough. And this dress would be fine.

Tessa rubbed Chapstick on her lips. She'd known things were wrong in her relationship with Randidly a long time before he broke up with her, only she wanted to work through it. Or, admittedly, she wanted to continue dating no matter what. It didn't seem like he did. In the wake of that, the System descended on the world, ripping away half of her building and all of her sense of security.

After both the breakup and the world-shaking change, Tessa curled up in her bed and cried herself to sleep, trying to ignore the screams. She felt oddly comforted that other individuals were just as miserable as her. Until she woke up the next morning and saw the bodies.

She realized she shouldn't have been hasty to dismiss the strange notification that appeared in front of her.

Not that Tessa felt too guilty about her ignorance. She had other things on her mind. She blamed Randidly for springing the breakup on her without asking for her opinion. They'd been dating for almost a year and it hit her hard to lose him, even if she had her own dissatisfactions. Not harder than adjusting to the System, but still.

The preceding month blended together in a desperate blur of short-term jobs and sleazy guys like that patroller, Alex. He was always trying to isolate and tempt her with cheap beer and free food. Even Tessa's boss Missy had dropped some comments that if Tessa wasn't willing to expand her responsibilities, her shifts would start to dry up. The world hadn't *quite* descended to lawlessness due to the monster attacks, but more and more people were willing to turn a blind eye to certain behaviors.

And now, just when she was wavering over whether to let it happen, Randidly showed up. If that wasn't fate, she didn't know what was.

Noticing the time, she hurried down the steps. She pulled up the hem of her flowery summer dress so it didn't drag through the dirty hallways. To her surprise, Randidly was already there waiting on a bench, munching on a hardboiled egg, when she walked outside.

"Oh! I'm sorry, did you wait long?" Tessa asked, instantly nervous when she examined his stoic features. His green eyes turned to regard her and a flush of heat ran through her.

Randidly was a good-hearted person at his core, but he did have something of a moody streak. Not that he would do anything about it. Tessa didn't want grumpiness to interrupt their reunion. Today had to be *perfect.*

To Tessa's surprise, Randidly's gaze remained completely even while he considered her. His eyes calmly looked her up and down.

"No, I just got here."

Maybe he's matured a bit? Tessa wondered. That made some sense. She'd heard stories from other refugees who hadn't started inside of Franksburg and were forced to flee from monsters. Some of the stories—

A memory of looking out her dorm room window and seeing an oversized falcon guzzling a professor's intestines flashed to the forefront of her mind. Tessa forcefully suppressed it and focused on Randidly. It was clear he *hadn't* just arrived, but he also didn't seem to mind he had waited.

That was a big change.

Tessa tried not to let her anxiety show. He still had the habit of keeping his face blank while lying, which was slightly relieving. Even so, why did he lie about something so simple? He always lied for the dumbest reasons.

Although this definitely was the same man she dated, he seemed almost completely different.

The change was a hard one to pin down. Everyone else on the street were hurrying around, like each one of them were in some sort of stage of worry or desperate business. And Randidly... there was a weight to his stillness. Something strangely compelling.

Tessa tried to banish those thoughts. "So, uh, I have some food tokens saved up. I can show you around the city..."

She trailed off when Randidly gave her the look and her cheeks flushed. It was the look he always gave her when he already knew what he wanted to do and was about to tell her what they *would* be doing. He still had his unreasonable streak too, then. It was annoying a lot of the time, but there were some other times...

"Actually," he said. "I had a question. What do you know about the university lectures here?"

Sam grunted, turning over the breast plate on the worktable. The metal steamed when it pressed against the wood of the table. Over the last month, he managed to set up something of a forge, enabling them to experiment with shaping metal. The whole ordeal was vastly simplified when, around a week ago, Daniel purchased the Supply shop. They could now purchase bars of smelted iron for relatively cheap.

Sam and Mrs. Hamilton had some pointed questions about the supply chain, but Nul refused to answer. For now, it was enough that it worked.

The prices of the modest supply shop were far cheaper to obtain than the weapons and armor they would become in comparison to the other shops installed by Nul. The only issue left was shaping the metal. He examined the breastplate closer.

Novice's Breastplate Level 2: *An early attempt by a Novice.* **The materials have been poorly utilized. +7 Health**

The bonus would be barely noticeable, though it was better than nothing. He looked to the maker. "An improvement is an improvement. Good work."

The man who ran the smithy, Ceth, chuckled bitterly. "It was several fucking long hours of work too. I need to get some more points into Stamina and I should be able to make things like this pretty regularly. As my Metal Working Skill improves, so should the quality of the armor. I hope to get beyond the snarky descriptions soon. There's even specific Skills for each body piece, so when we figure out a mold for a helmet, it'll go even faster. We're moving in the right direction, Sam. Why the rush?"

Sam's scowl was powerful. Why did so many people in Donnyton now want to start taking things easy? "Don't say something like that. You know it's bad luck to—"

A notification popped up, silencing him.

Congratulations! Your **Newbie Village** has been upgraded to a **Trainee Village.**
The chance of obtaining superior Classes is slightly increased. Raid Bosses spawning in your area have a slight chance of spawning as a Tier II Raid Boss at Level 30. Dungeons in your area will become active more frequently, spewing out waves of monsters. This cannot be prevented.
Due to your Tribulation remaining, the Tribulation has been strengthened. Be careful of your impending Tribulation.

Due to being the first **Trainee Village** on your world, the **Soulskill** of **Your Village Chieftain** has been strengthened. **The Skill Level will be reset, but all of the gains shall be retained.**

Due to being the first **Trainee Village** in your **Zone**, you have become **Earth's Nexus Seed** for this **Zone 32. Some small part of the benefits of the Nexus are open to you. Searching for an appropriate matching Village...**

Match found! Village is the first **Trainee Village** in **Zone** in the world, and third in your batch of Worlds. **Nexus portal has been founded near the center of your Trainee Village. In 7 days, the portal between your, and your sister Village, will be opened.**

Warning! In 21 days, a **Level 35 Raid Boss** will randomly spawn on either yours or their world. **Good luck.**

Sam's glare toward Ceth deepened as though his comment alone caused this change. He snorted and left the smithy, heading toward the village center.

Daniel owed them all an explanation for this. The talk of benefits was nice, but if Sam learned anything in the past month, it was that the "benefits" of the Nexus all came with steep prices.

The Black Tusk Wolf Raid Boss narrowed its eyes at the forking, looping black track made by the denizens of this world. Strange metal boxes littered the periphery, hinting at the prior use of this place. Rather than the details of the world, the Raid Boss was more concerned with the barrier in front of it. "We cannot go through there, although fresh meat is waiting."

The shadowy figure smiled. It reached with unnatural long, humanoid fingers and stroked the barrier. A ripple spread outward. "Normally, yes. But I have recently been empowered. And also... hehehe, that young man, carrying that item, acts as a 'key.'"

The ripples rapidly spread, causing the entire barrier to tremble. The shadowy figure gestured. "Go. Eat to your heart's content."

Hunger and an ever-present fear toward this shadowy humanoid warred in the Raid Bosses' heart. Ultimately, it bared its teeth and forced its way through the barrier. Almost immediately, it felt the energy of the barrier press against it. It began to whine and writhe, and its bones cracked. It had been tricked and would die here.

The Raid Boss *popped* through the barrier. Panting, it twisted around to look for the shadowy figure, but it was gone.

The barrier *had* reasserted itself. Its body was suppressed back down to Level 15. But otherwise, all of its capabilities remained.

The Black Tusk Wolf let its tongue loll out of its mouth. First, it would find weaker monsters to devour. Then it would lay eggs. And soon, it would feast on the flesh of the original inhabitants of this world to its heart's content.

Randidly glanced around at the students listening to the professor's lecture. This was the third lecture they'd sat through. Honestly, most of it was trash. More hurtful than helpful in regards to System knowledge, although not in any permanent way. The first professor recommended gathering as much PP as you could and spend it all at once to increase the effectiveness of the Stat gains.

Which wasn't so bad, but it ignored how useful it was to improve your Stats now, in case you encountered a threat. Plus, Randidly was becoming increasingly certain that Stats increased his ability to earn the first dozen or so Skill Levels. High capability was generally beneficial.

The third professor speculated on the source of the System and whether God was involved. Randidly distracted himself with activating Root Manipulation and Meditation, unwilling to fill his head with such drivel.

Congratulations! Your Skill **Root Manipulation** has grown to **Level 37!**

It was the second professor of the day, a small Greek man, who Randidly found fascinating.

"Why is this happening?" he asked.

The classroom remained silent, and the professor continued. "And I'm not talking about the technical details of why, but the larger scheme. Why has this 'System' been installed on our planet? Why are we pushed toward killing monsters, growing stronger, and gaining Classes? There is no such thing as a free lunch. What are we losing in this process?"

A student raised his hand. "Our humanity? We're becoming desensitized to the value of life."

The professor waved that answer away. "Technically correct, but you are thinking humanity is the center of the universe. It is clearly not. Not when some organization or being has the capability to affect such a broad and fundamental change to our existence. Anyone else?"

"Money?"

"Resources? Precious metals?"

"Control," Randidly spoke softly, but his voice resonated, carrying over the other whispers.

The professor gave him a long look. "Control over what?"

Randidly shrugged. After a pause, the professor continued to talk, moving on to the resemblance between their current situation and role-playing games, and what that could possibly mean about the why.

After lunch, Tessa nervously smoothed her hair. "I... need to go. I have some things. So nice to just... have a normal day, you know? With you. Oh, but! I wanted to ask..."

She squirmed a bit and he simply waited for her to speak. His mind swirled with thoughts as he considered what the second professor suggested, even while he planned to depart Franksburg proper for a bit and do some training.

In the face of his distraction, Tessa said, "There... there's a concert tonight. I have enough tokens to buy us tickets, i-if you want to go. With me."

The mention of a concert pulled him from his thoughts. Randidly waved his hand. "Don't bother."

His ex-girlfriend visibly wilted but affixed a bright smile to her face. "Oh, then I should really—"

"Ah, Tess, that's not what I meant." Randidly scratched his head awkwardly, uncomfortable at how disappointed she became, and how unwilling she was to show her feelings. Even if he wasn't interested in her now, he still held fond memories of their time together. He didn't want to hurt her. "I, uh, was given these. So, what I mean to say is that you don't need to buy tickets."

He produced the backstage passes, and her eyes widened into saucers. Shrugging, he offered them to her.

She trembled as she rubbed the glossy surfaces of those tickets. "Oh wow! No, you keep them. I wouldn't want to lose them at work. How... how did you get these?"

Randidly coughed into his hand. "For... Sewing. I took a job last night, to try and... earn some food tokens."

Tessa's eyes fluttered in her confusion. Her brain hopped back to the prototype uniform she had hanging next to her mirror. It was difficult to imagine Randidly hunched over and pushing a needle through it. "Sewing."

"Yes. Is it really that strange I can sew?"

She burst out laughing. Tessa was willing to bet Randidly would prick his fingers and glower at the cloth in front of him. But she didn't want to insult him, even if the image was adorable. "No! It's strange that Sewing can ·get expensive passes! I didn't even know they existed. Where did you—well, never mind. I need to get to work. Meet outside my building at 8 p.m.?"

Randidly nodded, holding his gaze on her as she left, smiling at him over her shoulder.

Bemused at her timid attempts at flirting, he walked toward the nearby Job Cryer and swiftly obtained a job on a farm near the edge of the "patrolled" areas. After his shift ended, Randidly intended to wander around a bit.

Randidly proceeded across the city. He was surprised when he arrived on the outskirts to find an apartment building bursting with greenery. Leaves and vines stretched out of every window. This was apparently how Franksburg supported itself. With cutting edge vertical farms. Still, Randidly was relieved to find an activity he recognized.

I wonder if I can earn any Skill Levels through this different Farming method... Randidly examined the plants on his approach. *And... they won't notice if I swipe a few types of their seeds, right?*

CHAPTER SIXTY-EIGHT

*D*aniel raised his hands, helpless, with a smug Nul standing behind him. "I didn't know the Dungeons would start acting up more frequently! Or about Tier II Raid Bosses. How was I supposed to know? Nul wouldn't say—"

"You had a theory, however," Regina Northwind said, folding her arms across her chest. "That something would change if you upgraded the village. And you did it, without consulting any of us."

"I... yes..." Daniel visibly deflated in front of the older woman.

"At any rate," Donny said slowly, glancing around. Decklan was out handling a recently spawned Tier I Raid Boss, but the rest of the important people were here. Dozer and Annie, who had become head of the Archers. Regina and Sam's furious forms, him standing behind her in support with a glare at Daniel that could have reduced him to a slug. Mrs. Hamilton and her assistant. Ptolemy and Glendel, the representatives of their mages, and finally, Donny himself. "Glendel, it's only been a half hour, but what can you tell me about the situation?"

Glendel closed his eyes and reached out to the whispers of his bound ghosts. Although the Spirit Caller could only manage a finite amount, it did not seem Glendel had such restrictions on how many ghosts he employed. The spirits floated everywhere, giving them an almost perfect picture of what was happening in the surrounding twenty kilometers.

After a few seconds, his eyes opened. "Looks like incidences of Raid Bosses has tripled. There is already one directly between us and Turtletown, and it looks like another is forming to the south, along the route between us and Franksburg. Both Dungeons have exploded like volcanos. The monsters are numerous, but they're still only Level 12 or 13. We'll take the monster horde from one. It looks like most of the others will be soaked up by Turtle-town's machine gun nests and their infinite bullets."

Donny rubbed his head. Even in the best case, it likely wouldn't be for a few days more before the caravan to Franksburg attempted to return with more population. "I move that Dozer and Annie head south to remove the Raid Boss from the route to Franksburg. Immediately. Not that Randidly needs our help, but if the monsters ambush them when they don't expect it…"

"Seconded," said Mrs. Hamilton.

"Thirded and passed," said Daniel with a sigh.

Dozer nodded and stood, Annie sighing theatrically and following him.

"Monster incidence is also up, generally, both in Level a little, and quantity by a lot," Glendel added. "We'll need to either send out more patrols or keep NCCs in a smaller vicinity around Donnyton."

Donny rubbed his forehead.

Regina frowned. "Samuel, what is our perimeter like?"

"Well, Ms. Northwind," Sam said with an uncharacteristic bow. "Likely quite secure. The monsters have never had much success coming up over the mountains to our west, and we have small teams on rotation to watch out for such incursions. The Arena built up in the valley to the north converted very well into a small fort. Really, the only weakness is the road that leads directly through the mountains to the NCC village, and the new farming expansion down to the south, following the shape of the valley. We've built as well as we could to defend against the forest to the east, but that will likely need to be bulked up, considering these… developments."

"Thank you for your analysis, Samuel," Regina said with a smile.

"Anytime." His smile widened.

Mrs. Hamilton rolled her eyes and spoke to get the meeting back on track. "I move for Sam's men and four Numeral squads to move to the southern Farming expansion and clear the area of trees as quickly as possible. Extending the area double as far as the expansion was planned, and clearing the ground for a fort."

"Seconded," Ptolemy said after a small hesitation.

The rest of the table was silent. Every few days, they held short bouts between the squads. If the lower won, they switched places. If they lost, they stayed the same. Excluding irregularities, they now had thirty full time squads on call. They lived, ate, trained, and fought together. Four single-digit squads were forty of their best men, with an average Level of just short of 20.

"I'm not sure if I get a vote, but I think it should happen, and immediately. That's the direction of the Dungeon that will hit us hardest. They'll arrive in a little over six hours." Glendel gave Regina a nervous look.

After a sigh, she smiled. "Yes, you get a vote. And that makes three. The resolution passes. I move we send the Heavy Mages to set up a roadblock a little ahead of the NCC village, in case something nasty comes down that direction."

Their Mage squads were divided into two teams, the Heavy Squad, which was effectively leaderless without Clarissa. They focused on pure power, breaking through heavy lines of monsters with fire, thunder, ice, or poison.

Meanwhile, the Light team was led by Ptolemy, although Glendel featured heavily in their operations. They were primarily their Healers, support Spell Casters, and Hexers. The communication abilities afforded to them by Glendel and the other Spirit Caller were a nice bonus.

"Seconded."

"Seconded."

Donny and Mrs. Hamilton spoke at the same time, then looked at each other surprised, before smiling.

"Resolution passes," Regina said with a flourish.

Glendel closed his eyes, sending a ghost to whisper in the ear of the second in command of the heavy unit. Communication was another natural advantage of Glendel's new Class.

"You know…" Mrs. Hamilton said suddenly. "Perhaps ask Decklan his condition; if he seems fine after finishing his current job, point him in the direction of the other Raid Boss. You know how much he likes to kill the Boss-type monsters. Stealing growth rates is why he gets out of bed in the morning."

"Agreed," Regina said, turning with a smile to a shivering Daniel. "And now, perhaps you should explain to us all the new options we have as a Trainee Village. After all, spending large amounts of SP should be a *group* decision. Doesn't everyone agree?"

"Seconded…" Daniel said weakly.

Randidly finished digging his hole, wiped the sweat off his brow, and moved onto the new spot and started anew. The idea of this job was to dig a defensive ditch around the entirety of Franksburg. An intimidating notion. The process was simple enough, though Randidly wasn't sure how effective it would ultimately be at stopping monsters.

One person, in this case Randidly, dug holes to a predetermined depth at predetermined points. Another person would follow and clear out all the dirt between those two holes, working on getting it all down to that predetermined depth. A third followed later to make it even. Another crew would come in and reinforce it, either as a defensive trench or fill it with stakes.

Randidly raised his hand to his eyes and looked behind him. He preferred the role of the lead digger since it let him work alone. His second man was nowhere in sight, long left behind by Randidly's ridiculous speed.

It was a rather fruitful activity too. Randidly had gotten to Level 3 in Manual Labor, and Level 5 in Digging. Even Physical Fitness rose by 1 Level during the four-hour digging stint. It wasn't as fast as fighting with his life on the line, but it was certainly a welcome amount of Skill Level gain after the weeks following his fight against Ep-Tal.

To Randidly's pleasure, these Skill Levels were enough to finish his Apprentice Path.

Congratulations! You have completed the **"The Apprentice Path, Applicant of Ash"!**
You have walked a Path fraught with danger and ash, and climbed to the summit of the volcano. You peer inside and see a face in the lava, with closed eyes. And as you watch, they slowly open and observe you in return...

Be ready, traveler, for you stand to be tested before the Patron of Ash.

Commencing Teleportation in 10...
9...

Randidly's eyes narrowed. This was something he'd never encountered before. Did everyone who made it to the Apprentice Path get tested like this? He supposed it was possible. And of course, Randidly was the first to earn enough Stats to unlock the Apprentice Path and gather enough PP to finish it. Probably by a fair amount of time, with his advantage from the Dungeon.

If he'd been warned, it would be easy to prepare for in advance. He would've also gained a better idea of how to pass such a test if he had someone to explain it. In a self-mocking manner, Randidly looked down at his dirt-covered furs.

Hopefully, the Patron of Ash wasn't a stickler for cleanliness. Randidly ultimately felt he didn't really need to worry about that.

1...

The world around him blurred. He was suddenly standing on a huge slab of black stone suspended over a volcano. The surrounding land surged with lava. Large waves of cooling rock and liquid metal were the only landmarks in the distance.

Before him, high above the slab of rock, hovered a face of stone, its eyes white hot and dripping, and open maw cherry red and grinning.

"You..." It spoke slowly, almost surprised. "None have chosen me as a

Patron in a long, long time. Apparently, my standards are... too high. Many have failed my tests."

Its words rumbled through Randidly's chest, even as the face gurgled and spat up a blob of lava. "You are Level... you have no Level. That is... unexpected. Thus, your opponents will be... Level 25. Survive for ten minutes and you may experience my blessing."

The platform rumbled and began to descend toward the bubbling and swirling heat below. Randidly might be strong, but surviving exposure to actual lava was still a little bit ridiculous.

Note to self, Randidly thought. *Continue with the "hit yourself with Fireball" training...*

Around two feet above the lava, the platform stopped. A bubble of molten heat grew and popped, spewing liquid rock across the edge of the platform. Randidly grimaced in the face of the swirling heat. Though the whole of the area was relatively large, the very heat near the off-spray was almost unbearable. Randidly wondered if Fire Resistance also covered Heat Resistance.

A glowing form reached out of the murky depths below and gripped the platform, slowly pulling itself up. A Level 25 Lava Golem. Randidly removed his new Bone Spear from his inventory, spinning it lightly. The massive weapon shook the air with its passage. He would need to be fast with his strikes, because he didn't want to risk his spear melting.

A noise from behind made him turn. Four more Lava Golems clawed their way out of the lake of molten rock on the other sides, turning to face him with burning eyes.

Let's just use the length to keep them away... Randidly thought with a sour expression. His heartbeat quickened. He didn't need anyone to tell him what would happen if he failed this test.

CHAPTER SIXTY-NINE

*R*andidly grinned with the manic thrill of danger and activated Haste, dashing toward the Lava Golem in front of him. He used a normal stab to attack, wanting to see how strong it was in relation to his ability. To his surprise, the tip of the bone spear ripped into the golem rather easily. It was the immediate reforming lava around the wound that was troublesome. It lurched forward.

Frowning, Randidly backed off a bit. If he couldn't expect to use raw force, he needed to be smart. Just like he'd been by controlling the sphinx's movements. Golems were made of a substance, and usually had cores that animated them. On this golem, his right chest cavity glowed with heat. He looked toward the others.

Left eye, left knee, pelvis, right hand. In each of the molten golems, some areas were obviously brighter than the rest of the body.

Shrugging, he turned back to the first. Could it really be this easy? He slashed with his spear again, ripping into the golem's chest where the molten metal was more yellow than red. He felt it that time. His spear struck something else other than malleable molten rock and liquid metal.

The entire body of the golem shuddered, but then it continued on, incensed.

Randidly grimaced. The hairs on his arms were burning. The heat was really something. So much so that he was losing more Health per second than he regenerated. But...

Randidly twisted the spear and pulled, using it like a shovel and separated the core from the rest of its body.

The form in front of him collapsed, and the small, golden ball rolled across the ground, sizzling. Randidly crushed it with the butt of his spear.

Congratulations! Your Skill **Spirit of Adversity** has grown to **Level 28!**

Randidly turned to the rest of the lumbering golems. Three more had crawled out of the lava to join the growing horde on the platform. Their mushy faces were twisted into silent howls of fury. He shook his head sorrowfully.

Do you really think numbers will be enough? Randidly growled and spun his weapon. *I am Randidly Ghosthound. And I will not be dying here.*

While the adults of Donnyton ran around working, preparing for the influx of monsters to the area, the children gathered in a certain clearing. There wasn't an overly populous group of children in the village, but enough that talk of installing a schoolhouse had begun to circulate, a conversation that filled them all with dread.

Playing and earning Skill Levels was way more fun than schoolwork.

Luckily or unluckily, there always seemed to be another, more pressing project. The schoolhouse, to their delight, had not yet been constructed. Nathan and Kiersty were the youngest at eight. The rest were between ten and sixteen, not yet allowed to engage in any of the combat exercises or to obtain a Class. In a rare show of unanimity, the leaders of Donnyton agreed that no one under seventeen could obtain a Class from their village, although they were free to stay here.

Most of the older kids thought this rule was dumb, especially when Sir Donny was barely older than them. The rumor was that he received special dispensation from the Ghosthound, who the children talked of in reverent voices.

They secretly hoped they would run into the Ghosthound too, and impress him enough that he would order they receive a special secret Class.

For that very same reason, they found themselves standing in this certain clearing, at that moment. Because against all odds, the Ghosthound spoke to Nathan and Kiersty and told them to protect and nurture a special seed. They stood around that seed, which had grown into a charcoal grey sapling.

As they watched, a small smoking bud formed on the highest branch.

Slowly, infinitely slowly, the bud twisted, wiggled, and writhed.

Then, it fell still.

The bud parted and a single, burning leaf stretched outward and tasted the air.

"Praise the Dancing Tree!" Kiersty said, rubbing her hands on the sooty trunk and drawing lines on her face.

The rest of the kids looked at her with strange glances. Even Nathan gave her an odd look. Kiersty just smiled, focused on the notification that appeared in front of her.

Congratulations! You have been offered the Soulskill **Priestess of Arbor.** Would you like to accept? **Yes/No**

Kiersty eagerly clicked **Yes**. The flimsy leaf wavered and fell, as if blown off by a wind, and drifted toward her. Reflexively, she raised her hand and caught it. The fire burned, but she didn't mind. Instead, she felt something else. Pulses, coming from the tree.

She knew what to do. She needed to get more people here to worship Arbor.

Her brother Nathan looked at her with a doubtful expression.

Congratulations! Your Skill **Fighting Proficiency** has grown to **Level 36!**

Randidly moved quickly among the growing number of Lava Golems, expertly smashing their cores and moving on to the next foe before enough could cluster around him to melt his skin. Every drop of sweat he shed immediately evaporated. The golems were strong and basically invincible aside from their vulnerable cores. But they weren't that difficult to deal with.

That is, until they surrounded you and raised the temperature 150 degrees around their bodies.

Randidly hurried around at first, ripping them to pieces. That seemed to displease the large face. It began sending larger waves of Lava Golems climbing up onto the platform at once.

It was a number still within manageable limits, but it made Randidly sweat, literally.

He controlled himself and continued to fight while seeming to struggle against the amount. In addition to being smart in the individual foes, he had to keep in mind the broader battlefield to impress this giant face. Only when he seemed about to fail would the face remain passive, glaring at him.

Shal taught him the importance of thinking broadly and using his current strength to prepare a path for the future.

Congratulations! Your Skill **Haste** has grown to **Level 25!**

The time slowly ticked down. Randidly gradually allowed more and more Lava Golems onto the platform, trying not to think about the constantly climbing temperature around him.

Five minutes…

Four minutes...

Congratulations! Your Skill **Pain Resistance** has grown to **Level 17!**

Every now and then, there would spawn a larger golem, still Level 25, though with clearly better Stats compared to the others. Its movements were quicker, its limbs more dexterous. Randidly kept his mouth shut and systematically fought, knocking out cores and crushing them.

Three minutes...

Two minutes...

Three minutes...

Randidly gaped. The time... *increased*?

Narrowing his eyes, Randidly spared the face above him a furtive glance. It remained stoic and frowning. That wasn't a fluke. He said nothing, continuing on in his plight.

More and more flooded upwards, filling the stone slab. Randidly upped his speed to match, relying more and more heavily on Haste and Empower to keep himself from being overwhelmed.

Two minutes...

Three minutes...

Congratulations! Your Skill **Empower** has grown to **Level 28!**

A sinking feeling grew in Randidly's chest. A very familiar one. That whispering fear he did his best to bury in his heart returned. He remembered the long nights in the Safe Room and the vicious nightmares that assailed him. He remembered the horrible pain and darkness that almost devoured him against the sphinx, before Thorn had grown within his foe's body.

If the Patron of Ash didn't want him to pass the test, was there anything he could do? Could he report the issue to some higher power... or would he just die here?

Two minutes...

Three minutes...

Congratulations! Your Skill **Spear Phantom's Footwork** has grown to
Level 34!

Though it was suffocating, this feeling was familiar to Randidly.

The current him bared his teeth and fought. If he could not see the way forward, he would stop peering ahead and just look down at his feet.

One step at a time... As long as I keep advancing.

A huge, eight-meter-tall golem pulled itself from the lava, bellowing its fury. Randidly allowed himself a tight smile. It seemed the big guy was starting to grow impatient. *Well, fine, if you wanted to be serious, you should have just said so. Time for me to drop pretenses as well.*

Randidly had thus far been using the bone spear as a weapon to deftly scoop out cores. Now he lengthened his grip, bringing the full eight feet of Spine-Spear to bear. He swept it expertly back and forth, smashing the golem cores with accurate blows to clear out some space.

Congratulations! Your Skill **Spirit of Adversity** has grown to **Level 29!**

Hissing, the large Lava Golem rushed forward. Randidly raised the spear directly over his head. With all his strength, he brought it smashing downwards, splitting the Lava Golem in half and revealing a vulnerable golem core. Small hunks of molten rock landed on his skin and burned through the outer layer. Randidly couldn't afford to slow down. Lightning fast, a Phantom Thrust flashed forward, crushing the core to powder. The golem collapsed. To his annoyance, some lava splashed on his bare feet.

Fuck that hurts! Randidly winced and tried to imagine his toes didn't feel like they were melting off in that very moment. He stamped his feet to get the melted rock off of him. The rapidly cooling stone simply grafted onto him and would not budge.

Congratulations! Your Skill **Fire Resistance** has grown to **Level 10!**

The lava below the platform began to bubble and several more eight-meter golems heaved themselves upward. More disturbingly, an even larger, scaled creature moved, visibly shifting the lava as it swam closer.

Randidly pointed his spear at the giant face. "The ten minutes is up. Give me your blessing."

All the golems stilled. The face's mouth moved soundlessly as its eyes narrowed.

"Ahem, the time counter—"

"Has been reset and you know it. Honor the deal."

If the giant face refused...

Randidly tried to hide his trembling. His Stamina needed some time to recover and his Health was below halfway. He still had most of his Mana, but he doubted either Fireballs or Spearing Roots would be useful here. If he survived this, he was definitely warning everyone away from the Apprentice Path. Whatever rewards he received were not worth this torture.

Randidly still had a hunch. From the way Nul behaved, although he had free will with how he did things, there were certain things he couldn't do. And certain things he *had* to do. Perhaps the big face would be willing to quibble with a small amount of time. Since Randidly survived to almost double the length of the original test...

"Ah, right you are. You have succeeded. Now stand still and await my blessing."

A golden sigil appeared in front of the face's forehead and slowly began to drift downwards. In the meantime, the golems around Randidly started moving again, surging closer. The platform beneath him began to sink into the lava.

"Fuck this." Randidly ran toward the edge of the slab. Right as he was at the edge, he activated Haste, Empower, Mana Strengthening, and produced a Spearing Roots beneath him, launching himself an extra three meters, and leaping toward the steaming stone wall of the volcano.

The weird thing about Spearing Roots and Entangling Roots before it was there didn't need to be actual roots for it to work. There just needed to be soil or stone. Even though the roots instantly withered and caught fire, they still came into being, giving Randidly a foothold not on molten rock.

Burning through his Mana, he raced up the inside of the volcano, moving so fast, the giant face couldn't react. He leapt up and out, dashing across the rim before throwing himself at the giant face.

On his approach, Randidly's lips had twisted into a wild grin. The face was made of stone too. It took him all of three seconds to climb out of the volcano, dash across, leap, and rush up the face, leaving a trail of ash in his wake.

It was only three seconds later, when the face realized what was happening and his expression darkened with a frown, that Randidly leapt again, catching hold of the golden sigil within his hand. He instantly flickered out of existence and teleported out of the strange and deadly volcano world.

The face remained still for a long time as the golems disintegrated and fell back into lava. The stone slab fell deeper too.

The floating stone face's expression was unreadable. Then slowly, it smiled.

"Heh," it chuckled, and sank back into the volcano, looking forward to the next time that individual would return to its realm. Next time, it would be ready.

CHAPTER SEVENTY

$\mathcal{R}$andidly reappeared back in his freshly dug hole, smoking slightly at the edges. His nose wrinkled. Some of his hair might still be on fire, and molten rock clung painfully to his toes. Notifications popped up in front of him, but he was distracted by a voice.

"Oh! There you are, Randidly! Thank god. I honestly feel better to find you were taking a break. I thought you were a machine there for a minute."

Cesar, the man who was supposed to follow Randidly and connect his holes together, grinned down at him. He was a tall, well-muscled man with golden skin and blond hair. From the alacrity with which he got to digging, Randidly knew he had a high Stamina. It was just nothing compared to Randidly.

Although maybe it's just a difference of Regeneration... Randidly's slightly distracted mind offered.

"Honestly," Cesar continued. "I've put all my points into Endurance, to raise my Stamina, but it raises so slowly. Makes me feel like it isn't even worth it."

Grunting, Randidly raised himself out of the hole, holding his shovel. "Try investing in Vitality instead. It will increase your Regeneration, which will give you more staying power. Because right now, when you run out of Stamina, it takes a long time to regenerate, right? Then you can dig for longer, which will increase your Skill Level, lowering the Stamina consumption even further."

Leaving Cesar to his thoughts, Randidly moved forward to the next spot and dug. And again. And again. And again. Gradually, the burns on his body began to heal.

Within the hour, he once more left Cesar far behind, giving him the time to pause and examine the notifications he earned by escaping with the Blessing of the Patron of Ash.

Congratulations! You have obtained the **Blessing of the Patron of Ash! Its energy swirls through your body, slowly assimilating into you. Remaining Assimilation time:** *10,000 minutes.* You have gained the Skill **Incinerating Bolt Level 1.**

Incinerating Bolt: *Shoot a highly concentrated, high temperature, bolt of lava, possessing a high degree of piercing power.* **Heat and size increase with Intelligence, Focus, and Skill Level. Range and Accuracy increase with Wisdom, Control, and Skill Level.**

Congratulations! For surviving the first test of the **Patron of Ash,** you have gained **5 Levels** in **Fire Resistance.**

Your Path leads you deeper into the flames, and your Patron will not force you to proceed without protection. These will be added on to any Levels you already have in the Skill. If you do not already possess it, this Skill does not count against the Skill total for your Class. You do obtain PP for these Levels, as if you gained them normally.

Congratulations! You have completed the **"Apprentice Path"!**

You have come under the scrutiny of a greater power and emerged alive through the crucible. But the Path is long, and stretches ever onward. +50 to Health, Mana, and Stamina. +2 to all Stats.

The Path "Initiate of Ash I *0/75"* **is available to you!**

Randidly checked around him, and seeing no one, walked a little way out into the field he was digging across, until he reached a deserted road lined with empty houses. Strange dog-sized ant things skittered forward. One paused and chirped. A dozen others rushed out of the houses and surrounded him.

Thankfully, the test subjects here are quite obliging. Since Franksburg is all defensive, they haven't learned to fear humans. Randidly raised his arm and activated Incinerating Bolt.

A burning bar of lava ripped from Randidly's palm, catching the first ant in its thorax, punching a hole right through. The bolt continued through the limbs of four ants completely, burning sizzling holes through them before finally cooling so much that it simply smashed the face of the fifth.

Randidly raised his eyebrows. It was like firing a fist-sized incendiary round that melted flesh as quickly as it encountered it.

Randidly's expression fell, sensing his Mana pool.

At the cost of 100 Mana a pop, it seems. Oof, that's steep.

He fired several more, testing the Skill and dispatching the rest of the ants. They were content to charge him until they were all dead and twitching. He went back to his holes, checking what Skill Levels he missed during his time in the Ashen Realm and with this little test run of his new Skill.

He earned 1 Level in Mana Strengthening, 3 in Sweep, 1 in Phantom Thrust, somehow 5 additional in Fire Resistance, on top of the free 5 Level bonus, and finally, 2 in Incinerating Bolt.

The Mana cost was debilitative. And when he Leveled it, it would be, without a doubt, his most powerful single target spell. Finally, he obtained the sort of Skill he'd been searching for. For that alone, the trip to that dangerous Patron's world was worth it. The stupid sphinx would have been a lot more agreeable with a flaming hole in its throat.

He arrived back at the hole and picked up his shovel. According to his mental math, ten thousand minutes was just under seven days. He wouldn't really know what he received as a reward until a week had passed.

At least the bonuses from the Apprentice Path were noticeable. The 50 Health, Mana, and Stamina especially. It took a lot of Stat points to gather that much of any of those Attributes, let alone all of them at once.

The last decision he needed to make was what his next Path would be.

Watcher *0/??* | **?????** | **Heretic III** *0/???* | **Oathbreaker** *0/25* | **Fireball I** *0/50* | **Initiate of Ash I** *0/75*

He immediately discarded the Initiate of Ash, shuddering in his remembrance of the sensation of his toes burning. He had a sneaking suspicion that following that Path would lead to more encounters with the Patron of Ash, something Randidly was not keen on at the moment, regardless of the possible rewards.

Besides, he finally reached Level 30 in the Fireball Skill and unlocked a Path for it. Hoping for more Skills than he had gained from the Apprentice Path, he poured his leftover points into the Fireball I Path. He had 13 points, and received +2 Focus and +5 Mana after putting 10 PP into it. He supposed that was a normal return, but he was still slightly disappointed. He pulled up his Stats in an effort to cheer himself up.

Randidly was pleased to see his Skills had shifted their arrangement to be easier to follow.

Randidly Ghosthound
Class: ---

Level: N/A
Health(/R per hour): 390/424 [+2] (197 [+3])
Mana(/R per hour): 132/644 (80.75)
Stam(/R per min): 401/504 (72 [+1])
Vit: 58 [+1]
End: 39
Str: 48 [+12]
Agi: 66 [+12]
Perception: 33
Reaction: 52
Resistance: 16
Willpower: 70
Intelligence: 92
Wisdom: 46
Control: 75
Focus: 35
Equipment: *Spine Spear of Ep-Tal Lvl 30: (Agi +2, Str +10) | Necklace of the Shadow Cat Lvl 20 (R): (Vitality +1, Strength +2, Agility +7)*
Skills
Soulskill: *Spear of Rot Mastery Lvl 352*

Basic
Passive: *Running Lvl 23 | Physical Fitness Lvl 32 | Spirit of Adversity Lvl 29 | Dagger Mastery Lvl 13 | Spear Mastery Lvl 47 | Fighting Proficiency Lvl 36 | Mental Strength Lvl 14 | Edge of Decay (Un) Lvl 14*

Active: *Sneak Lvl 32 | Dodge Lvl 33 | First Aid Lvl 14 | Block Lvl 29 | Calculated Blow Lvl 19*

Resistances: *Acid Resistance Lvl 23 | Poison Resistance Lvl 16 | Pain Resistance Lvl 17 | Curse Resistance Lvl 3 | Fire Resistance Lvl 20*

Utility: *Farming Lvl 23 | Plant Breeding Lvl 9 | Potion Making Lvl 25 | Analyze Lvl 24 | Refine Lvl 6 | Pathfinding Lvl 18 | Mapmaking Lvl 7 | Sewing Lvl 11 | Cutting Vegetables Lvl 2 | Manual Labor Lvl 3 | Digging Lvl 5*

Stamina
Attack Skills: *Heavy Blow Lvl 26 | Sprinting Lvl 19 | Phantom*

Thrust Lvl 45 | Phantom Onslaught Lvl 11 | Sweep Lvl 21 | Round-house Kick Lvl 16

Boosts: *Iron Skin Lvl 27 | Spear Phantom's Footwork Lvl 35 | Eyes of the Spear Phantom Lvl 23 | Phantom Half-Step Lvl 12 | Haste Lvl 25 | Spear Deflect Lvl 12 | Empower Lvl 28*

Mana
Attack Skills: *Mana Bolt Lvl 30 | Spearing Roots Lvl 16 | Arcane Orb Lvl 23 | Magic Missile Lvl 6 | Healing Palm Lvl 8 | Fireball Lvl 30 | Pollen of the Rafflesia (R) Lvl 9 | Summon Pestilence Lvl 20 | Agony (Un) Lvl 9 | Incinerating Bolt Lvl 3*

Boosts: *Meditation Lvl 33 | Mana Shield Lvl 25 | Root Manipulation Lvl 37 | Mana Strengthening Lvl 15 | Wall of Thorns Lvl 5*

Unique: *Inspiration (U) | Blessing of the North (U) | Blessing of the South (U) | Blessing of the East (U) | Blessing of the West (U)*

Although he was beginning to collect some useless Skills at the bottom of his Utility column, Randidly was overall pleased. With an hour or two to burn before he would meet Tessa and go to this concert, Randidly continued digging.

As long as I keep improving... Randidly pressed his lips together. *I won't be a burden any longer. At least in Franksburg, I definitely won't expose these people to danger they aren't ready for... And that feeling...*

Is oddly freeing.

Sam collapsed in his bed, exhausted. Although you could improve your Stats a lot, you couldn't escape eventual exhaustion. Shifting around with a groan, Sam looked at his Stats Screen.

Samuel Hoss
Class: ---
Level: N/A
Health(/R per hour): 227/227 (92)
Mana(/R per hour): 70/82 (17)
Stam(/R per min): 6/140 (46)
Vit: 26
End: 27
Str: 25

Agi: 22
Perception: 28
Reaction: 21
Resistance: 9
Willpower: 14
Intelligence: 13
Wisdom: 16
Control: 30
Focus: 13

Skills: *Drive Lvl 4 | Running Lvl 11 | Physical Fitness Lvl 22 | Woodworking Lvl 14 | Woodcutting Lvl 37 | Animal Skinning Lvl 22 | Hunting Lvl 17 | Construction Lvl 28 | Manual Labor Lvl 9 | Cooking Lvl 9 | Crafting Lvl 29 | Harvesting Lvl 17 | Repair Lvl 19 | Sewing Lvl 16 | Tailoring Lvl 15 | Armor Making Lvl 23 | Axe Mastery Lvl 26 | Chop Lvl 15 | Heavy Blow Lvl 18 | Iron Skin Lvl 17 | Herculean Strength Lvl 14 | Dodge Lvl 17 | Mana Bolt Lvl 9 | Wide Swing Lvl 15 | Eagle Eye Lvl 5 | Heightened Perception Lvl 7 | Bone Shaping Lvl 19 | Smithing Lvl 4 | Haste Lvl 6*

He kept his point distribution through his Stats rather even, focusing on Control so he could craft and forge more effectively, and then survivability. Especially with the upgrade to a Trainee Village, danger was a constant presence in this new world. All in all, Sam felt like he had some of the best stats among the NCCs, if not the best.

Although even at the best of times, it was hard to tell how capable Lyra and Annie were. And they were his only real competition at this point. Most of the other men working under him were also Classless, but they were slowly folding, taking Classes after the success of the first NCC to switch. Daniel's guidelines for obtaining a useful Class were a powerful draw.

Although they weren't impressively powerful, the Classes they obtained were still in the upper tiers of Classes, which was incredibly tempting for the crafters. Especially now that they were hard pressed on every side.

The increased spawn rate of Raid Bosses and the more frequent monster hordes from Dungeons had quickly annihilated the spirit of careless ease that wormed its way through Donnyton in the past few weeks. Back were the frantic battles and the grim-faced Classers marching toward their next fight.

And today, the first big Dungeon Horde arrived. The combat against monsters had been heavy at all fronts. Everyone was tired and sore after a long day of stopping the flood of beasts. Despite that, casualties were kept in the single digits. Based on what Glendel could gather with his ghosts, this looked to be a daily thing. There was already a plan, backed by Decklan and Dozer, that Decklan's unit would stay on constant Raid Boss watch, hunting and killing them before they could establish themselves and cause trouble. Meanwhile, Dozer pushed for his unit to be sent into the nearby Dungeon, which was the main source of the problems.

Thus far, they managed to hem and haw away from that, just to keep the village safe. But if sending a team bought them time, it might be necessary.

Not that they decided to stay away from Dungeons without Randidly, necessarily. They had a kept Dungeon at Level 16, and another kept Dungeon at Level 5, which seemed fine. Just, without his presence as a buffer, the council was unwilling to send one of their best men into unforeseen danger. They wouldn't know what sort of enemies or location they would encounter until it was too late.

Not that Randidly would be much help with that, considering how he was barred from Dungeons without a Class. Merely having his presence brought them a measure of security. While he headed south, Donnyton was on its own.

Ptolemy was starting to balk at remaining passive, and would likely give their plan the third it needed to pass.

"Damn, we need to rehaul this whole council system," Sam muttered to himself, sitting up. He heard a familiar shuffling and crept to the window of his cabin.

Sure enough, Lyra danced outside, petals of glowing Mana swirling around her. Every night she would do this. Every night since she had seen Randidly casually shooting bolts of Mana out of his hands.

Sam's heavy expression softened as he watched her. Whereas Randidly was eminently practical, Lyra appreciated the beauty of Mana. She sought to learn the nature of it. In exchange, she was blessed with abilities the rest of them couldn't even begin to imitate.

As the gloom gathered from the sinking sun, the air around her would fill with new and different shapes, increasingly detailed and complicated. Waves and patterns of Mana spun out from her every gesture. Birds and snowflakes, wolves and blooming flowers all manifested and transformed through an unending cycle. For Sam, watching her mastery of Mana was a small moment of escape from the pressing dangers of their current world.

Lyra swayed among her shaped Mana with a grace that made Sam chuckle. Mostly due to how desperately Randidly avoided addressing the girl's feelings for him.

Randidly was a strange one. Which was why, Sam supposed, of all the people she met, before and after the System arrived, Lyra was so fixated on solely him. Recently, it was clear he had said something to her before journeying south that clouded her expression.

Sam only knew a little bit about Lyra before the System in terms of personality. What he heard from other people in the business, she wasn't a good person. Or rather, she was a figure that lost herself in her job and was almost... hollow, outside of that. She was professional and perfectly played her roles, but off camera, she became cold and quiet, preferring to return to her own lodging rather than spend time with the other cast members.

Currently, among those blue-white shapes, her wistful expression was so soft, Sam didn't dare make a sound, lest he startle her in this moment of vulnerability.

Sam watched the dance for a long time before heading to bed, begrudgingly preparing for tomorrow.

Lyra and Randidly's problems were their own. He didn't plan on getting involved. Not unless the fate of Donnyton was somehow at stake.

CHAPTER SEVENTY-ONE

*T*essa knew she was going to be late for the time she agreed with Randidly, but it was only partially on purpose. She told him a slightly later time so she could stop by a friend's place and borrow some makeup and jewelry. Not that it was anything close to a date. She wanted him to look at her and think she had her life together in Franksburg.

Even if every day felt like human vultures feasted on her entrails.

She hadn't accounted for the absolute swarms of people rushing around, setting up into a place by one of the many viewing screens the city was erecting. At its own expense no less, for free viewing of the much-advertised concert.

The concert was relatively expensive in terms of obtaining actual tickets. Tessa herself had been straining for the past two weeks, working double shifts every day just to be able to afford one. Buying two would have effectively put her down to zero resources, meaning she would have to work before she could eat.

For Randidly, she would have gladly done so.

Maybe not because of what they had once been... but because of what they could *become.* She had been teetering on a decision and there he was, as if to save Tessa from herself.

Either way, Randidly casually obtained two tickets, and backstage passes at that, leaving her shocked. With the money she saved, she'd gone shopping, acquiring a cute white sundress covered in blooming pink lilies. She was very conscious of the lack of accessories, hence the extra stop.

She was panting and panicking when she arrived. Randidly didn't seem worried, or even rushed. Nor did he acknowledge the fact that she was late. He just appeared focused, his eyes following the hundreds of people surging around, talking and shouting with each other as they headed toward the concert.

"Are you ready—" Tessa froze, looking him up and down.

For some strange reason, he was covered in dirt and smelled like he'd been marching through a fire. She thought it strange he was wearing furs around the city, but supposed that was just a part of living outside the boundary. But now, with the furs crispy and matted, she couldn't help but wrinkle her nose. And he still wasn't wearing shoes.

"You…" Tessa struggled to find words to explain what was wrong. The image of him sewing to obtain these passes became even more absurd. Sensing her gaze, Randidly looked down at himself and chuckled.

"I didn't even realize. Yeah, this probably isn't good apparel for a concert." He scratched his head in the way he did when he was feeling awkward. "I… really need a bath, don't I?"

Tessa was flummoxed, and hesitantly said, "There are bath houses that you can clean up at. But obtaining new clothes at this hour…"

"I… have other clothes. But they're just a bit more—"

"Oh, that's perfect then," Tessa bubbled. She didn't want him to feel bad if his other clothes were ripped and bloodstained. "The bathhouses do cost some tokens, but I can—"

Randidly held out a hand filled with a dozen tokens, an amount that would take Tessa almost a week to earn. "Is this enough?"

Her mouth hung open. "Yeah… f-follow me, I guess."

Breathing heavily, Decklan stood over the cooling corpse of the Tier I Raid Boss. This one had been a centaur creature that used a bow with deadly accuracy. In a frontal confrontation, he was probably extremely hard to deal with. He and his minions fled while shooting arrows at their pursuers.

For Decklan's squad, who specialized in assassinations and quick attacks, the Raid boss had been blasted and sliced up so many ways, it died with its face locked in a confused expression. It barely understood what happened to it. While the rest of his crew cut through the few enemies that spawned from the Raid Boss before they arrived, Decklan reveled in his stats, boosted by his recent position as Raid Boss Hunter.

Decklan Hyde
Class: Killer
Level: 25
Health(/R per hour): 198/319 (98.5)
Mana(/R per hour): 22/90 (19)
Stam(/R per min): 53/205 (33)

Vit: 25
End: 29
Str: 31
Agi: 73
Perception: 33
Reaction: 39
Resistance: 22
Willpower: 19
Intelligence: 15
Wisdom: 14
Control: 23
Focus: 9

Skills: *Sneak Lvl 29 | Slash Lvl 27 | Dagger Mastery Lvl 25 | Backstab Lvl 30 | Feint Lvl 17 | Dual Wielding Mastery Lvl 24 | Sidestep Lvl 28 | Decapitate Lvl 23 | Shadow Strike Lvl 14 | Obscuring Mist Lvl 8 | Sneak Attack Lvl 19 | Tracking Lvl 11 | Foraging Lvl 9*

Luckily, his recent Killer bonuses had gone to Vit and End, boosting his survivability and allowing him to focus his Stat gains on Agility, Perception, and Reaction.

Unfortunately, he only had two more non-Class Skill slots remaining due to his Class limitations. Overall, he was pleased with his kit. Obscuring Mist was his one Mana usage Skill, summoning just a little bit of cover for him to approach. Then, he chained Backstab, Shadow Strike, and Sneak Attack together to rapidly rip through the Raid Boss's Health.

His two direct subordinates, Tera and Ivan, walked up to him, Ivan licking blood off his knife. Ivan was Decklan's direct disciple, using a mentor stone to earn the Killer Class. Meanwhile, Tera obtained the strange Class of Juggler, which made her a magic-based speed Class.

She was his...

Decklan frowned and cast his mind about for the current word. She was his...

"What is it?" Ivan asked lazily. "Another Raid Boss spawn?"

"We shouldn't go after it. We need to refill most of our potions. And our Healer is exhausted," Tera said, sparing Ivan a glance. He snorted, as though these concerns were beneath him. The two had settled into an adversarial role, but both respected the other's strength too much to take it too seriously.

"No, we're heading back. The full council is being called. We're finally heading after a Dungeon." Decklan looked up at the sky. "Obviously, they had a hard time defending against the horde without us. It was apparently worse than anticipated."

Clouds brewed overhead with low rumblings coming from the north.

They'd been lucky in terms of weather so far. There had been some scattered rain storms, but nothing serious.

This one...

Thunder rumbled and a flash of purple lightning tore from the clouds.

This one wasn't natural.

"Alright, boys, we're going home," Decklan called and started jogging.

The rest of his team, tiredly joking and carrying various parts of their quarry's body back to the base for Sam, followed behind their loping leaders.

When Tessa and the cleaned Randidly arrived at the street in front of the stadium, the line was around the block, and a sea of people jostled to get closer to the gates. Large banners flew from the surrounding buildings advertising "RAINA!" in huge pink bubble letters. Meanwhile, a dozen men with assault rifles guarded the entrance, glaring at the rambunctious concert goers whenever they got too rowdy. The whole situation was almost surreal to Randidly.

The state of Franksburg was bewildering. Similarities to a dictatorship in the post-System world were all too obvious. The constant threat of force hung over everyone, even if they were hiding behind city walls.

For his part, Randidly did his best to enjoy the ambiance and gather more information about Franksburg. The crowd around them pulsed as they sidled their way past the general admission. Some brave individuals ran up against Randidly and rebounded, their difference in Stats showing, even though Randidly didn't exert any strength. More and more the people clamored forward, forcing him to extend his arms to keep Tessa from being crushed by the press of bodies.

She looked at him gratefully. His sharp Perception didn't miss the way Tessa eyed the form-fitting clothes he wore. Randidly couldn't help but wince. The outfit was made by Sam from the fur of the shadow cats. Even though everything was tight, the material was light and cool. Tessa leaned backwards into him, the length of her body leaving no room between them. For a moment, Randidly's thoughts shifted in a lustful direction. He hastily slammed those urges down.

Right now, I don't need another distraction.

So much had happened, changing him in far too many ways to imagine ever being intimate with Tessa ever again. Even if she was quite cute.

Besides, Ellaine and her voice. That dress in the moonlight...

Her lips against his cheek...

Randidly shook himself again. *We just had a talk. Yes, I think she's beautiful, but... that's it. She was just... thankful for my assistance.*

Luckily, a nearby commotion distracted him from this train of thought.

"Make way! Make way! Freedom Fighters, coming through!" a male voice boomed through the surrounding area, stilling some of the energy in the crowd.

Randidly recognized the voice, although it took him a couple of seconds to remember why. The speaker was that pessimistic man on the patrol, who talked about how there were two types of people. And that Randidly was one of the lesser ones, insisting it was useless to struggle against your role. Persistent in that all that mattered was obtaining the right sort of Skill.

Or something depressing and whiny. Randidly thought, recalling why he hadn't bothered to memorize his name, if nothing else. Honestly, he had a hard time recalling the man's exact complaint.

The whiny man shoved his way forward through concert-goers, followed by several athletic men and women in leather clothes. Pistols and a weird saber-style weapon hung at all their waists. At the center of the convoy stood an extremely tall man, almost two meters tall, with fiery orange hair. His arms were long and lanky, and at his side hung two of those sabers.

As he passed, the patrol man noticed Randidly and Tessa, but his eyes went straight to her, narrowing when he saw the way she was pressed up against Randidly. Something ugly curled across the man's face and he began leading his group toward them.

"Tessa! What a coincidence. Did you manage to grab tickets to the concert?" As the man spoke, he reached out for Tessa's shoulder.

Randidly knocked his hand to the side. Despite the fact that they were broken up, the part of Randidly that dated Tessa for several months did *not like* the look in his eyes. The man turned to glare at Randidly.

"Alex—" Tessa started to say as she stepped away from Randidly, but the man's face was already red.

"You fuck, are you trying to say you're better than the Freedom Fighters!" He jabbed his pointer finger at them. "While you're sleeping safe at home, while your government is too scared to move, *we* are the ones risking our lives on the front lines! You have some fucking nerve to think you are too good to show us respect!"

Randidly gave him a sidelong glance. The crowd quieted around them, drawing back away from the confrontation. Although he hated to actually deal with this worthless person, Tessa was here, and it wasn't like he would take this fool's abuse to avoid attention. That protective instinct drove Randidly to speak.

"Weren't you saying how struggling was worthless for us, just yesterday? You sure changed your tune fast. Now on the front lines? Very admirable. And since you are at the front... I'd guess your position isn't very senior?"

"You...!" Alex clenched his fists, eyes flashing. One of the bigger guys from the small group stepped forward, laughing.

He put his hand on Alex's shoulder and stared Randidly down with an intensity that at least said he fought against monsters. Compared to the Classers of Donnyton, he was nothing special.

"C'mon, newbie, don't be so tense. Hey man, I just think that's Alex's girl. She needs to come with us and everything is forgiven. Otherwise…"

The man smiled grimly, the threat hanging in the air. The crowd around them began to mutter, but otherwise, all eyes remained on the ground.

Randidly chuckled. *Be empowered by the things that I'm able to do…* "Do you think if you say things nicely, that changes them? You want to take an unwilling woman with you. That's kidnapping."

The man's eyes darkened despite his easy smile. "Haha, kidnapping? Now, now, now, don't throw around words like that. If it was a *kidnapping*, would all of these honorable people, the ones heading to a fucking concert during the biggest catastrophe the Earth has ever known, really stand by and just watch it happen?"

The crowd crept further back. The group of Freedom Fighters, aside from the tall orange-haired man at the center, glared, their hands shifting to their sabers. Over by the doors to the stadium, the guards with assault rifles seemed profoundly uninterested in the naked threat. If anything, they were glad the crowd quieted down.

Because at the moment, not a single person in the massive crowd spoke.

"Yea," Randidly said simply. "But what they do doesn't matter. Because I'm here."

Tessa was sobbing quietly, hiding her face with her hands. "I'm so sorry… I'm sorry…"

Alex leered at the two of them. "So, you think you can stand against the Freedom Fighters?"

Randidly didn't bother to answer. He turned to stare at the other man who stepped up to speak for Alex. His body remained relaxed. A confrontation like this… was not enough to move his pulse.

"Now, he's just a newbie," the man drawled as he patted Alex again on the shoulder. "But he's still a Freedom Fighter and afforded certain… protections. And one of those protections is against civvies like you stealing his woman while he's away, ready to sacrifice himself in battle on the front lines. And—"

Randidly's lips slowly pulled back to reveal his teeth and he flexed his hands. A few Roundhouse Kicks would end this farce. Another voice cut through the drawling Freedom Fighter before Randidly could strike.

"Stand down."

Randidly regarded the central figure of the Freedom Fighter group, the tall man with orange hair. He hadn't spoken the entire time, choosing now to intercede, his tone brooking no dissension.

The orange-haired man grinned and added, "The concert is about to start.

I'm not gonna miss Raina because we were fucking around with some girl. Move."

Unwilling, but ordered by their superior, the Freedom Fighters sheathed their sabers and pressed forward through the crowd. Alex hung back for a bit, eyes bulging, and hissed at Randidly, "You're lucky this time. Don't you ever fucking let me catch you again, asshole, or else."

Randidly, still bemused, shook his head, and moved to follow the group. The hole they made in the crowd was convenient.

"Randidly! What are you doing? They won't do anything now, but after the concert—We should go and hide…" Tessa's voice wavered.

Randidly yawned. His soft shadow cat suit tickled his skin pleasantly.

"No worries. I'm sure it will be fine. Besides, would you really waste these backstage passes?"

Tessa didn't move, torn. Randidly casually walked forward, pushing his way through people. She was forced to sigh and hurry after him.

.

CHAPTER SEVENTY-TWO

*T*he people at the gate were shocked when they saw the backstage passes, and directed them around the side of the stadium to another, quieter entrance. Randidly cursed inwardly as they moved back through the cramped crowd, wishing someone had bothered to tell him beforehand. He could have completely avoided getting stuck as the center of attention.

When they reached the back entrance, a man with a clipboard took their passes and checked them off of his list.

"Oh, so you're Cassie's guests," the man said, his face warming immediately. He looked them up and down, his eyes lingering on Randidly's suit a bit too long for comfort. After a few seconds of scrutiny, he extended his hand to Tessa. "And you must be the gifted seamstress that sewed the costumes. Did you do this man's outfit as well? Beautiful, absolutely beautiful. If you ever have some spare time, please consider making a gown for my daughter. I'll pay you handsomely."

Tessa gave the man a blank stare. Randidly politely disengaged the conversation and moved into the stadium, dragging a dazed Tessa after him.

"How... how did you say you got these?" she whispered.

Randidly frowned. "Sewing, I told you."

"Sewing *gowns*?" Tessa asked incredulously. She looked Randidly from top to bottom, as though expecting to find physical proof of the capability.

Randidly's frown deepened, but he didn't reply. He couldn't decide whether he should laugh or be embarrassed that apparently he could be a professional seamstress.

Daniel peered through the newly available options for the village, excited even after the exacting interview he just sat through with Regina.

Most of the new items available for purchase with SP were higher tiered versions of the shops they already owned. Weapons, Armor, Miscellaneous, Accessories, among others.

There were however, some notable, and expensive, exceptions.

One was the purchase of Gold Nexus coins, which could be used to found another Newbie Village. Although this didn't seem a practical way to handle things, it would allow them some way of making outposts, should the need arise.

In addition, Nul informed Daniel the golden Nexus coins had two other uses. They could be consumed by individuals with Classes to allow them to have another, extra Skill, above the normal Skill cap. This could be used as many times as they wanted, but at 5k SP, it was too expensive to be feasible for general use. Even concentrating a few on one person was bound to have a low level of return.

After all, they would need to first position themselves to learn a useful Skill, and then take several weeks to Level it up to where it could impact battle.

The second use was in bribing a random monster to act as your companion. In the case of rare monsters, you needed to be a higher Level and have beaten it until it neared death. Only then would it serve the user for the rest of its life, and it would continue to Level.

This option was mostly attractive due to the currently unused Ride Skill Donny and his knight mentees had. If they could gather a cavalry squad...

Aside from the coins, Daniel now had the option to purchase what he could only guess were higher-leveled buildings. Production-focused buildings, pre-made smithies and workshops, which Sam was already interested in. Watchtowers. A shop for rare crafting materials. A very expensive cathedral. Something referred to as a Nexus Array.

And, most intriguing to Daniel, was the Adventurer's Guild. The rest of the council were less impressed. They insisted on first purchasing several Watchtowers to help with the immediate threat of monsters, and a Smithy in order to advance the weapon and armor crafting past the basic stages.

Almost unwillingly, they agreed the Adventurer's Guild could be the next building. Eyes sparkling, Daniel looked at the 8k SP option, and to him, it meant one thing.

Quests. Real world quests.

After thinking about it for a long time, he was sure it could only be for acquiring quests. Or bounties. Or... something else game related.

Always the downer, Mrs. Hamilton suggested it might be possible that it allowed more individuals into their world, like the strange portal that sprang up and would open in several days. Daniel didn't think it was that likely. At this tier of village, their strange and confusing bond with another Trainee Village would probably be their only contact with other forces in the Nexus. Nul assured him it was definitely a special bond.

Still, even that contact posed interesting questions.

Daniel was very much looking forward to that portal opening. Perhaps they could finally discover some answers about why Earth so suddenly changed.

After a long walk down a deserted hallway, Randidly and Tessa emerged into a large, cluttered space full of people with glassy eyes, drinking straight from liquor bottles. The room was filled with low chairs and open coolers. At the far side was a small opening in the curtains, from which flashing lights and noises echoed.

"Oh my god! Raina is on already!" Tessa hurried forward, barely seeing the bodies sprawled around on the furniture, grasping and laughing drunkenly in the dimly lit room. Her eyes were only for the music.

A bouncer blocked her crazed charge before she could rush onto the stage, and pointed her to a side door, which would lead her to the general admission area. Heedless of Randidly, she rushed out, leaving him frowning and alone.

Being abandoned wasn't the reason his instincts were tingling. There was something strange—

His eyes narrowed. It was the same, albeit more subtle and slight, feeling he had gotten around the Village Chieftain of Turtletown. An insidious influence was present in the concert venue. While the other had been a harsh order, this was a gentle cajoling.

Have fun, be happy. Be free, live, enjoy yourself, everything is fine…

Randidly identified Raina's voice as the source. This had to be why such a large town could continue simply based on inertia. This voice could periodically wipe away their concerns, luring them toward staying.

This town was home to a siren. This was the sort of power that was valuable in the ruins of "civilized" society.

Randidly gave the bouncer a short glance. Although he seemed to be maintaining his cool much better than Tessa, he too was grinning stupidly and bobbing his head to the music. Sighing, Randidly sat in one of the many empty chairs and began to Meditate. Once he identified the influence, it was rather easy to resist it. Doing so did take a lot of the enjoyment out of the concert. Instead, he focused on understanding the way it affected him and the other people backstage.

Besides, compared to Ellaine's voice, this Raina isn't that special, Randidly thought.

Congratulations! Your Skill **Meditation** has grown to **Level 34!**

Congratulations! Your Skill **Meditation** has grown to **Level 35!**

Congratulations! Your Skill **Meditation** has grown to **Level 36!**

An hour and a half later, when the concert came to what sounded like a stunning conclusion, Randidly opened his eyes, inwardly torn.

This singer, Raina, possessed a dangerous power. Even though he knew what it was, and his Willpower was undoubtedly significantly higher than hers, he felt a slight, unnatural lift in his mood after the prolonged exposure. Randidly wondered how specific the messages she sent with her songs could be.

At the same time, the positive, uplifting portion of the song definitely contained side effects. Randidly gained 3 Levels in Meditation while he sat through the concert. It was similar to the strange golden potion that came from the origin banana in that way. If Raina's music truly had an effect like that, if harvested—

Randidly blinked. He'd been so focused on trying to learn Mana manipulation recently, he completely neglected to improve his Potion Making Skills. Finding the uses beyond a short-term boost for that golden serum might be the new perspective he needed to make a breakthrough.

Now was obviously a poor time to realize that. Later, though, if he could find the right equipment here to process potions...

The people around Randidly were still dozing and languid after the prolonged exposure to the singer's Skills. Even the bouncer slumped in his seat by the stage. Only the tech people remained lucid, hurrying around with noise-canceling headphones over their ears. As Randidly watched, several sweat-soaked people removed their earpieces and walked off stage, talking excitedly to one another. A few of the backup dancers were in gleaming one-pieces Randidly had helped to finish.

Last of those to leave the stage was a slim, buxom figure with blonde hair streaked with pink. Her body curved gracefully, almost impossibly proportioned. What drew Randidly's eye was her face. It was striking for sure, with large eyes and a mouth that seemed in constant motion. Although she would never be called unattractive, Randidly felt she would also never be called beautiful. She, overall, was perhaps only pretty.

Across the dark room, they made eye contact. She smiled reflexively, a tired smile of victory and a job well done. Randidly resisted the urge to smile back, looking at her contemplatively. *This... this is Raina. In all her glory.*

A pessimistic part of himself couldn't help but wonder how many steps away Raina was from becoming like the mad King of Turtletown.

Congratulations! Your Skill **Mental Strength** has grown to **Level 15!**

The immediate Level made Randidly chuckle. It meant Raina's Skills were more powerful than he thought, and not just related to her voice. He slightly expected it after being unable to find any trace of Donnyton's Tribulation. Raina was one more piece of evidence that the System provided power in many forms. He wouldn't slack off in his training. He also wouldn't forget that even Shal got stuck in a Dungeon because he didn't have the right sort of Resistance Skill.

Their gaze parted and she continued following her other performers. Randidly felt the direct beam of positivity she shot toward him fade when her smile evaporated. After she passed by, Randidly wandered over to the door to look for Tessa.

A few seconds after Raina reached the other side of the room, a cloud of confusion came over her and she turned back, searching, scanning across the position that Randidly just vacated. Almost unwillingly, after several long seconds of fruitless searching, she turned to face a man in a suit who emerged from another back room.

From the shadows by the far door, Randidly observed the situation.

The man brought along a gaggle of other people, who Randidly recognized. The Freedom Fighters. Most of them had dumb, glazed expressions. Especially Alex, who seemed to drool from his close proximity to Raina. The extremely tall man with orange hair still held a serious expression.

If he was simply wearing headphones to block the noise, that was one thing. If he wasn't...

Randidly grinned wolfishly. Then apparently, there was some strength in Franksburg after all.

Raina and the orange-haired man walked onto the stage and Randidly slipped away, heading out through the passage to the area Tessa had gone.

He found her almost immediately, smiling and leaning against the side of the arena, seemingly at peace with the world. Which, in a way, meant she was completely oblivious to her surroundings in a way Randidly found rather disturbing. She didn't even notice his arrival. It was all too obvious she was lost in the after effects of euphoria Raina provided.

"One more thing! One last surprise for my fans tonight!" Raina said, arms held high.

It was strange. That smile of hers. The entire structure of her face changed, shifting. It was the only thing you wanted to look at in the entire stadium.

Randidly's frown deepened. This woman was incredibly dangerous. Every day, he thought deeply about his decision to forgo killing that foolish king with a similar ability. At the time, the temptation of the Black Nexus Coin had been too much. But now...

Sure, the kept Dungeon he earned with that coin had been an invaluable tool for exposing the freshly raised Classers to danger. Still…

"Tomorrow is finally the day we have been dreaming of!" Raina announced. "Tomorrow, the Freedom Fighters will be wiping out the ant colony. Afterwards, with your help, the Freedom Fighters will establish a Newbie Village and vanquish the monsters!"

The crowd was practically frothing at the mouth, screaming in primal exaltation of her every word. Even Tessa looked up with fanatical eyes. Randidly supposed there would no longer be a shortage of volunteers for the mission.

Knowing that someone like Alex was allowed into the Freedom Fighters, Randidly wondered how many people would die to accomplish this grand task.

CHAPTER SEVENTY-THREE

*S*everal kilometers to the southwest of Franksburg was a massive lake stretched beyond the distance the naked eye could see. It was night, but all was not still. The water teemed with fish monsters and huge freshwater sharks. Along the banks, a ghostly white wolf dragged a massive bear closer to the water.

The eyes of the gilled monsters narrowed, considering this strange behavior. The wolf braced its forelegs against the grainy soil and heaved the bear another half meter, and then another. The gilled monsters gathered beneath the waves. They considered the short distance between the lake and the tree line, perhaps four meters. Could they pounce and eat this foolish wolf before it escaped?

The wolf tossed the upper torso into the shallows of the lake. Blood marred the reflective surface, leaking from the bear to darken the pristine shine. The gilled monsters could no longer remain still. As blood stained the surrounding lake, their eyes reddened. Their leader rose up and considered the open-mouthed wolf as it stared dumbly out along the shore. In the darkness, they saw no sign of teeth.

"It is a toothless wolf!" the leader bellowed, its system roaring with the taste of blood. It wanted more. "Attack, brothers!"

Nearly fifty of the creatures surged out of the shallows. The salamander-esque humanoids were less graceful on land, but they still scurried forward. As they did, the wolf turned.

A thrill of fear ran through the leader as its subordinates rushed onto land. It was not that the wolf did not have teeth. Its teeth were simply black.

Just like the tusks that jutted out from its lower jaws.

The moment the beasts had gone too far to quickly retreat, three hundred white shadows surged out of the nearby tree line. It was a slaughter.

While its pack feasted on the flesh of these weak monsters, the Black Tusk Wolf Raid Boss looked to the northeast.

One of its lieutenants padded up next to it. "Even if we must still avoid the humans, let us hunt the unruly ants! They dare trample on our dignity just because the barrier suppresses our strength?"

The Raid Boss dismissed the lieutenant's words, eyeing its subordinates critically. "Not yet. The humans and the ants currently fight freely. If there is a sudden change in the ants' numbers, would they not notice and investigate? Better to bide our time for now...

"And when we do strike—" the Raid Boss bared its black teeth "—we rip out their throats in a single stroke."

The rain made the night an extremely long one for the Classers of Donnyton. Wave after wave of monsters streamed toward the village. The Mage battalion held the road. The efficacy of their magic was greatly reduced by the damp, resulting in more and more of the reserve squads to be called there and reinforce their position.

Donny held the freshly raised southern defensive line. Weeks of fighting at the front worked great changes in this teenager, accelerating his growth into manhood. His hands felt strong and content gripping the hilt of his sword and the handle of his shield. He continually moved to the front, calling out orders and releasing the empowering glow of Aegis to protect the line.

Meanwhile, Donnyton's scouting teams roved through the forest, ambushing and retreating, thinning out the numbers of approaching enemies as much as they could. It never seemed to be enough. As the night stretched onward, they began to tire. Tiny mistakes turned into fatalities.

And for the entire night, the rain fell. Blood, dirt, and rain mixed into a horrible, sticky, stinking mud.

The healing division worked as fast as they could. With a limited supply of Mana potions, even those were swiftly rationed for emergency situations. Non-fatal or debilitating wounds were wrapped up and not fully healed. Health could regenerate on its own quickly enough, even if structural damage to the body would not recover as fast without the aid of Mana Skills.

"AEGIS!" Donny's voice boomed, and a golden shield appeared in the air above the defenders. For a brief moment, both rain and the tide of monsters were pushed back by that Skill alone. Eventually, the light faded.

It was likely the bloodiest night in Donnyton's history. While Dozer and Decklan and their squads rested in preparation to force their way through and assault the Dungeon, several Tier I Raid Bosses were able to set up shop and multiply, adding to the constant flow of monsters.

In the absence of a large chunk of their fighting power and the Ghosthound, several individuals set themselves apart in terms of bravery and skill on that long, rain-drenched night. Of those heroes, there were two who deftly changed the course of the night: Lyra and Annie.

When the northern fortress, the most heavily fortified and the location of the heaviest fighting, was breached by a rare fire-belching iguana, the defenders paled. The wall cracked and smoldered, increasing the angles their enemies could use to attack. Monsters leapt into the gap, squirming to get into the hole.

From nowhere, Lyra appeared, her typical grey hood pulled over her head.

Dozens of silent birds glided forward, and for the following five minutes, the only thing that made it through the breached wall was a thin misting of blood.

During that time, another squad hurried over after being transferred by Mrs. Hamilton, plugging the gap and stabilizing the defenses in the north.

Meanwhile, Annie stood atop the watchtower on the southern road, firing arrows like a machine gun. Even more impressive than the speed was her accuracy. Each shot signaled a pained yowl of an injured monster or the unnatural silence of a dead one. The production-focused NCCers stationed there began to dread her glare. It meant only one thing. She needed more arrows.

No one thought about complaining. They ignored their cramping muscles and continued to work.

Annie's eyes glittered as she took a rare break from firing and surveyed the surroundings. Corpses of beasts littered the ground, scaring away the second wave from charging forward. Annie smiled to see her attacks could kill so easily. Although her own Stats weren't high, she invested heavily in Strength and Control, giving her arrows quite the punch.

For as long as the night felt, dawn did come. Although the weather cleared, the monsters continued their incessant charge. And the light of day made the combat that much easier. With a heavy expression, Regina received the preliminary report. Eighty dead, and most of them Classers.

Those that survived were changed. The predictable monster hordes of the first week had been stressful, but they were largely related to the number of defenders. As long as the Classers weren't lazing around, they could handle them. Now with the Level Barrier fallen, the power of the monsters was becoming harder to predict.

Only now were they exposed to true strife and the true horror of war. But with struggle came power. Not just actual Level, but their Skill Levels sharply rose across the board. They could now invest in their Paths, which further increased their strength. Those Squads that had been resting in the middle of Donnyton picked up their weapons and prepared to fulfill their role.

Grim-faced, they watched Dozer's and Decklan's squads punch their way out, heading for their respective targets. The monsters would be repaid in blood for what Donnyton suffered that night.

Randidly worked as a cook in the aftermath of the concert, after escorting an exhausted Tessa home and asking a barely lucid Cassie to look for two people named Ace and Sydney. It seemed almost everyone who watched the concert felt sluggish. Business owners were desperate for individuals energetic enough to work, even allowing someone fresh off the street like Randidly to assist.

Unlike the rest of the city, Randidly felt wide awake. He practically prowled around until he found a way to vent his energy. The stark difference between his response to Raina and that of the city brought him face to face with something he had thus far avoided: he did not feel at home in Franksburg.

From the accumulation of trash in the streets in the wake of last night's revelries, to the sense that people were celebrating just to keep their mind off reality… The way the citizens here behaved left Randidly feeling exactly the way he felt the night he broke up with Tessa and the System changed the world.

But even if this isn't the sort of place I want to be, Randidly thought as he stepped around a man using a pool of vomit as a pillow, *that doesn't mean there aren't things I can accomplish here.*

They set up food stands around the city and lowered the food prices to catch the dregs wandering out from the concert. It worked like a charm. Being subtly influenced by a songstress was draining.

After fifteen minutes, Randidly gained the Cooking Skill and understood the basics of what his boss wanted him to do. He was making fried street noodles. When he had some down time, he cut scallions and carrots, and mixed garlic, ginger, and soy sauce into the stand's "proprietary" blend. Despite the ease of the work, there was something extremely satisfying about it. It scratched a similar itch Potion Making did. While Randidly worked, he felt at peace.

Randidly wiped sweat from his forehead and grinned as he waited for the weary customer to pull out money. *Plus, it doesn't hurt this stuff smells amazing.*

Another half hour passed and he already reached Level 3 in Cooking, pumping out noodle dish after noodle dish. With his high Stats, his limbs became proficient at the routine movements.

Seeing Randidly's crazy speed and consistency, the overseer for this block moved Randidly to a larger grill and changed his task. Now he fried eggs, meats, potatoes, and pastries. This activity was far more demanding. Each item had its own perfect cooking time. With the volume of orders, Randidly might have thirty things on the grill in front of him that needed adjustments at specific points.

As always, the noise and the smell of savory food was *extremely* fulfilling.

The manager's mouth dropped to the floor in witnessing Randidly's hands blur. Both seemed to act independently of the other, keeping the entire kitchen running smoothly. The food even tasted better than it had in a long time.

Furtively glancing around, the manager told his subordinates to get Randidly's information so he could be invited back to a permanent position. He hurried away, confident this location would be fine in his absence.

At around 5 a.m., even the most hardcore celebrants drifted away. The shops closed down and the business owners packed up, their eyes swimming in all the currency they gathered.

Randidly, now with a Level 10 Cooking Skill, promised to report for work as a chef later, but could only shrug when the workers inquired where he lived. After all, he wasn't about to tell them about Donnyton. It also seemed slightly rude to use Tessa's address as his own, considering he'd broken up with her. The more they pressed, the more hesitant Randidly became until he finally took his payment and fled.

Cooking was a satisfying experience. It also helped Level Haste and Empower 1 Level each, as he used his spare attention to work on his control of those Skills while Cooking.

For the first time, the city seemed quiet. Randidly enjoyed the peace of the tall, looming buildings. Even the Job Cryers were absent, although there were several people shouting for volunteers for the Freedom Fighters operation later today. The euphoric effects left a long hangover, and even the most dedicated volunteers were still struggling to get out of bed.

Shaking his head, Randidly trotted out of the main part of the city into the edges, sneaking past a guard and earning himself a Level in Sneak. He found an abandoned home past the vertical farms, and even further beyond the defensive line.

Although one day was fine, it wasn't good to go any longer without training certain Skills.

Randidly withdrew his spear, the large bone monstrosity made from the spine of the sphinx, from his Interspatial Ring and moved through the basic moves taught to him by Shal. He began to accelerate, moving faster and faster, until his body blurred, pushed to the limits of his physique.

When he tired, he took a short break and spent his Mana on Incinerating Bolts. Then he would return to the spear work, enjoying the physical exertion. All the while, he continued to Meditate to keep his regenerations high.

After a few repetitions of this, in which he gained 2 Levels in Incinerating Bolt and 1 in Spear Phantom's Footwork, he stopped and checked his satchel. He still had plenty of potion materials he gathered on their trip south from Donnyton. His idea about the origin potion still fluttered in the back of his mind. After working up a sweat, some Potion Making to cool down would be nice.

Honestly, Randidly was mostly annoyed he had been so stressed and focused that the only way he tried to improve his Potion Making was by refining these further. He'd been so fixated on this clue about Ace and Sydney and finding the Tribulation, he definitely lost sight of himself.

Still, he was taking steps in both directions. Hopefully, Cassie would remember speaking to him through the haze of the Raina hangover and assist in his search. Otherwise, Randidly was slightly at a loss about how to find them in such a large town. Even if they were here, among fifty thousand people... There were restricted areas, mostly belonging to the government and Freedom Fighters. Places they might be that would be tricky to go completely unnoticed within.

That was assuming they didn't hole up in some homestead at the outskirts.

Randidly chuckled involuntarily, trying to imagine the blunt Ace putting up with the swaggering attitude of the Freedom Fighters he met.

One thing at a time. Besides, his enthusiasm for finding them was diminished some the more he thought about the conversation he had with Sydney right before he broke up with Tessa.

Randidly still hoped they were safe. They had been a beacon that kept him focused through the Dungeon. But now that Randidly had some free time to consider it... when he found them, he would help them, but...

What would he say?

Randidly shook himself. His primary concern now was to survive long enough to find them. Although that didn't seem like it would be a problem, Randidly knew the thing that would be able to kill him wouldn't announce its arrival and give him enough time to prepare. He had to anticipate and prepare in advance.

Randidly left his small hideout and went in search of some necessary tools. It was time to return to the Skill that changed it all. The one that earned him the spot as Shal's Disciple and made him the man he was today.

Potion Making.

CHAPTER SEVENTY-FOUR

During his wanderings in between training sessions, Randidly made a disturbing discovery. He looked out from the cleanly split building, his face grim. He stood in a room he hadn't been in for almost eight months. A space still intimately familiar. Or at least, he was standing in the front six inches of it beyond the door, before the remaining emptiness dropped to a grassy field below.

Randidly checked the room number again, knowing he wouldn't confuse this place with anything else. This was Sydney's dorm room. The place that both Ace and Sydney had likely been. Curled up in bed, watching a movie like they did every Friday night until Ace dozed off and Sydney could spend time studying.

Of course, that Friday had been a bit special. Randidly had called Sydney out and talked to her at dinner. Perhaps he'd affected their usual ritual.

After his difficult talk with Sydney, Randidly went to Tessa's place instead of hitting up Ace and seeing what he was up to that night. Ace probably wondered why he hadn't heard from Randidly, but it wouldn't be enough to reach out. Not when they'd just hung out Thursday night. Or maybe Ace hadn't even noticed the extra forty-five minutes slip by without a word from him, absorbed in whatever it was they were watching on TV.

Either way, it didn't matter. Everything after those six familiar inches of her dorm room was empty space. Most of the room had been teleported elsewhere, at whatever location the other portion of Rawlands University ended up.

Cassie vaguely told him this area had been a source of the Rawlands professors in Franksburg. Unless there was another chunk of dorm buildings in the area, Ace and Sydney probably weren't here.

Fuck. And suddenly, when I dragged myself here and didn't find them, I want to drop everything and go out searching for them again? Rubbing the bridge of his nose, Randidly stepped forward and off into the void, dropping the seven stories to the ground. He hit the ground with a crash and staggered a little. He quickly straightened and walked back toward the abandoned high school he found nearby. That was the landmark Cassie gave him in his search. Now that he found such a stark piece of evidence, Randidly didn't want to stay near the Rawlands building.

Maybe one of them was in the bathroom… God, that would be… Randidly calmed his thoughts. He learned early in his experience with the Nexus that worrying himself into a panic was possible. He set small goals and reached for them, keeping himself on track. He accomplished what he could now by not letting possibilities distract him.

He moved onto the gutted remnants of the high school's football field and closed his eyes. He couldn't let go of a lingering question. What would he even say if he saw them now? Sydney's ultimatum still weighed on his heart. It was why he stomped through the underground pathway after breaking up with Tessa. He felt good making the decision to cut off pieces of his past he didn't want. It was when he turned to face the future…

Releasing a long-held breath, Randidly forced himself to smile. It was relieving, in a way. He knew for sure they weren't here in Franksburg. He had time to prepare his heart. The itchy fit between Randidly's time fighting in the Dungeon and the return to human civilization could be slowly resolved. He didn't need to agonize over this.

Randidly swore to himself he would grow strong. Strong enough to face them both. Not in terms of Skill Levels, but in terms of emotional resolve.

He opened his eyes and headed into the main buildings of the high school and directly toward the chemistry lab. The front doors were stained with blood and hung off the hinges. Randidly ignored it. Now was the time to embrace growth and progress, and continue to avail himself to developing.

There were three main reasons Randidly decided to spend the day like this. He had a gut feeling normal jobs would be scarce with the huge Freedom Fighter operation doing its best to devour all the free manpower. Plus, he was no longer sure he could find enough variety in jobs for it to be worth spending another day earning PP at one. Especially since he didn't need to search so hard for Ace and Sydney. And it could be said the real reason everything developed the way it had was due to his Potion Making.

He needed to get that portion of his growth back on track.

Everything truly started when he'd brewed the potion that dispelled the strange curse the shamans placed on Shal.

Since then, he left Potion Making by the wayside. Sure, he continually made better and stronger potions than Mrs. Hamilton's NCCers, earning him several Levels in the process. But the real growth in his Skill occurred while trying out new recipes. The spirit of experimentation, even in the hell of the Dungeon, changed his life.

His attempts in the past few weeks to find recipes all ended in failure. He was beginning to suspect it was due to his preconceptions getting in the way. Randidly originally assumed all potions were variants of the two base materials, Red and Blue Energy Shards. However, his brief stint as a chef got him thinking.

In a way, what the System did was simplify the inputs in life and quantify the outputs. That was, of course, in addition to breaking most physical limits and laws, but that was secondary. It made everything work in a tight and reasonable *system*.

What threw him off, Randidly reflected as he set out beakers, was the Origin Banana. The profound effect of the juice of that plant made him believe the two colors were the important factors. The more he thought about it, the more he realized that wasn't true. The Origin Banana was a rare exception, rather than the rule.

As such, in order to progress past this Level of Potion Making, he needed to identify the other base units of the potion system. He needed to experiment with other materials to create something unique. And once he had those base building blocks…

Randidly set those thoughts aside for now. He already had some theories about what they would be, but he wanted to try a few things first.

Kiersty looked on bemused. The strange Thorn creature crawled all over Arbor, wrapping his thorny vines around it. She could feel Arbor's annoyance and helplessness through the bond of her Soulskill, as it was forced to put up with its elder brother's teasing.

Satisfied, Thorn climbed down and wriggled toward Kiersty. She wanted to stumble backwards, but knew this was necessary from Arbor's whispers. Gritting her teeth, she allowed Thorn to come close. With surprising delicacy, it pricked her with a single thorn. It absorbed her blood cleanly and the creature shivered in the process.

As per the instructions from Arbor, she raised her hands over Thorn and used her new Skill, Blessing.

Congratulations! Your Skill **Blessing** has grown to **Level 5!**

Congratulations! Your Skill **Blessing** has grown to **Level 6!**

She felt a flash of pleasure at gaining 2 Skill Levels at once, though she still felt somewhat afraid of the thorny creature in front of her.

Small motes of gold flew off her fingers and landed on Thorn. It seemed immensely excited about this and dug into the ground, hurrying off in the distance, seeking the ample prey that wandered around recently.

Feeling abruptly tired after activating her Skill, Kiersty sat down in front of the small rabbit hole Thorn had left. *Being a priestess is exhausting... No wonder no one was doing it before.*

Nathan, who had been standing off to the side and watching the interaction between his sister and the plant beings, offered his sister a cup of water. She drank thankfully, but too enthusiastically. Some spilled over the rim of the cup and across her shirt.

"We should go," Nathan said, glancing over his shoulder. "If Mom finds us here…"

"I know," Kiersty said meekly, standing up and hurrying back. Their mom didn't like them hanging out with Arbor, the "creepy tree."

She didn't understand. None of them did, really. Not even Nathan. In a way that she couldn't put into words, she knew the tree could save them.

Kiersty's eyes glittered. It might be hard, but being a priestess was worth it.

Randidly looked down at the four small crystals in front of him, his expression satisfied. It took most of the day, but he finally isolated four base units. There might be more. At least for now, he found these to use in his Potion Making experiments.

The typical red and a blue crystal sat on the left, joined by a green and a purple one on the right. The end result earned him 3 Levels in Refine. A nice bonus.

The green one had been the ingredient he was most confident about creating. He previously made several basic poison potions as weapons that could be thrown at masses of enemies. How could he not, after Shal enthusiastically taught him how debilitating poison could be? As his capability with Mana Skills grew, this method had been swiftly outclassed. That didn't mean poison wasn't still powerful, in the right situations.

He gathered dozens of the strange mushrooms that grew wildly in the area and slowly boiled them down before refining them. He extracted the poisonous energy and condensed it into a crystal form. Poisons and medicines existed on the same spectrum, so he figured the result would be satisfactory. When he boiled out the relevant compound and refined it, he was confident the System would extract the base essence of poison.

He picked up the green crystal and examined it closely. It was, Randidly reflected, probably enough poison to even threaten him, condensed as it was in the sparkling green decahedron. Still, the crystal was almost useless in that form.

The second new crystal, the purple one, had taken him most of the day to rack his brain and create. In the end, it had been a strange, passing comment Randidly remembered Sam making that was the clue to set him on the right path.

Sam had been talking about the difficulty in harvesting parts from monsters.

"The trouble is," Sam had said, his face fixed in his perpetual frown, "that the bodies degrade pretty quickly. A bone or pelt you get an hour after they die is half as strong and tough as one from five minutes after it passes. The effect gets worse with the more superficial wounds it has, the more blood it's lost. It's like most of the Mana sits in the blood of a corpse for a while, but slowly dissipates after it dies."

Randidly captured ants and crushed their bodies to a pulp, gathering the juice. He boiled away the pus until only thick blood remained. And he refined, and refined, and refined.

He was forced to go out five times for more blood. The final time, he slaughtered his way through a warren full of the ants in order to gather enough bodies. As previously, this insect monster attacked Randidly without any recognition of how many he eliminated. He even earned a Level in Incinerating Bolt and 2 Levels in Agony.

And stubbornly, a thick molasses-like substance was his only prize in his endless boiling of blood.

Then he remembered the rest of Sam's explanation and his eyes gradually brightened.

"The trick we discovered," Sam said, scratching his head, "is to wipe a little of your own blood on it. It's like a signal to the System that you want the body. That's the reason we got the sphinx in such pristine condition, even after so long. You'd bled all over it. So, thanks for that."

Would doing something like this really change the quality of the energy I extract? Randidly wondered. He created a Spearing Roots and allowed it to draw a line across the skin of his palm. The blood gathered and dropped into the molasses of partially Refined blood within his pot.

With a sizzle, the outer layer of molasses crusted over and disintegrated, turning into a rancid-smelling ash. And there, at the bottom, lay a small purple crystal. Even more impressively, the crystal released a pulse of glowing light when it had been revealed, which steadily faded over time.

Staring at the four crystals now, Randidly couldn't wait to start experimenting. When he looked up and saw the setting sun, he grimaced.

In terms of efficacy, the new crystals he made were only of the basic level, which meant refining more of either would require quite a bit more of the raw materials than he had on hand. Randidly pondered while he watched the sinking sun.

He promised to return to the business owner and do some more work as a cook tonight. The manager promised he would allow Randidly to work with more complex recipes, considering his abilities.

Tsk... I wasted too much time on the blood crystal. Randidly twisted his mouth. *I intended to look in on Tessa today too, because of how aggressive that Freedom Fighter was. Well, he was probably distracted by their big mission... I wonder how that went.*

Ruefully, he placed the crystals in his satchel and walked out of the partially demolished high school. His feet carried him quickly back to the city. Cooking was enjoyable enough, and the PP certainly attractive, that Randidly was willing to put off Potion Making for now. It could be done at any time, now that he had the ingredients, after all. Besides, even if Sydney and Ace weren't here, it was worth it to monitor Franksburg. Randidly had no doubt everyone would be gossiping about the result of the Freedom Fighter mission today.

Randidly's eyes flashed, avoiding one of Franksburg's patrols. *Plus, Raina's powers are more than enough reason to keep an eye out.*

As Randidly scaled a building to avoid passing through one of the manned gates of Franksburg, he glanced around at the surrounding buildings. *Actually... what the hell happened to the rest of the people from Donnyton?*

Ugh, when did I become such an expert in missing persons...

CHAPTER SEVENTY-FIVE

*A*lana looked up at the small noise in the corridor, bored from their prolonged confinement. They were largely left alone and the charm of the group's company had worn on her. Devan's plan to wait until the blond man had taken some action against them seemed reasonable initially, but now, with two days passed, it was beginning to seem foolish.

During that time in the tight space, they gained no experience and barely managed to earn any Skill Levels. They were simply waiting.

It was not like there was enough room to practice with her spear.

Not even the guards provided much distraction. Although today, most of the guards seemed excited about something else. So much so, there was a life to their faces when they served the gruel, a slop the group didn't bother to go near.

As the sun set, all that bubbling optimism popped.

There was banging from the other side of the building, and then yelling, swearing, and finally, silence. The blond man who claimed to be in charge of the town stomped toward their cell, pale-faced, followed by three men. The first was tall and grizzled, his hair cropped short, total military type. He hovered around the blond man as though trying to protect him, glaring daggers at the other two.

The most eye-catching was a large man missing his left arm. Strapped to his back was a large metal disk that seemed to be part shield, part buzzsaw. He reminded Alana of an NCCer from back in Donnyton who was aiming to obtain a combat leaning Class.

The third figure was a portly man with glasses. He smiled at the group when he arrived, but otherwise stayed silent.

The blond man coughed, eyeing the way the "prisoners" clearly escaped their handcuffs and were enjoying a meal of dried wolverine meat. His expression twisted between fear and anger.

Eventually, fear won. He smoothed down the front of his shirt. "We... we have decided to believe your story, and offer you your freedom, in return for an alliance. At this juncture, humanity should band together against this unnatural threat."

Devan nodded serenely, as this was the most natural thing in the world. Alana could barely resist snorting. But she *did* manage it, barely. As the "leader" of the expedition, she needed to remain respectful, however pathetic these officials were.

"What sort of alliance?" she asked cautiously, not bothering to stand to address this man. "What can you offer us?"

The blond man's face fell, turning to the two figures who were clearly from another power in the city. They stepped forward. At the very least, it seemed the blond man was willing to do some preparation for this evening.

The portly man smiled. "Hello, it's nice to meet you. You are Alana, right? I'm Anthony, the man who founded a combat-focused organization in Franksburg, the Freedom Fighters. We are in the midst of an operation to kill one of the nearby Bosses and receive a gold coin, so we can gain a Newbie Village."

"At our suggestion," Anthony glanced at the blond man, "the Senator has seen fit to offer you your liberty in the city in exchange for your assistance in this operation. I assume you came here with a purpose, and as long as it's within reason, I'm sure we will be amenable to assisting with that purpose."

Although she was pissed off at being trapped here for so long, Alana felt some exercise would be just what the doctor ordered. It would mean they could finally recruit more actively in the city.

Still, she knew helping them gain a Newbie Village might be counterproductive to the recruitment efforts.

For a long moment, she was torn between helping them and the goal of the mission. Doing one seemed to hurt the other. She supposed they came with recruitment as a goal. Ultimately, it was just an assumed goal. They just wanted to help any families who were still surviving. As things seemed to have stabilized in the region, assistance and the development of a positive relationship could be considered a success.

For her pride, she would find a way to extract reparations, but that was for later. For now, she needed to equip these people with the tools to fight against the monster threat.

Besides, don't we have the example of the Ghosthound? If we help them accomplish this mission in a very public way... I believe some daring individuals will want to jump ship and follow us back to Donnyton. Alana reflected.

She gave her toothiest smile, bearing a closer resemblance to a wolf than a person. "That would be excellent, Mr. Anthony. Of course we would be willing to help you. We are all humans, after all. And afterward, we can discuss the prospect of trade between our villages."

"And honestly, I would do anything if you gave Devan a shower," Clarissa added with no withheld snark, her nose wrinkling. "It smells like stale animal sweat in here."

Devan chuckled, his face impassive as the Senator and his military aide looked on nervously, worried by the recent developments. Alana's eyes narrowed to see the split in Franksburg leadership. She would need to pay close attention to see the ways she could take advantage of the disagreements.

"Pan-seared, pan-seared!" the small Hispanic man yelled over the clatter of pans, spatulas, and stoves that filled the kitchen. When that didn't work, he snapped his fingers until Randidly looked up and then mimed a strange act. Randidly cocked his head to the side, and recalled the method earlier explained to him. He used a spatula to press down on the beef, or whatever red meat this actually was, before flipping it and repeating the same on the other side.

Pan-seared, Randidly mused, the sides of the meat slowly darkening.

He didn't press too hard, so as not to drive out the juices. With his Strength, he had to be careful not to break the kitchen appliances. When the meat was almost fully cooked, he took a pinch of ground spices and sprinkled them on top, raising the heat and putting the pan back down on an unused burner. Randidly pivoted left, removing the fish fillet from the oven.

His other hand began to throw butter, herbs, and garlic in a pot of simmering oil. When he straightened, he flourished a whisk and rapidly stirred the contents of the pot, careful not to let anything spill. He flipped the meat again, lowered the heat, and brought the sauce onto the stove.

The Hispanic man, Karlito, working to Randidly's left, passed him the vegetables. "You do learn quickly, don't you? Don't forget about cutting the meat. Smooth, even strokes! Be gentle. Love the meat, man."

On and on it went. A litany of demands and euphemisms. The kitchen staff ran before a tidal wave of orders from the front, resulting in a long night of movement and constant heat. The previous chef had volunteered for the Freedom Fighter operation and hadn't come back in time for his shift. That, combined with the ominous news from the front line, made the owner willing to let Randidly work in his kitchen, regardless of his lack of experience.

It also helped that he had a Cooking Skill of 10. When Randidly admitted that, the owner greeted him with a wide hug.

By the end of the night, that Skill had risen to 13. The constant stress of a long shift spent working the kitchen pushed Randidly beyond his comfort zone. Mostly, the small, cramped space started to wear on him. Though that too had its own benefits. He earned the Skill Grace, and raised it to Level 3 through the process.

Grace Level 3: *Passive Physical Skill.* **Increases the fluidity and control over movement. Also slightly increases coordination and balance.**

Randidly would trade a night of sweating for a flexible passive Skill like that any day.

Although it was a passive Skill, it seemed incredibly useful, even in fighting. Shal's spear methods emphasized assault and overwhelming, direct speed, without much use of feints. Randidly supposed he just hadn't reached the proper criteria previously to earn a Skill like this. Twisting in a single spot and sliding between other chefs had certainly been a work in mastery of his own body.

Randidly idly wondered how people managed to perform this job with normal Stats. He walked out of the back door and gratefully accepted a drink from Karlito.

Randidly drank it in one gulp. He grimaced as his throat tingled and his stomach heaved in displeasure. "Was that... tequila?"

"Of course," Karlito said with a smile. "Unfortunately, your resistance to alcohol rises with your Vitality... but still. There is nothing so wonderful as the burn of a good tequila. The stresses just fade away."

Karlito gestured to the unmarked glass bottle, winking at Randidly. "When there is no good tequila, we make do with what we have. Do not drink too much more, friend; overexposure to this swill is known to cause women blindness. Too much of this and even God won't know the sort of woman you will bring home to share your bed! Ha!"

Randidly shook his head, only slightly amused. He liked Karlito and his wild stories and exaggerated jokes. He was loud and abrasive in the kitchen, but Randidly didn't miss the way he'd been constantly trying to help him.

Every kind individual born under the System has to try that much harder not to let someone take advantage of them. Randidly sighed inwardly. *Every iota of kindness can be turned against you.*

They joked and laughed for a while longer, Randidly feeling strangely at ease, even as a part of him nagged to get back to the potion recipes. Before he could leave, their manager hurried out the back door. "Oh, thank god you two are still here. I'll pay double, no—triple! If you stay and make one more meal."

"But the kitchen's already been cleaned. You want us to go through everything again?" Karlito rumbled, his eyes narrowing.

The manager raised his hands in a placating gesture. "No! No! I'll handle all of that. A very important client came, and—well, for her, there are no such thing as *hours*. Please!"

As soon as the manager agreed to let them off without cleaning, Karlito's cheer returned. The change was so sudden, Randidly started to wonder if Karlito was more realistic than he seemed. Tying his apron back on, he called over his shoulder. "So, who's the bigwig?"

The manager's face turned starry-eyed. "It's Raina. The Jewel of Franksburg."

Derek Quinn had been a truck driver before the System came to the world. When everything changed, he crashed his truck into a column of giant mutant ants and received the Exterminator I Path. After his rig heaved to a stop, he stared at the wrecked bodies in pure disbelief.

His hands were still shaking when he realized what a mistake it had been to stop.

The ants pursued him with a vengeance, swarming and biting at his flesh with a horrifying single-mindedness. They ripped off his left arm before another driver on the highway saw his plight and beat them off.

He still remembered that extended hand from the other driver. Attached to it was a smiling, portly man, his glasses splattered with blood. The scene was gruesome, but it was also beautiful. "Hey there, buddy. I'm Anthony. You're gonna be okay."

Luckily enough, Anthony had some experience with first aid from a stint in the army, and managed to bandage his wounds enough to keep Derek alive. Unlike most people who were mutilated in the aftermath of the System's arrival, Derek didn't fall into a stupor and give up on himself.

He got angry.

That anger served him well as he threw himself into a crusade to slaughter as many monsters as he could find. By this point, he'd gotten up to the Exterminator VI Path, cutting his way through the ants to earn the PP to carry him there. However, no matter how many he killed, it never seemed to matter. There were always so damn many of them.

Even now, leading a convoy to the frontlines, he felt a horrible mixture of jittery nerves and helplessness. Franksburg was running out of ammo. And the ants weren't running out of bodies. If anything…

Derek spared a glance for the group of twelve people that trailed after them, wearing a mismatch of bone armor and fur. Their last, desperate hope. They looked more like historical re-enactors than soldiers. Most of them carried swords, but their leader calmly polished a spear as they moved to the edge of the ant colony. It wasn't obvious what sort of weapon the other woman possessed. She merely walked in the middle of the group, yawning.

He was slightly depressed when Anthony called him away from the front line to escort them. Now he was even more disappointed. Even with a Class, how could this relaxed group of a dozen people change the tide of the fight?

After all, the problem wasn't talent. It was simply—

They rounded a bend in the road and the battle stretched before them, almost endless. Thousands upon thousands of ants marched forward, rushing to attack the fortified position humans made within their territory. These hills had been empty eight hours ago. Bodies had since been piled higher than a person in some places.

"So you see," Derek said sarcastically, "a small squad like you would be perfect for this operation."

Alana, the leader, nodded seriously and turned to the weaponless woman, and the man who seemed like the vice commander. "So?"

"Doable," the vice leader commented. "As long as they don't possess any unique Skills."

"Child's play," the weaponless one said, cracking her neck.

Derek was about to say something dismissive until a small amount of lightning crackled across her fingers.

Alana turned back to Derek. "Alright, take us to the front. Don't let your gunners shoot us in the back. We'll handle the rest."

CHAPTER SEVENTY-SIX

*T*wo weaker Black Tusk Wolves lay on their bellies, watching the ants push the human lines back. When the wind changed, both sniffed and laid their ears flat against their skulls.

"The humans from the north," one hissed.

The other's tongue lolled out of its mouth. "The ones we are supposed to watch out for. We have found them. We must report."

As the battle below grew more intense, those two white wolves shuffled backward and disappeared amongst the trees.

Randidly's hackles rose at the mention of Raina, forcing him to calm himself. She wouldn't even be near him. She'd be out there, waiting for the food.

When they walked into the kitchen, there she was, sitting on the counter kicking her legs, the pink highlights in her blonde hair neon underneath the harsh light. Next to her was a serious-looking woman with pistols strapped to her waist. That woman's eyes immediately jumped to the new arrivals and she pivoted.

"Oh, Raina! I'm such a huge fan of your work," Karlito said, bowing.

"Now, now." The manager laughed and waved his hands. "Let's not bother Miss Raina and simply get to work. Now, Miss, if you will follow me to your table?"

Raina rewarded the dramatic Karlito with a sunny smile. "Actually, I'm merely peckish. Matilda here always craves fish tacos, and when it comes to tasty food, everyone says this is the place to come."

Matilda, who Randidly assumed was the guard, glowered. She looked excited about exactly nothing, fish tacos or otherwise. If anything, she seemed disappointed she hadn't yet been given an excuse to draw one of her weapons.

I wonder if I could survive a gunshot these days... Randidly thought idly.

Naturally, Raina's gaze moved past Karlito to Randidly, who followed him through the door into the kitchen. She ignored the obsequious manager and remained firmly planted on the stainless-steel counter. Randidly looked toward the ground under her examination, suppressing the urge to smile. Not that he knew anything about Raina personally, but just the nature of her Skills—

Congratulations! Your Skill **Mental Strength** has grown to **Level 16!**

At least she's good for Skill Levels... The corner of Randidly's mouth quirked upward and he moved toward the supply freezer to get the ingredients for fish tacos. He'd made the dish earlier, so his body knew the steps he would need to take to make the food. Karlito would handle the fish, so Randidly—

"Excuse me, were you at my concert last night? Backstage?"

Randidly paused, turning slow. Raina hopped off the counter and was studying him, something strange in her eyes.

Randidly considered lying, but there didn't really seem to be any point. Under the manager's worried glances between him and Raina, he nodded. "Yes, I was."

The silence grew, their gazes locked between his striking green and her soft brown.

Karlito chuckled uneasily, breaking the tension. "Honestly, who *wasn't* at your concert, Miss Raina? It was the event of the year! I wish I could get a recording. Your music speaks to—"

"Not everyone was backstage at the concert. It takes a talented or rich individual to earn those passes. And not everyone can gaze upon me with such mild eyes while I'm smiling at them, not since the System came to this world," Raina said, her voice light and musical. "In fact, I think I have yet to meet anyone else that can. Not even that zombie Lucifer can resist smiling. What's your name?"

To Randidly's surprise, there was no power or Skill in the question. No influence from the System pressed against him, urging him to answer. Hers was just a face filled with curiosity and a yearning. Most of all, loneliness. She'd laid down her weapons. Surprisingly, her expression felt familiar to him.

After an extremely long pause, Randidly answered. "My name is... Randidly Ghosthound."

One of the great reliefs of Randidly's life, in regard to the System, was no longer would his name earn him strange looks. Raina nodded, as if this were the most natural thing in the world. For her, the name did not earn any special attention.

"Well, Mr. Ghosthound," the popstar said, the corners of her mouth quirking upward. "Would you like to have dinner with me? Maybe even picnic out under the stars?"

"I'm working," Randidly responded slowly.

Raina glanced at Randidly's manager before drinking in every inch of Randidly. "I can definitely pay you more than he can."

Derek stayed back on top of the hill, scowling down at the foreign group proceeding to the front lines. He admitted they were disciplined, far above the level of even the regulars within the Freedom Fighters. They settled into a crouch and moved in formation. How much could a Class really help in a huge melee like this? The numbers were stacked against them.

The ants marched endlessly, climbing over the shattered corpses of their comrades without derailment. Even if those twelve tried to overcome the weight of the monster bodies, it was an impossible task.

Like a ghost, a tall, orange-haired figure appeared next to Derek. He spared him a glance. Lucifer, the only man in the Freedom Fighters that Derek held no confidence in being able to fight against. He was also the second in command in all but name, leading the most powerful battalion.

"Is that them?" Lucifer grunted, wiping blood from his sabers.

Derek nodded. "Let's see if Classes are really worth all this trouble."

The duo watched. The squad picked up speed, moving to the front lines of the battle. Then the last of the Freedom Fighters stepped to the side and lowered their makeshift spears and smoking-barreled submachine guns, gladly willing to let someone else hold back the swarm for a while.

Derek froze.

He expected a crash. Not the way they simply slid into the enemy lines, barely slowing. His increased Perception let him just glimpse each one of the ten shield bearers stab forward smoothly with a short sword, each time accurately driving their blade into the skulls of the ants.

They twisted their wrist and disengaged their weapon with remarkable precision. The bodies were shoved to the side and trampled on. The squad barely broke stride in their advance.

As the group penetrated deeper into the ant lines, more swarmed, recognizing this new threat. An eddy emerged in the current of ants flowing across the hillside. The spear-woman at the back was ruthless in her efficiency, breaking the ants' legs and leaving them useless.

But what was most shocking was the weaponless woman.

"Magic user," Lucifer mumbled next to Derek, his tone wondering. "If we could learn those sorts of Skills…"

Although there were individuals who used the Mana Bolt Skill, it was mostly just as a supplement to gunfire. After all, no one had a large enough Mana pool that it was feasible to train up the Skill to the point it could inflict damage as easily as bullets.

This woman raised her hands and forked lightning shot out, smashing into two ants and splitting into two more, and then another two.

Thirty-two ants collapsed after being hit by the Skill, and sixty-four staggered, stunned by the electricity coursing through their bodies.

With a pleased expression, the woman did it again, clearing another huge swath in front of their group, and then drank a blue potion from a crystal flask.

Like a well-oiled machine, the squad marched forward, barely breaking a sweat as they ripped through the enemies that kept the Freedom Fighters stumped. The speed at which monsters arrived only ever became the speed at which monsters died.

It was possible for an elite squad of Freedom Fighters to do something similar, at least for a time until they too quickly ran out of Stamina. Stranded in the middle of an endless number of ants, helpless to survive with depleted Attributes. Even Lucifer himself could only fight for ten minutes or so before he needed a break.

Derek realized the advantage of this foreign group was twofold. First, it was clear that Leveling gave powerful bonuses to Health, Mana, and Stamina. Otherwise, there was no way they could use Skills this recklessly.

The other advantage was professionalism. Compared to this display of unity, the whole Freedom Fighters outfit looked like a joke. Those small thrusts effectively killed the monsters, but he suspected they cost next to no Stamina. They were simply well-equipped and efficient. They'd studied and developed best practices for combat.

Derek felt a small tremor in his heart. He'd heard this group came from the north. These were likely the elites of whatever location they came from. And if they had several other squads like this…

Just how powerful was this Donnyton?

Karlito and the restaurant manager began chatting excitedly when Raina insisted they all go for a walk, their eyes becoming increasingly glassy as time passed. The night air was cool and the streets were deserted. They had made plenty of fish tacos that sat in a wicker basket Karlito carried, and

Randidly ate freely. Matilda began to smile, as Raina told wild story after story, but her eyes always scrutinized Randidly.

Looks like her Perception didn't miss that Raina asked me for a picnic... Randidly resisted the urge to rub the back of his neck.

Again, Raina's urging drove them in a new direction. She pointed upward at a high building. "Let's head up there. I bet the view is gorgeous."

"That..." The manager hesitated under the dark, looming twenty-story building.

Matilda was a lot less circumspect in her criticism. "This building hasn't been cleared, Raina. For all we know, it's a den of drifters and gamblers."

"Isn't that why I have you? To guard me?" Raina flashed a winning smile. Almost unwillingly, Matilda smiled back. "Well, unless you knock me out and carry me away, I'm going up there. It's a picnic! Let's have an adventure."

True to her word, Raina led the way through the broken glass doors. Matilda scrambled to catch up. Karlito shrugged at Randidly and followed the nervous manager into the dark interior of the building. The ground floor resembled a bank, but the further they were from the doors, the more shadows consumed the depths of the room.

Raina didn't hesitate, heading directly to the stairs. With such speed that Matilda yelped in protest, Raina dashed up the stairs. By the time they reached the roof, everyone but Randidly was panting with exertion.

"R-Raina..." Matilda said weakly around gasps. "You... you can't just..."

"Fine, fine." Raina waved her hand. Her blonde hair was oddly luminous in the dark stairwell. "You probably want someone to check it out before I barge out there, right? Ummm... Randidly, will you go sweep the roof?"

Randidly tilted his head to the side and eventually nodded. "Sure."

Randidly walked past the others and twisted the handle. For a second, it stuck, but Randidly "gently" bumped his shoulder and the rusted hinges groaned. The door swung open and he glanced around. His Perception let him know no one else was here. He walked across the gravel and looked out at Franksburg.

It was a city, but a city after the apocalypse. There were lights, but most were dim and clustered along the streets. The massive structures of the buildings, from this height, seemed to crouch above the remnants of humanity, ready to stomp on the last embers.

There was a click behind Randidly, pulling him from his complicated thoughts. Raina had followed him out, her hands on the door knob. She'd locked the door.

She offered him a warm smile. "So, we are finally alone."

CHAPTER SEVENTY-SEVEN

*R*andidly folded his arms, his eyes narrowing. His experience with the touch of the King of Turtletown was still fresh in his mind. He began to agitate the cool Mana in his navel. If she tried anything—

Raina's shoulders slumped and her whole demeanor changed. Tears formed in the corners of her eyes. Suddenly, he recognized the familiarity that shone through her gaze. Raina did not feel at home in Franksburg.

Toward that, Randidly held plenty of sympathy.

"I... I'm really glad I met you. You are the first person—you are the first person to really see me. To see *me*. Everyone else is just blinded by the Skills, and..." She sniffed, looking at Randidly with an odd expression. She took a few tentative steps away from the door, as someone, probably Matilda, began to pound on it. "I just... I know this is strange. I needed to talk to you. I've wanted to talk to someone like you for so long. How attractive do you think I am? Be honest. Please."

Randidly squirmed. In the light, her hair was blinding, the pink stripes turning vivid and garish. He turned back to the current state of humanity. Raina joined him, tentatively raising her hand to touch his shoulder, but lowering it instead. Give him a sphinx with infinite Mana any day. This aspect of life was something he was simply never good at. His experiences in the Dungeon taught him how to act in life, but never how to interact.

"Honestly?" Randidly said tentatively, and Raina nodded. He shrugged helplessly. He knew that listless feeling of being unmoored, and knew what she needed right now was not to be reassured. She needed truth. His mind was focused on a different woman in the moonlight, spinning and surrounded by glowing butterflies. "Honestly... rather plain. Your body is very... uh...

well-endowed, but your face... Although that changes when you smile. I can't be sure that's not the Skill..."

Raina leaned forward, her hair swinging to cover her face. Aside from the increasing urgency of the pounding on the locked door, the roof was silent. Even the wind kept its distance.

"That hurt more than I expected it to. I'm not—I mean, that's how I used to be, but ever since the System came..." She shook her head. "I've felt lost, though, unsure of who I was. What I wanted to be. What I had *become*. Thank you, you've helped me remember. Plain, ha."

Raina's smile was sad, but it still made Randidly want to smile back at her. Ultimately, that was what made him not trust her. She pulled out a business card and offered it to him. Randidly's eyes immediately went to the bright pink star on the side.

"This is my address. If you want, we can talk again. I'd really, really like to talk again. Please visit." To Randidly's surprise, she leaned over and pressed her lips against his cheek. His Perception had seen her coming and he had ample time to React. His Agility was so high, it would have been simple to evade her. He was simply too surprised.

Randidly had girlfriends before, and sex, but... those always moved slowly, building over time. This sudden kiss, even a mere peck on the cheek, left him at a loss.

What had him most stunned was the lack of familiar influence of her charm on him. It was a genuine moment, without a Skill. She was fumbling and clumsy, but genuine.

Raina pulled back and she tried to smile, but failed. Her eyes were watery. "You... you're not going to visit, are you?"

Randidly shook his head and his heart clenched. Maybe it made him weak, but this person with Skills that could influence so many... he could not trust her. Raina walked back to the door and opened it, allowing Matilda to stumble out on the roof. Raina kept walking in silence. Matilda shot Randidly an annoyed glance before hurrying after her charge.

Karlito walked out onto the roof, took one look at him, and whistled. "Randidly, man... on your cheek, that lipstick, did Raina...?"

Randidly walked down into the darkness of the stairwell, leaving the people behind. Feeling annoyed, he sprinted for several blocks and scaled a nearby apartment building, climbing twenty stories to the roof. Once more, his eyes fell on the dim fires of humanity at the base of buildings. There, he let out a long sigh.

He really needed to work on his people skills. If only the System had Skills for that...

A notification popped up, a welcome distraction from his current annoyance.

Congratulations! Your **Thorn Level 4** is ready to **Level up. Due to diet and influence, Thorn wonders whether he is a *Lone Hunter* or a *Team Trapper*.**

As he mulled over these choices, another notification popped up.

Congratulations! Your **Arbor Level 2** is ready to **Level up. Due to diet and influence, Arbor wonders whether he is simply a *Lonely Tower* or a *Pillar of the Community*.**

Randidly narrowed his eyes at the timing. It was strange enough both were Leveling at the same time due to the seemingly increased difficulty for his Soul Plants to Level, but they both had similar references. Were they developing a symbiotic relationship with each other?

That didn't sound right; otherwise, there would likely be more of a connection between the two Leveling options. Randidly supposed, without his presence, both were forced to be exposed to more humans. Perhaps they were simply wondering what their purpose was, in the grand scheme of things.

This was a lot more likely for Arbor, with its higher Brain Function, but still...

Because he wasn't sure of the effects of either, Randidly split the difference. Arbor... well, all he really knew about the thing was that it was vain. As such, it seemed to make more sense it would be a part of a community. Meanwhile, Thorn was designed to lurk and slaughter monsters, which meant Randidly preferred it as a Lone Hunter.

Satisfied, Randidly made both of his selections.

Thorn is now **Level 5. Physicality has increased by 3. Brain Function has increased by 2. Particularity has increased by 1.** Thorn has learned the Skill **Thorny Whip.**

Arbor is now **Level 3. Magical Aptitude has increased by 1. Brain Function has increased by 1. Particularity has increased by 4.** Arbor has learned the Skill **Aura of Arbor.**

Randidly looked at the ultimate results from the Level-ups, slightly aggrieved.

Thorn (Blood)
Level 5
Survivability: *8*
Physicality: *10*

Magical Aptitude: *2*
Brain Function: *6*
Particularity: *9*
Battle Ability: *18*
Special Skills: *Flexibility | Strangle | Dig | Thorny Whip*

Arbor (Attention)
Level 3
Survivability: *2*
Physicality: *1*
Magical Aptitude: *4*
Brain Function: *8*
Particularity: *12*
Battle Ability: *2*
Special Skills: *Elaborate Dance | Aura of Arbor*

Thorn's Level had gone how he predicted and was delighted to discover his Battle Ability increased to 18. That meant Thorn could handle himself around enemies at Level 18. Average enemies, at least.

Meanwhile, Arbor, the Soul Seed he'd never truly seen sprout, continued to focus its points in Particularity, earning the ambiguous "Aura of Arbor." It was probably useful, but...

Randidly sighed and shook his head. *Would it have killed the thing to grow a little in terms of Battle Ability? Well, it's planted in Donnyton so it might just not be exposed to much danger.*

Twenty Classers left on the mission and nineteen came back. Dozer, with enough of a beard to indicate the time he spent in the Dungeon must have at least been a few weeks, led the way. The leadership of Donnyton had been able to tell they were returning when the waves of monsters slowly diminished in the last several hours.

The missing individual was a punch in the gut.

No one spoke. The men cut a brutal path through the remaining monsters. Their armor was covered in dents and dried blood. Several had glittering, high-Level weapons obtained from within the Dungeon. The squad's sole Knight had two shields, one on each arm, rather than a sword strapped to his waist.

They marched in silent formation, the discipline brutally apparent, making clear the absence of one of their numbers.

Even more notable than the absence of one of his warriors was the midnight-blue kitten Dozer had cradled in his arms. Daniel looked at it curiously. To his surprise, Dozer dumped it on him. The big brute promptly walked over to Annie, picked her up, and carried her off.

Daniel opened his mouth to say something, but Regina put a hand on his shoulder.

"Leave him be. Glendel already reports the monsters from that Dungeon have ceased. They have obviously won. We don't need to know the details until he is ready to tell them."

"But what about...?" Daniel looked helplessly at the cat that seemed to suddenly come awake, yawning. It blinked violet eyes at him, then gingerly raised its paw and placed it against Daniel's face.

Daniel couldn't help but smile. The cat returned his smile, so it seemed, and flexed its paw, its claws sinking into his cheek.

Daniel's howls earned chuckles, even from the freshly returned squad, who collapsed, releasing all the tension that kept them wound through the journey. They made it home.

Nathan frowned at his sister. She was by Arbor, but also dangerously close to the strange, thorny creature that frequented the area by the tree. Both of the strange plants were glowing slightly. The thorn creature writhed on the ground and Arbor grew upwards, fast enough to see with the naked eye.

"What's going on?" Nathan asked.

His sister smiled serenely. "The Ghosthound has willed it, so they are changing."

Nathan thought his sister was being even weirder than usual. The light around Arbor dimmed, but the thorny vine creature thrashed more. Peering closer, Nathan could even see the thorns on the vines growing more twisted, longer, sharper. Those weren't the needles they'd been in the past, but were more like hooks, aiming to rip flesh.

"Why did Arbor stop growing if the other one still is?" Nathan asked, but his sister just smiled and walked back toward the village.

Surprised, but glad they could leave and go see the return of Dozer's squad, Nathan followed.

They wound their way through the coffee and banana farms, moving quickly to the main part of the village, being careful to remain on mostly unused paths or along the tree line. Although their mother hadn't forbidden them from coming here per se, it was getting increasingly difficult to escape her watchful gaze and visit the plants.

Returning to the farming area proper, they relaxed somewhat. This was the area that was relatively okay that they played in, although not usually so late in the day. Farmers and Potion Makers moved about, discussing rations and ingredients. They paid no mind to the two siblings.

Instead of turning upwards toward the Classer Compound, Kiersty kept moving toward the middle of the valley, where the Mage battalion guarded the road coming through the mountains. The distinctive sound of spell casting evidenced the proximity of the front lines.

The men sitting around taking breaks at campfires drew a few stares toward Kiersty and Nathan, mostly because of the presence of children, not because any of them planned on stopping the kids.

Still, Nathan was suddenly quite nervous. To his relief, they stopped, almost directly next to the watchtower, right behind the spot where the relief squad waited, ready to assist their comrades. Kiersty pointed, and Nathan's gaze followed her finger.

Erupting from the ground was a grey, ashy piece of wood that looked like an exact duplicate of Arbor. Faster than any plant had a right to move, this Arbor clone sprouted from the ground and grew upwards. It kept on until it was the same size as the original Arbor's new size back in the field, about as tall as a grown man. Its branches spread, curling upwards.

Four flaming leaves bloomed. The relief squad turned to gaze at the tree with wide eyes.

Notifications popped up in front of Nathan that he tried to read, but made his head swim.

You are under the influence of the Skill Aura of Arbor. This allows you to make use of a Gift of Arbor. Regeneration is also passively boosted by 10%.

Gift of Arbor: *The next active Skill used will use 50% of the normal amount of Mana or Stamina.* **Gift of Arbor grows at a rate of 1 per hour per sprouting. As long as you are within the Aura of Arbor, Gifts from any sprouting may be used.**

"There might only be two now," Kiersty said, her voice loud and a little shrill. She spread her arms like a prophet offering alms. "But soon, this place will be covered in them. May the blessing of Arbor be with you all!"

The adults regarded the children with looks of mute confusion.

CHAPTER SEVENTY-EIGHT

*R*andidly spent the past hour carefully separating the four different-colored crystals he'd refined, creating thirteen different recipes. Randidly admitted to himself he simply didn't have enough of either the purple crystal or the green one to mix them with each other and try out all the possible combinations.

The first twelve recipes could be considered two groups of six. First the purple with red, 25/75, 50/50, and 75/25. Then the same, purple with blue.

The second group of six was the green crystal, rather than the purple one, but otherwise, the same ingredients in the precise ratios.

The final recipe was equal parts of all four crystals, ground down and mixed. A ghost of a smile fluttered across his face as he worked.

Randidly started with purple, because honestly, although he understood what the poison was generally, he wasn't sure what this crystal refined from the blood of a monster would do, and was more curious about its effects.

His hands moved to the 50/50 mixture, purple and red. Careful to get every small ground-up crystal, he dumped them into a glass container. The potion mixed and turned a dark maroon color. Curious, Randidly examined it.

Lesser Potion of Health Level 18: Increases your maximum Health by **180** for **20 minutes.**
If, after the time runs out, your Health is below 180, your Health will be reduced to 1 and you will obtain the status effect Overdrawn, which reduces regeneration by 90% for an hour.

At his Level, it might not quite be worth it. But as his Potion Making Level increased, he could raise the bonus...

Health was a valuable commodity underneath the oppressive System.

Curious, Randidly did the same thing, between purple and blue, obtaining a Level 23 Potion of Mana, increasing the Mana pool by 230 for 10 minutes, but otherwise largely the same.

The current boost was about the same as his highest-tier potions, but they were made with the least refined ingredients. After a bit of experimentation, if he could obtain a Potion of Mana to increase his Mana pool by 460 for 10 minutes, the increased spell-casting burst would be highly effective.

The night was long, and there were still more recipes to try.

Derek straightened abruptly, pausing from the constant fighting to wipe sweat from his brow. Many of the other Freedom Fighters were with him, methodically working their way across the hill, pushing the ants back. It was difficult for any of them to believe it, but they weren't willing to let this chance slip through their fingers.

The change came to the ants about an hour ago, around three hours after the squad trundled on down and into the ant warren. The ants began wandering away, the once directed swarm lost and leaderless.

Without a concerted attack, the ants were quickly beaten back. After all, they were quite weak individually. Even the volunteers, let alone the Freedom Fighters regulars, could handle a lone ant. Morale spiked upward as more and more ants were slaughtered by the enthusiastic fighters.

For a long time, there was no sign of the squad. Derek glanced toward the warren on the hill and sighed inwardly. Had they perished in the attempt?

And there they were, walking casually back, continually slaughtering any monsters that stepped in front of them like this was just another day at the office. When the group reached him, Derek Quinn didn't know what to say. He thought he'd worked hard and found strength.

In his heart, he knew this was partially because of the Classes that they had this advantage, but at the same time...

They moved cleanly, with a proficiency and professionalism that made him helpless. His pride as a powerful member of the Freedom Fighters had been completely trampled. It made him realize something.

While Franksburg tried to keep the outside world back, maintaining the status quo, these men and women had gone into the outside world and changed themselves to thrive in it. They had forsaken their previous humanity and found a new strength within the new world ruled by the System.

Alana cleared her throat and put her hands on her hips. "Take us to Anthony. We'd like to talk conditions."

Randidly considered the potions in front of him.

The purple 25%, with red and blue at 75% created two more intriguing potions.

Lesser Mana Regeneration Potion Level 25: Increases Mana Regeneration by **250%** for the next **5 minutes.**

Randidly pondered the implications. Especially when taking into consideration the non-Mana option. Mana regeneration, even with a build like Randidly's where he'd focused a lot into the regenerations, was still so slow. He would only receive an extra 200 Mana per hour with this concoction. Taken down to a five-minute time period, that was only an extra 15 Mana.

The Health potion was more impressive, but still slightly lackluster. On Randidly, it would restore 40 some-odd Health, a pretty insignificant amount.

What truly got his attention was the Stamina potion. He wondered whether a regeneration variant could be made for that. With unlimited Stamina, not only would it increase training speed at certain key intervals, it could be used to make individuals unstoppable for a short period of time.

Having the ability to completely ignore Stamina costs... Randidly shivered at the pleasurable thought.

In addition, there had been talk from the potion makers that they found a method to delay the time a normal Health potion would heal you over. If that same method could be used to extend the time the regeneration was increased, even if it lowered the bonus...

Unfortunately, he didn't have enough materials on hand to experiment. That would have to wait until he returned to Donnyton. At the thought of his village, Randidly tensed, struggling about whether he should feel guilty for remaining down here and exposing them to possible attacks from the lurking Tribulation.

Although helping the town had been a bit of a hassle at first, they were swiftly growing into something useful. They could be used to effectively gather the materials he needed for both the green and purple crystals. Otherwise, he would need to drain dozens of mushrooms or ants every time.

The purple 75% were his current favorite potions.

Congratulations! Your Skill **Potion Making** has grown to **Level 29!**

Lesser Hungry Flesh Potion Level 23: Gain **Healthsteal** for **5 minutes. 2.3% of the Physical damage dealt will be recovered as Health.**

Lesser Hungry Soul Potion Level 27: Gain **Manasteal** for **5 minutes. 2.7% of the Magical damage dealt will be recovered as Mana.**

These were undoubtedly useful. It would take a certain type of fighter to use the Healthsteal, but the Manasteal intrigued him. Again, though, the concept of Staminasteal would be the most effective, if it existed.

Satisfied with these, Randidly turned to the green crystal mixtures.

The 50/50 splits turned out to be direct boosts to stats.

Lesser Physical Tonic Level 24: +5 to all **Physical stats** for **10 minutes. After that, -10 Physical Stats for 30 minutes.**

Randidly grimaced. He wasn't a fan of these. Unlike the direct boosts to Health or Mana, these had demerits no matter what condition you were in at the end of the time period.

The green 25% yielded a strange result as well.

Congratulations! Your Skill **Potion Making** has grown to **Level 30!**

Lesser Physical Fury Potion Level 27: Gain **Physical Fury** for **27 minutes. Physical damage taken slightly reduced. Physical damage dealt slightly increased.**

Mana was similar, except flipped. It was the green crystal at 75% that really surprised him in terms of the poison potion results.

Congratulations! Your Skill **Potion Making** has grown to **Level 31!**

Lesser Health Fire Level 28: Deal **.56%** of afflicted targets current Health per second for **30 seconds, or until the fire is put out.**

Lesser Mana Fire Level 24: Cause target to lose **.24%** of target's current Mana per second for **30 seconds, or until the fire is put out.**

Both would be extremely dangerous, if discovered. They were designed to fight against a person with superior Health and Mana. Even Randidly, if afflicted with them, would have difficulties surviving. Classers especially would be vulnerable to the effects.

Taking extra care to study the description, he realized they were vastly more dangerous for mages. Though their spells contained more power than similarly Leveled physical Skills, magical Stats were useless without Mana. A tank with low Health still had his or her high physical stats and could struggle to survive.

But a Mage without Mana...

Chuckling, Randidly straightened and cracked his neck. He supposed it was good he was noncommittal and insisted on being good at everything. A potion like this would only strip away his magical weapons. In which case, he could reward the bold opponent with a domineering thrust from his spine-spear.

He refocused, considering the final pile of ingredients. These would combine all four crystals.

Moving carefully, he ground the crystals into a powdered form and began to mix. He activated Eyes of the Spear Phantom to enable him to watch the ratios closer. Only when he was 100% confident did Randidly mix the powders together and pour the final result into water. The potion glowed briefly, then settled into a swirling blackness. Small flecks of light emerged, almost like stars, that slowly dissolved the black coloration. After a few moments, the liquid cleared, turning back to...

Congratulations! Your Skill **Potion Making** has grown to **Level 32!**

Congratulations! Your Skill **Potion Making** has grown to **Level 33!**

Well, water.

When Randidly peered closer and examined it, his eyes narrowed.

Viscous Liquid of Possibilities Level ???: *Higher-tiered base crafting material.* **Can be refined to a more stable form.**

Randidly decided to trust the notification and focused his whole being on the clear liquid, and began to refine it. Over and over, for an hour. Until he held a small, clear marble.

Stone of Possibilities Level 42: *A stone that holds a sea of untapped potential.* **Can be used to store 42 Health, Mana, or Stamina, which can then be syphoned back from the stone to yourself, should the need arise. Reusable.**

Randidly's eyes were bright as he considered the possibilities. *Having 42 extra of any Attribute isn't much, but if I make several more of these... Having some bonus Health, Mana, and Stamina all have their relative benefits.*

Randidly sat back on his heels and stretched. Over the course of the night, Randidly gained quite a few benefits. Not the least of which was pushing his Potion Making over Level 30. In addition, he earned 6 Levels in Refine. Since the capacity of the stone was likely influenced by those Skills, he knew his next attempt would be able to contain more than 42 of an Attribute.

That was for later. He lamented the additional grinding he would need to do, grinning at the possibilities. There were still a few hours until dawn. Hopping off the building, Randidly prowled toward the edge of Franksburg, searching for more crafting materials.

Randidly wanted to check in on Tessa, to see if there were after effects from exposure to Raina's song. He felt slightly guilty that he ignored her all of yesterday, but his pursuits today were rather distracting. Better late than never.

Shrugging, Randidly put it out of his mind. Better to focus on the present.

CHAPTER SEVENTY-NINE

*A*lana's demands were simple and fair. Establishing a small base within Franksburg that they could use for trade, a share of the various supplies Franksburg had access to due to its size prior to the System, specifically of tools and clothing, and the chance to appeal to the populous, seeking residents to move up and settle within Donnyton.

Although they were better equipped and highly trained, Alana explained there were far fewer of them. Donnyton housed about 3,000 people. Anthony informed them Franksburg had a population of 42,000, at last count. And the last count had been loose.

Anthony, with the blond Senator's bemused support, was only too happy to agree to provide these things for their services in obtaining the golden coin. They were less willing, however, to listen to Alana's recommendations on how the Newbie Village should be constructed.

"You should wait," she advised. "Or at least limit the amount of people you allow to receive a Class. A monster horde will come based on the amount that have a Class in the Newbie Village. We also believe, based on the population, but that is more of a 1 to 1 ratio. The number of Classers multiplies the monsters by 10—"

"Look," Anthony said in a smooth voice. "I appreciate your concern. But I assure you our deficiencies are primarily in assault. In terms of defense, we are more than capable. Snipers, machine gun nests, walls; we have it all. We have been working tirelessly over the past month for just such a moment. We really appreciate your concern, but will take it from here."

Devan moved to step in, but before he could speak, both he and Alana saw something that made their blood chill. The golden coin turned to powder and disappeared. A small scorpion flashed into existence on the ground. It was red, with a crimson stinger.

It flickered and an unassuming-looking woman, with black hair to her shoulders, stood in its space, the crimson pupils of her eyes taking in each person present.

"You've made an excellent choice," the woman purred. "I will be the spirit of your Newbie Village, Elena. Without Classes, you cannot find power. But with them…

"Well, you can rule this world. And others," she said with glittering eyes.

Randidly frowned at the notification about the Newbie Village. Sure enough, a pillar of light rose above Franksburg. This would certainly accelerate their timeline for recruitment. Which meant he should probably head back soon. Just to make sure the Tribulation hadn't taken advantage of his absence.

Oddly, he found himself grimacing. *The time I spent in Franksburg…*

The sense that he didn't belong had only grown stronger over the past several hours. But it had been a chance to relax, which helped clear his head and led to his breakthrough on Potion Making. The message Ellaine told him in the meadow hadn't truly been absorbed until he took a step back from Donnyton. In those moments, he could consider his role based on what he *could* do. He also gained a lot of Skill Levels in random activities, which were useful for PP, but didn't have the opportunity to lead to useful higher-tiered Skills.

It was almost a mini-vacation. After the frustration and inaction of the previous four weeks, it was exactly what Randidly needed to rediscover his drive. Without a constant threat looming, he felt somewhat lost. His goal was clear now. Randidly needed information about the System and then act on it. He would do his best to grow and insulate these villages from the growing threat of the System. As the "lucky" one who had been teleported immediately to a Dungeon, he would ease their transition into this new world.

Randidly looked down at his hands. He would not baby them, but he would still do his best to keep the unknown from crushing them.

They might need to weather their monster hordes, though he would not let a Tribulation break them. Once these villages expanded, he could gather more connections, using Donnyton as a base. Information both on the System, concerning Skills, Classes, and survival.

And the locations of other survivors.

Randidly took in the pillar of light thoughtfully and turned away. There was something Randidly wanted to experiment with, but first, he had a few other… errands.

First things first. Randidly recalled the notification he received earlier, as the PP he earned for Potion Making was enough to finish the Fireball I Path.

Congratulations! You have completed the **"Fireball I Path"**!

As you tread down the path of fire, the ground may be hot beneath your feet, and your hair is wet with sweat, but strength fills your limbs. The Path may stretch ever onward, but your pace accelerates. Mana +50, Mana Regen +10. You have gained the Skill **Circle of Flame Level 1.**

Circle of Flame: *Conjures a circle of flame that expands outward from the caster.* **Damage is highest close to the user and drops off as the Skill travels longer distances. Costs 150 Mana. Size of flames determined by Control and Skill Level. Heat of Flames determined by Intelligence and Skill Level. Speed of spread determined by Wisdom and Skill Level. Duration of circle determined by Focus and Skill Level.**

Randidly was pleased with the nice boost in Mana and Mana Regeneration. He grimaced when he saw the Mana cost of the new Skill. He would need to experiment more with the Skill. At least he had an area of effect spell and a single target spell in fire, which would keep his options open during an extended fight. Even though the cost was debilitatingly high, improving the Skill Level would do a lot to increase the effectiveness, making the Mana spent worth it.

Or at least Randidly hoped so. After all, it was possible it was already extremely powerful. It just didn't seem like a good idea to check while strolling down the street toward Tessa's apartment.

Sidestepping around a mom and five kids staring up in wonder at the pillar of light, Randidly checked his possible Paths.

Watcher *0/??* | **?????** | **Heretic IV** *0/??* | **Oathbreaker** *0/25* | **Initiate of Ash I** *0/75* | **Potion Making II** *0/35*

Randidly was slightly curious why Heretic continued to increase, but he wasn't willing to invest his PP into it to find out. Not when there was such an attractive option as Potion Making II. There might not be very many Stat points, but it would likely end with learning a Skill he could use for the creation of potions.

His recent experiments reminded him how valuable they could be at giving humanity an edge. Even if he might not use them, they would definitely be a boon to Donnyton. Randidly put the remaining 5 points into Potion Making II and earned a point in Focus.

Right afterwards, Randidly found himself standing in front of Tessa's apartment building. Since returning from the Dungeon, Randidly's sense of time had become somewhat fuzzy. The first week out, the arrival of the monster horde had done a lot to help with that, giving a standard time. Since then, he noticed his lack of normal sleep hours made him commit several interpersonal oversights.

After all, he brought Tessa back from the concert two days ago and hadn't really bothered to check on her. Randidly didn't even know when she had to leave for work.

Still, he was here. Randidly tried to laugh at his own behavior, a sense of inadequacy washing over him instead. He was all too aware of the other people hurrying past him, going about their business on the street. *Should I just go up...?*

Even though it had been so long, in his mind, since he broke up with her, this short time spent with her made him less sure things were so simple. The year they'd spent together had been enjoyable. But he'd still make the same decision. The real engine behind his feeling of being adrift ultimately had nothing to do with her.

Since he'd already struck out on the clues about Sydney and Ace, she was probably the person he was closest to in this strange place. Because of that, he wanted her to move to Donnyton, where she would have a larger measure of protection.

Although, depending on the results tonight during the monster horde, perhaps Franksburg would turn out to be a relatively safe place.

He shifted his weight from foot to foot, torn on how to proceed. Randidly wouldn't mind some time focusing on Meditation, but there would probably be more fruitful times to do so. Better to just head up.

When his feet remained stuck to the ground as though glued there, he gritted his teeth. *Why am I letting this stupid thing bother me? Just... go upstairs and ask around.*

What was immediately surprising was the state of the hallways inside. Trash lined the walls. People lined the walls too, lying on those piles of trash and sometimes bundled up in blankets. The elevators weren't working, so Randidly climbed the stairs, which luckily were clear. Nervous people who wouldn't meet his gaze hurried around him in every direction.

That was nothing compared to the surprise that awaited Randidly when he left the stairwell and headed onto Tessa's floor. A tall, scarred man with long grey hair pulled up into a ponytail blocked his way and held out his hand.

"Rent," the man grunted, seeming bored.

"I don't live here."

"Then scram." The man flicked his fingers and turned away. Several other well-muscled men chuckled, leaning against the walls further down the hallway. Randidly thought things were slightly off with this floor. Besides the strange grouping of thugs, there weren't any of the other grungy hall tenants Randidly had seen on the other floors.

Maybe Tessa can actually afford to live on a floor with... guards? Randidly speculated. He wrinkled his nose at the thought of relying on these grimy men for protection. When another man spoke up, his negative feelings deepened.

"You trolling around for pussy, kid? Well, fuck off." The man sucked his teeth at Randidly and shook his head. "These women are all property of someone you can't afford to offend."

Ultimately, Randidly realized he would enjoy doing this the hard way. The fury in his chest didn't care about the consequences after this man referred to Tessa as property. He smiled lightly at the guys hanging around and activated Pollen of the Rafflesia. It was a Skill he hadn't really worked to improve recently, mostly due to the long amount of time it took to affect the enemies. After all, it was much faster to stick a spear down a monster's throat. While in Franksburg, Randidly supposed he should be more... subtle in his approach.

Content to stand under their harsh eyes, Randidly remained in the doorway, waiting for it to take effect.

Mr. Ponytail had a decent amount of Vitality. His bored expression swiftly descended into a frown, his eyes remaining clear. "Why the fuck are you—"

His words were interrupted by the sound of one of the guys vomiting behind him. The man spun, more concerned about this new occurrence than Randidly's continued presence.

He took several shaky steps forward and braced a hand against the wall. "Come the fuck on, if you knew you were sick, why—"

Another man swayed and collapsed, his face pale and mouth foaming. Another man backed away from Mr. Ponytail, his eyes wide, shaking like a leaf in a storm.

Another on the other side of the hallway vomited, spewing bile across the floor.

Randidly's smile widened when Mr. Ponytail spun around, dumbstruck by this turn of events. It seemed his Intelligence of 96 did a lot to speed up the time it took for these people to fall under the Pollen's influence.

Congratulations! Your Skill **Pollen of the Rafflesia (R)** has grown to
Level 10!

CHAPTER EIGHTY

*B*efore the system, Ezzie worked as a bartender. It wasn't a sexy or exciting life, but a satisfying one. Now, after the world fell to shit, he worked security on the housing for the girls who worked at the Carp Twin's "Gentleman's Club." Normally, this meant shoving away the bottom feeders that followed them home or attempted to break into their rooms after hours for a place to sleep. Occasionally, he needed to escort one of the girls somewhere or keep a close eye on one for Missy Carp, the more business-minded of the Carp siblings.

It wasn't a fulfilling life, but it was a stable one.

After all, life with the System made things dangerous. Stability was an important factor to consider when choosing a line of work.

Nothing had ever happened quite like this, where his fellow guards collapsed around him. With a strange fear in his chest, a growing nausea, and a sliver of disbelief, Ezzie turned back to the slim man.

"Did... did you do this?" Ezzie hissed.

Tall, muscular, but not in a bulky way, black hair, and green eyes. His features were as sharp as his smile was mild. Something instinctive, deep within Ezzie's gut, told him this man was dangerous and not to be trifled with. As soon as he acknowledged that feeling, a notification popped up in front of him.

Congratulations! You have gained the Skill **Sixth Sense Level 1!**

Whereas previously Ezzie had been nervous, now he was petrified. The Skill activated and the prickling of danger became a pounding violence hanging over him. The very air he breathed seemed suffused with some strange harm. Ezzie stumbled back and away from the man, coughing and sneezing, desperate to clean out his lungs.

He raised his sleeve to his mouth, trying to filter the air, but it was already too late. His vision swam. He struggled to remain standing. His back was sweaty. He collapsed backward against the wall, barely managing to remain upright.

Congratulations! The Skill **Sixth Sense** has grown to **Level 2!**

The man calmly stepped forward, moving around the moaning and writhing men, his bare feet avoiding the pools of vomit. Strangely, Ezzie could feel the man stopped doing whatever it was that caused this, and the oppressive feeling in the air was slowly thinning.

But the creeping dread grew stronger the closer he approached.

"I'm just here to visit a friend," the man said, regarding Ezzie carefully, a small amount of surprise in his eyes.

Ezzie was pretty surprised as well, leaning against the wall for support. His eyes wanted to drift shut, but he forced them open.

Congratulations! You have gained the Skill **Sleep Resistance Level 1!**

Congratulations! The Skill **Sixth Sense** has grown to **Level 3.**

Each increase in Sixth Sense's Level brought with it a reinforced certainty that this man was dangerous. This green-eyed phantom held within his hands the power to kill him. Ezzie backed up further, driven by his raw and fresh instincts.

"You… you can't. These girls work for the Carp siblings. You know what that means, right?"

The man frowned. Ezzie felt some relief in his heart. Perhaps if he at least was afraid of the Carps, this whole situation could be avoided.

"Honestly, no," the man said, shrugging awkwardly. "But I think you'll find that doesn't matter to me."

Ezzie collapsed, succumbing to the sickness in his veins.

Tessa frowned at the door. Had someone just—

The knock came again, in the same even rhythm. Her roommates had fled back to their bedroom, fearful of who would dare disturb them. Usually, news at the door was worse when the knocking was calm than when it was violent.

At least the violent individuals vented their frustrations and left. Someone who was calm always had a very specific plan for them.

If this was one of Ezzie's goons coming to harass them again...

Firming her resolve, Tessa opened the door. To her surprise, Randidly stood there, looking curiously past her and into the apartment.

"Hey," he said in that slow, a beat too late, offhanded way he had. To her, it was like he sometimes became so focused, he forgot to speak. When he finally did, it was only because he felt guilty about his silence. "I came to find you. There's something I wanted to talk to you about. Are you free?"

Tessa hesitated and forced out the word. "Yes."

Alana paced back and forth, thoroughly annoyed. As time passed, the knot in the muscle of her shoulders twisted itself tighter and tighter. In a show of generosity, Anthony decided to limit the number of people who could get Classes on the first day to 500. He made a great show of how torn he was, and how ultimately, he really valued the growing relationship with Donnyton, and that was what swayed him to listen to their advice.

He added that he hoped they would remember his understanding in the future. It made Alana want to vomit. They weren't doing this for their own benefit; they were doing it to protect Franksburg.

This toad couldn't see past the political edge he could gather. He was blinded to the very real threat the System posed.

Even Devan seemed somewhat disgusted by Anthony's slimy way of handling the situation. Only Clarissa appeared unfazed.

"Just seems like there are going to be a lot of monsters to kill, which will Level my Split Lightning faster. What's not to like?" Clarissa said with a shrug.

Alana sighed. These RPG types were the worst. They threw themselves into growing with the System like it was a game, flippantly disregarding the dangerous reality. Yes, there were benefits, but people in Franksburg would die tonight.

Clarissa had never been disrespectful of the dead, nor did she ever endanger the squad. Maybe Alana just wanted to lash out.

"Devan, come here."

The entire group spun around. They were located on the roof of a rather nice house deep in Franksburg, that Anthony had given them to use. As if it was the most natural thing in the world, the Ghosthound stood there, beckoning. After vanishing for the past several days, he was back, looking just as at ease as he had when they parted.

Hopefully, his adventures here were more productive than ours were. Alana thought.

Devan stepped forward and the Ghosthound put his hand on the man's shoulder.

A long moment passed. The two men gazed deeply into each other's eyes. There seemed to be some sort of powerful connection occurring in front of her, some sort of intimate bond. To her surprise, Alana found herself blushing.

What… what sort of situation was this!

After around ten seconds of this, Devan looked at the ground and said, "I… I would prefer not."

The Ghosthound nodded, even though he pursed his lips. "I understand. It is a lot to ask without being able to tell you exactly what it means. And maybe… well, Alana, come here."

Alana's blush turned into mounting horror. Devan would prefer not? And now the Ghosthound wanted her?

As if he could read her mind, the Ghosthound rolled his eyes. "I have a special Skill I'd like to test. But to receive it, you have to sacrifice your Class. A strange stipulation, but I suppose the Skill is pretty strange in itself…"

"You can give me a Class? Right now?"

The Ghosthound seemed to ponder that. "I don't know. But I do think what I'm giving you will be powerful. Do you want it?"

Alana hesitated, but only for a moment. "Yes. I want it." Alana's eyes blazed, remembering the casual carnage left in Clarissa's wake, and the brutal efficiency of Devan and his squad. "If it's power I can grasp with these hands… I want it."

Randidly put his hand on her shoulder. A red notification, which was a strange departure of the regular blue kind, floated in front of her.

Warning! Randidly Ghosthound has initiated the Skill **"Blessing of the South (U)"** on you.
This will create a permanent bond between you two. Should Randidly Ghosthound perish, all benefits gained from this bond will be retained, but the growth of the bond will cease. Do you still wish to accept his blessing? Y/N

Alana clicked **Yes**, although she frowned. Why did it say warning, instead of the usual congratulations?

Warning! This bond is permanent. Are you sure you wish to proceed? Your Class will be lost upon the acceptance of this Blessing.
Y/N

Now this was getting annoying. This must be why it had taken so long. There were so many pointless notifications… Alana pressed **Yes** again.

Warning! This is your final warning. A portion of this bond's strength will be drawn from Randidly Ghosthound. Are you sure that you wish to accept this bond?
Y/N

"Holy *fuck*!" Alana swore, pressing **Yes**.
This time, the familiar blue notifications appeared.

Congratulations! You have received the **Blessing of the South!**

Calculating Blessing…

From Randidly Ghosthound, you have received the Soulskill **Blessing of the Distant Southern Mountains.** You have gained access to the Class **"Spear of the Broken Ridge." As you do not possess a Class, speak with a Town Spirit to obtain this Class.**

Your Skill **Spear Mastery** has been changed to **Spear of the Broken Ridge Mastery Level 1. All previous benefits have been retained. Spear Thrust** has been changed to **Sun Strike Level 1. All previous benefits have been retained.** You have gained the Skill **Hot Blooded Level 1.** You have gained the Skill **Child of the Sun Level 1.**

Hot Blooded Level 1: *As your current Health drops in relation to your max Health, you receive a small boost in all physical stats.* **The boost increases as Skill Level rises.**

Child of the Sun Level 1: *Regeneration of Health and Stamina increased while under the Sun.* **At night, your body glows, slightly illuminating your surroundings. Regeneration increased by 2% per Skill Level. Illumination increases with Skill Level.**

"Oh wow…" Alana whispered, scrutinizing the notifications with fervent zeal. She had no idea how good the Class would end up being, but the changes to her Skills obviously seemed to be changes for the better. She couldn't wait to try out her new Skills. And these weren't even the Skills she would get when she got the Class!

She selected the option to display the notifications publicly. The Ghosthound carefully read through every one of them.

At the end, he sighed. "So, only really useful for people without Classes, huh? Still, that leaves us some options. Anyway, don't die before we return to Donnyton and get the Class. I want to see the Stat gains."

"Wouldn't it be easier if I just got it here?" Alana wondered aloud, but the Ghosthound immediately knocked down that idea.

"The place you get your Class... some sort of weird connection is formed there. I'm not sure what it does, but we shouldn't take it lightly. Just keep Leveling up Skills for now. After all, the efficiency of grinding for PP is increased now that you have a Soulskill. If it works the same way mine does. You get a bonus every 5 PP spent. Devan, just don't let her die, all right?"

Devan nodded seriously. The Ghosthound walked to the edge of the roof and jumped, disappearing into the night. Alana chewed on the inside of her lip. *I wish you wouldn't keep talking about my death like this. Was the creation of the bond a show of faith... or was it just because I was the only person without a Class?*

Devan walked up beside her and looked after the Ghosthound for a long moment, the sun sinking toward the horizon. He turned to her and said, "Time to get to work. Ready to join the defenses?"

Tessa stared at the ground.

She didn't know what she expected from their talk. She reunited with an ex-boyfriend, *the* ex-boyfriend, and in spite of the crazy change that occurred, they went to a concert together. And he came to her apartment to talk. He walked into her life right when she needed it. She thought it was fate.

Although she didn't necessarily expect him to beg to be back together, what she really hadn't expected was for their relationship not to come up at all. Instead, Randidly urged her to move north to a different town.

She hadn't realized there *was* a different town. A town in which Randidly had quite a bit of sway. Tessa had been under the impression Franksburg was all there was left.

While sitting on the couch, pondering their conversation, the apartment door opened and one of her roommates came back, practically bouncing with excitement.

"Tessa! Did you hear? People came from out of town! Like out, out of town. Like, thirty miles north, out of town. And they want people to resettle with them. How crazy is that?"

Tessa blinked. "That's... crazy."

She clenched her hands into fists. He claimed he wanted to protect her, but would taking her away from here change anything? Especially when she was so close to finishing her uniform prototype? No, this was just Randidly Ghosthound thinking he knew better than she did. Though her nerves buzzed, she found herself moving. She was going to find Randidly and say all the things she'd held in her heart for far too long.

Sam kneeled on the floor of his workshop, trembling.

The pressure from Raid Bosses evened out somewhat recently, and Donnyton was instituting several new policies in order to raise preparation for the possibility of it happening again. One of those policies was the official formation of five new Squads.

Sam already completed the work on the pendants, to give them their mark of pride, but more squads meant more and better equipment needed to be made. Armor was important, as the extra 50 or so Health it provided would mean a lot. If some Stats could be added, so much the better.

In addition, the high frequency of combat meant there was equipment in need of repairs. When it came to skill, Sam stood at the top of his crafting association.

But at the moment, he did nothing.

Instead, he frantically struggled to move, overcome by a strange bout of weakness. None of his Skills would activate. His hands trembled, unable to even maintain a grip on the small hammer he'd been using to work.

Over the past few weeks, there had been a few scattered moments of lightheadedness where he felt strangely empty and light, as if all his strength left him.

Initially, Sam worried it was age. Except Rickman, their official whiskey brewer, had been seventy-nine before the System came, a doddering old man. After slowly Leveling his various Skills and using the points to increase his Vitality and Endurance, Rickman's strength returned. He had salt and pepper hair, looking as though he'd just turned fifty.

Because of this, and other examples of the elderly recovering at least some strength, if not their youth as their Stats rose, and because no one else seemed to be suffering from these strange bouts of weakness, Sam ignored them. He focused on his work, assuming it was a sign of mental fatigue.

But now, as he trembled on the ground, unable to move, he was profoundly afraid. There was so much they didn't know about the System. So many pitfalls they might blindly walk into. If he died here... Randidly... Lyra... Even that fucker Kal over in Turtletown...

And Regina...

Sam breathed slowly, trying to calm himself. The bout of weakness receded.

Five minutes later, he stood, feeling just as vigorous as he ever had. When he looked at his hands, a hint of fear stabbed through him.

What was happening to him?

CHAPTER EIGHTY-ONE

*R*andidly looked out over the ruined suburbs surrounding Franksburg as the cool fingers of dusk spread across the sky. The corners of his mouth quirked up as he examined the "defenses" on this side of the city. Unfortunately, the leaders of Franksburg had been rather loose with their Class allowances. Almost seven hundred people had been given Classes. That was about as much as Donnyton had. Of course, the difference in quality of the Classers was obvious, but still...

It made it a little hard to imagine Donnyton becoming the superpower he wanted it to be, enabling him to use the superior political power for leveraging information. Their higher capability in Crafting and Potion Making would hopefully be enough to maintain their trading partnerships, with Donnyton likely coming out ahead with its higher-end products. In terms of fighting strength, though, in the long run...

If Franksburg wants to threaten Donnyton's position of dominance in the region, they need to survive this night. Randidly examined the meager weapons and armor of the defenders with narrowed eyes. Each group had about thirty people. Two of those hefted machine guns. Most of the rest had either iron bars, repurposed trash can lids, or hatchets.

Beneath a wave of monsters, once the guns were out of bullets, these groupings would be devoured.

Based on the information he'd gotten from Alana, the town housed 42,000 people. The population portion of the monster horde became much scarier than the Classer portion that threatened Donnyton. The monster horde was about three times what Randidly had ever seen attack Donnyton. Just below twenty thousand monsters were coming.

If seven hundred people had Classes, that meant the NCCs would count for a little more than half a monster to push them up to the 20k total. It seemed NCCs only counted for about a third of a monster in terms of the horde. Randidly was relieved, in a way.

Not that he wanted the horde to be big enough to threaten the city. He wanted Franksburg to feel fear and rely upon the goodwill of Donnyton. In addition, Randidly wanted to be out among the horde, Leveling his Skills. Especially the high area Skills, Circle of Flames and Pollen of Rafflesia.

He could slow their advance without inflicting enough damage to the horde as a whole to make it too easy for Franksburg. Basically...

Randidly could run wild.

Humming delightedly to himself, Randidly sat down, brewing his various new potions while he watched the monsters amass in the darkness.

The Black Tusk Wolf Raid Boss looked at its thousand fellows. "We know their smell, the humans from the north. We know them. We can avoid them. Tonight, we strike..."

The wolf bared its black teeth. "And finally, we feast on the soft flesh of humans."

As one, the wolves raised their heads and howled.

Alana gripped her spear shaft so tightly, her knuckles cracked. The monsters came in a thundering wave. She only had a brief chance to look at Franksburg's defenses. In some places, it was barely more than a chain link fence reinforced with metal siding.

The perimeter would undoubtedly be breached. The question was where and how much time would pass before they noticed.

And yet, Alana could not deny the bubbling excitement within her chest. After their display of earning the golden coin for Franksburg, the individuals from Donnyton were given the central vein into Franksburg, a two-lane highway that had been painstakingly cleared of cars and developed as a warehouse center.

Even now, monsters wandered down the road, the runts driven off from the main horde. Alana licked her lips as she studied the long stretch of concrete in front of her.

She wanted to see how far the changes in her Skills would carry her, even as she remained Classless. Once she returned to Donnyton and obtained a Class...

Alana understood the arguments that certain NCCs put stock into. Sam and Regina both chose to focus on raising Skill Levels for now. Alana had thus far taken the same path, and focused on polishing her Spear Mastery and gaining various other Skills for PP.

Now that she had a Class waiting for her in Donnyton, and a powerful one at that, it was hard to resist the allure of the strength it could give her. Above all else, the possible bonuses to Health, Mana, and Stamina changed the entire dynamic of her fighting strategy. Where NCCs have to rely on Endurance and Vitality for their Stamina pool, a Classer holds a naturally high Stamina pool just due to Leveling. This led to increased battle proficiency and increased length of training sessions, which in turn led to higher PP hauls.

Alana shook her head, focusing back on the situation at hand. The sun disappeared and Franksburg's defenders began to light torches. Soon, the attack would come.

Randidly leapt off the roof of a squat apartment complex, crashing into the middle of the flailing horde. He was out beyond the defensive groups of Franksburg, cutting the largest groups of monsters to pieces. This clump of enemies was mostly composed of skeletons with grimy rags hanging from their bones. They would do for the initial test.

"Circle of Flame," Randidly whispered.

A bright heat burned in his chest that soon exploded outward away from him in a wave of flame, smashing the nearby skeletons backward. Most of the ones within a few meters shattered to pieces. The concussive force was too strong for them to resist. The layer of skeletons beyond that howled as their bones charred and weakened, slowly falling apart. Beyond that, the skeletons were sent stumbling.

Congratulations! Your Skill **Circle of Flame** has grown to **Level 2!**

The flame circle dissipated into nothing. Although it was hot and dangerous near him, that power swiftly dropped off after the Skill was used. It currently was nowhere near the Level he wanted it. In terms of heat, the bones survived easily. It was the concussive force that knocked the skeletons out of commission.

Almost three hundred skeletons twisted around, their glowing eyes drawn by the explosion of light and color in the dark night. Randidly ignored them. With a dissatisfied expression, he focused on another skeleton a good distance away. He stepped again, using Phantom Half-Step. As soon as he appeared, another Circle of Flame exploded outwards, ending around twenty more skeletons.

Congratulations! Your Skill **Circle of Flame** has grown to **Level 3!**

The power of this explosion improved marginally. He wondered if that was confirmation bias. Randidly stepped again and activated Circle of Flame. With the potion that boosted his Mana pool for a short period, he activated the Skill freely. Over and over he continued, taking small breaks every four or five Circle of Flames to down a Mana potion. He left a trail of craters in his wake, like the footsteps of a flaming giant, even as his own form was quite small.

He wondered if the defenders could see his small explosions.

After what must have been his thirtieth Circle of Flame, Randidly casually turned around. He'd reached the back of the monster horde after cutting his way through it. All marks of his passage were already erased by the flood of monsters trudging on toward Franksburg. The skeletons didn't bother to chase him. Their attention spans were too short. They simply followed the prodding of the System driving them to attack the Newbie Village.

It looked like the front lines reached the outer Franksburg perimeter. That fighting would begin in earnest soon. Tonight, they would learn how unforgiving this world was. Even Randidly's presence could only do so much. Given enough time, and a lot of potions, sure, he could make a noticeable difference.

Luckily, the past two days had been quite productive, potion-wise.

After drinking both a Mana and Stamina potion, Randidly removed his spear from his Interspatial Ring. He admired the oppressive height and size of the bone weapon. He could still imagine that fearfully powerful sphinx. If it hadn't toyed with him for so long...

Randidly flicked the shaft, feeling it resonate. *The sphinx might have been able to defeat me at the start, but it toyed with me and let the situation develop out of control. By the end, when it unleashed its strange milky pain Skill, it was already too late.*

Randidly raised his spear and looked out at the skeletons before him. *That's why I need to move now, to strike before the situation gets out of hand.*

He tightened his grip and accelerated forward into the densest gathering of skeletons. They wheeled around with their rusty weapons, but even with a massive spine-spear, Randidly was too quick. He chopped and cut, sundering collar bones and shattering spines.

The noise of his offensive strikes attracted more of the creatures into the area. That just made Randidly grin. His body fell into the familiar cadence of spear combat. He practiced his spear Skills a little in Franksburg, but truly he had been focused on other things. To be able to let loose and fully engage in battle...!

I've missed this. Randidly released a breath through his teeth as his spear shattered a skeleton's skull. All the strange anxiety that tightened around his throat during his stay in Franksburg vanished. He spun around and swept the legs out from two others attempting to sneak up on him. Randidly laughed, accelerated forward, and body-slammed another. He planted his feet and used a Roundhouse Kick to shatter one unfortunate monster's knees.

Congratulations! Your Skill **Roundhouse Kick** has grown to **Level 17!**

Congratulations! Your Skill **Fighting Proficiency** has grown to **Level 37!**

His huge weapon of bone swept outward as Randidly began walking back through the horde, cleaving six monsters in half in one blow. Randidly's strength made their bodies seem like paper. The skeletons spun around, angrily clattering their jaws. The next stroke of Randidly's spear silenced them forever.

He pressed forward, faster and faster, cutting through the army, heading toward the section that was composed mostly of goblins. Skeletons were fine.

What Randidly really wanted was to grind other things.

Congratulations! Your Skill **Phantom Thrust** has grown to **Level 46!**

He burst into the columns of goblins in an explosion of mangled flesh, his spear sweeping back and forth. Finding a rather thick clump of armored enemies, he leapt over and unleashed a Spear Phantom's Onslaught, reducing most of the goblins in the area to paste. By the time he landed, the goblins had scrambled back in fear.

Randidly shook his head and advanced. His arms burned from the exertion, even as his Stamina slowly depleted. His spear was almost *too* big to use with the delicate spear-work. The blade of the spear ripped the torso of a goblin in half. Still, Randidly threw his attacks forward with wild abandon, barely trying for delicacy when the goblins leapt at his back.

The corner of his mouth quirked upward.

Twisting, his spear swept across, smashing them out of the air and into the ground. Humming a soft tune to himself, Randidly activated Pollen of the Rafflesia and began ripping quickly through the goblins as those nearby the already dead began to notice his presence. They screamed at him.

He continued, striking and moving on toward the deeper area of the horde. The ones in front were cut to pieces. The ones behind became drowsy, ill, or confused.

A walking catastrophe, Randidly strolled forward, focusing on his form.

After defeating a relatively powerful Goblin Warrior, Randidly climbed a nearby building. Even though it was dark, his eyes cut through the surrounding space. He examined the situation on the battlefield.

Congratulations! Your Skill **Eyes of the Spear Phantom** has grown to **Level 24!**

Randidly hummed to himself in contemplation, considering the state of the defensive lines. *Those toads over there are pushing forward... likely with poison attacks, which makes them difficult to resist. But also...*

Randidly's gaze turned to the south, where a sleek column of white-furred wolves circled the edge of the battlefield with genuine intelligence. *Well, well, what have we here?*

He rushed to that area.

Only to find nothing.

Randidly glanced around. All the wolves he'd seen had vanished. There weren't even that many monsters wandering around over here. All that waited for him here was a dry riverbed, and—

Randidly's eyes narrowed when they landed on the shattered bars of an old water drainage tunnel.

Alana was annoyed.

She lost herself in the vicious cycle of pushing back enemies in the central highway. Too soon, it became obvious having the entire Donnyton group here was a waste.

She left Devan in charge and took a group to another side of the perimeter to reinforce the struggling area. Alana's hands were soon sticky with sweat and monster blood. The first hour was slow. The monsters stalled out on the fences. As the flimsy defenses caved, their work swiftly became cut out for them.

It was only ten minutes ago, after they beat back ice spewing bats, heavily relying on Clarissa's superior magic, they received a new order.

The runner leaned over with his hands on his knees, panting. "You need to retreat to the headquarters."

"Why?" Alana demanded, furious Anthony was being so tight-lipped about the information. "Why the hell would we abandon the line when you *know* right over there is civilian housing!"

The runner trembled, helpless. Alana opened her mouth to continue venting her frustrations, but luckily, the young man spoke first. "The head-quarters went radio silent ten minutes ago. We thought the short-wave radio they use might've malfunctioned. But since we still haven't heard anything…"

Clarissa wandered over. "Uh-oh. Is that… a fire? From Franksburg?"

While the rest of the team remained to maintain the walls, Alana rushed back, hoping to find… well, that it was all an annoying, but ultimately harmless mistake.

Unfortunately, the deeper she moved toward the city, the more the sounds of chaos greeted her. The positive aspects of the situation were that it didn't appear to be monsters. The people were looting in this section of the city. She took profound pleasure in breaking the nose of a man who looked her up and down and leered at her as people chaotically ran around, their screams filling the night.

The outlook turned grim the further in she went. Although there weren't any definitive signs of monsters, people were flying away from the center of the city, panicking. They kept smashing into Alana and rebounding, surprised to find her thin frame so sturdy. Other people stared at her, apparently noticing the soft glow that filled the air around her. It was still light, as her Skill Level was low, but it was definitely visible.

A grinding noise caught her attention. She turned to find the manhole cover to the sewer slowly rising up. With a ringing noise, it popped off all the way. A white wolf leading several goblins scrambled out, chittering in their strange language. The wolf glanced around then dove back into the sewer.

As if this was a signal, a wave of goblins exploded up, waving their small daggers with glee.

The people around Alana froze. All at once, the citizens screamed, clawing their way in any direction that wasn't filled with chittering goblins. Foot traffic in the surroundings screeched to a halt as those who saw the threat struggled against the confused ones who hadn't. At least it gave Alana space to raise her spear. She tore those shocked goblins to pieces so fast that their faces hadn't even registered her presence.

Congratulations! Your Skill **Sunstrike** has grown to **Level 4!**

Frowning down at the open manhole, Alana considered what to do. It didn't appear there were all that many enemies that had come through the space, but the small groups were sending the average citizens into a panic, and—

A strange clicking noise interrupted her train of thought. A soft voice sounded out throughout the town through loudspeakers.

"People of Franksburg, don't panic! We can fight our way through this!" the voice said.

The people around Alana stopped, all turning to look up at the speakers in wonder.

"If you have the will to fight, come to the stadium! If we stand as one, we will push through this challenge!"

Even Alana felt the draw of that charismatic voice. She knew there could only be one source—Raina, the Siren of Franksburg.

CHAPTER EIGHTY-TWO

*R*andidly tried not to think about the lack of noise ahead of him. He stored his massive spine-spear and focused entirely on speed. With his System-strengthened body, Randidly bounced back and forth from wall to wall, bounding down the low-ceilinged tunnel. Two half-meter-thick ledges ran along the side of the cement passage, with a flow of indeterminate liquid in the trough between them. Randidly hadn't bothered to check how deep it was.

At the moment, time was of the essence. If this waste water tunnel led right into the heart of Franksburg… This city wasn't ready for the waves of monsters. If some managed to make it into the populated areas, the average person would be slaughtered. And if the panic spread—

His heartbeat quickened. The more distance he traveled, the more he accelerated. He practically blasted out of the side tunnel and into one of the connecting sewage lines, skidding a meter along the slimy ground. There wasn't much light down here, but the claw marks on the concrete ledges were enough to give him a direction.

Whoosh!

From a dark alcove, two crouching wolves launched themselves at Randidly's back. He planted his foot and attempted to turn, only to slip on the slick surface, his knee hitting the ground. The first wolf sailed harmlessly past, but the second slammed into him.

Randidly accepted the sudden jolt of momentum and rolled sideways with the monster. It twisted as they tumbled off the ledge toward the murky river running below the city, trying to latch on to Randidly's throat with its fangs. Randidly grabbed the ledge and kicked the wolf down into the liquid.

By the time he hauled himself back up, the other wolf had regained its footing and howled. It scampered forward and leapt. Randidly grinned mani-cally at the aggressor.

"Circle of Flame."

Congratulations! Your Skill **Circle of Flame** has grown to **Level 5!**

Despite the low Level, the wave of flame that blasted from his body crashed against the wolf, rendering its leap motionless. Its charred body thumped against the ground just as its companion hopped out of the sewage, sneezing and whining in displeasure.

Before the monster could recover its faculties, Randidly gathered Mana into his palm and released a bright Incinerating Bolt. The projectile lanced through the wolf's spine and the monster crumpled.

Randidly accelerated once again. The stone walls, oddly reminiscent of the underground passage in which Randidly started this wild experience with the System, blurred around him. Those wolves were only there to slow him down. Something intelligent had to be leading them in a directed plan to cause damage to the inner city.

With his power, Randidly intended to let them do neither.

The second ambush came on the heels of the first. Five wolves swarmed out of the darkness from both sides. He slid forward, this time bending his knees to absorb the variance from the fickle footing. As the first wolf snarled and howled, Randidly's fist smashed into its snout. He felt the cartilage shift and snap.

Congratulations! Your Skill **Fighting Proficiency** has grown to **Level 38!**

He faced the others, cool Mana once more collecting to a point in his chest before exploding outward. Circle of Flame flared. The singed wolves yelped and tumbled backward. Randidly didn't bother to stay and finish them off this time.

The tunnel became wider and the grimy shadows were pushed back by a light leaking out from the main passage. His stomach twisted. The fact that electricity ran through here practically guaranteed this would take the monsters right to the heart of Franksburg.

The familiar clattering of undead monsters clanged from beyond the corner, alerting him to the oncoming ambush. He slowed his mad dash and produced his spear. A score of skeletons shambled out to block his path.

Randidly's hands tightened on the shaft of his spear, not liking the impli-cation that whatever led the wolves through here was also bringing other varieties of monsters with it.

The clacking bodies pressed closer, waving their rusted weapons, and largely just occupying the path into the main sewage line. Heat flared in

Randidly's chest as he channeled his Stamina. He used Phantom Half-Step on a skeleton at the back to materialize in the middle of them all.

The muscles of his shoulders and arms tensed. Randidly mobilized his high Strength and brought the heavy spear around to smash the skeletons against the wall. Randidly hopped over their collapsing bodies, stored his spear, and pulled out a Stamina potion to chug. He emerged into the well-lit area, where the stone walkways were large enough for several men to walk abreast.

His eyes flashed. He caught the distant sight of fleeing wolves to the left, and trailing them was at least a few dozen Level 9 Red-Palm Monkeys.

Congratulations! Your Skill **Eyes of the Spear Phantom** has grown to **Level 25!**

He dashed after them. The Red-Palm Monkeys peeled off from the wolves and glared at Randidly with vicious eyes. His expression twisted into a scowl. Their evident cruelty brought back sharp pangs of fear from when he'd tortured himself against the Howler Monkeys in the Dungeon to spur his own growth.

The hotheaded, aggressive personality of the Ghosthound surged upward and took control of Randidly's body. Even though the Stamina potion had only just begun to refill his Stamina pool, he activated Phantom Half-Step twice to all but eliminate the distance between himself and the closest monkeys.

Congratulations! Your Skill **Phantom Half-Step** has grown to **Level 15!**

Randidly produced his massive spear and swung it sideways. The Red-Palm Monkey's eyes widened, succumbing to fear even before the attack landed. The Ghosthound was filled with a wild glee.

He cut down the first monkey in a single stroke. His spear flashed upward on a diagonal line, shearing off half of another Red-Palm Monkey's hand. Stepping forward, Randidly unleashed a flurry of blows back and forth, wounding and maiming the unfortunate monsters in his path.

This is why I trained. This is why I struggled. This is why I cried myself asleep and woke to nightmares. His Stamina dropped dangerously low. He was only halfway through the panicked column of monkeys, but he dared not slow his blitzkrieg. *So that when I stood between innocents and monsters, I could protect them.*

For a brief moment, Randidly's mind flicked back to that moment in front of the Giant Serpent, when Shal knocked him out of the path of danger. Though he couldn't repay that debt directly, Randidly could do the same for someone else.

His body trembled with the effort to keep himself moving forward. He brought the spine-spear horizontally across his body with a Sweep, knocking two Red-Palm Monkeys to the side. He took one more step forward, sinking down to single digits in Stamina.

Spearing Roots erupted from the ground, cracking the stone and ripping through the legs of the unfortunate monkeys. They collapsed into fits of wild screams, leaving Randidly to waltz through the last several meters with enough spare time and attention to store his spear again and pull out two more Stamina potions.

Congratulations! Your Skill **Edge of the Decay (Un)** has grown to **Level 15!**

Randidly spared the monsters behind him a glance. Each one that met his gaze flinched. The Ghosthound chortled. *Most are just injured, but my Spear of Rot Soulskill will not let them off easily.*

By the time he turned back, his Stamina had risen to acceptable amounts. He loped casually forward, drinking one more Stamina and Mana potion for good measure. Randidly didn't want to be caught unprepared, not at such a critical time.

A few times, he caught sight of a single Black Tusk Wolf leading a dozen or so goblins down a side tunnel as he rushed onward. He was tempted to pursue, but those weren't part of the main group. He followed the growing cacophony of growling, snarling carnivores further ahead.

He rounded the corner and his eyes widened. Wolves scrambled up a ladder and out through a manhole, with at least a hundred others circling below, waiting their turn. Their black fur seemed especially ominous beneath the buzzing fluorescent lights of the sewage tunnel.

Frantic screams echoing down through the asphalt was a frozen dagger to his heart.

For a second, Randidly couldn't breathe. He took one step, then another. Each time, his stride lengthened and his gait became a little more bounding. The Ghosthound forgot all about conserving Stamina. Through the haze of desperation, he poured every ounce of his being into stopping these wolves from escaping the sewer.

A slender wolf's ears flicked and it raised its head to stare right at him. It opened its maw to sound the alarm. Randidly bared his teeth in response and activated Phantom Half-Step.

"Circle—" He landed at the edge of the thick cluster of wolf bodies, his momentum carrying him forward and shoving several wolves to the side. "—of Flame!"

Congratulations! Your Skill **Circle of Flame** has grown to **Level 6!**

Heat and kinetic force exploded out from Randidly's body, burning through the nearest wolves and knocking those in the surroundings off their feet. Unfortunately, the Skill was only Level 6. Most of those that weren't directly burned were quickly able to get back on their feet.

He ignored their snarls, his eyes on the movement of wolves scurrying up the ladder. One wiggled its way up the last few rungs and scampered out onto the streets above. Another wolf was already carefully bending its claws over the metal to ascend.

The screams grew louder.

A wolf leapt at Randidly from behind. He twisted his stance to smash his knee into the side of its face, but three more approached. A bead of sweat trickled down his temple. Perhaps with infinite time, he could Roundhouse Kick and smash his way through, except every second he wasted down here released another wolf onto the streets above.

Grimacing, Randidly barreled his way toward the ladder. A wolf raked his calf and left it spurting blood. He ignored the wound, knocking wolves out of his way with his bare hands. A wolf jumped over its comrades, attempting to tackle him from the front. Randidly brought his hands together, interlaced his fingers, and swung his arms wildly across his body.

The blow cracked the wolf's neck and sent it tumbling. It was dead before its body hit the ground.

Congratulations! Your Skill **Spirit of Adversity** has grown to **Level 30!**

Of course, the brief digression earned him a gash across his forearm and a bite on his opposite elbow. Randidly planted his feet and leapt through the air, beginning to mobilize all his remaining Mana to end this snarling wave.

Another wolf hopped up from the crowd to intercept him, but Randidly activated Phantom Half-Step on the wolf about to escape and avoided the meddlesome monster entirely.

Congratulations! Your Skill **Phantom Half-Step** has grown to **Level 16!**

Randidly underestimated his momentum, crashing into the back of a wolf lower on the ladder. Its legs were forced between the rungs and it whined in protest to being the cushion for Randidly's leap.

Randidly shoved the stunned wolf to the side, grasping for the ancient iron ladder before he tumbled down after it. His fingers momentarily slid along the rung, wet with his own blood, before his grip held.

The wolf on the ladder above Randidly flashed its black teeth at him. Randidly yanked on its tail, reducing its snarl to a yowl when he flung it to the side.

The wolves below circled, attempting to bite at his legs as he hauled himself up the last few feet and seized the edge of the manhole opening. He forced a smile.

"Why don't you just stay down there forever?" Randidly coalesced all his Mana into a chilling surge, focusing it into one attack that exited his body and left him feeling vaguely spent.

Randidly heaved himself up through the hole just as one particularly aggressive monster bounded up the ladder. The wolf raked its claws, catching nothing but metal and throwing itself off balance. It chomped down on the metal bar to steady itself just as the old bricks attached to the ladder exploded outward, undermined by the determined work of Randidly's Root Manipulation. The wolf frantically tried to ascend, but the heavy bricks creaked, tumbling onto a half dozen of the tightly packed wolves.

Congratulations! Your Skill **Spirit of Adversity** has grown to **Level 31!**

Randidly heaved the manhole cover back in place and the shouts of the surrounding civilians washed over him. It wouldn't keep the beasts out of the city for long, but keeping the situation from escalating now was the most important. He spotted about a dozen monsters rushing in various directions after fleeing civilians, bounding over shredded corpses splayed across the street. Shrill cries of pain and voices begging for help echoed from nearby streets all around him.

The other monster groups were revealing themselves.

Randidly caught sight of a lone monster surveying the chaos from a far corner. It regarded him with evident shock. Randidly was just as surprised by what he saw above its head.

Black Tusk Wolf Raid Boss Level 20

How the hell is its Level that high? And a Raid Boss? His mind scrambled to make sense of its presence in that strained moment of recognition between them. The Newbie Barrier shouldn't allow this beast within its border. Unless monsters from the first Newbie Villages could wander into other safe areas?

The wounded Shadow Cat that led him to Turtletown's Tribulation popped into his thoughts. He wasn't sure how, but Donnyton's Tribulation was likely at work here. This was the beast he'd really been after in those tunnels.

The beast shook its furry head, opened its mouth, and produced a voice. "One of the Northerners? Cheh. Your presence here changes nothing. In this city of fresh meat, with our numbers—"

Roots cracked open the sidewalk beneath the Black Tusk Wolf's feet and slithered up around its legs. The monster hopped out of the way as soon as the threat showed itself. The wolf growled and flicked its nose at several of the subordinate wolves around it. Four rushed Randidly, their matte-black fangs bared.

As well trained as a fucking army. Randidly's chest seethed, his heart walking the precarious tightrope between anxiety and rage. He produced his spine-spear and hefted the weapon. *I wonder...*

To his surprise, and relief, the wolves wove between each other and settled into a familiar shape. Randidly sidestepped, predicting their formation and attack strategy after pushing through so many ambushes in the sewers.

When the wolves leapt, *they* were the ones surprised by Randidly's diagonal sweep with his spine-spear. The first wolf's forelegs were severed and the second couldn't even cry out as the spear's blade sank into its skull. The remaining two landed behind Randidly on his left and right, ready to follow up. Randidly released his spear and used the momentum of the swing to keep spinning to his right.

The waiting Black Tusk Wolf raised its head and howled. Randidly's skin tingled. It unleashed a curse Skill, but Randidly's high Willpower weathered the attack without any difficulty. His fist crashed down on the wolf to his right, splintering its skull and driving it into the asphalt.

The final of the subordinate wolves threw itself, fangs first, at Randidly's back. But he was used to their speed now. His right hand snaked out past its snapping jaws and seized its throat. He flicked his wrist, snapped the offending wolf's neck, whipped the body around, and sent it spinning back toward the Raid Boss.

"Gonna need to try harder than that," Randidly gnashed his teeth and picked up his spine-spear just as the subordinate's body rolled to the feet of the Raid Boss.

After witnessing the display of Randidly's raw Stats, the orchestrator of this tragedy turned and fled.

Unfortunately for it, Randidly was firing on all cylinders.

Randidly didn't bother wasting energy on turning as he chased it around the corner. He slammed into a defunct streetlight, denting the thick shaft to adjust his vector. He activated Sprint and gained ground. The monster ducked to the left at the last second, clambering through the broken glass front of a shopping center.

Franksburg's speaker system buzzed on and a familiar voice echoed out over the sound of screams. "All able-bodied individuals, head to the Stadium for assistance as monsters are loose in the city! I repeat, monsters are loose in the city."

One thing at a time. Randidly's foot pushed off so violently, the skin tore. He ignored the sting. He was right on the Raid Boss's tail. It fled across the deserted remnants of a food court, aiming for the thickest cluster of tables.

The wolf squeezed its muscular body beneath them. Randidly's heavy spear smashed the obstructions to pieces.

They were soon out of the desolate food court area, heading toward the edge of a balcony that overlooked other portions of the underground mall.

Randidly licked his lips. He'd finally caught up.

He spun his spear and raised it for a Phantom Thrust. The Black Tusk Wolf whipped its head around and unleashed an ear-piercing howl. For a brief moment, its eyes glowed red. Wolves swarmed out from every shadow, over deserted countertops and garbage-strewn booths. Their movements blurred into each other.

They crashed toward him in an overwhelming wave, as though the fur, and claws, and fangs of the pack had become liquid and the wolf dam had broken.

Congratulations! Your Skill **Mental Strength** has grown to **Level 17!**

The illusion shattered. Randidly stood above the Black Tusk Wolf as it attempted to create some distance between them. His spear flashed down and pierced the monster's back leg.

Randidly twisted the weapon to damage its mobility further, but it managed to wrench itself free and hobble the remaining three meters to the edge of the balcony. Randidly raised his hand and gathered the Mana for an Incinerating Bolt.

"Randidly Ghosthound!"

Randidly blinked and turned around. Across the broken and cracked floor, inexplicably, was Tessa. The thug Randidly confronted at her apartment stood beside her with a bloody meat cleaver in one hand and a scratched trash can lid in the other.

"I... I'd better go see if Madam Missy needs any help," the thug gulped loudly and backpedaled away after a single glance from Randidly.

Randidly's eyes moved back to Tessa.

The sound of the Raid Boss hopping off the balcony brought Randidly's attention whipping back to his quarry. His eyes reddened. He didn't know why Tessa was here, but this Raid Boss, with intelligence enough to lead its fellows and other monsters alike into Franksburg, was his main priority.

Without a backward glance, Randidly vaulted off the balcony after the wolf. In his descent, he barely caught sight of Tessa's form dashing for the frozen escalators but pushed the knowledge away. With his Stamina recovered enough, he used Phantom Half-Step to shift his position midair. They sailed over the barren husk of a sunglasses kiosk and an Auntie Anne's, heading directly toward a massive dried fountain that was the centerpiece of the lower plaza.

Randidly brought the shaft of the spine-spear smashing down toward the wolf's back. It twisted at the last second, likely to avoid having its spine shattered, but Randidly felt its ribs crack.

The wolf bounced across the dried basin of the fountain. Randidly hit the ground running. He smashed his foot into its wounded back leg and sent it sprawling again into the wall of the fountain.

Congratulations! Your Skill **Edge of Decay (Un)** has grown to **Level 16!**

The Raid Boss struggled to stand, the flesh on its leg beginning to blacken and swell. Randidly raised his spear.

"Randidly! Don't you dare kill that animal!" Tessa shouted, shards of broken glass crunching loudly underfoot, alerting him to her nearing approach.

He was once again stunned enough that he hesitated, but he didn't dare look away from the monster for fear of another illusion. The Black Tusk Wolf panted as it stared at his raised spear with wide eyes. Randidly couldn't believe it'd merely lie down and give up. *What game are you playing, wolf?* Was it waiting for Tessa to come closer and use her to distract him to escape? He had to make her see the ridiculousness of her interference and leave before she got herself hurt, or worse.

"Don't kill this *animal*?" Randidly asked when Tessa was only five meters away. "Did you see the bodies in the street? This thing led those monsters—"

"You told me you and the people from your village allowed us to buy into the System and get Classes," Tessa interrupted. "So didn't *you* bring the monsters here?"

Randidly tore his gaze away from the wolf and just stared at her, unsure of how to answer.

Tessa took his silence as license to continue. "I'm not coming with you to your village, I have a life here. This isn't one of your games or novels, Randidly. The world... Well, everything is crazy right now, but what you're doing is wrong. Embracing killing so quickly means letting go of your humanity. There are other ways we could handle this."

The determined way her eyes fixed on the wounded Raid Boss filled Randidly with a bad feeling. His grip tightened on his spear. "You can't be serious."

Perhaps the only reason he didn't attack, as Tessa clambered over the edge of the fountain and approached the Raid Boss, was the intensity in her eyes. Her actions blindsided him and left him bewildered.

"Tessa—"

"Can you, for once in your life, listen to someone else?" Tessa barked, and gestured vaguely to his bloody feet and massive spear. "Is this really what you want? You know what, don't answer that. I can tell you for sure that it's *not* what I want. I don't want to have to fight all the time. I don't want violence to become normalized. If we would have just continued to ignore the System, everything would have been fine."

"Do you really believe that?" Randidly snapped. "The monsters—Tessa, just stay back! I can't protect—"

"You don't need to protect me. That's the point," Tessa insisted. "And I'm going to prove it to you."

Shal would have ruthlessly mocked Randidly's immobilized staring over the past ten seconds. He just couldn't believe that the gentle and mild Tessa could suddenly become so bold. Tessa walked right up to the Black Tusk Wolf and extended her hand. Randidly could far too easily imagine it lunging straight for her throat.

As meek as a trained dog, the Raid Boss lowered its head and licked Tessa's fingers. Randidly pressed his lips together. He didn't believe this for a second. That creature was playing her for a fool.

Tessa rounded on Randidly with a bright smile of triumph. "This is what you don't get, Randidly. Your way of life is not one that most people would choose. Don't you dare assume that everyone else is like you.

"My decision regarding how I want to spend my life is just as valid as yours." Tessa took a step forward, interposing herself between Randidly and the monster, her bottom lip trembling. "So what if I'm weak? So what if I need to stay in Franksburg all the time? You don't get to make that choice for me, just like you cannot force me to live a life where I have to justify killing."

"Do you think I wanted this?" Randidly asked, the volume of his voice rising. "To fight all the time? To ache and bleed? I don't have any choice, Tessa. Monsters are here and they are definitely trying to kill us. Don't fall for how cunning this Raid Boss is—"

"Then answer me this." She took another step forward, her brown eyes bright, getting right in Randidly's face. "If you didn't enjoy this, why were you smiling as you were about to kill this poor creature?"

Because killing it would mean that I protected this city. Because accomplishing that would mean I'm strong.

Randidly didn't dare vocalize either of those thoughts, partially because Tessa's previous words made him realize she wouldn't accept them, and also because they were a bit disingenuous.

Tessa trying to pin Franksburg's current difficulties on him was misguided, but she did hit on one true thing: a part of Randidly enjoyed the changes that had been wrought by the System.

"Exactly." Tessa jabbed her finger into his chest. "And you know what the worst part of all of it is? The costumes. Do you remember how many times I invited you to join me in the sewing circle and you told me it was dumb? An entire year's worth of spurned invitations. And then you had the nerve to take a job sewing and did well enough you got fucking backstage passes!"

Randidly blinked several times. "What are you—"

The Raid Boss moved. Randidly was only a hair behind it. He cast aside his huge spear and thrust his arms out and around Tessa. He caught the bared jaw of the Raid Boss as best he could. Its sharpened tusk lanced through the meat of Randidly's palm before its sharp teeth could sink into her back.

"Ahhhhh!" Tessa screamed, flinching away from Randidly and toward the open mouth of the drooling wolf.

Randidly was done giving her the chance to endanger her own life. He lifted his arms and twisted, bringing the yelping wolf up and over Tessa. He torqued the monster's neck through the arc until he heard it snap, and slammed its body against the ground.

Congratulations! Your Skill **Fighting Proficiency** has grown to **Level 39!**

Randidly put his bleeding foot against the monster's torso and pulled his hand free of the tusk of the Raid Boss. He produced and drank a Health potion as he turned to face Tessa. He winced. She had a thick spatter of blood across her legs, likely from his hand.

She collapsed to the ground, face ashen. "That... that thing just—"

"Tried to kill you. With no prodding from me," Randidly said. "That's the way the world is now. Look, I know it's not easy. I... shit, Tessa. I'm so exhausted from all of the killing. But it really is the only way."

That stubborn expression returned as she looked up at him. "No, it isn't. But you... the way you live is the problem. Can't you see that? Your lifestyle makes it necessary for poor creatures like that to behave irrationally. Because *you* brought the Newbie Village and made everything go to shit for Franksburg. *Your* existence forces this! Most people want nothing to do with all this blood. Which is normal! I'm perfectly normal!"

There was a muffled crackling in the distance beyond the space of the food court. The melodic word that followed as the sound system across the city activated was extremely clear.

"Fight."

Randidly looked at Tessa with tired eyes, even as he acknowledged the emotional tug contained in that broadcasted word. He could see her panic, her desperation, her fear. Each of those emotions had broken Randidly down to desperate sobs in the Dungeon. Tessa hadn't yet had the time to adjust to the newness of the System. Franksburg had done far too well at insulating her from the shift.

She might even be right about his influence. Things wouldn't have escalated so quickly without his presence. But for now, he folded up that knowledge and stored it in the corner of his mind. He had to focus on the current situation.

Franksburg's sound system chirped again. "Fight."

The emotional tug was stronger this time. Randidly turned away from his ex-girlfriend and closed his eyes. "I need to go. Maybe—well, definitely things could have been different. Should have been different. But right now, this is the way things are. Monsters are loose in Franksburg. Whatever else I might be, I'm a realist. I'm not going to let ideals stop me from addressing the injustice in front of me."

Raina peeked out around the curtain, looking at the swiftly filling concert venue. The sound of panicked and desperate talk bubbled upward, filling the space with unease. Raina tried to remain positive. The fact that so many people made it here was a good sign for their ability to survive.

More chilling were the intermittent pops of gunfire and shouts of anger from around the doors to the stadium. Her security detail was manning the doors, keeping monsters away. It was becoming difficult as more and more people pressed in, desperate for a port in this bloody storm.

Her main bodyguard and friend, Matilda, and her manager and costume designer, Cassie, stood next to her at the curtain with similar expressions of worry.

"What do you plan on doing?" Matilda asked in a low voice, her eyes bouncing between the stadium and the frantically scrambling men backstage.

Normally, the concert venue got their power from the small power plant the government of Franksburg ran. However, that had become quite fickle in the last few hours. Her production team was scavenging the nearby area for generators. If there wasn't light, someone would trip and break their neck in the dark stairwells without a monster even needing to injure them.

Raina even brought the one that powered her own home when she came.

"I… don't really know. But…" And truly, Raina didn't. These past few weeks, she'd become increasingly reliant on the Senator. He essentially told her what she would be doing every day. It was nice, in a way. Her life was simple and filled with music.

And yet, she couldn't get the voice of that strange, stoic man out of her head. She could still picture his face on that rooftop when he told her he couldn't tell what about her was the Skill, and what was not. Sighing inwardly, Raina plastered on a bright smile and continued to speak. "But we couldn't do nothing. Once word gets to the military, they'll send—"

"No, they won't," a cold female voice interrupted Raina.

Raina was shocked to find a blood-soaked woman holding a spear standing near their group.

Snorting, the woman pulled a towel out of nowhere and wiped her face. "The perimeter is full of holes, there is no one they dare spare to come assist you. I brought a few of the Classers from Donnyton, but—"

A shout of panic interrupted her words. A bellow and a wolf's howl cut through the stadium air. The talk died and something much more dangerous began to bubble.

The woman hesitated, her face scrunching up. "Well, hopefully, we'll be enough. I'm Alana."

"You..." Matilda tilted her head to the side and gave the other woman a measuring glance. "You are from that other village, to the north. The people who came down with Classes? Did you know this would happen when they founded a village!"

Alana grimaced. "We did warn them; they simply didn't—"

"Enough, it's fine," Raina said coolly, giving the woman Alana a short glance before turning back to the stage. "For now, let's focus on surviving. My song can help calm people—"

A scream distracted her. Raina twisted to see several large toads hopping in from a side hallway. They spat poison and the coated walls and floor slowly warped and melted. An acrid smoke wafted upward, turning the air murky.

Alana blurred, racing toward the toads. Several turned and spat at the approaching threat. Spinning her spear, she knocked the strange liquid to the side, except for one fat glob. It arced slowly through the air. Raina watched it with wide eyes.

It's inevitable, she thought. *My body won't even move.*

Matilda realized what was happening after it was too late to intervene. Her face flickered between expressions. From calm, to shock at the frog's appearance, to relief as Alana moved, finally settling on mounting horror.

The acid took Raina fully in the face. She barely managed to close her mouth and eyes in time.

There was nothing but the sensation of liquid splashing over her. Raina couldn't help but shiver. It clung to her jaw like jelly.

Then there was pain.

Her entire world was on fire, concentrated on her face. Every overwhelmed nerve-ending lit up like a torch. The fire started to spread downward through her neck.

Collapsing, Raina heard people swearing and rushing around her, dumping water on her face. The pain persisted, ripping deeper. Her mind stuttered and began to slow.

"Fuck, open your mouth, you foolish girl!" a voice next to her ear hissed.

Raina drifted off into darkness, her only regret being that she—

Someone punched her in the gut. Reflexively she opened her mouth, gasping for air. A strange, warm liquid was poured down her throat. She choked and began to cough, but almost immediately, the pain on her face faded from life-threatening to a burning ache.

"Mixed by the Ghosthound himself, not that you'll appreciate it," the woman, Alana, said waspishly.

Raina shivered and took several shaky breaths as her once weakening body was filled with vitality. More water was poured over her. The pain decreased, down to manageable levels, even as she felt tears forming in the corners of her eyes.

Slightly woozy, she managed to stand, gripping tightly on to Matilda. Slowly at first, but then committing to the effort, Raina opened her eyes. The skin above her eyes twisted and twinged.

Raina blinked several times, somewhat surprised they hadn't been overrun with monsters yet. The sounds of fighting were growing louder. It appeared Alana swiftly killed the frogs. No one else, other than Raina, had been harmed, which was a blessing. Except Matilda and Cassie were looking at her with deep wells of sorrow in their eyes.

"Is... something wrong?" Raina asked, wincing when her lips moved. Even the skin of her cheeks felt tight and raw.

"Oh... it's... it's nothing. Just... a little scarring..." Cassie stammered.

Alana's snort was almost painfully direct. "Girl, that acid sorta fucked your face up. It's not something makeup can fix."

After fumbling for a second, Alana produced a small mirror. For several long seconds, Raina looked at herself. Then she began to laugh.

It was a low chuckle at first, until it twisted and grew dark. She wrapped her arms around her chest and shoulders. Her skin was cool as a plastic mannequin.

"Plain... he said I was..." she muttered to herself, which set off another fit of giggles. What she wouldn't do to be just plain right now. Would her Skills be enough to overcome this?

"Cassie, do you still have that embroidered mask he made?" Raina asked.

Cassie ran to a trunk and grabbed it, bringing it back.

Alana's eyes narrowed. "So now—"

"Now we fight," Raina said, a small, smoldering coal of hatred burning in her heart. Although that man hated thinking a Skill affected him, drawing him to her, he was clear on one fact.

When she smiled at him, he liked it. And now even that was gone. Raina wondered whether he would accept her with these scars, but set that aside. First, she needed to survive. And she only had one path for that—her music.

She took the mic offered to her by a trembling crew member, his gaze on the ground. Ignoring the looks and the not-looks by the crew who witnessed her disfigurement, Raina put the mask on and walked onto the stage. The crowd cheered raggedly. Filled with desperation fueled by the howling of wolves growing closer. From the stage, she saw quite a few couples having sex right there in the seats, driven by their fear and panic into an animalistic frenzy.

She pitied them.

She pitied them more for what was about to happen. That small coal spread its flame, igniting the whole of her being.

Raina raised the mic and sang a single word into the receiver. Softly, crooning it to fill it with as much of her Skill as she could.

"Fight."

She did not bother with lyrics, or any of her songs, or any tune. She didn't wait for the band to come out and join her. There was no need to package this message. The hot rage boiled inside of her. She used her persuasive Skill to give it a vicious and desperate voice. Even after she had spoken only once, the air changed.

The ambiance was still wild, but some of the fear began to dissipate.

"Fight."

She sang for every friend or acquaintance who was likely dead, killed by monsters. For every hollow-eyed fan who crowded her concerts, starving themselves in this city in order to afford the ticket. For her dream of being a successful singer finally coming true, while everything about it felt so wrong.

"Fight."

She raised her voice, stressing the word, dragging it out and adding more musical flair to her imperative.

People in the crowd looked upward as she sang, a glassy look appearing in some of their eyes. They breathed and moved as one, slowly aligning with her rallying cry.

"Fight."

She heard them mouth the word, but knew it was not enough. She moved to the edge of the stage, standing right above them, her arms raised to the sky.

"Fight, Fight, Fight."

Slowly, they joined, their chant following hers, their eyes slowly narrowing and turning red.

"Fight! Fight! Fight!"

She shouted it now, clutching the mic with white fingers. Hating the monsters but loving them too. They crushed her old life while giving her this brief month of being on top of the social circle. Even if she was nothing more than a glorified mouthpiece for a pompous Senator. No matter how twisted it was, at least she was loved.

The System gave her a Skill that made even that stoic boy struggle to resist her smile. And just as quickly, the System had taken it away, leaving behind its grace in the form of scar tissue. For that, at the moment, she wanted to bring it all crashing down. And so, she sang, howling her dissatisfaction.

"FIGHT!"

Raina continued to shout her call to action. Her Skill-imbued voice echoed over most of the town. Some people were already insensible at this point. Vicious, their vision tinged red, they stumbled outward, gathering poor weapons to hunt down their enemies.

When they found monsters, they threw themselves at them with wild abandon, not caring for their lives.

Because they heard a beautiful voice.

And it told them one thing: Fight.

Men and women attacked each other in their haste to find and kill a monster. They surged out of the seats and streamed toward the entrances of the concert venue. The weaker among them lost their footing and were swiftly trampled. The crowd cared not. They were scared, weak people, and Raina had given them something to cling to. In her strange magic, they found strength.

Not their own strength, but the strength of a vicious, hungry, mindless mob.

CHAPTER EIGHTY-THREE

*R*andidly stretched, cracking his neck as the moon rose over the city.

Unlike the attacks on Donnyton, this monster horde came soon after sundown. Around six hours later, when the monsters were too thinly spread to be considered anything more than the usual amount, the survivors collapsed, ready to rest for the "rest" of their lives.

He couldn't help but laugh at his own joke on his journey back to the city. When he looked around at the piles of bodies, he sobered up somewhat.

Surviving the first monster horde carried a bloody cost, more so than Randidly expected, due to the weird wolves that led monsters directly into the city. He'd hunted them down and slaughtered their leader in the dark sewers, but the damage was already done. Without the protection of its machine guns, Franksburg was a sitting duck.

Of course, even if they had just charged straight forward, most of the monsters would have avoided bullets anyway. Randidly could only shake his head at the foolishness of Franksburg's leaders. *The ammo stores were running low before the horde. Did they really expect the leftovers to slow twenty thousand monsters?*

Even if they kept the number of Classers low for tomorrow, the sheer number of people here meant the hordes would always be large. Surviving would be tough. Briefly, Randidly considered remaining to assist for a while longer.

He pushed his mind away from that line of thought. He could not help every village grow. He was here to create an advantage for Donnyton. And the advantages in recruiting they would gain after Alana's performance last night would be more than enough.

In addition, Devan told him about some of the dangerous notifications he'd received a few days prior. Donnyton apparently had advanced to a Trainee Village. Hopefully, this also meant Nul would relent and allow Randidly to learn more Skills from his Skill Challenges. And maybe, just interact with him in general.

At any rate, it was time to head home. Or at least it would be, tomorrow.

Over the course of the night, Randidly accumulated quite a few Skill Levels he hadn't noticed. He gained 3 Levels in Spear Mastery, 1 in Phantom Thrust and Spear Phantom's Footwork, 2 in Phantom Half-Step, 2 in Heavy Blow, 2 in Phantom Onslaught and Sweep, 4 in Pollen of the Rafflesia, 1 in Agony and Eyes of the Spear Phantom, 3 in Circle of Flame, and finally, 1 in Physical Fitness.

Randidly did not yet distribute his PP. Instead, he walked through the depressed city, heading toward the location of his Cooking job. This would likely be the last time he would be here, so he wanted to join in the work. It was not nearly as impactful as the fighting he'd done outside of the view of Franksburg's citizens, but Randidly liked to be part of the clean-up in some small manner. Especially when they were offering free food to the survivors in an attempt to keep up morale.

The catharsis of his conflict with Tessa and the city's answer that had emerged through Raina obliterated his uneasiness about this place. His power was not the power of the city, though power mattered here too.

The System had changed the entire world. Probably not for the better.

Plus, this will be my last chance to grind Cooking. Randidly mused. He looked down at his bloody knuckles. *I'll need to find a place to wash up a bit first.*

Luckily, or unluckily, for Franksburg, the Senator survived the skeletal ransacking of the headquarters. He locked himself in the closet and cried himself to sleep during the worst of the fighting. Most of the previously intimidating "military presence" that flanked the blond man fled, leaving him alone to man the communications room by himself.

For that, at least, Alana decided not to tear down all pretenses of civility between them after the disastrous first monster horde.

The Freedom Fighters as a group searched for him and found him. Satisfied, everyone wandered to find the nearest bed. Even Anthony, who only commanded the battle, had red rims around his eyes and was starting to slur his speech due to exhaustion.

Alana supposed it was only natural. This was their first beast horde. They'd fought monsters before, but were wildly unprepared for what it was like to fear for their lives. And to think they had nowhere to return to.

Internally, Alana admitted it was slightly cruel, what they were doing. Without their assistance, they wouldn't have acquired a Newbie Town for a few more weeks. At that time, their average Level of Strength would have risen another Level. She felt a slight amount of guilt for depriving them that chance to grow.

Admittedly, not to the point where they could have survived what came for them last night, but still…

Shaking her head, Alana searched out Devan and his squad, only to find another group of three had crept up on them.

"Still awake?" Alana said with false casualness.

She was slightly afraid of the masked woman in front of her. Alana felt the pull on her will when Raina chanted for all to fight, but she resisted it. Once the conscious choice was made, it was rather easy to push its influence aside. She was forced to watch as people had their arms cut off, stuffing their bloody stumps down the throat of a monster to kill it, their eyes gleeful.

It was a dangerous power when not wielded with wisdom and empathy.

"Yes," Raina said simply. "And I know a place that is giving out free food to survivors. I… know a chef there. I'm sure you're all famished. Won't you join me? I have something to discuss with you."

Raina explained cautiously, trying to push through Alana's hesitation. The powerful spear user rubbed her chin as she considered Raina's request.

"Are you sure?" Alana asked carefully. "That you really want to abandon what you have here?"

"Yes," Raina said, for the first time realizing what a boon it was to have the mask on her face. Even though everyone assured her the scarring would heal, she would likely keep it. Right now, the other woman could not see the change in her expression. "Things are fine now, but I expect there to be backlash for what I did to all those people."

Though Alana remained silent, her gaunt eyes meant she had seen it too. Most of the lives lost at the end were not due to people being overwhelmed by monsters, but rather for fighting without any care for their lives. Throwing themselves into danger in order to inflict wounds on the monsters. If they had fought more prudently, the number of casualties would likely be noticeably lower.

The rest of the walk to the restaurant continued in silence. Raina admired the professionalism of the people who came down from this village to the north. The head of the squad, who Raina heard was a Knight, marched with his squad members following behind in formation, even now prepared for a sneak attack. Their equipment looked well cared for and practical, especially compared to the eclectic Freedom Fighters.

She wondered idly what they had gone through to get to this Level of Skill.

Raina saw Randidly as she walked up, working the front of one of the outdoor stands they set up. One hand blurred as he cut food before moving it to the pan, all the while speaking with a customer. His movements were liquid and smooth, while everyone around him hurried back and forth, struggling to keep up with the mass of people pressing forward for the free food from such a high-class restaurant.

Not ten feet away from the stand, piles of people were lying around, snoring next to their half-eaten plates. The entire area was a chaos of human bodies, with people torn between biological needs and psychological release.

"It's here," Raina said, stepping into line. To her surprise, all the people from Donnyton had extremely strange expressions when they gazed up at the food.

Raina ignored that and tried not to worry over how Randidly would react to her face. Would he even recognize her with the mask? Of course he would. He'd made it for her in preparation for her big concert.

After what felt like an eternity, their group reached the front of the line. Randidly's stoic eyes slid up, appraising them. Raina froze, unsure of what to say. How to say that him calling her plain had finally woken her up from a strange stupor she'd been in since the System arrived.

What she didn't expect was for Randidly to largely ignore her, turning to the others. He tilted his head and addressed them in a sharp tone. "Fatigue level?"

"Moderate, but no injuries," Devan said smartly, saluting Randidly.

Rubbing his hands on his apron, Randidly nodded. "Good. This Level of enemy shouldn't give you pause. Also, this is convenient. All of you come back here. Devan, you take orders. I'd rather just cook. And you, how are you at cutting vegetables?"

Raina's jaw, hidden by her mask, remained dropped as these stalwart warriors, who even the toughest of the Freedom Fighters treated with awe and respect, dutifully trotted behind the counter of the stand and began to help Randidly cook and clean.

"Alana? Tell me about the Soulskill you received. Did you get enough PP to activate its benefits? Well, unless you took a nap last night, you definitely did," Randidly continued, rapidly stirring a sauce in a pot, smelling it, and adding a pinch of something to adjust its flavor.

"Ah…" It was a slight comfort to Raina that Alana also seemed to think this whole situation was strange. "There are four things that rotate; I get one every 5 PP spent. 5 Health and Stamina, and then 1 Endurance, followed by 1 Strength, and finally, 1 Willpower."

Randidly grunted, turning his attention to Raina. "Alright, Miss, Devan will take your order."

"What will it be?" Devan said, his face serious when he stepped forward. Randidly began to turn away, but Raina ripped off her mask, trembling.

Randidly stopped, slowly turning to look at her. He gazed at her for several seconds without comment, a curious sadness in his gaze.

"H-how do I look now?" Raina asked, desperate to end this strange silence, smiling as well as she could with her stiff facial skin.

To her surprise, Randidly chuckled and raised a hand to scratch the back of his head. "Still plain. But... more genuine than before, for sure. Are you feeling alright? If your face is still scarred, that must be fresh."

Raina frowned, yet she felt oddly jubilant. Why had everyone else acted like her face was ruined earlier if Randidly was just going to ignore it? Now she felt slightly hysterical for inciting a mob over the incident. "The only reason I was feeling down before was because you called me plain."

Randidly smiled awkwardly and shrugged. "I really didn't like your Skill. It seems whatever happened has let you control its activation. It's... nice."

"I have a question," Alana interrupted, unwilling to remain silent any longer. She sniffed the roast porkchop with cream sauce Randidly had just finished plating. "When the fuck did you have time to learn to cook like this? This is fucking delicious."

Shrugging, Randidly turned away and walked out to where the shop-keeper kept supplies.

"How do you know him?" Raina asked, turning to Alana.

Alana blushed. "He... he's my... Our town's..."

"Something like a guardian angel," one of the squad members supplied, tying an apron around his waist and moving to skin potatoes. The rest of the Classers from Donnyton nodded in agreement.

"He's the Ghosthound," Devan said, his face completely still and disinterested. "I would love to chat, but there are more people to take orders from. If you don't mind, please step aside until you make your decision so we can service other customers."

Alana still was thinking. "It's not like he's in charge. But he's definitely got the support for anything he wants to do... and he's the most powerful."

"Some people..." One of the other squad members hesitated to say the words, but pushed past that and said, "Some people really revere him. Worship him, almost."

Raina almost couldn't believe what she was hearing. But it was the absolute surety in Devan's tone that left her speechless.

"That's true. He is, after all, the Ghosthound. That man is the sole reason we've all come this far. And that's why he came down to Franksburg too," Devan spared Raina one last glance. "Because he wants to help."

CHAPTER EIGHTY-FOUR

*A*s Randidly finally allowed Devan's squad to leave and get some rest, he examined his notifications. Cooking today, he gained 3 more Levels in Cooking and 2 in Grace.

He was all too aware of the strange glances from Raina while he worked and ignored them as best he could. Still, his heart was heavy with guilt when he saw her. If he'd chosen to pursue the acid-spitting frogs instead of going after the white wolves on the frontlines...

Well, she will heal, Randidly assured himself. After hearing from Alana that she wanted to head north to join Donnyton, he wasn't sure what to think. Without the added danger of her looks, there was definitely some appeal in trying to recruit her to come back to the village, although that sort of depended on what she could accomplish with her voice.

Shaking his head, Randidly focused on his PP. Even though he didn't want to stay and help the town too much, it couldn't be denied that nights like this were certainly wellsprings of PP. He supposed that was half the reason monster hordes were sent against Newbie Villages, to encourage Skill growth.

Only, his combat Skills were already pretty well-developed to begin with. He had to rely on ancillary Skills like this to earn PP. He accumulated 42 PP, 20 of which were used to finish the Potion Making II Path. He earned 12 Focus getting there, as well as a notification.

Congratulations! You have completed the **"The Potion Making II Path"**!

Battle is not the only path to strength. Understanding the world's mysteries and using them to your own advantage will greatly increase

your chance of surviving. For ahead of you, the Path stretches ever onward. Effectiveness of bonuses from Potion Making Skill Level have slightly increased.

Congratulations! You have learned the Skill **Extract Level 1.**

Extract: *Separate the composite parts of a substance or mixture.* **Speed and thoroughness of extraction depend on Skill Level. Purity will increase as Skill Level rises.**

As Randidly expected, he received a Skill for the completion. He couldn't currently think of any uses for it, but he supposed as he encountered more materials, he would find something that could use the Skill.

The remaining 13 PP sat there while Randidly frowned at his Path options.

Watcher *0/??* | **?????** | **Heretic IV** *0/???* | **Oathbreaker** *0/25* | **Initiate of Ash I** *0/75* | **Spear Mastery II** *0/75* | **Path of Carnage I** *0/???*

The obvious choice was to go for Spear Mastery II. It was still the bread and butter of his close combat techniques. Would probably provide a new Skill as well. At the same time, he was oddly drawn to the Path of Carnage choice.

Both the surety of Spear Mastery II's usefulness and the question marks in the amount of Path of Carnage made Randidly hesitate. Ultimately, he decided the safe option was best. At least Spear Mastery would likely result in a positive outcome, even if it took a while.

Randidly poured his PP into that Path, earning himself a point in Perception at 5, and Reaction at 10. That, combined with the bonuses Randidly received from his Soulskill, added up to a significant boost in his raw Stats.

After allocating everything, Randidly looked at his Status Screen. What he saw there made him smile. *See me now, Shal? I'm getting stronger.*

Randidly Ghosthound
Class: ---
Level: N/A
Health(/R per hour): 390/432 [+2] (209 [+3])
Mana(/R per hour): 132/769 (90.75)
Stam(/R per min): 401/544 (76 [+1])
Vitality: 62 [+1]
Endurance: 39
Strength: 49 [+12]
Agility: 70 [+10]

Perception: 36
Reaction: 53
Resistance: 19
Willpower: 70
Intelligence: 96
Wisdom: 46
Control: 79
Focus: 50
Equipment: *Necklace of the Shadow Cat Lvl 20 (R): (Vitality +1, Strength +2, Agility +7) | Spine Spear of Ep-Tal Lvl 30 (+3 Agi, +10 Str)*
Skills
Soulskill: *Spear of Rot Mastery Lvl 437*

Basic
Passive: *Running Lvl 23 | Physical Fitness Lvl 32 | Spirit of Adversity Lvl 31 | Dagger Mastery Lvl 13 | Spear Mastery Lvl 50 | Fighting Proficiency Lvl 39 | Mental Strength Lvl 17 | Edge of Decay (Un) Lvl 16 | Grace Lvl 5*

Active: *Sneak Lvl 33 | Dodge Lvl 33 | First Aid Lvl 14 | Block Lvl 29 | Calculated Blow Lvl 19*

Resistances: *Acid Resistance Lvl 23 | Poison Resistance Lvl 16 | Pain Resistance Lvl 17 | Curse Resistance Lvl 3 | Fire Resistance Lvl 20*

Utility: *Farming Lvl 23 | Plant Breeding Lvl 9 | Potion Making Lvl 33 | Analyze Lvl 24 | Refine Lvl 15 | Pathfinding Lvl 18 | Mapmaking Lvl 7 | Sewing Lvl 11 | Cutting Vegetables Lvl 2 | Manual Labor Lvl 3 | Digging Lvl 5 | Cooking Lvl 16 | Extract Lvl 1*

Stamina
Attack Skills: *Heavy Blow Lvl 28 | Sprinting Lvl 19 | Phantom Thrust Lvl 47 | Phantom Onslaught Lvl 13 | Sweep Lvl 23 | Roundhouse Kick Lvl 17*

Boosts: *Iron Skin Lvl 27 | Spear Phantom's Footwork Lvl 37 | Eyes of the Spear Phantom Lvl 25 | Phantom Half-Step Lvl 16 | Haste Lvl 26 | Spear Deflect Lvl 12 | Empower Lvl 29*

Mana
Attack Skills: *Mana Bolt Lvl 30 | Spearing Roots Lvl 16 | Arcane*

Orb Lvl 23 | Magic Missile Lvl 6 | Healing Palm Lvl 8 | Fireball Lvl 30 | Pollen of the Rafflesia (R) Lvl 14 | Summon Pestilence Lvl 20 | Agony (Un) Lvl 12 | Incinerating Bolt Lvl 6 | Circle of Flame Lvl 6

Boosts: *Meditation Lvl 36 | Mana Shield Lvl 25 | Root Manipulation Lvl 37 | Mana Strengthening Lvl 15 | Wall of Thorns Lvl 5*

Unique: *Inspiration (U) | Blessing of the North (U) | Blessing of the East (U) | Blessing of the West (U)*

Randidly had some decisions to make. For now, both survivability and Mana Skill damage weren't an issue. In addition, his Mana and Stamina were increasing to the point he could use his high-cost Skills and spells multiple times in a row. Not many without potions, but enough for an extended fight.

Randidly was torn whether to drive up his Agility, increase his Strength for more power, work on the supporting Stats of Perception and Reaction, or finally address the glaring weakness that was his Resistance. There were merits to each position and each had their own consequences.

Randidly first considered his Resistance of 19. He supposed it was only so glaring because of the height of his other Stats. Most put points into the physical defense Skills. He likely had a relatively higher amount in that Stat, even compared to most non-Knight Classers, who generally built themselves the tankiest.

If there was a way to beat him in a fight, it was to hit him hard with spells. He was getting by in his spars with Clarissa due to his high Agility, but that wouldn't always be an option. Some attacks could only be endured.

After rubbing his forehead, Randidly climbed to the top of an abandoned apartment building. Although he was gaining a lot of PP, they did not translate into distributable Stats as much as they used to. The points usually flowed to a Stat relevant to his current Path. And Randidly hadn't yet encountered a Path that was specifically related to Resistance.

The annoying part of it all was he couldn't know what kind of threats still remained. There were obviously enemies Resistance would be necessary against, but if those enemies never came, it would essentially be a useless Stat.

Something occurred to Randidly. He did know of one enemy they hadn't yet accounted for. One who would likely know magic. Donnyton's Tribulation. If anyone were to prepare and use his weakness to magic to defeat him, it would be that creature.

Shivering, Randidly resolved himself to raise his Resistance. He looked north, toward Donnyton.

Yeah, I've searched for my past down here long enough. It's time to head back and face the present.

EPILOGUE

"*H*ey."

Lyra stilled, recognizing the voice, but barely able to believe he was here. She bit the inside of her cheek, trying to disguise any sort of physical response, and to keep the verbal ones quiet. Not only that, this was her secret spot. Deep in the forest. How did he...?

She turned, facing a smiling Randidly. More than any other time she'd been around him, he appeared kind and affectionate in the way he grinned at her.

Something clicked into place in her mind. Resisting the urge, she smiled back. "Hello."

Randidly stepped closer, his gaze turning serious. "I'm sorry to follow you like this. I'm sorry for everything... After I left, heading to Franksburg, I realized something. I need you—"

Randidly gazed down at the glowing sword of Mana sticking out of his chest. Lyra had cut halfway through him. She didn't bother to strike the rest of the blow. She realized immediately that harming the physical form of this *thing* wouldn't be enough.

"What gave me away?" the creature taking on Randidly's shape inquired. Its eyes faded from emerald to pure black, showcasing motes of shadow drifting away from the corners of its eyes.

The answers were obvious.

There were the Mana fluctuations she sensed the entire night Donnyton dealt with the Dungeon horde. The fluctuation came from different monsters, but they all hung back the same distance over the course of the battle. The fact that Randidly would never—could never—sneak up on her. The dumb grin it posed to charm her. The sweet lines it used.

How she sensed nothing but deadness from this creature. Whereas Randidly burned with a strange, musky emerald life.

Not that I don't want him to look at me, Lyra reflected sourly. *I want to feel like I've done something... something that makes me worthy of finally acknowledging me.*

"The apologies. I've never heard Randidly apologize, even when he's being foolish," Lyra said softly.

The Randidly-form dispersed before her very eyes, leaving only a shapeless blob of grey-purple lying on the ground. The same wisps of shadow that permeated its eyes radiated outward from its entire body.

Above its head floated a foreboding label.

Kim-Lath, the Tribulation of Many Faces Level 35

"Would you like to fight now?" Kim-Lath asked, its voice oddly flat, as if a computer read a script. Randidly reformed, this time holding a spear.

Lyra shrugged with forced looseness. She was an actress. Her character did not feel fear.

"If you want. Though... it really is good to see him."

Remaining calm, Lyra approached the shapeshifter and touched his—its —face. The movement might have appeared casual to anyone viewing from a distance. That was far from the truth. Her attention was stretched to its limit. If this Level 35 Tribulation turned into a threat, she was prepared to blink away.

The fake Randidly tilted its head to the side.

"Would you like to share a meal?" it asked, its voice no longer artificial, but also not quite Randidly.

With as much grace as she could muster, Lyra accepted.

THANK YOU FOR READING THE LEGEND OF RANDIDLY GHOSTHOUND BOOK ONE

We hope you enjoyed it as much as we enjoyed bringing it to you. We just wanted to take a moment to encourage you to review the book. Follow this link: The Legend of Randidly Ghosthound Book One to be directed to the book's Amazon product page to leave your review.

Every review helps further the author's reach and, ultimately, helps them continue writing fantastic books for us all to enjoy.

Want to discuss our books with other readers and even the authors like Shirtaloon, Zogarth, Cale Plamann, Noret Flood (Puddles4263) and so many more?

Join our Discord server today and be a part of the Aethon community.

Facebook

Instagram

Twitter

Website

You can also join our non-spam mailing list by visiting www.subscribepage.com/AethonReadersGroup and never miss out on future releases. You'll also receive three full books completely Free as our thanks to you.

Looking for more great LitRPG?

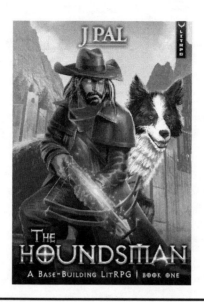

Have you been dreaming of a LitRPG with kingdom-building, flashy skills, and evolving dogs? Well, you just found it. The next series from the hit author of *They Called Me Mad* is here! Grab your copy today.

Get The Houndsman Now!

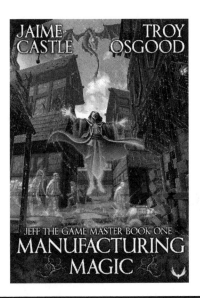

Jeff Driscoll becomes the only active Game Master for the VRMMORPG Infinite Worlds after a rogue patch turns the game into a buggy, dangerous mess. Can he fix it on his own and save the players?

Get Manufacturing Magic Now!

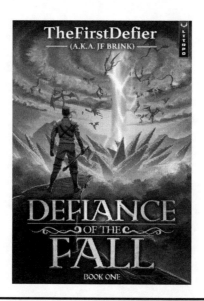

About the Series: Jump into a System Apocalypse story that merges LitRPG elements with eastern cultivation. Class systems, skill systems, endless choices for progression, it has everything fans of the genre love. Explore a vast universe full of mystery, adventure, danger and even aliens; where even a random passer-by might hold the power of a god. Follow Zac as he struggles to stake out a unique path to power as a mortal in a world full of cultivators.

Get Defiance of the Fall Now!

For all our LitRPG books, visit our website.